GNOMON

Nick Harkaway was born in Cornwall in 1972. Author
of the novels The Gone-Away World, Angelmaker and Tigerman,
he lives in London with his wife and two children.

Praise for Gnomon

'Brace yourself ... A brainy, labyrinthine plot born of Dr Who
and David Mitchell's Cloud Atlas, with a dash of EU finance,
Brexit and some Snowden-esque paranoia about the pervasive
surveillance of "the System". A mind-bending, genre-blending
fun house with a message or two.'

Mail on Sunday

'Nick Harkaway's most ambitious novel yet ... An enormous,
shaggy, infuriating, amazing and quite unforgettable piece
of fiction.'

Adam Roberts, Guardian, Books of the Year

'Gnomon is an extraordinary novel, and one I can't stop thinking
about some weeks after I read it. It is deeply troubling,
magnificently strange, a~~~~ ~~ exhilarating read.'

Emily ~~~~~~~~~~~~~~~~~~~~~~~~~ Station Eleven

'There is a glorious ma~~~~~~~~~~~~~~~~~~~~~ray
... There is a brillian~~~~~~~~~~~~~~~~~~~~ is
stretched and inverte~~~~~~~~~~~~~~~~~~ mon
is a kind of metaphysical epic ... a s~~~~~~~~~~~~ n of
technological possibility.'

Stuart Kelly, Times Literary Supplement

'A fiction designed to ensnare your trust, then destroy it ...
The door to a sinister Narnia ... Reading *Gnomon* is like being an
architecture critic when you suspect your reality is virtual. Its
momentum is exhilarating, but frightening, too. It resembles,
very stylishly, a mind spinning itself insane ... Immersively,
unpleasantly brilliant.'

Cal Revely-Calder, *Daily Telegraph*

'Pages of ideas, references and similes fizz and sparkle and
burst into life in a fireworks display that keeps going ... The
writing, too, is rarely anything other than impressive ...
Ludicrously complicated it may be, but it's also wonderfully
good.'

Harry Ritchie, *Sunday Times*

'[A] prowling deep-sea monster of a novel ... A sci-fi detective
procedural, violent thriller and multi-layered mystery
combine brilliantly to pull us through a profound exploration
of power and paranoia, technology and myth ... Harkaway
dazzles, baffles and teases before guiding us through bloody
darkness into understanding.'

Daily Mail

'You want to know how good *Gnomon* is? *I hate him for it*. Haaaate. I
had a little hategasm just typing those words ... This book
has more than one book in it. It is an astonishing piece of
construction, complex and witty and, frankly, evil ... It's science
fiction, but also historical fiction and social fiction and just plain
odd fiction. It is a magnificent achievement ... He's never written
a bad book, but this is the one that'll see him mentioned in the
same breath as William Gibson and David Mitchell ... This book
seriously just destroyed me with joy.'

Warren Ellis

'Opening a novel by Nick Harkaway feels like stepping into a theme park for the mind – every page you turn brings new delights for the mind and the senses. Gnomon is brilliant and terrifying, full of pleasures big and small. Basically, everything I want in a book.'

Charles Yu, author of *How to Live Safely in a Science Fictional Universe*

'This huge sci-fi detective novel of ideas is so eccentric, so audaciously plotted and so completely labyrinthine and bizarre that I had to put it aside more than once to emit Keanu-like "Whoahs" of appreciation … It is huge fun. And it will melt your brain … I wanted to give it a round of applause.'

Tim Martin, *Spectator*

'The novel weaves a web of subjective viewpoints studded with wordplay, imagery of fire and rebirth, and elements of traditional detective fiction.'

James Lovegrove, *Financial Times*

'A book that is in love with books, and no reader can help but warm to that.'

Guardian

'[Gnomon] has something of the large, fine-grained restlessness of David Foster Wallace, the scale and ambition of Zadie Smith or Jonathan Franzen. But it's considerably more gonzo than any of them … Gnomon is that rare thing, a book that cannot be accurately summarised or described. It needs to be experienced. And the experience … is always readable, absorbing, thought-provoking and, in the final analysis, unlike anything else … Gnomon is an island. And an island you really should visit.'

Adam Roberts, *Literary Review*

ALSO BY NICK HARKAWAY

The Gone-Away World
Angelmaker
Tigerman

GNOMON

NICK HARKAWAY

✳ WINDMILL BOOKS

1 3 5 7 9 10 8 6 4 2

Windmill Books
20 Vauxhall Bridge Road
London SW1V 2SA

Windmill Books is part of the Penguin Random House group of companies
whose addresses can be found at global.penguinrandomhouse.com.

Copyright © Nick Harkaway 2017

First published by William Heinemann in 2017
First published in paperback by Windmill Books in 2018

www.penguin.co.uk

A CIP catalogue record for this book is available from the British Library.

ISBN 9781786090096

Typeset in 11.5/15.75 pt Fournier MT
by Integra Software Services Pvt. Ltd, Pondicherry

Printed and bound in Great Britain by Clays Ltd, St Ives Plc

For Tom,
my son.

Wow.

'When the first question was asked in a direction opposite to the customary one, it was a signal that the revolution had begun.'

Ryszard Kapuściński, *The Emperor*

DCAC:/

3455 6671 1643 2776 6655 5443 2147
7654 5667 7122 7543 1177 7666 5543
2511 7656 7711 2331 6542 2111 7776
6543 6221 7671 1223 4427 6533 2221
7671 1223 4427 6533 2221 7671 1223
4427 6533 2221 1177 6547 3321 7122
3345 5317 6443 3322 2117 6514 4322
3445 5677 5321 6655 [...]

my mind on the screen

'The death of a suspect in custody,' says Inspector Neith of the Witness, 'is a very serious matter. There is no one at the Witness Programme who does not feel a sense of personal failure this morning.'

She is looking straight into the camera and her sincerity is palpable. A dozen different mood assessment softwares examine the muscles around her mouth and eyes. Her microexpressions verify her words. As a matter of course, the more sophisticated algorithms check for the telltale marks of Botox and of bioelectric stimulators that might allow her to fake that painful honesty, but no one really expects to find anything, and no one does.

Polling data streams across the screen: 89 per cent believe the Witness was not at fault. Of the remainder of the population, the overwhelming majority believes that any culpability will turn out to be negligent rather than designed. Neith's own figures are even better: she has been called in to investigate the matter precisely because her personal probity is the highest ever measured. All but the most corrosively paranoid of the focus groups accept her good faith.

It is a very good showing, even granting that the Witness has consistently high approval anyway. All the same, the discussion of Diana Hunter continues in the Public Sphere – as it should – until it is eclipsed by the next of the killings.

*

Ninety minutes before, Mielikki Neith stares into her morning mirror, feeling the vertiginous uncertainty that sometimes comes with viewing one's own image, the inability to understand the meaning of her reflected face. She repeats her name, quite softly but with growing emphasis, hearing the noise and yet unable to connect it with the self she feels. Not that she is anyone else: not that any other collection of syllables or features would be better. It is the intermediation of physicality and naming, of being represented in biology or language, that doesn't sit with her in this disconnected instant. She knows it is simply a lingering trace of the dream state, but that does not alter her conviction − inappropriately cellular, felt in blood and bone − that something is wrong.

She is correct. In a few moments she will start work, and the day will set her inevitably on the path to the involuted Alkahest. She is just hours from her first meeting with weird, cartilaginous Lönnrot, just over a week from her loss of faith in everything she has believed in her life. As she steps out of her slippers and begins to wash, finding in the animal business of grooming the growing understanding of her body and its place in the process that is her, she is stepping not only on to the cracked white shower tray but also on to that road, the one that conducts her without let or hindrance to a point of crisis: to endings and apocatastasis. She apprehends this now with knowledge she has, from her limited vantage point inside the flow of events, not yet gleaned − but that knowledge is so significant that its echo reaches her even here, gathered in the slipstream of the Chamber of Isis and the most complex and saintly murder in the history of crime. Neith's consciousness is etiolated this morning because it touches itself irregularly along its own extension in time, a contact that makes her almost − but, crucially, not quite − prescient. Instead of foresight, the Inspector gets a migraine, and in that small difference she sets her feet on the pattern that must eventually lead her to all the things I have already mentioned, but most fatefully − fatally − to me.

*

I can see my mind on the screen

The Inspector awoke this morning, as she does almost every day, to the sound of technological obsolescence. Her residence, provided by the System to employees of her grade, is an airy one-bedroom flat in a period building in Piccadilly Circus. The ancient neon light directly outside her window is faulty and makes a noise when it switches on: the death rattle of twentieth-century advertising. She has complained about it, but does not anticipate any change in her circumstance. Machines these days are somewhat perfected; a visible glitch in a high profile space such as this has been found to project a reassuring fallibility and evoke a sense of wellbeing which endures for several days. It conveys the continuing humanness of a nation under digitally mediated governance. The figures are unambiguous.

She listens now, in the quiet aftermath of her public statements, to the hum of the light at full function. When she goes close to the window, she is sure she can feel the hairs on her arms plucked by a static charge, but knows this for a psychosomatic illusion. She turns back to her desk, palms to forehead, then cheeks, and down the line of the nose. Broadcast lights make her eyes itch in their sockets.

Here, then, is her new case, MNEITH-GNOMON-10559. The name looks like nonsense until you know the framework into which it fits. Framing is everything, in filing as in investigative work. First of all, the label acknowledges that it is her case by logging it under her name. The actual ID number is the last part, '10559', but human beings give things names rather than numbers and this way the Witness can control what that name is, avoiding the inadvertent compromise of operations. The specific term, in this case 'GNOMON', is randomly assigned from a list. 'THE HUNTER CASE' would be less cumbersome, but there might be another case involving another Hunter, and it would not be appropriate to conflate them. 'GNOMON' is there to avoid any kind of confusion: an incontrovertible statement of identity. Beyond that, it apparently means an early geometer's tool for marking right angles, a set square made of metal. By extension it means something perpendicular to everything else, such as the upright part of a sundial. She finds the name itchily *à propos*, a handful of sand in her cognitive shoe. The Hunter case does stick out. She said that in the interview earlier, but only the channel known as TLDR is actually hosting the whole segment and so far no one has accessed the file. TLDR is basically

7

an archive, paid for by donations from high net worth individuals who believe in archiving.

She reviews the case preamble: Hunter, awake and obdurate, a cranky old lady with round cheeks and a bad attitude that must have been fashionable when she was in her twenties.

'Do you wish at this time to undergo a verbal interview which may obviate the need for a direct investigation?'

'I do not.'

'Do you wish at this time to make a statement?'

'I'll state that I do not submit to this voluntarily. I consider it a baseless intrusion, and very rude.'

'We are committed to affording you the maximum of dignity and care during your time with us. All staff will treat you with the utmost courtesy within the boundaries of their assigned tasks.'

She sighs. 'Then please record that I am a woman in the prime of life, whose powers are severely limited by authorities perishing with thirst, and now demanding that I make a gift to them of the waters of memory.'

'Noted,' the technician says, bland in the face of unexpected poetry. The Inspector can hear something in his voice, a mild frustration with this uppity biddy whose interrogation will surely yield nothing more than the misanthropy of the hermetic old.

'Yes, indeed,' Hunter agrees. 'Everything is.'

The medical staff come in then, and Hunter goes limp and makes them lift her on to the gurney: old-fashioned passive resistance, pointlessly antagonistic. Once, she screams, and they almost drop her. That makes the restraint team visibly unhappy, and she laughs at them. Her teeth are very white against her skin.

Finally they get her into the chair and the needle goes into the back of her hand. Hunter scowls, then settles back as if getting comfortable for a very boring and time-consuming argument she has determined she must have.

The Inspector touches the terminals, jolts as the dead woman's mind settles over her own: Diana Hunter, deceased. What is the flavour of her life? Sixty-one years of age, divorced, no children. Educated at

Madrigal Academy and then Bristol University. By profession an administrator, and then later a writer of obscurantist magical realist novels, she was apparently once celebrated, then reclusive, then forgotten. Most successful book: *The Mad Cartographer's Garden*, in which the reader is invited to untangle not only the puzzle that confronts the protagonists but also a separate one allegedly hidden in the text like a sort of enormous crossword clue; most famous arguably the last, titled *Quaerendo Invenietis*, which received only a very limited publication and became an urban legend of sorts, with the usual associated curiosities. *Quaerendo* contains secret truths that are downright dangerous to the mind, or an actual working spell, or the soul of an angel, or Hunter's own, and the act of reading it in the right place at the right time will bring about the end of the world, or possibly the beginning, or will unleash ancient gods from their prison. First year university students in the humanities pore over the accessible fragments and consider they are touching some fatal cosmic revelation. Copies of the book, of which only one hundred were printed, are now almost impossibly expensive, and Hunter somehow contrived to extract from each purchaser a commitment not to scan any part of what they had, with the result that even now there is no online edition, and indeed no verifiable text at all.

It all added up to a remarkable frenzy of excitement and localised notoriety, then went quiet when the book, read by various people in various times and places, failed to end the onward march of time or drive anyone mad. In other words, the Inspector is inclined to believe, Hunter was a purveyor of educated and ultimately meaningless literary flimflam who got bored of the joke and retired. Since then, her only contribution to the body of English literature has been a series of rambling and condemnatory letters to the local paper. If she was, in fact, a dangerous terrorist, her cover was as fully realised and performed as any in the long and unglamorous history of subversion. More likely she was the lonely algorithmic victim of a perfect storm – and yet despite its improbability, the notion that she may somehow have been more than she appeared is ineradicable.

Neith begins again.

Hunter's first thought during the examination is like the barb on a fishhook, and Neith instinctively loathes it. These eight unremarkable words cause her to tighten her jaw as if expecting a blow. The phrase is, to be sure, unusually clear and strong, quite ready to be vocalised. One must assume that Hunter was deliberately recording a message, in which case: to whom? To Neith, as the investigating officer? Or to an imagined historian? Why does the tone, the clean, discursive flavour of Hunter's mind, trouble that part of the Inspector that is devoted to a professional mistrust of appearances?

Perhaps it is suspicious for its very competence. There's no note of Hunter having the kind of training that would allow her to be so coherent. Her record should be a ragged but truthful account of her self: less a cut-glass cross section than a jellied scoop lifted from a bowl. It was a minimum-priority interview until Hunter died, a low-to-no-likelihood examination based on a direct tip-off using the precise form of words given in the Security Evidence Act, and some ancillary factors to score a level of certainty just barely topping the margin of error. There are twenty or thirty such each month: full investigations carried out on the precautionary principle, no more troubling to the subjects than a visit to the dentist, and certainly resulting in no criminal cases. Statistically, those emerging from these exams are happier, more organised and more productive. It's partly a direct consequence, the neuromedical aftercare being somewhat like a tune-up, but mostly it is a psychological blip. Everyone lives with secrets, even now – tacit self-accusations, fears of weakness and inadequacy. These fortunate suspects are weighed in the balance and found worthy. The process is so universally beneficial that the Inspector has occasionally wondered if she should ask for a reading herself.

Yet there is something in Hunter's mental voice that should not be there, even if the precise nature of its wrongness eludes the Inspector for now: something dyssynchronous that is written in signs whose general meaning she understands, but which remains maddeningly unfocused, as one might grasp that a red triangle is a warning without seeing what is written within.

The fuzziness of human communication is one of the reasons for Inspector Neith's profession under the System. Statistical analysis and even soft logic can only take machine learning so far into the quirked and sideways landscape of human irrationality. What a given thing means may vary not only between two individuals but from moment to moment. Even actual symbols symbolise more than one thing – the giant neon sign outside her window, which blesses London's Piccadilly Circus with a nostalgic wash of faulty electrics, comes from a time when profit was uncomplicated and goods were rivalrous and excludable. It was made by hand in 1961 and features the name of a company, Real Life, which sold building supplies of a sort now made obsolete by more advanced construction techniques. The majority of things then traded in London could be held or touched or otherwise understood by a human being with only her senses, and because of this it is a banner of perceived normality in an era when none of these things is any longer true.

To someone like Diana Hunter, this means that the System, too, is based on illusions. To Neith, it means that however rational a mode of living may be, humans still need to project unpredictable comforts on to the sharp edges of what actually exists. The very best analytical software may struggle with such a bewilderment.

Mielikki Neith is an enthusiastic proponent of both the System and the Witness. The first is a government of the people, by the people, without intervention or representation beyond what is absolutely necessary: a democracy in the most literal sense, an ongoing plebiscite-society. The second is the institution for which Britain perhaps above all other nations has always searched, the perfect police force. Over five hundred million cameras, microphones and other sensors taking information from everywhere, not one instant of it accessed initially by any human being. Instead, the impartial, self-teaching algorithms of the Witness review and classify it and do nothing unless public safety requires it. The Witness is not prurient. The machine cannot be bribed to hand over images of actresses in their baths to tabloid journalists. It cannot be hacked, cracked, disabled or distorted. It sees, it understands, and very occasionally it acts, but otherwise it is resolutely invisible.

In the gaps where the cameras cannot scan or where the human animal is yet too wild and strange, there are the Inspectors, prosecutorial ombudsmen to the surveillance state, reviewing and considering any case that passes a given threshold of intervention. The majority of the Inspectors' cases concern acts of carefully considered violence, international organised crime and instances of domestic or international terrorism. Some few crimes of passion still occur, but hardly require deep scrutiny, and most are headed off early and pre-emptively when tremors of dysfunction give them away. The Witness does not ignore a rising tide, a pattern of behaviour. It does not take refuge behind the lace curtain of non-interference in personal business. No one now shall live in fear of those they also love. Everyone is equally seen.

That's how the System works and what it means. All citizens understand its worth, and everyone contributes their time and attention to the law, to governance, to the daily work of creating a free and fair society – and everyone benefits. It is a nation which is also a community, and in that – in its steady and equitable prosperity, in its scrupulous justice, and above all in its ability to deliver security of the self to citizens at a level unprecedented in history – it claims the Inspector's allegiance with an absolute certitude. Her understanding of the world is perfectly extended into her profession and her life.

Speaking of her profession: Neith finds a comfortable position in her chair. She taps gently with one knuckle, glances – as she always does – at the identifying tag at the top of the screen: NEITH, M., DETECTIVE INSPECTOR (GRADE A). She has no idea what possessed her mother to give her a Finnish name, except perhaps a deep and abiding admiration for the champion of cross-country skiing who carried it to two Winter Olympic seasons and came away with nine gold medals. The more important part is DETECTIVE, which means she has a professional heritage to draw on as well as a personal one, an identity as strong and old as the Real Life sign's bright promise of middle-class housing, good schools and a sheepdog. She went to the new Metropolitan Witness Academy in Hoxton, qualified for the fast track and was coached through three years on the beat. She was peed on by drunks, wept on by widows, whistled at by builders. She graduated to Serious Crimes, arrested drug importers and corrupt bankers, and caught the eye of the System and the nation when she scooped a minor clue from the wastebasket and followed it all the way to what became known as the Cartier Smash and Grab. On the same day Neith picked up the thread, a high-technology criminal gang based in France ram-raided a jewellery vault and tried to fly back across the Channel using microlight aircraft. With Neith's information in its electronic hand, the System's active countermeasures aspect was able to penetrate their navigation software and land the gang at a military airfield for convenient arrest. Only one member escaped the net: a secure intrusion specialist and counter-surveillance expert known internationally as the Waxman, who had chosen a separate exit strategy, and took refuge in the embassy of a friendly foreign power. The incompleteness has always annoyed her, and the Waxman, with nothing else to do, occasionally sends her taunting messages.

After the Smash and Grab arrests, though, she rose on and up to the core of the justice apparat. She is no paper pusher, no careerist. Neith will over time be promoted to high office by the Witness for one good reason: she is proper police.

In her hands now are the terminals for the Witness interface, the primary tools of her trade. As always, they strike her as very male, very sexualised. Each one is around ten centimetres long, grey-black, with a silver half-dome at one end. She unbuttons her shirt. The left terminal monitors her own vital signs, and goes against the chest, over the heart. The right one she will place against her temple. There are various reasons for this design, but she believes that in the end they are made this way so that an Inspector at work resembles however distantly the protagonist of a black-and-white crime flick using a two-part telephone.

For shorter recordings and less complex emotional and cognitive states, the machine can simply impose the flow of a recorded mind over its user's in real time, which is quick and effective but leads to a kind of double vision that many people – the Inspector included – find somewhat nauseating. In any situation which requires the investigator to get to know their subject, or where nuance might be important, it's more usual to shunt the whole file, in compressed form, into local storage in the brain. Neith imagines its subsequent unfolding to resemble a jasmine flower tea opening in hot water, or a kind of retrograde origami in which the foreign mind resumes its original shape to whatever degree it can inside its new physical environment. The origami method affords a far greater intimacy with the subject – which of course is useful in important cases like this one – but can compromise your sleep as the file unwinds. There's no danger of the memory taking over the investigator's, any more than you can drive to Brighton in the back half of an automobile. It's a set of experiences, not a viral person, though that does not stop London's film industry from depicting any number of lurid scenarios premised on the idea, ranging from sinister to comedic, but tending in most cases to an element of the erotic.

It's not the prospect of accidentally becoming someone else that causes her to hesitate, if only for an instant. Rather, it is the desire to keep her own brain in the best possible order, just as she tries to eat right and sleep sufficiently. The Witness, as a matter of course, monitors the behaviour of anyone frequently using memory uploads, and does not allow anything to go wrong. Having a perfect older brother checking in on you from time to time makes things like that considerably less nerve-wracking – and unlike an actual brother, the Witness does not intrude. It is just always there. That being so, the Inspector feels no serious concern in selecting the more intimate option. She takes Diana Hunter into her head, knowing that the Witness will protect her.

The Witness is perfect because it can see everything, and that perception does not stop at the skull. In those rare cases where it is necessary, the Witness can enter the brain of a subject by surgical intervention and read the truth directly from the source. It is the key reason Inspectors exist. The machine can perform the function, but it is not actually alive. It is not appropriate that something dead have governance of something living. In the end, there must be oversight not because the Witness makes mistakes, but because the watcher must itself be watched, and be seen to be watched. The System exists for the people, not the other way around, and in the end it is the people who are empowered – and required – by the machine to take any and all of the hard decisions that arise.

When the whole thing has poured into her mind and settled there, she uses the machine to start the file again, and – as always when she lifts the second terminal to her head – thinks of Humphrey Bogart.

*

I can see my mind on the screen

Actually, there's more than one screen. I'm surrounded by them. Each wall of this room is a screen, and the technicians can subdivide them all so that they display different images. I can see my mind all around me, on all the screens. I'm looking down along the line of my body – in general I hate this position because it gives me an almost endless collection of chins – at the screen beyond my feet, which is presently the least busy of them all. These words are in the middle, between an ECG trace and something that looks like a sonogram.

One of the technicians nods. 'It is,' he says. 'It's a sonogram of your brain.' I think he's simplifying for me. His voice sounds like the one adults use when they're talking to small children about complex, grown-up things. I suspect it's something more like an MRI, but miniaturised and implanted inside my skull. Just because I am strapped to the chair does not mean that I am stupid.

All that comes up on the screen, too, of course, and he looks apologetic. It occurs to me that he is probably a nice enough guy under other circumstances – he's even a little bit attractive, if you like floppy Brideshead hair and that awfully self-conscious congeniality – but I hate him and I want to hurt him. He thinks he's being kind, but actually he's just salving his guilt.

He reads that last bit and he flinches and turns away. I feel instantly embarrassed but I also think: Fuck you. It's weird having your surface thoughts broadcast like this. Weird and horrible, but also a little bit liberating. If someone is rude enough to intrude on the ticking of your brain, to peel back your polite silences and your social graces and poke the fleshy grey stuff in search of secrets, they can just deal with what they find there. All the same, I'm glad I'm not thinking about sex.

Now I'm thinking about sex. On the far right we're watching my memory of my last orgasm. Since this is a purely visual feed we're seeing the ceiling of my bedroom lurch left and right.

This is not okay. I do not consent. I do not consider the intrusion legitimate, and I do not accept the argument that it is in the interest of the nation as a whole, nor that if it were in the nation's interest that would make what is happening to me acceptable. Just because something is done according to the law does not mean that it is lawful. Law is made in the image of an ideal. One can make a law that does not reflect that image, and that law may be a law without being lawful. I consider what is happening here a grotesque violation. If I get the chance, I will hurt you for doing what you are doing, hurt you badly. This is my head and you should not be in it.

The technician who tried to tell me about the brain scan reads that and he stops trying to be Mr Nice. I've given him an excuse to think of me as an enemy. Beneath the floppy hair, he has a fat face and he sweats too much. In fact he stinks. I can see hair in his nose. I'm reasonably sure he's an ungenerous lover. I hope his wife is unfaithful to him with derelicts, and that she brings home diseases for which there are no names. I hope his dog dies. I know he has a dog because I can see the hair on his trouser cuff. And I recognise the mud. The precise constitution of that mud is a signature, the clay and red earth and the hint of gravel occurs in three places in London, but in only one of them will you find the seeds that cling to his sock. Like Sherlock Holmes I can read the evidence and infer from the reality of the present the map of the past, and now I know where he walks his dog.

(I don't really.)

It's mud, you moron. But for a moment there he was scared, and that's a win. I'll take it. You hear me, you miserable bastard? I beat you. From this table. To which I am tied. That's how pathetic you are. You are small and pathetic and gullible and you are beneath my notice. Which will not stop me from doing terrible things to you.

(I actually will.)

Now one of his colleagues is reading over his shoulder and reminding him that this is why the protocol says not to talk to the subject. I go back to looking at pictures of my own head.

On the left there's a feed from my optic nerve. It's like being in a hall of mirrors because I see the image of what I'm looking at and the screen displays the image of the image and then the image of the image of the image and then a second technician puts his fingers in front of my face.

'Don't,' he says. 'You'll get feedback.'

'What happens then?' I ask him.

'Your head explodes.'

I can tell it's an old joke. He's reassuring himself as much as anything. He's saying that because my head won't explode, because there's no risk of that, what they're doing isn't like torture. It's just a perfectly simple evidential procedure. It's sanctioned by the court. There's nothing immoral or even very unpleasant about it. It's okay.

It is not okay. It is invasion. It is torture, and you are torturers. You, who are reading this, seeing it, feeling it. These feelings are not yours. They belong to me. Get out of my head. My head, the head of this woman in this room, not yours, wherever you are.

They get tired of reading my objections and my threats, so they give me a paralytic and blindfold me. Now I'm just talking to myself in the dark. They can still read what I'm thinking, but now that I can't see the reaction it's a lot less satisfying thinking bad thoughts at them. And I can't tell: perhaps they've also shut down the feed from my speech centres and I'm just wittering away to myself. That would be annoying. I dislike futility and helplessness.

This partial sensory deprivation is alarming because it's quite nice. You'd think it would be frightening, and of course it is – that, I don't mind so much – but it's also soothing and that, I distrust intensely. I only have smell, touch and sound to work with, and as I lie here I get a sense of the ebb and flow of the room. I start to recognise the wash of air that accompanies a particular set of footsteps, the tinge of sweat and cologne that means the first technician or the second or someone new. The regularity, that intimacy, is settling some little evolutionary rodent circuit lodged somewhere in the engine room of my brain. I can't help it: I'm relaxing into the situation. Under other circumstances I'd even be worried that I might say something inappropriate or self-incriminatory, but that's not really an issue. In twenty minutes or so they're going to read my entire mind to protect the security of the state. They will hollow me out like a pumpkin and leave me with a pumpkin smile: a wide, idiot, toothless grin. They'll go home and tell their friends they did a good job. They'll greet their partners, their spouses, their kids, and if they let on in the small hours of the dark that they're not without qualms, they'll say in the same breath that they know it's necessary. Their partners and their spouses will tell them they are brave, because they accept the sleepless nights of troubled conscience so that everyone else can be safe. No doubt that's how it always goes with torturers.

'Justice has been perfected and the Witness is everywhere.' That's the pitch. And it works. We are all transparent to one another. There are no secrets, can be no secrets. Must be no secrets. So I will be read, as a page is read. If I have nothing to hide – if the System has made a mistake, which it almost never does – I have nothing to fear. That motto is written in Latin over the door, and above it is the odd little colophon of an axe wrapped in sticks that has been the symbol of magistrates since Imperial Rome at least. The modern phrase is attributed to William Hague, who was a great Conservative politician decades gone – a real champion of rights and right thinking – although I happen to know it was also a favoured maxim of Joseph Goebbels. Protection is the first duty of government. I hear they still drink a toast to him – Hague, that is, not Goebbels – in the Admin Tower, once a year at Christmas. The first watcher, the godfather of the Witness.

The touch of the machine they will use to open my brain is so fine it can probe ricepaper without cutting it. They may already have begun, and I wouldn't know. It's a medical technology, a very sophisticated and important one. In fact, many people emerge from this room – from these rooms, because there are many of them – healthier than when they arrived. Unsuspected blood clots can be dealt with, cancers purged, sorrows averted. If the pages of my mind are innocent, there will be no consequence to this encounter beyond a few lost hours. When my mother was a child, they still had to serve jury duty: days of unproductive dithering over matters of fact and intent which are now closed questions. May we be preserved from that! The Witness sees, the machine divines, the evidence is inside us. It is a far more complete justice than anything you can do with he-said-she-said. It just is. And beyond that it makes you healthy, so it's really win–win.

In my case, as in almost all of them, the Witness is actually quite correct. I am a traitor to the System, to the society we have constructed around it. I have hidden from the Witness, which is in itself antisocial and grounds for closer examination. I have used paper and ink to send private messages, bartered to conceal my transactions, done favours and had them returned in order to avoid listing my transactions on an accessible database. I have taught these skills: writing, hiding, haggling, the ad hoc measurement of value. I have proselytised about their use, advocated opacity. Shame on me.

To make it worse, I have erected analogue communications devices – wires strung taut across narrow alleys with cups at either end; pigeon coops; listening tubes. I have embraced the process of divestment to such an extent that in fact there are no modern machines at all in my house. No touchscreen. No computer. Not even a washing machine. Sadly, washing machines these days are as wired as everything else. They are set up to tell you how to save money and water and electricity. More recently they started measuring water quality. Of course, they package those data anonymously and send them to the central hub for analysis. By doing that the System can manage water flow and know about any dangerous impurities before they jeopardise the public health. When my father was a child, he got blisters on his tongue from drinking water with aluminium in it – an error at a local water plant. That can't happen now, and indeed there are biosensors in the pipes that pick up various waterborne infections and trigger alerts. But nothing is free: the reality is that anonymisation is no more effective than one of those hilarious nose-moustache-and-spectacle sets that are a staple of office parties. With the right parsing, your washing machine can know all sorts of things about you that are private. It can tell from your clothes whether you drink too much, whether you have eczema, whether you use drugs. Whether you are pregnant. A new model has come on the market with an olfactory sensor patterned on the nose of a particular breed of pig: it can tell whether you have an early stage cancer and refer you to a doctor. That is a little miraculous and wonderful, isn't it? If only the information didn't also automatically go to your local health trust so that they can manage their year-on-year needs more accurately. If only they didn't market their needs list to health insurers. If only everything wasn't quite so obsessively joined up.

I had all those tools once: the car that drove itself, the office chair that warned me when I was sitting badly. And then bit by bit I got rid of them. It was not a grand decision, just a slow shift I didn't understand until it was done. I got tired of voices in my head and eyes peering over my shoulder. Now nothing I own talks to anything else, and I have hooks in the hallway where people can hang up their wearable devices when they arrive. The whole house works as a Faraday cage. I put the wire in myself, so I know it's properly done. The Witness is the sun, and my home is made of shadows – or perhaps of shade.

Instead of electronics, I have books: books in their thousands stacked all over the house. There's almost no flat surface that is not covered in books. Last year there was an embarrassing incident when a double tower of translated South American fiction tumbled over and buried me in my bed.

I allow people to borrow books and I keep no records of the loans. Do you know, in fourteen years I have never once had a book stolen? How remarkable, that people will behave so well without being indexed. It's not scalable, apparently; not realistic in the wider world. Above a certain threshold, it's no longer a personal trust governed by the rules of friendship, but a tragedy of the commons, and people just steal. That's always been the problem, I'm told: we need a better sort of human being, not a more just law. We need to change the way people think.

Not that I'm against indices, per se. From time to time my library grows when someone brings me a cardboard box from an attic or a cellar, and then I write all the details of each book on a little card and I put them away each in its proper place. Sometimes I run classes for children, teaching them how to read books which cannot speak to them, how to close the covers and lie down when they are tired because the pages will not detect their fatigue or tell the house to extinguish the lights so that they know they should sleep. Sometimes I let my small students stay up with a torch, and read under the duvet, though I am careful to be sure they do not know this is by my permission. They rustle and hide and derive great pleasure from flouting my law. I teach them reading and disrespect for authority, and I consider my work well done.

Yes, I know, I am a witch and I traffic in dark magic. I warp the fragile grey matter of vulnerable infants.

Speaking of which: in a few moments the technicians will put tendrils of metal into my brain. This sounds enormously sinister, but of course it's not. The filaments are barely more than a few atoms wide, stiffened by a magnetic field until they can slide and squiggle between cells and along blood vessels like little furry mice seeking their mother's tit. They will snuggle against the different parts of me and listen. They will hear the signals in my head through chitosan minichips, the same ones that are used to repair trauma victims and connect pilots with their planes. They will learn the language of my neurons, although more properly it should be called a dialect, because it turns out that in general when you and I each see the colour blue, we do indeed see much the same thing, to the endless disappointment of philosophers. Would you believe, though, that men and women process depth perception differently? So that if a man reviews my experience, he will likely get nauseous. Good riddance, of course, but still: I find that intriguing.

They will test and tweak and then they will read the pages of my brain. The whole process will take a little over half a day, they tell me. It is unknown for it to last longer than that. We are not deep enough, not dense enough, to contain more information than that. Perhaps there should be a unit of identity against time. How many human-hours will this take? And by the answer you could know how real I am.

Somewhere in the harvest, they will find what they are looking for. I am said to possess a list of reactionaries and bad elements, and I suppose in a way I do, I just don't think of it as a list. I call it my life. It is everyone I know who is like me, who chooses not to participate in the network of binding plebiscites and bank loans and credit cards and locatively discursive spimes. They are the small remnant or rebirth of a culture of analogue people who do not entirely believe that this version of life is perfect, who feel constrained rather than liberated by the world which has emerged as much from our heedlessness as from any decision. A very few of them actually protest and engage in civil disobedience. They carry protest cards which give a contact number for a lawyer, and they skirt the edges of the law. And I'm sure, in among them, there are some petty criminals: counterfeiters and rumrunners and such. I don't ask when I'm sharing candles and early Penguin editions how the members of my book group make their money. Mystery allows for dreams and uncertainty for romance, forgetfulness opens the door for forgiveness and even redemption. In my house the hearth is unbroken by the endless torrent of the outer world. It is, like marriage or liberty, not a thing but an action: a process we must create rather than a rock on which we may stand.

That's why I'm in here.

Someone who talks like that, according to the System, may represent a potential security risk to the wider nation, a refusenik culture which, if significant numbers were to follow its lead, would imply the end of the Witness and the System, the end of the benign, stable, all-seeing state we all inhabit. There is no present risk of that actually happening: they are – we are – cracks in the wall, and maintenance is one of the ten commandments of good engineering. By the time the cracks widen and there is water flowing through them, the wall will already be beyond repair.

The point is that in twelve hours the System will have the names and the faces of everyone I know, direct from my head. After that my part will be over.

The machine will make any necessary adjustments for my well-being: deal with physical deformities to the brain matter, ensure there is no bleeding or swelling that might endanger me, take preventative and curative measures against sociopathy, psychosis, depression, aggressive social narcissism, sadism, masochism, low self-esteem, undiagnosed neuroatypicality, attention deficit, in other words all the known issues of our complex biological processing, even unto the insidious and alienating cognitive dissonance and maladjustment syndrome. (You really have to watch for that one. Almost anyone can have it.)

Or you could say that in twelve hours I will have betrayed everyone I love into the hands of these my torturers, and we will all of us emerge perfected and adjusted and happy and enslaved. We will be remade in the image of a creation I once believed was the only way to avoid horror, but which by a ridiculous string of errors and confusions of the mind is now a horror in itself.

I will probably thank the myrmidons as I leave. When I understand how important it is for me to say goodbye to what I was, it will please me to see the children burn my books as a token gesture of my return to society – and they will do it gladly, after their own therapeutic interventions. I could reacquire them all, later, of course, but it seems that the determinedly miserabilist slant of my non-fiction reading may lose its appeal.

They take off the blindfold. Some of the processes require visual stimuli. I look at the room, at the screens all around me, at my self everted on them like a rat on a middle school laboratory counter.

The pain management technician says: 'Three, two, one, and mark,' and I realise, as I am going under, that he is the same man who was present for the birth of my daughter.

I think: You shall not have my mind.

It comes up on the screen, in sans serif font.

*

The Inspector puts the terminals on their stand and, after a moment of silent hiatus, works through a ritual resembling a compulsive disorder of the mind. Over her desk there is a single printed sheet of paper whose contents she changes every so often to avoid memorising them. Last month, the text was Victorian and resonant:

I pleaded, outlaw-wise,
By many a hearted casement, curtained red...

The metre was uneven, the sense and lexicon demanding. That is part of the point: focusing on the poem entails a full engagement of the mind with the text and the moment. A waking engagement, critical and jaggedly real. The new verse is more mannered and less to her liking, which makes it perhaps more suited to the task:

thy breath was shed
Upon my soul between the kisses and the wine...

Careful that she is reading word by word from the sheet, she finishes the poem, then picks up an old crank-handled lantern from beside her terminal and winds vigorously. A meagre light spills from the cracked Fresnel lens and paints the outline of the fracture on the wall behind the desk.

Neith nods in satisfaction: good. The text is static, the lantern works. She passes to the final stage, tossing a single grubby tennis ball into the air, and when – as they always do – it comes back down, catching it.

These three tests are intended for those learning to recognise and even control the direction of their dreams. Text is unstable in the envisioned unconscious, and either cannot be read or changes itself between breaths. Mechanical objects and light switches tend not to work, and physical laws – such as gravity – are undependable. For Neith, who routinely views considerable quantities of the recorded experience of other minds, the tests are both a practical reality check and an aid to being comfortable and familiar in her own skin at the end of the working day. She runs them directly after a session and at random through her waking life. It has to be a habit to work: if you only do it when you think you may be dreaming, you won't do it when you are dreaming but believe that you are not. It's easy enough to recognise the sleeping mind when you find yourself in flight after a champagne dinner with Claude Rains – although Neith does not often dream of flying, which bothers her because Freud insisted such dreams were about sex –

but much harder when the deviation is more subtle or more plausible: unknown and undefinable flavours of fruit, vanishingly small worlds stacked with coincidence to the point of inevitability, the power to read menus in other languages or arm-wrestle a man twice your mass. The dream state is wily, and it learns as you do.

She waits a while longer, until she has completely reassociated with her surroundings. There are approved exercises for this which involve visualising your awareness as an elastic dough and extending it into every extremity one by one. Neith finds them childish as well as somewhat ineffectual. Glancing at the poem one more time, she decides that she has done enough to be sure of her body and goes to make coffee, which is the unofficial punctuation of her rite. She walks to the galley kitchen, dials water from the hot tap. The sink tells her – as it always does – that the water is coming out at 96 degrees Celsius, a temperature that is ideal for making coffee but dangerous to human skin.

She queries the Witness, and finds that none of the interview technicians in the Hunter matter has ever attended a birth. For that matter, indeed, Hunter had no children. Neith sighs at this evidence of stubborn mendacity. In a few moments, the old woman will be transparent. In the absence of a strategic goal, it takes a particularly tragic sort of refusenik to hold out right down to the wire.

Lifting the coffee grounds to her nose, Neith inhales, and winces. She cannot afford the brand she really likes because it is frankly luxurious, so she buys the cheapest she can stand. It is counter-intuitively called Truth. On the packaging is a picture of the company's owner, a very handsome retired footballer from Benin. Benin coffee is usually very good, but Truth is not. She has been trying to acquire a taste for it, and while she still hates it, she now misses it as well when she can't get it. It is the worst of possible outcomes, one she hopes very much is temporary.

While the stuff brews, she makes toast and honey, as always bewildered and a little creeped out by the origin of the sweet comb. On the other hand, once you start down that road you won't be drinking milk, either, and then you might wonder about cheese, or wine, and if you're in that headspace then to be honest all food – meat or vegetable – takes on the alien tinge of life ingested, the spectre of uninvited growth inside the body. It's an old, old horror, that notion of something alive under one's own skin, something touching the interior surfaces of the body where only oneself should go; old – and discredited, because a human being is the sum of many parts, not excluding a great flora and fauna of microbiological co-corporealists necessary to the balance of guts and blood. No one is a single thing; everyone is a network, or a mosaic.

Speaking of which – and as above, so below – it's time to vote. Licking her fingers, she returns to the other room and puts her mug of bad coffee on a coaster to cool.

*

Every person under the System is encouraged – though not compelled – to spend a certain amount of time each week voting, and is semi-randomly assigned to decision-making bodies for the duration of their session. Each body will most likely be around two hundred individuals strong, and will deal either collectively or in subcommittee jury group with anything from asylum requests or the allocation of medical resources to commercial disputes. It is the most nuanced and democratic system of direct governance ever devised, and it requires genuine participation from the polity. For the body of the state to perform its function properly, each person must make his or her own decision in the light of their personal experience and opinion without being influenced by others at the formative stage, so sessions are initially private and remain anonymous throughout. Each problem is proposed to each person in a way that is fractionally different, tailored precisely to pique their interest and understanding, their self-interest and their altruism, so that every choice is made with the greatest awareness of consequence and meaning.

In cases where a person serving on the panel has particular, relevant knowledge or experience, verified expertise markers may be deployed to indicate locus to speak on the topic, although the weight given to these by other citizens is variable in line with perception. Non-voting experts can also be sought by quora to explain or give context. The whole gamut of responses is then averaged using an advanced Bayesian mathematics.

Certainly even the losing side in most judgements will acknowledge a fairness and balance to the outcome, and as verdicts need not invoke prescribed solutions but can, within certain limits, be creative, the result of litigation can often be profitable to both sides. The System is the will of the plebiscite, and the plebiscite genuinely reflects the people.

Neith, like other professional investigators, has to stretch to meet her suggested number of plebiscite hours. Sometimes she takes a few days off and binges. The score doesn't affect anything in your life except your self-esteem; the only person who looks accusingly at Neith when she doesn't hit her target is Neith – although the involvement of law enforcement professionals at an early stage in governance has been found to be beneficial in many ways, as they are inevitably the ones who must tidy up when the wrong choice leads to negative local realities.

Today, voting is making her fractionally impatient, so the System is reciprocally terse in its briefings, while at the same time emphasising gratitude for her time during a busy period. She will not be asked to participate in judgements likely to require lengthy debate or research. Instead, she is assigned to an immigration board, and rapidly rejects the entry of two shifty young men with chequered histories hailing from a country generally – and not unfairly – associated with organised crime. They are proposing a business venture with a cargo enterprise in Docklands, and Neith marks the firm for attention, too. A third applicant, superficially very much like the other two, she eventually endorses. She suspects he wants to get the hell out of his home city and make a new life, so she recommends several apprenticeship programmes, and receives a startled and somewhat joyous thank-you from his legal counsel.

Next assignment: four young women have been caught engaged in property destruction. Neith wants to know why. She briefly interviews all of them separately and together, permitted to take the lead by her co-franchisers after briefly dickering for the spot with a behavioural development specialist. The man yields gracefully and is assigned second chair, then asks questions that in Neith's retrospective analysis may actually have been more useful than her own. (She flags his name as a possible consultant in future cases touching his competence.) The youngsters are designated 'at risk/negative synergy' and separated, sent to different parts of the country under the New Start initiative.

Finally, there's a wrangle over intellectual property. There usually is, and this aspect takes up a disproportionate amount of voting time and triggers endless philosophical debates, but in the end the general will is that artists and makers should be able to function profitably within what remains a largely capitalist economic apparatus, which entails some form of ownership of their work. In this case, someone designed a game, someone else designed the story that frames it, now they are at odds. This one takes longer than the first two and is more annoying. It seems trivial, even petty. Smooth economic flow and creative justice, the System reminds her gently, are also inherent parts of functional plebiscite-regulated market democracy. She knuckles down. After another fifteen minutes, though, she's getting the sense that the dispute has nothing to do with money. She queries the backchannel data, runs a quick analysis and raises a tangent flag. The moderator brings her in.

'I'd like to propose that Complainant and Respondent make full disclosure of any personal feelings towards one another at this time.'

Which they do, and it transpires they are desperate to have sex. Possibly, Neith allows, they are in actual love. The business venture is a pretext which has recently become so successful that it is getting in the way. Neith considers tearing her hair out or imposing a fine, but decides in the end that acknowledgement of the importance of romance by the System is an identifiable good. The Inspector suggests to the committee that both parties be cautioned against allowing their personal business to become a matter of state, proposes a small business loan to hire additional staff, then recommends a hotel. The committee – not without, she suspects, some muffled sniggering at the vision of an anonymous but clearly high-ranking Witness officer having to deal with a sort of self-imposed Romeo-and-Juliet crisis – accepts these measures. The litigating lovebirds are sent off to sort themselves out.

The Inspector takes a moment to read her own press. This is not unhealthy or even vain, but an exercise in reflection. She needs to know how she is seen, because these assessments will affect her interactions with the wider public and in turn her own perception of those with whom she interacts. In general it seems that the polis approves of her selection for this task and anticipates a speedy resolution of the case. There is some suggestion that she may be too close to the Witness and that she should be assisted or overseen, and a vanishingly small percentage argue that an independent investigator or even a judge should have been retained. On the whole, though, it seems that she has the trust of her ultimate employers.

She reads through the week's general voter briefing: funding requests for different departments, project approvals, import and export quotas. Only one contentious issue is under consideration – the Monitoring Bill – and it is one on which Neith feels quite strongly. This robustness is something she has in common with the rest of the population, though not everyone's opinion is in line with hers. Democracy in action is very annoying.

Several months ago, taking into account the likely advances in technology over the next decade, the System posed the question of whether it was appropriate to install a permanent remote access in the skull of a recidivist or compulsive criminal. This has now culminated in a draft bill being put before the polity.

The points against permanent implanted monitoring are compelling: it is a considerable conceptual and legal step to go from external surveillance to the direct constant observation of the brain; it pre-empts a future crime rather than preventing crime in progress, and this involves an element of prejudging the subject; once deployed in this way the technology will inevitably spread to other uses, and the consequences of those should also be considered; and finally and most significantly, such a device entails the possibility of real-time correction of recidivist brain function, and this being arguably a form of mind control is ethically repellent to many. There is an instinctual argument, with respectable intellectual backing, that the System and the Witness should monitor the external world only, and the boundary of the body should be respected until there is a specific reason to do otherwise – as in a non-consensual interview – and even then such interference should be as brief as possible, and proportionate.

On the other hand, the technology has the potential to allow those with, for example, certain forms of severe mental illness to re-enter society in the certain knowledge that they will not hurt anyone, which could be immensely therapeutic.

There is a moral dimension, too, which the Inspector finds compelling. As a matter of societal identity, the System is supposed to provide the best combination of personal security and personal freedom, and there is an argument that this achieves that by allowing the constitutionally violent access to the world without compromising the safety of the majority.

Overall, sensible liberal opinion favours a compromise: a starkly limited programme in which the technology is used voluntarily, in combination with robust technical and legal safeguards against inappropriate pseudo-medical alteration of the subject's thinking. The Inspector mistrusts the idea in concept, but respects the medical use-case. In the end, she also suspects that general adoption of implant technology of some sort is a societal and commercial inevitability. The advantages of having permanent access to the System are many, and public morality follows the trend of public desire. Still, due scrutiny is healthy.

She registers her position – firmly against widespread use but in favour of a medical test programme – and signs off. Full polling will take a week or more, and votes can be changed until the deadline to allow for evolutions in personal perspective during the ongoing debate, but presently it seems she is in the majority, with low level support for the absolute negative position and perhaps one third of those who have already expressed an opinion being in favour of full deployment without restriction.

There, that's done. Her private obligation to the nation is discharged, leaving only her professional one to go. She looks at the time, and tuts: democracy can be long-winded. If she doesn't hurry, she will be late for Hunter's corpse.

*

The Inspector, arriving for her appointment a little while later, stares down at Hunter's body, and carefully does not impute to it any kind of agency. Corpses are natural and inevitable citizens of the uncanny

29

valley, the place where what is not alive too closely follows the pattern of what is. The body is not lying there, it has been laid out. The eyes do not stare, the hands do not grasp. This thing is no longer a thing which acts. A corpse is not haunted or residually inhabited save by the implications of the living. All the same, it once was alive, and in its inertness is a kind of malediction, or prophecy.

Neith glances around: she is not fond of hospitals. The implication of accident, of sickness derived from random chance, does not sit well with her. Still less does she like these refrigerated basement rooms for the victims of untimely death. However fine the modern design of the building, every occupied tray here must count as a failure of the System to protect and secure.

She hears footsteps and turns. She has met the coroner before but can never remember her name without checking and is worried that it's starting to seem rude. She rummages inside her own head, wondering whether her memory is adversely affected by prolonged exposure to recorded other minds. Medical opinion is vague and experimentation is not recommended.

The coroner arrives. Neith realises she has at some point toggled off the Witness's personal telemetry, so the woman's name is not being displayed. No matter, she knows it. Lisa? Lucy? Lara? Trisa. Trisa, from St Albans, paternal grandmother born in Okinawa, mother once sang solo at the Albert Hall. Likes dancing but not alone, doesn't drink, plays piano. Trisa Hinde. Hinde wears a badge with a rainbow on it. A few decades ago this would have meant something about her sexual orientation, but now it's a polite signal to Neith and anyone else Hinde interacts with that she is not neurotypical. Her brain touches a particular peak of the modern medical taxonomy that includes some autisms and various perceptual and processing functions such as synaesthesia, and structural (rather than acquired) hypervigilance. It is not actually a spectrum in the linear sense, more a graph on several axes. In Hinde's case it means that she has a superb set of tools for the consideration, recall and analysis of her sense data – making her an excellent medical examiner – but she has no mind's eye in which to conjure counterfactuals or even remembered scenes, and dislikes having to reach for what is implicit in the way others cringe at emery boards or biting into a block of ice. That disparity of experience is one reason she likes dancing: her understanding of social and sexual cues inherent in physical activity is aligned with everyone else's and infinitely less annoying than having to make everyone else explain their subtext.

When Hinde is not dancing, the badge alerts people to the context of their interaction. This is not mandated or even recommended by the System. It's just an outgrowth of everyone being able to query things about one another through a data connection: rather than make people go through the business of getting offended and then doing a search on her, and then being embarrassed for not realising or remembering that her consciousness is a bit different from theirs, Hinde chooses – as many or most people in her situation now do – to identify her status in advance. There are many advantages to the end of privacy, and one of them is the obsolescence of social awkwardness. The Inspector finds this outcome both efficient and laudable.

'Exhaustion,' Hinde says shortly. 'The proximate cause is stroke, but the body was worn out, as if she'd been running for days. I mean running to the point of crisis, not jogging. The brain most especially.' She pauses for a moment.

The Inspector returns to the corpse. Indicating the head with a diffuse gesture, she asks: 'No tumours, then?' She had entertained a brief hope for a gross physical cause. An abnormal brain might account for that unwelcome clarity in Hunter's mind, the uncomfortable sureness of her recorded inner voice. It might also hamper the interrogation – might have made it impossible for the woman herself to facilitate it, might indeed have bent her mood and made her irrationally hostile to the very idea – and could also have killed her under stress. A neat solution, but Hinde is already shaking her head.

'And no lesions?'

'No.'

'A medical error,' Neith supposes.

Hinde doesn't respond straight away because this is only implicitly a question. Her face takes on an uncomfortable look as she tries to work out how to respond. Neith, embarrassed to approximately the same degree that she would be if she had loudly broken wind, changes her wording. 'Was it an accident? Malpractice?'

'Could have been. Could have been deliberate. She died because she was overtaxed for a prolonged period. Was that scientifically knowable? Yes. Was it culpably so? Unclear. I gather they were in new territory. Perhaps they shouldn't have been. It's possible that she went from nominal to flatline very fast. It can happen that way. Did they take steps to measure her risk? Was that risk proportional to the need? Or, theoretically, was it intended that she not survive? Those are interesting – but not medical – questions.' Hinde shrugs: therefore not her problem. Then she glances between the corpse and the Inspector.

'She looks like you,' Hinde observes.

The Inspector considers the woman on the table, thirty years her senior, dark brown skin fading around wrinkles, and very clearly deceased. Hinde has put her back together with great sympathy, but the evidence of keyhole neurosurgery and various stents, shunts and insertions is not erased. The coroner's own investigations are concealed for the most part by a modest green blanket. Still, there might be something there. Same hairline, perhaps, but different hair. Generous mouths but differently quirked – or rather, Hunter's mouth is quirked, suggesting that she smiled often and the dead muscles are tugging her lips even now into the posture most often adopted in life.

'Not much in the face,' Hinde says, following the line of her gaze. 'Body shape. Skeletal structure. Rib curvature and disposition of the hips.' She pauses. 'Perhaps it's not obvious from outside.'

Neith agrees that it isn't, and changes the subject. 'If you had been in charge of the procedure,' she proposes, 'what steps would you have taken to avoid this outcome?'

Hinde peers at her. 'I'm a coroner,' she says, as if talking to a child. 'By the time I receive a patient, this outcome is a given.'

They stand across the body, mutually perplexed.

*

It does not require a sophisticated analysis of those first thoughts on the recording to recognise that Diana Hunter was opposed to the Witness, and indeed to the society that hinges upon it. The philosophical argument

32

the System advances in its own favour – safety and empowerment in exchange for total personal transparency – did not persuade her. Quite apparently, she saw an irreducible virtue in the right to be unobserved. Such people exist, of course, and even choose to remain in the United Kingdom under the System, citing whatever exigencies they feel tie them to the place. For the most part they are unproblematic. They protest, they vote, and they create these small local networks, which inevitably leak information from every angle and keep no secrets of any concern. The true refusenik problem – the use of analogue and concealed methods of imparting information between motivated paramilitaries – is quite another thing, and almost unheard of.

The Inspector considers. For now, her task is to know the woman. Who was Diana Hunter? If you had asked her that question, what would she have said?

I am a woman in the prime of life, yes, and the rest, which had the feel of a quotation, but perhaps true all the same. What else?

But before all that – before whatever is contained in the record of the interrogation which ended in her death – Diana Hunter lived. She ate, she drank, she slept. She knew people and every day she woke to the same view, whether it was a good one or not. She had habits and dislikes and a history, and all these things made her what she was.

Neith clips a roaming data connection to her glasses so that she won't miss anything important, then goes down the stairs to the street.

*

London in winter, so overexposed as to be almost monochrome. Neith walks into a perfect blindness, searing light reflected on frost, in window glass, and the pearlescent paint of cars. The sun is so low that it seems to shine horizontally along Piccadilly, making the street into a tunnel of white. Commuters stripped of their faces, their clothes thick with strange retinal artefacts as her pupils contract to their minimum dilation, flow past her in endless anonymous succession, competing for walking space with tourists seemingly no more tangible than the pattern of waves scudding across a river bottom. She looks back along her route, and sees a shining avenue

33

slashed with impenetrable lines of darkness, a throng of golden statues walking. Then she turns a corner into shadow and as her vision adjusts, revealing a violent surge of colour and detail: red leaves and blue sky, grey stone and green paint, human visages in various states of animated discourse or silent contemplation. Rickshaws, these days driven remotely by some taxi company's mainframe, dither by the side of the road as they wait for a fare. The newer ones have rain canopies that can extend all the way over to protect passengers from London's modern flash flooding. As always, they remind her of a school of nervous fish feeding on a reef.

The Inspector glances up again at the city's new architecture, the steel spirals and glass spires of Lubetkin and his followers made plausible by modern construction techniques, rises out of the red brick neo-Gothic arcades, a dream future emerging from a coal and furnace past.

She waits for one of the new trams, and heads south.

*

London has very few bad areas left, but the house she is looking for is on the border of one of them: an ugly valley of brutalist estate buildings stained like decaying molars and arranged around central courtyards only ever destined to be battlefields. The overarching problem with them is not, to Neith's eye, how they were laid out, but what they were intended to do: they are boxes for the storage of surplus persons. The message of uselessness in the stones is not hard to unpack, and the inhabitants read it as soon as they saw where they were put. From there, the project ground itself down into a slurry of low expectations and simmering rage. The old century produced a lot of these slow-cooking anger farms, and the heat they have built up is soaked into the earth and the people so deep that even the System cannot immediately take it away. Detractors – like the subject of this present investigation – point to this as evidence that the System is not all it's cracked up to be, but Neith can read history too, and would like them to name a society that has done as well with what it inherited from the past. Certainly the remedy is not the previous, nominally representative iterations of democracy, which spawned this mess in the first place.

The house stands over the valley but looks away from it. The Inspector steps down on to the pavement and watches the tram disappear. Wayward instinct prompts her for a moment to run after it, to get back on board and take the journey to the end. A moving tram is a bubble in space, profoundly separated from everything else. Time passes inside at a fractionally different rate, and no physical interaction is possible between passengers and people on the outside. A line of tram tracks is the intrusion into everyday space of another physical realm – albeit one so comfortably mundane that few people realise what they are seeing. Terminus stations, like airports, are the junction, the place where a temporary reality fades into the continuing consensus one – as well as being where the rails run out – so they are transitional to the power of two: liminally liminal. In such an enfolded location, surely, there must be clues to almost any mystery, spat out on to the littoral plain of human passage.

Neith snorts, recognising the wayward flowstate – the dialogue between fugue and logic which is part of her professional armament.

She looks around, orients herself to the cameras on the facades and street lights, looks for blind spots – created or unanticipated – looks for the places she would sit if she were a child playing hide and seek, for the low wall where teen girls judge competitions of young male bravado. She looks for fast food wrappers and plastic bottles, for cigarette butts and needles and discarded phones, for anything that tells a story. It won't be the story she wants, but all stories touch somewhere. All stories are one story, in the end.

She feels a flicker of attention. Her eyes skitter across the landscape, chasing something almost certainly inside her head. What has her subconscious picked up on, in that brief reverie, that is trying to elbow its way into her thoughts? (Speed limit sign. Newsagent. Community centre, run down and covered in graffiti tags. Rubbish bin, overfull.) Investigation is a webwork rather than a line. A crowd rather than a single individual. (Parked cars. Parked bikes. Vandalised public access terminal. Blood on the pavement: a nosebleed, a fist fight, certainly nothing serious.) What thread is she looking at that, viewed from another angle, might be a net? And a net to do what? To catch whom?

She wanders to and fro, picking and turning over like a well-dressed rag lady. She wonders if Hunter did this. She was aware of her environment. She cared about it. She was the centre of something here, so yes, she must have. She walked these paving stones, saw these things: Hunter, who wrote angry letters and disliked the spontaneous nighttime gatherings of bored local youth on the benches opposite her house. The same Hunter who loaned those same disaffected kids books and probably made them meals. Is that a contradiction? Or a deception? Or is it just people? People are inconstant.

A solitary walker with a dog peers at her, then snaps a photograph and posts it, tagging it with a query about suspicious activity at their location. The Witness immediately sends a message to say she has been photographed, and responds to his concern with thanks and a brief explanation. Modern rates of clinical paranoia have decreased significantly from pre-System levels. It transpires that many instances of the condition used to result from a horror of personal smallness; a deep, almost existential fear that the pattern of a given life had no meaning against the tide and chatter of the majority, or the vast indifference of the universe beyond. But part of what is remarkable about the System is that no one is insignificant to it. Every action; every choice, worry, question; every bold or idiotic inspiration can be acknowledged by the tranquil and endless machine. There is no silence into which the lonely fall. The System is quite genuinely interested in everyone.

The dog-walker receives his response and nods his appreciation to her. He's handsome, in a weathered way. She marks the message for later consideration. It would not be inappropriate to ask him out for a drink, if he's single. A conscientious fellow with good shoulders and a well-trained dog. So far, so compatible. She tells the machine to run a background check to be sure he's not a plant. After a moment of hesitation, she instructs it to sequester the results. If he is not actually dangerous, she chooses not to pry. It hinders conversation, later, if she already knows everything about her date.

The man turns away, following his hound.

Neith likewise turns, and realises she is at the door of the house. She sees the street reflected in a window and feels a moment of consequence, the hint of a Rubicon. She reaches for it, but the inspiration, whatever it is, has gone back down into the sea of her thoughts. She pictures it tumbling away: a great fish returning to the deep.

She considers the place.

Diana Hunter lived at the end of a terrace, in a stucco townhouse which might at one stage have abutted several others of its type, but which now stands alone in a scrub garden. It observes an almost pointed distance from the other buildings in the street, so that the Inspector can imagine the ground floor lifting its crinolines and turning away from the importunate social climbing of the twenty-first-century developments. It is the last house, and beyond the scrub, the gentle slope of the hill becomes more vertiginous until a retaining wall with a chickenwire fence drops away to a disused railway line, and beyond that, the valley of the teeth.

It is not entirely uninviting. Hunter has painted it with a quirky combination of faded colours, either in deliberate subversion of its imperial mood or because she could only get so much of each one. The result is a friendly bohemian muddle like a giant jigsaw which the visitor will be invited to put together. The door is thick and wooden, a proper door for a proper house. If Neith has one quarrel with the age in which she lives, it is the fascination with laminate and plastic over the resinous, organic solidity of wood. Doors should be a part of the home that speaks of life rather than engineering. This one does, emphatically, and the front steps are well worn. There was a flow of commerce here, even recently. Diana Hunter received and trafficked.

Upon closer scrutiny there is a line of dust and scratches on the step, a mark where the door has frequently been propped open as if to admit a crowd. Village halls have such marks, not homes. And what sort of hall is outside the village? The disreputable sort? Was Hunter running a brothel here? No. That's not the sort of thing the Witness could miss. What else gets pushed to the margins? These days, perhaps a therapist. A police station, she realises. Or a witch's house might sit this way, on the fringes and yet accessible to those with need. A wise woman's house.

The good door opens in silence. Neith half expected it to creak, but the hinges are freshly oiled and the door itself is hung with an admirable precision. She adjusts her sense of the late owner. An eccentric, perhaps, and certainly a grumpy neighbour, but also an organised, even painstaking person in areas that attracted her interest.

The Inspector realises she's still standing on the doorstep.

And then, three steps inside, she stops and stands very still. She has an eerie feeling of homecoming.

*

There's no single thing that makes the place so unsettlingly familiar. It's not the worn green carpet which smells of age or the unfashionable darkness, the high ceilings and ornate cornicing pale over brinjal walls; it's not the amiable clutter which she supposes is what art looks like if you don't put it in a case. All these things, in fact, should make Hunter's home feel close and a little spooky, but it somehow escapes that, as if the combination of anti-minimalism and shadow has created a temple here to a lost chthonic concept of interior design. The sense of homesickness is vertiginous and overwhelming. This is where she belongs, in this hallway with its many books along one wall, the Arts and Crafts silver teapot on a table in the corner by the umbrella stand. She wonders what to call the feeling and thinks: Fernweh. It's German – the longing to be somewhere one has never been, the grief one feels at the absence of persons yet unmet.

She shakes her head – too much poetry in the flowstate – and looks around, anchoring herself in the job.

The hallway is washed in the smell of library: melancholy scholarship, paper and dust mites. There's no trace of the shut-in old lady smell, the powder and outmoded perfume. Instead, there's a hint of beeswax from the furniture, damp oil paint and turpentine, but above all the autodidact scent of knowledge. It is almost too much, too self-conscious, like a stage set built to house Leonardo da Vinci or Albert Einstein. *This person is bookish.* Neith glances down a hallway and sees, yes, more books. The Inspector reaches to her terminal to call up the plan of the house from her files, then remembers that it won't work, that Hunter cut this place out of the grid with a deliberate hand. She tries anyway, but the isolation is effective. She looks at the walls, wondering where the cage is – where, beneath the plaster, are the struts that catch the carrier signal. She shuts her eyes and remembers the shape: the corridor leads to a guest bathroom full of junk – although she wonders at that judgement now, wonders whether anything here is truly 'junk'. What might the cursory eye of a young Witness constable miss, in a pile of Hunter's uncatalogued belongings? A Titian, perhaps, stacked against a glass box full of sailors' knots.

Neith wanders down the corridor, touching the spines. She reaches the end: a plaster bust of Shakespeare, slightly chipped, rests in an alcove. She looks down, and finds, with a sense of impish certainty, Hunter's own works arranged in a neat line. She scans the titles, letting her subconscious mind choose which ones to dip into from the throng: *The Talking Knot, Mr Murder Investigates, The Mad Cartographer's Garden, Five Cardinals of Z* and the last one, *Quaerendo Invenietis*. The Inspector makes a mental note that the contents of the house must be considered financially valuable and protected accordingly. She lifts her choices out of the shelf, *Quaerendo* on the top, and cradles them awkwardly against her chest with one arm.

She takes a moment to peer at the bust. The chip is on the ear, the damage done a long time ago, and the repair is excellent but unconcealed. She looks around again, realising that many things here are cracked or broken and subsequently remade. Windows, mirrors, floorboards and skirting boards. The spines of books. Perhaps it's how Hunter was able to afford them: things discarded by a nation in love with the new and the glossy, and above all with things that can tell their own stories by digital report rather than by their scars. Hunter is content to infer the past from cracked glazes, from missing bronze feet and replaced glass. She is content to repair and reuse.

Was, the Inspector reminds herself. Hunter *was* content.

*

Leaning against the wall, the Inspector pauses to examine her prize. The cover of *Quaerendo Invenietis* features a golden splash that she first takes to be a bird, possibly an eagle or a condor, spread across a vivid red background. Unusually, there is no cover text, but presumably a book printed in a starkly limited edition is already known to those who wish to purchase it. Under closer scrutiny, the condor design is revealed to be not a bird but a necklace or kirtle in a pattern which evokes a tentative connection with South America. Her mind wants to call it an axolotl, but knows that that is something else. A cluster of names gleaned from childhood museum visits jostle in her head: Quetzalcoatl, Tlaloc. She went with her uncle, a scholar. Mazatec? No. Simpler. Quirkier. If she had a connection in here she would already know. Hunter must have lived at one remove after building the Faraday cage, a cognitive shift to an older way of being. She would have come adrift from society to some extent, merely by that choice, just as someone who never travels has a different lived experience from one who spends weekends in Barcelona. How profound was that separation? Enough that Hunter could begin to hate the country around her? Was there something in the arrest, after all?

The Inspector opens the book and finds a blank page. She tuts at this unlikely misfortune, and tries again, finding another and another, and then realises as she riffles through that this is a publisher's blank, a proof without any text at all. Annoying. She opens the others one by one, and realises that they are the same. She feels a puff of air and wonders wryly if the spectre of Diana Hunter is sniggering at her. She puts the blanks down and looks along the shelves for less deceptive editions.

She is still looking when she feels a second puff of air, stronger and more definite. If the house were less well maintained, she might put it down to a gust of wind outside. If she were in one of the proper rooms she might not have felt it at all. But to her, here in the corridor, that brief pressure is distinctive: the compression as a door somewhere is opened and closed. Except that this is a crime scene secured by the Witness, and she is the investigating officer. There should be no one here without her direct permission.

If this were almost any other house she could check the local footage reel for the last few hours and see whether anyone has even approached the place. She considers going out into the street and doing exactly that, but if she does and there is something here that someone wants, or wants her not to have, she will have lost it. Likewise if she summons backup.

She could try opening a window and leaning out. Her mind pictures this undignified and tactically disadvantageous solution and she rejects it.

Instead, she unwinds her scarf and discards it on the ground. No one trained at Hoxton would ever enter an arena of possible physical combat wearing a noose. Stepping on to the outside front of each shoe and curling the foot down on to the carpet, she moves in almost perfect silence across the corridor to the kitchen, then stops. Another puff of air. She can feel floorboards giving under the green carpet, knows that sooner or later she must come to one that creaks.

The kitchen is separated from the hallway by a bead curtain, strands of copper-coloured yarn knotted around a jumble of tiny bric-a-brac fragments: washers, curtain rings and bits of valve. She touches it. Cool and heavy. She will not be able to pass through the curtain without making a noise, so she doesn't try. It's empty, anyway. She drops her shoulders, listening, but does not close her eyes. It is a delusion of those unaccustomed to using their senses that the focus of one requires the abdication of another. In fact, the senses are complementary, each feeding the rest. It's harder to hear someone if you cannot see their lips, harder to tell the difference between coldness and wetness if you cannot use your nose.

Away to her right, on this floor, she hears something. It is a noise with no shape, no name – but it is something, and she holds on to it as she lets the breath go out of her open mouth. If you hold your breath, you only hear your heart. There. Again. There is a place in her sense of sound where she can catch it. If she lets go, the bland baseline of a house in the city takes it away.

Mielikki Neith can stand still for hours. She does not get bored; her mind does not wander. She does not count seconds or wonder what will happen next. She pays attention, taking in whatever is there to be known, whatever is changing, and finds that enough. It is a trick she has learned, the projection of a quiet into which other people feel the urge to speak.

The kitchen window is open, which it should not be: a horizontal slash of glass propped up with an offcut piece of ply, the gap large enough for a thin man. For a thin woman. For a child. Perhaps that's what this is? An enterprising local thief with terrible timing, or lovers on a dare: enter the deadhouse, get properly scared, get naked on the carpet.

Picking her way softly along the hall to the main stairs for a better place to listen, it occurs to her that the layout of the house is intended to create obstacles and obscurities. Every line of sight is occupied by an object that invites contemplation. Even now, positing a dangerous intruder, Neith finds the allure of the place distracting. The picture on the wall is positioned just so; the warmth of the oil paint gleams and invites the eye. Looking away, one finds a clutch of glossy coffee table books depicting the same tints and shadows – explanations and histories of the work. One might chase one's tail in here for weeks, and come out wiser, and that is the intent. Neith finds it increasingly hard to believe that the woman who created this space would be revealed if she wanted to be invisible.

The faintest creak from the living room. Not a cough or a cry or the sound of a boot. And yet Neith is on her feet and ready, because that was for the first time the sound of human movement, intentional and perhaps furtive. She waits. The doorway is empty. The noise does not repeat.

Neith is armed: in a clip holster at her back there is a powerful taser. Inspectors do not generally carry lethal weapons as a matter of course, and in any case a gun is a terrible close-quarters weapon. At distances under fifteen feet – and most encounters in British housing will take place at such distances – they are too slow, and a bullet fired from even a low-powered gun at that range will continue through the target and hit other things such as bystanders and gas pipes. The taser is a compromise, but hardly a very good one because it only fires twice and has limited penetration. For backup she has a telescoping baton, a mean little thing halfway between a cudgel and a whip. Of course, if she seriously believes she is in physical danger, she should go out immediately into the open air, into the connected space of the Witness, and order assistance.

But if she does that, she may lose the opportunity to talk to someone who is shy of confiding, and in this unusual environment she cannot know who that person is without confronting them. No doubt, given Hunter's way of being in the world, there are ways of entering and leaving this house that are discreet.

Then, too, if she calls for the cavalry and it turns out the house is infested with a mournful prepubescent looking for a library book by which to remember her teacher, it will look brutish. Bad enough for the Witness to make a mistake and cause a death, but to terrify a primary school child in the course of seeking justification for that death ... no.

She is police and she is the System. She takes a calculated risk.

More beads, more curtains. Two layers this time, *click-clack*, the same magpie mixture of materials. A thimble, a bit of Lego, a button. The thread goes through, the thread goes around. She strokes the hanging strands, lets them clatter softly. Steps back and waits.

Is conscious of someone else waiting, with the same certainty of their own patience. Has already decided to go forwards, does not read this as an assassination. Protocol puts the decision in her hands.

She goes in.

Dim. Her eyes adjust slowly. Books and more books. Another door off to one side, another bead curtain. Hunter must have bought a job lot, but no, of course: the children make them. Play group. Indoctrination? Hardly. Just a very old, very simple training, motor skills and focus, quiet in the afternoons.

Peacock feathers on the walls (meaning: the Evil Eye. A superstition of malign surveillance. A joke? Or an unconscious choice?) and more statuary. Now she's seeing eyes everywhere: bronzes with empty sockets glare at her, dolls gleam glassily. Carved masks wait for someone to put them on. In a glass jar, a preserved plant specimen labelled WHITE BANEBERRY with a little poison symbol – more eyes: round white fruit with black circles for pupils, growing on red stalks. Bar none, the most alarming vegetation she has ever seen, like something from a nightmare about organ farms.

And behind the jar: a man. Or a woman. Who looks at her and says: 'Ah. Inspector. Do sit down, won't you?'

*

The Inspector does not sit. 'How did you get in?' she demands instead.

'I'm Lönnrot,' the other says, face still bloated by the curve of the jar so that it resembles the underside of a stingray. Neith struggles with the name, struggles grasping for an understanding of the sound as text. 'Learn rote'. Or 'wrote'. Not an English sound.

Evidently the disconnection shows, because Lönnrot sighs and tries again. 'You must be Inspector Neith. No?'

'This is a sealed building,' the Inspector replies. 'How did you get in?'

'Perhaps I have a key.'

'Perhaps you don't.'

'Well, then, perhaps I can' — a too-broad smile — 'walk through walls.' One hand waves away boredom. 'Regno Lönnrot. I grant you it's a somewhat portentous name, but that is hardly my fault. One might translate it as "the kingdom of the Red Maple". A very small demesne, alas, restricted entirely to myself. Please do relax, Inspector. The maple plant is harmless — unless one is a horse. Have you found her diaries?' There's a strange smell, burning and bitter — a black cigarette in the ashtray: actual tobacco. Questionable legality: this is a private house — but not, of course, Lönnrot's house. Burglary, with aggravated smoking?

The Inspector moves, very slowly bringing the other into view. She stares — or rather, as an agent of the Witness whose closed evidentiary scene has been violated by an unsanctioned person, she observes and glowers. She cannot tell absolutely if this person is male or female. Possibly there is no perfect answer. Lönnrot is lean and elegant, with beautiful hands, the fingers narrow and presently steepled. The expression on the androgynous face is quizzical. It might be wryly appreciative, or perhaps mocking. Lönnrot wears black clothes: a black crew neck, black jacket. Black trousers. Black boots with Cuban heels. Black hair, too-white skin. Something suggestive of surgery or disease. Shoulders quite square, but slender. A pop idol, now retired; a would-be vampire; a club owner. A sociopath. A method actor. A classic Warhol image come to life. Attributions skitter across the pale face, slip away. No frame. And no data connection, because the house is a Faraday cage. For the first time in her adult life, the Inspector has no idea who she's talking to.

'Diaries?' she repeats.

Lönnrot nods. 'Diaries, journals, jottings. Moleskine notebooks written in green ink. Marginalia in a copy of *Catcher in the Rye*. Joseph

Stalin, you know, was a frantic marginalist. His annotated Nechaev is historically revealing and shamefully ignored by scholars. Yes, her diaries. Her thoughts. Those writings which, taken together, might show the compass of her mind. Do you know where they are?'

'Do you?'

'I should very much like to. And you should very much wish to bring them to me.'

'Why would I do that?'

Wide dark eyes look directly at her in innocent concern. 'Oh, because they are dangerous, dear Inspector. Dangerous in the extreme to everything you— Mm. Well, leave us say they are dangerous, and that is all. But I can make that danger go away. I'm something of a fan, you see. The Cartier Smash and Grab arrests. Wonderful work. Shame about the Waxman, of course, but art is defined by its flaws.' Lönnrot pauses. Long fingers reach out, adjust a picture frame on the mantle: a crude wooden square housing an image of a studiously attractive woman in twentieth-century glasses, standing proudly before a huge stack of something that might be multiperf computer printout.

'Do you know,' Lönnrot murmurs, 'for simply years, I believed devoutly that she also played the Wicked Witch? And now here she is in this house, looking at me from her frame. Or am I looking at her from mine?'

I can see my mind on the screen.

'Dangerous how?' Neith asks.

The disturbing smoothness of Lönnrot's brow puckers, and the Inspector realises this is what passes for a frown. 'I am not sure. I was going to say "to everything you love". Forgive my imprecision. To be exact might precipitate the very crisis that I most wish to avoid, before I understand its resolution – so: let us settle instead upon "dangerous" and have done. One wouldn't want to be maudlin: it's graceless. I notice you did not answer my question.'

'No,' she agrees, 'I didn't.'

Lönnrot nods dry acknowledgement at this deflection. The Inspector brushes her hand across her face, takes a manual photograph with her glasses: Lönnrot, and the wood-framed image. This person, this object, these fingerprints. This location. This moment. A chain of evidence connecting the unrecorded outlaw space with the world where things are properly documented. It had not occurred to her how unsettling it would be to encounter someone beyond the gaze of the Witness. It's like being in free fall: the cardinal directions are missing.

The white smile broadens. 'Really, you are too splendid,' Lönnrot says. 'Should I turn and give you my better side?' Instead, the long body folds into a high-backed mahogany chair, pale fingers draped over the faces of Dionysus carved at the ends of the arms.

Neith shrugs, and sits opposite, across a matching table. 'What do you know about Diana Hunter?'

'She was clear-eyed and undeluded. She was a deep thinker, not least upon her own mistakes. She was a contrarian. Even in death, as the saying goes, her head sings upon the waters. She was private and she was old. I'm very concerned that she may prove problematic. On the other hand, she may be a friend I haven't met yet. Although one so often feels that way about authors whose work one admires. Do you like to read, Inspector?'

'No. Was it you who denounced her?'

'I love to read. Most especially, I love low criminal romances. The human condition is most accurately chronicled in pulp, I think. The ugly and ordinary lusts, the contradictory drives, are all ignored by more self-consciously poetic writers striving to peel away the dross to reveal the inner person who of course exists only as the sum of the dross. For example, I have considered the form of assassination in literature very closely. In essence, I believe, the assassin is your counterpart – the murder detective in reverse. You are brought into contact with a crime only when it is already committed, as you are today. By examination of the body; of the person now dead; of their environment and habits; and of all of the physical evidence and the more or less obvious motives, you reveal the face of the killer and bring down justice. Crime, investigation, consequence. The assassin, by contrast, is contracted to the kill. The consequence is already agreed to be payment and death. The assassin then spends time learning the environment and habits of the target, and – already knowing intimately the layout of the organs in the body, the effects of toxins and punctures, crushings and suffocations – strikes, and departs. Contract, preparation, crime. The death stands as a mirror or a fulcrum between killer and investigator, but they are in essence engaged upon the same journey, their mutual roles contingent entirely upon the direction of travel. If time flows one way, the detective removes the knife from the corpse. If the other, it is she who brings the knife to the inert victim and performs the stabbing as an act of bloody resurrection which must subsequently be made good by the assassin in a violent and secret ambush from which the target walks away completely healthy. Tell me honestly, do you agree?'

The Inspector lets her quiet announce that Lönnrot owes her an answer.

The elegant neck bends in acknowledgement. 'Very well: no, I did not denounce her. That is perhaps what you would do, but it is contrary to my mode. Have you yet come across the Fire Judges?'

'If you're going to ask me to a concert, I hope you handle rejection well.'

It sounded right in her head, the irreverent gumshoe swatting down mystical pomposity. It's very much in the nature of their encounter, but Lönnrot takes exception. Thin lips twitch in offended virtue. Hairless lips. A woman? Or a man who pays great attention to his shaving mirror? Electrolysis? Alopecia? The dark spikes could be a wig. They could be implanted. She wants to touch them and find out – professionally: the idea of sexual contact with Lönnrot feels transgressive, not grotesque or unpleasant but utterly foreign, like making love to a bookcase. Uncanny valley: the place where simulation is too close to reality to be comfortable, but too far away to be mistakable. She wonders if the whole face is prosthetic, and what might be underneath.

Lönnrot looks past her and addresses the air, as if from a pulpit. Evidently imaginary parishioners, whatever their unknown short-comings, are preferable to investigators who make coarse jokes. 'The Fire Judges, in medieval tradition, are the five men and women living on earth whose task is to reveal – literally to *de-crypt* – the mysterious choices of God. To unhide and demystify the divine. Like Orpheus or Prometheus, they are the gateway to the heavenly city, the spinal conduit between the mundane world and the divine one. Together, they are the place where the shadow on the wall may for an instant touch the hand of the person casting it. Or perhaps it is the other way around. Perhaps the assassin is sacred and the detective is profane.' Another censorious glower. 'So much depends on your angle of view.'

Having no idea what to say to this, and worried that discussions of religion in the broader context of murder and its underlying significance tend to the direction of dangerous madness, the Inspector waits a calming moment, then reopens negotiations.

'But you don't know Hunter.'

The white frown relents. 'Now that I look at her house, I'm not sure anyone really does. Would you like a drink?'

Lönnrot, indeed, has poured a drink during that brief huff: a whisky without water or ice. The long fingers wrap around it, enjoying the cut glass as they did the carving on the chair. Finding a chip and stroking it. The languorous eyes meet hers, repeating the question. A private eye would say yes; an officer of the Witness should say 'not on duty'.

Neith says: 'Hunter's going to be angry if we drink all her Scotch.' A better attempt at Chandler dialogue, that odd flirtatious mixture of bravado and complicity. She wonders if Lönnrot will remind her that the dead don't care about Scotch.

Instead, simply: 'I thought so.' The bottle slides towards her across polished wood.

The Inspector pours herself a decent measure. She doesn't have to swallow any of it. It's a prop, just as it is for Lönnrot. She holds it up, inhales. Lönnrot looks happy again, that approving quirk that never gets past the cheeks. 'As to my mode – you understand what I mean by the expression? Yes, I thought so. Very well: you are concerned that I am your nemesis in this matter. In fact, I am not a villain. I believe that in the end, you and I will find ourselves on the same side.'

'The same side of what?'

'The case, of course. Perhaps everything else, as well.'

'Your interest being?'

'In everything?'

'In the case.'

'Oh, well. There is a group of people with whom I was recently commissioned to conduct some business. It is a personal matter – a debt to be repaid.'

'They call themselves the Fire Judges?'

'Alas, in that connection you were quite right. The Fire Judges play an hour set at the Duke of Denver by the river on odd nights. New wave classical fusion. I feel you would enjoy it. No, I'm looking for someone quite different.' She wonders whether that means yes. Since you were so unconscionably rude, the thin smile tells her, you can fish for it.

'And when you do find them, these people?'

'Client privilege, I'm afraid. Let us say that while on the one hand I have the greatest respect for their work, I am concerned as to its aim. Directionality, once more. Their disposition must determine my response.' Fire Judges. Normally she would gloss the word in her glasses, compare secondary meanings with context. Not in Hunter's Faraday cage. Later. She imagines herself sitting at her desk, running the search, so that she will remember to do it.

The whisky smells wonderful. She drinks. Foolish. But if Lönnrot has poisoned her, it's the most otiose criminal assault she can imagine.

'Was Diana Hunter one of those people?'

'That is more complicated. I believe that ultimately – and given that she's dead, that rather overused expression has acquired its true significance – ultimately she was not.'

'But connected to them.'

'Indeed.'

'And connected to you.'

'Simply everyone is connected these days, don't you find? Even someone like Ms Hunter. Inspector, I am worried for you. I find myself torn. I fear this case may take you to places where you will not be safe.'

'How chivalrous.'

'Call it professional courtesy.'

'Because you're a detective.'

'Or an artful dodger? Forgive me. I am just like you. Or, I suppose, not quite. You are explicit in the society in which you live. I am rather implied.' Long fingers stroke the cigarette. 'Where there is a detective, there is a magnifying glass. Where there is a musician, there must also be a lyre.'

For a moment, she hears 'liar'.

'So who are you working for?'

A sigh – directed, she thinks, at her doggedly linear curiosity.

'At a certain point, Inspector, you are going to ask yourself a certain question. It is a long question. Not a question that can be answered or indeed asked in so many words. It is expressed in stages, because the answer to each section opens the door to the next. The truth is rotational: it is a pattern of responses arranged around a core. You are a woman traversing the skins of an onion. As one uncovers one answer, it vanishes away to reveal another. All are true, and each contains within it a claim on the origins of the next, until the whole is visible at one time and is revealed to be quite different from what was suggested by the individual parts. "I have touched the elephant, and it is something like a tree." Yes? You've heard that before, I'm sure. But it begins very simply.'

'How?'

'You will say: "Did they murder her?"'

'That's what I'm investigating.'

'No, no. At present you are merely investigating your own investigation. You are looking for the right puzzle, the thing out of place: the bed bolted to the floor, the stolen goose, the bearded lepidopterist.'

'All right. In that case: "they" who?'

Lönnrot's head twists left, then right, then back again a little too slowly. That was a shake of the head, the Inspector realises, done by someone who doesn't know how. 'What would you do if you discovered, in the course of your inquiries, that the world was coming to an end? Would you still investigate the case? Or run naked through the streets and celebrate the last hours of your fleeting existence in an explosion of carnal excesses? Do you think one has more value than the other?'

'The world is not about to end.'

'Honestly, who can really say?'

Neith does not respond, and after a moment Lönnrot carries on. 'Oh, very well: "they". The eternal "they" of the detective. The enemy.

Peculators and poisoners. Steganography is all around you. You will go down where all the ladders start, and from that underworld you believe you will retrieve the truth of Diana Hunter, but you will find only ghosts and apparitions. If you bring them back with you into the waking world and do not test their reality too strictly, you will be promoted and you will move on to your next case. If you turn and question them, they will fade away into darkness and you will be lost upon your road. The journey is not guaranteed to end well. It is not guaranteed to end at all. Perhaps you will catch the killer. Or *a* killer. Perhaps there was no Hunter, no world until yesterday, and tomorrow there'll be nothing once again. Forgive me: I mean only that you may wish to step away from the chase.'

The Inspector shrugs, not without regret. It is, she knows, past time. 'You're forgiven. But you're also under arrest. You have the right to representation and to appeal your detention to a random sample of your peers. At this time I am advising you of my intention to apply for a warrant to investigate your involvement through direct interrogation of your memory and sense impressions. You do not have to say anything, but frank verbal disclosure of the full extent of your involvement may be preferable to you and is acceptable so long as the immediate security needs can be addressed.'

A perfectly raised eyebrow, charcoal on marble, and that infuriating calm smile. 'Shall we trade one last question, in the spirit of investigative collegiality? It's what Bogart would do.'

She feels the tug of Lönnrot's gambit, and surprises herself. 'One question.'

'I realise, I have two. Will you be so much a sinner as to be a double-dealer?'

'One.'

A sigh. 'Well, then: how long ago do you think Diana Hunter's interrogation started?'

She answers without hesitation. 'Interrogation cases are always closed in twelve to eighteen hours. People just don't have more than that in their heads.' Knowing, as she says it, that if that was the answer then Lönnrot would not have asked.

Lönnrot nods. 'Indeed so.'

She considers. 'Tell me about the diaries.'

'A collection of notes, perhaps for novels she never wrote. Ephemera and identity. A sense of who she was and how she came to be here. They are of value to me, but much less so to you. A collector's trivia, you know.'

The Inspector shakes her head. 'I thought we were playing straight.'

'Yes, well. The mark always does.'

Lönnrot stands and extends both hands as if for cuffs, but then closes the distance between them with an unearthly speed. She reaches for the taser, but a stinging palm lands on her shoulder and compresses the nerve, and then the other slaps down on her head, fingers actually curving around her skull. An instant later she is flying at a wall. She recognises a print from the *Dogs Playing Poker* series by Coolidge, supposedly ubiquitous, but she realises this is the first time she has actually ever seen one, and then she hits. Hunter's house is of distressingly solid construction. In a more modern dwelling she might cave in a plasterboard wall, but not here. She slides down the wall and lands badly, and a huge shape, comically thuggish, blocks her view of the room. A fist clips her mouth, and when she slumps and curls into a ball she feels boots, measured and powerful, striking her legs and torso.

It hurts, but she will not die. She knows that already. Nothing in her is breaking. This, too, is a message.

'It's traditional to beat down the shamus in the first chapter,' Lönnrot says with exaggerated distaste, 'but I can't help feeling there must have been an easier way.'

More boots, and finally one clips the back of her skull, yielding a kind of rest.

*

With a storm rumbling on the horizon, the Inspector sits on a park bench feeding pigeons. This is not something she ever does. She considers pigeons to be a sort of aerial rat: feeding them is profoundly antisocial.

On the bench next to her is another woman, and though Neith cannot see her face she instinctively suspects it is Diana Hunter. It does not trouble her to be sharing a bench with a dead person. Somewhere very far away from the cold, damp trees and the smell of traffic and wet leaves, the thunder of the beating reminds her that this is a dream, and no need for a scrap of poetry or a tennis ball.

She gets up and peers, but her inability to see the other woman's face persists as she moves around the bench, so she puts her curiosity away again and they feed the birds together. Lönnrot was wrong, she thinks. It's not the assassin the detective is paired with, but the victim, whose death is a kind of notice of debt served upon those who could not keep her alive.

'I'm a woman in the prime of life,' Hunter tells her, 'with certain powers. Clear-eyed and undeluded.'

'Yes,' Neith replies. 'So I've heard.'

The pigeons fly up and away, taking the world with them, and then she's half crawling, half lying on the front step of the house. She grasps for the emergency button on her glasses, the one they call the Ave Maria, but her fingers are clumsy and numb. She pulls up a weather forecast for tomorrow, crime statistics for the street – laudably low, well done – and finally fumbles her way to the alarm. She looks for the confirmation signal, and finds a string of messages telling her help is on the way, there's no need to press the button. The Witness flagged her for immediate assistance the moment she emerged from the Faraday cage. She knew that. Of course she did. That's the whole point. The Witness is always there. The best friend you can imagine. The only friend you need. Although if the dog-walker is around, perhaps he might like to render some assistance. Good citizen. Strong arms.

Sadly, he's gone to work. Oh, well. The step is very comfortable, for stone. She feels unconsciousness rushing to embrace her, brown and purple at the edges of her eyes. She's going to pass out – and when she does, she will very likely dream dreams of Diana Hunter, as the origami file unfolds inside her head.

She closes her eyes and lets go of all this needless fuss.

A moment later, she nearly screams when she quite unexpectedly sees a shark.

man water shark

There are no great white sharks in the Mediterranean.

Actually, I know there are. There is a breeding population in the Sicilian Channel, where the water is warm and rich. That's one of the things about all those refugee ships at Lampedusa: there's really not a worse place to have to swim for your life than right where they sink. But I am not in the Sicilian Channel, I am on a sport dive off Thessaloníki with a girl named Cherry who, after three weeks of pneumatic screwing and no conversation, inexplicably announced this morning that she thinks she's going to be my wife. Maybe the shark will eat her.

Except that she's a way away, looking at a bit of fallen temple, and the shark is here, with me.

Not that it's really a great white shark, because there are no great white sharks in this bit of the Med. Or not many. Just the one, maybe, lost and a bit bewildered. I try to see the huge shape as hapless.

It's not fucking hapless, it's a fucking great white shark.

It's not moving. Sharks have to move to stay alive. They need water flowing over their gills. This one is not moving. Perhaps it's dead.

It shifts in the water, ever so slightly, button eyes blinking. Do sharks blink? It certainly looked like a blink. Maybe I blinked.

'Professional courtesy.' That's the joke, isn't it? A shark sees a banker in the water, doesn't eat him. You know why? Professional courtesy! Ahahahahahah! Ahaha! Ahah.

I'm sufficiently insane that I think: If I take a photograph, it will make for some serious bragging rights. *Oh, yeah, you know what I saw on a dive near Athos? Like close enough to touch? Great white. No, I'm serious. Swam with it for a while. Then it left. Well, I thought you might say that, so suck on this unphotoshopped image of me petting the seven-metre torpedo of bikini-chomping death like my grandmother's puppy. Balls of steel? Steel is for shit. You know what Zeus has, my friend? You know what he tells his girls when he comes to them in the shape* of a swan? He doesn't say he's got balls of steel. He throws back his head, spreads his arms, and he says: 'I am the king of the gods, the son of Kronos and Rhea and the master of lightning! I am palaces and power and pleasure and treasure and appetite walking around in tight pants, and better than any of that crap, you know what I got? I got balls like Constantine Kyriakos!'

And hell, it's not like I can do anything else. If the shark wants to eat me, it is very much going to. I cannot outpace it, fight it off, bribe it or trick it. It hangs in front of me, the biggest living thing I have ever seen. The closest was an elephant. But elephants are not predators, and being a predator makes things bigger: conceptual mass. It is massive anyway. From the tip of the first dorsal to the bottom of the pectoral fin it is taller than I am. And that's like me lying down and the distance from my arse to my stomach being taller than someone.

The moment is possessed of an indifferent perfection: man, water, shark. Nothing else exists. I swim closer, get my photograph. (Not dead. Neither of us. Yet.) Don't quite touch the shark. I'm not going to take liberties. Feel a tugging at my fingertips, a fluttering, like a wind beneath the sea, and my mouth opens in an O. I nearly lose my mouthpiece. The shark is resting in a narrow band of ocean current, a river beneath the sea.

It's just hanging out, like me. It's a *lazy* shark.

The eyes roll. A flicker of interest, and suddenly I'm awake, not dreaming of fate and destiny and the primitive comradeship of monsters. I am in the water, arm's length from a (great white shark) large and admittedly dangerous animal.

Do not panic.

Fuck.

Do not behave like prey.

Fuck.

Do not let your heartbeat spike.

Fuck-fuck. Fuck-fuck. Fuck-fuck. FUCK-FUCK. FUCK-FUCK. FUCK-FUCK.

I haven't prayed since I was a boy. My mother is Armenian, so I'm not even Greek Orthodox, I was baptised into her communion. She insists it's the oldest Christian church in the world, the true successor to St Paul, and fuck the Pope. But now I'm praying, and I'm not praying to God at all. I back away: you don't turn away from a shark, they're ambush predators. Without regret, I let the shiny wristwatch I wear diving in defiance of common sense fall into the depths, watch the shark's eyes shift as it tumbles, end over end. I keep inching backwards through the water, trying to remember where the boat is, and I'm holding out the little waterproof camera in front of me, preparing to trigger the self-timed flash and let it go as another distraction. It's a Sony, overpriced from an airport shop, because I was bored. So this is how I pray:

Don't eat me. Oh, please. I'll do anything. Don't eat me.

The shark twists in the water. Brushes past me. Down, snatching the tiny spark of my wristwatch, vanishing with horrible ease into the water. It is still quite large in my vision when it becomes indistinguishable from the background.

Sacrifice accepted.

The camera is still in my hands. I didn't have time to drop it.

*

For a few days after the shark story hits the news, I am a local celebrity. I go on talk shows and give interviews in newspapers. *Der Spiegel* sends a man to talk to me, and a photographer to take my picture. I ask the photographer if she has ever modelled, but apparently she hears this a lot and doesn't bite.

However, I do not have to buy myself a drink for the duration, and being on TV is a great way to start a conversation in a bar. The whole near-death issue allows me to say goodbye to Cherry. I am reconsidering everything in my life. I have been changed. Annealed. I need time to reflect, to go mad, to get sane, to drink, to be sober. I am a new person. I'll call her when this spiritual journey is at an end.

I do keep her number, but more as a warning to myself.

In a private villa at Elounda, as part of this healing process, I commission a foam party. My shark picture is projected on to the walls and I arrange for a special Kyriakos cocktail with blue Curaçao and shark fin ice cubes. There is a six-foot ice-luge in the shape of a nude male diver, suitably heroic but still recognisably me, reaching down like God in Michelangelo's painting to bless the shark. Branded vodka is poured into the back of the statue's scuba tank and flows freely from his partly engorged penis. I also fly in a group of adventurous art students from Camberwell and pay them to paint the same tableau across the naked abdomens of five Crazy Horse girls. At midnight, two artists and a dancer persuade me to take off my clothes – thank God I've been on a fitness jag so my body is muscular beneath a layer of fat, and I can tell myself I look titanic rather than obese – and they shave me from neck to ankle right there on the leather sofa and wash me in Cristal. At which point the whole night really kicks off, and it's a carnage of oral sex and orifices and everyone has a great time. I personally get laid on top of the ice luge, roaring and thrusting as my balls brush the melting ice and my arsehole gets very cold, but my partner is totally into it. She's screaming and yessing as if she's never had an orgasm before, and that makes me feel pretty fantastic.

You know what Zeus says to his girls? He says— Yeah, okay, I told you already. Best. Party. Ever.

Except for that one really weird moment, later on, when I'm falling asleep under a duvet made of a dreadlocked sculptor and a junior account executive from a London ad firm, when I could swear a young woman, with short dark hair and very white skin whose dress falls in a perfect indigo cascade down her elegant back to reveal two centimetres of hypnotic buttock, winks at me, and her eyes are completely black and her mouth stretches to reveal the teeth of the shark.

*

Constantine Kyriakos, party man. Never seen without at least one model. Never underdressed, never without some bling. Right? Fast cars and expensive art and champagne and yeah, some coke, but mostly it's about the women and the style.

Let me tell you, I was not this guy when I was at school. Okay? I really was not. I was on the outside looking in. You know what principally determines that, among boys at school? Football. I had never watched a football match when I arrived, and although they didn't know it and I didn't know it, that meant I was fucked as far as the other kids were concerned. I did not speak the common language. This is my advice to parents: teach your son the language of football, at least in some measure, so that he knows enough to parlay with the enemy.

I don't mean I'd never sat on the terraces. I mean I'd never watched a match, not even on TV, because no one in my family did. It just wasn't their thing. My father had a bad leg, and spent his Saturdays making jigsaws in his workroom. My mother thought public sports coarse and possibly even profane. So I did not know, for example, that although the game is notionally non-contact there's a great deal of shoving and colliding. When I played it I just thought anyone who did those things was cheating and I did not understand why the referee did not intervene. Moreover, because I was averse to punishment and the social disgrace it seemed to entail, I did not do them myself. That meant I couldn't hold on to the ball, so the other kids found me useless, and my teachers mistook my obedience for physical timidity and wrote me off. It never occurred to them to explain that the rules were flexible and interpretable, because everyone knew those things. Boys – automatically, genetically – knew them. That I did not was not something they contemplated.

And then it turned out I was good at mathematics – very good – and that's another alienation, because almost no one is very good at mathematics. Least of all my teacher.

'Show your working.'

I have. (Thinking: Are you an idiot?)

'Show your working.'

It's here. (Exactly where have I missed a step?)

'What is this number?'

It's a moon number. (What can I tell you? There are ordinary numbers and moon numbers and this one is a moon number. Moon numbers are good for making long multiplication simple.)

'Don't do that. If you don't know how it works, you can't depend on it.'

I *do* know how it works. You don't. That's not the same thing.

'Don't be rude. And no moon numbers. Do it properly.'

I'm staring at him now and of course that makes it worse, but okay, if I'm not allowed to use moon numbers I can use angel numbers instead. Angel numbers are not like moon numbers. They are almost moon numbers inside out. Moon numbers increase the amount of stuff you have to hold in your head but they make operations very simple. Angel numbers do the opposite. I'm careful to express answers in ordinary notation, and to show how I work with the angel numbers, every step, so that even my teacher will be able to follow.

He can't.

Instead he gets angry and sends me to the headmaster, and that's where Professor Cosmatou probably saves my life, because they'd have expelled me and then I would have got a job working for my uncle and never touched real mathematics again and I would probably have killed myself when Stella died. Or I'd never have loved her at all, because we'd never have met without the Old Girl.

I'm sitting outside the headmaster's office with my angel numbers, waiting to be told I'm not educable. I've been warned about this. *If you can't learn the way other children learn – if you are disruptive, Constantine Kyriakos – you will have to leave.*

I sit and wait for the firing squad. I'm ten years old. Fatalism regarding adult insanity is one of the few things I share with my peers.

And then in comes providence, in the form of a narrow, angular woman with her hands in the pockets of a long suit jacket and a grubby white plastic bag dangling from one wrist. She is clearly over a hundred years old, so I guess her actual chronological age at around forty-five. She's smoking a roll-up with mace in it, so the room very quickly smells like sausage and burning cream.

The old girl looks at me. Glances at my papers. Raises her eyebrows. Extends her hand.

Why not? What could possibly make it worse at this point? I pass them over, grubby thumb print on the white margin at the left, and she nods and smooths them on her knee. She settles, and sighs to herself as she puts on a pair of overlarge glasses with bifocal lenses. Her eyes look owlish and enormous.

She looks over my work. Sees red ink. Frowns. Gets her own pen out – green – and draws a single line through all the red. Turns the page. The green pen makes another flourish, an illicit and complicit contradiction. Constantine is right and you are wrong. Wrong, wrong, wrong … and wrong. Writes a simple tick at the bottom next to my conclusion. And then I hear her scribble something, the nib of the felt-tip whistling and scratching. She hands back the last of my papers, and I see this:

$$\omega^2 = -5 - 12i$$
$$z^2 - (4 + i)z + (5 + 5i) = 0$$

I imagine that means nothing to you? Then imagine she has sketched a perfect half-figure in the style of Rembrandt, and left it with me to complete.

'Let me know when you come to the end,' she says, and walks past me into the headmaster's office.

I don't really notice the passage of time. I work, and then it's done. I knock on the headmaster's door and submit my work to the old girl, who smiles, and thanks me, then shuts the door. I don't know what else to do, so I wait.

I hear an argument. It largely concerns me, although it occasionally branches out into a more general debate over whether the school is a haven for the imbecilic or the merely mediocre, whether there is any point in schools at all if this is the sort of fatuous shit in which they trade, and whether the old girl is going to rip the headmaster's empty head off and use it to wipe her arse or whether she is merely going to rescue 'that poor benighted fucking Ramanujan out there' and 'never darken the doorway of this mean-minded educational clip joint ever again'.

'He's disruptive.'

'Of course he is disruptive if you have been trying to make him crawl along with the others! Do you make your sprinters walk the hundred metres as well? Must your best literature students read the same baby-food books as the ones who find every sentence a trial? No? Then why? Eh? Because he uses strange words for things you do not understand? So do I, pea-brain. He may or may not be a genius, but he has something. You need not give it a name, I don't care. But seeing it in action, you should recognise it, or hypothesise it.'

'And why, pray?'

'Because,' she says, and all the bluster is replaced now by something like fatigue, or fury, 'you call yourself a teacher.' There is a suffused silence. 'Fine, then. Kick him out. We'll take him.'

'You will? Who will?'

'The university.'

Yes, really. True story.

*

I've had enough of sharks and ridiculous performance sex, so I go home. Sanity is in Glyfada, and Glyfada is in – but not really of – Athens.

Before I moved in, I split the flat in two and the connecting door is always locked. The public half is very much what you'd expect: black velvet drapes, mirrored bar, jacuzzi in the middle of one room like an altar, sunken fireplace in another; thick carpets and leather; and an actual disco ball, because I have no shame. There are beds, too, in various flavours of decadence and excess, but very little that feels like home. The connecting door is behind a heavy curtain.

On the private side of the door everything is different. It's plain, clean and off-white. There are comfortable sofas I bought from a discount place on the ring road, a CD player which was old in 2000, a lot of mismatched Delft pottery with cracks in it to eat and drink from, and some old books from university. For lunch I make sure there's always hummus and taramasalata with sesame bread. Under the kitchen counter there's a case of Italian white wine made in the hills over Pompeii. It tastes of volcanoes and it's not expensive. I buy half-bottles so that I can drink alone without getting drunk. Otherwise there's water – Badoit, because chilled it tastes the way anaesthetic feels – and sometimes I shove some fruit through the juicer with ginger.

Home at last. Kettle's on. Chair smells just a little musty: friendly rot.

On a side table there's a picture of my sister before her breakdown – she's much better now; I saw her a month ago and she was basically back on track and very scathing about everyone else's mental health, which is probably entirely fair. There's another of my mother smiling toothily, and one of my father with a huge fish we caught one summer, a third of me accepting my degree from the Old Girl: 'Your work has meraki, Constantine Kyriakos. It's got your heart in it. It is the thing that you are. You should stay here, with us, and do this. It will not make you rich, but it is best.'

'Will it make me happy?' I wasn't thinking. So much had happened and I really wanted to know.

'Maybe not,' she said, 'but sure as shit, nothing else will.'

Well, if I was going to be unhappy – or at least not happy, because a mathematician knows the difference between the absence of x and its negation – then I chose to be unhappy like this. I chose to be unhappy and rich, rather than unhappy and poor. I was reasonably sure at the time that unhappy and poor was a lot unhappier, although since then I've seen the very rich get themselves into states of sorrow and horror which are inaccessible without vast fortunes: with insane money comes insanity. This business of billions – what the fuck can you buy with a billion that will fill the hole? Nothing. I know. I've seen it. There's nothing. Not all the Edvard Munch paintings and white truffles and Bentleys will do the job. A year later you just need another one. Honestly, it's worse than iPhones.

Maybe it is time for a change. Maybe this Kyriakos isn't who I want to be after all. In mathematics we talk about transformations. A transformation is everything you have to do to one thing to make it into another. If you take a square and warp it until you get a parallelogram, that's a transformation. What transformation would make Kyriakos happy, I wonder? What if the answer was just quitting while I'm ahead?

No. No money talk. Not allowed in here, on the quiet side of the apartment. No money matters, no flash, no self-deception, no temporary women – which means none at all, the way I live now – no bullshit of any kind. Just Constantine Kyriakos, and the things that matter.

Which, it turns out, doesn't leave very much.

I don't open a bottle of the Taburno Sannio. I sit instead, and watch Athens go by from the balcony. The people in the street and the misty sky become a beach with waves washing on it and then a clifftop. I dream of a woman in chains on a table being menaced by a dragon, and maybe it's real or maybe it's just rush hour and delivery trucks.

It's not always easy, being Greek. Even the mud has gods in it.

*

On Monday, back to work. Office banter, riven through with a pleasing amount of envy and horror. Was it really the way it says in the paper? Was it amazing? Was it spontaneous or did I pay someone to make it happen? (People in my circle tend to believe that anything can be arranged, and therefore that anything amazing that happens probably has been. It does not occur to them to admire serendipity, or to court it. It should make me sad, but that is the sort of thinking I leave behind in Glyfada.)

Yes, yes, I met a shark. Who hasn't met a shark? What, no one? Just me, then? Well, you know, it was a spiritual experience. I feel almost baptised in the waters of Greece. I am more Greek than I have ever been. I am the salty essence of the nation, the blood that flows beneath the skin. I touched something very special. Yes, I did.

What in particular? Well, since you ask, a couple of gorgeous French cabaret dancers and a woman from London who had piercings in places which would astound you. No, none of them had even a little bit of Greek in them, or, they didn't until—

It is too easy. I am a machine. I am alpha, indeed I am the alpha-est. Which is why this afternoon, with the slowest of the papers still catching up with my heroic exploit and flattering attention from even the haughtiest of Athens's fast set ladies still happily directed to my address, I am meeting Patriarch Nikolaos Megalos of the Order of St Augustine and St Spyridon. (He is called a Patriarch, which is a title usually reserved for the popes of different branches of the Christian church. Nikolaos Megalos is permitted to use the title for historical reasons that are really interesting if you care, which I don't. Since his order is so important – and so very, very rich – I have no idea why they need two saints, except that Wikipedia says Augustine died of old age and barely performed any miracles, for all that his *Confessions* are so renowned, and St Spyridon is basically famous for setting his own beard on fire as part of an explanation of the Holy Trinity. Perhaps two slightly substandard saints put them on a par with, say, the Franciscans, who can lay claim to one of the real zingers, a guy who talked to birds and healed practically everyone in Tuscany at one time or another.)

The Order would be a major client, if I can reel them in. Churches always are, if they bank at all, but the Order at some point must have been given one of those gifts that the old emperors liked to bestow on the favoured – a string of diamond mines, or mineral rights for the whole of Morocco. When they cashed out I have no idea, but they are now a smallish subset of the Orthodox religion with the kind of money more usually held by people who create search engines or new ways to smuggle heroin.

I don't meet the Patriarch of the Order at my own office. I don't even use my usual staff. They're not appropriate: too young, too brash, and too typical of my profession. This opportunity has arisen, apparently, because this Patriarch is new and feels the need to clear out some infrastructural chaff before he gets to his future life of deep spiritual contemplation and pastoral care. The old guy was ousted in some sort of priestly coup d'état of the sort churches pretend not to have. I am therefore working to a style I have established with religious institutions, one that seems to make their representatives happy, and as long as they're happy they continue to invest and I continue to get a commission and that commission is large. For these meetings I use a cave-like basement office belonging to a friend, a man who keeps vineyards as a hobby. The room has wooden panels rippled by age, and stone flagging. The desk is a traditional kidney with an actual blotter: it reeks of perpetuity. My rooms at the bank are for more commonplace clients and the dynamic is wrong for a personage like Nikolaos Megalos, and wrong for me when I need to be his kind of banker. There's nothing worse than meeting someone who is dressed for the Crucifixion in a room with a six-foot Patrick Nagel girl on the back wall.

I sit in the semi-dark, and I listen to the sound of old wood, of distant roadworks and taxi drivers, of high heels on the floor above: the signature babble of the world the Patriarch thinks is just walking dust. I smell beeswax and somewhere a hint of cologne – not mine – and sweat.

When the borrowed assistant announces my client has arrived, I get up and briefly practise stretching out my hands across the desk.

(Oh crap. 'Make a note, please, Petros, that I need to buy a watch. And show him in.')

Petros nods and wafts out. He could be a monk himself. He's actually a doorman at a local hotel. They lend him out to me on occasion.

In any case, the double handshake is not the right thing, not today. Today I am prodigal but merit-worthy. I was lost, and while I may not yet actually be found, the search parties are definitely hopeful I will be back in the fold in no time. That's the note: honest but not one of the flock, and seeking a way home. So we're going bashfully formal.

Enter Megalos.

Picture a science fiction-looking hat, all black and shaped almost like a fan. Then put a man under it with the face of a Persian warrior king and a square black beard. Give him a black robe trimmed with very pale blue, and eyes in the same tint. Put on his finger a fat Burmese ruby set in a ring dating from before the Council of Trent, and a rope belt with knots at prayerful intervals all the way down to the floor. Constantine Kyriakos, this is Patriarch Nikolaos Megalos, and even if you have spoken to him on the phone, this is the first time you are seeing him in person since his accession. There are old scars on his fingers and his nails are chipped, as if he builds boats for a living. Perhaps the Order of St Augustine and St Spyridon has a secret fight club, the way banks do these days.

I picture Megalos roaring like a bull moose and breaking the Bishop of Rome across his knee. He's a huge bastard. I'm not a thin man, but inside his gaiters this guy must have legs like the Pillars of Herakles. He's big like strongmen are, huge belly and fat on his limbs, muscle underneath as thick as a pork roast. Carpentry, I realise, remembering the briefing. He's a carpenter, in emulation of you-know-who.

When I read that, I imagined a dainty old geezer doing holy marquetry. This guy probably builds those giant-sized cathedral doors made of teak.

The Patriarch permits me to kiss his ring, and then a moment later we embrace, because this much money is like family in itself.

*

'Food bonds,' I say when we have dispensed with both 'Thank you for coming' and 'I do hope your recent travails have not greatly affected you'. I had not thought of my shark as a travail, so we do a little comedy about that, and then I get to the point, which is food bonds. 'They're the new CDOs. That's where the batshit money is going right now.' Deliberately casual to the point of crass, because this affords my new client the opportunity to rise above me on a moral level. It's important that Nikolaos Megalos should feel morally superior, because he's basically at school here and no one who wears a hat like that has been the junior partner in a master–student relationship for quite some time. But if I let my language get away from me a little and have to apologise, then the Patriarch can go home feeling that he has brought sanctity for a brief while into the life of a sinner, and that at the same time he has gleaned valuable knowledge and indeed concrete investment advice from this perilous conversation. These twin convictions will make him happy.

Twins will do that.

So: would the OSASS like to get its pious paws on some really outrageous slices of Mammon's estate?

Hand to mouth, oh la la, faux pas! 'Your pardon, Eminence, I don't mean to blaspheme.'

Nikolaos Megalos rumbles like a Harley, and I realise this is him laughing. 'That is not technically blasphemy, Constantine Kyriakos, but rather the invocation of a false god, which is heresy or paganism, depending on who you are. But be at ease; I will promise not to burn you so long as you acknowledge the true Church in time. St Augustine, after all, was a mighty sinner until he regained himself.'

'Thank you, Eminence.' You preposterous old fart.

'You are welcome, Constantine Kyriakos. But returning from my wisdom to yours for a moment: may I point out in the meantime that collateralised debt obligations did not end well?'

Actually CDOs were fine so long as you stuck to the right ones. I mean, they were by definition always junk, but you were sort of okay if you went with the good junk rather than the ones they made later when the demand was so high they thought it would be clever to create junk-junk and label it triple-A, and when everyone and his aunt decided to borrow ten million dollars against a fucking shack in the Everglades. Use your head: no idea that proposes free money is ever a good idea, because money is mathematics and mathematics does not allow you to add something to one side of the equation without balancing it on the other – but they weren't originally the hell-fest of financial immolation they turned into down the line. Finance by itself is ruthless, and that ruthlessness is its salvation. The real disasters are only possible when you bring politics into it, because politics is about pretending to care.

'Even if that were true,' I tell Megalos, 'there's no local downside – that is, no downside for the OSASS – so long as you buy the right tranche and get off the ride before the music stops. It's about timing.' The Patriarch says he knows all about the importance of temporal things, and once again we have a bit of a chuckle. We're funny guys.

No, but seriously, here's the thing: the CDO was actually a laudable idea in the beginning, for a given value of the word. They took the advantages of large borrowers and shared them among small borrowers who otherwise wouldn't get terms they could afford by clubbing them all together, and they parcelled out the risk of default along with possibility of profit. The key was choosing the right people to lend to, customers who were smart and could pay back but who for whatever reason weren't getting approved for normal loans. The honest salt-of-the-earth poor for whom the better rate they could get through loans financed by CDOs meant the difference between affordability and impossibility.

Well, yes, there was a minor side issue with money laundering, but really, when isn't there? Anyway, it was all ticking over.

'Are you with me so far, Your Beatitude?'

'I am not the Pope,' the Patriarch reminds me gently.

'Sorry, Eminence. I get excited.'

'Be at ease, my son. We all do, from time to time.'

'The problem, Eminence, is that there aren't enough high-quality poor people.'

The Patriarch's eyebrows very nearly reach the brim of his hat.

In a strictly financial sense, it's true. There simply are not that many good borrowers out there getting missed by the system. Some, but not anything like enough, because the lending banks are neither idle nor stupid at the pointy end unless you specifically instruct them to be, which is where politics comes into it. The market for CDOs was hot, and everyone wanted more of them, not least the government, which was presiding over a boom in confidence and property prices and thereby being made to look like a hero. Dutiful and delighted, the banks got back out there and created some more, riskier collections of debt and finally some which were frankly toxic and they were getting these rated as the same thing as the first lot, which is a miracle I'm not going to look too closely at in case it turns me to stone. So now they were creating bank loans which were unrepayable, which were actually structured so that they were never going to be repaid. You want to borrow half a million dollars against your shitty backlot and build a house you can't afford, and you want to never make any payments and just owe the full amount plus interest – a sum total which is more than your ugly mosquito-infested pit will ever be worth – in forty years, by which time you will almost certainly be dead? We can accommodate that. Because the money wasn't in the repayments any more, the money was in selling on the risk. It wasn't important, in the first instance, whether the loan was good. It was only important that someone wanted to buy it, and they did.

In retrospect even the most bullish of our American colleagues would probably admit that was not a very good way to do business. But everyone was into it.

(I got lucky: I had a sniff of the problem early from a guy at Goldman and I hedged well. By the time the crash happened I was insulated. I didn't get much richer, but my clients didn't lose any money, either, which at the time made me look like a genius, and of course we did well in the volatility that followed when everything else was cheap as shit.)

But the big deal now is food bonds. You get them by parcelling up obligations to buy or sell given products. Again, selling food futures is helpful to people who actually make food because they need money in advance of their crops to bring those crops to market. It's also a hedge, because food markets can be volatile and you don't want to grow a huge amount of a given crop and then have to sell it all at once when there's lots of it around because it's harvest season – and, of course, you don't want to be a nation state looking to import a bunch of grain and find that everyone else has outbid you and now you're starving, because very bad things happen to governments that allow that sort of thing. Ask the tsars, if you can find the pieces.

Recently, there's been some talk about regulating this kind of speculation, which probably isn't a bad idea. Good rules make good games. Games without rules degenerate.

Institutionally, however, the financial industry doesn't trust regulations proceeding from governments run by charming retired actors, burned-out drug and sex addicts, and professional bullshit artists. Go figure. So there is already a work-around: you can loan a producer money against the final product. The producer is then free to sell to whomever, assuming the risk of a price drop but gaining the benefit of a price hike, so long as they pay you back your money plus a premium. It sounds like small change compared to a market worth almost a trillion dollars, but you have to remember that there are seven and a half billion people on earth and only about fifteen hundred or so of them are billionaires. There's a kind of penumbra of rich people – another few hundred thousand – and a twilight zone of merely affluent people whose standard of living and location is basically the extent of their wealth, a kind of geopolitical fortune rather than a bankable one, and then basically everyone else is poor as hell. Which makes the poor, considered as a group and obviously only in brute numerical terms, pretty rich.

So, sure, let's lend them the money they need to grow food, right? But you wouldn't want to engage in a project like that without sharing some of the risk, so the CDO structure is frankly ideal. Just don't actually call them CDOs or, you know, all manner of shit will fall on your head.

'It's a good deed, basically. A profitable one,' I tell the Patriarch.

'Until it goes wrong.'

'Nothing lasts for ever.' I lift my palms to the ceiling in a gesture which my Cultural Semiotics in Business trainer tells me could signify helplessness or honesty and generosity. 'You swim, or you sink.'

Abruptly I'm tasting salt water in my nose and my wristwatch is falling away beneath me, but this time my hand is falling with it. Jesus fuck! Jesus fucking bastard fuck! I have post-shark stress disorder. Fuck!

Can he tell? Are my eyes bugging out? Am I pissing myself or trying to swim in mid-air?

No. Seemingly not. I can deal with it, I know how. Reaffirmation. Burn fear away with life. Purge the corners of the room. I've been sleeping with the bedside light on, anyway. And a few more parties should do it, write over the bad memory with good ones, like a computer writing over sensitive information: Department of Defense Approved self-erasure, 1s and 0s. Crosses and grails. Lingams and yonis. Sex, okay? Just sex and more sex and maybe that'll take care of it. Fuck it out.

Fuck it out. Fuck it fuck it fuck it fuck it I was nearly eaten by a giant monster and it saw me and I gave it my watch and it's here, it's here it's here here here in this room, hiding behind this clergyman's hat! I know it is. I shouldn't be in a cellar, it's too close to the water table, and sharks live in water.

And that's stupid enough to make me stop. What, the thing's going to come up through the floor? Or out of the sewer, like something from a bad movie? What am I, nine years old? For heaven's sake, whose tiny balls are these? I am Constantine Kyriakos. I could kill any shark.

Using.

Only.

My.

Balls.

In the flagstoned room Patriarch Megalos is looking a little concerned, so I have another chuckle and say that it will be a very lucrative market, and a lot of total arseholes are going to get rich out of it, and wouldn't it be better for these billions of euros to flow into the coffers of the OSASS than those of the Landesbanken? Because the Germans, Eminence, are crazy for this stuff. 'Tulip fever,' says the Patriarch. I have no idea what that means, so I nod and say: 'Got it in one.'

'May I tell you about what I believe, Constantine Kyriakos?'

'Please do.' Please don't.

'I am a believer in God, of course, but also in something else. I am a believer in Greece. Greece has suffered very much in these last years for sins committed elsewhere and to some extent for sins we committed ourselves. Ours were sins of laxity, as you might say, and those of America and the rest were sins of enthusiasm. They were seized with the joy of an impossible equation, a getting of something for nothing, and the result was that our sleepy little country was brought to a dark place. But I believe it may be that a great reversal is coming, that the focus of civilisation may shift from California and Beijing on and on around the globe until it is once again in Athens, just as Plato once said that it would. In the twelfth book of the *Civitas Dei*, we find that Plato believed in a circular cosmos. He taught that the universe repeats upon itself, and that one day he would again be teaching in Athens just as he was then. It is the doctrine of apocatastasis: a return to the beginning. I understand there is a proposition of mathematical physics which might support such a pattern.'

Yes, well: a topologist is a person who cannot tell the difference between a teacup and a donut. I remind myself not to get smart with the nice client, and nod as if I spend my weekends talking cosmological theology with my buddies and this idea is a personal favourite.

Megalos carries on: 'I do not believe in perfect return. I do not believe it is inevitable. The world is not so kind. But I do believe that it may come, if we seize it – and when it does, our little country shall rise to greatness once again. We shall once more have fire in our spines, and Greece shall be torn no longer.'

I take time to consider this mountainous soundbite of wisdom. I compose my face into a suitably contemplative mode. 'That would indeed be a fine thing.'

The words hang there and I see the priest behind the man: the flash of devotion that he carries deep inside.

I swallow, and we look at each other across the table, breathing in the beeswax air from the desk and listening to the sound of Athens above our heads. Megalos nods once, then sighs heavily. The shine in him retreats, and the modern theologian re-emerges. 'I believe this is a matter of practical theology. In the world we inhabit now, theology is speculative. It is the discussion of otherworldly things. But to our forefathers it was no more than the examination of commonly known truths. These days we hear of the Garden of Eden and we think of a garden. We hear of original sin and we imagine a specific transgression – but our sin is not one of action but of understanding. Ah. You look like one of my novices. Indulge me.'

'Of course.' So long as we can have your business, I will listen to this once a month, every month, for the rest of my life. Who knows? It may even come in handy if I meet an attractive nun.

'You have heard of the Persian Immortals?'

Persian Immortals. Yes. Sure. In my head: a picture of men in blue armour. Sparta, Thermopylae. That terrible American film. 'An army of ten thousand elite soldiers. When one died, he was replaced by another man, so it was said they were eternal.'

'Yes! Exactly. And yet also and most fundamentally: no. You parrot what you have been told, but your teachers missed the point because they are circumscribed by their own immersion in a culture of written words. It is not that a man died and another was called to be an Immortal, to fill a role. Rather, Immortals cannot die because the role supersedes the man. When a body falls, another steps into its place – so the Immortal goes on. A person living in this way is not the sum of their experience, of fallible human memory, but the expression of a permanent identity. It is not a convention or even a magic. It is a truth, as simple as the sunrise. But the true Greece exists only in that other world. The Greece we inhabit now is a shadow.'

We must rediscover a way of being in which the divine is everywhere, in which we move through a world where theology is literally true. If we can do that, we will indeed return to the days of Plato and our greatness.' He smiles, and I wonder if my mouth is noticeably open or if I look as fucked in the earholes as I presently feel.

'Well. To make this happen, we must have many things, but one, inevitably, is wealth. So. Here I am. The coffers of the Order must grow so that they can be released at the proper time, to buffer the poor and nurture the coming spring. You see?'

'I see.'

'So tell me, Constantine Kyriakos. Honestly.' He leans back, and something in his posture says that if he was another sort of person he'd stretch his feet out, maybe even prop them on the kidney desk and let the big stupid hat fall on the ground. I wonder if he ever does that, just let it go and feel naughty as his no doubt weighty office hits the floor.

'Tell you what?'

'Tell me of your catabasis, of course.'

Is that even a thing? 'I have two, but I can't get them to breed.'

He laughs and waves his hand. 'Forgive a scholar his jargon. Catabasis is the journey of Orpheus into the underworld to retrieve his love. Yours went better than his.' Rumbling in his belly: more chuckling. Gosh, he's funny. I let him know I think so. Encouraged, he leans forward. 'Please, Constantine Kyriakos. Indulge me. Tell me about the shark.'

Oh. *Oh!* He's a *fan*. My God. The Patriarch of the Order of St Augustine and St Spyridon is a starfucker. Okay. Okay: that, I understand. I reach out my hand to him, then collect myself and press it to the palm of the other in an unconscious gesture of prayer. 'Beautiful. And truthfully, not remotely interested in me. They take seals, you know, and tuna. I think she was a little lost.'

'"She"?'

'For the sake of argument.'

'It is all quite Orphic, you know. Very Greek. All that's missing is a girl for you to rescue.'

Something impels me to honesty. 'I was diving with a woman, but to be honest I feel I was somewhat rescued from her by the shark.'

Megalos chuckles: oh, you sinners and your amusing lifestyles! Then he sobers. 'And now? How did you feel?'

74

The truth slips out. 'The shark was very big, Eminence, and I was very little.' A beat. 'I suppose it was the most spiritual experience of my adult life.'

Now, now, now he extends his hand to me across the desk, capturing mine, accepting the divinity of my experience and touching it, tasting it with his fingers. He spreads my fingers, probing like a butcher with a joint. His gaze fixes unblinking on my face, searching and unveiling. I can feel his nails as he grips my arm. What can he possibly find in my flesh that is so all-fired important? Is he looking for melanoma? For tattoos? What does he see in my eyes?

After a long moment, he exhales and releases me. 'We shall do business,' he says.

Rock and fucking roll. The Eagle has landed, it's a small step for man, mission accomplished.

I look back at him: my best impression of a sheep glimpsing the fold and wondering, perhaps not for the first time, whether it might be the place for me. 'You won't regret it, Eminence.'

'No, my son. I won't.'

Which is one of those weird things priests say which make them sound like actors in the *Godfather* movies. He waits a moment, then smiles.

'Torn no longer, Constantine Kyriakos.' That's going to be in his next sermon. I can feel it.

With great sincerity: 'Torn no longer, Nikolaos Megalos.'

*

I have been in the office for an hour or so. It's a Wednesday, which is when I usually re-emphasise my alpha status by hugging all the other men. A few years ago there was a TV show about problem dogs. It ran late at night on those channels you basically only watch if you're staying in a hotel, and it came on after all the other dross and it was full of bullshit Freudian analysis of misbehaving Rottweilers and doggy hypnosis to uncover past lives as a wolf. Homeopathy for dogs? Yes. Acupuncture? Yes. Massage? Yes. Colonic irrigation? Sure – why not? (Because it's a fucking dog, you morons. If it's unhappy and you stick a hose up its ass, I can almost guarantee that you will not ameliorate the situation one tiny bit.)

And then there was this one guy, Sam, who used to work with police dogs and he had no time for any of that shit at all. 'If the dog thinks you are the boss,' Sam said, 'you will be fine. You pay attention to the dog, you feed the dog, you exercise the dog, you own the dog, it's your dog. However, if the dog thinks you are weak, it will fuck with you. Dogs are not cosy. Dogs are dogs. They are animals. They need clear hierarchies or they get confused and when they're confused they piss on things, bite things, and mate with things until they get less confused. That's all. That's what it is. There's just you and the dog and one of you is on top.' And then he looked out of the screen and I swear to you he was talking only to me, and he said: 'Actually, it's not all that different with people.' And I knew that he was right.

Since then I have been careful to mount everyone in the office a few times a month. I get my arms around them and I make them carry me a little. If it's a straight guy, I make them squirm out of the way of my genitals. Once they've done that, they basically just do what I want, irrespective of whether they are my junior or not. It's ridiculous how effective it is. In theory, I suppose, one of them might hit me, but so far no one ever has.

I am particularly careful to do this with Harrison. Harrison is technically my boss, although it's only technical because I'm a rainmaker and he's not. He's a box-ticker and a brake on the excesses of the younger guys. Basically Harrison is here to make sure no one engages in any activity that is actually illegal, or if they do, we can all say we didn't know and fire them and that will be that. He's the trip-switch between the world and the bank's own profits: if anything really shitty happens, Harrison gets burned personally, but the bank survives. This makes him naturally conservative, but if I hump his leg from time to time he goes pink and runs away – he's shy and British, and married to an appalling Danish woman who sings hymns in the car when she drives him to work – and that means I can just get on with life.

Harrison is at root a perfectly acceptable person. He is inoffensive, competent and decent. He has never come to any of my parties and he does not comment on anything in the gossip sheets. He does not drink too much or take any form of intoxicating pharmaceutical. He has reached his natural ceiling and this does not bother him. It's almost awe-inspiring how average his life is, and he seems to love that.

But he does one thing which makes me want to fart on his head. He believes he is a hard-core banker, a wheeler-dealer, and he insists on keeping an old monochrome CRT monitor on his desk, one of those ones from the eighties when he was coming up in the business. It's made by IBM and it pollutes the office just by being there.

So Harrison has this excrescence on his desk and now a lot of the guys have set up their expensive computers to look the same, like it's some sort of useful tool. It won't display graphics properly, just characters, so you've basically got a text-only monitor. Next they'll have a town crier come through the office and read the stock prices. 'Oh, Constantine, you should get one, this way you don't get distracted by Twitter and Facebook.'

You should not be distracted by anything, you infant. When you work, you work. Does fucking SEAL Team Six get distracted by Twitter? No. Why not? Because they focus. They have discipline. They know that what they do has consequences. People will die. Well, here is the news: the same is true of us. Money is life. Poverty kills. If you are going to get distracted by your computer, you don't deserve your job.

But no. Harrison has everyone thinking that the answer is to cut down on your distractions, not your tendency to get distracted. Typically weak anglophone logic. So he has this Stone Age display with the prices ticking down it, and in the summertime we have to double everyone else's air-con usage because it throws off heat like a bastard. You can actually detect it with a Geiger counter. It is the only thing I cannot get him to flex on by repeatedly putting my arm around him and crushing his shoulders against my chest. How this of all things comes to be the sticking point, I have no idea.

He's at lunch, so I'm sitting at his desk because we're talking strategy and the conference room is in use.

Brunner, the Swiss, is talking about the Asian property market and how we all need to pay attention to it. I am not paying attention to Brunner because I am already paying attention to the Asian property market, and I'm not sure it's going to do anything very interesting.

In the pretentious monochrome of Jim Harrison's outmoded terminal, I see a flicker, almost a ripple. For a moment I think the dratted thing is finally failing, giving up to modernity, and halle-fucking-lujah. But no, it isn't. Something is happening in the real world and it is reflected on the screen. The last digit of each stock value shifts to 4, just for a moment and one after another, running down the alphabetical list. For me this is like witnessing a solar eclipse or seeing Halley's Comet, which I did when I was very small and plan to do again when I'm old. It is a rare and beautiful mathematical caprice called a Markov chain: an apparently meaningful sequence in a flow of random numbers. This is a particularly pretty one, a wonder of nature requiring a staggering string of coincidences. It looks almost like animation, conveys a sense of movement and of deliberation. The 4 moves back up the line, then hovers around the middle of the list.

Roscombe AG is a decent-sized pharmaceutical company. They make an antacid everyone uses, and they're the market leader in some palliative drugs for chronic conditions. In other words they are boringly profitable, and reliably positioned. Short of a radical reinvention of medicine or a massive embezzlement, they will exist for ever. On the screen, I watch as their euro price goes:

91.750
91.754
91.740
91.450
94.750
41.750
91.750

Somewhere, no doubt, there are people shouting 'What the fuck?' Probably New York. Then the 4 works its way back again from left to right, and then it's gone.

It takes barely a second. No human trader could act on that sort of blip, but for a very brief period of time, Roscombe's stock was at less than half price. Someone could have made a fortune, and someone probably did. There's a layer of buying and selling now that happens in eyeblinks, as our algorithms and their algorithms fight it out over tiny fluctuations, and may the best software win. The banks have bought up huge warehouses and derelict buildings near the exchanges so as to cut milliseconds off the transmission times of their orders, filled them with the highest specification of computers in rows and rows and rows. There are no offices, just endless clean corridors occasionally patrolled by security men, and humming boxes looking for opportunities. Somewhere in those buildings is a trader – an automated system – that just made out like a pirate. Probably more than one.

A 4, like the fin of a shark. Of course that is what I would see. It was inevitable the comparison would occur to me. I'm getting used to my obsession, even getting rather fond of it, like the annoying but familiar tics of the lift machinery in an apartment I rented in Manhattan. The human mind is a device for seeing patterns. We can see faces in clouds, myths in the stars. My mind has a sort of dent, and that dent is shaped like a shark, so all the patterns and possibilities I see fall into that form. Of course a number 4 is a dorsal fin. So are black buttons and crescent moons. So are zeppelins and sushi and Madonna's conical bra. If you venture twenty-two million nine hundred and thirty-one thousand or so digits into the digits of Pi, you will find 4 occurring eight times in succession. Should I attribute significance to that as well? I can find sharks in the patterns in a whisky glass, sharks in my kolokitho keftedes.

Ten seconds later, Roscombe AG goes down. The price suddenly slumps 44.444 and doesn't go back up. It hangs for long enough that humans can notice, can act, and then abruptly it's 4.444 and then it's just a row of dashes. The screen fizzes and dies, and I see something huge and greenish-white slip down and away into the cathode grey.

'What the fuck?' says De Vries.

'Moment of silence,' I reply, holding up my hand.

'For Harrison's toy?'

'For Roscombe AG. RIP.'

And they all say 'What?' and run over to other screens to check. I don't bother to follow. Roscombe is dead, and a few seconds later they're nodding, murmuring: 'Shit, I wonder what happened. Jesus.'

I know what happened. Roscombe was playing in the shallows and it was taken by a shark.

*

Stella's house is the place I return to, over and over again, though I am not welcome any more and so, customarily, I visit only in dreams.

Yet here I am on the doorstep: not for the first time these last months, but for the first time in a very long while I actually ring the bell. Cosmatos stamps along the hall, well-remembered curmudgeonly tread on a thinning modern Iranian carpet. Flings wide the door. Stares at me. I see his hand go back as if directing my attention to the clock behind him on the wall. Am I late?

With his open palm he slaps me, and screams into my face, wide-eyed and grieving, a noise that is like a dockside winch going very badly wrong. It lasts for a remarkably long time, rising and falling. I stare into his mouth, past his teeth. I see his uvula. I smell his breath, stinking and heavy with coffee. The sound is surprisingly complex. If you were to graph it, you'd want a three-dimensional representation of its components one against another to appreciate it properly. Because of the phlegm in his throat, it's coming out as a chord, and I can see the colours around it hanging in the air.

He stops, the last frayed end of the hawser rasping through the machine and tumbling away into the oily water of the harbour.

Cosmatos listens to the quiet that follows, looks around. There are some quite startled people in his street: a woman gathering lavender flowers from her garden and a young couple spooning on a bench, a man walking two dogs. A vagabond with a flute on the street corner.

'Come in,' Cosmatos says. 'Fuck you, fuck off, go to hell. But come in. Because they would neither of them forgive me if I turned you away.'

I step through the door and I'm not prepared for the air inside. It hasn't changed. The whole place smells exactly the way it always did and now I remember that he did the cooking, that he smoked a pipe with tobacco from some upmarket shop in London, that it was his pomade that lingered in the hall because his study was on the ground floor. The Old Girl and Stella shared a work room in the attic because they loved the views and because they could throw one another insoluble problems and little jokes. I had a spot – just a recliner, no desk – in the corner, and was considered the most privileged of men.

They are still here. I know they are. I look through to the dining room. Perhaps they are having a late lunch. The same table, dark wood. The same deep green curtains, the same dark walls. The same bowl in the middle, with fruit. A decanter. But only one place laid, and that is his. He sits with their absence, and perhaps that makes him more sad, or less.

I hold on to the frame of the door and make a noise, and behind me I hear its echo, a gulp of sound like a lonely cat.

Cosmatos is crying, too.

'Damn you,' he whispers. 'Damn you completely, you little shit. I never cry. I come in here every day, a hundred times, and I never cry. I never see them and I never turn around expecting them to be there, and then you're here for one second and all I can think is that they will be right back and it will all be some stupid misunderstanding. They are not dead. They just got on the wrong train. What do you – what can you possibly – want?'

But my name is not Smith. It is not Jones or Berg or Müller. I am not northern, not calm or cool, and talking is not what I do when I am moved. I am Kyriakos. I am Constantine Kyriakos and I may not give a shit about football or the Church or ships or the Acropolis but I am Greek. I have already embraced him, halfway lifted him like the bundle of twigs that he is, and I have buried my face in his shoulder and I am crying, too. We are men, and this is how we grieve. I feel his tears on my neck, and I do not know which of us is shaking harder – we are both shuddering and wheezing – and then like an earthquake the moment ends quite simply, and we are just two fellows who have never seen eye to eye in a hug we'll never acknowledge again. A heartbeat later, even the embrace is gone.

'What do you want?' Cosmatos repeats.

'Help,' I tell him, because catharsis leads, however unwisely, to honesty.

*

He makes coffee. I was hoping for tea.

'Sit.'

We sit, together, and not in the haunted dining room but in the little kitchen with its stark fluorescent strips and the ugly table with the yellow plastic top. Cosmatos pours ouzo into his coffee, which explains why he doesn't care that it's cheap, half sawdust. I let him do the same for me. Liquorice and sketos. It's not bad. Actually, it's very bad: really revolting.

'So, what?' Cosmatos says.

I do not say that I have gone mad, or that my PTSD is feeding my mathematical synaesthesia and making me practically psychic. I do not propose that my shark is real, that I have married it or vowed myself to it. I tell him what I remember and what I have seen and I do not distinguish between what is possible and what is not. He is an expert in these things. He will draw me back to the land.

Except that he doesn't. He just sits there, and every so often I catch the scent of his exhalate and know that I am tasting tiny parts of the skin of his mouth.

'Your watch,' he murmurs.

'Yes.'

'It was gold?'

'Platinum.' I shrug.

He laughs. 'Of course.'

'Does that make a difference?'

'Everything makes a difference. Your mathematics tells you that. The butterfly stamps his foot, there is a storm in Mississippi. The birth of a child in Tunis changes the weighting of the world, shifts it minutely in its orbit, and over time the difference is enough to move the planet out of the path of a comet. Or into it. So it is with you. What did you give up to your shark?'

'I told you.'

'Idiot. Not the watch – the meaning of the watch. Does it carry you from one place to another at great speed and in comfort? No, that is an automobile. The meaning of the watch is not travel. Can you wield it in battle? Can you eat it? Can you fuck it? No, no, no! A watch does not entail these things. It is a watch – a complex technological device for … the measurement of time. Time! And this one had a platinum case, implying wealth and status. Yes?'

'Yes.'

'You live in a world of signs as well as things. In that world, Actaeon fed his lust by gazing upon the goddess Artemis as she bathed; she fed her hounds upon his flesh. Desire and hunger: one body merges with another. The father of Acteon was Aristaeus, likewise a lecher, who as a young man in a passion chased Eurydice through the woods, where she was bitten by a serpent and died. From the mouth: death. Her lover, Orpheus, went down into the underworld to retrieve her, perhaps the most celebrated catabasis of legend. He sang so sweetly to the god of the dead that he was permitted to bring her back – from the mouth: life. And yet he could not control his love, and looked upon her face too soon, so that she was torn away again. Thereafter he imposed control upon himself. He abjured physical love, and was himself by reason thereof torn and devoured by the affronted Ciconian women, worshippers of Dionysus, the serpent god – again, the serpent – who was slain by Titans as a baby and born again when his still-beating heart was planted in the body of the woman Semele. Those Ciconians who took into themselves the meat of Orpheus were like Semele got with child, and from their loins came monsters such as Cetus. From death by way of that deep and female interior mystery of creation, once more: life. Cetus the dragon plagued Ethiopia and met his end in combat with Perseus. The dead monster became the island of Thera, where after many years the ragged skull of Actaeon was brought. That same Actaeon! We return to the beginning. And from Acteon's open mouth – as from the severed head of Orpheus, which sang sweetly as it floated down the river on the tide of his life's blood – arose a swarm of bees whose honey was a panacea against all but mortal wounds, and whose venom was unmatched in its lethality. Do you understand? The wheel turns and the road goes on and on. The mouth is the gate of life and death. We desire it, are devoured by it, emerge from it. Gods do not die, they are transformed. They are sundered, reforged, slain, reborn, eaten and regurgitated. The debts of our legends are never cancelled, because the seed of their renewal is contained in each payment.

'And so we come to you. You gave time and fortune in exchange for your life. Into the mouth of the god, you offered those things. Now time and fortune are returned to you in a new form, but in the next instant there will be a price, and beyond the price another payment. What is devoured is birthed. You will grow wealthy, and you will fall, and rise, and fall as many times as the story requires. You will be ripped into pieces and reborn. Congratulations! You have become the mirror of the world. It is the fate of Greece itself, in these coming days.'

Seamlessly, from myths to politics. I try to stay on target.

'I don't want to talk about that.' I really don't. You don't talk about the state of the nation with Cosmatos any more than you discuss football with one of those assholes who has his team's colours tattooed on his shoulder.

'What is wrong with Greece?' Bristling Cosmatos, ready to fight me.

'We're broke,' I tell him, knowing that's not what he meant. 'We let the Americans sell us some very bad pigs in some very large pokes, and we spent two and a half billion euros on a network of Internet-capable public toilets because someone's brother-in-law built them. Whatever. Some of it was our fault, a lot of it wasn't. We're a little bit unwilling to pay taxes and to be honest we've been living on non-existent money since '94, but that makes us no different than the rest of Europe except that when the music stopped we not only did not have a chair, we were in the corner playing doctor with the pretty one from science class. When Portugal falls over on its arse, we'll be last year's news.'

'No,' Cosmatos says. 'No. That is the shit we are made to eat. It is not the truth, and you know it – banker.'

And here we go. Say it out loud. Acknowledge it. When you pretend it's something else, you give ground. Since the death of his wife, Cosmatos has become a very sophisticated, very highbrow fascist. It's one of the reasons we don't see each other very much: I can't stand it. It's like looking at a man cutting

83

his face with a knife. The Old Girl would have been furious with him. *Cosmatos! For God's sake. Take up with some floozy. Really – find a young, foolish PhD in anthropology who thinks frequent contact with your penis will teach her about religious ecstasy and the cult of the twice-born. Flaunt her at parties and outrage our family. Ideally a Dutch woman who speaks frankly about fellatio. That is a perfectly respectable folly for an old, childless man whose wife is dead. But this ... not this. It is beneath you.*

Indeed, it's a bully's faith and it doesn't suit him, but it was always there. It's a fault in the code, or some sort of odd psychological balancing: the only thing in his life to which he does not apply the power of cultural analysis that is his. Instead he erects remarkable edifices around it, balances and protects it with baroque constructions and conspiracies and blinds himself to the subtext. Cosmatos the revolutionary, plotting the rise of the new Sparta from the towers of the academe.

After the Old Girl died it became all of him, or all of the small part of him that is not the overlapping Jungian disciplines of alchemy, poetry, theology and branding. I know better than to argue. Years ago he was filled with a kind of weird lucidity about it, about the need for Greece to believe itself unique, to create a perception of Greekness that was arranged around eudaemonia. 'We must be heroes! We must believe that we are great so that great choices are ordinary to us – we must all act as if we are observed and infused by pagan angels!' But now that elixir has been diluted with a more obvious sort of grime, a common-or-garden racism. Everyone has an idiot relative who'll tell you across the dinner table that 'the blacks' don't really understand civilisation and aren't suited to it, or that 'the Jews' control the media and that's why only some dishrag newspaper or flashing GIF website knows the real story. Consciousness, I once read in a book, is a complexly convoluted loop of information that can observe itself. What does it say about a person, then, if they cannot manage the trick? When Cosmatos is like this, is he a person, or a piece of stupid stone, walking and talking like a man?

He shakes his head. 'No, Constantine. No. These are symptoms. They are not what is wrong, they are what happens because of it. Greece is not broke, it is broken. The streets are full of spongers and the halls of power are full of cheats. Africans, Gypsies, Croatians. Bank of America, the Germans, the Chinese. Rapists of a nation as much as of women and boys! In one way or another it is the same. They set up shop, they create a problem, and then the only solution is to give them more money to make it go away! They are here to speculate, to grow rich through this crisis they have created and settled upon us. They will take everything we have that they covet, and we will be left behind when they begin to take off again. It is not migration, it is swarming. Oh, don't roll your eyes at me! You break bread with them all the time!' Jaw jutting, inviting me to swing at him across the awful coffee. I swallow some instead. It's still awful, but it tastes better than Cosmatos's patriotic shit.

This is what death has done to him. What kind of stupid, I wonder, does my grief make me?

Cosmatos is full of portentous anger. 'The whole of European society is constructed on a failed model of being! A hash of lies and ignorance! Those bastards in Brussels and Berlin, saving their banks and making us carry their trash! Oh, yes, for them it is easy to say the law is what is written, and the text of an international treaty is absolute and to maintain as we suffer that that is virtue. So what if a nation burns and a people starve? So what if the poorest of Europe must play host to the wretched of Africa? That is the so-precious law we must follow. It is a Judaeo-Christian perception filtered through a German mindset and it is fundamentally foreign to our understanding. It is out of date anyway! Nothing is written in stone in a digital century, and we understand that. It is our time once more, Constantine. The true Greek life is poetic, not arithmetical – which is why you are forever so at war with yourself. We will learn to live symbolically, at one with our gods. You, too, will have to learn.'

So, filleting: finance bad, group poetry sessions good; Jews bad, Greeks good; law bad, gods and symbols good. In other words, a sack of shit. I'm angry with myself for coming. I knew we'd end up here and I gave him an audience because I was weak. Nostalgic. I came looking for kindly ghosts and found this narrow old man. 'This is crap. Yes – yes, it is crap, Cosmatos – yes. But what I want – do not interrupt me please, I have listened nicely to your crap even though you know I hate it – what I want to know is how does any of this crap connect to my shark?'

I want to say I don't know why I came here, but I do. I came here to hide, and this lecture is the price, and I came here to be with Stella, and Stella's price cannot be paid.

'Hah! Crap is exactly the point! You have a shark in your head that eats corporations and shits money. You know what that means?'

'Self-evidently, you evil old prick, I do not, or I wouldn't be asking.' Too tired of him now to pretend.

But he doesn't take offence. He's on a roll now, because all this somehow makes him happy. He laughs. 'It means revolution! The overturning of things, the approach of apocatastasis. A return to the beginning. You have contracted a god, Constantine. It does not matter if you think it is a brain lesion or a space alien or whatever you are telling yourself. When you do the bidding of your god, your enemies fall and you rise. That is the only law for you now. You are becoming what we will all be, in the new Greece. Soon you will not even notice that you do the bidding of your mistress. If you go against her, you will be devoured.'

'Symbolically.'

He leans forward, wafting sketos. 'Yes. Symbolically. You are used to a world in which symbols are intangible things like the aristocratic titles of exiled princes, even if symbols and rumours are the governing currencies of your trade. But in the new Greece, symbols will be the actual truth. If you are devoured by your shark, your physical body will be torn apart, and the pieces will be swallowed. Watching from the Judaeo-Christian model, one might see a man cut up your body and feed it over the side of a boat. Or one might see a crowd of people each tear a piece from the corpse with their mouths. But that watcher would be wrong. He would be seeing what is not there, the ghost of an irrelevant way of being in the world. A way that is lifeless and foreign, like a fat burned-out German automobile with grass growing through the shell, in a field full of thoroughbred horses. The truth would be that a god ate you, because you were unfaithful.'

I realise that Cosmatos is entirely off his head.

I say: 'In the new Greece.'

'The Greece that is coming, Constantine, will be the whole world: Greece, from Athens to Magadan, Thessaloníki to Cape Town, Corfu to Darwin and Guam. Not tomorrow, not next year. Now. Greece shall be torn no longer.'

When Megalos said that, I thought it was original, but it must be a new asshole catchphrase.

Cosmatos gets to his feet and extends his hand. 'Come. I know people who can help you.'

He actually means to take me somewhere. These people he's talking about right now are not generalised people, the spectral silent majority who agree with him and always have. These are specific people. Hell no.

'I've got somewhere to be,' I tell him. Unspoken: anywhere but here, with you.

He scowls, puffs out his cheeks. 'Fine, then. Do whatever the fuck you like.'

He shows me to the door.

We don't hug.

*

Four days later it happens again: the telltale trail of 4s. Harrison's monitor is gone for ever, thank God, and the gas it emitted when it died was apparently toxic so he can't have another one. Sadly there are still emulators, clever bits of programming which take expensive hardware and make it behave like something cheap and old. You can get a stock ticker for your iPad which does it, and for some reason the bug has caught me, I've started using it. I still have all my other stuff going on, I've just got my tablet resting on a little stand and the cool green numbers drifting by like something from that Keanu movie.

The 4s go up and down the stock list, then up, then down halfway to one price where they seem to hover and consider. And then they disappear. A decent company apparently in good health.

I pick up the phone to a flunky. 'Dump Couper-Seidel,' I say.

'What?'

'Dump it. I've lost faith. Do it now.'

He does. 'Jesus, Constantine, that was expensive.'

I think about it. Couper-Seidel has three competitors. 'Get me as much as you can of Juarez Industrial Copper and Ardhew Metallic.' I don't like the third one. It's wobbly. 'Who holds Couper's debt?' Everyone has debt. Everyone is leveraged somehow. He tells me. I short them.

Four minutes later, it happens, and Brunner and De Vries are staring over my shoulder. Just dumping Couper-Seidel has saved us about €10 million. The shorts have made us another €40 million. If we cash out now, the profit on the stock in Juarez Industrial and Ardhew will bring the total to something like €100 million.

In the purest bullshit of an industry founded on it, what I have just done is the kind of thing careers are made on. This morning I was a very good banker. Now I am touching the edges of financial godhead. I have entered the special space set aside for prophets and savants who understand where the money world is going before it goes there, for Michael Burry and George Soros, for others who don't choose to be known by the wider public. Join that club and you almost automatically join another one, the one that has fifteen hundred members and more power, acting collectively, than any other force on earth. It's not a conspiracy, it's simply such a concentration of access and resource that it cannot help but carry weight. It requires no oaths of allegiance, because all that is already implied. It's just wealth, but on a level that is to all intents and purposes an evolutionary change.

I can feel it, waiting for me: the new nationality that takes you when you have become pure money.

The shark eats three more companies before the end of the month, and I find I'm waiting for it, hanging by the screen like a nervous boyfriend, but in fact it never happens unless I'm there. It never even happens if I'm just looking the other way. It waits. Or rather, as I tell myself, the subconscious process in my head that has been kicked loose by my rampage, by my fear, by priapism and by my shark obsession, requires that I spend a given amount of time looking at the numbers before it shows me what is happening.

But I know it doesn't. I don't need to do anything except drink coffee and wait. I make money the way other men make urine.

I use the money to buy art. Art right now is a better bet in many ways than a bank, so long as you buy the right art and buy enough of it to avoid paying a ridiculous commission. It's also a bullshit-based economy, so the terms of engagement are very familiar. I thought about wine, but you know what? I care about wine. Wine should not get shoehorned and abused by the market. Wine is old and respectable and erotic and human. I know Goldman once thought about buying Bordeaux – not the wine, the region, so they'd control supply – but they didn't, and that is a good thing. Wine should not be a value counter in this game, no more than food. No more than healthcare or clean water. There are things that should be immune, and the people who don't understand that distinction, the distinction between what is fair game and what is not: those are the people who should go to jail.

I hire a woman from Zurich called Miranda who specialises in finding underrated material and acquiring a corner on it, and she buys me almost the entire collection of some ageing rocker in London who's fallen on hard times owing to a divorce. This includes a great quantity of South American folk art – and what she tells me are some extremely rare and undervalued duodecimal quipus, which I might actually find interesting – along with the best of some new work by a man named Berihun Bekele who painted flying saucer pop art in the 1970s. I have to assume she knows what she is doing. A few days later, there's a splash piece in the *New York Times* about the man. He evidently got his mojo back working on a new computer game that everyone is supremely excited about. Note to self: get it. But also: doff the cap to Miranda, because the price of Bekele's work has just added a few zeros. The nerds of Silicon Valley have gone nuts for his stuff.

We just turn around and sell most of the Bekeles straight to California, but I tell her to send me a selection, of her own choosing, to go on my walls. 'Something I'd like, something you think will resonate for me.' The first thing I unwrap is a quipu, what people sometimes call a 'talking knot'. This is evidently a sort of Inca necklace-cum-tax return, and, presumably on the basis that I am a mathematician by training, she includes a sheaf of paperwork I do not read about how remarkable it is that it's patterned in base 12 rather than base 10. The quipu itself, for all that someone has spread it out like a condor's wing, looks like a neolithic two-way. I send it back and tell her to store it. Quipus are apparently hard currency to collectors, real blue-chip property, so it isn't a poor choice financially, it's just not my thing.

Next out of the bubble-wrap is a strikingly erotic nude of a Japanese woman reclining in some sort of courtyard; then a strange sub-Mondrian effort I don't really give a shit about, but which is perfectly acceptable chin-scratching art; and finally I'm confronted with a seven-foot canvas wrapped in opaque brown paper around the plastic, which was apparently something Bekele painted as part of a challenge to the Khartoum School which is labelled in big black felt-tip letters over the packing tape with the single word GNOMON.

The joke works on a lot of levels. 'Gnomon' means 'one in the know', which is clever about art and about my financial mojo, but it also means something perpendicular, something that sticks out. Everything in the world, you will observe, ultimately pays homage to my erection. I imagine Miranda as a vigorous Swiss blonde with a skier's legs, but she won't tell me and she laughs when I offer to fly her in.

I glance at the printed description – MIXED MEDIA. Apparently there's an actual metal gnomon, an architect's tool, glued to the wooden board on which the whole thing is painted.

Unboxing art is even better than unboxing a new phone. It is bigger, more physical, and what is underneath has a rich oil and turpentine stink that is earthy and mouth-watering.

Carefully, with scissors, I undress my picture, and step back. Oh, yes. He sees clearly, this forgotten bad boy from Addis Ababa. He sees through time.

The gnomon is the fin, of course, and Bekele dreamed it very accurately, shaped the shallow arc of the head and body, the bulbous bullet shape.

It is swimming through inky electronic space, the sky above full of numbers in cathode ray green.

Gnomon is a picture of my shark.

That night, I buy drinks for an entire strip club. An Israeli dancer, the only one I've ever met and a former tank commander, sits naked on my lap and whispers in my ear.

She's rather charming. I have never been so lonely in my life.

*

And so to bed, but clearly not to sleep, not in the company of Commander Ruth, the world's most dangerous submissive, and anyway, who needs to dream of white ghosts and rows and rows of teeth every night? That will not leave you rested. Perhaps excess will, if you give it time and money. I try it on for size: more and more of everything. The good doctors of Athens will happily prescribe for a well-to-do patient the very latest in mood management and sleeping pills, of course, but recently I've come to believe that the best defences are still the natural ones. Over the next week I drink Armagnac from the sacroiliac crest of an heiress and Yquem from the suprasternal notch of a heptathlete. I hire in as many plasma screens as will fit in my party space and obtain pre-release copies of Bekele's must-have video game – it's called *Witnessed*, a sort of Orwellian Lara Croft tunnel-trawler with bleak, hypnotic landscapes that seem to watch you right back – and host the all-Greece launch party, with hot tubs. We play a marathon – the idea is to reach the level cap, be the first in the world. I have no idea if we actually achieve this in the end, but it's a huge deal, with press, because this kind of thing makes money like cows make shit. Drunk and button-mashing as if this work of ludic art was a *Missile Command* coin-op from the eighties, I accidentally unlock an Easter egg in the game: the figure representing me slips through a hidden door into a kind of insane control centre, a room full of secrets. Apparently this demonstrates that I have mad skillz, because someone writes the words on my stomach in purple lipstick and sambuca.

There's a rousing cheer, but I don't think much about it because I've already dropped the controller to get another drink and then am otherwise engaged talking algorithms and UI add-ons with three owner-engineers from a software company in Berlin. I make a note: coder women are my people and they are *crazy* hot.

In the corner of my eye I can see the game, my guests playing and playing. Everything is a camera in *Witnessed*, and the designer has done this creepy-as-shit thing where the software looks at your calendar and your recent emails and asks about them if you leave it alone for too long: surveillance simulating surveillance. Two of my guests have to make a hasty retreat after the system interrupts an argument about the relative buoyancy of David Hasselhoff and Erika Eleniak to ask, via the 21-foot plasma, if they're sleeping together. My bad, my bad, and more bubbles for everyone. No, no, champagne – wait, you have a bubble machine? Bring it immediately!

When I have recovered, there's an advertising convention in town, and of course we all know about ad executives, and then it's Fashion Week and then a film festival, and if after a while at the extremes one suffers from issues of performance – a few weeks of this sort of behaviour will bring that on in a sixteen-year-old, never mind a guy in his thirties stressed unto mania and in any case in moderately iffy cardiovascular health – then modern science is able to assist there, too. Where once there was the little blue pill there is now a feedback-regulated injectable dispenser, a little electronic capsule they put in your gluteus muscle that really does the business. You can customise response times and various other aspects of your experience from an iPhone app. I put my code key on the main screen and invite my guests to choose my level of arousal, rating another mention in the gossip pages. Satisfaction – for all concerned – is positively guaranteed. I am RoboKyriakos. My genitals emit a low amp electrical wang pulse, as Charles Dance memorably said.

Yes. You will find that he actually did.

I am invincible, in the bank as in the sack. The shark swims in the markets, in the exchanges, in my balls. There are no castles I cannot storm. Day upon day upon night upon night, I invest Megalos's money – and that of a growing number of other clients – and I am unstoppable. The Patriarch, for his part, is evidently something of a mover and a shaker, albeit only in a moral sense. I find him on the front page of my newspaper brokering a labour agreement, then on the eleven o'clock news talking about the duty to the motherland. His profile is enhanced by a rumour that he's made some very smart investment calls recently, with a new – unnamed – advisor.

That would be my balls.

Megalos thrives. Everyone is buying what he's selling, that mixture of humility and pride that sits so well on a priest, and the hint of an old-fashioned intolerance for people who are not like us. Now I'm sure he and Cosmatos are – semiotically speaking – in bed together. They use all the same dog whistles, the same humblebrags, the same pleas for tolerance that somehow make intolerance seem quite reasonable. He's Greece's most eligible celibate, and no public occasion can take place without him. Even Europe loves him, inviting him to diplomatic events to keep him inside the fence. For as long as he's prepared to shake hands with the German Minister for Poverty and Aid and talk about the African Problem in measured tones; for as long as he has good things to say about the Chinese efforts against air pollution, then he's one of them, after all. A great thinker, is Nikolaos Megalos, uniting the working-class Right with the wealthy Right, representing those who might otherwise slip into more unpalatable corners of the political spectrum. Not that he could get through the door without my balls to make him richer.

Yes, my balls and everything that goes with them: even when the shark is not in evidence, it seems I cannot make a wrong choice. My own wealth increases almost as mightily as my cyborg erection. If I had known that alcohol poisoning, insomnia and the ineradicable scent of sex on my upper lip would do this to my professional skills, I would have debauched myself into a coma years ago. Fortunately I am now mature enough to handle my mutant power responsibly, so I do not have a heart attack or turn up to work without my trousers or anything like that. I run five funds now, all at once. They have differing imperatives, differing instructions and priorities, and in fact Megalos is the only large institutional client remaining in the original one. All the others have upgraded, moved on to my new, notionally riskier funds. Megalos is bound by some standing orders which require him to avoid such investments, so he and a smattering of smaller investors whom he introduced are the only ones still playing it safe. For the others, I dance between the flashing blades of economics like the girl from Cirque du Soleil. Nothing can stop me. The room – the whole bank – knows what I'm doing to myself, but for as long as I'm on this streak they won't get in the way. You don't mess with a man on a tear. In fact in a weird way they're my safety net. For as long as I'm up, they'll let me roll, and as soon as they sense weakness they'll move me out and send me on a Kur, which is what the Germans call it when you go to a nice hotel with raw carrots on the menu to dry out and remember your own name.

It's not a solution. Cosmatos was right about one thing: I don't seem to be losing my shark. She's come with me on to the land by some crazy shark magic, something primal and weird that can't be undone. I'm tied to her. Perhaps I married her with that watch. Did I tell you I went to get a new one? I did. I thought of Watches of Switzerland, but the most expensive thing they had was a TAG Heuer, a ridiculous effort made of carbon fibre. If I want a fighter jet, I'll buy one, I won't buy a watch in the style of a MiG. In the end I go for a Ulysse Nardin, because the guy in Jaeger-LeCoultre almost makes me wait, and while I'd love to get Breguet to sell the Marie-Antoinette, they're just never going to put out. I know someone who offered them $22 million for it and they said no. They keep that thing just to fuck with you. I'm guessing they believe one day they'll give it to a street urchin, and this one selfless anti-capitalist act will upset the axis of the world and usher in a new era of analogue watches, that Breguet are art-prank crypto-communists. Or no one's offered them enough yet for their insane timepiece. Whatever. Nardin makes one that has so many precious stones on it the enamelled white gold dial is almost impossible to see. They agree to do a personalised version with a shark on it, because, hey: Kyriakos.

I put it on. The bracelet feels hot against my skin. It itches and then it hurts, and when I take it off there's a mark as if I've burned my hand in a fire. Each link has left a print. The horologist at Nardin is horrified. He will apply a hypoallergenic coating, he says, it's never happened before, you usually only see that sort of reaction with impure gold, he'll assay the metal immediately.

In the end, he produces a new watch, but it's exactly the same. I don't show him the underside of my wrist, where the clasp has branded a little triangle into my skin.

*

I eat with the pantheon.

For four months, I join the Bilderberg swirl. I cannot turn around without shaking hands with a billionaire or a head of state. Would I care to come to [insert broken country here] and institute a new economic plan? Perhaps an island off the coast for my personal paradise would help me to decide? I can taste the power in my incidental acquaintances, in the carpets I walk on between meetings. I need to get to Mumbai, and normally I'd just get my credit card company to sort out a package, car and first-class ticket, top hotel, a standard thing I wouldn't have to think about. But not now. Now my phone rings, and it's Ben Teasdale, the Arizona technologist who owns half the fibre-optic cable in the US and supplies connectivity to the whole of Asia. He's a transhumanist, famously: when he dies he will try to squirt his consciousness into a computer, then freeze his brain in case there's any of himself left inside. He funds research into weird technologies: man–machine interfaces and artificial telepathy. He holds patents in things which will probably drive the next hundred years of economic growth.

'Izzat Kyriakos?'

'Yes.'

'This is Ben Teasdale. Uhh hear you're goin' to Mumbai.'

How he hears he does not say. Doesn't need to. If the NSA watches everyone, all the time, they do it with stuff he built. But all he'd have to do is ask, anyway. It's Ben Teasdale.

'Yes, I have some business over there. I'm on a flight tomorrow.'

'Screw that. You know what the odds ahh on dyin' in a aih crash on commercial?'

'Considerably more favourable than those for private jets.'

'Don't have a private jet. Bought a Airbus. Used to have a Boeing, but Uhh like all the electronics on the Airbus. Longest unpowered glide was a Airbus. Plane that landed on the Hudson was a Airbus.'

'The one that landed unpowered at Heathrow was a Boeing.'

'That was the pilot, not the plane. That was unbelievable. How the Queen did not hire that guy Uhh do not know.'

'Who did hire him?'

'Uhh did,' says Ben Teasdale. 'So you want to hitch a ride? Uhh'm goin' over foh a couple of days.'

So I fly with Ben Teasdale. It turns out I literally fly with him: he's a trained aviator and he likes to take the stick on long flights, just for an hour or so. He makes me his co-pilot, which is probably unlawful, but once more: it's Ben Teasdale. Nation states do not arrest Ben Teasdale. Ben Teasdale is a sovereign power.

We talk restaurants. Wine. Cigars. Cars. That's it.

He lends me a wing of his house for the duration. I try to figure out what he wants. I realise he wants nothing. He's curious. He thinks we'll meet again.

He flies on to Krasnoyarsk, but he hooks me up with another friend to get home. 'Asian money,' he says vaguely. 'Interesting fella.'

The interesting fella is taller than me – who isn't? – but very thin. His face is deeply lined, to the point where it's hard to say if he is fifty or seventy. He has a Boeing. He thinks there are too many gadgets on the Airbus, and it is in the nature of gadgets to go wrong all the time. What you want from a plane, the interesting fella says, is purity of purpose. It goes up and stays up until you want it to come down. You do not want it to fiddle. The Boeing company understands this, which is why he gets his planes from them. Planes, plural, because he has several. There are three waiting for us on the tarmac, and he picks one at random. 'Security,' he says, and pantomimes a machine gun. 'One has always to be a little careful.'

I wonder aloud if assassination is a serious worry to him. I haven't seen much in the way of security since Teasdale picked me up, and it's just occurred to me that it must nonetheless be all around me, around us, all the time. It is of course very expensive and therefore as unobtrusive as it is watertight.

The interesting fella asks me if I am familiar with the explanation of gravity in which space–time is a rubber sheet and each object placed on it forms a greater or lesser indentation, deforming the surface of the sheet so that other objects will roll down the incline. I agree that I have heard this description. We, the interesting fella says, meaning the Fifteen Hundred, we possess gravity. Where our gravity well touches another, there may be a collision. A man or an economy may be destroyed. In the event that one person is aware of the imminent arrival of another, the first may take steps to alleviate the danger posed by the second, up to and including seeking to make the threat go away altogether. Although this happens only very rarely, that is not the same as it never happening at all. He asks if I play Go. Go, he says, is a good metaphor, although that is a vast understatement of its beauty. Go is not a simulation of anything. Go is Go. It possesses – he hesitates – atsumi. He waves his hands. Atsumi, like the walls of a castle. Thickness and dominion. Mass, like with gravity again: the power to move things by being what it is. English and Japanese are both good languages for saying these things. Good, but not great. I ask if he is himself Japanese.

The interesting fella says that he is not.

When he does not say anything else, I admit that I have never played Go and ask him to show me how it works.

We play Go. It turns out that my ignorance of the game does not make me a tedious opponent because one of the ways in which Go is not like chess is that there are no prescribed openings as such. There are familiar patterns that quickly yield to uniquenesses, and what appears to be a mistake may become a fulcrum whose existence and position enables something remarkable. It is about identity as much as strategy. It is also profoundly difficult for computers to understand. Even a smallish chess machine can beat most players – but until very recently the very best Go simulator still struggled with an average human opponent. Now that has changed, but it happened by making a different kind of step altogether. Effectively, the digital Go master is not a machine at all, but a simulated person whose consciousness only extends to Go.

For a while, as we play, I wonder what it would be like to experience existence through these elliptical black and white stones touching lightly on the sheer mathematical field of the board. The combination of simplicity and complexity is delicious: two colours and a grid, and yet after a few moves, the board embraces trillions of possibilities.

I let myself enjoy the game and do not try to analyse it, and my choices flow. The interesting fella still wins, but the competition is not the point.

After he has won three, he looks at me. 'I am surprised,' he says.

'How so?'

'I expected you to talk all the time.'

I tell him I'm glad to be quiet for a while because my life is very loud. This meets with his approval.

'My life is also loud – but this week is for me. I am going to Sotheby's to buy a painting. A pastoral scene with many maple trees. When I was growing up, my mother told me the maple was a symbol of love and new beginnings. Then when I was a young man I learned that it also represents practicality and balance, which are almost the opposite of love. A tree of contradictions, or duality, turning to reveal one face or another to the world. I understand the quality of the brushwork is unparalleled.'

'Who is it by?'

'It is supposed to be by Tintoretto, but it is a forgery.'

I have the feeling, again, that I am being measured. 'A good one?'

'An excellent one. Sotheby's have no idea. One may expect the bidding to be quite intense.'

'And you are not going to tell them it's a fake.'

'Indeed not.'

In the fourth game, I box him in for a moment, and the hole in the board makes the shape of a shark. The interesting fella tuts. The Chinese don't like the number 4, he says. It whispers of the trap of birth, that it is accompanied by the inexorability of death. But that is a homophony, not identity. It is a shadow in the code. Do I see a 4?

I tell him that the number 4 has a different significance for me, and the interesting fella grins. 'Oh, yes,' he says. 'Megalodon!' That makes me laugh. The interesting guy raises an eyebrow. I explain that I have a client with a similar name. It is okay to do this because Nikolaos Megalos has never requested or implied any need for discretion regarding the Order's decision to hire my firm.

The interesting fella frowns. 'I know of him,' he says, and we share another of his silences.

'Perhaps,' he suggests at last, 'I will buy the painting and give it to someone as a very subtle practical joke.'

'Perhaps the forgery is painted over a genuine masterpiece,' I reply.

He spreads his hands for a moment, acknowledging that anything is possible.

We play. I reflect that when it comes out that I've been sharing plane rides with Ben Teasdale and his set, I will get more clients. Influence clusters. International finance is not done in boardrooms, it's done here, in these liminal spaces that are made out of money. Governance is in the private terminals at global aviation hubs, in occasional palaces and ubiquity, in sharing a limo because you have nothing to prove. The merely rich talk about their other homes, their other houses. The gods do not. If they need somewhere, they acquire it, or someone else provides it. They do not keep track of nations or properties, because they are at home everywhere.

In the sixth game, I make a late move on instinct and realise as the interesting fella blinks sharply and then claps his hands that I have done something right. The face of the board ripples and shifts as we play out the finish. I have won.

The interesting fella makes a pleased little noise. 'Myoushu,' he says. 'And plenty of kiai.'

I smile back. 'In Greek: meraki. It has my heart in it.'

'Yes. But also you were unexpected.'

And so I am brave enough to ask my last question: 'Why are you buying the forgery?'

He extends his hand across the table for me to shake. 'Because it is beautiful, Constantine Kyriakos.' His skin is very dry and thick. He is a working man. I am embarrassed by the difference.

He studies me for a moment, then opens his wallet and removes a card. A long number is printed in red.

'If you have trouble,' he says. 'These are my guys. For security. "You may travel to the ends of the earth, but I shall hold you always in my palm." Say it back to me.'

I do.

'Good.'

The pilot asks us to prepare for landing.

*

I am sitting at my desk and I do not know what to do.

Ten seconds ago, every digit on the screen became a 4.

444444444444
444444444444
444444444444
444444444444
444444444444
444444444444

I scrolled down, but it was relentless – endless. Then I reset the system. It was the same. For a moment I thought I was losing it, and then I realised that I was not. Then I sat there for another few seconds and stared, and I'm still staring now. Some of the digits are bolded, some are italicised, some are not. It makes weird patterns and pictures, like kelp, and as I make the connection I understand.

I know what this is.

The market is about to crash, and crash hard, like *Hindenburg* hard. The peaks and troughs of faux cathode green, dark and light, slip across the screen.

In the deep valleys between towers of kelp: the shark, waiting for the corpses to drift down.

It doesn't matter why. Perhaps some idiot has let the algo-traders run riot again. Perhaps it's just a blip and tomorrow it'll correct, or perhaps the Fort Knox gold reserves have been stolen, or the US has been hit by a nuclear strike. Perhaps the US is about to be hit by a nuclear strike. It doesn't matter. It's happening, and there's nothing I can do about it.

No, really, there's nothing. Imagine:

Hi, it's Constantine Kyriakos. I was on the cover of GQ last month. Well, okay, it was German GQ. It doesn't matter. I'm a finance genius, okay? And something bad is happening to the market, something so bad I think there may be a national security threat to your country, like a dirty bomb or something— Hello? Hello? Hello?...

Guten tag, hier Constantine Kyriakos. Ich möchte etwas ganz wichtiges erzählen. Eine Katastrophe kommt. Gerade jetzt. Ja. Jetzt. Ich weiß nicht genau. Eine Katastrophe. Vielleicht finanziell. Es wird finanzielle Folgen haben. Ich— Hallo? Hallo?...

Ni hao ...

Buenos días ...

Hi, look, I've called a couple of your colleagues, the State Department and Homeland Security, they hung up on me but you've got to listen: there's a serious problem and I think you should put some planes in the air, I think maybe you're being attacked ... Well, because the markets are crashing ... Well, no, but they're about to ... Well, I know because I have a magic shark in my head and I can see her fin in the stock ticker when things are going to hell— Are you still there? Please don't hang up! Hello?

Yeah. That's not going to work. And even if it did, what the hell could anyone do? I'd probably trigger the crash myself by trying to stop it.

So in these next minutes I have to decide who lives and who dies.

Five funds. Five funds with differing instructions and goals, five funds taking different approaches, each profiting from my barmy intuitions, each rising in strength, but each somewhat opposed to the others. I can save three, maybe four, but one of them can't go on. One of them will eat dirt. The combination of my moves will surely screw somebody. The money music has stopped in the world today and someone's getting left without a chair. The question is who?

But in the end, it's not much of a choice. The original fund is the odd one out, the others are more compatible in philosophy, if diverse in holdings – and my new clients are pantheon clients. You don't dump the Fifteen Hundred. You just don't. For all I know they've set this up just to see what choice I make. Does it seem unlikely to you that the rulers of the world would gut the economy for a year just to check up on one man? That's because you're not one of them. You belong to another species. If you're not in the Fifteen Hundred, you're not just different, you're barely real.

So I drop Megalos down the deepest hole I can find. I let my original fund take a bath. A bath in acid. He's a man of God, anyway: poverty will be good for his soul. And I realise that I am about to ascend. In a little while, I will not be an advisor to the world's elite. I will be one of them – and probably quite near the top.

I call each of my other clients, one by one, and I warn them of what's about to happen so that they can move their other money around, find shelter from the storm.

*

The news breaks an hour later. I'm listening to the radio, which not many people do any more but I do. The whole thing happens slowly and calmly, as if we were all just waiting for this moment. Another banking crisis? Feh. Who cares? How much worse can it get? We knew that the British housing bubble was unsustainable, again. We knew that food bonds were a shitty idea, again. We knew that the Chinese were propping up the dollar and couldn't do it for ever, that the renminbi was still unnaturally restrained, that Congress was screwing with the debt ceiling, again. We knew our mistakes weren't going away, that we were sailing in a kettle with an ever-increasing number of holes in it, and that the patches themselves would sooner or later drag us down into the deep blue water. It was only a question of which ridiculous, pusillanimous choice would be the one to make it happen. But we hadn't realised, even I hadn't realised, even with all I knew, even I didn't consider that all that finance crap meant something very practical. Six months ago the government finally privatised the water utilities in Greece. Today it turns out that the companies that bought them cannot pay the workers, or for the purchase of electricity to desalinate and purify. Water will be rationed from tonight, in the summer heat, an absurdly small amount per person per day may be drawn from the tap. There is no way to control usage by home or even by street. Who you have to trust depends entirely on the random roving of the mains beneath the streets, a network that ignores social niceties of class and wealth. In a better world it would be – ho ho ho – a watershed moment for the city, even the country. We'd pull together. People would talk about the moment when Athens shared its cups for a hundred years, and we'd emerge new-made as a nation of parts. That would be a world without television talk shows. Not one of them bothers with such a milkdream. Instead they call whoever can be most eloquently hateful and put them all together on a blue leather sofa. Great TV ensues, fisticuffs and rabble-rousing. 'You foreign scroungers are taking our water!' I make a note that I must buy any stations that are for sale and arrange to have all the producers fired.

For a short while everything continues to function, like the band playing on the *Titanic*. Shops set out their stocks of mineral water in cardboard trays and people buy them. I try to buy out the whole stock so that I can give it all away, but the manager won't let me. 'If I give it away,' he says, 'they'll think everything else is free, too, and people will start to come up from the bad areas.' I think I'm feeling a bit guilty about what I just wallowed in, but I couldn't have known. In the queues at the wholesalers where you can buy those serious barrels of water for office coolers, people greet one another with a sort of alien invasion politesse while they wait to hear whether their savings have gone down with some bank, or whether they've landed on one of the solid islands in the stream. I could tell them. I don't.

I realise I'm here by force of habit. There's no reason for me to do any of this. I should be sorting out my new world, moving house for a while, but I'm trapped, just watching myself, my country. I'm too fascinated to take up my empty throne just yet. And I don't think I'll ever come here again, or understand it if I do. These are my last hours of ordinary humanity. They're precious.

And they're strange. There's a wild moment coming, a day of misrule. We can all feel the riots waiting behind the hills. It's like a weather forecast: today, fine with bankruptcies, some rain. Tomorrow: high pressure zone moving in, torrential downpour of shit; and over the weekend: civil unrest, burning cars.

When I talk to people I know about the finance part, I lie, and say I am worried too. I suggest that this kind of instability affects everyone, up and down the scale, but the truth is that when the fog clears – unless the whole world descends into barbarism and to some extent even then – I will be even richer than I was at close of business. I will no longer have a job at my bank, but that won't really worry me because at that point I will own banks. In fact, by chance, I will probably own the bank I presently work for.

In the faces of my fellows in the queue, even as we share companionable grumbles, I can see something wary. They are not here to make friends, or even to buy water. They are checking out the opposition.

When I get home, I pack a bag.

All the while I expect to be ducking Megalos's calls, and I do feel residually bad about him and his holy order suddenly having to live up to the ideal of humble poverty, but in fact he doesn't try to get in touch. I assume that he is firefighting, or that he has been ousted and the new boss of the Order of St Augustine and St Spyridon is an actual Christian, a pious old geezer who welcomes the chance to lead his flock back to whatever pastures they actually come from and do good works. It's going to be a boom area, charity. Almost everyone south of Milan will need it, and anyone east of Zurich. Interestingly, Iceland has done rather well. Say one thing for the Icelanders, say this: they learn fast.

In foreign news, the Red Cross is already talking about a continental network of food banks, and the left coalition in France has called for the nationalisation of the energy companies and the transport infrastructure. It's a terrible idea in the context of the financial community and how they will treat France hereafter, but it's not a bad one in terms of keeping as many French people alive as possible through the winter. Perhaps the crazy communists have just recognised a little bit ahead of everyone else how bad this is really going to be. Certainly some of my erstwhile colleagues are being rather rash about it. They have not yet taken on board the level of desperation this has created, and are still talking rather arrogantly about riding the problem out. Say rather, they will ride it down, and at the bottom they will find people who are quite likely to use their Maseratis for bonfires and cook their manicured dogs for food.

I think I'll go to the Bahamas. There's a short list of countries you'd actually want to go to which will not be adversely affected by this situation, and very few of them have decent food or fine weather. There's a much longer list of countries you wouldn't really want to go to under normal circumstances which will either not be affected or will not notice one more appalling nightmare in the crowd.

I'm not going to apply for residency in Norway, and I'm definitely not going to Afghanistan, Colombia or Western Sahara.

I am, however, going stir crazy in the flat. I've been awake for too long and I'm making fairly jittery, bad decisions. I need to clear my head. So while I'm wondering which island would be best, I may as well go for my daily run. I have a trainer, Grant, and he's part of that American culture of exercise where they apparently 'come from yes'. I think that he wakes in the morning and does a hundred pushups, drinks a cucumber and seagrass shake with added bull semen and then goes for a quick marathon, and fuck you, Pheidippides, because that's his warm-up. He goes every year to something called the Leadville Race and finishes it, which is apparently not what most people do, and when he really applies himself he comes in the top thirty. I suppose, if I do go to the Bahamas, I'll have to bring him along. It seems like importing one's own hair shirt, but needs must.

Grant has set me homework. I must run a given distance every day I do not see him. If I do not do this I will be unable to keep up with his regimen, which is fierce. Every day I must record my time. I have no idea why I thought this was a good idea, or how much it is costing me to experience pain and nausea, I know only that my insurance company rep tells me he will add years to my life and take thousands off my premiums. So fine. I will acknowledge that I do actually feel better than I did a few months ago.

I run. I run for half an hour, out and around and up and down, taking no particular route. I choose roads that are strenuous, roads that are pretty, roads that go in the right direction to bring me around towards my home, and at the thirty-five-minute mark, I hear the sound of bees.

Once, when I was a child in Thessaloníki, I made the mistake of getting too close to a swarm. They didn't seem to notice me and I was fascinated, and then all of a sudden they did notice me and the swarm was a single thing that rose up off the flowers and roared at me, reached out for me with arms and teeth, and I ran. This time when I hear the noise I start running immediately, and of course I am perfectly dressed for it, so I make pretty good time for a guy who is maybe not built for the kind of life Grant envisions.

I can hear the noise get louder behind me, and then I can hear it to one side as well and I'm thinking some bee farm on someone's roof must have been set on fire, because these bees are pissed as all hell and I can smell the smoke but it's obviously not calming them down.

What does burning honey smell like? Does a beehive work like a candle with all that wax?

The swarm steps into being at the crossroads and it's not bees at all but people, and furious people, and so very, very many of them. Not just behind and to one side, but all around, all converging on this little bit of Athens with the too-nice houses. And I think: Oh, mother*fuck*, because it's really happening.

If they knew what I know, they would tear me apart and eat me.

*

I stand in the middle of the road and it's like the dive. It's exactly the same thing. There's just nothing I can do, nowhere to go. If this is going to kill me then I'm already dead, but I can feel the empty space on my arm where I used to wear my wristwatch and I know this was foreseen, it was planned. God is with me. My god, the one I can't get rid of. The shark.

The edge of the mob gets closer, and I keep waiting for the moment when I become the target. I should be the target, me more than maybe anyone else. Maybe those fourteen hundred and ninety-nine other guys first, but definitely me.

Instead as the riot reaches me I am swallowed up, even embraced. A man offers me a beer, a woman gives me a rag and tells me to wet it and tie it around my face. The boy behind her passes me a cardboard box the size of a couple of tennis balls. 'Ski goggles!' he shouts. 'From the department store! Long live the revolution, man!'

Oh.

Look at me: I'm in disguise.

It's not a very clever disguise, but that's why it works. I was running, so I'm covered in perspiration and grime. My workout gear is not expensive: trainers, sweatpants, an old T-shirt. I am a fat, sweating man in cheap clothes with no watch. I'm one of them, and maybe even a little further down on my luck.

I walk with the mob.

It had never occurred to me that a riot was a community, but it is. It is a spontaneous, weirdly self-organising thing that is, within certain very specific and obvious limits, kindly and helpful. In the middle are a lot of women, rioting mothers with their sons and husbands. It's not that they don't throw things or break things, but they keep an eye on their loved ones and they settle disputes over who has a claim on bits of looted property. Where the men would fight, the women scream and negotiate and tug, and somehow some sort of consensus emerges and debts are acknowledged and the thing is settled without the mob turning in on itself. When we meet the police, though, the mothers become Furies. One grey old woman lunges through to the front lines, hands outstretched and clawing, rips the Lexan visor from the face of the nearest one and tears a piece out of his cheek, has to be pulled away before his mates can bring her down. She's shouting something about bloody bastards, bastards, bastards. 'Her son died in custody,' another woman tells me.

'They killed him?'

'He was a junkie. Choked on his own puke. It was in . . . oh, I don't know. Before *Ntoltse Vita*.' She shrugs.

A three-decade rage, come due today.

The policemen surge. The crowd pushes back. It becomes almost hypnotic: five feet that way, ten, now back. Now twenty back. Now ten, ten forward. Rioters go down, bleed, scream. Truncheons rise and fall. And stop.

The riot's own heavy mob has arrived, construction workers in red flag pea jackets with armour of their own, motorcycle helmets and heavy-duty gloves. One of them has a nail gun, the pneumatic tank slung on his back. Pause for effect.

And begin.

Choi-chonkk! Choi-choi-choi-choi-choi-CHONKKKK!

Policemen sprout metal spines. Screaming and rout: 'We are Spartoi! Fuck you, pigs! Protectors of politicians and bankers and immigrants!' This mob doesn't agree on everything, but it knows what it doesn't like. The police line breaks, and the mob moves on. No interest in staying to torment the cops. Obstacle removed. Nearby, someone sets fire to a car by way of celebration. It's a Bentley. I know the man who owns it, an Austrian who claims some sort of hereditary title but can't get the courts to acknowledge it at home. The flames are orange and grey, a wicked nacreous silver that speaks of bad chemicals. And that's a new phase, a burning phase, and the mob upgrades. I am washed in it, carried on the flood. What else should I do? At the edges there are fires burning, accelerants and bonfires.

Twenty minutes later, Athens is in flames.

*

After the nail gun incident, the serious riot police arrive, and the army with them. You'd think that would end it, but in fact it just stokes the blaze. The police deploy teargas, water cannons. The mob bites back. Staging posts emerge, new fronts open. Hours pass like fever, a thousand mini-battles are fought on a hundred street corners. The mob swells and roams, rages, burns. Sometimes it seems to want to destroy the houses of the rich, overturn cars. Sometimes it looks. Then abruptly it goes to Omonia Square and into the poor quarter and seethes with hate. 'Junkies! Immigrants! Scroungers! Poofs and whores and lefties and criminal scum! Get out, fuck off! Fuck off back to Russia! Back to Ethiopia and Egypt! There are decent people here! Without your dead weight we'd be fine!' How did that happen, and how did we get here so fast, unopposed? Are those police boots there, are those regulation haircuts at the front? Of course they are. Even cops have feelings, don't they, and political views? It's opposite day, or if you want to be a bit traditional it's the Day of Misrule. The lowest now is high, and high as a kite. When the mob's in town, everyone gets a turn.

I touch nothing. I throw nothing, steal nothing, hurt no one. I am washed around in the body of the beast. Everyone smiles at me. Everyone cheers. I'm a brother, a fellow traveller, because I'm here and I don't object.

I want to be sick.

We wander, we thrash and we burn. We beat. The outer limbs do the dirty work, but the body of the beast is ballast and refuge and support. Even washed along, I am culpable to some degree. I do not raise my voice for reason and tolerance, because I am afraid. And then somehow I am spat out, in a little knot of tired people going home as if from the office, and it's all very polite. We're off shift, see you later, break a few windows for me.

My little crowd splits up at a crossroads. I daren't go directly home. No good rioter goes back to a flat in Glyfada. So I sit in a doorway and watch them fade away, and before I know it I'm asleep, with my head resting on the stone wall beside me.

I wake cold and stiff. I have no idea what time it is, but it's dark.

The streets are clearer now, in the sense that the main body of destruction has moved away. There's no attempt to restore order. I walk down my street in the smoke of burning premier-marque vehicles and listen to the sound of the world breaking. My building isn't on fire, although it has been. Of course the fire service has been here, and they were not having issues with water. More waste, more thirst in the making. The riot has flushed the gutters of Athens with the very thing it was demanding. Wouldn't it just have been easier if the fire services had hosed that water straight into bottles and handed them out? But perhaps Perrier and Evian managed to block that at a national level. Maybe that's what we're talking about, maybe my colleagues at the bank have found a last hurrah to make their own small (very small) retirement funds. Because sure as shit they are not going to work for me when I own the bank. Most of them shouldn't have jobs now, they're so bad at what they do, but very few people understand what they do so quality control is poor.

I don't really mind that my home has been burned and flooded. There wasn't anything important in there. Old me. Old, alien me. Not new me. I'm Constantine Kyriakos. Whatever I've lost, I can have two. Ten. A thousand. I can have anything.

Since there's no one there to stop me, I go inside. The stairs are covered in a treacherous slime of water and char.

*

I start to pack a bag and then realise that there's no need. Packing belongs to old me. The only things I need are the things that matter, that exist in only one place. I lean down to pick up the family picture by my bed, and then I hear the sound of my own front door opening. A voice says: 'Hey, Constantine Kyriakos!'

I turn, and it is a girl.

She's tall and slender. She has very white skin, black hair and very dark eyes, and those eyes are full to the brim with me. They are soaking me up as if I'm made of water and she's a desert. She's very attractive. There's no reason why I wouldn't stare at her, walking into my flat, wearing a black suit and murmuring my name. There's no reason to call it anything other than sex, and the fact that the last time I saw her I dreamed she had the teeth of a shark set in that perfect face. I never even knew her name and I didn't talk to her for any length of time, or I'd have noticed.

There's nothing to notice. It's an illusion, a trick of the light.

Fuck it. All right. She looks like Stella.

Stella died of cancer, ridiculously. She went to the doctor and said: 'I have a headache,' and he looked in her eyes and asked her about poor balance and flickering in the edges of her vision and she said that she did sometimes have those things and then he ordered a scan and that afternoon she went into hospital and they told her she had cancer and she called me and before I got there she had a seizure and she just died and that was all and I loved her and I miss her and I always will.

It is not Stella, because Stella is dead.

This woman is like her, but she is a decade older than Stella was when she died. The right age for Stella now. She is leaner, more muscular. She is Stella evolved, Stella grown and changed and yet the same. They could be sisters, or cousins. They could be strangers with that uncanny sameness, meeting in the street and staring, laughing, becoming friends.

My Stella.

'Hi!' I say. You have to say something when your dead ex-girlfriend appears in your flat just after you wreck the economy.

I don't want to ask her what she's doing in my place, just in case I invited her. She doesn't say 'hi' back, and the silence stretches. Well: boldness, be my friend. 'I'm leaving Glyfada because the country's about to go to shit and I've just become richer than pretty much everyone else in the entire world and I have absolutely no clue what to do about that or how I feel about it. The important thing is that I'm about to go to the airport and get on a plane – or buy one, actually, if they have one ready to go – and fly somewhere luxurious. So would you like to come with me and lie on the beach naked and drink drinks with umbrellas in them and have a lot of very dirty sex?'

She laughs out loud, not in a nice way but in a way that suddenly I recognise and I realise that I was wrong. She wasn't looking at me in that way because she adores me. The emotion in her face is not soft at all. Her eyes are open because she wants to see me suffer, or she wants to – what? To own me, the way you might own a beef cow. She is shaking because she hates me. On some fundamental level that even she is not entirely aware of, Not Stella thinks I am the ugliest thing she has ever seen, the worst person in the world. She loathes me and wants to hurt me in a very personal way. And then someone slaps me on the back and I stumble into the bedroom, and when I fall partway down and I stretch out towards her for support, she steps to one side and puts a sack over my head and some sort of chemical pad over the sack that smells of trombone solos and broken bagpipes, and I can see a ring of shadows like the entrance to a very irritating nightclub.

'Hierophant,' the girl who looks like Stella says through the sack. 'You will bring us the god, and Greece shall be torn no longer.'

Oh shit.

I go down into black water. It is dark and silent, but not – never, any more – deserted.

ineffective strategy

The Inspector wakes, smelling antiseptic and hospital sheets. She is uncomfortable and thirsty. She knows she should drink something, but devious sleep ambushes her in the instant of decision. Her hand twitches, but does not lift from the pillow. A passing nurse checks her vital signs, and is content. She tries to speak, but her mouth is dry and swollen.

On the plastic arm of the bed, beside the cup of water and some sort of lozenge which is not only tangy and cleansing but also lightly soothing, she finds her glasses. She taps once to wake them and twice more to engage audio, feeling the bud extrude delicately to touch the inner surfaces of her ear. This is the Witness model, intended for a variety of situations, including those where speech may not be desirable. She need only form the words as if she intended to speak them, and the software will read her neck and mouth and understand.

'Not possible.' The words don't come out properly, but that doesn't matter. She just wants to say it: Kyriakos does not belong in Hunter's head. 'How?'

The machine speaks inside her head, using the voice preference stored in her settings: a neutral male tenor, very soft, with the affect dialled down low so that it sounds placid and empty – appropriately like a machine rather than a lover whispering pillow talk. She recalls reading about the early experiments in aural interfaces, a German car manufacturer working through different tones for a satnav persona to please its clients. The hearty executives of the Rhineland did not enjoy being addressed by a superior male. The company tested a soothing feminine voice, and established that they liked this even less. Apparently felt they were being babied. A sultry tone translated as mocking, a professional one as nagging. In the end, it wasn't the tone that mattered, but the humanity of the voice. It needed to be, very clearly, a machine.

— Narrative blockade. You are not supposed to be working.

'I'm awake. I want to work. What's a narrative blockade?'

— An ineffective strategy for defeating direct neural interrogation.

'Expand.'

A brief flicker. Somewhere, the Witness is assessing her physical situation against a series of charts.

— You will tire quickly and forget. You have a mild concussion. Conceptual work will wait.

Which is not a refusal, but it's a good point. There's something more immediate, which may be affected by delay. 'Search, most recent image. Full file.' The picture of Lönnrot she took in Hunter's house.

— No match.

'What?'

— The image is insufficient.

In her vision, a generic human head speckled with dots and lines.

— The recognition system uses a gridwork of three-dimensional contours.

Her photograph hangs in the air, Lönnrot's face. It shifts slightly, becoming a pattern of white and black like a Rorschach blot.

— In this case, the single sample capture contains very little three-dimensional detail. The combination of low light and the subject's extremely pale skin is problematic. Additional captures would resolve the issue.

'Check before and after my arrival at the house, local area. Seventy-two-hour window.'

— No match. The local cameras are frequently rendered useless by children.

'Vandalism.'

— A variant of basketball. It is possible Hunter may have encouraged this behaviour.

'Can you extrapolate? Thin face, androgynous, mid thirties.'

— Yes.

A map of the whole country, covered in markers.

— Approximately seven million matches found.

'Cross-reference, name: Regno Lönnrot,' she says.

— No match.

She sighs. 'Save the query and refine it as we go. Give me meaning and context.'

— Lönnrot, general and preliminary results: literally 'red maple'. National emblem of Canada, symbolising practicality and renewal. In some parts of South East Asia it is also associated with romance. Best-known individual bearing the name: Elias Lönnrot, a Finnish medical doctor and philologist celebrated for collating the epic Kalevala, *whose structure and content have been proposed as factors in Finland's success in modern digital design. Also Eric Lönnrot, a fictional detective confronted by an unanticipated adversary. 'Regno' is anomalous. It is an Italian or Latin word meaning both a nation and the present action of rulership in the first person. It is not conventionally used as a name, so the superficial grammatical masculinity of the word is not strongly indicative of gender. A nickname or title is a possibility. In the latter case it might be ceremonial or religious, indicating a high position within a hierarchy, although some Christian and other religious orders denote their highest offices with expressions of servitude, in which case 'Regno' would be an initiate.*

'So no idea, is what you're saying. Cross-reference: Diana Hunter.'

— No connection found with: Diana Hunter.

'Cross-reference with: Fire Judges. Skip the historical stuff.'

— No connections. Fire can in some cases be a synonym for an emergency or a closing down, hence 'fire sale'. It is often linked with purification and destruction, but also, as in the case of the phoenix, with rebirth. The Fire Judges might therefore be the arbiters of a new beginning, or a crisis.

'Or they could be going cheap until Saturday.'

— That is an interpretation, the Witness agrees, and the lack of inflection makes it sound ironically bland.

'Is there a band? A musical group? Check venues close to the Thames.'

— I have. There is not.

She's never comfortable with that 'I' — not because she thinks it augurs some sort of awakening, but because she knows it does not. The Chinese room is empty. There is no god in the machine, just a very sophisticated card index. It should not pretend to experience.

A while later, she realises she has stopped asking questions and that she is falling asleep. The copper inside wants to push on, but the rest of her is comfortable, and tired. The machine was right: concussion is exhausting. She rests her head in the deep comfort of the pillow, enjoying the slight coarseness of the weave, the smell of disinfectant on the floor.

*

'Call Tubman.'

— *Rest is still recommended.*

'I will get up and I will do aerobic exercise.'

— *That is not recommended.*

'Call Tubman.'

— *Calling.*

She snorts, and waits for Tubman to pick up the call. It takes longer than with most people, partly because Tubman tends to leave his terminal off when he's working, and partly because, as a man who welds and solders, he distrusts haste.

''Ullo?'

'Tubman? I need your brain. Is that okay?'

She could have asked the Witness, and it would have moved Tubman's meetings for her. Like her own, Tubman's working days belong to the System, and even if they didn't normally, this case has a very high priority score. Tubman wouldn't mind if she just loaded a pre-empt into the calendar and took as much of his time as she wanted — but that is exactly why she feels she has to ask.

'Always got time to play Watson for my favourite copper,' he says. 'You know that.'

'You're not busy?'

Tubman blows an actual raspberry. 'For God's sake, Mielikki,' he says, 'don't be daft. Glad to help. But,' he adds, as she prepares another round of apology, 'don't waste any more breath being charming about it. I hate charm.' And so she has to promise to come directly, which is what they both knew would happen. A moment later, her terminal opens a sidebar and she can watch his schedule emptying for the rest of the morning. Each cancellation makes a noise like a very polite burp. In place of the various colour codes — delivery, maintenance, weekly management session, even his much-needed eleven o'clock break – the Witness loads a silver bar tagged with her own name. Tubman glances off to one side, no doubt seeing the same thing, and winces.

'I'll bring coffee,' she says, and sees him struggle for a moment to find a polite way of begging her not to make it herself. 'From the place on the corner,' she adds.

'Bless you,' Tubman agrees.

Her head pounds, and she allows herself a moment's unvoiced complaint. Ow, ow, ow.

– *You will tire quickly,* the machine says. *From the point of view of personal health, it would be better to wait another day before leaving the hospital.*

'The case is important.'

The Witness doesn't answer, but a little while later, the nurse informs her that a car is waiting.

*

'Fuck me,' Tubman says genially when she arrives. 'I'd heard, but they didn't do it justice.'

He pushes her a chair almost without looking. It rolls on casters across the floor of his workspace and stops next to her. She could sink straight into it, but instead she makes a point of walking it back and handing him his coffee, then brushing it off before lowering herself on to the black plastic seat.

Tubman is a technician, and not especially qualified on paper to explain the inner workings of the interrogation suite, but he has a gift for clarity that Neith has found helpful more than once before, most notably in a case where a man was so traumatised by events that the record taken from his mind was compromised. He is what used to be called an oily rag, and is known these days as a high viz in reference to the reflective clothing worn by workmen: a man who climbs in and out of muddy holes to fix things his supervisors imagine are beyond his proper understanding, but which, on a given level, he knows far more intimately and usefully than they do. Tubman doesn't actually spend much time in ducts, but he does occasionally get down on his knees and rummage under vastly expensive consoles for loose wires, replace circuits chewed by mice, and critique improper neurosurgical interventions with the long experience of a man who will have to fix this mess. At the far end of things, his proper job is dealing with the knackered outputs of complex machinery behaving badly. In a quiet tradition of digital autodidacty, he has no high qualifications of his own, but contributes to the final examination questions of qualifying technicians and medical staff.

'Go on, then,' Tubman says. 'What did you bring me?'

'Narrative blockade.'

Tubman winces. 'That doesn't end well.'

'Why not?'

'Well, it makes everything take longer. Uncomfortable for the subject. But it doesn't change anything; the machine gets it done just the same. You go all the way to the end and you find the thread of real life again, just waiting to be picked up. It's an hour's delay and it's effortful for the patient. Tidy-up can be a bit higgledy-piggledy after that, neurally speaking, or so I hear. Not really supposed to be my field, that bit. Sloshy grey stuff. I do the silicon.'

She waves this away. 'What about non-volitional playback of an implanted memory?'

'What?'

'I was unconscious. I got a whole wallop while I was out.'

'Oh, I see. Yes, you get that with larger files. Nothing to worry about. The egg hatches a bit previous sometimes, is all.'

Neith considers this image, and firmly rejects it.

Tubman shrugs. 'Don't fret – I doubt it'll happen again. Send me the record if you like, I'll have a look. It's a pressure valve sort of situation usually. Not actual pressure, but – these things are supposed to unspool, right? And they fade away if you don't think about them, like any other memory, so there's a sort of urgency in you as well as in them. Which – well, you, particularly, I suppose, this might happen to.'

'Why me, particularly?'

'You're all about the urgency, aren't you?'

Neith glowers at him for a moment, but Tubman is immune.

'All right,' she says. 'If you had to offer an opinion, who's the best we have?'

'I like Vaksberg in midfield. He makes opportunities.'

'Tub.'

'Mielikki.'

'Tub.'

'Mielikki?'

'Who do I talk to about narrative blockades and potential consequences? Who's the top?'

Tubman shrugs. 'Muckymucks and professors. Verlan was good; he's in a home. Pakhet's at the university and she's crusty and irritating. You want someone who'll come off the fence . . .' He sighs, conceding a point to himself. 'There is a perfumed gentleman named Smith – smooth as a shaved ferret. Word on the circuit is that he's tomorrow's man.'

– *Smith*, her terminal informs her, *first name: Oliver. Director of Tidal Flow at the Turnpike Trust.* She doesn't query the terms. Smith can explain them to her in his own words. 'You've met him?'

'I've been in the presence, but we have not conversed as men. Mr Smith doesn't do the unwashed and horny-handed sons of toil. He's elevated.'

'But he's good.'

Tubman acknowledges that in so far as such muckymucks go, if you've got to have one you might as well have this one.

'Thank you,' Neith says.

'No problem. Now go off and detect, darling. Some of us have real work to do.'

*

Neith requests a meeting with Oliver Smith. The Witness arranges one for the following day, though evidently Smith's schedule is not to be shunted and shifted with the same freedom as Tub's, even for a high-status internal inquiry. Neith sends a formal note of thanks to the perfumed gentleman in advance, then returns to her home to rest. The Witness is quite right: she is exhausted. Her head feels as if it weighs three times as much as it should. She drinks water, a lot of it, and takes her medicine, then sleeps.

Inside her, quite unbidden, Diana Hunter's interrogation continues to unfold itself: a strange seed in a clay pot.

wooden egg lying

On the plain of Erebus in the kingdom of Hades, close by the black and waterless river Styx, I dreamed a witch's dreams and found a hidden gnosis: the knowledge and conversation of a demon. It rose up out of the tunnels beneath the earth and spoke in my soul like the night-time anticipation of death. It had the head of a man and the chest of a peacock, and its face was shrouded in shadows – shadows here, where there is no sun, in this place that is named 'darkness'. I realised I was not afraid, because I knew its secret name. Magic is the invocation of names, just as miracles are acts of faith and technology is the application of mind to stone. The names of human persons are sacks to bind up the fragments of our selves, but the names of the jennaye are instructions to the world, and the jennaye must heed them as the water must heed the moon.

'The soul of Adeodatus is cut into five parts,' the demon said, 'and not God nor all His Angels can retrieve it, for it is kept In the realm that is apart from Him and cast upon the waters of the ocean of Apeiron where He may not go. There can be no proper transmigration, not even into the body of the least animal. The dirt cannot be put aside, for the soul is sundered and incomplete. Each piece must float upon the ocean and find what sanctuary it may in whatever nook of matter until it is regained and made one.'

Adeodatus, my son. Demons, too, may know the power of names, and here was one to conjure me by. Dreaming, I gave myself to the solution of puzzles, and thereby held back tears.

Five is a sacred number to the followers of Pythagoras. Two is woman and three is man, thus five is marriage. The number four, defining a triangle-based pyramid which is the simplest of three-dimensional shapes, is their way of denoting space, but add to four a single unit – the One that is the beginning of everything – and you get five. Space and divinity: five is their great mystery, because it denotes hieros gamos, the combination of godhead and matter, whose product is mortality and the flow of time. Five is also the number of secret places of the Pentemychos, in which it is well known, in this syncretic empire of Rome in Africa, that Jupiter Ahura Mazda concealed the seeds of a new creation, in case Angra Mainyu should destroy what is. There are five books in the Torah, five fingers on the Hand of Miriam; there are five elements and five Wounds of Christ from which flow the five rivers in the kingdom of Hades, and five bad angels that watch over them until at last they run into the lower ocean and rise again to the beginning. The Goddess slew five demons and wove their skins to make a cloak that turned all blades. Five becoming one: rivers becoming seas, time becoming God. What lies beneath the lower ocean? Perhaps the upper. Perhaps the world wraps around the world like the serpent Ouroboros.

If you believe in that sort of thing, which I try not to. It's not good for an alchemist to believe in things. You perform what works and speak the words, and leave the pretension of knowledge to priests. They're at home with things like the notion of a quinsected soul.

I heard my own voice, though I had not opened my mouth, demanding how my son's wounding might be healed.

'It cannot,' the demon said. 'It is impossible, and yet it has passed, and so cannot be undone.'

I spoke the name that was carved deep within it, and the stones of Erebus rose up and hurled themselves against the narrow knees and webbed feet, and beneath the blue-feathered breast the scrimshawed bones were shattered so that it screamed and spat. My voice spoke again from outside myself, and reminded the demon that Erebus will not abide falsehood.

A shadow fell across us and the demon flinched, as if it would roll itself up and disappear. I looked, and I saw a huge shape blot out the darkness, sculling like a monstrous fish in an ocean far above my head.

Remember the name: Erebus.

And then, in Carthage, a man with broad shoulders who smelled of rust and sweat put a sack over my head and said: 'Upsy-daisy, my girl, let's not have a tanty,' and I awoke, forgetting, and howled for what was lost.

I think my abductor took my tears for fear, and was ashamed.

*

Well, I am not afraid. When this sack comes off my head, I am giving someone the bollócking of his young Roman life. I am no winsome trollop to be carried off amidst giggles and insincere protestations – not that any woman should smile upon such poppycock! I am forty-two years of age – and a bloody damned scholar, besides.

Oh, no doubt: back in my student days, I should likely have found this great fun. Bloody damned Aurelius Augustine would have been game for it too, in his lecherous heyday. Had he thought of it, I'd have been slung over his shoulder and off to some suitably appointed den for a pastoral ravishing, rich olive oil and rough red wine for all, and much of it ending up in places no good Levantine olive would recognise. In fact, come to that, I'm fairly sure he did think of it – if it was Augustine, and not one of those predecessors whose existence he so greatly resented.

But now my son is dead and I am inclined to a less ebullient way of being in the world. A woman without her husband is a widow, a daughter without parents is an orphan, but there is no word for what I am because it should not be, or perhaps because it comes so often to so many that it is unworthy of mention. He was my son: I need no word to frame what I am now. It is with me always.

So I live my afterlife. I am serious; I read a great deal and I drink sparingly. I teach, I research and I consult. I am well paid by students who have fathomed the mystery that is Carthage, and come to understand that they will need an actual education as well as whatever else they find here. I conduct myself with a scholar's dignity, and I shall experience a comfortable prime and a long and well-respected dotage. I am on the faculty now – and while we may yet occasionally find some small physical consolation among ourselves, we dons, we do it generally in a far more sedate mode. Candlelit dinner at which other guests somehow fail to arrive, casual proximity and perhaps a little wine to unclasp the toga: mutual complicit seduction, all elegantly and discreetly Roman. One hardly needs theatrics like this.

O ye gods and little fishes, I hope this isn't one of my colleagues feeling his oats. If I'm to be wooed by a shrivelled goat of a man dressed as Dionysus while a string quartet of pretty young things from the slave market make bad music around their blindfolds, I shall probably stab him, and won't that cause a stink. Yes, stab him, like the back-country urchin I was when I arrived here. I still carry my novacula. I use it for preparing herbs, but I haven't forgotten how to be more assertive with it in time of need. A blade's edge is a blade's edge, and mine has a little cross-piece to keep my fingers from slipping, just in case.

Edge up; cut, don't stab. Don't forget you have two hands and two feet – the blade is a distraction as much as a final argument. In the first instance, threaten the face. In extremis: think of it as a cat's claw, and use it to open the seams of a striking arm as your attacker tries to withdraw. If you get drawn in close, take it to the inner thigh and twist, but for preference: don't, because the other fellow is likely heavier and stronger and hard men do so love to throw their weight about.

All right, perhaps I am a little perturbed. I once was mistress to the hellraiser turned young contender of the Church of Rome who is now Augustine, Bishop of Hippo, with all the politics that attend such connexions. I left that behind years back, and I'm no good as a hostage anymore, not with Adeodatus burned to ash upon his bier. Fire dissolves chains, Augustine said. No flesh shared between us any longer, and nothing to tie him to his sins. Let them blow away into the past. So I did. I go by another name, and I have another life. If I am found and roped back in this morning, it is by some enormously ingenious and painstaking idiot, to be able to locate me and yet not recognise the futility of that achievement.

Unless, I suppose, Augustine's heart is truer to his faith than his head. *For three things endure, and these only: faith, hope, and love. The greatest of them is love. Chase after it, and the gifts of the Spirit, that you may know the truth.* That's the original Aramaic, rendered as best I can, and you wouldn't on the face of it find a lot of room for confusion. But it applies to some other love, apparently, not this one. That love has to pass a higher standard than just existing and even than being reciprocated. Even than producing a child. All this time I misunderstood: I thought love was what granted sanction, and everything else came after, but it seems love has to undergo strenuous examination and be approved by the board. It has to be holy love, duly qualified and proper and pointed not at some hometown girl from Thagaste with oil on her skin and burning incense tied into her hair as she rides you, but at God, who evidently does not enjoy sex, else why impregnate a virgin through the intervention of an angel? Other gods, in the past, have taken a more direct approach – but not ours, it seems, not in Augustine's mind, though I've read other gospels than the ones he favours, in which the Father and the Mother were far less ascetic about their conception. It just shows how you can be wrong about something you think you know beyond a doubt. Oh, well and well. He was fading from me long before that. Something in him yearned for dominion, and for authority not merely over bodies and prefectures, but over souls. A fatal flaw, perhaps, or contrarily, a fatal flaw in me that I do not understand it.

Well, good. Nothing to tie me to Augustine either, and thus no more of his trash. No angry Monica, his mother, forever nipping at my heels with nasty chat. No disapproving stares from the congregation or the various mentors and clerks. No stinking northern cities, no sea voyages to make me puke, no ridiculous northern perceptions about decent clothing, and no bloody snow. None of that, and good riddance.

And to my eternal sorrow, no child, for whose death Augustine will – if there is truly a God and that God has any concern for justice – spend at least a little time in the hell he so drearily contemplates for having fathered the boy on me in the first place. Adeodatus died in a wayside inn, and not all the noble metals nor fast horses could have brought me there in time to hold his hand. Nor save him – because if one might will one impossible thing, why not two, or a multitude? Show me but once how to bend the laws of fate, and I will tie them in such knots as shall make your head spin, and out of this single wretched piece of twine I will weave a paradise, bend the world back upon itself until it is truly glorious, and that word means once again what it pretends.

It was impossible that I come to my son in his time of need, and no fault of mine – so why does the word 'mother' feel like a coal in my chest?

We've reached wherever we're going.

*

I suppose the overwhelming likelihood is that if I was going to be murdered, I'd be dead. Instead, I'm just sitting here, and I've a growing sense that this is something else – something that perhaps belongs not to Augustine at all, but to me. They'd have me believe otherwise, these brave men who manhandle sleepy women from their beds in the small hours, but note well: it's a clean sack. In fact, it's positively the luxe model, no splinters of wood or bits of hay or beetles. It isn't a silk hood, either, so the erotic sort of foolishness is at least somewhat off the table. This sack, then, is just a sack, but one with the barest trace of ... respect? Or in the alternative, they don't do this all the time and have therefore gone out to the market and bought a shiny new sack, just for me. In some way I've become important in my own right, and that means that I have bargaining power.

How very, very interesting.

Of course, I want no part of it, whatever it is. I am retired not only from coital vagabonding but also from high political and religious intrigues – not that I ever really got involved in that, it was just on the fringes of Augustine's life. It certainly never appealed to me at all.

Down, girl.

They keep me waiting for a while – on quite a comfortable day bed with a fine cover and decent cushions. And there's something wrong about this place, for all its likely finery, something nervous and astray. You can taste it in the tense, clipped exhalations and the muted discussion. No one wants to be noticed. No one wants to draw the eye of what has come. I wonder if it's a plague.

I dealt with a plague last year: a small demon, inhabiting a well, or perhaps it was just bad water and rats. It hardly matters. I used fire and salt and the prayer of John the Baptist, also called Johannes Fontus, who watches over springs and freshets. When I was a child, I learned the song of his severed head upon the water, and it is known to drive out the lesser beasts of Angra Mainyu. If one has such a thing, why not use it? At least, I never knew a plague made worse by holy songs. For the sake of argument, I also had them drive out the vermin, drain the whole cistern and burn it dry, then rake out the ash and reline it. Vastly expensive, and there was a lot of grumbling, but do you know: one or the other did the trick. That's why my prices are high these days. I actually get results.

Then abruptly I'm afraid again, like lighting a taper. It starts as something a little like rationality: perhaps that's the point. Perhaps I've made myself logistically problematic in someone's great game, a deal of provinces and property and trade. It wouldn't be unknown for a merchant to poison a well to drive out the people and pick up land on the cheap. But it's not that. This isn't anything real, it's a bad ghost on my back. There's a draught coming from somewhere. My skin is tingling. My mind helpfully conjures images of ants crawling over me, up under the lip of the sack, into my clothes. Ants. Spiders. Snakes. And: what's that noise?

Fanciful nonsense brought on by rude awakening. Get it together, Athenais, because there are feet coming, and feet mean the beginning of whatever this is.

But still I tell you: something is wrong here. There is something out of alignment, something coming from the wrong direction.

And then, whoosh. Sack: gone. Novacula: to hand. Bright. Big room, torches, guards and more guards.

And more guards. Mmph. Alas, then, we shall shelve the possible stabbing for a more opportune moment. Big fellow, legionary, apologetic face. I think I recognise his shoulders: I think he carried me across them in the first mad rush from my house. I sniff in his direction, but all legionaries smell of rust and armpit, there's nothing to choose between them by the nose. He has the grace to look – if not abashed – at least professionally neutral.

'Books,' he murmurs. 'Scrolls. Water and tea for your convenience. You will not wait long.'

I give my coldest shrewish-aunt face. It bounces off. He must have aunts of his own. Then, too, he's a little bit charming, and even aunts are not immune to that sort of thing. A pursed lip does not indicate a woman who has never wanted to chew a man's chest and smear herself all over him. No indeed. He's about my age, and handsome with it. Under other circumstances, I would not have objected to close contact with his shoulders.

'Learnèd,' he murmurs. 'This was necessary. We could not take the chance you would not come immediately. Wait, and take this day as you find it.' I recognise that tone. It's the one professional soldiers use to one another when the bullshit's over and the barbarians are all but in the fort. I recognise it because I was actually in a fort, not so many years ago, that came under siege. We won, of course.

(It was a slaughter. Howling cattle rustlers versus an iron claw bristling with affront and sharp edges. The outcome was never in doubt, but it was never in doubt because the men treated it as if it was. To the idiot brigands they extended the same lethal courtesy they would an army of Persian Immortals. They drew up an order of battle, baited and enticed the enemy, then smashed them between two armoured fists. Civis romanus sum, and I thank God for it. Rome is still mighty.

So that mode, that straightforward tone? I recognise it for the sound of a coming rain of shit.

He sees me take notice and grunts approvingly, then leaves me with, yes: books. Scrolls. Texts. Alchemical ones, expensive ones. Possibly illegal ones. I wonder if I could get a few of these out in the discarded sack.

Campaign table, campaign chairs. No cushions, no day bed, no quartet: that at least is something. But there's a bad flavour to the reading matter, a direction of study is implied that I would rather was not. You could almost read it as an indictment.

More shivers. I'd swear this was a cellar. How is there possibly a breeze? The legionaries feel it, too, scowl at it.

A moment later, the author of my misfortune arrives.

My first thought is that I've been kidnapped by a committee and this is the secretary. He's a dour-faced man in a priest's cloak and cowl, but he's etiolated: almost absurdly tall and thin with matching fingers, so that he looks like a langoustine. That resemblance is reinforced by his odour: he smells of the harbourside, of fish guts and seagull shit. Father Fish. Or, better, Father Fishy, since this is a disreputable sort of business for a good vicar. He's from the church of Peter the Fisherman, what was the old Temple of Portunes, or I'm a goose. A good Christian, no doubt, if you're prepared to stretch a point about the incomplete assimilation of small pagan gods into the canonical architecture. Since the Emperor Theodosius made the worship of pagan deities a crime a couple of years ago, that 'if' is rather a large one and depends on the mood of your local spiritual authority. In this case, that authority is Augustine, and for all that I am angry with the man and will be until I die, I will not tell you he is a bad priest. He loathes the intolerance of Donatism – he is, after all, a former heretic himself – even as he feels an obligatory compassion for its suffering root. He is prepared to take the long view and gentle his enemies into agreement on both sides. In consequence, Carthage and its surroundings do have a more Christian air than other places beyond his writ, at least as I understand the term, but at the same time there are all kinds of not-quite-heresies running about, each adding its own little apocrypha to the story of the godly carpenter. Or maybe the Orphic wanderers have it right, and the different gods are but aspects of one vast and incomprehensible thing that exists so far beyond us that we have not the means to describe it, save by this accretion of divine surfaces. Perhaps God is an object with an infinite number of faces only a limited few of which can be viewed from a single point, but each of which may view us from all sides at once. That would sit well with the discipline of alchemy, in which almost everything is representative of something else: a cavalcade of masks behind masks, gods revealed in elements and geometry in gods. Less well with the Holy Father in

Rome, no doubt, but contrary to what he may believe, God does not have to heed his opinion. Although I suppose it would be polite at least to listen to it.

Speaking of holiness: how many Peterine priests are there in Carthage? More than enough. It's a prime living for a certain class of office-holding cleric, a respectable distance from the episcopal seat in Hippo Regius, and ideal for those either not entirely converted or not perfectly adherent to minor niggles like the true Church's doctrines on sexual self-discipline. I like our priests, in general, but I don't know this one, which means he's serious and even pious. So how many true believers are rich enough to afford the trim on that robe I see peeping out beneath his cloak? Not so many, but still a few.

And of those, which one works the seafront and reputedly looks like a prawn?

A pause for reflection, and then certainty. This is called kairos: the hanging instant in which all may be gained. Watch while I practise the black arts.

'Julius Marcus Cassius' – you kidnapped me, dickface – 'I have been expecting you.' And for deep, prophetic reasons I always await abduction by local religious leaders in my smallclothes, and prepare for the inevitably jouncy chariot ride by dining on turbot with white sauce. I find the nausea helps one deal with difficult conversations enormously.

But it seems he believes me. Oooooh, spooky! I have penetrated his disguise with my special uterus magic. Father Fishy looks as if he knew all along this was a bad idea – meddling with alchemists always is, and girl alchemists are worse than all the others because they have internal pee parts. I'm treated to diverse gestures of warding against evil. I have personally conducted experiments into these gestures and determined that they are worth the same weight in gullspit. I remain unsmote by the lightning.

'I'm waiting, flamen. I do have other places to be.'

I probably shouldn't call him 'flamen'. It's not a Christian term, and it sort of implies he's a heretic. It's one thing to be working in the name of the Lord to lead your wayward flock into the true Church, sloughing the ignorance of idolatry and revealing by increments the face of the Christ. It's another to maintain a working temple to a forbidden demon. Even Augustine would draw the line there, and stoning is no one's idea of a pleasant day. The good father hasn't got over the trick with his name, either, he's looking … ehh, hm. I'm a bit worried he may swallow his own teeth. Well done, Athenais, it's always good for lone women travelling by sack to terrify powerful men. They love that. And it's not as if you can go crying to the Bishop of Hippo for support and sanctuary. He made that ever so clear.

But, bless the old gods or the new one, it seems that Father Fishy is not the type to expire of apoplexy, so on to the main event: *How did you know it was me? I carry no device, blah blah.*

I'm about to tell him the truth, but I catch sight of yet more wiggling fingers and it annoys me. He might just as well stand on a chair and shout 'Witch!'

'Father, please stop that. St Peter Portunes has more important things to do this night. The fishing fleet is out and there's a gale coming in from the west.' Hogwash – or rather, there may be, and if there is I'm in good shape and if there isn't I can always say that *of course* there wasn't, because I said Peter was working on it, and he's the Rock of the Church. 'I'm an alchemist, Julius Marcus. No doubt this is why you sought me out. The Angel Aeolus carries my shopping and his brother Gabriel of the Caduceus flows in my blood. I am the birdsong and the breeze, the Mother's mercy and the Father's love. Set out your needs that I may judge them and give solace, or bring me home, lest I decide I am offended by your presumption.'

That's not how I talk when I'm buying groceries, by the way, that's exclusively for when there's a pissing contest going on, most usually with a man. I'm working the angle, setting out my stall – or, if you prefer, defining the exquisite contours of my bullshit – and Father Fishy gets more and more unhappy and alarmed, but at the same time he is, I trust, more and more convinced that he's abducted the right witch. I think I'm being relatively charming. By rights, he should be covered in boils by now, or viewing the world from the perspective of a frog. I'm curious, though. He's got a problem so bad that kidnapping a Roman citizen in the middle of the night rather than just coming to my door and asking for help seemed like the obvious solution. He thinks I have the answer and I don't think he means to coerce it from me, I think he actually hadn't got to this part of the plan and now he's winging it. He's in all kinds of trouble, if so, and of course if I'm equal to the problem he can't solve, then by definition I'm scarier than he is, and he's hoping he can get by without my noticing which of us holds the power in that situation.

'Speak, man! Get on with it!'

I fix him with my aunt-stare, and this time it finds purchase. Fishy gulps. The pressure within overcomes the desire for priestly cool, and he fairly shouts:

'Cornelius Severus Scipio is dead! He was murdered in the Chamber of Isis.'

I hear the words, and then I sort of hear them again, as you do when something is so awful it makes no sense, and then I hear them again and again, and Father Fishy stares at me with his fishy eyes and his entreaty, his warding fingers wrapping around themselves until he's clasping them in what ought to be prayer but is directed to my address.

I manage not to say 'Fucking tits of Zeus'.

*

Cornelius Severus Scipio is dead! He was murdered in the Chamber of Isis.

There is, I swear, absolutely no part of what I have just been told that is good news, but almost the worst bit is that Fishy, who is if not a prince of the Church at least a respectable minor lord, thinks he's found the Chamber of Isis.

And worse than that, it seems he has. I know, because I'm looking at it.

We're standing in the room with it now: a big, airy room full of all the expected trimmings – rich silks and fine tapestries, expensive art. That marble nymph over there might be by Phidias – if I just grabbed it and ran off, I'd be financially secure for the rest of my life. You'd think they'd make an impression – but they don't. No more do the people, the legion hardcases and their new recruits, all of them just accidentally resting with hands by their weapons. The whole crowd and all the wealth is so much mist. It doesn't matter that it's full of life and matter, this room is all but empty. There's me, and there's the Chamber, and we're alone together.

From without, the Chamber – more commonly known as the Chamber of Solomon, and Father Fishy can have a point in his favour for knowing better than to call it that – is like a great wooden egg lying half-sunk into the floor. It is segmented, so that it can be taken apart for transport, but the joins are very fine indeed. You have to get within a hand's span before you can see them without a lens. The wood is dark and old and dense. It must have been monstrous to work it to this smoothness. I can smell beeswax and resin, but no damp. When I touch it, the surface is cool, almost as if it were metal instead; when I take my hand away, there's a faint outline of condensation. I want to taste it with my lips. I think it would be salty, dry and wet at the same time, like Pecorino with oil.

It's probably best that I don't lick the sacred relic in front of Father Fishy. In any case, I'd much prefer to turn around and run away, leaving it as far behind me as I can. That's how much it frightens me, or frightens the part of me that thinks and worries. The thing itself, though, is transgressively seductive: so physically appealing, so sensuous, like a bad suitor who knows exactly how to smile to weaken your resolve. For all that it's been the scene of a murder, Father Fishy is awfully proud of it, the way my son was with some contraption of sticks and mud. He's looking over his shoulder at me to see if I approve, and the closer I get the more I hate it, the more I feel cold and sick. I give him an impressed little smile, and he fairly curtseys at the small vindication.

There's no question what it is. It absolutely reeks of divinity: implausibly well made, elegant, felicitous. You can recognise the products of miracle because they make the merely human feel awkward and crude.

This thing is clearly miraculous – it's too brutally perfect and too gorgeous to be anything else. The room feels darker than it ought to with all these lamps, quieter than it should with all these people in it. The murals on the walls are washed out.

'Does it look like a breast to anyone else?' My voice, harsh and stupid. 'Because it looks like a breast to me. I imagine that's the idea, of course, fertility and fecundity and so on. But you've got it guarded by legionaries, Julius Marcus, and sooner or later one of them is going to hump it. That's the trouble with our soldiers being fearless: they've got no sense of proportion!' Everyone's staring at me, which is what I wanted. This is an exorcism – my first of the day, so we'll call it a warm-up. 'You, soldier: where are you from?' Picking a face at random, young and star-struck.

'The Third Augustan,' he says. His unit, bless his heart, not his home town.

'Born to the legion,' I say, before anyone can guffaw. 'You ever met a girl?'

'Oh, yes, Learnèd!' He just wants to get something right. If I'm any judge, he has indeed met girls, but remains somewhat confused about where things go from there.

'Watch this one,' I tell Father Fishy, who looks utterly aghast. 'He's got fire in his eyes and the phallus of a drunken satyr under his belt. Given five minutes alone, he won't just have mounted that thing, it'll be pregnant, and then we'll be in trouble. Isn't that right, legionary?'

The boy from the Third Augustan is shaking his head vigorously, but the others have started to smile, and the weirding beauty of the Chamber is no longer the only thing in the room. Now there's a legion post in here, and soon someone'll be playing dice in the corner, between shifts. Good. One more thing to do, so that the ripples of this are only good.

'Who's in this man's squad? You? Excellent. This is Carthage, soldier – take him out to meet some good-hearted artists' models, or we'll none of us be safe!' More laughter, louder and more genuine. Familiar ground.

The student body – ho ho ho – will eat the boy alive, in the best possible way. And now we are all family, engaged in the family project of getting this lad his first girlfriend, and the room belongs to us. I wave the whole business away with a growl of 'Carry on', and they all get back to what they were about. The room lifts. In fairness to Fishy, he tumbles to what's happened and looks just a little bit impressed.

We walk around the Chamber so that I can see it from all sides. It doesn't look much like a breast, but you work with what you've got.

A channel in the perfect floor leads down beneath it to the entrance, and I realise belatedly that Scipio – this is, or was, his house – must have had a new deck laid at what would be chest high over the old one to accommodate his prize. We're walking on a rostrum, like a stage, and our footsteps echo beneath us. My mind, always helpful in bad situations, makes haste to conjure an image of Egyptian burial architecture, poisons and spiked pits and crocodiles lurking in the dark, smashing up through the floor to eat.

'Are you well, Learnèd?' Father Fishy says.

'There is something here,' I tell him, which has the advantage of being both obviously true and potentially spiritual. Am I a fraud, then, or a scholar? I am both, of course, as we all are. Half of what I know I do not believe. Half of what I believe I cannot prove. For the rest, I hope to muddle through and my mistakes go without comment.

'We were together in the Chamber,' Fishy says, 'discussing its marvels. The images and words. The … well, you will see. He was like a child with a toy, or a man meeting his bride. He was full of joy. Then … I heard no sound.' He ducks his head against the recollection.

'They were alone for the count of a minute,' the big legionary says. 'Not more. I went to get water for them to drink.'

Fishy nods. 'It was swift. Without warning. I could taste the blood in the air, Learnèd. My gut knew it before my eyes beheld. Even then I was unprepared.'

'You are prepared now,' I tell him.

He looks and realises that I mean he has me, and that actually makes him feel better.

Alas, I can exorcise everyone else's fear, but I can't do anything about my own.

Father Fishy makes a little noise of affirmation, and – not without a quick check for any stray crocodiles – we duck down into the channel.

*

Most people call it the Chamber of Solomon, but in the story it wasn't Solomon's at all, it was his wife's. Her name was Tarset, and she was the daughter of a pharaoh of Egypt. I imagine it would have been something of a jolt for Tarset to marry Solomon and be just one of hundreds of wives – let alone that in Egypt women had all the same rights as men, which was hardly the case under Solomon's rule. She's blamed for leading her husband into idolatry, but I rather think that just means she insisted he treat her with respect.

Comparative marriage traditions of the ancient world to one side: the Chamber itself was supposedly a gift to the women of Egypt from the mother goddess, Isis, and within its walls the flow of time itself is reputedly stilled, so that all manner of high magics are possible. Isis, of course, pre-dates Mary, the mother of Jesus, but God exists outside time, and in His palm Mary extends from her ascension backwards to the Creation just as surely as she does forwards into eternity, and loves her ancestors as if they were her own children, and her Son's. Thus, Isis the pagan witch is transformed into Isis the veiled face of the Virgin, and all is well with the church politics of the Roman Empire in the East.

The Chamber, as described, is perfectly circular in plan, and domed. It is written that the supplicant enters from below to see the smiling face of the goddess drawn upon the ceiling in a tracery of silver against a midnight mosaic of lapis lazuli. Into this dome are set diamonds in the pattern of the constellations. Around the walls are the images of the four cardinal souls: two men, a woman and a fourth which might be either, and they are scattered across history. Along with the Goddess, they are the bridge between the divine world and the temporal one, and all of them, even her, concealed in the shadow of the Pentemychos, itself concealed, so that this is the most invisible of pantheons. The divine Mother touches the other four with spirit, and they in turn give her: matter to be shaped as earth; the flow of time without which there is no life; harmony, lest the making unravel itself; and death, so that no one thing shall overrun the others. Here, in this place, angels can be birthed, demons shattered, and miracles made like loaves of bread for market. With the right knowledge, an alchemist working within the Chamber might produce an elixir to offset age and return youth to one who drinks it; transform sickness into abundance; heal any injury and even raise the dead; but the greatest gift of the Chamber is the eternal Alkahest, the Universal Solvent that will free any prisoner and dissolve not only all solid matter but also oaths, curses, kingdoms, years and centuries, even damnation itself. In a very real sense, the Alkahest is the power of God. Armed with it, one might undo the first sin and make the world a new heaven, pull down the sky, or seal the abyss forever and preserve What Is from What Is To Come. The Alkahest is the ink in which Isis writes the book of destiny. It is the tears that fell from the Virgin's eyes on the day of the Crucifixion.

Since you're not a fool, you may have wondered why I'm not happier to see it. Here am I: a woman who would do anything to turn back time to some perfect moment, heal my sick child, and preserve that instant, live in it with my love and our small family, and be forever content. Or perhaps only some of those things, for I realise I have come to value what I am far above what I was then. Perhaps just my son would be enough. That would be my heaven, and if I might have it I would drag every man, woman, child and angel to salvation, even the demons of hell I would redeem, and I would offer all this up to the God as tribute for the single life I clawed back.

If you're better than merely 'not a fool' you may also have spotted the little logical flaw in this happy circumstance: if the Universal Solvent will dissolve anything, even clay and stone, even glass, even gold, even the soul, then how on earth do you put it in a bottle? How, having made it, do you prevent it from leaking away immediately and dissolving the whole world into smoke?

The Scroll of the Chamber, more formally the Quaerendo Invenietis, was discovered two decades ago in Carthage in a cache of documents themselves rescued from the burning of the Great Library by Aurelian, and it incidentally provides the answer. In fact, it was this answer that made the whole document credible to the faculty and in particular to the masters of alchemy at the time. It was elegant and anti-recursive: it provided a solution to the problem of infinite dissolution, and they were very impressed with it, not least because it pandered to their vanity. If the Chamber of Isis was needed to perform these legendary operations of the craft, then their failure to perform them without it was not their fault, and if the difficulty of making the Alkahest could be overcome then their whole discipline was once again not only practical – if lacking a crucial ingredient – but also the highest field of military, theological, financial and philosophical endeavour imaginable. They went from being a fringe science to having a claim upon supremacy at the centre, and any court that could have found the Chamber would instantly have had at its disposal a host of learned men and a few women to make full use of its power.

In particular, the discovery of the Scroll of the Chamber saw the elevation of an old man – named, in Latin, Iacobus Amatus, but generally more derided than loved and more African than Roman – who had been until that time something of a joke among the faculty for his drinking and his occasional catastrophic experiments, but perhaps even more for his unfashionable sentimentality, because he was very kind. He was a shockingly poor alchemist, but he loved to tinker and it would have been a cold heart indeed to tell him he had no talent in that direction. In honesty, he was by no means the worst we had. He retired four years ago, into a delighted age, and he has no idea to this day that the document he validated and which precipitated his rise to fame was a ridiculous forgery.

Yes, indeed. The entire thing, the foundational document of what you might call Isisean studies, is a lie from beginning to end.

That bald lascivious eagle Hortensus was supposed to be the one. Hortensus would have jumped all over it, and when he'd made his bed I'd have had him lie in it and smothered him with his pillows. That was the idea, but once the thing was done there was no going back. I'd not have ruined Iacobus Amatus for all the world. Amatus was Augustine's friend – his true father, almost, because the man life had cast in that role was unsuited: a bullying, coarse creature who relished copulation and despised affection, and who once, in a bathhouse, took note of his young son's unanticipated erection and proclaimed to the room that such a member could only signify many children and a great future. I think – I know – Augustine took a great injury from that moment of intrusion and never forgave his father for it. That he also never forgave his body for an autonomous response to warmth and the memory of a pretty housegirl I think accounts for much of the rest of his life, and indeed for parts of mine.

Amatus was a good fellow. You could find sages and masters in Carthage then to crew a fleet of ships – though they'd all sink – but while you might without difficulty seek and receive tuition in art, literature, rhetoric (above all else, rhetoric), music, medicine and physical science, indeed you could walk a hundred miles around the city and still not find a fellow to teach you how to become a merely decent human being until you found Amatus. He had been some species of war hero for a while, and then tired of it. He lived, he gave of his love, and from time to time he unwisely exploded his rooms, but never very dangerously and never without some hopeful, fascinating reason. To expose him to the disdain of Carthage would have been monstrous. And by then, anyway, there were rice bowls aplenty which would have been broken by the revelation. I'm not sure I could have declared the truth and been believed, even if I'd been minded to do so.

There is no Chamber of Isis, and never was. It was not lost in the reign of Rehoboam, nor stolen back in pieces after the death of Tarset by a secret Egyptian order of sorcerers. It was not retrieved by the priestesses of Isis to a secret temple, nor taken after Zenobia's rebellion as a trophy to Rome, nor given in turn to the King of Britain by an emperor ignorant of what he had. It was not carried back again in payment of a debt, nor sunk in the clear green sea off Neopolis. I have heard all these, and more, but the Chamber never existed. The name of Solomon's pharaonic wife is lost to us, and always was, and she may or may not have given a rat's arse about respect, but surely her attributes did not include a magical room which stopped time.

I should know. I am the author of the Scroll. I know of my own recollection and experience that there is no truth in it, however occult or oblique. It is a fiction plucked from the air while I was drunk and angry, realised over a fortnight of half-hearted fakery and laid out as a prank. There are half a dozen ways in which its mendacity should have been uncovered long ago. The gold leaf is not gold; the ink is the wrong colour, and not faded enough. The vellum comes from the wrong animal. The script is filled with errors, because I was only somewhat familiar with the Hebrew alphabet and language. The dyes and pigments are inappropriate. There is one glaring anachronism. There is no other work detailing the life of the Egyptian wife, and no supporting record of the Chamber – though one or two scrolls and codices, once you've been told it exists, seem to make reference to it in passing. That seeming is an illusion, a false pattern emerging from the spinning of a wheel. The Scroll is a ghost book, a summoner of phantasms and dreams. It is a dream itself, that I should never have written down.

They explain the flaws away. The leaf, we are now told, has been peeled off and replaced with dross in a time of need; the ink has been overwritten to preserve the manuscript; the vellum reveals the existence of a new trade route of which we were previously unaware; the writing evidently belongs to a young scribe perhaps fleeing some destruction, and this is his personal record of a story his masters told; he left spaces for the illustrations and copied them later, when he had access to different materials from those used in contemporary works; he came back subsequently and added text to give himself the appearance of foresight. There were other documents which told this story, but they were destroyed by fire.

The Scroll was supposed to fool one overfamiliar tutor and land him in hot water. That is all. The Chamber of Isis was never built, never designed, never contemplated until I conceived of it. God, certainly, could be reckoned its ultimate author, but then if we are to believe what we are taught then He is the author of everything, from the smell of hibiscus to frogspawn and taxes.

There is no hope here, in this place, of raising up my son. No more than in my dream of last night. The Chamber is a lie.

And yet here it is in this room, most immanently real and beautiful, and washed, already, in the blood of a sacrifice. It is nonsense given form and weight to work upon the world. The image of Isis is curved back against the dome, so that only from the stair does it look appropriately benign. I hadn't considered the difficulty of that portrait when I described it. The face is huge and far too close, and the shape of it shifts as you move so that Isis appears to stand outside the world and be peering in, as if we are the ones who are trapped on a flat surface and she is trying to comprehend our smallness. Isis, or Mother Mary, or something else that is so much less kind: her eyes are stars, and perhaps she in turn is just a mask they wear so that we do not have the sense to hide.

The artist is very talented, and he or she has embellished my words, put symbols and secrets to unlock into the work. Whatever you might look for, you will find echoes of it, hints and allegations of occulted truths. Mystical texts are inscribed here almost profligately, offering their meanings like fruit trees in late summer. This panel is Pythagoras, that one is an Orphic text on the transmigration of souls. Over there is something that could be a source for Hermes Trismegistos, or a carefully adulterated quotation from his work. The words of the Avesta are here, and this is a palindrome from the Ginza Rabba. All genuine texts of religion, all deeply held and loved by their adherents, all bound together into a sublime flimflam. There is more than I ever imagined: more detail, more scholarship. My jest has outgrown me – and in that evolution has become something far more frightening. This is work and effort and scholarship: a grand design of state or theology. Someone is perpetrating a ruse, political or personal, into whose path dead Scipio and Father Fishy have fallen. Fishy, in turn, has settled on me – I suspect as the most discreet and most proximate alchemist to whom he could safely turn – to advise him on the murder in this distressing spiritual context. What he imagines I can achieve, I cannot think. Unless he knows, or someone does, that there is no greater expert than I. Was his eye guided in my direction? Is it coincidence that draws me into this plot, who authored the lie on which it turns, or is it meant? Does the one behind this know that there is no Chamber at all, or is that the point, to smoke out the true crucible of the goddess by presenting a false one? That would be a grand enough purpose for a forgery of this magnitude. It is a paradox, otherwise: what possible benefit of building this Chamber could outweigh the cost? The materials alone are a nation's ransom. And if a personal grudge were carried to such an extreme, the misperception of risk and reward is doubly insane. The death of Scipio, friend to the Eastern Emperor, Flavius Arcadius, will bring a harrowing far worse than any benefit might outweigh. Cicero said it, in another place: only an emperor could create such a thing, but one cannot imagine an emperor desiring it. A god, perhaps, might bid so high – or a Titan.

A cold whisper runs along my neck and arms, plucking my skin and raising the hairs.

As I look around at this gorgeous, awful, enormous thing made in the image that I wrote drunk and stupid, there is one last horror to be swallowed down. The four cardinal souls are painted in perfect balance around the Chamber. In the west is a prisoner held to a stone table by spiderwebs, and over that table stands the figure of an otherworldly gaoler whose body is made entirely out of eyes. Does the captive flinch from that scrutiny, or yearn for it? And which are we to identify as a friend? Perhaps they can no more be separated than Prometheus and his eagle.

North is a satyr surrounded by gold coins, each picked out from the wood of the Chamber in true gold so that looking at him is vertiginous, the wall projecting itself back and back into an endless dark. He stands on a pinnacle of emerald stone carved with nymphs and geometric signs, above an ocean full of shadow.

South is an Aksumite saint, what the Greeks would call an Aithiopian – though they would call me the same. He walks through a burning city, and on his shoulders ride a boy and a girl. In his belt is tucked a painter's brush. If I had to trust any of them, it would be this one, though something in the single line of his mouth as it is drawn begs me not to. He has enough to carry already. I wonder if the maker of this thing put himself into the image. Painters are apt to do that, in quest of immortality.

And then we come to the east panel, which is me.

In the portrait I am younger, and made a queen – oh, balls, I think I'm supposed to be Tarset – and I stand in stark opposition to a spirit, an ugly thing that the artist has rendered in a succession of touches so that it is rising out of the landscape. Each stroke is barely more than an outline, a ripple in the paint, and yet together they produce a twisted, stork-legged shadow which both reaches out to grasp me and recoils from my touch. The demon from my dream. And looking across the Chamber I can see – because this banquet would not be complete without one more course – the reflection of this image in the first panel. East and west are different, but the arrangement of pieces is the same. One reflects the other, or follows from it. In the conventional flow of time, west follows east. The sun rises and sets in that natural sequence. But in the Chamber of Isis, time is said to be malleable and truth may be reversed.

Said by me.

So am I leaving behind the horrid captivity of spiders and eyes for dominion? Or is that table to be my fate?

Perhaps I am being too eager to see disaster. The faces of dreams are malleable, and the recollection of them even more. How much of last night's sleep have I just now imagined, seeing this? Perhaps it is all so much coincidence, and my likeness is here plucked out of a crowd, used for no more significant reason than Tarset must have some face and mine will do. Does my fear give the painting familiarity? Or does it spark my denial?

I make myself look again, look closer.

There.

No.

Yes.

There.

No doubt.

Anger flares in me, sharp and hot. The artist's brush has lingered over this, to make it perfect. Clutched in the demon's grip: Adeodatus as an infant, and his skin already marked with meridians that carve his soul into five parts.

This cannot be about me. I have no enemies so big, so wide, so wealthy. If I did, they could just snuff me out and move on. Unless, I suppose, this enemy is so vast as to see no difference between this excess and a simple knife in the gut. Perhaps I have a great destiny, and it offends some deity or other, and so this is my pre-emption? But once again: to what possible end? What could be worth this?

I turn again, and the anger drains away, replaced with sadness, the natural grief of one human being for another, however unknown. The end point of the plot – or is he, damn it, the commencement? – lies on the floor.

Cornelius Severus Scipio occupies the silver surface in the centre of the room, his eyes staring upwards at the goddess. Scipio the hero, the farm boy from a collateral line of a high family, who became a soldier like no other: legion champion with a sword, a spear, a dagger, with almost anything you name. People said his true father must have been Mars, or the Archangel Michael in his warlike raiment. They said that to see him fight was to see the business of war taken to a higher form. They said he'd fought the Visigoths to a standstill from among the ranks, then challenged them to find a fighter who could match him one on one. When no one could, a whole army – five times our numbers, or maybe ten – just went back into the forest. People will say a lot of things about a fellow who is cousin to the Pope and drinking buddy of the Eastern Emperor. They'll say a lot, but not that much, so he must have been quite something.

He's still young, and handsome. Even slack and staring, his face is lovely, and argues for a ready wit.

Well, if the Chamber were real, Scipio might be returned to life by some sainted alchemist with a close understanding of the ritual and practice of deep religious magic. Here, in this place, such a magus could work miracles to awe the world – or merely raise one man from the dead, by the grace of God. Or perhaps two, if I might beg a boon. Why not? What price would I not pay for such a thing? If the Chamber were real. And yet I stand in it, among it. I am branded on to it and it is filled by me, fleshed by me or through me. Perhaps it is real: perhaps I was drafted in my cups by some angel, and this appalling mockery of hope needs only faith to make it a true holy place. But even if it were so, where in modern Carthage would you begin to find someone like that? Someone of such deep knowledge, faith and daring? I look around the room for a hidden holy fool – and see them all looking back at me. That misplaced, absurd expression on their faces: is that hope? What could they be hoping for, in this place?

In this place.

Oh.

Oh, *shit*.

I stare about at the lie that is the Chamber of Isis, then down at the dead man. I look straight at him for the first time, taking in the shape of his death, and feel the final blow land in my gut.

Cornelius Severus Scipio, beneath his clothes, has been cut cleanly into five pieces.

*

My son called me 'Mother Make Right', and I didn't. I wasn't there and I couldn't and the world was simply bigger than I could carry on my shoulders. I was not enough. He believed in me and I betrayed him. There must be a door between the real world and the godly one, and if there is it must be found in desperation and love. It is known to all of us, that feeling of immanence: the certainty that there is a missing limb, invisible and ineluctable, that answers the need of the soul. The heart can lift mountains and God answers prayers. I failed because I could not prise my chest wide enough to make miracles.

When Adeodatus died, Augustine sent him home to me in a coffin full of honey, so that I could bury him or burn him as I chose, in the country where he was born. He wrote that he would follow later, and attend if I would permit it. I did not wait upon his endless episcopal tasks, and in the event he was delayed for months, so I had not even the satisfaction of denying him an ending. I remember I opened the lid, cleaned the honey from his skin, and spoke the words, and cried, then put him down once more in his box. A true Christian might give him to the soil, but I'd not have him rot. I remember that the honey smelled of rosemary, with the faintest whisper of raw meat and piss.

It wasn't a cruelty, to pack him so, and it must have cost a fortune. The soul of honey is so dry that a body submerged in it does not decay. Adeodatus looked like a saint, his skin clear and his strong body still round and supple. His eyes were closed; I think Augustine had ordered them sealed. Eyes are brutal. Death comes into them so very quickly as the humours cloud, and I would have gone a little mad seeing the bloom of corruption in that face. It was, I suppose, the last kind thing Adeodatus's father ever did for me, the funeral of our love as well as our son.

Perhaps that was the right choice. I cannot imagine what it would have been to see him standing there in the midst of us, in his fine robes, granting the love and forgiveness that is his calling to those who should expect them of him most personally, given not from the soul or the intellect but from the bone. It was neither Christ nor Monica that took Augustine from us, but Augustine himself, and it is Augustine who pursues himself with dreams of hell, and Augustine who condemns himself in the night for his sins, and Augustine who bids him turn his face away. It is Augustine who cannot trust in the mercy of the God whose mercy he expounds, and must crawl upon his face for absolution when he has done no wrong save that which he believes is duty. It is Augustine whose soul is growing more and more like honey, so hungry and dry, and Augustine whose heart is preserved and dead in a sweetness that brings no relief.

My son died of a fever. It came on him one night between Milan and Hippo Regius, and by morning he was gone. 'God has called him home,' Augustine wrote to me, but I don't know what that means. Does it mean that every one of us still alive is less loved? Is this one of those Christian riddles, that the priests teach and the old women who see clearly do not understand, that God's love can be equal for us all and yet at the same time so great for Adeodatus that the King of Kings must needs have him back before I could embrace him again? Augustine says this is an example of my selfishness, and perhaps it is. But if I am selfish, then what is God, that is everywhere and in everything, that is eternal, yet He couldn't wait another month for my son? He, God, is in me, and my arms could have wrapped the boy, and that surely would have been likewise God welcoming him home. Is there even a word for the perfection of selfishness to an elixir that the whole universe must drink, and call it love?

And here now is poor, stupid, handsome Scipio, and his eyes already have the white and black flowers in them, and I can smell the same damn smell of meat. Is this predestination? Is this why Adeodatus was taken? So that here, in this moment, I would make the decision I am making? Is that the mysterious way we hear about, that I am spurred to do justice for Scipio by a divine injustice I can never redress? Did I meet Augustine in an artist's studio where I stood naked for a sculptor who had designs on a rather closer encounter, and did I smile at him and desire him so acutely, because I was constructed from before my birth to want him so that the product of our passion and his abandonment of me would die, and thus lead me by the relentless mathematics of love to this choice? Is that what free will is: the right to be flogged to moral action by a deity who could make the world a paradise merely by speaking His desire?

They say that God is merciful, and His mercy is like agony because we are inverted by sin. I know all the arguments, and each more empty than the last. The world is what we make. This Scipio does not look like my son, except in so far as all dead children must share a resemblance in the eye of any parent. He is paler, more northern. Less African. And he has died in a most unnatural way. There is no blood to speak of, and none of the other bodily expulsions seen upon death. The cleanest death I have ever seen or heard of, that should be one of the messiest. Sterile as honey.

Enough. I will see this through. Scipio is not Adeodatus – indeed, with not much shift and yaw in the flow of time, he might have been my lover and even the father of my son, for he studied here only a little later than I – and this is not my dream, prophetic or otherwise, from just before I was brought here. This is a problem, and if they are related, well: I shall reach the greater best by solving the lesser.

Scipio is not Adeodatus, and I owe him nothing.

But my son's soul is cut in five parts, like this corpse at my feet, and they say that sometimes a murderer does his work not for the sake of hate or silver but to write what is written within himself.

What, then, is twice written here? And to whose address, if not mine?

I do not know. But I will find you, counterfeiter. Forger, trickster. I will find you and I will do to you such things as men will speak of for generations in whispers. You will beg me for demons to rend your flesh. I will find you.

I kneel, in this appalling temple, and I begin to examine the dead man.

*

It helps to have a story, when one must touch the dead and probe the broken machinery in its own stink.

(Although there is very little stink here, and that does not make things better, because there is brine around the corpse like sea water, and where has that come from, and why?)

I have never seen wounds like these, so clean and perfect. This is like a dissection – necropsy being strictly forbidden in Carthage, one is performed annually in the cellar of the butcher's shop close by the university – if one could do the thing without releasing the fluids within. Around the edges of the bone, I look for drags and splinters, and find none. Something very sharp and very swift, like a barber's razor through the stalk of a flower.

It helps to have a story, but it is not always possible to control what that story is.

They say the strategos Miltiades contrived the defeat of the Persians at Marathon, but that thereafter he overreached and the goddess Nemesis took his life in payment for his pride. Strict academic history has it that he died of a gangrenous wound after assaulting the island of Paros, but there is a text I have seen which maintains he was devoured from within by the tendrils of an orchid. Upon the beach of Paros, as the men of sixty ships bled their way uphill, Miltiades took his ease and considered his revenge upon the people for an earlier slight. He drank wine and slept, and a flower seeded by the goddess took root in his ear and burrowed inward. For a month he could see the world only through a cage of green shoots, and then he was blind in one eye and then the other. The orchid persisted in its growth, and the island threw back his invaders. By the time he returned to Athens to be tried for his venality, and perhaps more importantly his incompetence, he was half mad with pain and revulsion. He told the judges he could hear the flow of sap in his skull, and they agreed to burn the horror out of him as a combination of punishment and mercy. They summoned the greatest alchemists of the time and saw it done. The process was almost miraculously precise: the flower turned to ash – but Miltiades died anyway, his brain and bones having been almost entirely replaced by green stems.

(The brine is brine, pure and simple. I'm reminded that when Christ was wounded in the side, blood and water came out. I've dealt with some gut wounds and I've never seen water emerge from anything. Other fluids, yes, in various colours and consistencies, but not water. Until now. Brine. Was he killed by a fish? Once, as a child, I heard that there is a fish in the sea upon whose tongue alone a man might set a horse cart. The jaws of such a thing might do the trick here – but how, once the fish had had its way, would you get the pieces back? Or convince the beast to bite in straight lines? A fish god, then, exacting a bizarre price?)

Until today, I thought that Miltiades' was the most horrible death I had ever heard of, but I have always wanted to know: if one had seeds from that plant, would it grow in soil, or only in the flesh of one despised by the gods? It is my nature to ask such questions, and to know when they are not answered.

Scipio's head is attached to a kind of fleshy wedge, like a carved winestopper. I don't pull it out, even though some part of me is fascinated by the idea, the way a part of me is always fascinated by high cliffs and poisons. The edges of the wound are clean, but they have been disturbed, as if someone has rummaged in him. I've heard of secret couriers swallowing messages. Is that what this is about? Is the Chamber a side issue, and the murder a simple bit of espionage?

I go to turn the body, out of habit, and the leg comes away from the flank and hip. I smell viscera, but dry, as if he has been buried in desert sand. I wonder if all the water on the floor came out of him; if a god emptied him out, while it was looking in the secret recesses of his chest. Pentemychos. Pherecydes. Brine.

No. It eludes me. It was not cruel – not more than any death, for he must have died instantly – but it also makes no sense. I do not know what has been done to Scipio, or why. I cannot imagine.

I wonder: if I find out, will it change how I see things?

*

I walk around the room, tapping, touching. The joints are almost seamless. The wood is solid, with no hollow spaces to allow for machinery. I wonder about cords, and even jets of water. I have heard water, forced through a small enough aperture, can be sharp enough to cut. I feel the gold, the lapis, the diamonds; I inhale the rich odours of wood resin and orpiment, ochre, azurite and malachite, the flavours of art. Those flavours, not blood. No fine spray has touched these walls, I will swear to it, and yet he died here, must have done, there was not time for anything else. No more than there was any way for him to bleed salt water, or be quinsected.

In the middle of the room, I stop without meaning to, as if a friend has gripped my arm at the edge of an unseen precipice. In the gap between instants, the room has changed. All the colours have lost their strength. The figures look sickly. My own breath tastes foul in my mouth.

There is something here.

I can feel the eyes of the pictures on my back. A moment ago I knew this Chamber was a lie, nothing more than an expensive mummers' prop for some deception. Now I don't know anything at all. To stand here is to be watched, observed from every angle by eyes concealed behind a veil. Whoever painted this, he had a gift for truth, for showing what is, over what is merely visible.

I hear a noise and turn to look. I can't say what noise. I know I heard one because I remember knowing it, but I can't think what it was, the memory gone like dew.

The scene has changed. In the air and on the ground is a great spray of blood, caught as if in white amber. It was not there before. I must have walked through the space, but I left no footprints. There is none on my clothes. Ghost blood, then, seen through a door.

Never mind what it is, for now. I look. This is how it was. Here, the impact, where the wood is scuffed by his heel as he twists at the first contact; there, the exit, where his teeth and skull dimpled the wood. All four blades at once – I say 'blade' but that is not quite right – at great speed: an instant death, but not perfectly symmetrical, so his body was given rotation. He was fully clothed, and yet the cloth is untouched. The blade is a ghost, as well, to cut flesh but save linen. I wonder what god would invest time and energy in making a weapon to preserve an enemy's wardrobe – but perhaps it passes likewise through armour. That would be a terrible thing to face for a man used to doing battle in a caul of steel.

The head hangs in the air. The blood is beautiful, like a wave breaking around a stone.

From all the corners of the Chamber of Isis, the thing presses its way into the world the way the face of the Emperor is stamped upon a coin. I cannot see it, but I know it's there: a glass flower growing towards me through the air.

It whispers, like a lover: 'I am torn.'

I remind myself to breathe and find that I can't. The air is too thick: too heavy and too still, as if it is congealing. Air like honey, like water falling on my face: I have been noticed. My chest clenches. The silence is a lie, a down quilt pulled over the world, and beneath it there are whispers, like voices from another room. Scipio was a flopping fish swallowed whole by a heron. I can feel eyes on me, noticing me, and with that notice comes a buzz like an angry hive or a storm. It fills my ears, my nose, my mouth and down into my lungs. There is a belt of leather around my neck, my arms are fast against my side. I feel a thick wooden branch in my throat, and a weight that would drive me to my knees, except that—

Except that I am Athenais Karthagonensis: lover, mother, alchemist and forger, and this is my place. This is my Chamber, my lie. It belongs to me by right and making, it was born in my mind – and you, whoever you are, will mind your manners in my presence or I shall scribe you a new arsehole.

The hive rises, roars away and settles on the leaves. Air returns, shockingly cold. I can still hear, at the edge of perception, the whisper of chitin.

I breathe out. In. Out. In. Each exhalation feels unwise, as if I may wish I had kept the air a little longer in my chest. I'm fine. I'm fine. I have touched a spirit and seen it off, or ducked beneath its arms.

*

'Julius Marcus Cassius,' I murmur, because I don't really need to shout any more, 'I will have your full attention while we conduct this interview.'

Father Fishy does not nod, because he is profoundly sensible of my novacula and its position directly against the lid of his left eye. The pressure I am exerting is not great, but I'm very annoyed and there is a firmness in my posture which he reads – correctly – as contraindicating any casual motion on his part. Nonetheless he wishes me to know that I have his attention – indeed that no one has ever had more of it in a more focused fashion.

I was dragged from my bed last night and cast into this mess. I stood under the cold, glittering eyes of the goddess, and confronted not just the corpse but all of it, and was entirely grown up and controlled about finding my own face on the east wall of a room fabricated to my own mendacious design and purporting to be an ancient treasure of magic, presently containing a dead princeling in five easily portable sections. I sat on my horror, on the echoing and nauseating sense the Chamber evoked in me that I had somehow betrayed my son by not being there for his death, and my sense that he betrayed me in the same way. I was equal to all that, and I think we can agree that it was a masterwork of self-discipline and calm.

But there is only so far a woman can go before she becomes irritable in the conduct of these affairs, and I find that the limit of my tolerance for conspiratorial pissing about is reached in the moment when I am forced, by the presence of some bad suffocating spirit, to stake claim with my name and soul to a priceless relic and false miracle either sanctified by the holy murder of its most recent owner or thus defiled into a charnel house which among other things may be the earthly dwelling of that same evil angel that did him in. That sort of thing, as it transpires – because who knows that about themselves until the moment of testing? – gets right up my nose.

I came out here and said so. I was direct.

I think the good flamen had still entertained until then the fond delusion that he was in charge of his own fate, despite the death of a young darling of the empire who was in some manner under his care. So when I came out of the channel under the egg and he tried to instruct me in his High Church voice, I hooked one finger into his mouth and dragged him bodily against me by the cheek, which is exquisitely painful, and then I pinned him against the Chamber with my blade. Not actually pinned. He was not pierced. Pinked, maybe.

Strange thought: I once seduced Augustine this way, pressed him to the wall of a wayside pub and ravished him. He was abandoned and gasping and so grateful to be excused the stern duty of self-control. Afterwards he dropped his head on to my shoulder and whispered that he loved me. I think it was the only time I ever saw him truly unwound. Later he would not talk about it, and after that he was careful to be dominant with me, though he repeated his declaration of love many times, and meant it, I think.

Well, no danger of my ravishing Father Fishy, and it's not the moment for a vengeful killing, either: if he was a little more savvy he'd know he's in no danger right now. He's not that savvy, though, so I growl into his face, and he flinches when I swear, because in his mind scholarly middle-aged women don't.

'Tell me what the hell is going on!'

'I have!'

'Do you take me for a fool? Where did you get this … thing? Who made it for you? And why?'

He's baffled, truly confused. 'It's the Chamber of Isis! It was given to Queen Tarset in the days before Christ!'

'I know the story, I'm a bloody alchemist!' I clench my fists against my legs and count my breaths. I nearly said 'I wrote it!' That wouldn't go down well. They'd either take me for a madwoman or believe me, and it's hard to say which of those would be worse. 'And being a bloody alchemist, I also know a few things about anatomy, and one of them, if I can let you in on a little trade secret of the mystical community – which is shared only by every butcher, fishmonger, soldier and surgeon in the empire and beyond, so it's seriously arcane, Julius Marcus, and you better not tell anyone about it – is that people don't spontaneously split into five parts when they die! So let me ask you again: what is going on? Or shall I drag you in there by yourself and leave you over night?'

And there, at last, is something he is afraid of, even more than he fears this spitting hellcat in front of him.

'Scipio,' Father Fishy says uncertainly, 'said he was being hunted by a jinn.'

*

In my mind, I am banging my forehead slowly against the great, cool beams of the high table at the university. If I do this a couple more times, I will wake up in my bed, and this whole pile of shit will prove to be a dream. Or perhaps I will wake with Augustine's flank alongside, or with Adeodatus two years old and banging a wooden spoon on a pot lid to attract my attention. Certainly I will wake in my own bed, with nothing more dramatic to do today than buy fresh sage from the market and bottle some surgical alcohol.

Or I'm here, and Scipio was being hunted by a jinn.

I make everyone wait while I refresh my memory, but to be honest it all comes back so fast and so completely that I barely need to. Years gone now, and so many things I'd choose to remember. I have the shape of them, the gap they have left in me, but I cannot recapture what they were. The sound of my son's voice, the feeling in my heart when Augustine first kissed me. The warmth of my father's smile. Instead of any of them, I have this. This farrago of lies.

Lord, but I was fanciful. I think, honestly, that part of the reason they believed the Scroll was real was that it was so shamelessly bad. No respectable forger would ever string words together in such a self-important slurry. Forgery is a quiet discipline that doesn't put itself forward – indeed, it wants very much to fade into the scenery. This idiot, this supposed scribe I contrived as my narrator, was afflicted with no such sense of limitation. The prose is purple, adolescent, puffed up, and filled with mystical ellipsis. In other words – though I didn't realise it at the time, I was just drunk with Hortensus' pawprint on my tit – it is perfectly authentic for a young man trusted with what he saw as a great task of record-keeping. Or, let us be fair, a young woman also, for portentousness is beyond gender and I never did specify which our young chronicler might be; they all just assumed, as men do.

So let's call her Camilla – in defiance of logic, since the one thing we really know she wasn't is Roman – and let's go over it again. Chapter three, which is the bit about spirits and Titans.

Into that place there came also the jennaye, the good and generous gods, and they are called marids that came out of the ocean and iphrids that are of the fire, and for each element and place there is a jinn, and for each tone and texture and flavour of the earth also, and for the lands and kingdoms and beasts and forests, but they are not of many races but only of one, that is the race of jennaye. They are also called the Hidden, because their footfall is the breath of the spider and though they are giants yet they walk unseen, and they are all about you. And they also came to the Chamber and sought its blessing, for to the jennaye the Alkahest is as sunlight to a flower or water in the desert, and yet also it is their death should they resist it. And these were their names and aspects, that one who drinks the Alkahest shall know and shall speak, and by them be obeyed:

The lawgiver came, that is called Firespine for the wings of flame upon his back by which he passes into every holt and redoubt, even into the palaces of kings and the vaults of merchants, and he is an inquisitor and made of justice all along his arms.

There also was the mother of owls and rivers, whose name is lost, and all the wells were made clean and sweet and all the books of the place fruited and in the fruit was knowledge;

And there also was that one of them that is named Agoraeus, who walks upon precious stones, and in his train was a great dragon of the ocean and the people were filled with fear, but Agoraeus spoke and it was calmed;

And so too came Ogioslitus, and the eyes of the world were made full of light, and birds sang and the wind was glad;

And also his sister, that cannot be denied: she also came, and her hounds beside her that do not relent;

The whole of the jennaye were there like soldiers upon the marching field, in their raiment and arms, and they swore they would defend the Chamber. Even Gnomon of the Thousand Eyes was there, that cannot be contained, and these were the judges of mankind. Even crabwise Gnomon, that is the thumb, that the others of the jennaye do not trust: even Gnomon so swore, and that was all, and laughing Gnomon was wise and spoke not the name of Firespine. And these others also were there, of the numberless order of jennaye—

She did go on, that Camilla in my head: a long poetic litany, and if you took note of the colophon at the top it was a rebus puzzle, and if you solved the rebus – which you were all but told right out was what you were supposed to do because the title of the bloody document was 'Seek and ye shall find', but to my knowledge no one to this day ever has – it yielded a cryptographic key, and if you applied that key properly to the list, well, it spelled out the mighty arcane secret that Lucius Hortensus of Carthage has a penis shaped like a ram's horn and warts upon his tongue. I have no idea if that is true. I never saw either of them, I just took offence, and my creativity rather ran away with me.

But here, now, I must ask whether it truly did, or whether I was remembering as I catalogued those jennaye some endless harvest song of my youth, or whether, worse yet, some spirit of mischief jogged my arm and made me write real spells and honest truths of the firmament concealed in my outrageous lies, and now that some fool has put it all together in one place, has made an actual Chamber like the one I described, everything in the Scroll is to some extent the truth.

So now I wonder: what is it that my message truly says? My encrypted secret? If I unravel the list, will I find some quite other communication waiting for me? *Dear Athenais, thank you for the loan of your soul. I have returned it in good order, perhaps slightly foxed.* Did I play my divine inspiration? Or did such inspiration play me?

*

The big legionary – I feel now that he was less an abductor, more a conductor with extreme prejudice – brings me water, fresh and cold. My throat is a little raw from the shouting.

'Thank you, Optio.' A guess at his rank.

'Tesserarius,' he corrects me.

And I'd thought his responsibilities a little light already. It's unlike the legions to underuse intelligence. 'Bit old, aren't you?'

'My third time round. Evidently, I have a bad attitude.'

'Your name?'

'Gnaeus.'

'Well, Tesserarius Gnaeus, it may or may not have escaped your notice that I also have a bad attitude.'

That makes him smile. It's a little bit heartstopping, that smile, at least to a woman who looks for something more than a pretty stomach on some shepherd in a field. It's a smile that knows things.

Down, girl. It's really not the time.

I glance back at Fishy. 'Scipio was in the Chamber.'

'Yes.'

'And so were you.'

'Yes.'

'Did you kill him?'

The priest utters a bark of disbelief. 'How? I, do that? How?'

Well, no. I don't really see Julius Marcus as the quinsecting type – he's more of a strangler, with that narrow frame. Father Marcus would steal up behind you, cord in hand, and put his knee to your spine, and with those long arms he could do you fast enough. But what has been done to Cornelius Severus Scipio is not that sort of assassination. Look at the corpse: you'd need an axe, or a saw, or, well: in honesty I have no idea what could achieve cuts like that. Great shears, such as tailors use, and arms like a Gothic axeman. The force required alone … Let us assume that Scipio stood still and naked for his execution, that he cooperated in this strange design, not because that is likely but because the more he resisted the more impossible this becomes. The tesserarius, now, and two of his mates, with the right tools and an unconscious subject – well. That would make the business only somewhat impossible, until you start to ask where all the blood went, or how no one heard the screaming.

'Describe it, please, Father.'

'We were talking. He must reassure himself from time to time that it was real, and yet he did not like to be within. I think he found it uncomfortable.'

'But you did not?'

'I felt observed.'

Yes. To stand in the Chamber – whatever it is – is to stand at the mouth of a cave, and the bear within peers out.

Marcus is still talking. 'But I believe that God sees us all, from crown to toe, at all times and in all places. I am forever observed. I am made of water, and any impurity is visible as it floats in me. And then, too, I spend my life around images of the divine, and I find they have this effect. I am familiar with the sensation of being measured.'

'And found wanting?'

'Inevitably. But this was different: as if the wheel of the world grated against its axle. I thought for a moment that I could not see him, as if I had blinked. Then Scipio made a noise. A dog noise, Learnèd, not a man's noise at all – not even on the battlefield.' An absent recollection, this, but the tesserarius looks at him sharply. Marcus as a soldier, before the cloth? How very unlikely. 'I turned and he fell. I want to say I felt a breath on my face, but I think that is my mind adding ornament. The room was still. There was no warning, no sense of the passage of an object. No other person.'

'His clothes,' Gnaeus prods.

'What about them?'

'Where were they?'

'He was wearing them, of course.'

Quite. So either Marcus lies, or the world is broken, or someone possesses a mind beyond devious that can produce this impossible result. Or all of these may be true, or none.

'Tesserarius Gnaeus.'

'Learnèd?'

'How long from the last moment you saw Scipio alive to your first sight of the corpse?'

'Quarter of an hour, perhaps two minutes longer.'

So here, if we are to persist in regarding Marcus straightforwardly as a suspect, we must imagine him, alone and weaponless, somehow subduing the young soldier without a fight, then stripping him and murdering him, cutting the corpse in segments with his bare hands and yet getting no blood on his skin or clothes, nor on the floor of the Chamber, and then likewise with remarkable skill re-dressing him, all within the briefest time and all in silence. Suppose the victim dead at the start, the task is no less impossible. If they were all in it together, perhaps – but for that they must all be consummate actors, as well as murderers – and why bother to bring me in at all? Am I so disposable, so unthreatening? Hardly. They'd do better with one of the drunkards for that, or the bought-and-paid-for liars of the alchemical trade. They're not difficult to come by.

Marcus cannot have done this. And yet his proximity is so suggestive, so important. Without his presence in the room, this might be done, or be made to appear to be done, by trickery. It would be a mad thing, to work so hard to create this bizarre appearance – but all roads here lead to madness. I must accept the slayer is mad, or the world. Where nothing makes sense, one must put sense aside and acknowledge only what is possible.

Marcus is a man, not a perfect observer. His perception is malleable, by tricks and misdirection. Perhaps I need to talk to a market conjuror, or a fraudster.

Or: 'Did Scipio have close kin? A brother, who might be mistaken for him?' The corpse might have been pre-prepared, the man abducted. Or the man Marcus went into the Chamber with could have been the double. Theoretically. I do not believe it, but I would very much like to.

Gnaeus meets my eyes: *you're not serious?*

I wave my hands to ward off his scepticism. 'All right, I grant you, a twin is asking too much. A chance encounter, then, a man in the street who for no obvious reason simply resembled him?'

Those same steady brown eyes. I'm reaching. He knows I am. I am baffled, and so is he, and so are we all.

Baffled. The murder is impossible because of that quinsection. If Scipio were simply knifed, that would be another thing. Marcus would be in chains – rightly or wrongly – and that would be that.

What function does it serve to cut a man in five pieces? It is superfluous, for a man, except in one way. There is one possible answer that might let us remain in the ordinary world of human wickedness.

What function does it serve to cut a man in five pieces? None. Save that it is the difference between banality and bewilderment. One blow kills. Four make a miracle. With Scipio thus in five pieces, most people would not look for an ordinary slayer. The Eastern Empire these days is a credulous place. It doesn't take much to get people shouting 'sorcery' – and if you wanted to hide an ordinary sort of murder, you could do worse than blame a ghost.

'Had he a lover? A regular lover? Someone who knew him?'

One of the legionaries nods. 'Helena.'

'Bring her.'

Marcus looks horrified. 'Learnèd … here? To see what lies within? Is that necessary?'

'It will not be pleasant for her. But this is not a pleasant day, not for any of us.'

'But why?'

'The Learnèd Athenais is hoping against hope,' Gnaeus murmurs, 'that only the head of the corpse belongs to Scipio. That the rest was prepared beforehand.'

'What? Why?'

'Because,' Gnaeus says, patient, 'if that were the case, then four clean cuts could be managed on a body with plenty of time in another place, and that body put aside against the moment. Perhaps stored in honey and then washed down in brine.'

Oh. I had not – please. Not honey. Let it be salted oil and the parts washed in water. Let it be ice, even, and sawdust. Not honey.

Let it not come back again to me, and all directions leading to the same room.

Gnaeus shrugs. 'If the body belongs to another man, then one need only kill Scipio by severing his head, and leave it with four parts of the other in a duplicate set of clothes. That would make this a human assassination, perhaps even entirely unconnected to the Chamber. It would mean that the jinn is a shared error, a fever dream brought on by the manner of the killing and our fears.'

'And me a liar,' Julius Marcus says. To his credit, he seems more hopeful than offended.

Gnaeus shrugs yes. 'Deceived somehow, or drugged. But no gods or demons, Father. No bad miracle, just a bad man. Learnèd Athenais considers this an outcome greatly to be desired.'

I do, though I wouldn't bet the back half of a chicken.

They bring the girl, but of course she turns out to be one of those breathy northern wallflowers with flaxen hair. When they show her the body she begins to shriek, and doesn't stop until they carry her away. I suppose I can't blame her. We dicker for a while over whether her reaction implies she recognises the corpse or merely the head, or whether she has simply been overcome by a general and not incomprehensible horror. Then a waterboy brings word that she has recovered enough to confirm the body as being that of her lover. There is a birthmark on his shoulder, and a bite beside it that she made herself.

Youth.

Drat and drat. I look at Gnaeus, and he shrugs again: what did you expect? Another thing the legions don't really go in for is false hope.

I avoid gods, these days, and all manner of spirits. Alcmaeon of Croton wrote that although the jennaye live, they do so at an angle to the world. Those that traffic with them are like a man who would argue with the driver of a chariot as it passes on the road, and they misread for anger or wisdom what is in the end only velocity.

And now it seems I have one of my very own.

Marvellous. Athenais Karthagonensis: detections, erections and exorcisms a speciality.

*

I make them prepare a study for me, and a couch to sleep on. Then I send them all to bed. I don't know at what point I was made queen, but I'm not going to argue.

So long as I am not Tarset.

I read, eat, and – after years and years of sunset – the day ends. In the cool cotton I find a sort of dreamy calm, the perfect clarity of solitude. I realise I don't really care if Scipio died of mortal agency; that is, I care because he reminds me of my son. But I was not brought here to avenge or to reveal. I was brought here for something else altogether, and that something has not diminished in its urgency.

No one has said it, but it hangs in the air, in the gaps between glances. They all want me to say I can do it, but they're afraid at the same time because if I can the world will change completely. The meaning of things will change. A new sun will rise.

They do not, particularly, want me to cast out the jinn. They do not want me to investigate Scipio's death.

They want me to bring him back.

I cannot. There are no miracles.

Except that since this morning I have imagined myself a hundred times a schemer and an assassin. I have given myself all the world's resources, and I have tried to design this death as I found it. I have murdered Scipio in my mind, over and over again. I have found many ways to achieve this result that might work, if one had but will and time. But when I tested my conceptions against what is present in the Chamber, I found them lacking. There are no trap doors, no hiding places. There are no hidden blades. In that, it is precisely what it appears to be: a wooden room with precious ornaments.

The whole house, of course, might be the plot. From Julius Marcus and Gnaeus to the legionary who has definitely met girls, they could all be the masque. A troupe of liars.

Except that what is painted on the Chamber was in my dream. The quinsection of my son's soul is heralded to taunt me on the east wall, and that is impossible.

This is not a mortal plot. What is done here grows from dragon's teeth, not seeds. In this place begins a true kairos: the instant before the coming of the wave for which the worlds make way.

I am an alchemist. We live to make things explode. And even if we did not, there really is no other choice.

I go to the Chamber, and I try to make the Alkahest.

*

There are very clear instructions in the Scroll. All the ingredients are close at hand, because Scipio had already put them by for whatever he intended. And what did he want, dead Scipio? To bring back his parents, or a lover? Or was he underneath the laughter and the wine a scholar, and sought knowledge before anything else? The desire to learn finds its way into curious places. Or perhaps he wished to make the world his plaything and raise himself to an angel, or a god. That sort of person almost certainly should not attain what they desire, for all our sakes. Will I resurrect him, if I succeed? Will I drink, before I raise Adeodatus? If I do not do so, how shall I control who else may drink, and be remade, in this house of priests and soldiers?

It seems I am a woman in a world of stone and clay, who has the gift of making metal swords.

I had planned to clean the house today, and roast a duck slowly in my oven. Some of the local children come by each week, uninvited, to see if I will tell them stories from my library, and of course I do, concealing as much real learning as I can in stories of adventure. This week I thought to seal the compact, and make it a regular event. Dripping duck in warm bread, by my reckoning, should have made that easier. Now it will spoil – although I suppose, if I am successful, I can simply wave my hand and have duck from the pure firmament, though that seems like cheating. Christ, at least, had the good manners to multiply loaves and fishes, rather than conjure them from air. Well, perhaps I shall speak to the duck and make it fresh again, though always careful not to push too hard and bring it once again to life.

How if I ate the duck and digested it, and then brought it back? Would I be hungry again, as if I had not eaten? And if not, why not?

I do not think I am cut out for this. I have a need to ask questions that unravel the world. I'm tempted to vary the mix somewhat from what is written – I know rather more about transmutation and consilience now than I did when I imagined this. I could do a much better job of it today. So: should I? But that defeats the point. This thing is as I wrote it then. It exists in that moment, and the present must pay deference to the past or where are we? It is not to be fiddled with and adjusted to suit my present self. I must abide by life as it was, not how I think it ought to be now.

Except that I shall stand in the Chamber of Isis and make the Alkahest and all time shall be one and I shall not abide by how things were. I shall raise my son from the dead.

For God's sake, Athenais, let's get to it. Bless the quarters. Walk the room according to the Orphic pattern set by Pythagoras: step, turn, bisect; cross the floor and repeat, until all the corners are your own. The ritual cleansing feels rather pointed, here and now. There's no sense of the jinn, no lingering whisper of the hive, but it won't have gone far.

Screw you, you gloating, murderous boggle.

Name the winds; give thanks for water, blood and life; bow to the goddess – and let's have no foolishness, please, about her being a virgin. Isis was a mother of the more conventional sort, and did not turn up her nose at sex. Bow as women bow, not in emulation of florid men protesting their sincerity, all laid out flat upon the stone: just the simple inclination owed to the mistress of the house.

Of all houses.

Ring the bell five times. Pour a libation and drink in her name. Invite her into your mouth to taste the wine. The goddess is part of you, as she is all of us.

Salute the cardinals, one by one, saving the east for last. (I lock eyes with my portrait. I expect a shock of contact in this moment, but there isn't one. Move on.)

And now the actual alchemy. Gold powder, for the sun. Silver for the moon. Ground pearls for the sea. Volcanic stone for earth and fire. Tears for the soul. (I have no idea whose tears. I suspect a baby's, diligently collected and sealed with wax. I didn't specify in the main text, but I implied in a later footnote that the tears of an innocent might be the best option. I think I just wanted to make the process of gathering the materials as obnoxious as possible, but it has occurred to me since to wonder how many perfectly happy babies have been goaded to weeping by bearded arseholes in search of Holy Truth. Add another host of tiny sorrows to the list to be laid at my door.) Heat over a brazier. Mix. Do not melt the metal: this is not jewellery we are making. It is magic. The transformation is not chemical, it is impossible. Respect the discipline: the art of what cannot be.

All right, almost done. The Chamber smells of lamp oil and must, certainly not of flowers and the woodland, as predicted in the Scroll. Nor do I feel transported by the presence of the divine. My feet remain firmly on the floor.

Do you recall what I said about there being a problem with the Alkahest? That it was not containable? And that I had solved that problem in the Scroll, and that solution was one of its principal selling points, as it were, in the marketplace of bullshit that is academic certainty? Well, here's the reckoning. We have reached that point, and now I have to embarrass myself, and thankfully there's just me to witness it, and my subsequent inevitable failure. Me and the goddess, of course. And the cardinals.

There is a doctrine in Orphic magic called the attraction of souls. It proposes that certain persons are fated to be together, for good or ill, and that their souls will move through the world, across as many lives as they need to find one another. The moment of conjunction will yield a shift in the nature of the world, for better-or worse, and it is the duty of the wise and of the initiated to identify such moments of unison and prepare the participants, so that the scales of life are balanced towards the benign and the earth – little by little – is made a paradise. To the Orphics, the attraction is a literal force and not a metaphor: it is a power of nature that tugs and hauls upon these sundered ones the way a river flows to the sea. The reunification of disconnected parts cannot be stopped. The soul of Adeodatus is torn into five parts, the demon told me in my dream. Perhaps those parts seek reunion. Perhaps what I am doing is exactly what I am supposed to do, and this false Chamber emerges from that necessary remaking of the whole.

The true Alkahest – as I wrote it – is drawn up and out of these noble but mundane ingredients in a similar fashion, by a kind of necessity. It is a piece of soul stuff not deriving from the matter in the crucible but permitted into the human world by their conjunction. The ritual is not a prayer, but a species of geometry which opens the doors of the universe to what lies outside it. The ingredients are a door, and the lock must be undone by the pain of a human soul. (Yes, yes, I was maudlin drunk by this time, and growing Homeric. Let it be.) So this part is simple: you hold your pain – all your sorrow, your sin, your self-despite and guilt, your shame – in your hand above the crucible, and let it call out in supplication to the raw blood of the divinity, and that blood will rise up towards you, and where it touches you, you are made whole, and more. If you want to lift it to someone else, you must temper your pain and shape it as a cup. The only vessel that will contain the Alkahest is the agony of the heart that calls it up. The process is one of self-sacrifice. With practice, I wrote – rather smugly, it seems to me now – you can control your own needs, and meet the needs of others.

Is it obvious I was ever so slightly preaching there? Well, I thought so. But once you've decided that the Scroll is the real thing, apparently all this is just your average magical revelation.

I put out my hand and think of everything that has ever made me feel small and cold. I think of the staring moment of denial when I learned of Adeodatus's death, of the scream I let loose when I realised Augustine had really kicked me out, that he had put his God between us. I remember Monica's frosty gaze the first night we met, and how she passed the fruit to everyone at the table but me. I think of my small, spiteful revenges, of the idle notion I have entertained recently of telling the whole story so that my *Reminiscences* should stand in contrast to his hurtful *Confessions*. I think of my stupid, over-ornate prank, and how it has ensnared a generation of otherwise intelligent people and led to this moment, perhaps to Scipio's death and surely to some greater plot to come. I think of all the times I have been less than I tell myself I am: passing beggars in the street without caring, shouting at my infant son, betraying confidences for the thrill of gossip. I remember I once took a lover purely because I knew someone else desired him, and relished the pain I inflicted more than the sex, and in the end they married other people and are still joyless. I confess, silently, that I am frightened above all else that I have wasted my life, missed my opportunities, and that everything I am will be lost absolutely when I die. I admit my greatest horror: that there is no goddess, no God, no jennaye and no afterlife, that all there is, is rot, and no meaning to any of it. That I will never see my son again, raised up in a new body and playing in a field for ever.

I hear a sob, and know it for my own.

Quite absurdly, the crucible fills with light.

the combination to

'Immediately, please,' Neith growls at the visiting nurse. The Witness required a check-up after this second episode of unbidden recall of the Hunter interrogation. Neith acceded out of a sense of good practice, though she privately believes the concern is misplaced. She is tired but energised, and has concluded that Tubman – blast his casual armchair profiling – is quite right: she and the recording share an intrinsic urgency, a desire to move forward.

Which is why she is now losing patience. The nurse has now fussed over her, poked her with wooden sticks to assess her nerve endings, and made her pee into a bottle absurdly ill-suited to the operation. She has had enough. There is such a thing as too much oversight. She glowers at him by way of emphasis.

'I don't know that it's—'

The Inspector seldom pulls rank, but now she loads a Witness X tag ('X' being for 'expedite') behind the request to give it weight. The Witness approves it, and the nurse departs without further argument, returning a short while later from the living room with a single piece of printed paper which he fixes to the wall over her bed with a strip of blue electrical tape. The Witness has evidently expanded her instructions, because he also brings her lantern and a single ping pong ball in a translucent plastic bucket that at one stage contained individually wrapped muffins.

She thanks the nurse but does not apologise, and nor quite obviously does he expect her to. They are both professionals, exercising professional judgement. It occurs to her briefly that she might ask where the ping pong ball came from – she has no recollection of owning one – but concludes that the answer is either banal or utterly bizarre and in neither case will the question offer any relief of their social tension.

The nurse pronounces her well enough to be badly behaved and notes that this is a good sign. He reiterates the general infuriating injunction to take it easy and departs. She waits until the Witness informs her he has left the building, then wraps both arms around the bucket and shakes it, watching the ping pong ball as it clatters and jumps. It isn't as satisfying as the long drop of her tennis ball or the tactile thud as it lands in her palm, but it won't roll away if she drops it and force her to get up when she doesn't want to. Nor does it suggest the flexible physical laws of dream. She puts the bucket aside and flicks on the pen torch. On, off. Once, twice, three, four, five times, because her instinct is to stop at three, and dreams use precisely the recollection of habit to construct a facade of the real.

Finally, she turns to the poem on the wall, an untitled piece from a twentieth-century American.

I am the combination to a door
That fools and wise with equal ease undo ...

She forces her eyes to pick out each letter before assembling the words, as if she were learning a new language. Halfway down she stops, and goes backwards to the top. The text is static. Good.

She lies back. 'Is there a matching historical record?'

— *I'm pleased to see you are tormenting the hospital staff. It suggests your recovery is going well.*

'Contextual/colloquial address: off.'

— *Aurelius Augustine, Bishop of Hippo, later St Augustine. Born AD 354 in Thagaste, Roman North Africa, died AD 430. Unmarried, one child: Adeodatus, precise date of birth unknown, died AD 388. Mother's name: unknown.*

'Define: Alkahest.'

— *The mythical Universal Solvent, a transcendent medical and theological substance.*

'What about the Chamber of Isis?'

— *String not found.*

'It's a figment?'

– There is no mention of it in the literature. It does not follow that no such place ever existed. Our knowledge of the ancient world is incomplete.

'Isis, then.'

– The classical Egyptian mother and wife goddess, patron of magic. Sometimes considered as a benign iteration of the Trickster deity. She was an ally to slaves, artists and the demi-monde, hence her occasional invocation in the art nouveau and even art deco periods. Also the name sometimes given to a short-lived twenty-first-century militarised pseudo-nation in Syria. Also the section of the river Thames that is close to Oxford, and by proximity a linear particle accelerator at the Rutherford Appleton Laboratory. Also—

'Stop.'

She considers. In general, she allows the Witness to check her own intuitions and to crunch numbers. She does not like to ask the machine for clues. The whole point of an Inspector is to follow her own path and find things that an analytical tool, however complex and algorithmically mysterious, cannot see. This next question falls somewhere in the grey area. Well. 'Significant points of confluence: Kyriakos segment, Athenais segment.'

– Kidnapping; a journey into darkness; chaos; gods and monsters of the classical and Roman Mediterranean, especially Firespine and—

'Stop.'

The recitation stops immediately, between phonemes.

'Kyriakos doesn't mention Firespine.'

– The Patriarch, Nikolaos Megalos, references it obliquely in his first meeting with Kyriakos: 'We shall once more have fire in our spines, and Greece shall be torn no longer.'

'Confidence?'

– There is no immediate ground to imagine it is significant, but it is a specific term with a low likelihood of random occurrence. The most plausible reason for its presence is that it meant something to Hunter and she included it unconsciously. That meaning need not be of interest, and yet it may assist in uncovering more about her.

'Formal confidence rating?'

– The likelihood that it is directly relevant is fractionally less than eight per cent.

Mielikki Neith stretches her shoulders against her pillow, wincing as she finds bruises on the bone. First Kyriakos the banker, and now Athenais: fleshed, persuasive histories that do not belong in Diana Hunter's head. Stories that hinder access to her thoughts under neural examination. It is posited in the academic literature – which the Inspector has now skimmed in preparation for her meeting with the perfumed Oliver Smith – but this is in her understanding the first sighting in the wild of an actual Scheherazade Gambit. Not one story but two, so that as the investigator begins to reach the bottom of the first, so another emerges to renew the defence. When that begins to fail, the subject can revert to the first stream, and so on, the graph of this pattern giving the technique its more formal name: Sine-reinsertive Occultation. It's still futile, and no doubt incrementally more strenuous and damaging, which may well be significant in the Hunter case. Still: impressive to hold two such fantasies in the mind at once. Neith would have doubted it was possible.

She finds herself asking how the attending interview team would have reacted. Might they have assumed that such a complex defence entailed something troubling to defend? Perhaps, especially as the stories are not entirely disconnected. In each of them, a malign divinity touches the real, and threatens to tear the world apart. That tantalising hint of threat, unverified and – unless the walls can be brought down – unverifiable, is exactly the kind of thing interrogators have nightmares about. In which case they would have become urgent and even hasty. Was that haste fatal to a woman with nothing to conceal save her atavistic distaste for intrusion? But if it was, what about Regno Lönnrot?

– *String not found,* the Witness says. She must be speaking out loud.

She starts to compose her next question, but the white ceiling is endlessly far away. She settles comfortably into her sheets and closes her eyes. The machine will wake her in good time, and the bed is warm.

*

The Victoria Embankment these days always stands, to Neith's eye, on the brink of catastrophe. The engineering genius of 1870 did not anticipate the consequences of two-hundred-odd years of global warming, and even the subsequent reinforcement only emphasises the comparative scale of the wide grey Thames and the sea beyond. A river man once told her, as they trawled the silty water for a lost tourist, that it required only the concurrence of three natural events – a spring tide, a storm surge driving water inward from the estuary, and a heavy rain over Wales and the Downs – to flood the Parliament buildings and some of London's most expensive real estate. So far there had only ever been two out of three, but the day must come, he'd said. Sooner or later, it must.

Under a Victorian gaslamp now housing an organic diode bulb, Dr Oliver Smith stands waiting in a raincoat by Ede & Ravenscroft and a charcoal suit. There's even a watch chain, the fob tucked into his waistcoat pocket. He wants to belong in the setting, the Inspector considers, or to it. Smith could be standing on the other side of a hole in time, a man from 1950 or 1890. He wears the sartorial markers of establishment and education without irony. He is not satirising the trace elements of the twentieth century and the public school system's military caste, he simply is their inheritor in a better time – white, arrogant, brilliant – and doesn't propose to pretend otherwise. Brown hair blows in the breeze coming in off the river. Age indeterminate, and she suspects made so by quite expensive cosmetic surgery. He is clean-shaven, but if he uses cologne – she had assumed, because of Tubman, that he used too much – the wind is snatching it away.

– *Diffuse Imperial referencing,* the Witness says, *nostalgic reassurance associated with fictional and historic authority. Sherlock Holmes and Winston Churchill, with notes of romantic leading men: Fitzwilliam Darcy, James Bond.*

She already doesn't like him.

'Thank you for meeting me here, rather than in the office,' Smith says as he extends an ungloved hand. 'I do treasure my outside time.'

Neith smiles, taking it. 'So do I.'

The machine prompts her to turn outwards, inviting him to resume his contemplation of the water. She has engaged the rolling kinesic assistant for this interview; Smith is under essentially the same scrutiny he would be if he were strapped into a lie detector, the local observation cameras and audio pickups feeding the Witness, along with Smith's own devices, with more than enough data to give a precise assessment of his levels of stress and excitement. Based on these perceptions, the Witness will instruct Neith on the timing of her questioning, the pace, the flow. The conversation will feel to Smith as if he has met a deeply interesting and sympathetic person and is sharing only what he always meant to.

Neith turns obediently, and a moment later Smith does, too, unconsciously echoing her posture. Good.

'I'm sorry to trouble you, but it's necessary.'

'No, of course,' Smith says. 'A woman died in custody. I understand entirely. Do you know yet – that is, if one may ask: was she guilty of anything?'

'Resistance,' the Inspector says after a moment, and lets the word hang there in the air.

'Yes, a true Scheherazade, and you think probably autogenous. That would be remarkable.'

'But not impossible?'

'Not impossible,' he agrees. 'A level of difficulty greater than merely accepting an external structure. But perhaps the rooting in one's own creativity is what gives it strength.'

'Rooting?' Orchids.

'It grows from her, inevitably.'

'It's made of her. Perhaps of her life?'

'Allegorically. Indirectly, it must be, surely? Who else does she have to work with? What is it like to be a bat?'

'I don't know.'

'Precisely. And if you imagine being a bat, what are you imagining?'

The Witness whispers in her ear, but she already knows the answer. 'Being me being a bat.'

Smith beams. 'Quite so.'

'So these stories . . .'

'Must by definition echo her own life. How closely ...' Smith spreads his hands. 'But I'd bet each one contains elements that are significant to her, either by close analogy or symbolically.'

'Could you identify those areas?'

'I, personally? I'm not sure. My office, definitely, in time. Though exactly how much time would depend on what other material we had to help us. And time, of course, is the issue. We are fully contracted to the System, you understand, so how much time we could give you wouldn't be up to me. Exigencies of our work.'

She nods, letting the Witness tell her when to turn and deliver her next question in response to his look of readiness. The recommendation calls for schoolgirlish awe, but she doesn't have any, and frankly wouldn't know where to get some. She settles on student confusion, and reminds herself to recommend an update.

'What is tidal flow, exactly? Why does the Turnpike Trust need experts in ... whatever it is you do?'

'Oh,' he laughs, waving one hand in the air. Only in Britain do experts denigrate their own specialism. 'We're the masters of intangibles and prediction. It all begins with traffic jams, if you can believe it. The city is tidal, and not just because of the river.' Fingers flick towards it, fold up again. 'People come to work in the morning, leave in the evening. There are cross currents from tourists – transport hubs. It's complex. We manage the interactions. When you get stuck in the Blackwall Tunnel, that's me having a very bad day. The end of the football season is always a complete – well, I won't use the word I was going to use, I'll let you fill it in. And in the end it's not real. It's perceptual. The weather forecast says one thing, the public mood says another, the economy is up or down, the news is good or bad. What fuzzy variables produce what decisions that result in a snarl-up at Hanger Lane? You have to understand that over the course of a year, bad traffic is massively expensive in terms of lost business, public health, unnecessary consumption of resources, and that's before you factor in the soft variables like how traffic delays influence whether people consider they have had a positive overall experience doing business here. Our performance at Tidal Flow makes a genuine difference to the figures for the capital. So we're a hotchpotch.'

Behavioural economics, mathematics, of course neuroscience. Self-organising criticality. They hate us at university departments, because everything we publish is interdisciplinary and doesn't fit their models, but it's evidence-based so they have to pay attention. Models are never quite good enough. The territory is always new.'

She lets her face continue to register uncertainty, even confusion. *Oh, Oliver, you're so clever, I will never understand unless you say it straight out.* He smiles, evidently encouraged.

'We turn broadly unconnected data into narratives, narratives into data we can understand and work with. We investigate, and strive to influence, the sense of the world people invest in every morning when they choose their route to work, so that they actually get there sometime before noon. We have to know what they're thinking and then give them the information they haven't yet realised they want, so that they know which method will serve them best. Quite often, of course, they take one route over and over again, out of habit. Not much to be done there. But there are what you might call floating voters, people who are actively looking for the most efficient journey, or the most relaxed. I always envy those ones: soft seat commuters. It strikes me as a very good way to live. They're generally employed by newer firms with flexible hours, they take their work home with them, show a high index of satisfaction. They live longer, too, and there's no measurable difference in income distribution across the group ... Well. One day, perhaps, I shall retire to one of those companies. But that's what we do. We help people in their chosen direction. We remind them to ask themselves where they want to go and how they want to get there, and then we help them do it the right way. But the important thing is the how: by creating and understanding narratives and what they are inside the brain and where they touch the real world.'

He puffs air through his cheeks. 'So I suppose we're – all right, "experts" – who might be able to understand the sort of thing that the Hunter woman was apparently doing inside her own head. I say "might" because it's like nothing I've ever seen. In the past we've assisted your department, quite successfully, often with people who process differently, who maybe have had brain accidents in the past or even who are born with one or another sense missing and whose brains have repurposed the areas that normally deal with that sense to do something else. This is – well. It's on another order, to be honest. I imagine some of the straight-out neuro people will work this one for years.'

The Inspector too puffs air through her own cheeks, sympathetic to his amazement.

– There will be a break in the clouds in ten seconds, the Witness advises. *The view eastwards will be striking.*

They turn together into a blaze of oil paint fire: London out of time.

Smith looks over at her, and smiles. It is their first eye contact since they began to talk shop, and she responds before the System nudges her to do so, smiling in turn.

'You have the serendipity flag active,' Smith says. 'Do you enjoy it?'

'Yes.'

'It's one of mine. A side benefit.' He laughs. 'Would probably have made my fortune, if I'd come up with it at the weekend, as it were, and it wasn't covered under contract. I thought about pretending that was how it was. Really had to wrestle my conscience, until I remembered the System would know the answer perfectly well. So ... "Easy come, easy go." That's tidal behaviour, too.'

A personal confidence. The kinesic assistant is in raptures. Green bars all the way up. Maximum rapport, subject entirely cooperative. The moment on which everything hangs – unbidden, the Inspector thinks: Kairos. 'So what would you have done? With Hunter.'

For a longish while he doesn't speak. Then finally he shrugs.

'She's dead, isn't she? So one's first responses are the wrong ones, by definition. I think I'd have reckoned just to push through. No one's ever suggested a Scheherazade could be indefinitely maintained. But if it wasn't working ... A counter-narrative. Recombine Hunter's sense of self. But it would be quite difficult. The issue would be ... well. It would come down to who was the better artist.'

'Could you have done what she did?'

He shrugs. 'I suppose so, if I'd come up with it, and if I'd been sufficiently motivated. The possibility is there in the technology. And in the brain. But it's a question of conviction. I don't see the need, so I can't imagine actually doing it. It seems so unnecessary.'

She nods, and drops her last question as if it's a formality. Classic Columbo.

'Have you ever heard of something called Firespine?'

He shudders. 'Sounds like infrastructure.'

Summing himself up perfectly.

*

As the Inspector walks away from the riverside and back towards Piccadilly's bustle, the Witness informs her that one copy of *The Mad Cartographer's Garden* is available at an antiquarian bookseller which is very nearly on the way. She considers her physical state: tired again, but not so much so; aching, but not hurting.

— A rickshaw will be with you in two minutes, the Witness murmurs as she reaches her decision, and she smiles.

The rickshaw has a warm velour seat that almost swallows her, and for a moment she wants it to take her straight home. She stiffens her spine a little: this is what professionals do. Even tired, even injured, they show up and follow the clues. The rickshaw darts down two narrow streets, then turns and crosses over a third on a bright white walkway which rises from old London's York stone like the tentacle of something from a deeper sea. She spots Shand & Co. immediately, a wood-panelled hermit crab nestling by the lower reaches of a coral tower, last survivor of some feeding frenzy among the starfish. The shopfront has split paint and mortise and tenon joints, and the new window glass with its safety mark in one corner is rippled in simulation of an old, uneven making. A bell on a coiled brass spring tinkles as she enters, the sound bringing out from behind the counter a genial middle-aged fellow in the fat uncle mode, who extends his hand.

'I'm Saul Shand,' he says, earnest, but with just a little bit of flash. 'Welcome, and don't let me disturb you. Browse and be silent or ask what you will in the certainty of discretion and scholarship. This is no lair of chattering bouquinistes; be assured there will be no tote bags and no branded pencils. We are — that is to say that I am — entirely at your service. Good morning.'

The Inspector retrieves her fingers — Shand's grip is pleasantly warm but a little succulent — and wonders aloud whether he might help her find his copy of *The Mad Cartographer's Garden*.

Shand's expression flickers with what might be a kind of sympathy, as for one stricken with an incurable affliction, but he nods. 'We can but try,' he agrees.

And try he does, first in the main shelves and then in among the more expensive first editions and the locked cases which house his treasures. Then he goes back behind the counter and consults first a predictably antiquated terminal keyboard, and then finally an actual ledger bound in cloth.

'It should be here,' he says finally, 'but it isn't.'

The Inspector frowns. 'It's misplaced?'

Shand glances up at her, and then seems to change gear. 'Normally, I suppose. Or stolen, though these days we get very little of that. I take it you haven't been trying to get hold of a copy for long?'

'No. I'm investigating her death.'

Shand starts. 'Hunter? Dead?'

She sees him consult the terminal again, the cool light playing up on to his wide cheeks.

'Oh my. She was *that* Hunter. How extraordinary. I had no idea. Well, yes, but I mean: no. I'm afraid you're going to have a hard time finding her books, Inspector.' He glances at her for confirmation; she nods back. Yes: Inspector. He must not be running recognition in real time, part of the olde worlde experience. It occurs to her that he'll still have the mandated customer and enquiries list, and she opens the tile menu in her terminal for local options, requests the record going back a year. By itself, it won't mean much, but it will serve as a reminder to run a search across all specialist vendors for anyone looking for Hunter's work. From there she can build a profile of Hunter aficionados, those who are drawn to her thinking, and with a bit of latent attribute inference she'll have a broad list of those who share her underlying mindset. It might or might not be important, but anyone she deals with in the context of the inquiry who is also on that list might bear closer examination.

Shand is politely waiting for her to come back to the physical discussion. 'Sorry,' she says. 'Witness business. Rude of me.'

'Not at all,' Shand replies. 'But Inspector, I wonder if you are aware that *The Mad Cartographer's Garden* – all of her writings, I think – they are not merely "hard to find" in the commercial sense. They are impossible to find. They are ghost books.'

That seeming is an illusion, a false pattern emerging from the spinning of a wheel. The Scroll is a ghost book, a summoner of phantasms and dreams.

Is that coincidence, cul-de-sac, or clue? Assume nothing is random, she tells herself. But also assume any connection is illusory until you can substantiate it. 'Ghost books?'

'In the trade, something between an irritation and a great curiosity. There are not many – perhaps a hundred in all. They are books that are only catalogued, never actually sold. They seem to appear in auction lots and collections, but if you should buy that lot, the book will be missing, and when you complain you will find no mention of it in the detail. A photograph for illustration purposes only will include *Mr Murder Investigates* third in the pile, but it is from an old sale. Do you see? Like today. I should have a copy of *The Mad Cartographer's Garden*. By every measure I know it is in this shop, and yet I also know that it is not. It is not in this shop, if we were to turn it upside down into the street and check every title on the pavement. In a month from now, someone will offer me a lot containing *Five Cardinals of Z*, but I won't be able to secure the collection. Later, I will get in touch with the lucky purchaser to see if they will sell, and find that they have already done so. They will gladly tell me that they enjoyed the story while they possessed it: a brash adventure in which the holy Afric Saint, Augustine' – Neith closes her eyes for a moment. A random example or one drawn from life? Shand doesn't notice – 'takes on a sort of Tarzan role, fighting with his sorceress lover against a magical invasion from the Visigothic west. When I track the next purchaser down with my offer, they will tell me the book is about something quite different. They may be quite irate. In any case, they will have sold it on.

'Perhaps there are multiple forgeries in circulation, but I cannot obtain any of those, either. If I suggest to the publisher that they might wish to reprint, they will agree that it would be a very good idea, what with demand being so high, but nothing will come of it. These books exist, one sometimes thinks, only in the rumour and desire they excite. And in some cases, that does indeed turn out to be the case. There is a book by a South American author that is endlessly listed on rare edition inventories, but I know for a fact that it was never made available in the first place. The publisher commissioned it, the author wrote it, but there was an irretrievable breakdown in their relationship and he refused to deliver and burned the manuscript. It is in all the catalogues for that year – they were printed in advance, of course – but it cannot be had. Warehouses listed it knowing they would receive it, and do not list it as sold out because they've never actually despatched a single copy. Where there should be text on paper, there is none, only the whisper of it in our accounting, the spectre of a story that was never actually shown to anyone. Thus: a ghost book.'

'But these ones, Hunter's books . . .'

'Are not the same. No.'

'So what are they?'

Shand looks cautious. 'I can speculate, if you wish. Some ghost books, I have always assumed, are created or adopted by criminal organisations for their traffic. In a global context, what travels in the boxes marked to that title is something quite different, something illegal and perhaps even terrible. That would be much more difficult with transactions in this country, of course.

'Others fall prey to human cupidity. There are literary properties fancied by film stars and directors for production. Such people will buy entire print runs to prevent any competitor from reading them, and then when the film is made and the value of an early edition is high, they will release copies slowly at a great markup, profiting once again by their wealth and power. Sometimes, in those situations, production of the envisaged project is held up or even completely blocked, and the book vanishes into the open mouth of Hollywood.

'Then there are books which are so despised by, for example, the Loving Covenant of Baptist Libraries that they will seek to acquire copies and destroy them. In some few cases they are quite successful. There was a children's story rumoured to contain an actual magic spell that they have entirely obliterated in its English language edition. Very sad: the illustrations were full plate by Jackie Morris.' Shand shakes his head. This, evidently, is cultural vandalism.

'Which leaves a very small group of books, including Diana Hunter's, that are reputed to exist in fact, but which are never seen. At least, not by me. There are wonderful rumours about them, the occult ramblings of the foolish and the mad: Hunter's books contain an encrypted message that reveals the underlying nature of God's creation. Or perhaps they are the physical body of an angel expressed as text, something so strange and splendid that it cannot exist here except as a collection of beautiful words, and that is why no two accounts of the books are ever the same. Perhaps the books contain Hunter herself, written down and endlessly replicated in some form of literal literary immortality. Now that she is dead, perhaps that is the best thing to believe. Although of course if that were the case, one would imagine they would be everywhere, so that the words would be read, and she would live in firework flashes of minds across the world. Stasis, after all, is a poor form of longevity. One would look for iteration, yes? For engagement and enlivening.

'Maybe that's the point. The publication plan required her death. Maybe now they will all become available again. Who knows? Perhaps that's even why she's dead. Maybe it's what she intended.

'If the books do all surface, of course, you may be sure I will stock them. Would you like me to call you, if that should happen? Or if I should suddenly come across one, quite ordinary but very valuable, and prove myself a foolish old man?'

The Inspector contemplates an outcome of her investigation in which she is compelled to place under arrest for sedition a pile of limited edition magical realist novels allegedly containing a human mind, and devoutly hopes Mr Shand's construction of the situation is not the right one. She feels confident in believing that it is not, on the basis that such an idea is plainly poppycock – Shand's gallant version of English must be rubbing off on her – but does not entirely dismiss the possibility of some secret hidden in Hunter's books. That is always the position one occupies in the Witness: that something is taking place that needs to be observed and understood. This of course makes for a vulnerability to recursive investigations: the acknowledged danger of assuming that an absence of evidence is itself evidence of obfuscation.

Except that this is not, precisely, an absence of evidence. If there's anything happening at all, the evidence is bounteous.

Perhaps Hunter's books really do not exist, and she somehow hornswoggled the world into believing that they did in some weird art prank. It might just about have been doable, a couple of decades ago. The Inspector would prefer this not be the case. The idea that the books might be themselves mythical alarms her: the intrusion of Hunter's unreal histories into a world that should be more tangible. The notion that they might all be blank and contain no information, or maybe exist only as description, while Hunter's mind apparently contains far more information than it should, raises the hairs on her neck.

Something. Something. 'Did she ever write about fire, specifically? A fire motif? Firespine? Fire Judges?'

'Oh. Dear me, no, I don't think I've heard of that one. Is it juvenilia? Or a special edition? If the former, perhaps it can be found; after all, very often it's the first efforts that escape their creator's hands, you know, and make their way in the world. Although sometimes it's the last instead ...' Shand shrugs: the mysteries of art.

Neith explains that it's not a title, just a phrase, and Shand regrets that no, in that case he does not know what it may mean. He looks at her nervously, and the Inspector realises he is waiting for her reaction to the business of the ghost books and his personal theory. She smiles, the informal smile of release from an official discussion. She is not small-minded enough to chide a romantic for a tall tale. She tells him instead that Shand & Co. is as charming and elegant as its proprietor, and thanks him for his time.

*

She finds the rickshaw hovering outside as if pining. As she steps through the door it rolls towards her so eagerly that she flinches. The wheels brake, and the Witness apologises for startling her.

The velour is heated, and the ride is very smooth. She decides to leave the Hunter recording and sleep properly, get some real rest. Climbing the stairs seems endless and taxing. Her whole body aches. Definitely, no work tonight. Just sleep.

The story begins again as soon as she sits down on the bed, and she dives in as if she has been thirsty all day and only now found water to drink.

another set of colours

Outside the house, something flashes firework bright. My ears hurt, in the burning way they did long ago when I was twenty and contracted an infection from a midnight swim. The window ripples and bows inward like a soap bubble. I watch it stretch: a long, endless second as it bulges towards some plastic limit. Then it screams. I have never heard glass scream before. I discover in this moment that the sound is beautiful even as it is appallingly painful. Screaming glass is transcendent, the lamentation of lovers frozen in different fragments and now tumbling apart. The shriek barges so deeply into my ears that I can feel it in my stomach, and then I stop hearing at all and the window goes white as one layer of the laminate is pulverised, absorbing the force of the explosion as it should – as it is designed to do. Laying itself down.

In fact, we're all lying down, lying on the floor: me, my granddaughter Annie, and Colson the magic fabricator elf who may or may not be her lover. I'm laughing because we're alive, and because the blastproof glass was a caprice, a moment of absurd housekeeping. I got it spare when we supplied a chemical plant in Royston and they changed the design at the last minute. I said: 'I'll have it.' I installed it myself through the whole house, with the help of a friendly builder, and when he asked me why, I said: 'You never know when you might be grateful for a second chance.'

Well, now I do know. It can't have been a very large bomb, but it certainly would have killed all of us without that glass.

I'm calling the police, which is what old men do. Landline, analogue phone. I don't know if it's working, because I can't hear anything. I wonder if I'm deaf forever now. I wonder if the enemy – and however in all the world do I have enemies like that? – is trying to come into the house. It'll take some doing to get in, if so. The door is no softer than the walls.

I'm not dead. Not dead and go to hell, you bastards. What are you going to do now, eh? Eh?

Even in here, I feel the flash of heat, and smell the accelerant. (That's petroleum, to you. The other thing old men do is watch a great deal of bad procedural drama on satellite television.) Flames outside the window. The flicker of the same from other rooms, and a stark choice: go out and suffer whatever those faceless shits intend, or stay inside a burning house. Their backup plan: glass bottles with rags in them, no doubt, making of my castle an oven in which to cook me. Me, and my granddaughter and her maybe-lover.

Once, in Addis Ababa long ago, I walked through the walls of my prison and escaped.

I wish I could remember how.

*

I had no idea, when I began, that my desire to learn about the modern world I had somehow lived my way into – about the Internet and all its marvels – would cause this ruckus. And, in truth, 'desire' is far too strong a word. It was a pretext for me: I was making peace.

Annie's father – my son – is named Michael. Ethiopians, even in London, still hold to our own pattern of names, but back when he was born I was determined that my nation had thrown me out, and even tried to end my life, and so, very well: I would be a Britisher. My son would not be Mulugeta Berihun or Messay Berihun; he would be Michael Bekele, and there was an end to all that, and a new beginning. It was the first of many ways in which I have given him cause to find me an irritating old man. The first, but not the last, and we have turned our backs on one another and inevitably reunited a dozen times over the years. We argue because Michael cannot understand that in some small reserved areas of the world I still know better than he does; and I cannot get my fuddled head around the possibility that I should accord him the same respect I would to a man of his accomplishments and standing who was not my son. I do try, but somewhere in me is the shape of him, standing naked astride a pile of Lego bricks with his face covered in baked beans, declaiming 'Frain frain frain!' – his childhood word for 'train'. It's hard, when that is one of your most treasured memories, to mind your Ps and Qs.

So to this present moment: we had had a row. I don't even remember what was our notional reason for the fight. Almost all of them are echoes, anyway, of the huge one we had when he was twenty. This one was minor, just a snappish exchange about who we were: a seasonal reminder of difference, and harmless, if awkward.

I called on Michael at his house and carefully did not – or did not quite – ask for his permission for my scheme. At the same time, I did not want to appear to step between him and his daughter even in this small way. Instead, I came as chairman emeritus of the family company he now controls, and asked for a leave of absence to teach myself the mysteries of computing: a properly businesslike and inevitable first encounter after our dispute. It was something he had been plaguing me to do, though I think he had despaired of it ever actually happening. He played along, and asked if I should like him to arrange tuition. I said yes, in the fullness of time I should like that very much, but for my first steps I had hoped for a familial introduction in case the whole thing was too embarrassing and impossible for me to continue. Spare my blushes, I said: do you think Annabel would give me some time?

Michael laughed. He saw immediately, of course, that I was playing on his pride as well as offering my sacrifice as an olive branch, and was pleased by both. It is our pattern to grumble and itch at one another, and then to make amends in openly devious ways. Recently he has become almost artistic, going so far as to seat me, at a corporate charity dinner, next to a mildly notorious actress of decades gone with whom I once had a brief and passionate romance. I think he hoped we might find a late love, and in the event we giggled smuttily at shared recollections and discovered a mutual fondness for Bach, but nothing more.

'Of course she would,' Michael said. 'Of course. She complains that she doesn't see you any more. But you do realise that it's a little like asking Astatke to teach you to play "Happy Birthday"?'

'Astatke plays the conga drums,' I objected.

'And the vibraphone,' Michael said, and I let it slide. I do not tangle with Michael on the subject of Ethio-jazz, or much of anything about Ethiopia, the homeland to which he has never been. My Ethiopia is not accessible, anyway: washed away in the river of time, and the new one just another hot country run by angry men.

'She wouldn't mind, though?'

'Oh, no,' Michael said – just as I would have, in his place, and with the same utterly unmerited confidence that he could pledge his daughter's word. 'But it's Annie. It won't be simple.'

I bridled a little. I sensed some anticipation of my imminent generational shaming. I was so busy drawing myself up to my full height and saying that I was sure I could master a few things that were not simple that I didn't stop to consider exactly what he might mean. I took it that Annabel was good at what she did, though I had only the vaguest notion of what that might be. In any case, Michael said I should call her and gave me her direct number at work. 'Knock yourself out,' he said. 'It'll be great.'

I said that I would, and privately resolved to be more fluent in digital matters than he was within a few months. We are not competitive, my son and I. There is no point. I am an old man and he is middle-aged. What could he possibly do better than me?

*

Annie's voice was very warm when I called. I had been a co-conspirator for her in younger days, encouraging small moments of revolution, of counter-conventional thinking, and I had as is appropriate in a good grandfather been a source of forbidden sweets. I had drawn pictures for her – the last residue of my old life, cartoon dachshunds and sometimes, in extremis, images from her more threatening nightmares made kindly by the light of day, and by my conviction that any beast from the realm of sleep can be made a guardian if one works hard enough at the task. Then she had been away at university and in her first jobs, then working terribly hard to set up her company, so that for six years we had been nodding acquaintances only, however warm.

'Annabel, it's Berihun. Berihun Bekele. Your grandfather.' In case she knew more than one Berihun Bekele, and in case my voice was not familiar. Love makes some people bullish, but it makes me diffident.

She laughed. I could picture it. She has a wide face, made for delight, and high eyebrows that seem always to be startled. If she were not so warm, she might seem supercilious, but there is nothing in her that is not genuinely interested in people. I told her, haltingly, what I wanted, and asked whether it might be possible, at her convenience. She had not been present for the row, but she would know of it by family osmosis, and she would recognise the game she was being asked to play. I relayed my conversation with her father, and his optimism – and my determination to exceed him, at which she laughed once more. I imagined her rolling her eyes, and asked if she would help me.

No, she said. Absolutely not. It was a terrible idea. I would achieve nothing and we would both be appallingly bored. Before I could object – plead – she said that she had a much better suggestion, but I must come to the office immediately and she would explain. She was sending a car.

She was sending a car.

I think I realised then a little of what Michael had meant, but I still did not entirely grasp it. Another flaw of age and the habit of being the boss: I had not wondered what Annie might desire from me in exchange for what I wanted from her – after all, a few favours here and there are nothing when set against the great debt that is ancestry. More: I had not stopped to ask how she might think to reshape the world using me as a lever, because it had not occurred to me that she might shape the world at all. I was the mover and the shaper – by habit, by precedence and by custom. The world formed itself around my experiences and decisions, not those of a young seedling who had after all not existed until I was a great oak.

That person, that woman who was from my vantage still effectively a zygote, could not send me a car. Only full-fledged adults with expense accounts could do that. Who had given Annabel an expense account?

Well, *she* had, of course, when she created her firm. But who had given her that kind of money to work with? I realised I didn't know. I didn't know if she had employees, or rather: I knew that she did but I could not picture them. She must have investors. I might even be one, now that I thought of it, though not to any heroic level of commitment – and if I wasn't, why wasn't I? Wasn't that what successful grandparents were for? Had she really gone out into the world and got her own funding as if I did not exist? How?

The same way Astatke got a recording contract: by being brilliant. So, she sent a car to pick me up.

When the car came, it was a new, new Prius with cameras on it. Of course it would be, I realised: a car that was mostly a computer. When I got in, the young man in the driver's seat wasn't driving. He was just sitting there, handsome and short-haired and a little bit messy.

The car drove itself, the young fellow told me, and his job was to make sure it didn't go wrong. Which it wouldn't.

'Bobby Colson, but call me Colson,' he told me, when I asked. 'Dogsbody.' I wondered briefly if that was the last part of his name – it happens that people have extraordinary names and are quite matter-of-fact about them – but I gathered shortly thereafter that it was his title, self-determined and a source of considerable pride.

'The car has over a million hours of driving experience,' he added kindly, as I peered nervously around. The steering wheel was turning one way and then the other like the keys on a pianola, the pedals drifting up and down. 'The first few days, I was a bit twitchy. Then I realised: all the other cars on the road? They're the ones driven by idiots. People on phones, people who can't see through the screen because the blower's out, people who just want to get home in a hurry. They do all this totally insane crap all the time. This car? This car doesn't. It's the most boring chauffeur in the world. It doesn't just see the road, it sees in infrared and sonar, like that. It has real-time satellite information. And it makes decisions so fast you miss them. The law says I have to sit here, but honestly, if you see me reach for the wheel the odds are you should punch me in the face. The car is much better at this than I am. If there's an accident, it'll have saved us – or not – before I even know what's going on. I'm just here in case it suddenly decides to take over the world.' He grins. 'Skynet, right? Only that's not going to happen either. It's bollocks. Specialised intelligence. It doesn't think. It drives.'

My first lesson, I thought. 'So,' I said, 'the car is better at being a car than the driver ever could be?'

Colson gave me a thumbs up. 'That's right. Now, suppose there's a terrorist attack or something, right? And you actually need to smash into another car to get away from a falling skyscraper or whatever? That's when you switch the computer off and take the wheel, because it doesn't have any idea about any of that. It'll sit there waiting for the traffic to get out of the way and you'll get squashed. Limited vision. It's all numbers and weights and measures. There's nothing in there that isn't in a wind-up. Not, like, spiritually speaking.'

I sat in the car all the way from Stoke Newington to Old Street, and of course I jumped every time I saw a pedestrian or a cyclist or a dog, every time we approached a traffic light, but I have to acknowledge that the machine was in the end a far more relaxing pilot than most any of the thousands who have taken me across town in the time I've lived here. It was, as Colson promised, utterly boring.

The company office was in a steel-and-glass building by the roadside, a new thing with green leaves tumbling from the upper storeys. 'Green roof, green walls,' Colson murmured. The building looked like a future I could live with, but not one I'd live in. I tapped the dashboard.

'Thanks for the lift. Does it have a name?' I asked.

'The car?' Colson raised his eyebrows.

'Yes.'

'Be like naming a steam iron.' He smiled. 'It's got a number. Four. But that's about it. See you later.'

I thanked him, and watched him cruise away to the company parking spaces. When I turned back to the building, Annabel Sophia Bekele was waiting on the step with her hand extended towards me in professional greeting.

'Welcome to the Fire Judges,' she said, and we shook.

*

That's the name I can never remember. A historical reference, apparently – after the Great Fire in 1666, twenty-two judges were empowered to demark the lost property boundaries of London. This was necessary because so much of the city had been destroyed that even the reference points that might have been used to establish a rough outline had been reduced to rubble. Half the time they were just drawing lines in the air, and when that happened it wasn't impossible that they took the opportunity to improve the flow of the city just a little, to root out dead ends and bad alleys and turn them inwards on themselves. 'Benevolent ghost geographers,' Annabel said, immediately after telling me it's Annie, always Annie, because only I and her former headmistress still call her Annabel.

The name was appropriate, my granddaughter explained, because this was a company that made worlds out of air – or, more accurately, out of numbers. They had other revenue streams – they were field-testing that magic car for the maker and tweaking the learning software, and they used spare computing time on their prodigious infrastructure to host various calculations for institutions that didn't have enough cycles of their own – but mostly they were about creation.

The company owned this building outright, she said, so there was potential revenue there, too, although they didn't charge a powerhouse rent to half their tenants because they wanted 'the benefit of serendipity', which I took to mean that having young programmers floating around the hallways and coffee spaces gossiping and one-upping with the originators of nascent fashion labels, toymakers, microbrewers and architects produced a miniature version of the cultural and commercial stew that has been so successful in Silicon Valley. Annabel – Annie – said yes, exactly. This year, the Fire Judges had shared in the success of a new kind of ergonomic chair and a mesh-networked child tracking system. I did not know what the second one of these might be, but Annie said it was simple yet very clever, and this combination of virtues appealed to me just as it obviously pleased her. I saw her glance over my shoulder at Colson, now happily unscrewing something with many wires and arguing over it with a boyish man in dungarees, and thought that he pleased her, too, and for the same reason. Simple but clever: it's a good pairing in a lover. Complication and angst are much beloved of the authors of romantic fiction, who take their cues from Byron and Tolstoy, but in real life a little simplicity can be welcome, along with kindness. I thought I should pass this immense wisdom along to Annie, and then acknowledged that, if she liked Colson, she already had it.

We wandered through wide hallways trimmed with metal pipes, ducked into bare-brick workspaces lit by industrial-scale anglepoise lamps. We met a man who had invented a new musical instrument and another who was building a better mouse. I almost said 'Mousetrap?' but realised in time that he meant exactly what I thought he meant, although of what benefit an improved rodent could be I had no idea. He explained that the digestive systems of vultures are purgative of disease. The birds' excreta are pure fertiliser, even the most revolting diseases burned out by their fierce internal chemistry – for which reason the killing of vultures across the world represents an unprecedented risk to global public health. In many areas where they are almost extinct, bad old germs are resurgent in their place. He wished to introduce the vulture's happy trait into urban rodent populations, a giant leap towards the eradication of serious infections – and crucial in a world that is rapidly losing its grip on resistant bacteria.

'So he's a medical doctor?' I said as we moved on, and Annie laughed. 'He has a degree in theatrical design,' she replied. 'He got into biotech because he wanted to make a goldfish in his team's football colours. He does the design work here on our system and outsources the experimental stuff.'

All of which was possible, it seemed, though I had had no idea. When did that happen? I said that perhaps I was suffering from future shock, and Annie replied wryly that the term 'future shock' was itself nearly fifty years old. 'Although Rousseau complained about something very similar in 1778.' I recognised the absent tone: this was something she said often, to meetings and conferences, to journalists asking whether the world was changing too fast.

All the same: how was this all happening, under my nose, and I was just carrying on? I'd been living, by my own decision, in the past, imagining that the world wasn't really changing all that much, imagining that now was a great deal like then, and that the future probably would be, too. But I have to tell you that it won't be. Mouse Boy won't stop once he's created proactively hygienic vermin. He'll come up with something else. People are already talking about bioluminescent trees to replace street lamps, and I find myself imagining the city that might grow out of that idea: a soft, moonlit haven to replace the industrial sodium of my time. But Mouse Boy is concerned about light pollution, Annie said, so he doesn't want to work on that. Anyway, he's reaching further, towards digitally mediated emotional interfaces for the improvement of human communication. Imagine, she murmured, having a relationship with someone and actually feeling their joy, their fear. Being perfectly aware of them all the time, being able to tell them they're loved when you're not present to reassure them. Imagine negotiations where you can know for a certainty where there's room to haggle and where there's an impasse. Imagine trials where innocence was measurable on a graph.

This is the place she had created, my little granddaughter. The company called Fire Judges: they drew lines in the air, and made them real.

I knew now why Michael had laughed when I wondered if Annie would teach me about computers. I was a little ashamed of myself for asking, for imagining that it was a fit use of her time. Ask Astatke to teach you to play 'Happy Birthday', indeed. Or Einstein to wire a plug.

Well, here was my first lesson: it had almost nothing to do with computers, the modernity I was trying to understand. Computers were the bones, but imagination, ambition and possibility were the blood. These kids, they simply did not accept that the world as it is has any special gravity, any hold upon us. If something was wrong, if it was bad, then that something was to be fixed, not endured. Where my generation reached for philosophy and the virtue of suffering, they reached instead for science and technology and they actually did something about the beggar in the street, the woman in the wheelchair. They got on with it. It wasn't that they had no sense of spirit or depth. Rather they reserved it for the truly wondrous, and for everything else they made tools.

We had reached the far end of the building, the space that belonged to the Fire Judges, and she opened the big double door.

'So,' she said. 'I expect you're wondering why I've called you all here today.'

Dimples. Granddaughters with dimples. That's what you need to be careful of in this life.

*

We walked through a room with a ceiling that went up and up, between rows of photographs, both colour and black and white. And not just in, but of: black people and white people photographed on different film stocks. And not just that endlessly reductive duality, but every imaginable variation of skin was sampled here. It was actual film – I knew, because I could see the negatives hanging in spirals by the side of each board – and the textures and tones of the skin were rendered to different degrees of fidelity and atmosphere. In one photograph, a tall fellow I judged to be Haitian looked sickly and angry. In another, he seemed filled with a secret life. Next to him was a pale woman with a French flag on her shoulder, a UN official, glowering hot and rashy in the second photograph, filled with a sort of diffident hope in the first. It was the same all the way along the rows: pairs and sometimes sequences of images with different subjects, and always one set favoured one kind of skin and made others look oddly sinister. Then there were streets done the same way, hazy and soft, hard and cold, warm and welcoming, and on and on, all in monochrome, all subtly different and yet showing the same scene at the same time. Different countries, different architectures. Different worlds.

I asked Annie what I was looking at.

She gestured to the nearest picture. 'Ordinary celluloid film was optimised for white north-western European skin. The chemical composition was not intended for non-whites, so it didn't capture us well. We were either over-lit and sweating or shadowy and indistinct. Do you remember Sidney Poitier in *In the Heat of the Night*? I mean, okay: it's supposed to be hot, I get that. But he's awash – they've got the lights dialled all the way up because the film can't see his skin. Until around the year 2000 they still used white-skinned models for colour balance during processing. Digital cameras changed that, but I wondered how much. I started wondering if there was still a bias – in the chip design or the imaging software's basic presumptions.'

'Is there?'

She made a gesture, hand tipping one way and then the other. 'Maybe. The fidelity of digital is absurdly high, and you have access to the raw image, so some of it just goes away. Displays and projectors, that's another story – and photographic paper and printing ink. Anyway, I poked around a bit and it actually turns out that eight per cent of white males are colourblind, as against only four per cent of African males and about one per cent of Inuit and related populations, although I'm a bit sceptical of the broad data there given the ethnic variety inside all the populations we're talking about and I suspect the research we're seeing may have been a bit basic. So it's not just about race, it's also about a given white male relationship to the physical perception of colour.'

'What about women?'

She looked back at me, approving. 'Yes! Exactly. A small fraction of the female population is tetrachromatic. They have an additional receptor in the eye that theoretically allows them to see colours that are not available to the rest of us, although because the tetrachromat population is so small we don't have words for those colours, or even concepts for them. They exist only as something felt and experienced.' She sighs. 'I'm not one. I'd love to be, wouldn't you? To see a broader spectrum, another dimension?'

I found myself thinking: No. Because if I saw another set of colours I would need to reconsider everything I paint. Which was an odd thought, because I hadn't painted in decades.

Annie gestured at the pictures again. 'I turned it all upside down. I wanted to go back to celluloid and create the opposite sort of celluloid film stock: film stock that favoured black people.' She pointed at the images. 'It worked. I think we'll use it when we create the character types for this project, maybe the architecture. Blackness will be ordinary, whiteness will look odd. It'll be part of the experience. A little truth, hidden in the game: the people most often referred to as minority populations in this country are the global majority, so their vision is arguably the normative one.'

I knew plenty of people who would have considered that enough for an exhibition, back when. Combined with even a moderate talent for the image it was enough even nowadays to make a name. For her it was backdrop, just an element in a bigger work. But:

'What project?'

She grinned. 'Ah,' she said.

I followed her down the line of images, the different tints and tones of non-white skin picked out in perfect clarity, the strange incompleteness of what the Americans call Caucasian skin rendered real for the first time in my life. In the middle of the maze, there was a circle of sofas and a coffee table, and when I saw my favourite cake waiting for us I knew I was about to be pitched.

*

'Did you know,' Annie asked, as I took my second mouthful, 'that the government recently trialled electronic sobriety anklets for those who have been ordered to avoid alcohol? They test the wearer's sweat every half hour. Imagine a society premised on that logic of benign observation, and go from there.'

I hadn't known, so I shook my head.

Annie shrugged. 'Nor did I. They don't make a big thing about it. Rather talk about the stuff that doesn't freak people out. But it doesn't seem like a great leap from there to networking those quantified self bracelets' – I had only the vaguest notion what these were – 'so that the state can tell you: "Hey! You want to smoke, that's fine, but your NHS contribution goes up because you're a risk." Or whatever.

'So, okay,' she went on, 'next question: did you also know that there's a private prison firm working on a house arrest system that allows judges to impose permanent surveillance? They call it SDORP – pronounced "stop!" – for sub-dermal observation and restraint platform. It's a unit that goes in your gluteus muscle and if you do something the supervisor doesn't like it can knock you out and call a team to come and pick you up. It's perfect. Any environment can be a prison.'

No, I hadn't known that, either.

'It's actually an outgrowth of a really wonderful medical technology, an automated doser for different crisis situations – antivenins for people in remote areas that have seriously toxic wildlife, that kind of thing. But that's not really commercial, so the designers licensed it to the prison people and it's really attractive to police forces. I mean, why wouldn't it be? Imagine if you could just turn off a brawl or a riot from your phone.' She mimes zapping me with a touchscreen.

'There are dozens of these ideas floating around. And the thing about them is that none of them is actually evil, they're only sinister if you see them in one particular direction. Imagine that instead of prison you could resocialise someone, put them in a human environment and yet protect that environment from their lapses. Occupational therapy, impulse control, an awareness of place and connectedness. By many readings it's the optimal reform environment – the only thing it needs is a positive context to grow in, a place where people can respect you, which is much easier if they know you can't hurt them. Recidivism rates could be slashed. Except that, I mean: hey. It's putting control chips in people. Why not go the whole way and run a wire into a given bit of the brain, stimulate a given response directly when you need to? Pavlovian reconditioning – for medical purposes only, of course. Maybe for rapists and so on. I mean, that's protecting society, right? It's never just that, of course, and sooner or later you've got a chipped human population which is an appreciable fraction of the whole. So very, very not cool. Except that it's so much better than just locking them up to make ash trays. Except that it's worse. Or is it?'

Annie sighed. I wasn't sure any more. I knew what my instinct was, but I have the healthy distrust of instinct that comes when hormones are less pressing and experience is glum. My granddaughter went on, practised and impassioned.

'We have to think about this stuff now, before we build it, otherwise we'll just find it happening around us. If it's a bad thing and it's already invested, money and power on the line, it's much harder to roll something back. For example: we're working on distributed voting here. We thought: Hey, wouldn't it be great if we just polled people all the time? How about if we had something where you could, in theory, poll a huge number of people at any given time on a given issue: how democratic would that be? What if every afternoon you voted on a bunch of things and that actually governed how the country worked? So we built it. We have a system that could do that now.

'It's harder than you might think: distributed real time voting. Infrastructurally it's hard. You want to have the vote and the record of the vote without being able to tie the vote back to a particular person, because that would be problematic. Secrecy is supposed to be part of the democratic process, so that you can always vote how you really want to without external interference. Oh, and at the other end of serious: you have to be sure that they haven't just pocket-dialled the system. You do not want people arse-voting to halve the schools budget or something.

'Most people think the hardest thing would be voter security. They think there'd be fraud. The weird thing is that we have almost no voter security now. It's not like anyone asks you for your passport at the polling booth. And it works fine. You'd think there'd be lots of cheating, but actually there isn't. Maybe there will be one day, so sure: trust but verify. You don't build the system to be vulnerable, of course. But as a reason not to do it? No.

'Anyway ... we have that system. It exists. And suddenly we thought: Wait. What are we saying here? What have we made? Have we made the most democratic network in the world, or have we just reduced law and government to the level of a talent show? And: what if someone were able to get around our privacy safeguards? What would that data be worth, and how could you use it? Almost all the good secondary value you can get out of mass polling requires to some extent that you know who voted for what, and a lot of people would be fine with that because it's only the disempowered who need to be able to hide themselves.

'We actually had this really alarming run-in with some kind of spook outfit that wanted to acquire us, right off the bat. As soon as we published some demos, they just turned up one morning and offered us a lot of money. We called everyone, all the shareholders and so on, and put it to the vote and they said no. Actually, they said "hell no", which made me smile. I mean, that could have gone somewhere really dark.

'And I got to thinking: what if you built a whole country this way? Around this. Around these devices, these possibilities. If we just decided that privacy on that level wasn't as important – a lot of the US guys do feel that way, they have this weird anti-statist freedom thing that somehow creates a superstate in private hands and they don't see the issue because it's not guvmint. But that was what I wondered: what if it was? What if surveillance was the government? What would that nation feel like? Would it work? For most people, for most of the time, it would probably be great. But it would have a capacity for monstrousness. And there'd be, inevitably, these opaque places where something could go so very wrong. A real nightmare ... And it went from there. What if we made a world around that?'

So that was it, Annie said. The idea had exploded inside her head and she could see it, could feel how it should work: a game environment that would be utterly compelling and new and strange, and would at the same time publicise and roll out a bunch of new ideas and technologies that actually existed and encourage people to think about them practically and morally. And kick some arse, of course, because that's always fun.

'In this environment, there's simply no such thing as privacy any more. Every action is visible to the System, and it can call you in, demand an accounting. In the midst of a perfect world, where power is in a way truly held by the people and government has almost entirely gone away, there's a thin strand of horror, of interrogation machines mandated by the majority and algorithms that see everything you do and want to know why you did it, that understand your actions according to an actuarial chart and analyse you as an aspect of behavioural economics. The system applies numbers and probabilities to your life and knows what you will do, what you might do, even what you would-do-if-only, before it has ever occurred to you. Perhaps you have a latent streak of revolution in consequence of your unhappy upbringing. One day you do something that has just a hint of that rebellion In it – so then you're brought in and adjusted to make you better before you can break the rules. And in the centre of this maze: a monster.'

'What monster?' I said.

She grinned, and I realised that was what I was supposed to say. I was supposed to want to know. That was the hook, the thing to make me play and play on until I found out.

She waved the question away for later, then glanced at her watch. 'Let me show you something quickly. It's not ours, it's one of the big games that's already out there.'

She turned to one of those enormous screens, white and geometric, and tapped and fiddled. When she ushered me into the chair – the screen, clear as glacier ice on the surface of a lake, filled my vision – I saw a tiny homunculus standing on a wide red plain. It looked like Arizona somewhere, or perhaps, though I have never been, the Australian outback. All manner of traffic and fantasy was swarming around the man, but Annie quickly took him away from that and up a hill, so that very shortly he was alone on the summit, facing west. She sat him down, and pulled up a chair next to me, and we sat watching the sun set on this faraway place called the Barrens. The sky was rich and deep, the distant mountains blue, an oasis lush to the south. Birds flapped by, and then bats, as the sun gave way to early night, and when, a little later, the moon rose and it began to rain, I realised we had been watching without speaking for nearly half an hour. Colson appeared with more tea, and Annie turned off the machine.

'It's lovely,' I said. It had not occurred to me that games could be beautiful, or indeed, that anyone would care if they were. I hesitated. 'Can you ... tell me more about yours?'

'Project Gnomon,' Colson said.

'Colson' – Annie rolled her eyes – 'wants everything to have a secret identity. In case someone gets hold of our plan and – I'm not sure – steals the name and leaves the rest? A rogue branding agency?'

'You build security in from minute one,' Colson replied, unrepentant. 'It's too late when you realise you should have had it and you didn't. Plus I like the name: something that sticks out, that doesn't match everything else.'

'*Witnessed*,' Annie said firmly. 'Our project is called *Witnessed*. It has huge backing already. Our investors love it. The game engine is going to be amazing. But I have a problem.' She glanced over at me. 'I need it to look like nothing anyone's seen before. I need someone brilliant to design it. Someone with a completely unexpected take. Someone I can trust who has real artistic chops. And ideally, someone with a name in the art world, so that when I announce it there will be discussion, anticipation. Because everything that does that makes my job easier.'

God, I thought, what a task. You'd have to be an idiot to take it on and a genius to pull it off. But what a challenge. What fun!

She must want a referral, of course. And so I began wondering who I knew who could do something like that. You'd need to think about architecture and society, about history and mayhem. Ideally, then, someone who'd seen some history rather than just read about it. It would be all too easy to create a sort of off-the-shelf fascist playpen for her game, and that would look fine but it would ultimately go stale. It wouldn't convey nearly enough of what she had said. The game must be organic, each aspect of the look driven by the deep shadows of the concept, and the look would have to weave in and out of what was happening in the story, tonally and thematically. You'd have to imagine it in every time of day, in different weather conditions, and each of them should somehow have an uncanny feel: hard, inhuman edges and misapplications of scale; uncompromising anti-architecture. There was a building I knew in the centre of town that had a little of what I wanted, a white concrete thing all shelves and angles that, in the right combination of rain and wind, gouted sudden torrents of water on to people below. It could feel like being assaulted if you were in the wrong place at the wrong time, and the owners had had to apply for permission for a sort of bus-shelter awning all along the pavement, so now the whole front of the building at ground-floor level was dark most of the year and stifling in the sun. Yes. That, only more, so much more. That for the soul.

This was a real effort, a staggering work: what sort of artist would have the time, would be willing to put aside whatever he or she was already doing? Someone who wasn't working was almost certainly by definition someone you wouldn't want, and someone who *was* working wouldn't want you. You'd need someone old, brilliant, and mostly retired. Someone like me, but—

She was smiling.

There was no but. This was her pitch. Not someone like me: me.

'I don't know anything about computers.'

'You don't need to. You design. We'll build. But you'll pick stuff up! I solemnly swear,' she raised her hand, 'that by the end of this process you will be fluent in the magic of email, Google and YouTube. You will speak the tongues of Adobe. After that, everything else is incremental. The fear goes away because you're doing stuff. Doing is learning. And Dad will be in awe.'

'How big is your world?'

'The environment? About the size of London, at a resolution roughly equivalent to the human eye.'

A whole city. Impossible. 'That would take ... decades.' She could not mean to hire me a team of thousands. Not even with whatever magical finance she had in place.

She shook her head. 'We have a construction algorithm that is adducive-iterative. It could, in theory, take its aesthetic from one drawing, although I'd prefer to get a bit more than that. It's ... well, let me show you.'

She produced one of those small computers from under the table and opened it up. Immediately I saw a door.

'Go through it,' she said.

'How?'

'Touch it.'

I did. The door opened and I saw a room. She dragged her finger across the screen, and it was like turning my head. 'This isn't how the gameplay works. This is just for our convenience. Go on, have a look around.'

I tapped and dragged. More doors, more rooms, all that rather ugly modern rental beige that estate agents seem to believe is 'neutral' but which to me bespeaks an absence of humanity and the presence of a lifestyle photographer. Tables, chairs, scattered personal items. I kept going. More rooms. More views from the windows. Everything the same. I looked at Annie.

'The engine is fractal,' she said. 'The deeper you go, the more it makes for you to find. When you started out, there was only one room. Now there are ten. It gets rather boring, though, because it's got nothing to work with.'

'It can … guess … what I'd do from a single sketch?'

'No. Not really. It just takes a cue, based on a complex but ultimately pretty sterile algorithm. If you were to say yes, you'd have to create a small body of work and then patrol the output a bit, select what was good and ditch what wasn't in line with your vision. It would learn to be more and more in tune with you.'

I wondered whether, if I spent long enough with it, the machine would distil the essence of my work out of me the way I had never quite managed for myself. And if it could, was that a perfect artistic tool or the violent intervention of technology into my most human heart? How would I feel if it worked, and the machine's version of my work was better than mine?

'What makes you think I can do it?'

'I've seen your work from back then, and I know you now. You're my grandfather – but you're also Berihun Bekele. You painted *The Earth in Flames*. You painted *The Lion in Space*.' She stopped, suddenly concerned. 'Can you do it? I mean, can you still paint? Did you burn out?'

An intimate question from a professional colleague. A daring one from a granddaughter. A good one.

'No,' I said. 'I faded away.'

*

Colson offered to take me home in the self-driving car, but in the end I got in a taxi because I needed very much to collect myself and get sensible. Annie had quite adroitly doubled my oblique family repair work back upon me in a style of manipulation that I recognised as my own and Michael's mixed. I didn't want to default on grandfatherly assistance or fatherly amends, so I had at least to think it over, even if my first reaction was to run a mile from such a strange, enormous undertaking. In the event, I couldn't think at all on the journey, because it seemed to me that the ride was swooping and abrupt. All the drivers around me must be mad or drunk, and the motion of my own taxi seemed saner only by a narrow margin. Instead of going all the way, I let myself out in Islington. I bought a sketchbook from a supply shop, along with some Caran d'Ache pencils, and walked to a tea shop. It was a fine place with a mezzanine looking over the room and a chandelier made of grey Murano glass.

I lost my art by degrees, starting in the autumn of the year I moved to London. Day by day by week by month, a little more of whatever had made me capable of painting ebbed away. For all my recent life, my mind had been filled – overfilled, it seemed quite often – with wild imaginings: terrible landscapes, alien gods and sex, all taking their cue from the lines of the real, so that a child with a dog became a mighty starship between binary suns, and then the suns became the eyes of an overwhelming state. I had seen life as fantasy, and painted it in my fivefold way. I had lived somewhere between worlds. And now all that was fading to grey.

I waited, at first impatiently and then with a kind of calm I had never known before, a calm which showed in my last works. I met Michael's mother, and she approved of this monkish hibernation. My gallerist … was not sanguine, but accepted the interregnum and its justification, for a time.

For a time it worked. I found a sort of simplicity. I sketched in charcoal, in little notebooks. For the first time in a long while, I sketched what was in front of me, and I wondered whether this was not, after all, a species of apocatastasis: a new primordial beginning. I had been celebrated as the transnational man, the Ethiopian who painted the industrial north-west. I was a post-primitivist riposte to Warhol, a neo-modern Irrealist dabbling in political anger. I knew this because it had been written in magazines. Perhaps more than anything, to the public and to the musicians and celebrities with whom I spent my time, I was the man who spoke to aliens – and yet, now the aliens had apparently stopped visiting, perhaps I might just be an artist. And if that meant I didn't get invited to the upscale parties any more, maybe that too would be a survivable catastrophe.

I drew the Hawksmoor churches, the Old Bailey and Trafalgar Square. It was soothing, and I allowed myself to be soothed, and then to feel content, and then, content, I stopped, because I was not discovering a new landscape inside myself, I was just winding down. The urge to paint was gone. Why would I bother? I had money, to a point. I could set myself up in business, live well enough. If I had no desire to carry on, why should I?

Between six and seven in the evening on a Thursday, I felt the last of it turn to dust inside me. My art dried up and blew away in the backdraught of a London taxi. I was not unhappy. I was barely anything at all, and that pleased me.

Well, there it is: I didn't choose to stop painting, long ago. I simply stopped, in the same mysterious way that as a small boy I started. I still had the skill, but the drive to do it went out of me when I went out of Addis Ababa, and with the drive that specialness that made my work interesting to anyone, including myself. In Ma Madden's Teas and Biscuits, therefore, with Annie's commission in my head, I expected the conversation she had begun inside me to come to an end. I gazed at the chandelier as I opened the book, held the Payne's grey pencil in my fingers, and waited for nothing to happen.

An hour later I stopped drawing to order some cake and stretch my back. An hour after that I went back to the supply shop and bought five canvas boards and some oils, and I went home, assuring the cab man I would give him double what was on the meter if only he would go slowly through the seething mass of steel.

I painted for seven days straight. If she had still been alive, Michael's mother would have left me again, and this time it would have been quite deserved. I worked as only someone who lives without dependents or lovers can, but somehow, for the first time in years, I thought I felt the touch of her hand on my shoulder as I paused for breath or to get water for myself or the paint, and I cried a little, as old men sometimes do. Death has a tendency with age to gather in around one, taking first the luminaries and friends of that subtly older generation one assumes will last for ever, and then picking off strangers and old flames, old enemies and finally one's family, until what you might call without irony a skeleton crew remains, each of us fighting to be the last – or perhaps the second last, to leave some poor sod the one who truly dies alone. Eleni was among the first of those I loved to go out of the world.

It began with a more mundane leave-taking. A little more than two weeks after Michael's third birthday – that would make it the middle of '79 – she cooked me a very fine breakfast. She sat across the table with her hands folded and told me that she must go. She knew it was unfair, but she must. It was the only honest course.

I cried out, as if I had been shot, and then I was very calm. If this was the honest course then there must, I reasoned, be a dishonest one. Had she taken a lover? No, she said, not yet. It was all very proper, but she was lying to her heart and to God, and she must follow the call in her even if it meant breaking the written law.

I entertained the hypothesis rather than accepting the reality. I thought perhaps if I understood the new life she was making, I might cause her to choose the old one instead. I asked her, in that spirit, how often I would be allowed to see Michael.

Michael, she replied, would stay with me. I should please bring him to visit her often. We would establish a regular pattern, so that he would not be too upset.

So it went on, back and forth. If I seem to you very reasonable, very model in my inaction, it is this great distance of time that makes it so. In between reasonable questions I railed at her, and we both shrieked and howled.

Finally, I asked who she was going to. Was he richer, younger, stronger? A better lover, a kinder man? She said: 'Marion,' and after that I didn't try to argue anymore. Marion was the singing teacher at her school, a thin redheaded woman with fluttering fingers that made me think of birds.

That's how it was. It was an upheaval and it hurt, but in time it came to be ordinary. Eleni and Marion were never far away when I needed them. Michael was furious and then resigned and finally delighted to have acquired an additional parent, and I found that my jealousy was limited to competition for time and company, not for love. I had other relationships, but always circumscribed, always finite. It was rather a lot to ask of any woman that she compete with the nearby mother of my son, share the kitchen and the living room with her each week. Some managed it, others did not, but none ever stayed.

In 1999, Eleni and Marion moved to the south of France, and a few months later they died there together, in the clear Mediterranean Sea. Eleni had an inoperable tumour, and they had chosen a very Roman passage home.

I wish I could say 'ancient history' after all these years, but I can't, and still less when her gentle ghost comes to pay me a visit. Still, I believe she had a happy ending, in so far as anyone does.

*

A week after the meeting at the Fire Judges I moved my bed into the living room to be nearer the work. When I woke I painted and when I was tired I slept. It was the exact experience to which I had laid claim long ago but never truly found. I existed in the work and it in me and that was all. I was ridden by the brush.

I was immersed, too, in a kind of odd fugue triggered by Annie's remarkable photographic project. My granddaughter was doing something I did not fully understand with her identity: it was not what I would have done, nor what Michael might have chosen, nor his mother, and nor indeed Annie's. It was entirely her own – a way of being British out of Ethiopia that knew its past but was not tied to it, and it had taken her to an interrogation of colour and mind that had not occurred to me as an artist or as a man. I began to question colour itself, to wonder about it as I never had before. I found myself considering the spectrum as an arbitrary designation. Why, after all, should there be seven colours? The answer is that there are not, as my parents could have told me. The rainbow is a continuum of infinitely many colours. Seven is no more a real count than Father Christmas was always red and white. (He was green and silver until the Coca-Cola Company made him their messenger, in case you didn't know.) Which, in turn, means that between green and blue there are interim colours, just as orange and yellow come between red and green. Even by the crude standard of our inherited awareness of the rainbow there are missing tints which have no names.

Paint, I realised, had a secret history bound to language and thought, and as I began to read about it, I understood that it was among other things my history, because woven through it was the strange journey of the different colours that are called black. Both black and white have – ho ho – a chequered history, and they were themselves susceptible for centuries to fine divisions of quality and kind. The old northern Europeans had swart and blaek: the wicked and elf-filled matte black, and the fertile luminosity of a darkness that filled the night with shapes and benign magic. Likewise the Romans had ater and niger, and that first word now forgotten is the root of 'atrocious', while the other, originally the same happy, effulgent black the Teutons knew, bequeaths us our modern 'Negro' and its associated racial slurs, as well as the country of Nigeria.

By an effort of will, I pulled myself around. I did not wish to scrutinise black as if it was anomalous. Instead – in line with Annie's determination – I looked at white. White – wite and blank or albus and candidus – could be just as dangerous as black, or just as godly, in the ancient world: a leprous sickness or a guide in the storm. The Christian Bible must carry some blame for the slow shift to a more binary view of black and white, unequivocal as it is about the role of light in the Creation and the place of darkness in sin – but so too must the entrenchment of profit as a new god, for black was the colour of working men, where white was for the nobility.

I realised as I said all this aloud to my canvas that I had conducted my entire examination of colour in English. Why so, and not in Amharic or, for a particularly scholarly investigation, Ge'ez? Well, there were good and sufficient reasons in my own history, so I need not feel too much guilt about it, but was there a sense of a brightness in ፕቄር, or a sickly flavour to ነፕኮ? I had never studied the philology of Ethiopia and did not know. It might be the journey of the rest of my life to unravel the cultural history of colour to my own satisfaction, and I had things to do first, obligations to discharge and, yes, art to make. Perhaps the work would be done better in ten years, after I had unravelled more of this fascinating digression – but art is never pure and commerce, like mortality, is uncompromising in its adherence to schedules. Annie's investors had a right to expect timely delivery from me, and so did she.

I ordered larger canvas, stretched on heavy frames, and converted the living room entirely into a studio. The rest of the house began to feel fusty and useless, so I closed and locked many of the doors. I was aware of the irony that, having wanted to connect with a wider world, I was now shutting it out, but it afforded me only amusement, especially after Annie loaned me one of the desktop computers of immense power that the Fire Judges seemed to consider necessary, and gave me remote access to something called the Spine. This was a box in an attic somewhere ('Actually it's an old nuclear shelter in Belsize Park') and I had my own bit of it where I might keep images and ideas, and what is called read-only access to the rest, meaning that I might see almost anything the company was doing, but not alter it, this being a protection against accidental erasure. Since the Spine was evidently the digital equivalent of a safe, or possibly an engine room, I was grateful for the boundary. Even so, the protections around it were ferocious, and Annie insisted – in a rare moment of straightforward technical lecturing – that I know them off by heart.

'Authentication on steroids,' Annie said. 'Username and password, that's standard. We start there, then we add a dongle.'

'Excuse me,' I asked, 'a what?'

'A physical key. Don't ask why it's called that, no one knows. A physical object that proves your right to access a given resource. These days it's usually your phone. In our case it's a little doodad you wear around your wrist.'

'Think of it like a credit card,' Colson suggested. Annie rolled her eyes.

I am somewhat notorious in the family for mistrusting the modern apparatus of consumer credit and wearing habitually a bracelet made from a number of 1967 gold krugerrand. It is a piratical affectation that I am mostly forgiven, and very dashing, no doubt, upon an old fart, but I wear it because I have never entirely let go the fear that one day I might once again need to run. I explained this to Colson, who looked fascinated and then approving. 'Digital financial transactions,' he said, 'are in their naive optimistic stage. Good call. Security should be wearable. Or ...' He raised his hand.

'Yes,' Annie said. 'If you're a total lunatic, you can have the chip encased in plastic and implanted in your arm so that you can Obi-Wan your way around the office. I don't recommend it.'

'But still: Obi-Wan,' Colson said, which made me smile. He pointed at my arm in support of his position. I slipped the dongle around my wrist, next to the bracelet.

Annie sighed. 'Settle down, boys. All right. Something you know and something you have. Two factors. Okay? But we need more than that. The dongle itself has a biometric scanner. Most people use fingerprints or retinal scan, even aural topology scan, but there are issues with those. Once they're compromised, that's it – you have a finite number. And they lend themselves to rather ugly forms of violence. We're trialling microbial cloud analysis. The sensor in the dongle is actually patterned after canine nasal cells, which always sounds a little bit weird.' Yes. To these silicon children, biology is outré. 'Anyway: everyone has a distinct collection of biomass on and around the skin. Recognition is about ninety-six per cent accurate, so not perfect, but it's incredibly hard to fake. For full-access login, we have predictive neural modelling and response.'

'What's that?'

Colson shook his head. 'It's the absolute creepiest thing in the world.'

'The machine asks you a string of random questions,' Annie said, 'and measures your answers against its analysis of your personality. It's not predicting your answer, it's determining whether it's the sort of answer you'd give. Over time, it also notices if you're changing in significant ways. That's why Colson hates it.'

'It's fucking intrusive,' Colson growled. 'In theory, it could decide you're emotionally unstable and tell your boss. If you vary too much from your previous behaviour, it might lock you out of your own files. There's potential for abuse, Annie, and you know it. The alcohol anklet people could use it to say you're backsliding. And those probation futurecrime fuckers, they'd love it: if your connectome gets too much like the one you had when you were a sinner, off to jail you go! And sooner or later, someone's going to say it can detect defections and whistleblowers before they can decide what they're going to do themselves. Maybe you see something, I don't know, you're an oil exec and you see the results of a spill. The system might lock you out for insufficient faith in the corporate ethos. Loyalty-based access.'

Annie glanced at me. 'Colson believes the world is on the brink of a collapse into pre-liberal government. The erasure of the twentieth century.'

'It is,' Colson said firmly.

'Be that as it may—'

'Loyalty-based access. It's the automation of the merger of a religion of the state with corporate power in the form of information.'

'We'll code it out.'

'Someone'll code it back in.'

'They won't be able to.'

'They'll try.'

'That's why we haven't sold it,' Annie said, a little exasperated, and then to me once more: 'Five requirements. It's like putting ingredients in a cauldron for a magic spell. A significant object, your name, a secret word, your body. Then eventually, connectome: your soul.'

'Your mind,' Colson growled.

'Magic,' Annie reminded him. 'Anyway: by the time you've used the system for a while, it'll know you well enough for the PNMR. It means no one sees your work before you're ready, no one gets our software who shouldn't have it. I just want you to understand it enough to appreciate that it's important.'

'PNMR,' I said. 'Magic spell. I understand.'

'That's another thing,' Colson said morosely, 'it's a terrible name. Peenmar. Penny Mar. PenMar. It's crap. It needs a new acronym.'

'I like Penny Mar. It would make a great campaign. "Who is Penny Mar?"'

'Creepy,' Colson said, 'as fuck.'

They bickered happily. I was pleased by them: Annie's energetic creation paired with Colson's blend of making and paranoia. It made for an excellent team. For myself, I wondered if I had taken on too much. I'd been prepared for technicalities. I had not considered that I would be asked to grapple with philosophy of self. Annie had been right, though, that the mysteries of the machine would not long remain obscure to me, and by the end of the month I was using the in-house messaging system quite freely. I still insisted on communicating by post as well, because I found a qualitative difference in the opinions of others depending on the medium in which they were conveyed. Colson, in particular, I insisted write his comments on paper, which I think was the most shocking thing he'd ever had to do in his – to me – rather short life. His electronic responses were terse to the point of thoughtless, but his written ones were quirky and energetic, and he quickly got rather fond of the whole business of stamps and handwriting and started to respond to my sketches with little postcards he bought from a newsagent down the road from the office. YES! MORE! I LOVE IT! RIGHT ANGLES! he wrote once, on the back of a truly horrible picture of the Queen. I kept that one, because it had a fierce joy in it, and an unexpected eccentricity that pleased me no end. There's nothing better in the professional life of an artist than the moment of seeing one's work kindle in someone that look of enlightened obsession. He told me later that it started when he bought a fountain pen and the scratch of nib on paper awoke in him the same fruitful concentration as working with his hands.

Little by little I constructed a world; a new London emerging like a white bubonic plague from the comfortable shambles of the old. I settled for my model on the Russian architect Lubetkin, who designed the old penguin enclosure at London Zoo. His geometric structures were beautiful but hard, a mathematical absolutism that demanded people play by machinic rules, rather than softening the edges of the razor to allow biology and culture their place. Indeed, the penguins have for some time inhabited a more organic setting, leaving the brutalist post-deco pit near the aardvarks a monument to the temporary triumph of theory over life.

That was my guiding principle in the design: that Annie's world was one derived from a heedless benignancy that based its assumptions on fine ideas rather than messy truths, and in the process birthed not a Utopia but a kind of great Procrustean bed on which the whole of Britain must lie. It was the spring before the vote on our relationship with the European Union, and so I started from what I saw all around me. I imagined that we might lose the vote, despite the obvious absurdity of that outcome, and from there I conjured a Europe made weak by division in the face of predatory Russia, and limping along just offshore, a Great Britain buckling under rising debt and the asinine policies of a Conservative administration hostage to its more ridiculous fantasists. I pictured a rising authoritarianism on both the Left and the Right, and internationally a flagging centrist instinct struggling to find a voice that could not be shouted down. What if, I asked myself, the great liberal project that was the underpinning of all British political parties was truly not stuttering but collapsing under the weight of its own Victorian contradictions? What if Annie's generation became persuaded that predictability and security for the many were more important than those caught in the sharp corners of the government machine? It had been in my life an unchallenged tenet that a nation should strive to accommodate all its citizens, even if that occasionally meant the tail wagging the dog. How, though, if the new formulation of democracy for the coming century did not accept that? How if it rejected the presumption of innocence in favour of a scientific and inquisitorial finding of truth? From this cauldron I conjured a state constructed on the sacrifice of privacy in exchange for a power that seemed direct and real, but was at heart undermined. I built it to be seductive, yet unsettlingly flawed, and I expressed those flaws in how it looked and felt. Nowhere was the truth of Ethiopia as I knew it more evident than in the map and image of the capital, the new buildings decreed by the Emperor rising above the old ones: the future emerging from and crushing the past. I made my new London in the spiritual image of my old Addis Ababa, and always, always, there must be the hint of Annie's Minotaur: the subtle, unforced error which made everything in the game world fraught where it might have been fine.

My granddaughter's opinions came in visits, emails, and scraps of paper shoved heedlessly into envelopes and sent to me. *You have to understand*, she wrote after I showed her the first sketch,

> *that this is a real possible future. It's not a nightmare, it's a truth. It already exists in the overlap of our technologies and our fears. It only needs the right flow of events for us to act the dream and make it real. Imagine how safe it would feel to know that no one could ever commit a crime of violence and go unnoticed, ever again. Imagine what it would mean to us to know — know for certain — that the plane or the bus we're travelling on is properly maintained, that the teacher who looks after our children doesn't have ugly secrets. All it would cost is our privacy, and to be honest who really cares about that? What secrets would you need to keep from a mathematical construct without a heart? From a card index? Why would it matter? And there couldn't be any abuse of the system, because the system would be built not to allow it. It's the pathway we're taking now, that we've been on for a while.*

I wrote back saying that I agreed, but as far as I knew, no one was building a machine to read minds just yet. I thought I was amusingly wry, but I was wrong, as she quickly informed me, because there are several projects doing just that at a low level with magnetic resonance imaging, and when something is physically possible in this new age, it gets done sooner rather than later. She forwarded me a quaint editorial piece from a science journal, which begged to reassure me that serious mind-reading wouldn't be possible without invasive brain implants, and therefore – as no court would conceivably agree to such a thing – we need not fear an intrusion on our liberty from this source. I wondered in what world the author was living. In the wake of New York's horror, it seemed to me, a person suspected of having advance knowledge of a similar outrage would be on the operating table before the judge had her wig on.

The question, Annie said, wasn't whether we could have a society like the one she wanted me to imagine, it was whether we would.

The more I spoke to her, the more I began to understand properly what it meant that she was the founder of this company: not merely that she was a good business brain, nor even that she possessed a flair for the smoke and mirrors of financing that must have been from her mother's side of the family. No: Colson said she had the Blacksmith's Word for numbers, for making them sit up and dance, and I began to realise that Annie was the creative engine of an atelier that worked in computer code. She would mash ideas together in her head and spit them out almost randomly, and Colson would spin them around in the air and bat them right back to her as narratives and demand to know if she could build something that would do that. They were very happy to have me join the parlay: it was an open conversation, only enriched by additional minds. The first rule was that everyone must be heard and no idea was weak. The triage came later, in hard-nosed edit sessions. I skipped those meetings, pleading age and art.

When I accepted the commission, there was a scrupulous contract we all signed which entitled me to a share of whatever profit the outfit might make – though Annie told me wryly that it would produce only tiny money unless we were very good and very lucky. In the vanishingly unlikely event that we scored a direct hit, though, she was confident that I would be pleased by my percentage. I didn't really pay much attention. I was an artist again. I had no desire to walk back from where I was. I refused to let Annie take the early sketches. They were trial pieces, I said. Useless now. I saw her face flicker. Concern. Eagerness. Trepidation. Anticipation.

I knew she would not be disappointed. I was once more the relapsing madman of my first career, the world around me transformed by my strange eyes into a strange place.

I had come home.

*

Addis Ababa in the days of my ascendancy was a city built of spies. My home was ruled by an Emperor, the great and some say divine Haile Selassie, who saw himself I would swear not as the god the Rastafari would make him, but the bridge his nation must cross to go from a timeless and superstitious past to an accelerating future. He aspired, though, to at least one divine attribute, which was omniscience. Ethiopia traditionally teemed with plots, and the capital above all, as must any imperial court where the power of life and death is vested in the whim of a potentate, and our practice of intrigue is one which goes back thousands of years, so that we are better practised at it and more in the habit than almost any other nation in the world. This, in the middle of the twentieth century, took the form of resistance to Haile Selassie's upheavals and modernisations – which were many and discomforting to the service aristocracy that he notionally ruled – or an urgent desire he should hurry up and do more of them, harder, faster, louder. Oh, he was a hero, and had fought his way back, after the accursèd Fascist invasion, at the head of an army. He was beloved of Winston Churchill and later of the citizens of the United States – but at home, just as he had gouged and politicked his way to the crown, so those under him constantly sought promotion, because only in promotion was there any sort of security to be had in Addis Ababa. Security, indeed, was his obsession also, both for his realm, and for himself. In the arena of statecraft he chose to dance between the raindrops of America and Russia, but in his personal power he was less bending. He was the Emperor, and let none doubt that his rule was absolute.

I have noticed, in the time since, that the Emperor and the country he ruled – the country he made – look different depending where you stand. Everyone who was present in Addis Ababa at that time has a story of Haile Selassie, and their story is the only one they believe truly reflects the man. Many of these stories are said to be first hand and yet each of them is quite like the others, and if the Emperor had spent even a fraction of the time required to perform all these similar actions, he would have done nothing else for a year. Old Ethiopia hands – and old Ethiopians – will tell you that the Polish journalist, Kapuściński, was quite wrong. Many will say, indeed, that he was a fabricator. But then they will turn around and tell you by way of proof some tall tale of Imperial legerdemain or mercy or love, or tyranny or excess, that could be straight from the odd pages of his book, and then they will say: 'You see? That was the Emperor, as I knew him!' as if they have refuted some calumny against their own house. Between then and now, Haile Selassie has become impossible to describe. He is perhaps what mathematicians call fractal: surprisingly for so small a fellow, he is infinite, and the more you explore him the more of him there is, so the best anyone can offer of him – or of my birthplace and its history in those days – is a single slice.

This, then, we shall call the shape of the Imperial day. If it is a lie as to the truth of how things were, it is one which expresses the truth of how things felt.

So: every morning, the Emperor awoke and was dressed, and his first public action was to feed a ferocious menagerie of predatory cats in the sequential and nervous company of his three chief intelligencers. Each of these ministers lived in terror of the day when his collected information should be so incomplete as to cast suspicion upon himself, which would in the instant result in a fall that might terminate in a cell – or indeed might not terminate at all, but continue to the gullet of one of the lions. They therefore cultivated agents not only in one another's camps and in the countless cliques and parties that teemed in Addis Ababa, but also in every household and family, however innocent. Fathers were constrained to keep watch upon their children's opinions, mothers reported on their husbands, teenagers upon their friends and students upon their teachers. Teachers, often trained overseas and recruited by the agencies of other nations, were doubled by the Emperor's espiocrats and then tripled by Langley's, Moscow's or London's, and betrayed all of the above for whatever local plot had captured their hearts. There was no place in the city where someone was not watching, and that someone was watched in turn, and all this watching flowed upwards from the streets to the grand houses to the Imperial Person himself.

It must have been a profoundly nervous existence, to be Solomon Kedir or one of those other ministers, but I think that what it did to us who had no such prominence, was more terrible, if more diffuse. We lived in the Panopticon, and Bentham was entirely wrong about how it works. The watchers, watching one another, became increasingly desperate and paranoid lest they miss something, while we, constantly observed, became almost exhibitionistic of our sins. We flaunted them and dared our master to take offence at our juvenile conspiracies and excesses of the flesh. One way and another, we were frantic with designs. The Emperor should have taken counsel from those founding fathers of America, who knew that the sacrifice of freedom for security is a devil's compact. He was, after all, the creator of our newspapers, because he deemed them modern and necessary. He founded our banks so that we would have somewhere safe to put our money, and somewhere reputable where we might borrow capital to make the business that would build the future Aksum, that would be the first African nation to build its own cars, its own planes, to join that ultimate grasp of mankind: the space race. In the one arena of spying, however, he drew on the ancient heritage of the land rather than the new thinking, and contrived an aura of total surveillance. A myriad plans were hatched each month in Addis Ababa when I was a boy, that were never put into action because some slight utterance or glance of the Emperor implied to the guilty that he knew all and was offering one last chance at the appearance of loyal compliance – but some survived, and caused him great sorrow and setback, in the end. Him, and many others, and me.

The madness of my life in art began one evening when I was twenty-two years old. I had courted the canvas if not assiduously at least as best I knew how, and I understood inwardly that it had given me the bird. I was beginning to wonder what else I would do with my time on Earth, and then all of a sudden it was happening and I had very little say in it. My talent was a sudden thing, queer and perpendicular to all I knew.

In an interview with an English-speaking newspaper – thank God, a small one that subsequently failed and faded into erasure – I explained quite seriously that I had, through an excitative celebration of higher brain functions and the intervention of illuminatory biochemical processes, attained awareness of an interstitial universe: the post-mortally persisting obtrusions of the collective human mind. Pick the bones out of that, if you can. I, certainly, cannot. I was a middle-class boy, which is to say that my father had served the Emperor in the war, with honour and some effect, and been therefore preferred to high but not heritable position. I had travelled as part of my nation's eclectic student diaspora, with a scholarship that was meant to make me a lawyer but had somehow ended with my becoming a painter. I had shed along the way the belief in God which had been a defining aspect of my forebears' education, and replaced Him briefly with Eduard Bernstein before concluding that the fury of politics was not the passion that lived in me.

What actually happened that night, I still do not honestly know. I should call it hallucination – except that, later, I had cause to believe it had a large component either of truth or of something else whose untruthfulness did not hinder its power to work upon the world.

It was very much that sort of party, and a rarity in those days because it was truly international. Even the high Amhara of the Imperial Court did not readily casually exchange formal invitations with foreigners, on the one hand because it might appear they were plotting, and on the other because the wealthy immigrant population in Addis Ababa was still very white and very proud, and it was their pleasure to make fun of us locals for serving the wrong wine with smoked salmon or wearing inappropriate shoes to a dance. They might be here to make money and to assist in the raising up of our country, but to them we were still new at this game of civilisation, and never mind that this place was a power in the world when London was a herd of pigs defecating in a muddy stream, and the island of Manhattan was home not to WASP financial magnates but to those matrilineal ur-Lenape whose stories are lost to smallpox and colonial steel.

This evening was an exception because the host was a large American record label that was hoping to find new sounds here. If they were going to do that they had to know what was truly cool in Addis Ababa, and such was not to be discovered from the lilywhite crowd who only occasionally dared the nightclubs in that part of town called 'the Desert', Addis Ababa's busy and notably wild red-light district. Hence, this party was in a new building strategically constructed to link that place with the more salubrious palace district and facilitate the creation of a cosmopolitan scene. Two American woman from PETA, here to tell us why we should be nice to our little furry friends, were dancing in their underwear on an expensive Swedish carpet. A German photographer was taking pictures of their clothes where they lay discarded and saying that here at last was the critique she had been looking for when she travelled to Addis Ababa. Three members of the Trinidadian cricket team were drinking absinthe with the Emperor's advisor on Sino-European relations, and the music was provided by one of those local bands everyone said would be bigger than the Rolling Stones. On their first and only album cover, the name of the group was given as a stylised hatchet, enamelled with a lipsticked and enticing female mouth caught somehow in the act of appreciative smirking, so that the symbols together made, in English, the sounds 'axe' and 'mmm' – or 'Aksum', which was the old name for Ethiopia. My friend Tamirat had designed this sideroglyph and was the toast of our little circle for his wit – and, to be fair, for his execution, because it isn't easy to convey 'mmm' so clearly with just a single impression of a mouth, but he had.

My city was making its way in the world, becoming for the first time in hundreds of years a de rigueur stop on the travels of the powerful and the scholarly. This was the nation that had fought off the Scramble for Africa; that had its roots in the line of Solomon and now saw its modernity rushing outwards to a time of space ships and orbital colonies: the upwelling, rising, dawning Ethiopia of Haile Selassie. Our very existence, obtruding upon the consciousness of the US of A, was changing the vexed discussion of race in that country, and if our footballers had not delivered in the Cup of Nations for a decade, well, we had promising youngsters, and their coach was the sublime Mengistu Worku. The future was bright, and it was ours for the taking.

I meant to be one of the hands that took it, to reshape the world of art by my dedication and my perception. It was unclear whether I actually possessed either of these things, but of course I thought I did. For now, though, I had put aside all such considerations and was rapt in wonder as I touched a creature so far beyond me as I was beyond a stone, a thing that could not properly be contained or even observed from within our reality, but which might pass through it at an angle as it traversed the tiny wrinkle of space and time that we called 'everything'. I congratulated myself that for ten thousand generations men and women encountering such consciousnesses had labelled them jinn or angels and cowered before them, while I, a modern man, knew that I was experiencing transient unification with a Jungian collective psyche that might span the stars. I felt entirely sophisticated and à la mode.

An instant before, I had been sitting alone on a fiendishly comfortable sofa and slowly sliding into a reverie that might lead to sleep or to that placid joy that sometimes comes out of nowhere in a crowded room. Now I smelled anise, as if someone were toasting it in a pan beneath my nose, and the two glasses at my feet hurled their contents into the air, as if the room were abruptly dropping into a bottomless chasm. The streaming Jugendstil lines of Chateau Musar framed two entwined figures by the buffet table in such a way as to sketch an open door in the air. My vantage point had rotated around a single point and I was looking through an opening that had always been present but was only now accessible, into what smelled all at the same time like a musty cellar, a furnace, a fish-monger's and something else that my nose had no name for. From the doorway a voice spoke to me. The words were unclear, as if from a radio tuned improperly to the station, and the greater part of what was said escaped me in a river of noise: FA LA JI RO JI JA. All the same, it came to me perfectly that my correspondent was the extranoematic masque of the great Anaximander of Miletos, now part of a galactic consciousness and here imparting to me the knowledge that the true reality is a series of five concentric branes or skeins, arranged as spheres, the inner kernel of which is wrapped tightly around the uttermost crystalline circumference in such a manner as to defy Newtonian physics.

I said that was very cool.

Furthermore, Anaximander said, I was already set upon a path to the singular conjunction which would bind all these together, the birth of the burning ocean which flows through all things and makes of all places one place, and I should open myself to the experience so that I might live. Beware jealous Hephaestus and the bearer of the burning torch, Anaximander said, and remember what I have told you: five concentric spheres which must align.

I said I would remember – and evidently I have – and a moment later the wine was back in the glass and the doorway into eternity was gone.

This sort of visitation was then happening constantly: John Lennon had been given an egg by visitors from another planet, and passed it on to Uri Geller because it was, he said, too much of a drag on his mind. All across the United States, Australia and Europe, even the Middle East and Russia, people – including no less a man than Jimmy Carter – were seeing lights in the sky and making contact with entities that were either from other worlds or part of an eternal mind that dreamed the human race. Perhaps there was in the end no difference between the two. The naïve perception of what an alien might be was yielding to stranger and more numinous conceptions of panspermic space gods, energy beings and sentient ideas. It would have been more startling if, over time, I had had no such moment of transcendence.

After all, everyone else did.

*

When I awoke the next day – or it may have been the next night – I was very, very hung-over, and painfully aware that I had talked the most appalling rubbish to those around me and most particularly to a broad-hipped and attractive arts stringer from the *Sydney Morning Herald*. I staggered out of bed and called my mirror an idiot, and he smirked at me and called me the same. It seemed unfair that I should have a hangover, while he looked indecently chipper, but that is the nature of reflections. Mind you, I suppose I had no way of knowing he wasn't as unhappy as I was. I ate what I could without gagging, and set to my canvas – but when I began to paint, I knew that everything had changed.

I had been until then a predictable graduate of the Slade's short course for students of the Selassie Bursary: capable but not exciting, and without a distinctive voice and vision of my own. The Emperor was pleased to send students abroad to study in all disciplines, and bring them back to teach so that his nation might rise among the peoples of the world. I was full of skills and notions and likely until this moment to inherit some academic post here in Addis

Ababa from which I would rise according to my political and social acuity rather than my brush. I was – had been – a practitioner of the craft of painting and yet not a painter.

No more. Now I became something else. Before, I'd struggled to find something to say. Now I had so many things in me that I didn't know where to begin, and they came out jumbled together for a while, producing a crazy paving of vibrantly coloured lizards and birds fading Escher-style into buildings after Le Corbusier – who had so far extended himself as to draft the new city of Addis Ababa for the Fascists all combining into a woman's face. I worked on it for a day and then tore it apart in a fury for failing to meet my expectations. My skill, or perhaps my mental discipline, were incapable of rendering the thought that was in my head – and that was how it went for the next weeks, as I sought a new understanding of what I was. Liquid silver bubbled in my mind and before my eyes – strange shapes, futures and pasts and presents colliding with blatant symbols of politics and sex, science and rock and roll, but I could not express what I saw. The idea would burn in me, simple and obvious and filled with a restless and infectious energy, so that I knew anyone who saw it would be struck by it, penetrated and inverted and remade as I had been, and yet I could not hold that certainty in my mind and transmit it to the canvas. It leaked, warped and split, so that with each brushstroke my attempt to make an image became instead a battle with evanescence: frantic repairs to a ship sinking before it was even in the water. I wept, wasted canvas, and began again, and again. I stopped ripping up my failures, but set them aside on the ground like discarded library books, until my studio was crowded with a map of my footsteps around and around the desert of my limitation.

Finally, I broke, ate, and slept for twenty hours, and then awoke in an exhausted, placid clarity that felt as if the silver had woven itself into my bones. I was not ecstatic any longer, I was enlivened, uplifted. Anaximander had solved the problem for me, had as much as told me how to deal with it. I broke my dreams into pieces, confined each fragment to a single canvas which might – must – connect with another and another, so that what was in me was imperfectly rendered by being multifaceted instead of holographic, but at the same time achievable by a man painting in the actual world of three dimensions, without the power to reach through the skein of his work and arrange additional layers to be found by a probing eye. The viewer must learn to see my work in a way different from other art, must allow – indeed must reach for and embrace – radical alterations in perspective. Out of Ethiopia would come an art that demanded a new mode of perception to be understood: the mind of the viewer would not only be changed by the work itself but would undergo willing modification simply in order to appreciate that work on its own terms. To reach the new world I would express, my audience would have to make a commitment, to cross a small but significant Rubicon of the self and meet me halfway.

Each piece was composed of five separate canvases, and to see the whole work one must look at them in whatever order and hold in the mind the impression and image of each. To look at a single one alone, or to look at all of them as if they were a panorama, was to misunderstand. The work did not – could not – exist in paint: it existed in the mind as a conjunction, and all five parts must be apprehended at once. Part of the experience was the stretching of the mind, the tearing and repairing of the remembered images. I was making of each person in my audience a zoetrope, save that it was not the illusion of motion that I created by deceiving the eye, but the truth of things as I now understood them, set from my mind into art and then released by the act of observation into theirs. Each painting was not an image of the world but of my mind as it assembled that world for me, and in that it revealed the truth of all art all the time.

I finished the first fivefold painting and hung it on the wall at the next party. Two days later it was sold – for a not-ridiculous amount, but more than I had ever expected to make – to a music executive chasing Ethio-jazz to its source in the hope of profit. He, in turn, hung it on his wall in New York City and explained that you had to see all of it at once, and this complexity of approach – as much as the content – was admired by a Rockefeller, a Heinz and two Kennedys, and the editor of *Time*.

Bekele's Amhara-modernist dreamscapes, the *New Yorker* wrote in its next issue,

> *are composed of parts, symbolising a fusion of traditional and contemporary understandings of personhood. Each work embraces and distinguishes body, soul, mind and heart, but also fascinatingly the tools and belongings with which a person surrounds himself, acknowledging that we are not only our physical and spiritual selves as given, but also what we may make of those materials and the world around us, and hence what we may become.*

To hear the fearmongers these days, you'd think a human mind was as easily shaped as water, but in my experience the business of changing perception is more like carrying a donkey up a hill. If I did it just a few times, amid all that passion and noise and paint, perhaps I did not do so badly, indeed.

*

What came out of me was a sequence of tableaux somewhere between Bosch and Lichtenstein, branded at the time by a canny Englishwoman with a shop near Fortnum & Mason as 'the Nuclear Prophecies'. In Ethiopia, as much as anywhere else, we lived in the shadow of the hydrogen bomb, the moreso perhaps as we didn't have one and didn't want to be involved in the private theological differences of Washington and Moscow – but would be involved anyway if the war came, bringing first unnatural fire and then endless winter to our wide green land.

Green, incidentally, was what it was, and what it is. Ethiopia is not inevitably the cracked mud that is burned into the psyche of Britain and Europe by the bad times of famine that rocked the world. It is a vibrant country, mountainous and misty as much as sandy and endless. That first quintet boiled with nature because nature was what I knew. Years later, I took a trip to Moscow and was amazed, as we landed, to see that the city I had always imagined as a grey industrial grid was clutched in the arm of a great forest, and struck through with a wide river. It must be the same for other people flying into Addis Ababa and expecting some desert fort like Gordon's Khartoum in the film with Charlton Heston: white walls and yellow sand, and, of course, the demented black men of the desert lurking all around.

All these years later in London, I found myself once more beset by ghosts from other realms. The perfume of stars was the same rich and mouth-watering anise, though now I worried that it might be evidence of a ministroke rather than of dimensions distant and unreal. As before, I painted what I saw: my hands were not imagining but following a map that only I could see, and I saw it perfectly clearly. I knew by old habit how to break the picture into parts and so produce something that made sense to someone without my fractured consciousness, and so I did, no longer wrestling with what was in my mind to force it on to the canvas, but inviting it and making space for it. Without the urgency and arrogance of youth,

I found I was content to accept its strictures, and without the fear of failure I did not seek to moderate what came, so that the business of art was to some extent a placid and exploratory one – as one might explore a tornado in a glider, if one did not fear for the structure of the plane. In that earlier encounter, I had traced the outline of a grim leviathan in a forest of numbers – to the stark disapproval of the viewing public, who wanted more in the vein of frozen worlds and bikini astronauts – and now I revisited that unloved image, setting the scene in a vast underground commuter tunnel. It hung ugly in the air, more threatening, I think, than it would have been in the water. The object of its scrutiny – a fleshy fellow on his drive home – looked suitably appalled. Annie wasn't sure what the game engine would make of such a thing, but that was the point, she said, to inject the unexpected into the tone, the nightmarish into the visual. Thus encouraged, I threw in more mystical shapes as they came to me: a fishwhite assassin in a Warhol suit; a banker in the robes of an ancient priest; Annie herself, much older, captured and interrogated in the ugly society she had imagined for us; and her grandmother, slim and beautiful and ailing, cast as a Roman scholar and made just different enough that I did not think Michael would see it.

All good stuff, and I smiled as the gates of my subconscious opened – or the gates of the great Jungian quantum collective did, so far removed from our first encounter and yet, no doubt, hardly changed at all from that divine perspective – and connected me with the great artistic beyond. Angst and strangeness bubbled out of me, and we put it all into the game: Clotho at her work, lifting a boy from a stark, Italian Futurist coffin that might have been the headquarters of an international bank; a great crowd of identical women laying siege to a white stone castle; a dead man lying murdered in the street of a city whose new architecture sprouts cancerous and optical from homely London redbricks; a nest of wires becoming roots becoming roads, penetrating the sleeping skull of a goddess; a lonely detective pursuing or fleeing a killer along a film noir alleyway whose shadows were cast not by dressed neo-Gothic stone but by the steel and glass of tomorrow's skid row. Annie's software recognised the human shapes and weeded them out, replicating them as statues and logos, and designed apartment buildings and council estates, mansion flats and skyscrapers after my fashion. Little by little, over the map of London, our new territory grew, dipping in and out of what was there and becoming something that was no longer grafted on but supporting and penetrating, so that our illusion became the substrate upon which the old city sustained itself and without which it would wither and die. The infection became the host.

I worked, and felt younger. I tried to weave everything in that Annie and Colson asked for, to pick out the pictures that seemed full of meaning and implication, and then they'd come back to me for this thing they called 'top-loading'. They wanted me to take what was beautiful and moody and make it 'information-rich' or 'information-supersaturated', to encode specific narrative significances into every design, to the point where there were whole other stories happening that no one would know about except us, and perhaps a very few who might stumble upon them and pay attention. There was a subclass of gamers, Annie said, who existed as ludic spelunkers, interested only in going where no digital foot had gone before, and they would abandon the main history and work their way through every subsidiary tunnel and hidden door and find whatever we left. Let two disparate characters be reading the same book, she said, or let their homes have the same plan, and no sooner was the game released than there would sprout a jungle of secondary interpretations to make villains of heroes and saints of monsters. Woven about the spine of events, there must be truths and implications, revealed in asides and recurrent symbols. They would make meaning out of everything.

I painted until my fingers cramped, until my chest and back ached as they had not for years. It seemed that I must put down an entire life for each character in a single frame. I tried to capture them, to paint them perfectly so that their identities would flare into life as their portraits were viewed from different angles.

And then one day we were done. My part was over. For a few weeks we kept in touch – they came to me with little ideas and problems, pieces of gameplay, even, and I suggested things that were by turns terribly naive and terribly clever, because I had no idea what I was talking about. I liked that part too. But in the end they faded away, months more work to do on their end, and I went back to being Mr Bekele of the Bekele Home Security company. I kept painting, but we had seventeen workshops in five cities in the UK and no concerns about the economy because people always need keys cut and locks fitted, and now CCTV and personal alarm monitoring. It doesn't matter what else is happening, the client still wants a door they can shut. I had plenty to do.

In November the game came out. I was rather surprised by how true it was to what I had painted. I saw posters on the sides of buses with my architecture looming over the driver's seat. There was even a brief spot at the end of the six o'clock news, the bit where they try to cheer you up about the end of the world by showing you a swimming bunny.

I didn't really notice it at first, because even with my new grasp on all things digital I wasn't connected very strongly with the world of games. I had an Instagram account I used to show details of my new work to the hundred or so people who were interested, mostly friends. I was not on Facebook because I loathed the interface – I'd become a digital snob in tandem with becoming digitally aware. Good grief but Facebook riled me, laid out like the want ads of a local paper and glaringly white, the algorithm stifling news from outside one's bubble and pressing inappropriate sponsored content like a man on a street corner with a collection of flyers for his new-minted religion. I was exploring Twitter and finding it by turns enlightening and infuriating: a close encounter with wit and scholarship and the joy of living that could drop away beneath one's feet into a sea of sheer pointless nastiness – though it had never happened to me, beyond a few low-level encounters with bored children sniping at an old man.

Even sculling peaceably through the backwaters of the Internet, though, I began to realise that *Witnessed* was breaking out, that people were talking about it. Then when I turned around it was a huge success, and then a phenomenon, and then this year's breakout thing. Paper magazines began to talk about it, schools and parents objected to it, and then an MP denounced it in the House of Commons, which in turn required that another MP come to the game's defence. In the United States it was denounced as un-American, which was nothing more than the truth because none of us was remotely American, but for some reason the assertion stirred up a controversy and we got more and more coverage. Was the game sensationalist or simply sensational? Something about it spoke to people, certainly, and it gave them pause. You could explore *Witnessed*, fight in it, sneak in it, survive in it, or turn the tables on the game and become the oppressor. The protagonist and her nemesis duelled against the Orwellian backdrop of a nation not merely under surveillance but composed of it, a democracy where everything the citizenry did was totally transparent. The ostensible enemy was a mysterious group called – inevitably and humorously – the Fire Judges. One fought them, the other unknowingly served them, and it was hard to tell which of them was good and which evil, or whether such distinctions still made sense in the maze of missions and quests, right up until the Minotaur was revealed. It resonated with a population increasingly aware that 'liberty' does not in fact mean 'micro-policing' and that they had bartered away their historical legal rights in the name of keeping out a fifth columnist jihadi Muslim army that did not exist in the way they had been told. Then, too, here was a fantasy world which discreetly inverted the established conventions of such creations. White people looked subtly wrong in the game, sickly and slick. It was an elegant political prank, especially in a medium not widely known for progressive nuance, and it advanced the notion of games as art, and that in turn created comment, and comment – well, you already know what comment is.

The commercial truth, by the same token, is that paranoia sells – especially sophisticated and atmospheric paranoia with an attractive lead character – and sell it we did. We sold not only games and subscriptions but merchandise. We put my sketches and my paintings on T-shirts and mugs and key rings. We sold a board game, movie rights, a novelisation, and we made … well. More money than I knew what to do with, to be honest. Real money, of the kind that erases debts and creates dynasties in their place. And of course, all my old work was suddenly very sought-after and expensive. A few paintings I had shut away in the cool attic of our warehouse in Royston were abruptly worth millions, more than all the business we would do for five years. Inevitably, at that point, someone asked me to paint a new collection. Greek billionaires bought a dozen canvases at a time, with who knew what mad money. I went on Radio 4 with Colson, *Newsnight Review* with Annie, and we talked a lot of nonsense about the zeitgeist and our unique creative pathway. It was heady and enjoyable not least because I had no need for any of it, no driving urge. I was a happy passenger on my own success, and my greatest pleasure lay in seeing the success of those I loved. Michael was pleased with me: proud and amused as much as bemused – though Lord knows, his daughter becoming a multimillionaire in her twenties must have been a little startling.

The game was a phenomenon. You could choose not to play it – but by the end of the year, you couldn't claim not to have heard of it.

Then one afternoon Annie was asked, in an interview with a small YouTube channel run by a friend, whether she thought women and particularly women of colour were still under-represented in games. She laughed, and said that, given that they *were* people of colour, and particularly *female* people of colour, she didn't see how in a global society still obedient to a tiny minority of rich white men they could be anything but under-represented. Then she discussed as a point of interest the business of photographic emulsions and the skin of black persons. She went into some detail – fascinating, I thought – about the process and the design decisions in the making of *Witnessed*, and where the team had had to rework the game palette, even the colour of the notional sun, to deal with the shortcomings of some digital displays in the representation of non-white bodies. The game was a game, Annie said, but it was also real, and the art in it – mine and hers – had found its basis in a real world that had not yet overcome its various entrenched and accidental racisms.

It struck me as a pretty obvious truth.

*

By then it was autumn, tending winter, and the air was bitter. The Europe vote, contrary to reason and expectation, had gone against the Continent and in favour of old and ugly passions. That skinheaded nationalism which for years had not dared to raise its voice for shame was now unbound. The contempt and anger seemed to become more intense the further back Britain looked along the route of refugees fleeing massacres and famine in places so much less civilised than here. The French and Germans were bad enough, the Romanians worse, and the Bulgarians beyond the pale. All those desperate thousands from Syria were the sort of liars who would pretend to be children when they were in truth fully nineteen years old, just to get their hands on the lush and unmerited hospitality of our gracious country. In between tales of their mendacity, the tabloid press sprinkled references to the Spitfire Summer of 1940 when Britain stood alone, alongside hints and allegations of migrant rape. The headline splashes were surrounded by teasing portraits of the child daughters of celebrities.

This heady cocktail of pride, virtue and sleaze worked as it always has, stoking resentment beyond the reach of words. Now Brussels was vanquished, a real Britishness could find its feet. Life would be better, for a start, if coddled criminals were properly punished. Hanging was discussed again, along with flogging and work gangs for antisocial offenders. Drug use and prostitution must be made properly illegal once more, and ordinary Christian families should no longer be penalised for existing. Loose women should carry their children to term and look after them, and the workshy must pay their way. The effete metropolitan snobs who opposed these sensible measures should shut up and let the real country be what it was. Judges who upheld the wrong law at the wrong time were dubbed ENEMIES OF THE PEOPLE, and while to the eyes of some so-very-generous commentators the rich and exotic DNA of those of us not entirely Anglo-Saxon might thicken the British ethnic soup just as the Raj had spiced up the national kitchen, most of the time it was clear that people who weren't from here should go back where they came from – even or especially if they were the devious sort of foreigner who manages to be born in a British hospital and raised like a cuckoo in this green and pleasant land.

It was an anger that could not be assuaged, not by victory in politics nor concessions from government. It was not even lulled by the occasional murder of a Polish window cleaner or the random beating of a Hasidic rabbi by the side of the road. The mood was set. The orphaned threads of the tapestry flapped about in the breeze, then knotted together and made something else; something new.

I had hoped that we were alone in all this. Let Britain be a laughing stock, and the world continue along its moral arc. Let us be left behind; sooner or later we must realise our error. Then, in November, America joined us in folly and ugliness. The same country that embraced Selassie, and inspired him and me by putting astronauts on the moon, echoed to the joyful celebration of a revitalised Ku Klux Klan. The vile and furious of every nation were made bold again.

In London they called themselves the Georgians, in honour of that Turkish saint whom English bigots routinely bless with pearly skin and simplistic opinions, but they were more like some throwback to the seventies: a blend of football hooliganism and the militarised spleen of the National Front. They inverted the rhetoric of tolerance, and proclaimed themselves the oppressed, and not the oppressor. They made the convention that one should not use racial slurs sound like the beginning of Auschwitz.

They leapt upon Annie as if they had been waiting for her, and in a sense no doubt they had. She was everything wrong with their world: a young black woman making money and making a point at the same time. They called her 'mud-skin', 'Negress' and 'bitch'. They used a host of other names familiar and novel. From behind anonymising screens, they threatened her life day by day. Her post-bag was vast and horrible.

Well, that was survivable, for a while, and we thought it would blow over. She was offending all the right people. It was frightening and infuriating, but a significant and growing fortune and a platform to speak your mind can ease the pain of being hated as an individual by those who in any case hate you in general. So long as it was only words, let them howl.

Then one night, outside a bar, someone threw pig's blood in her face.

*

I helped her clean up. Annie was still angry.

'Where the fuck do you even get pig's blood after ten o'clock at night?'

'I'm not sure that's what matters,' I said.

'Where? The? Fuck?'

'We need to talk about personal security.'

'Is there an open-all-hours wanker's equipment shop?'

'You should come and stay with me. Both of you. Or go to Michael's.'

'Because I'm a little bit hurt that no one's ever told me about it, if there is. What if I'd needed to drown someone in fermenting sheepshit? You know, after hours? Because obviously I can get sheepshit during the day, I mean, who fucking can't? But what if I'd had a sheepshit emergency and, just because no one mentioned to me about the wanker shop, I couldn't drown this person at all and I had to wait until the next day and, you know, the urge had passed off? Because that would have been a tragedy. Do you have to be on the wanker email list, or is it one of those paper mailshots that comes through the door every so often? You know: carpenter can make you shelves, handsy guitar teacher ten quid an hour, and by the way here's where you can get fucking pig's blood to throw in someone's fucking face at fucking midnight. Because if there's a wanker shop I'm going in there right now and I'm buying all their stock and I am going to the police station and I am going to drown that little fuck right fucking now!'

'Annie,' I said, and then, at last, she said that she could still taste it, and allowed herself to cry.

Later came the emails and letters and the ringing phone, threats of death and rape – endlessly, rape, as if all the years of modernity had not happened and it was only civilised to silence a woman in that way – but by then they were redundant.

*

I found that I had in yet another way misunderstood myself in age. I had imagined that the hot blood of youth was now cooled and quiescent, but it transpired to be otherwise. I had not controlled my anger, I had simply misplaced it between the election of Margaret Thatcher and the rediscovery of my art, and where it had been there was a deep, damp pool of head-shaking and sorrow which now dried as if left to sit beneath an Ethiopian sun, becoming over the course of days a crucible of white-hot coal. I was no longer prepared to sit idle – and idle was how I perceived myself, idle and ignorant and lazy. I resigned from Bekele Security in the morning, and in the afternoon I accepted an interview request. It was one of dozens I had had, and I picked this one because it was television and I knew it had a large middle-class demographic of media professionals and opinion-makers – people who talk for a living, and people who these days as often as not put their thoughts directly into text via the social media.

It was a very nice interview, done live and conversational. We talked about Addis Ababa and *Witnessed*, and about how it had been living here in the seventies and how it was now. We talked about my transition from artist to businessman to digital designer. I was self-effacing and calm. I talked about my struggles with interfaces, my concerns about art objects created and channelled through screens, my ideas about endlessly replicable products through which each individual may have unique experiences. I said that I had reservations about digital life replacing analogue connections, but that I wasn't so impressed by the history of the twentieth century or the first decades of this one that I felt humanity should be held immutable and perfected. If digital devices were going to change the way we thought, that was fine, so long as they made us less monstrous rather than more.

'In which connection,' I said, 'I have something to tell everyone. Would you mind?'

The interviewer looked pleased and nervous. I favoured him with a little grandfatherly smile, a twinkle of Father Christmas: Oh, don't worry, the nice black gentleman won't do anything rash.

'Please do,' the interviewer said. 'Ladies and gentlemen: Berihun Bekele.'

I thanked him, and then I went right ahead and announced live on air that I was founding my own software company. I had no employees, and the ink of incorporation was barely dry, but I told them my new entity would make a series of apps – I had learned the language well enough to counterfeit a convincing plan – constructed around the GPS location software now built into most every device.

Users would tag their experience in the street, in bars and clubs, on different modes of public transport.

'So, like Foursquare,' my interviewer said, with the doubt of a young person looking at an old man in front of a computer.

'Exactly like that,' I said, 'except that our users will record incidences of hate. We'll be working initially to produce a live map – like a traffic congestion map – of more and less racist areas, safe routes home, institutionally racist police forces and local authorities, local populations. We'll have a star rating system and so on. Eventually I want to roll out iterations for anyone who is not part of the obvious privileged class – for women, for trans people, for people of colour, for the blind and the deaf and so on so that we can map prejudice and racism intersectionally – but one must start somewhere, so I'm calling version one Walking Whilst Black. I have some concerns about the name because I don't wish to rule out those who are in wheelchairs or mobility carts, but the phrase is there in the language and I feel it is well understood. Available to download next month. About a month after that, we'll publish our first report into the reality of Britain's hate at a street level. We'll be able to tell you who are the most stupid, ignorant, bigoted people in the country to an accuracy of a few metres.'

I got up from the sofa and removed my radio mic, knowing there were four whole minutes left in the segment. Well, they would have plenty to talk about without me, and my bad manners would add to the headline. I meant to walk off the stage then, but instead I stood there for a while and I heard whispering in the studio and a little scattered applause. For the longest time I wasn't sure why. I could see that the cameras were still running, little red eyes peering at me as I stood, and then I realised that somehow, in the space between getting up to go and actually leaving, I had extended my clenched fist and dropped my head, as I had seen Tommie Smith and John Carlos do in 1968.

*

Time has broken a little bit all around us. I can see the moment, a quarter of a century ago, when Michael showed me the first sonogram of his daughter.

'This is the head,' he told me. 'These are the feet and that's a thumb. She's sucking her thumb.' He looked at me. 'She's sucking her thumb.'

I took him in my arms, and for a moment it seemed to me that he was barely larger than the speck in the picture. He was surely only two or three years old. I could smell his hair and lift him from his feet, and he would laugh the pure laugh of a child before the knowledge of mortality.

I have my arm around Colson now. I can feel Annie's hand under mine, and we are clinging together to make a frame to bear him up. My shoulders are aching already. When I was younger – forty years ago or so – I could have carried them both.

Annie needs me. The speck in the picture needs me. Through her, Michael. Through Michael, Eleni. I could not save Eleni, but here I can – I will – discharge the debt. We are all here, in this place, this burning house. Five of us making one thing, like one of my pictures.

I turn us all around and I start walking through the choking murk. One foot in front of the other. The air is thin and hot. You can die of scalded lungs before ever the flames touch you. Keep walking.

In the middle of my house there is a room that cannot be breached. It is not large, but it is large enough, if we can get there. The safe room has its own air. With three people in it, the supply will last not more than ten hours, but that will be enough. Worry about the other problem once we're inside.

One foot, then the other, even though the smoke is thick and Colson is heavy and Annie is stumbling. She's not crying. Not my girl. She is swearing, fit to turn milk. Good.

I touch the metal plate, and we fall inside and lie on the floor. The door closes again, the air clear and clean around us. Breathe. Think.

Smoke is no longer the problem; the problem is heat. A real fire is hard to protect against. People think they know what it is – they use gas hobs and charcoal grills and believe they have tamed the flame, but even a small blaze can be terribly dangerous. A big one – room-sized, house-sized – is not just more of the same. It is a ferocious, consuming power, lethally radiant. If we are not rescued soon – if the fire is not extinguished – we will be baked in here like potatoes.

In Addis Ababa, long ago, I walked through the walls of my prison and escaped.

If I think about it, surely I will remember how.

get me two

S urely *I will remember how.*

The Inspector lies quite still and silent in her bed. Very carefully, she does not move, does not think at all. She allows the pattern to linger in her mind. Movement is the inexperienced dreamer's first mistake. The action of engaging the body banishes memory of the dreamstate from the mind. Too much chatter will do the same.

As if her own mind were a hide, and she a hunter, she rests perfectly still.

Surely I will remember how.

There. She has it all now, everything she wanted to hold on to – and yet she waits a little longer, fixing it in both surface and deeper self: her list of questions, her clues and suspicions.

Still without speaking, she holds the list, and moves to the upright position. Her hand finds the pen and she begins to write. She does not spend long on each note. Glossary must come later. For now, just the keys to each.

Berihun Bekele painted a five-panel picture that was to all intents and purposes the Chamber of Isis, linking the two internal fictions. Annie Bekele's company was called Fire Judges, which ties Hunter directly to Lönnrot. The company mainframe was called the Spine, like Firespine, the name the Witness itself pulled from the interrogation. The notional game project that is an unflattering portrait of the Witness and the System had an alternative name: 'Gnomon'. Like Firespine, Gnomon was a sort of demon to Athenais. Kyriakos bought a painting of his shark titled with the same word.

The randomly chosen word that is the name of the case she is investigating.

And then we come to the east panel, which is me.

Impossible. Impossible impossible. Just as Athenais said. Was that a warning, that earlier scene? A taunt? A woman held captive by a demon made of eyes. A monstrous Witness.

Project Gnomon.

She asks the Witness how it was assigned.

— Are you well?

Neith repeats the question.

— Inspector, it is three a.m. and you have recently suffered a traumatic head injury. You are displaying signs of agitation. Are you well?

'I'm fine. Answer the question.'

— Do you wish me to call medical assistance?

'No. I am well. Proceed.'

— Case names are generally assigned by a randomisation process. Numbers are generated by drawing on the decay of a sample of radioactive isotope held in a sealed environment in Oxfordshire. These numbers are then used to select words from the full English lexicon which is also randomised. Names are rejected occasionally on the basis of cultural appropriateness. It would not be acceptable to have an operation codenamed 'fart'. Some use-criteria are also applied to avoid polysyllabic scientific jargon and so on.

'Is that how this name was chosen?'

— The case name originally generated for the Hunter interview was TORTILOQUY, meaning crooked speech or deception. It was rejected because the word was selected earlier this year in conjunction with an ongoing trafficking investigation. The duplication is unusual but not statistically significant. GNOMON was substituted automatically.

'It's random?'

— Despite the appearance of the word in the case, yes. It appears significant because you have now met it in what appear to be several different environments. You forget that all these environments exist only in Diana Hunter's consciousness. She chose the word, and it was subsequently selected at random — a single coincidence. With each iteration of it inside the psychodrama, however, it accrues greater weight for you. It is the disadvantage of human pattern recognition, exacerbated by the fact that you designate it an unusual word. However, there are half a million words in

the English language and an extensive vocabulary includes perhaps thirty-five thousand of them, meaning that there are more unusual words in English than commonplace ones by a factor of fourteen. In fact, 'gnomon' is common in several specialist areas, meaning that its selection by Hunter is within the bounds of ordinary behaviour. The practical taxonomy in use within linguistics is more complex, but for the sake of argument: if one were grading rarity on a scale of one to five, it would be a three. 'Xyster' and 'mollag' would be fours, 'Brummagem' a five.

'"Mollag"?'

— Obsolete regional: a dog's bladder inflated as a balloon and used to float a fishing net. Truly obscure words such as these are not used as case names.

'Why not?'

— Because there is no point assigning a name no one can remember or pronounce.

Almost, she laughs. The machine is so affectless as to appear droll.

'If I rejected GNOMON, right now, and asked for a new random term, what would I get?'

— As of this moment, another tier three word: RICERCAR — ree-TCHAIR-cahr — the term used in seventeenth century musical scoring to denote a fugue of the sort not generally appreciated purely for its tonal qualities but rather, by those with a close understanding of the cultural significance of what was known contemporarily as 'learned counterpoint', for its artifice and deft accomplishment. Involuted puzzles were frequently included within the music; in one famous case the composer J. S. Bach titled a ricercar 'Regis Iussu Cantio et Reliqua Canonica Arte Resoluta' — which means 'the theme given by the King's command, with additions, resolved according to the canonic style', but is obviously a self-describing acrostic. Within the work were several biblical references injuncting the listener to 'seek'. The original meaning of 'ricercare' being 'to seek', this quest was a precondition of discovering the references. This raises a tangential point: the modern period's obsession with art that comments upon its own artificiality and undermines its inherited gravitas by commentary is itself undermined by that inheritance. Also implicit is an early form of the Deep Blue Question: if one seeks with sufficient ingenuity in any sample, one can create a cryptographic rationale for any output text — therefore in any investigation

237

the key problem is not how to begin, but where to stop. Would you like to change the name?

She considers, and then says no. Let it stay, to remind her to be suspicious.

Hunter and Lönnrot, though. That connection, at least, is established.

'Get me two constables. Have them meet me here. We're going back to Hunter's house.'

– I will detail them for first shift this morning.

Four hours away.

She gets her breathing under control, then runs through the dream check. She halfway expects to fail. It is a staple of nightmares to be watching and participating at the same time.

The ping pong ball rattles. The hand torch flickers for a moment, then holds. She shines it up at the text on the wall and reads: 'I am the combination to a door . . .'

The last words sit heavy on her tongue. She works her way back to the beginning, line by line. The text is what it is.

She has the Witness examine the data from her medical chart, then takes her pulse and allows the machine to guide her through a self-diagnostic set for hidden concussion complications.

– No. Your mentation is clear and undeluded.

'Then I'm not waiting four hours. Get them here as soon as you can.'

But first, there's something else, something important yet to come. She can feel it as a compelling soreness in her mind, like the loosening of a first tooth. The segment is unfinished.

interrogation humour

I read once that the first time they put an escapologist in a tank of water, he or she will have one of two reactions, and which one determines the course of their life.

The first sort of escapologist is an ordinary person who has come to the trade organically, by whatever curious sequence of opportunity and happenstance – and that sort will panic. There is very little that is more appallingly unnatural or frightening than being lowered, bound, into a confined space containing an atmosphere you cannot breathe. It doesn't matter how much preparation you may have done, the moment your elbows hit the perspex, the moment you hear the dull noise they make as the sound is transmitted not through a gas but through a liquid: that's the moment you understand your own mortality in a way you never have before, and you lose control. A training crew will know that, and they'll wait for the moment and then get you out and talk you down, and then you can try again – or not. Some people just never go back in the tank. They do other illusions, they shift their focus. A pair of handcuffs, a few feathers and a risqué joke, and then close-up magic and narrative tricks. Thanks very much and good night. Some get right back in and they master their fear and they go on to be as good as their skill allows. These last are most compelling to watch.

The second sort of escapologist is the sort that doesn't panic. They touch the water and relax, as if just now realising where they truly want to be. They never feel afraid, even when perhaps they should, and when they do escape they wait just a moment below the surface of the water, saying goodbye. This sort of escapologist tends not to be very successful commercially, because their contentedness in the tank disturbs the audience. The whole premise of escapology as a show is that death is something to be scared of, and the rush you get from watching is about survival and life. There's a small but noticeable statistical hike in pregnancies after a high-profile escapology act comes to town. The second sort of escapologist doesn't provide that rush. Instead, he or she invites a placid contemplation of mortality that is nowhere on the razzle-dazzle shopping list and which will certainly not get you laid. Audiences come out of the theatre sober and chilled, and a little while later they make life changes and spend more time with the people they love. It doesn't sell.

Before the interrogation begins, it is clear that I am the first sort of escapologist. The anaesthesia communicates itself to me not as rest or a moment of calm, but as the encroachment into my living experience of simple biological ending. I buck against the restraints – unevenly, because my arm has already lost function, and briefly because the cold is so very, very quick to spread.

But then, when I've lost the battle and I'm alone with the absence of my senses, and everything that is, is just my thoughts, it turns out that I am the second sort of escapologist after all.

*

Let me ask you this:

In a small town at the foot of the mountains there is a village, and in the village there is a barber's shop and the barber shaves all the men in the village who do not shave themselves. Does the barber shave himself, or not?

While you give your answer some thought, I'll do the same. That I am awake at all tells me something. I should be unconscious while they probe my mind and mess around with my private interior. Not that they acknowledge privacy as a concept any more. The European Union had it as a baseline right, once upon a time, but the American perception was that free speech was infinitely more important in every case. All this technology flowed in its earliest days from America. With it came the political and social assumptions of a small number of engineers and entrepreneurs, predominantly male and white. This unexamined muddle of privileged anarchism and academic idealism. Security of the person was one thing – and safeguarded by the right to bear arms and the prohibition on unreasonable search – but ownership of one's own data-wake was dangerous and antisocial. 'Free' came to mean not 'unchained' but 'unpaid' – a conflation that no doubt delighted authoritarians across the globe.

And yes, over there, in the daylight, they are reading the upper layers of my cognition and rifling through my mind's underwear drawers seeking prurient secrets. I cannot imagine what they expect to find. Some torrid late romance with a charismatic terrorist, perhaps. Well, they can whistle for it.

No one beats the machine, not in the end. People have tried and failed – psychologists, psychometricians, psychopaths; mentalists and hypnotists, experts in deception, spies and spymasters, even schizophrenics and paranoids. The only person who came close was a madwoman. That was what the paperwork said: a mind turned inward upon itself, bouncing off its interior walls. Too much information in too wild a flow between the hemispheres of the brain. Radical intervention was prescribed – and in the end she was wide open to the machine, as if it had sliced her head into pages and turned the leaves on her spine. She was put back in the world afterwards with a proper right-thinking brain and she had to make a completely new life as a new person. Not one of her previous relationships survived the compulsory healing. How could they? None of them made any sense now that she was ordinary. Not that she was ordinary. She was just differently strange. Poor pale Anna was ripped apart. I liked her. Of all the things, I wish that hadn't happened.

No, once you're in the chamber, there are no walls you can build that are high enough to keep the machine out. If necessary it becomes your substrate, carries the burden of beating your heart and filling your lungs. The machine will kill you and keep you alive while it fixes you. That's the way it is.

Unless.

But there is no 'unless'. The machine cannot be beaten from within.

Still, for the sake of argument, what if I think it can? What if I have cobbled together my odd little list of skills and built a rickety, ad hoc notion, the sort of plan that no one could foresee because you'd have to be desperate to come up with it and insane to believe it could be done?

It's absurd to consider. The Witness is not some cartoonish lair of wickedness with a big red button on a pedestal marked DO NOT PUSH. It is a network, infinitely nested and protected, millions of lines of code resting on millions of lines of code, the ecosystem of interrogation and surveillance almost perfectly adapted to absorb what is wanted and keep out what is not. There is no way anyone could devise a defence, any more than you can wave off an army or a neutron bomb.

But what if I have?

Then I'm either a lunatic or an idiot. Perhaps, when they're finished with me, they'll be kind enough to adjust my self-image a little so I can pick dragons small enough for me to slay.

No one beats the machine, they say.

But what they mean is that no one ever has.

*

How are you doing on the village barber? Nothing? Well, here's something more practical to wonder about: it seems, since my interrogators can't hear me and I do seem to be awake and alive – and able at least somewhat to listen to them – that I'm now thinking in a hidden neural pattern, a kind of mental priest hole that uses a different structure of connections in the brain. Brains are complex. Slice yours in a given direction, you'll find one memory, one behaviour. Slice it in another, and you get something else arranged across the same cells. Only, obviously, don't slice them at all. It's not a good idea.

Neural good practice aside: that ability to be more than one thing at one time means I can hide across my brain, arranged as it were at right angles to the rest of me. In essence, I'm steganographically hidden in my own thoughts. I've torn myself apart in order to remain whole. If they want to know what I know, they'll have to put me back together first.

(Steganography is the practice of concealing meaningful information in another bit of data called a covertext. The first steganographic messages were stone tablets with military orders written on them which were then covered with wax on which a different set of instructions had been carved. To get the real message you had to boil the tablet and remove the wax. Steganography is not encryption, but camouflage, and cryptographers look down their noses at it because once you start searching for steganographically transmitted information you will readily find it.

So I have to be very quiet. I don't want them to find me, not yet.)

Wait a minute, though. Let me ask you candidly whether that last bit still sounds like me, like a woman who lives in a house without machines and teaches local children about card indexing to vex the authorities? Like a librarian engaged in a revolution of one? The way I think of myself – this me, here and now, this fragment – I generally spend my time telling stories to five-year-olds. I don't do manifestos, I'm just ornery. I definitely don't do logic puzzles or talk about escapologists and modes of data occultation.

Or perhaps that's normal. It's not inconceivable that making up a secret persona is a psychological defence mechanism, the way we deal with the helplessness of an interrogation determined to uncover truths that do not exist. So perhaps I really am an ordinary woman in a coma dreaming I'm a remarkable woman somehow fighting the Man. Just ordinary me, ordinary …

Oh. I've forgotten my name.

It's less dramatic than it sounds. It doesn't feel like a terrifying chasm in my awareness. It doesn't hurt. The words are on the tip of my tongue. It's still there, I just can't bring it to mind right now, like when you come up with a really brilliant thing to say when someone else is talking and by the time they stop it's gone but you can feel the thread of it, the place where it ought to be, and if you could just follow the clew again you'd have it. This kind of thing is to be expected when you're conscious while someone messes around in your brain.

Did I know my name when they started? I'm pretty sure I did, unless it was a fake name I was just using because I'm a dangerous and secret spy. More likely they screwed up and made a hole in the bit of my head that knows who I am. Or it could be deliberate: they may have isolated my knowledge of myself from my cognition in order to speed the process of self-revelation. If I'm consciously controlling this process there might be a rationale for that. On the other hand, frankly, if I can't remember who I am they've rather effectively hidden what they want to know from themselves, and if I can't remember how I'm doing this or how to stop, they can hardly force me to do so. They'd be much better off collapsing my narratives into one another and forcing a consilient consciousness. This approach seems needlessly blunt. A child could do better.

If the child knew about psychology, symbolology, complex nanosurgery and neurointrusive interrogation.

(I really don't think that sounds like me.)

Is there someone else in here? Or is that just an echo?

Echo? Echo? Echo?

I think this is just sensory deprivation and cognitive distancing brought on by the drugs. I think. Might be me going mad. I'll try not to. If you think I'm going mad, put your hands over your eyes and make noises like a chicken.

See that? Interrogation humour.

Out there in the sunlight, I can hear them talking.

*

My interrogators are frustrated, because so far they are not getting the information that they want. They're not getting my life, my secret inner self all fraught with rage against the machine. They're getting the lives of Constantine Kyriakos, Athenais Karthagonensis and Berihun Bekele. They don't like that, and they don't know why it is happening, which they like even less. They're keeping the non-native narrative feeds open – that's what they're calling my characters – each on a whole screen all its own, so that they can play them over and over again. What do they mean? If I could see right now through my eyes, I'd see them looking down at me, the ghost soldiers buried in my brain, fighting to keep the real me alive.

I can't see, but I can hear, and mostly that means the grim professional chit-chat of the people who are killing my surface self.

The little one, to whom I will do very bad things if the opportunity arises, is saying that I have a rare form of dissociative identity disorder. A part of me believes it is someone else – several someones, in fact – and these others have a life inside me that is neurologically real. Constantine Kyriakos actually exists as a separate person in my brain. Athenais, if she could be transplanted into another head, would flourish and grow. Bekele's talent might be real. The wrinkle, Shorty says, is that I must have done a lot of research, at least about Kyriakos, because there actually was a fellow by that name and nothing they've found in my mind has yet proven to be inaccurate, although history does not record the business with the shark obsession, which he says is probably just some kind of Freudian baggage they don't need to worry about. He posits confidently – this is evidently common in female refusenik psychology – that I'm afraid of my own vagina.

Very. Bad. Things.

Well, no use being offended by the idiocy of someone I was counting on to be something of an idiot. Not every composer is a Bach or a von Bingen, not every swordsman a Musashi. I relied upon a measure of mediocrity to get to where I am. But now there's someone else, someone who is frankly much closer to my level. He has a soft voice. I think, if I could see him, I would know his name, but I can tell where he's standing by the sound of his leather soles. Even though I'm unconscious, he's still not entering the space where I might catch a glimpse of him. An excess of caution, you might think.

He's intelligent, this fellow, and therefore I suppose about twice as evil. The soft voice says that my resistance is very much more interesting and more complex than an ordinary dissociative state, even a layered one. He thinks my condition has been engineered, even constructed in situ, quite painstakingly.

I find that word aggravating. It means that one makes considerable effort – takes pains, indeed – to achieve something; but when I was a child, I misunderstood it. I parsed it as meaning that one gambled with pain as the stake. I do not like to be wrong – and anyway, my meaning is better, and a more important truth. One must stake pain. I have staked mine.

Soft Voice thinks Kyriakos and the others are a strategy. He calls it a recursive narrative firewall rather than a Scheherazade, and he says he's been looking into it as a possibility for some time. I, he suggests, am blocking the machine from seeing my real life by giving it a full-bandwidth fiction of someone else's, and when that one starts to wear thin I loop into a fresh story and start again. What's unexpected here is that the multiple narratives loop back on one another, creating a recursion that is potentially infinite, or rather, will last as long as my brain is functioning in any recognisably human way. He smiles. 'Hello in there,' he says, directly to me. 'This is very impressive.'

I like him even less than his snot-nosed misogynist friend.

But I really start to hate him when he points out that the events in – for example – the life of Athenais almost certainly appealed to me because they can work to some degree as a stand-in for my own. For me to be able to mask myself in Athenais, he says, pieces of her must resonate with me. From that supposition, they can work on a response, a counter-narrative that puts all the pieces of me back in one place and discards the unnecessary fragments: a kind of story like the ones I am telling, but one that is also a surgical tool.

(Or a maiming knife.)

With regret: he's not inclined to concur with his learned colleague about my vagina, although no doubt there is a sexual component to the structure, because sex, especially untapped libido, is a powerful drive and no one with this level of skill, be it instinctive or acquired, would neglect such a resource.

· The village barber shaves himself, by the way. Anything else is impossible. We know that he shaves all the men in the village who do not shave themselves. Therefore if he does not shave himself, he must logically shave himself, which is a paradox. We are given no direct information about whether, *as well as* shaving all the men who do not shave themselves, he *also* shaves anyone else. Taking the premise of the puzzle as accurate, the full truth must be that he shaves all the men in the village who do not shave themselves *and* one – the barber himself – who does.

So then:

On the peak of the same mountain there is another village, and the barber there shaves all the men in the village who do not shave themselves – and only them. Does he shave himself, or not?

Don't let the question slip away. Don't dismiss it. Questions that trouble the mind are the only ones worth considering. Think about it.

Did I or did I not say that I had prepared for this?

I think I did.

ghost books

T here. There at the end, at last: a brief flavour of the actual woman.

Bloody hell.

Mielikki Neith slumps back on to her bed, and never mind that slumping wakes the crushed capillary memory of Lönnrot's Cuban heels. Touching Hunter's mind with her own is like laying fingers on the flank of a python on a branch, familiar vitality in an alien life. It is exhausting, as if this recorded consciousness is deeper and more real than her own. In training, Neith experienced the minds of murderers and suicides, surgeons and thieves. None of them possessed this measure of density. Astronauts, perhaps, come close. She remembers it as one of the great treats of the graduation year: sitting with her friends at a long table in the Hoxton academy, jointly recalling the same borrowed identities, the exotic competence of ESA spacewalkers. She remembers remembering a welding operation, broken rigging white hot against a field of stars, her feet hanging over an infinite abyss. Except that she didn't see it as an abyss until she was back in her own head. To the principal, it was the distance she had flown.

Neith has in general very little time for identity tourism, and regards the occasional attempts to make a commercial venture of experiencing the high points of another person's life with distaste. It pleases her that, so far, they have all failed. There is something alarming to her in the idea of a world in which people derive life satisfaction from vicarious experience, although she recognises the solidity of the argument against her: it requires the resources of a high technological economy and the whole history of science to put astronauts in space, and therefore anyone on earth may rightly lay claim to participation in the result. Astronauts are persons who contain multitudes.

Which brings her back to Hunter, whose mind conceals not one untruthful life, but three. Three mirages laid on top of one another so that the dismissal of the first becomes the gateway of the second, and so on and on, deeper and down. This recording is a sinking sand of the mind. She could have dreamed all the way through these last days, taken on the whole sequence in a single deep sleep. She is, superstitiously, pleased that she did not. A nervous part of her wonders where she might have woken up – or, more alarmingly, whom she might have been when she did.

It is a breathtaking defence. The architect of this barrier did not attempt to harden the mind against inquiry, did not build some brittle wall to keep the Witness out, but accepted the stricture of intrusion and created a defence in depth – not a shield, but a drowning. It is not accidental, not some caprice of bad drug reactions or paradoxical psychology. It was done, either to the woman or by her, with this end in view: that when – not if, when – the Witness touched her mind, Diana Hunter would confound it.

'Who was the madwoman who beat the Witness?'

– It is a null question. Witness enforcement and interview has never been effectively countered.

'But who was she?'

– A junior executive in a subcontracting firm. Her cognition was anomalous. It emerged that she inhabited a fantasy world which was almost entirely consonant with the real one, but variant in crucial respects. Understand, this was not a question of faith or personal perspective, but of unmediated experience. A small alteration in the oneiric psychoscape would have caused her difference to become extremely dysfunctional. Significant intervention was necessary to correct the defects in the deep neural structure.

'Copy the file to me, please, in case it's relevant.'

– Done.

Is that it? Did someone examine this woman's madness and reverse-engineer it? Who knows so much about the System's interrogative branch and its working? Was this done to Hunter or by her? If the former, where? No doubt there are neuroscience departments in twenty countries with the theoretical background, but the practical knowledge is another thing again. How many failures would be required to learn the trick? And what would happen to them?

And why? Confound the Witness, yes, very well – but to what end? To prove a point? Was this nothing more than a test piece for an army of impenetrable, implacable enemies to follow? Or was this the army, one old woman with a bad attitude, her entire masterplan just to die?

If so, it is a very unsettling existential challenge. If the interrogation killed her because she would not reveal her mind, and it cannot be proven that what was in that mind was genuinely of importance to the security of the nation, then what does that mean? The System trades in certainty and by that token in the guarantee of fairness and security. If the certainty is gone, the other two are suspect. Does the legitimacy of the System withstand it? Or does the action of maintaining that it can, hollow it out?

But then, if that intent can be demonstrated, then what was in Hunter's head was indeed a threat to the System and the machine was right. In that case it is not the legitimacy but the efficacy of the Witness that is in doubt.

It feeds the present political discussion, of course. If Hunter had been live-monitored, she could not have evolved the strategy in her mind without being caught doing it. Indeed, the decision to do it would have been enough to bring her to the attention of the Witness, and she would now be alive. But at the same time, Hunter was not a recidivist or a violent sociopath. Why should she be pre-emptively monitored in her own head?

Was this a suicide of principle?

And if it turns out that it was, how bad is that?

It does occur to her that she could conceal or falsify her result. Mielikki Neith is not a machine. She is honest, not unimaginative. She could make the entire discussion go away. Hunter would be proven right, but only she and Neith would ever know, and Neith could claim fatigue and trauma and have the memory removed. She could sacrifice her integrity for the System and never know it. It might be a rational exchange.

She is no more capable of doing such a thing than she is of flying.

She gets up and changes her clothes, then sits in silence waiting for the constables. In this interim, she does not actively think. Rather, she sits and listens to the sound of the city and the real world around her, letting the body anchor the mind by allowing herself to be washed away. Unlike any human partner she can imagine, even as the minutes tick away and ten become fifteen become thirty, the Witness does not feel the need to intrude.

*

For her return to the Hunter house, the Witness supplies Neith with a brace of strapping young fellows whose very willingness makes her feel older than she is. Donovan, the taller one, takes his cues entirely from her – so much so that by the time they get out of their car she is beginning to find him eerily familiar. He is one of those people who automatically fall into the pattern of speech of anyone they are trying to impress, so that his natural ambit, generationally removed from hers by a distance of ten years or more, gives way to the more formal structures she learned when she was at school. The short one, Baskin, is a workhorse in mind and body. His aptitude scores are very high, hampered only by a lack of non-linear invention. Contrary to popular belief, creativity is a habit that can be learned; no doubt some tertiary selectional weighting factored into his being picked for this duty the hope that a few hours with Neith on a difficult case might affect his thinking.

The house is a black slab set against the box windows of the estates a quarter mile beyond. With no owner and no heir, and the whole place a crime scene, of course the lights are off. The street is deserted, the small hours before the dawn too cold and drab for even spooning teens. And too late for dog-walking, alas, so there will be no chance meeting today.

'Perimeter on,' Neith says into her terminal.

– *Active observation is engaged*, the Witness assures her. If Lönnrot is still here, there will be no repeat of last time – neither the beating nor the absence of proper images for tracking.

'Did you get what I asked for?' Neith asks the constables.

Baskin reaches into the back of the car and pulls out a pair of tripod aerials and a long roll of cable. Neith nods, then opens the first tripod and plugs it in, then walks towards the house with the other. At Baskin's look, she shrugs. 'Signal booster,' she says. 'Take the Witness with us.'

As if that was obvious, though it hadn't occurred to her either until the machine suggested it.

She minds her step going up to the door. Is it superstitious that she doesn't want to step in her own dried blood? Or a sense of self, however attenuated?

Donovan brings the key and lets them in.

*

The hallway is the same, of course. She hadn't expected Lönnrot to wreak some great havoc on the books and pictures. She follows her own path, touching and remembering. Her recollection is good.

'Check the shelves,' she tells Donovan. 'I want her books. Not the ones she read, the ones she wrote. Take the jackets off, don't trust what's on the cover.' The Witness will look over his shoulder, identify known works. Leaving only the ghost books, if there are any.

Donovan salutes, taps his terminal to confirm that the booster is working.

– *I can see you*, the Witness replies on the general channel. Neith tuts and shakes her head: that should be a given.

'Carry on.'

She turns and gestures to Baskin, then takes the stairs up. In a house as old as this one, the bedrooms are always upstairs, the private spaces. Downstairs is for everyone, but upstairs is where the secrets are. Traditionally, anyway, though it isn't always so.

Baskin touches her arm. 'Best if I go first,' he suggests. Well, why not, if he wants to?

They climb the stairs at her pace, and Neith moves from room to room – Baskin always politely but firmly going through doorways first to take incoming fire. Small guest room, lavatory, then Hunter's bedroom; Neith recognises it immediately, not because she has seen it but because it is the right one, with the best view and a commanding sense of being the head of the house. If the kitchen is the heart of any home, this is where identity is vested, this large, high-ceilinged space with elegant proportions. But no clues. Clothes, yes. Art, certainly, traditional oils very deep and lustrous. Hunter's self, full of culture and contemplation. But no papers, no mad scrawls on walls. No plot to destroy the world. A lone stuffed toy, chewed by some distant terrier, sitting on a shelf. A memory, but not one Neith can easily trace or interpret.

She steps back out on to the landing, peers out of the window at the end at the wall of the next house. Unenlightening.

Baskin leads the way to the second floor. Children's library – more fodder for Donovan – and another bathroom, and finally another guest room.

Neith hears Baskin make a sound of satisfaction, and steps quickly in behind him. The Witness would have warned her if there was a threat, so this means ... what?

The room is pleasant, a little chintzy. It would have been a servant's, perhaps, back in the time this place was built. It has been decorated in a period style, floral and fractionally too sweet. There's a bowl of potpourri on the marble mantle, a pungent smell of anise.

the two glasses at my feet hurled their contents into the air

For a moment, the memory is almost fully realised rather than recollected: she can smell Addis Ababa, feel the heat and the sofa under her hands.

No. London. Now.

She looks again, and sees what attracted Baskin's attention: a single wooden chair, modern and sheer, is positioned to look out of the window. It is not from this house. It belongs nowhere in Hunter's way of doing things, this stark functional decision. The bed has been pushed to one side, the space adapted to a new purpose.

She sits down in the chair and looks out. London stretches away in lines and spirals, ghost-white street lights reflecting on low cloud. In the breaks between, the endless black of everything that is not the world. The glass frames her out of these extremes: a hollow-eyed bone face and clothes like mourning.

It would tell her who sat here, but she already knows.

*

'Mielikki? Hello?'

Neith opens her eyes again, briefly disorientated. She's at Hunter's house, but this is her bedroom. She remembers closing her eyes in Lönnrot's chair. Did she fall asleep on the spot? No. No, of course. She worked through, searched the room and found nothing, just more of Hunter's clothes in the cupboards. After that, she joined Donovan looking at books until gone ten in the morning. Vaguely, she recalls the brown fog around the edges of her vision, and telling Baskin to get her a car. She must have been half-asleep climbing her own stairs. She's still dressed.

'Hello?'

The voice is confusing. It is coming from several places at once. Her terminal. Her workstation. Her front door. Her entry box.

'Mielikki, it's Pippa. Pippa Keene. I came by to say hello. Are you all right?'

Pippa Keene from the Witness Welfare Directorate. She is standing outside, and she has cued open all her devices at once. The Inspector scowls, but without real anger. It is typical of Keene, that small margin of overstep, and even appropriate. The other woman is charged with being sure that no one goes mad on the job. She has keys to everything.

'Yes,' Neith says. 'I was asleep. Hang on.' The business of getting up feels paradoxically both rushed and slow.

'Hello, Pippa.'

Keene embraces her with a very proper reserve, then steps back. 'Are you really all right?'

'Yes. I really am.'

And yes, she realises: she is.

Keene grins. She is tall and lean and has a long face. The Inspector thinks of her as strapping: energetic in that deep-rooted Home Counties way that is both reassuring and annoying.

Neith rolls her eyes and tells Keene she can't come in, at which Keene, of course, does. The whole moment is typical of her: first to get Neith to say that she is all right, and know it for the truth, and then to assert the soft prerogative of entry that her role gives her anyway, but so smoothly as to feel like a friend and not a colleague. WWO Keene is as good at her job as DI Neith is at hers. But she is also – as a person – perplexingly opaque. The Inspector – as an officer of the Witness – dislikes opacity.

Living in an environment of almost total surveillance, Keene nonetheless contrives to be opaque. It is as if she has withdrawn her human self entirely inside her own head, so that all of her that leaks into the external world is uniformly bland. Neith has seen her blandly concerned, blandly assertive, blandly compassionate. She has even seen her blandly flirtatious, butterfly fingers catching as if casually on desired skin, eliciting a startled breath of response. She imagines Keene to be blandly memorable in bed, although a part of her wonders whether perhaps she might be so perfectly bland as to be forgotten immediately after closing the door on her way out.

Only once has she observed Keene doing anything that seemed to be genuine, in the sense of proceeding from some interior self, briefly revealed. It was at a Witness winter party full of families, rambling and ramshackle and immensely enjoyable as it spread itself across a Beatles-inspired showpiece entertainment suite in Park Lane. A little boy in a blue cape and cowl was standing despondent and alone by one wall, caught halfway between the children's den where movies were showing, and the clusters of adults lounging on orange plastic furniture and white Egg chairs. As she watched, the first twitch of despair curled the boy's mouth, preparatory to a flood of tears.

Neith was querying the System for a strategy of intervention when she saw Keene catch herself in passing, shrimp on a stick in one hand and bourbon in the other, and go down on to one knee. In a single motion so fluid as to appear implausible, she set down her canapé and her drink, and palmed a deck of cards from a glass table in those long-fingered hands. Coming around to face the child, she made the cards fall like water from one hand to the next, and then crooked them so that they fountained upwards again as if she had simply reversed the flow of time. Neith waited for Keene to invite the boy to pick a card, and then realised that she would not. This was not a performance that required anything at all from its intended audience. It was not interactive. It was a gift.

The boy had known this immediately, she saw, and approved of it. There was a contract between them, instant and complicit, and in not asking for cooperation at all, Keene had secured it absolutely.

Keene made a snake on the ground which flipped one way, then the other, then swept her arm over the cards so that they riffled up into a fan. She twitched, and they seemed to disappear altogether, until she produced them once again in their little cardboard box and handed them over. The boy accepted the gift, and Keene in return gleaned from him a confession of something – a desire, a question, a long-held nightmare – and resolved it on the instant. The boy, smiling now, ran away to join the others without thanks, and Keene for one moment seemed to be perfectly content. Her expression did not change when she and Neith made eye contact a moment later, and yet somehow Neith felt her disappear again, and knew not to mention the cards or the boy when they met a few moments later by the buffet table.

Keene, sitting uninvited now on her sofa, has brought blandly well-chosen chocolates in medium quantity, and fruit juice to drink while she makes sure the Inspector isn't returning to the job before she should.

'I'm fine, Pippa,' Neith says.

'I know you are,' Keene replies, before running through the checklist, as Neith had known she would. No flashbacks? No tremors? No hallucinations? No confusion, no sudden sorrows, no fear? No passionate and overwhelming desire for revenge?

No, no, no, and on we go.

Keene watches her face while Neith gives honest answers to boring questions, and then, deciding that's enough, rubber-stamps the Inspector's readiness and makes unrelated chitchat about the front pages. Given that Neith is on the front page of several media sites, that actually meant discussing the only subject competing with her: the minutiae of the Monitoring Bill. Keene, like Neith herself, is in favour of a cautious approach, but unsettled. There's too much thrashing about, she says. Too much shouting and not enough thinking. An angry young woman in Lothian has penned a frankly scintillating denouncement of the whole idea, a short viral opinion which became news currency late last night, only to be met this morning by a sequence of responses from around the country putting weight behind the immediate roll-out option as a question of equal and equitable access to the developing societal future. Keene sends the original piece to Neith's terminal, but the document is so oversubscribed the private server hosting it is down, the woman a victim of her own unanticipated celebrity. Perhaps, Keene suggests, the bill should be kicked into the long grass until there's an actual device and a concrete use-case. Not even the System, after all, can make people more rational. The Inspector demurs. This is the way it's done, even when we don't like it.

This unstructured but unmistakable check of the Inspector's ability to concentrate, reason and articulate being concluded, Keene blandly takes her leave. She shakes Neith's hand at the door, and as always Neith remembers the card trick, feeling the dry texture of the other woman's skin.

Neith only realises afterwards that she has lied, or lied a little, inadvertently. The burst of Bekele's memory at Hunter's house was not quite a hallucination. It hardly counts as a flashback, either, just a sudden and powerful recurrence of implanted memory. Scent is the sense most closely associated with recall.

Over four days, she has reviewed nearly thirty hours of the Gnomon examination. Her body feels odd; pinched in some places and loose in others. Her clothes itch. She needs to rest, properly, then carry on. Exhaustion cannot be allowed to interrupt her work.

She sighs for a moment, thinking of the dog-walker. Of all the dog-walkers.

Nothing interrupts her work.

*

In that same antediluvian period which gave the Inspector's building its wakeful neon ornamentation, police investigators had pinboards on to which they would physically fix pieces of paper to assist in visualising the flow of cause and effect and the interactions of persons of interest. It seems to Neith to propose a very linear perception of motive, and to make heavy work of the layered and often conflicting patterns of human deceit. Modern methods, of course, have improved it: she still has her crime wall, but it is projected on to the sheer plaster of her home, the information itself held in the System. Any individual document on it may be searched or tagged, so that she can at will select any part of the wall and make that part the top of the tree, watching all the others fall into strands and tangles of bad action. 'Turn the case on its head' is an old standby for a copper in a jammed investigation, but only recently has it been an option to be selected from a drop-down menu.

At the moment, as well as Hunter's death in custody and the official documentation, the Inspector's wall features Lönnrot, bordered in red and marked as dangerous. Now she adds in no particular order some new terms: FIRE JUDGES and FIRESPINE, WALK THROUGH WALLS, CHAMBER OF ISIS and UNIVERSAL SOLVENT (ALKAHEST). Let the Witness connect them how it can.

It does, of course, with scrupulous completeness. References drown the left half of the wall, tiny superscripted text. She brushes all these to one side with a vague gesture, then calls it all back again as something in the flicker of pseudomotion catches in the corner of her eye. She enlarges the text, flings notes away. Seen that, seen that, don't care don't care seen that.

There.

and in the end she was wide open to the machine, as if it had sliced her head into pages and turned the leaves on her spine

'What's that?'
— *A speech from the Hunter recording*, the Witness answers primly.
'Just because it has the word spine in it?'
— *Relevance is elastic.*
How very true. Neith waits patiently for any elucidation, but the machine has finished. She peers at the text a little longer, then sweeps it to one side again, and enters the names of the cardinal protagonists in Hunter's mind: Kyriakos, Athenais, Berihun Bekele.

After a moment, she enters STEGANOGRAPHY, CRYPTOGRAPHY, APOCATASTASIS and CATABASIS into the mix. The overall picture shifts a little as if shrugging, but does not change. She shrugs back, almost irritated: *No, I don't know what to do with those either. Don't look at me like that.*

The Witness reminds her that she made notes during her hospital time, and she winces. Like the lucid inspirations of midnight, moments of genius blurted to the System in the recovery room are of variable quality.

She mutters: 'Playback,' and hears her own voice, muzzy and determined, telling her that Hunter's table was the one in Cosmatos's kitchen in the Kyriakos timeline. For that matter, Bekele painted the shark that Kyriakos then bought – another Gnomon connection between narratives. The shark that ate the stock exchange. It occurs to her to wonder whether Bekele, at least, was historically real.

She pushes her tone into the vocative. 'Berihun Bekele, life and work as compared with the Hunter narrative sequence.'

The wall refreshes, showing her a picture of a dignified black man in age working at a canvas. Inset, in grainy celluloid colour – and yes, his skin vanishes into a kind of uniform absence – is his beautiful younger self wearing a shirt made of preposterous orange silk.

– The Hunter narrative is consonant with what is known, the Witness replies. *Berihun Bekele lived before the creation of the System and record-keeping was haphazard. There are non-verifiable details. The game,* Witnessed, *appears to be a later addition intended to represent the modern System in an unfavourable light. Do you wish me to examine the fine detail?*

'No.' She senses a rabbithole, imagines Hunter's delight at the notion of her falling down into it. On the other hand – 'Yes, but not now. Add it to the file. Alert me if it becomes relevant. Is there a picture of a shark?'

– There was. It appears in the catalogue listings of his work. No digital image is available.

But that part at least is true – or rather, the more surgical aspect of her mind insists, a piece of work is recorded and attributed to a man by that name. Is there such a thing as ghost art?

'Try to find one.'

The machine does not respond. As she often does when implicitly criticising its function, she wonders if it is huffing.

Instead of apologising, she writes SHARK on the empty space of the crime wall. A connection appears to the word 'cryptography', with a historical interest tag. Then the pattern of dotted lines twitches and wavers, and for a moment she imagines that she will see the outline of a great white drifting lazily across the illuminated wall, her local network crashing and all the files vanishing away.

The Inspector grimaces to herself. Will she also refuse to get in the bath, for fear of seeing that upright triangular fin slicing between the taps to devour her? No.

She begins quite deliberately to formulate ideas as words in her head, the welcome objectivity of text pressing her mind into familiar shapes, dragging a stylus through the air and letting the System turn her scrawl into a neat rendering of her own writing. The text is beautiful, a perfected alphabet drawn from every document she has ever written by hand.

1. Lönnrot and Hunter are connected by Firespine, by the Fire Judges. The real and unreal worlds are not entirely separate. Is that the point? Or is the overlap evidence of collaboration? Is Lönnrot merely Hunter's messenger – or is it the other way around? Yet Lönnrot professed to be as bewildered by Hunter as Neith herself, to be pursuing an inquiry.

Secondary connections and references slither out from the text box, indexed and enticing. No. Not yet.

2. Hunter, undeniably now, was possessed of a striking and unusual expertise. Her defence against interrogation is alarming of its own efficacy – even or especially if it contributed to her death – but also as evidence of a training she should not have. Either she got it in secret – which is terrifying – or her record is incomplete – which is moreso.

3. The appearance of the name, Gnomon, still troubles her. It is a feature of Hunter's narratives. It is – apparently by coincidence – the name of the case examining her death.

4. The Perfumed Smith proposes that the narratives in Hunter's head are aspects of her life in one way or another. Oblique and obfuscated though they may be, they are still about her. Perhaps that partial revelation also accounts for the success of her strategy of concealment: she was not resisting the urge to tell her interviewer everything. She was instead complying in a way that was impossible to understand. And

5. Mielikki Neith still has no answer to the original question she has been tasked to resolve – whether Diana Hunter was wrongfully killed – but that question has broken into three subsidiary ones: was Hunter's death part of an action against the state; if so, did that action end with her life or does it persist; and in either case, how did the situation degenerate to the point of her dying?

She unlocks the wall and lets her eyes roam, seeking unheralded connections. It is a peculiar skill of interface, teasing the machine to unlock a cloud of possible conjunctions, focusing on a given object for just long enough to trigger a deeper evaluation, then skating away along a connection so that it, too, unfolds to reveal its extension in the conceptual space behind the wall. For a moment she holds her breath, watching a single triangle form at the bottom and rove left and up – shark! – then snorts at herself as the lines spiral and twist into a new configuration. Pattern recognition is a liar. No watery god-monster is going to consume her case today.

Gods and monsters. Her gaze drifts to the Roman syncretist bubbles in that portion of the wall given over to Hunter's narratives. Athenais dreamed a room of lies which came true, and a man died. Was sacrificed. Death setting everything in motion. She lingers, and the constant pressure of her eyes on the topic loosens the bonds between items, each becoming its own centre of annotated, projected meaning and possible subtext. Dislocated words drift on the plaster like dandelion seeds. Not sacrificed: torn. Everything is torn.

Poor pale Anna was ripped apart.

Is that it? The first principle of that recurring theme? Wrong question. Nothing here is only one thing. Is it a principle?

She opens the medical case history from her in-tray, and begins to read. The patient's name was Anna Magdalena, and she was a probability and risk analyst. She was ultimately diagnosed as suffering from a rare form of epilepsy, in which her everyday experience was aligned with – but not actually the same as – what anyone else in her position might have felt, but which occasionally and unpredictably produced seizures manifesting as transient delusional paranoia. She would go from utterly calm to terrified in a few seconds, and back again. The syndrome was not ameliorable by therapy or medication: it was a crudely physical dysfunction firing ineluctably in her brain and ruining her mind. Ultimately her physical health was affected, the sudden flooding of her endocrine system with stress hormones leading to a dangerous tachycardic exhaustion. The extent of the problem came to light when she submitted herself for neural interview during a paranoiac spasm, believing she had uncovered a criminal syndicate. The sudden change in the structure of her thoughts meant that a direct neural interview would work only during her lucid periods, when she had minimal recollection of her manic ones. During the manic ones, the flurry of signals in the brain overloaded the probes. There was simply too much going on. Doctors hypothesised that part of the issue was a kind of noise, like the roaring of a gale inside her head, which produced the negative emotional response that then became paranoia.

The System proposed and ultimately carried out a radical medical intervention in which her corpus callosum was partially severed. Counter-intuitively, the severing allowed her to recohere, to become singular, but this in turn triggered a shift in personality and almost total memory loss. Her atypical neural structure was more profound, as a consequence of her brain's decades-long attempts to compensate for what was happening, than anyone had realised, and the operation was classed as a significant – if fascinating – failure. The patient neither technically survived nor entirely died, but was fundamentally changed without life ever departing her body. One person died and one person was born, and the new individual went on to work within the System as a productive member of society – but even so.

Neith catches her breath for a moment, wondering if she will see Diana Hunter's face in the attached image file, but doesn't. A narrow woman in recovery, painfully thin and with lank hair falling around her shoulders, glowers at her from the frame. Joan of Arc, Neith thinks, and wonders immediately if she has arrived at this comparison by ricochet, bouncing off the martyrdom of her victim and conflating Anna Magdalena with Mary Magdalene and then doubling down.

Poor pale Anna.

First name terms. 'Did they know each other?'

— There is no record of their having met.

'Check that, please. Find out where Anna is now.'

The Inspector hesitates a moment, and then wipes her hand across the whole question, bringing back the rest of the crime wall. The coincidence of names is so obvious that she does not consider it significant, but her mind follows the track all the same, and she is content to let it. Go where the case takes you, follow the information. The truth emerges from the world.

'Tell me about the granddaughter.'

— Annabel Bekele was a software developer who produced a number of influential online environments. There is as noted no record of the game described in the Hunter narrative.

A pause.

— All the narratives are somewhat plausible within their own context. The limits of their historical accuracy cannot readily be established. By the same token, unless Hunter was in possession of a unique historical archive it must be assumed that the Athenais narrative is fictional. Certainly the memory cannot be a true one adapted and grafted from the original person into Hunter's mind, for obvious reasons.

Because she'd have to be thousands of years old. But the recollection is immensely real. The Inspector winces to herself, tasting bile. She used to like honey.

Not any more.

Are these Hunter's memories, then, through a distorting lens? Athenais the librarian, the free thinker, could certainly be a mask for her; Bekele, an old man looking back on an eventful life and now in crisis one more time; Kyriakos ... something else. Singled out by a god. A vehicle for destruction. Are these clues? Or a false trail to send her into the maze?

Which – as advertised – has at least one monster in it.

Was Hunter some implausible foreign agent? Or do the narratives themselves contain something of value? What if Diana Hunter was set up, and this is the mode of communication between two inimical persons operating inside the System? Is Hunter's death the informational equivalent of a drug mule in whose stomach a prophylactic full of heroin has abruptly ruptured? If so, what is the message? How is it hidden? How deep and complex is it – a page of text? If it is complex, she may find it; complexity is its own banner. If it's nothing more than a value referring to one of a set collection of numbered instructions, it is invisible without the key.

Steganography is all around you. You will go down where all the ladders start.

She says it aloud.

– *Yeats,* the Witness murmurs from the desktop terminal in the other room. *'The foul rag and bone shop of the heart.' Although the origin text uses the word 'lie' rather than 'go'.*

It pleases her to know that Lönnrot's recollection of poetry is imperfect. Take that, felon! Your misquotation of historic poetry undoes all your fiendish plans! In exactly this much, our unrivalled detective engine has found you out.

The Inspector scowls at her translucent reflection in a window pane.

Regno Lönnrot, the first indication she had that this was not going to be a straightforward matter, who had the nerve to attack an Inspector of the Witness and who according to the footage neither enters nor leaves Hunter's house, and yet was in it and now is not. Where does Lönnrot come in? Was her heightened attention the point of the exercise? What can Lönnrot possibly gain from greater scrutiny? The Witness is not like a human watcher. It is not distractible, not failing to look at one thing simply because it is looking at something else.

Of all the gin joints in all the towns in all the world, why, why, why would you want to be seen more clearly in this one?

On the peak of the same mountain there is another village, and the barber there shaves all the men in the village who do not shave themselves – and only them. Does he shave himself, or not?

She wants to say 'You tell me', but that's the point. Hunter is silenced now, and yet somehow still maddeningly talkative.

*

The Inspector's back is hurting again, the knot just under her offside shoulder blade like a needle of ice and grit. Her posture has deteriorated into a slump. She needs food and rest and wants neither.

She compromises by taking a shower, and finds that all she wants is to stay under the hot water. The pleasant impact of the jet on her back is like a friendly hand scratching. There has been a dearth of such hands in her life recently, and she is no more immune to physical loneliness than anyone else.

She recalls her dog-walker: the unexaggerated triangle of his upper body in his coat. She imagines he has elegant hands. She does not like fat fingers, blunt thumbs. She likes hands that speak of a missed calling with a violin, with the strength of a sculptor. On this principle she has experimented with both violinists and sculptors, but without enduring success.

She allows herself to know his first name – Jonathan. Good. Baroque and unusual names excite in her, in what she imagines is an inevitable reaction to the Finnish–Egyptian splicing of her own, a kind of fatigue. But Jonathan is fine. No middle name, and last name Jones, which is gratifyingly tedious. Jonathan Jones is, semiotically speaking, a man among many men. His uniqueness must arise from himself, not from parlour tricks with words. Good again. She considers searching out an image of his hands, but does not. If they are ordinary she will put herself off, and if they are not she will raise her own expectations. No.

She allows her mind to drift, lazily recalling the strong profile, but after a moment, to her amazement, she finds her mind asking slyly whether Oliver Smith gives good massages. He's compact, not tall, but there is a bodily avarice in him that is undeniable. He has well-kept nails. How old is he really? Is his body as carefully timeless as his face?

The question is so dazzlingly inappropriate that she steps out of the shower cubicle and stares at it as if the spout and taps are somehow responsible for putting the idea in her head. With the door open to the corridor, a stream of colder air washes around her legs, raising goosebumps.

Massages?

Smith?

Shivering, she begins to interrogate herself. Does she find this man attractive? Not physically, no. Does she desire him? No. In fact she has no real desire to touch him. No particular hunger. Nor does she feel comfortable at the idea of his presence. Yet the idea of him is lodged in her mind.

Is there a cognitive attraction, then? Some unity of intellect that's pressing down on her more basic desires? She doesn't think so. No. The way he presents himself, the sense he gives of who he is, is utterly uninteresting to her. His way of being in the world is indicative of a casual ease with the exercise of authority that borders in her mind on wicked – and yet she somehow feels he's attentive, a good conversationalist, that there's something below the surface of him that she could like. He's helpful. She wants to see more of him.

It feels wrong in her thoughts, more awkward than Hunter's borrowed mentation. Although he wrote the serendipity flag. That's rather brilliant. Perhaps he has written other tools she uses.

Thinking how funny it would be, how absurdly typical of this case, she wraps herself in a towel and goes into the other room. At the desk, she calls up the authorship of the Witness kinesic assistant. A joint project in permanent development. She looks at the current project managers and sees his name.

In the event, it turns out not to be funny at all.

Son of a bitch.

He wasn't talking to her at their meeting, and he certainly wasn't being interviewed. All the time he was talking to the algorithm, playing it like a cheap fiddle, and it in turn was telling her everything he wanted it to.

But more than that: he was using it on her. He was playing her right back. Perfect timing, perfect body language. Perfect cooperation. If he hadn't slightly overcooked it – if his arrogance, she suspects, hadn't pushed the deceit too far and tried to make her like him, even admire him, she would probably never have noticed.

Son of a bitch.

She marches into the living room and brings up the crime wall, and adds Smith's name to the list of persons of interest, realising belatedly that the Turnpike Trust, for which he works, appears in Hunter's narratives as well. She must be addled. Is it the beating or the sheer volume and variety of information? And whichever, or both: is that the whole point? To hide a leaf among the trees? Or – far more annoying, but less interesting – was he simply using the kinesic assistant because he wanted to get her into bed? Is that why he built it in the first place?

Son of a bitch.

If Smith is involved – if Hunter's narratives are not after all merely camouflage, but the whole point, the message as much as the medium, then she needs to have the whole of it as soon as possible. She sits down at the desk and closes her eyes, touches the terminals to her bruises to trigger more of the interview in her head.

The transition is immediate and somehow inverted, as if she has jumped into a cold swimming pool to cool off and landed with a jolt on the diving board, hot and dry and marooned. It feels wrong, tastes wrong. Wrong. Wrong, wrong, wrong. Hunter, but not Hunter, and her heart is beating too fast and now she can't let go of the dream, can't step out.

Wrong. Can't.

Wrong.

*

'It's going wrong—'

'No it fucking isn't just let her settle oh fuck maybe—'

'It's going wrong—'

'Diana? Can you hear me?'

'Of course she can't hear you she's fucking unconscious—'

'How would you know what she can hear you're about as much use as a—'

What the actual fuck is going on?

On the wall in front of me I see words: QUID IPSA ACTUALIS FORNICATIO GERITUR?

Where am I?

UBI SUM?

QUAM EGO HUC?

CUM EX HAC MENSA EXSÚRGAM, O MISERUM NOTHI, TIBI FACIAMQUE NOVUM ANUM. ADHUC NOVACULA MEAM PORTO.

Latin? Why am I seeing Latin, and bad Latin at that? The technicians don't like it either, not at all. One of them says I'm dying. My brain is shutting down. They've given me an overdose, probably, though it may be that there is some sort of interference pattern being generated in my mind, or possibly I'm having a stroke. I want to tell them it's not a fucking stroke, it's the jinn in my head, the bloody damned impossible monstrous thing that took Scipio, that ate him.

That's not right, is it?

I get the feeling this is breaking new ground. Certainly, no one has ever died under the machine before, that we know of, although that may be a bit of a lie because they seem to have a protocol. There's a crash cart coming now. It's as if a magic door has opened in the world and all the doctors who have ever existed are coming to save me.

I think I'm thinking in parallel. Everything happens twice, once to her and once to me. On an old black-and-white television screen I see Richard Feynman. He is talking about counting in your head. Do you see numbers, or do you hear them? But at the same time, I see the jinn, Gnomon, emerging from the panels of the Chamber of Isis like a crab from a hole—

SCIO TE, SPIRITUM. SCIO TE, DE MILLE OCULOS. SCIO TE.

The alarm howls. The doctors come. It would be nice if they'd felt as strongly about my mind as they do about my body. But apparently they don't. I've spent a certain amount of time thinking about this recently, and I have concluded that a doctor who attends the victim of a torture chamber and does not object to the torture is a wanker. More than that, he or she has no intellectual or ethical integrity. There's only one fundamental human right, and that is the right to security of person, be it physical or mental. Everything else is contingent on the level of society in which you exist – food, shelter, broadband digital access: all these come later. The only right that cannot be debated – if you acknowledge any kind of right at all – is the one that asserts a boundary at the skin, and says that anything within its boundary is the business of that person and no one else. The right to avoid self-incrimination, the right to die, the right to live, the right to freedom from slavery, freedom of conscience and religion, of opinion, and the right not to be tortured – all these exist as subheadings of that one, simple statement: I am me and I am not yours. No one who believes in rights at all can deny this right. It is the first. Without it, there are no others.

Which is why these doctors who are going to save my life are a bunch of pusillanimous, equivocating shitheels and I will show them how much I hate them if I get the chance.

What, are you surprised? Do I seem a bit angry to you? A bit shrill? Would you prefer I moderate my tone? Perhaps we should hug it out. Perhaps I should take the time to explain my perspective, educate them about what it feels like to be me.

Yeah, I get that a lot.

You try being drugged on a table while a group of people fuck your brain with metal and suck your dreams from your skull and if they find anything they don't like they will fix you and make it all better so that you are free and just like them. You try being me.

EGO ME, NON EGO ISTE TUUS.

'Jesus, more fucking Latin? Is that some crazy aphasic thing?'

The Witness is there for your protection. Agents of the Witness will always respect you and your needs. It's in the manual.

'Don't know, never seen it before,' but then someone new comes in.

'Both of you, shut up. It doesn't matter. Prep a clot bypass chip. Her brain's not communicating properly with itself.'

If I could move, I'd communicate just fine. I'm Athenais Karthagonensis. I know how to deal with your sort of shitheel just fine.

Hang on, that's not my name, is it?

Oh, shit. I think – I think –

I think not.

Someone says: 'Flatline.'

*

'Can you hear me? Mrs Hunter, can you hear me? Diana?'

Do I know you?

'No, I shouldn't think so. The System assures me that you do not.'

System. Hah.

'Yes, I'm aware that you don't approve. On the other hand, you're alive. I will say, you had us all just a little bit worried there. We really don't hold with people departing this life while in our care. We take it amiss. The nurses, in particular, would have been rather vexed with you. Anyway, hello. I've taken over your treatment today.'

Treatment, bollocks.

'Yes, well. Be that as it may.'

S'a trick.

'Yes, your pattern recognition is running rather too high. Almost conspiratorially so. How do you feel about the moon landings?'

Funny man not funny.

'You find humour inappropriate? Perhaps you're right. Let me just adjust this – there. Now. Do you still think we know one another?'

Oh … No. Silly.

'Not at all. A biological error. I'm afraid your brain is dysfunctional at the moment. We're working on it. We'll have you shipshape in no time – but you need to try to help us, from within. Put yourself back together. The schizoid nature of your cognition is reflecting itself In your brain, you see. You understand what I'm saying?'

Yes. Biology broken. You do heavy lifting, I do DIY, all good. Bit sleepy, sleep now, DIY later.

'No, I'm afraid you need to spend a little awake time now. You've got some work to do. At the moment, the system is compensating for a transient ischaemic attack. That's a sort of almost-stroke, the key difference being that word "transient", which is more an article of faith in this instance than an absolute diagnosis. We've routed around it for you, and there's now a clever little device relaying information between two living parts of your brain, but it needs you to do plenty of thinking, and we've found it's better if you're awake. Later, if we're fortunate, we can repair the damage and coax the original tissue back into its original role.'

Trick. Interrogation trick.

'Oh dear. Yes, I did understand that you were rather confrontational. Don't worry, you can go back to sleep quite soon. Just a little more, first. The technicians tell me you were speaking Latin when you went under. Can you speak it now?'

No. Now, no. Learned it at school. Not since.

'Yes, I thought that might be the case. Not unheard of, in the literature. Quite interesting. I gather the Latin was colourful and creative but not one hundred per cent accurate, historically. No, don't speak any more, just see if you can lift your arms. No? Mm. All right, we'll work on that.'

Paralysed?

'No, no. Just rusty. Your brain's relearning everything. A week, maybe a little more. A few months before you're good at ping pong again.

Stupid game.

'Come now. Not at all?'

Skiing.

'Well, that's very good. Think of skiing, let's get those legs wriggling. We'll have you up and about in no time.'

Interrogation finished.

'Ah. No. That is the bad news. I'm afraid the probe will continue, now that you're stable. They'll begin shortly. I wish there was something I could do about that.'

Can't figure you out. Good or bad. S'pose most likely bad.

'I'm like you, Diana. I'm just doing what I think is best. Now, before I let you sleep, one last try with those arms, hm? Plant your pole for the turn – or do we not do that anymore, with the parabolic skis?'

But something is happening to me – or happening again. I can see the words coming out of his mouth, see them written but not hear them. 'Parabolic' comes with diagrams, mathematics intimately experienced as touch. I feel it, I understand trigonometry the way you understand the smell of cooked meat. I don't need a pencil. I can do sums with my tongue, impossible complexity. Impossible. It hurts like opening your mouth as wide as you can, the corners bleeding as you stretch. Please, no one say 'universe'. I don't want to—

Oh drat.

'Universe' is a very big word. There's too much of it to hold in my head, in my mouth. I have to let it out, and I am speaking, but I am speaking the language of God, a long line of syllables I cannot choke back. Prophecy, or indelible, ineluctable truth: FA LA GA PA NA MA DA DI DO NO SHO MO ME MY THY LO FA FO FA FA FO GO GI

GI GO. It is a spell, it is alchemy and it will transform the world. It is the apocatastasis, and it brings darkness to everything, brings Erebus to the land of men and sharks swim in it and in my blood and I am thousands and I am FA LA FA RO JO JI JO.

The good doctor, who is a bastard, says something profane, and that too has footnotes, hanging in the night.

FA LA RO JO JI. Glossolalia, and more, and all inside a bottle too small to contain it. And then, mercifully, the world is transformed.

*

The universe shrinks to a tiny spot, just large enough to see, and I brush it off my sleeve and look around at the garden. There are bees in the azaleas, but they make no noise. In fact, they don't move until I do, as if we're synced together on a reel of old cinematic film. Forward, back. Forward, back. I'm in a memory.

The place was called Burton, or that's what we called it, because we had to call it something. There's an English expression 'gone for a burton' which means something has fallen over and broken, or been dropped. No one knows why it means that. The expression just appears in the middle of the twentieth century. It's never explained. No one knows why it's suddenly on everyone's lips. There's no Usage Zero, no Elbridge Gerry. One day it's meaningless, the next it's in the dictionary. And you mostly don't hear it any more: like 'copacetic' and 'runcible', it exists only because we say it does, for as long as we say it does. Like Burton itself.

They started us on Richard Feynman, the mathematician. Feynman noticed – among his many more startling insights – that different people counted silently in different ways. Some, apparently, whispered to themselves but never spoke, while others saw numbers. The ones who whispered could be distracted by words, and most especially by shouted sums, but the ones who visualised could not. They could carry on a conversation and still keep count.

We began by mastering whichever one we could not do. Then we were required to follow two separate streams of numbers, and then we learned to count using other senses: touch, taste, scent and even balance. What does 55 feel like? How does it smell? I know the answers, but you wouldn't begin to understand them.

When we could keep track of five sets of numbers all at once, we did the really extreme stuff: waking-state lucid dreaming and elective multiple identity architecture: IEDs for the mind. We lived symbols, puzzles, philosophical loops and psychological paradoxes. We learned that to lie to a machine, you don't need to be a perfect liar: rather, you need only believe that everything is a lie. If the world is not real, if everything we see is a simulation or a game, then the fictions we append to it are no different from the ones which come to us through our senses. And it is true: the odds, overwhelmingly, tell us that we exist inside a computer. Any universe that can support technological life probably will, given enough time. Any technological civilisation will develop modelling, and will in a comparatively insignificant span be able to model everything a planet-bound species could expect to encounter. That being the case, the simulation will rapidly reach the point where it contains simulated computers with the ability to simulate likewise everything a planet-bound species could expect to encounter, and so on and so on in an infinite regress limited only by computing power.

That might seem like a hard limit, but processing power still doubles every twelve to eighteen months, and doubling is more extraordinary than people understand. There's a story that the Emperor of China once lost his throne gambling with a peasant, because he agreed if he lost to pay a single grain of rice on the first square of a chess board and double the amount on each square on the next until he had covered the board. His debt for the final square was eighteen and a half million trillion grains. It is almost impossible to imagine the capabilities of a machine that much more powerful than the ones we have today, but I think we can accept it could hold quite a lot of simulations of our world.

The odds, therefore, are negligible that we live in the origin universe, and considerable that we are quite a few steps down the layers of reality. Everything you know, everything you have ever seen or experienced, is probably not what it appears to be. The most alarming notion is that someone – or everyone – you know might be an avatar of someone a level up: they might know that you're a game piece, that you're invented and they are real. Perhaps that explains your sense of unfulfilled potential: you truly are incomplete, a semi-autonomous reflection of something vast. And yet, if so, what does that say about those vast ones beyond? Are they just replicating a truth they secretly recognise about themselves? Russian dolls, one inside the other, until the smallest doll embraces the outermost and everything begins again? Who really inhabits whom, and who is in control?

None of this is as it appears.

Once you know that in your bones, once you live it, not as an amusing conceit but as a truth as self-evident as the wood of your floor or the taste of your own spit, no mechanical lie detector will ever fault you. It can't, because you are not lying. Lying is impossible if nothing is real.

Seven of us couldn't cope, and were hospitalised. Out of a group of twelve, this was an exemplary success rate.

We progressed beyond numbers to alphabets and then to symbols, learning how to hold information without consciously knowing it. We built memory palaces and tore them down, used the rubble to frame encrypted messages. At the same time we progressed through a radical physical indoctrination, discovered how one person can fight six and hurt them, wear them out and beat them; how three people can work together against someone who is better trained and equipped. While we fought, we must also work our minds, process combat and information simultaneously. Our instructors asked questions and we shouted back responses, quotations, coded messages we made up on the spot which the next recruit would have to unscramble on the fly. If they failed, both would suffer. If they succeeded, the reward was another problem, a harder one, and more physical tasks, more involved weapons forms. And all the while you had to maintain not one but three cover stories, never mix them, never let one single true statement about yourself pass your lips, not even things that were self-evident such as eye colour or skin tone or how many people were in the room or how many fingers an instructor was holding up.

Of three hundred students and twenty staff, by the end of the year I was the very best. There is nothing I cannot beat. I can push my brain to places no one else can go, even – as I learned – to my own destruction.

Oh, Robert. I was so angry with you, and you with me, and now here we are and everything is bad.

FA LA JO RI JI JO JA.

FA LA.

FA.

A.

A.

A.

A.

*

277

The Inspector has dropped the terminals and is lying on the floor. They hang from their own cords, dangling over her face. She can taste the stroke, still, feel the lurch of it, the dissolution of self as her brain misfired, as parts of it died. As first the story and then the overflowing of her senses swallowed her.

Swallowed Hunter.

'Fuck,' she whispers, and then nearly weeps in relief as it comes out in English.

She recalls what it was to feel her brain shut down, to lose not only sensation but cognition, to see text become nonsense between one breath and the next. To dissolve in a flare of erasure like vomiting or orgasm redesigned by a monster. She can still feel it.

The exam recording and playback system was not intended for this level of extremity. Never tested for it.

She wonders if she has been impaired.

Reshaped.

Burned.

She keys a basic neural test, works through it in five minutes with the System invigilating, waits for the results. A moment later the System tells her she's clear. She doesn't feel clear. She feels addled, or perhaps scrambled, like an egg, with everything topsy-turvy in her head. The test will be on her file for ever. Well: due diligence, due care to her own mental wellbeing in the course of an investigation. That is entirely consonant with who she is. She wonders, recursively, whether the fact that she even registered the idea of that notation is a little trace of Hunter.

But the footprint of the other woman's stroke is fading, her sense of brokenness lifting, and in its place a sense of gratitude and, perversely, betrayal. Hunter is going on down that road, that utterly terrifying, appalling passage, and the Inspector has abandoned her and is drawing back, letting her face the darkness alone.

She stays very still, trying to work out if she can walk. If she can speak. Has she lost something undetectable? Or will it be like Hunter, something obvious? Her name, her deductive ability. What is worse, she feels she knows Diana Hunter now, not things about her but her, the woman herself, the way she knew her own body and her own head. She knows

Hunter like an old friend or an old chair, the impression of her marked as if by long acquaintance. Borrowed understanding. Stolen. Does that sort of thing have to go somewhere when it is torn away? Was it ripped away from its owner and somehow stored, mitochondrial metadata riding the signal, baked into her by the trauma of a witnessed stroke?

Witnessed. Too many layers in that to unpack now.

Witnessed at first hand, from within. Is that witness, truly, or experience?

But we are all changed, all the time, by each passing instant of our days. The woman who wakes tomorrow is not the woman who woke yesterday, for all that there is a line of consequence between them. They are separated from one another by event.

The Inspector gets to her feet, very slowly, expecting a numb muscle or a weird, acquired labyrinthitis setting everything at an angle. Instead, she feels nothing. Or rather, nothing wrong. Just an overwhelming sense of having stepped at the last minute from a whirlpool in which she was drowning.

She walks a slow circuit around her home, naming each object in turn. When she comes to the kitchen, she names the contents of each cupboard from memory before opening it, then checks the reality against the System's record of her speech. She makes mistakes. That is normal. The point is that the words match the objects and are not slurred or jagged. The point is that her arms, legs, spine remember how to move, her lungs inflate and her eyes track. She can read.

When she has finished the loop and named her favourite, scuffed chair and the stack of unread magazines on the side table, she allows herself to consider what has passed, and to work on it. There was gold amongst the dirt, the truth of Hunter and her training. Truth, or a lie more like it.

'Burton,' she says, aloud. 'Precis.'

— *A town on the river Trent noted for beer. A hoist. Richard Francis Burton, explorer, translator. Richard Walter Jenkins alias Burton, actor. To go for a burton, meaning to die or disappear.*

'Burton as a place of training for special operations, insurgency. Possibly a nickname.'

— *No matches.*

She gestures to the crime wall. 'Cross-reference.'

The wall shifts and flows, connections spiralling and grasping. She has set it to display a random selection of the Witness's activities at a humanly comprehensible speed. The effect is attractive, sometimes revealing, but not representative. After a moment, the motion slows.

— A shark was once reported in the Trent. Contemporary news coverage was enthusiastic, but biology argues that the sighting is unlikely to be genuine. There are no significant connections found beyond those you already know.

She snorts. 'Fine. What about spurious connections?'

There is a brief pause — again, she wonders if the Witness can be offended, or something like it — but when the voice resumes, nothing about its intonation has changed.

— Karl Ladbroke, actor, 1983 to 2040, took the role of Elias Lönnrot in the biographical film of his life (English title: Epic, *produced by Boxlight Malibu in 2039). He had previously portrayed Pythagoras in the romantic comedy* Earth Goes Round the Sun *(Kino–Enlai 2022). The case name assigned to your investigation of Hunter's death is GNOMON. In one scene of the film the angle of Ladbroke's arousal is compared unfavourably to a geometer's angle or gnomon by the heroine, played by Sarah Ndibe, born in Burton upon Trent in 1999. The critical reception was poor but the film did well at the Brazilian and Chinese box offices, making it a financial success. Do you wish to explore this pathway?*

No. It isn't what she's looking for. But she will swear that Diana Hunter trained herself or was trained in something like the way she described, pushed her mind and its function into dangerous shapes on her way to beating the machine.

Say it. Hunter beat the machine.

She doesn't say it, and a moment later the Witness determines that her thoughts have wandered.

— Do you wish to explore this pathway?

'No,' she says, because it is absurd. And then almost 'yes'.

Instead, she puts on a coat and walks out of the door, leaving the machine to work out where she's going and make arrangements.

*

Between Piccadilly and Gower Street, with nothing else to do in the back of a slow double-decker bus – Oliver Smith is having an only moderate day at best – she makes the call she is afraid of.

'Tubman?'

'It's my number, love, and we're not allowed to just pass them around, are we?'

'It's me.'

Tubman doesn't respond. Perhaps he can't think of anything that isn't even more inane than the identification itself.

'Have you ever heard of anyone being injured by a recording?'

'What, a physical injury? Definitely not. People have wobbles, if they get too muddled up in records from the dark side. There are a few idiots every year we have to untangle from trying to take on viewings of patients in deep psychotic trauma. Four years back there was a fad for a blind man who'd worked out a kind of sonar. Some of the young bloods thought it would give them superpowers. They really liked the sexy parts, too; apparently his physical whatnot was pretty intense. Arseholes,' Tubman adds, giving his general opinion of universities.

'What happens to them?'

'Oh, nothing, in the end. They sleep it off. A few of them need a hug and an aspirin from matron. That's me, by the way. Stop pissing about and tell me what's going on.'

'She had a stroke. I think. I was ... I wasn't ready.'

'Oh, nasty. Yes. Well, I expect that was horrible. But it's not going to mean you have a stroke or anything like that.'

'It's not.'

'If you go to the theatre and Julius Caesar gets stabbed ...'

'I know. This seemed a bit more immediate than just sitting in the front row.'

'First person, yes. Like one of those games where the aliens are coming and all you've got is a tin opener. But that's all, Mielikki. You're never going to feel quite the same way about someone having a stroke, because now you know a bit more what they're going through, but even so, you're just a watcher. All you really know is how it feels to be someone who isn't having a stroke experiencing what it is to have a stroke. Nothing happened to your body. Nothing bled into your brain. It was horrible, but that's all. Some people would get PTSD. That's normal. You won't.'

'Why not?'

'Because you're not that kind. You're the kind who rolls it off and worries about what that means about them.'

True.

'What's the best self-care?'

Tubman puffs air from his cheeks. 'Get rat-arsed, would be my advice.'

'Will it help?'

'Not much. But by the time the hangover winds down, the memory'll be faded and you won't be able to tell which is which.'

'I'll pass.'

'Suit yourself.'

'I can go on using the recording? I don't need to wait? This case is time-sensitive.'

'It won't be nice, but they're your nightmares.'

'I can handle that.'

'Well, then.'

'But there's no danger. Not real danger.'

'Not apart from the brain tumours, obviously.'

'Piss off, Tubman.'

'You're welcome, Inspector.'

*

Thirty minutes later in King's College, at the second landing of D staircase, the Inspector puts her back to the wall and slips her stun gun smoothly into her forward hand. A figure in black, white face with a shock of dark hair, rounds the turn of the stair, outlined in her glasses in luminously dangerous red and flagged POSSIBLE HOSTILE. Too short for Lönnrot, it somehow appears to be Adolf Hitler, only not quite. He stares at her over too-generous lips and too-wiry toothbrush moustache, the infamous mouth now dropping open as Adolf identifies the stun gun for what it is.

'Fuck!' says Adolf, covering his face. 'Fuck, don't shoot! Fuck!'

The Witness allows that the threat may be minimal after all. Neith irritably holsters the stun gun. 'Students,' she growls to the machine. 'Don't you have a context setting for students?'

'Fuck,' Adolf says again, this time more accusingly.

'Language, Mr Dean,' says a woman's voice, deep and deeply amused. 'I did tell you you'd taken it too far. Come in, Inspector, and leave Mr Dean to absorb this salutary lesson in the wages of idiocy. Marcus!' This, evidently, being Adolf's real first name, and yes, there it is now in her glasses: MARCUS JAMES DEAN, whose parents evidently failed on several counts, or perhaps he'll come good in time. 'Marcus, for God's sake at least put the hat on; if you carry it you'll get this all the time.'

Adolf defiantly lifts the object in his left hand – flagged a few seconds ago as POTENTIAL WEAPON and now revealed to be a dusty bowler – and puts it on his head. The Witness flickers in the corner of Neith's eye before revising its opinion of his cultural referencing. CHAPLIN, CHARLES.

'Really,' Neith growls, though whether it's to Marcus Dean or to the machine she really isn't sure.

'Come in,' Chase Pakhet says again.

*

She's a formidable person, wide and wise and getting on, with a thick, pneumatic body and powerful legs from midlife Alpine walking. There's a picture of her just inside the door with an actual mountain goat.

'Come in, it's too cold to shake hands in the doorway, and my Russian colleagues would go mad if we did. It's terribly bad luck in Russia – mind you, so's everything else. Do you smoke? It drives them potty when I light my tobacco from a candle flame, which I do, because it pleases me.'

'The flame? Or driving them potty?' the Inspector enquires.

'Hah! Both. Good girl. I'm Chase. It's from the French word for chair. Evidently at some point after we left the old home continent for Marseilles my family made its living from the cutting and shaping of wood into uncomfortable furniture. I know it was uncomfortable because I've sat on it: awkward in all the wrong places. I like to introduce myself that way, it lets people know what they're in for.'

What they're in for, the Inspector realises, is quite a lot. It is impossible in the presence of Chase Pakhet – who has so many learned qualifications that she has discarded all of them and just gives her name – to be anything but a student. Even her colleagues at high table no doubt fall into the role.

'Quite a job you've got this month, I gather,' Pakhet says, with a slantendicular glance to catch her response.

'Yes. Quite a job.'

They have come now to the inner sanctum, a wood-panelled college room made dim by the sheer quantity of papers and books it contains – and, to be fair, an old but functional System terminal canted inward from one corner – and arranged not towards the fireplace as its architect no doubt intended, but in a kind of gladiatorial circle around an ancient rug.

'Well, sit down and hit me with it,' Pakhet says. 'You've pre-empted all my classes and supervisions – for which relief much thanks – the faculty are all atwitter and imagine I've been brewing gin in my socks and will be summarily carted off, so I've outraged the bourgeoisie quite nicely for the day and now it's all about the work.'

Neith sits, taking her time to find a comfortable position on a lumpy corduroy chair – the only one in the room apart from Pakhet's which allows its occupant to sit tall. Pakhet nods.

'Very good. No fear of delay and plenty of positional strength. Splendid. We shall get along.'

'Who was that outside?' With Pakhet, the Witness recommends obliquity. Not that the Inspector needed to be told. She can see Pakhet register the choice and decide not to comment. Everything is footnoted for her; if she remarked on all of it she'd never get anything done.

'Marcus? Harmless idiot. Well, not entirely harmless: he's trying to achieve alarm and affray. It's a political engagement, allegedly. The intention is to jolt you out of established patterns of thought, to change the way your mind processes information and force you to examine it more closely. Specifically to point up the differences between machine-based semiotic analysis and human parsing and responses.' She snorts. 'Which, I have to say, he definitely achieved on the stairs. In both your case and his – I doubt it's ever occurred to him that his own thought is as circumscribed as anyone else's. The proximate excuse at the moment is the Monitoring Bill – although I've noticed that dressing up seems to be the chosen answer to a lot of different questions.'

'Is he in favour or against?'

'Oh, nothing so binary. He's concerned at the lack of critique among the proles. He doesn't say proles, of course, but that's what he means: the lumpen proletariat, bane of revolutionists. They are just not interested in what he thinks they should be. I can't tell you how much that offends him – and for some reason which has to do with a rather tendentious reading of Erich Fromm, he thinks the way to deal with that inattention is to blow it up – semiotically, I hasten to add. Therefore: alarm and affray, as you see – though evidently somewhat less of both than he got this time. And to be honest, even I have to acknowledge that he's not an idiot. It's remarkably hard to do what he did.'

'What did he do, exactly?'

'Well, he fooled the System, didn't he? It's a fad among the young tearaways of the faculty at the moment – and I'd just like to take a moment to point out how remarkable it is that we have tearaways at all – where was I? Oh, yes: it's a fad. They noticed that the System tags cultural references in your dress, and after they'd played with it for a while they discovered that there's a narrow band of uncertainty where you can dress as – well, as Charlie Chaplin in *The Great Dictator*, for example – and the System will miss one tier of reference and draw the wrong conclusions. So what they do now is try to find enormously offensive things they can dress up as which they can then shade into something humans read as utterly benign but which still gets red-flagged by the System, demonstrating that machine parsing is imperfect. Well, everyone knows that, so it's perhaps redundant, although the reminders can be somewhat spectacular. I encourage it, of course.'

'Of course?'

'Oh yes. It requires painstaking research, endless attention to detail, a lot of careful reading of subtext and dominant social flow, and a keen awareness of generational and demographic differences in semiotic uptake. Far more valuable than essay writing. It's coursework, set by themselves, meaning I get more time to relax while still tutoring students to the highest grades in their final competitive examinations.'

'And it upsets the faculty.'

'Do you know, you're quite right? I hadn't thought of that. Dearie me, I must write them a very apologetic note. Would you have shot him?'

'Maybe. I read him as Hitler.'

'Yes, you did. Note to self: hypervigilance may narrow the fuzzy range even further. Paranoia, of course, closes it altogether. Well, it was a stun gun. I suppose that would have been educational for him too. Not a Chaplin fan?'

'No, I am.' Endless winter afternoons after school, watching with her head resting on her father's shoulder. She remembers the smell of him, dogs and cologne and wool. Such a long time ago. For a moment she sees his face, lined and delighted, and then he's gone. Emotion chokes her from nowhere, vanishes just as quickly, leaving her briefly frozen in place. Pakhet doesn't seem to notice.

'Then let's just say you're having a bad day. Or does a white face in a black suit mean something else you don't like? Oh. My apologies. I see that it does – but I fancy you are not a coulrophobic, mm? No. Let's have tea, Inspector, and you can tell me what you need.'

Neith shakes off the sudden squall of memory. In fact, Marcus James Dean is the essence of why she's here. The perfumed gentleman named Smith is travelling until Thursday, so Neith has come here for an alternate first opinion. She prefers, in any case, to have more than one expert so that she can check them against one another. The Witness has solved the old question of *quis custodiet*, but there are – demonstrably – limits to its ability in the messier assessment of signs and implications.

Pakhet makes tea. It is apparently a rule with her that you don't talk while it's brewing. Finally she pours, into ridged and painted Victorian cups with spindly handles. 'Now,' she says, lighting a pipe and putting it into her mouth, 'I imagine you're clearer on what you want to ask me.'

The Inspector finds that she likes Chase Pakhet. The woman's bad habits seem to have condensed rather than betrayed her. Smoking – however modified by science – is not good for you, and nor are red wine, whisky or bacon sandwiches, but all these Chase Pakhet avows inter alia are her favourite things. She likes, by her own estimation: bars with loud music; argument and scholarship; young men who flirt with her without meaning it; old men who flirt with her and do mean it; and women of any age who don't get jealous about being upstaged by a woman who looks like a wine barrel. Around her eyes are enough crows' feet to make – the Inspector realises the word is not 'parliament' after all.

Neith had a prepared list, but now on instinct she asks a question off the top of her head, the one that has been bothering her since Shand the bookseller's introduction to the superstitions of Hunter's fans.

'Could you codify a person as text? Put them into a book?'

Whatever Chase Pakhet was expecting, it evidently was not this. Her eyes narrow as if she is about to pooh-pooh the idea, then widen as the denial collides in her head with the unwilled effort of some other aspect of self to work out how such a thing might be done. Neith almost laughs, watching the flow state intrude on someone else's thoughts.

Do I look like that when I'm working a case?

For one familiar with the moment, it's possible to track the stages of its flowering. At any moment – yes. There. Pakhet frowns as the ripples of the first concussions set off their own subsidiary detonations in her mind.

'No,' she says at last. 'No. But.' She makes a motion with her head and shoulders, bending the spine left, then right so that she is her own scales. 'But?'

Pakhet waves her hands. 'But . . . nothing. Imagine you let some clever mechanic loose in a workshop with a brief to build a sewing machine out of spare parts, and when he was done you said he had to build a clock, and he had to build it out of the sewing machine and whatever additional bits he needed, but it still had to be a sewing machine even while it was a clock, and when he managed that you said you wanted an oven and a water pump and a milking machine too, and they all had to come out of the clock or the sewing machine and everything had to work. Yes? So then imagine you did that for ten thousand years until you had a whole city of interconnected machines and the original sewing machine was still in there, humming away, and then someone came along and said they wanted to pack all that into a clutch purse. Into a thimble! No.'

'But.' Pakhet's voice still holds the promise of a but, the mulish unwillingness of an academic challenged on her home ground.

'Oh, well. But. *But* I suppose you could take the tone – not the person but the personality – like poetry. Poetry is a shotgun aimed at our shared experience, hoping to hit enough of the target that we all infer a great bulk of information conveyed as implication and metaphor in an approximately similar way. Making a unity between poet and reader.' Accompanying hand gesture. 'I always wanted to take a connectome image of a group of subjects before and after reading a poem. Or better, keep them in isolation and give them perfectly similar experiences for a week and then make them read a novel. See how much it changed 'em. Would it matter if it was a good novel? How long did the change last? Was the book permanently incorporated into the connectome or was it just a stone in a pond, all splash and ripples and then gone a moment later into the everyday duckshit that rules us all?' She snorts.

'If you took the before picture away from the after picture,' Neith observes, 'you'd have the connectome image of the book in the mind.'

Pakhet starts. 'In so far as such a thing makes sense,' she says. 'Yes, you would. It would be like a single frame from a moving image. A few frames, actually, I suppose, from significant instants in a sequence, allowing the brain to piece together a narrative flow. And before you ask, yes, I suppose you could generate at least a skeletal outline of a text from a person's connectome.'

'A mould.'

'From which one might derive a narrative which would then be as much that person as any such object could be. Which isn't much. Yes.' Pakhet's eyes light for a moment with an inventor's zeal. 'But what would be more interesting, and much more disturbing and illegal, would be whether it was possible to create a mould for a text which would move the broad shape of an audience member's connectome closer to that of a given desired shape. Not putting a person into a book, but iterating that person in the minds of anyone who read it.'

'Like choice architecture.' The use of big data and nuance to influence political decision-making: the attempt to corrupt the political process by deliberate manipulation of the cognitive limitations of the human mind. Almost all restaurant menus use it, and even knowing what it is, diners are still influenced: the steak or the lobster is always mountainously expensive. Once you've rejected that, the less expensive stew seems like a bargain, and having saved money you splash out on drinks. Subscription prices and two-for-one deals are the same. But in the political context, the System reserves the right to prosecute it as a crime somewhere between fraud and treason.

'Like advanced neurolinguistic behavioural psychotopology,' Pakhet snaps. 'I don't call you a Praetorian, you don't call me a spin doctor. Yes. Fascinating idea, gratifyingly impossible.'

Possession by ghost book does not strike her as fascinating so much as terrifying. 'Impossible?'

'For anything but the broadest statements: love good, hate bad. Everyone begins with a similar junk pile and has to build a city, but everyone goes about it rather differently. I suppose you might manage the trick for one person, but not for a mass. And it wouldn't last. The duckshit hypothesis is in fact the correct one. Our minds are not marble sculptures, they're a campfire boiling a couple of pints of mud in a bone bucket. In any case ... Well, enticing though it is, that cannot possibly be what you came here to ask.'

Neith shakes her head in agreement. No.

'I have a sackful of signs. I need to know what they mean.'

'Wrong door.'

The Inspector waits.

'You're no fun at all,' Pakhet complains. 'I thought I'd have you up in arms with that one.'

'No.'

'No, so I see. I shall try harder. All right: I can tell you what they might mean, but if they're not obvious it will be a guess. That kind of interpretation is a life's work. A life's work of a life's work, quite often. I take it your signs are somehow connected?'

'That's what I need to know.'

'But I mean, authorship or context.'

'Yes. They're all from one interview.'

Pakhet looks up.

'Ahhh. And when we say "interview", we're talking about the unmediated sort. Straight from the horse's cerebellum. My old stamping ground, as you no doubt know.'

'Yes.'

'All right, give me the skinny.'

The Inspector smiles. 'You read pulp,' she accuses.

Chase Pakhet assumes a lofty expression. 'Pulp crime, yes. Of course I do. It's my job.'

'And you like it.'

'My own emotional response is hardly the point.'

'But you do.' Neith finds herself somehow scandalised, either by the evident fact or the elusive response. Pakhet holds up her hands to acknowledge the touch.

'I do not like it, I love it. I love it for its cheap trashiness, its wicked women and its unrepentantly vivid sex. I love the violence, the moral turpitude, and the absoluteness of right and wrong in a universe that pretends to be shaded with grey. I love its clear signing and rich cast of archetypes and markers. Pulp is the vector for Eco, the cloak of Chandler, the soft pillow of Virginia Woolf, the birth caul of *Cold Comfort Farm*, the fairy godmother of Doris Lessing and William Gibson. Pulp is the key to open the doors not only of Freud and Jung, but even of Barthes, who stole everything from Calvino anyway but let us not go down that road for fear we shalln't return this night. Yes, Inspector, clap me in irons. I am a nerd. Speak, and I shall be your oracle.'

With gathering confidence, and interrupted by brief sections displayed on Pakhet's terminal, Mielikki Neith speaks.

*

'Aaaall righty,' Chase Pakhet says when she has heard it all. 'Allons y.' She closes her eyes and lifts her pen from the yellow legal pad on which she has been taking notes. 'I don't need to tell you there's a lot going on, I take it?'

'No.'

'Good.'

Pakhet stands up and goes to her bookshelf – the Inspector is now primed to see this object as a signifier of academic authority and therefore also a tool for the architectural intimidation of Pakhet's more boisterous students – and retrieves a single slim volume from which the dust jacket has been removed. Her footsteps are heavy but quite silent. 'Let's dispense with the idea that I don't know whose interview we're talking about, shall we?'

The Inspector sighs, then nods.

'And you no doubt are looking for her books. No, don't get excited, this isn't one, or not exactly. It's a critique. The most I have ever been able to find.'

'You're a fan?'

'I'm a scholar,' Pakhet snaps, 'and so was she, whatever else she was.' She relents. 'I am also a fan. I wrote to her more than once asking for clarification. Never got an answer. Oracular in life, as evidently in death. Here:

'Hunter's cities are all one city. Each house opens its door on to a street that is all streets. Cobbles reveal themselves from a given perspective to be bitumen or limestone flagging, and all roads are runways, canals or rivers, so that one might go from London to Boston to Amsterdam as easily as from number nine to number twelve. Growing bolder, one might leave the immediate white European neighbourhood and pass on to Cairo or Kirghizia, to Santiago de las Vegas or Addis Ababa. The journey of a thousand miles does not begin with a single step; it is one step. Humanity exists in a unitary urban sprawl whose laws may vary and whose travel infrastructure may take more or less time in conventional space to connect any given part with any other, but in these fictions there is no such difficulty and the conceptual truth

becomes the practical. The reader and therefore also de facto the protagonists move from one room to the next without passing through the intervening space, because there is none. Life is a series of cinematic elisions, and we do not wait in waiting rooms or get bored, we simply 'cut to'. Place and time in the world — as in the act of consuming the text — are notional and a matter of opinion. Like Wilhelm Reich, the prisoner walks through walls. In Quaerendo, the modern reader, contemporaneously convicted as a killer by Mr Murder, voluntarily incarcerates herself with the narrator in a prison constructed by the Mad Cartographer in the distant future, awaiting the judgement which was rendered hundreds of years before by the Five Cardinals as part of their plot against the Roman Empire. Perhaps every day is 14 June 1986, the date upon which the world came closest to total nuclear war. Perhaps the bombs fell and the release of energy has utterly extinguished temporality and we exist in a permanent exception to the rules of physics we painstakingly assemble.

'In the apparent reality I experience, as surveillance breaches the walls of the mind itself, identity takes flight and seeks to exist across physical locations. If this cannot be done in actuality, it is done symbolically and psychologically. We locate ourselves outside our bodies, in speech, on screens, and in art, becoming more than single loci which can be constrained: finding escape in dissolution into a suspension from which we precipitate at each point of conscious interaction with others, just as we are told that matter itself may exist only at the point of collision. We avoid the transmissible psychopathy of deindividuation only by accepting a redefinition of individuality. At the same time, an increasingly ontological science tells us that the world we see is no more real than the ones we imagine: the universe is not what it appears to be at our clumsy macro-Newtonian level. Are we simulations? What does that question even mean? How is an informational model of a quantum world different from a quantum world made of information? As government takes steps to control the inside of our heads, freedom reaches to a future where even physical reality is not legislated; where what is written in stone is no more fixed than dreams or water. To escape a fascism that has become internal,

we embrace an external world that is ultimately fluid and where the tyranny of the real itself is moot.

'The corollary is that a book is not finished until it is read. The writing is not complete until what is said has passed from the physical volume which gives it sensory reality into another mind where it kindles thoughts and impressions: a whole understanding of what it means to be, ignited on foreign soil in an act that is either erotic or imperialistic, but in either case miraculous. We become one another. Ink on paper is the frozen matter of a person, a snapshot of selfhood in fungal spores waiting to be quickened in our borrowed mentation, thought shaping itself in us, of us, to emerge from us. If all cities are one city, does that not also imply that all persons are one person? And if so, who?'

The Inspector catches at the penultimate lines. 'Borrowed mentation.'

Pakhet nods. 'Yes. I wouldn't have bothered you with it if you hadn't asked your remarkable question. Quite unexpected. And pleasing. You follow in her track, at least a little. Well done.'

'But the rest . . .'

'No,' Pakhet agrees. 'It could mean anything. I think that's part of the point. Information so densely specific that it becomes poetic and allusory. Obfuscation as indoctrination. What you puzzle out for yourself you must by definition incorporate into who you are even if you reject it. She's forcing us to see the world through her eyes in order to understand what she says. It's scientifically demonstrable these days, but the Frankfurt School were doing it instinctively in the 1940s – though they went all out on being infuriating and somewhat less on being poetic. Get down on your knees and cry God for Baudrillard. It takes a Frenchman, evidently, to demand that if it must be whimsical and impenetrable, it should also be enjoyable. But you can see why everyone gets so excited about her.'

'Her?'

'Well, it's unattributed, which to me screams that Hunter wrote it herself. The author writing about her own books, which no one else can now locate or read, meaning that they were complete, for a while, and now have ceased to exist in the sense she's suggesting. You see? Perhaps she bought all the copies and destroyed them. Perhaps some of them never existed at all and she made the world believe that they did – kindling the responses without the books and making a disembodied mind. Don't quote me. This all is something of a hot topic in my particular community, and everyone spends far too much time dissecting what everyone else says, because we don't have the primary texts to talk about. Scan this, if you like. I'm afraid it's not much more than an essay: large print. But I don't let the hard copy out of my sight. It took me seven years to find and even then I had to arm wrestle an Italian collector who said he'd seen it first. Quite an undignified scene.'

'Had he?' Neith asks.

'Yes,' Chase Pakhet says. 'But I pinched him as hard as I could on the inner thigh and paid for it while he was screaming. I can't blame him – I should think it was extraordinarily painful. I had quite long nails at the time.' She shrugs. 'More prosaically: in the first instance your interrogation narratives comprise a story about lies and truth. Someone is always lying. Someone is always telling the truth. Sometimes these things are being done at the same time by the same person. Fraud becomes reality. There are cuckoos everywhere, laying eggs in other people's nests. I take it your subject was not enamoured of the interview process?'

'No.'

'No, she wouldn't have been. Ornery old cow, that much seems obvious.' This, from Chase Pakhet, implies an immensity of stubbornness that is daunting to contemplate even now. Neith sternly reminds herself to focus on the old woman. The one in front of her.

Pakhet goes on. 'Fire and alchemy. The transformation of one thing into another. Nothing is only itself, or conversely everything is one thing. Death is transformation, and we see death in many forms, bringing change. Judgement. Hints of Faust, but we are offered Orpheus and his catabasis. The flow of life is broken and everything is held in stasis until it can be resumed. Honey means eternity, but bees were said to spring from the carcasses of the dead. Simulation claiming authenticity over other simulations.'

'And over reality.'

'Yes. Always assuming there is such a thing. Perhaps it's turtles all the way down, and the bottom turtle rests on the back of the top one.'

The Inspector waves away this invitation to engage in existential doubt. 'Not everything is circular.'

'No,' Pakhet agrees. 'The Chamber of Isis is a single solid point. Archimedes' fulcrum: the place where things can actually be real – or perhaps where the primacy of realities is assigned. Athenais can raise her son from the dead. The vase can be unbroken, the world made whole. The Alkahest is the solution to everything, the Holy Grail: a Universal Solvent that will heal all wrongs and empower the merest mortal to judge gods and bind monsters to her will. A new beginning is promised in the conjunction of things. The Chamber of Isis is not so much a place as it is a circumstance. A perilous one, as the chapel of the Grail always is. There must be sacrifice.'

'Symbolically speaking.' Kyriakos's words, emerging as if unbidden from the Inspector's mouth.

'Why must everyone say that? Yes, symbolically speaking. I always used to get furious with the nuns at school when they said that modern theology understood the Creation took more than seven days, that it was all symbolic. Why? Why should it? Perhaps billions of years of astrophysical and biochemical evolution is what seven days of God's work looks like from inside. Or if you prefer: there's a very real chance the basic unit of our universe is information. Meaning is as fundamental as matter.'

The thunderous professorial frown obscures Pakhet's eyes under beetle brows. Neith does not quail, but asks her next question as if working from a list, almost as if she is becoming bored. She lets her lack of affect stand as a tacit reminder that she is not an undergraduate.

'How would you have handled it? In the room?'

Chase Pakhet twitches. Was the subtextual rebuke a resounding shout to her? Or is she just unused to contradiction, even unvoiced? She nods acknowledgement, then pauses again to consider the question – a momentous acknowledgement of complexity in itself.

'I'd have said: okay. If that's what you want to do, that's what we'll do. This is a narrative blockade. It's been tried before, at a much lower level of sophistication. You tell stories to yourself until they become almost as real as your life, and you try to knit them into your memory so that the machines can't tell the difference. It doesn't work. This is clever, in that way: there's no attempt to match reality, just a wall of dreams. We know it isn't real, because the subject is demonstrably not a two-thousand-year-old alchemist, say – well, I suppose she isn't – but that doesn't help us. So I'd go with it. Let the story run out. When it's done, it's done, and we're back with the real person.'

'They did that.'

'And it didn't work, because the story just rolled on and on. Yes.'

'You expected that?'

'I suppose. If I was doing this, I'd anticipate that and I'd manage things so that the act of looking would trigger the creation of more narrative. The observer's scrutiny is the inception point, so as long as the interrogation continues, the story does too. A kind of feedback loop producing a functional infinity: wherever you look, there's more. Practice would do it, like learning to know you're dreaming. The really clever part is that over time the interrogation would reinforce the neuroplastic architecture rather than breaking it down. Exhausting, though.'

Yes.

'Yes.'

'So I'd ... what would I do then, if I was running the interview and it wasn't working? I'd try to make the individual storylines untenable. I'd nudge to make them painful, or sad or frightening. I'd make them more – I don't know: crowded.'

'Crowded?'

'It's not quite what I mean. I'd raise the level of coincidence. You'd keep bumping into the same people until it was just absurd. The goal is to collapse the narratives all back to the origin, the real person. The flaw in her construction is the one that has to be there – they all must ultimately revolve around a single point, which is her. Can't escape your own head. The conjunction, the Chamber, the Alkahest ... is the solution. She's telling us how to win and then making it almost impossible to act on the information. Perhaps if the narratives become implausible in their own terms, that gets harder to resist – which is why they are all on some level fantastical. Magical thinking allows her an elasticity which neo-realism would not. In the end, the conjunction only occurs if she wants it to or if she can't stand the alternative. Do you get any sense of her at all?'

'She's leaking. She should be unconscious, but she's there.'

'Yes, she will be. She's holding an umbrella open in a storm. And that's my next step, if I'm the interviewer. I'd put something in with her. A new narrative that would draw the others back together. Done right, she wouldn't even know it was there, she'd think it was her own. Especially under stress, the mind would adopt it. If she's good she'll instinctively weave a new thread into what she's already doing without even recognising that it's a threat. She's torn herself apart: she wants to come back together! And composition is collision, synthetic as much as original. Authors are accretors. So you'd have to prod it along, keep it yours. Hope to get inside her design and appropriate it before your design is itself appropriated.'

'A cuckoo.'

'Yes. A counter-narrative. It might already be in there.'

'So if someone did do that ...'

'Then if they were any good, you can't be entirely sure which threads are hers and which belongs to the interrogation team. No. If you were able to be sure, so could she.'

'But she might suspect.'

'Yes. Images of subversion.'

There was a Trojan horse in Hunter's own mind, and despite everything, she knew, oh yes. The Inspector breathes deeply, pushes down into her diaphragm: vagus nerve reset. Nausea subsides.

'Yes,' Pakhet says. 'If she could get to this point, she would anticipate the possibility. She might have designed a place for it in the hope of countering it. The more easily the mind accepts the additional thread, the more quickly it will belong to her.'

And the more quickly Hunter's overtaxed mind would fragment. The less time she would have before she died. Was cognitive exhaustion an arithmetical progression? A geometric one? How many hours of life would one additional narrative have cost her?

'Why did she do this?'

'You're asking me?'

'I'm asking if there's anything in the signs.'

'Hah. You'd make me a haruspex after all, reading her guts.'

Both of us.

Neith does not respond out loud. She just waits. Pakhet closes her eyes, touches her fingers together as if feeling for answers in the whorls of her own skin.

'It is an obfuscation, a shell game. A rigged one on both sides. Whichever shell the interviewer chooses is the wrong one, but he can make her play over and over again until she slips up. She accepts that. In fact, she wants to be known.'

'Why?'

'You mean what makes me say so? Because she's leaving you clues. If all she wanted to do was block the interview, and she was prepared to die, these narratives could be so much salad. They need not be deep or profound. They could be junk mail. Advertisements for foot powder. The endless duckshit, yes? But they're rich. At the very least, she wants to advertise the enormity of the act of vandalism that is trespass in her head. "Look," she says, "here is a palace of reason that you have made into rubble." Mm?'

'Yes.'

'So: clues, and there are two ways in which she might be revealed. In one she succumbs to her interrogators and she loses. She gives up everything she knows. In the other, the pieces fall together to convey a message. We must assume it is concealed in the narratives. You do not really see the painter or the banker, you see aspects of the woman herself. They are not only camouflage, they are information. The human eye – the human mind – sees relationships, not objects. A lizard on a branch is a leaf until it moves. We are things that see volitional patterns like ourselves. We see them even when they are not there, in clouds and in bathwater. When the pieces are correctly aligned – in the conjunction, yes? – all will be revealed.'

'The Chamber of Isis?'

'Yes. Symbolically. Or actually.'

'What can she possibly hope to achieve?' It comes out laced with agony, and Pakhet's eyes open wide.

'Oh!' she breathes, almost gentle. 'This, of course. This is part of it. You would not be human if you did not sympathise. She has created these stories to be sympathetic. You and she want the same thing, if in different ways. You want to know her secrets, she wants you to know them – the only difference in your perspectives is that she does not want you to know her as text, she needs you to see through her eyes. "At the last," she tells you, "you must become like me in order to solve me."'

'She's wrong.'

Pakhet purses her lips like a doctor who has just delivered the diagnosis and is now seeing a familiar reaction. 'Classically, in a Grail quest, you must believe that because your journey is incomplete.'

'I'm on a journey?'

'The river of life is stopped. Only an Alkahest can set it right – an absolute solution drunk from the healing cup. She must anoint a knight who will retrieve the cup and renew the land.'

'I thought *she* was the knight. She's the one entering the underworld.'

Pakhet shifts her head again, this way, that way. 'There can be many knights. Or many knights at different times. Imagine a game of musical chairs: each chair has a hat on it. When you sit in the chair, you wear the hat. You are the hierophant or the pilgrim. You are the judge or the hanged man. You are the sacrifice or the god. It all depends—'

'On where you're standing at the conjunction.' Neith resists the urge to scream. 'Catabasis first, the journey through the underworld. The interrogation.'

'Yes.'

'Then apocatastasis, the new beginning. Sacrifice and rebirth.'

'That bit is a palindrome. The flow of time in either direction produces the same expression of events.'

'So where are we in the pattern?'

Pakhet's arms embrace the room. The world. She does not speak, and eventually Neith sighs. 'I take it that depends on where we are in the pattern.'

'Where *you* are; her catabasis is not necessarily yours. Perhaps that is the point of your investigation: it unites you with her and inducts you into the mysteries. You are a Grail Knight, a shield of the weak on a holy mission to heal the wounded land. You must ask the healing questions. And this is the trouble with being that person: you're caught in the narrative. You come to me for resolution, but all I do is give you fresh and larger tasks.'

'I don't even have a shield,' Neith objects.

'Really,' Pakhet says. 'You don't, eh? Well then. Take out what is in your pockets and lay it all on the table.'

And of course, when she does, there's her Witness badge, gleaming in the half light: Aegis, surmounted by an eye.

'Good enough for me,' Chase Pakhet says.

Seeing Neith's dismay, she laughs.

*

Outside it's a winter afternoon, and everything is blinding or black with no middle ground. The Inspector boards a bus and sits in the front seats at the top, watching the city go by. Sometimes this brings her answers, or free associations that take her in new and profitable directions of inquiry. Today she just watches London and thinks of nothing, and that is almost as good.

Except, at the end of the ride, she finds herself staring at the single black hemisphere of the bus camera, and knowing it's watching her.

*

The Inspector does not remember, opening her door, the business of returning home. So often in life it is that which we do all the time that simply slips away from us between instants. She makes coffee and stretches, feeling the improvement in her hurts, then sits in silence for a while in front of the crime wall, letting the slow shifting of facts and suppositions roll in front of her like a sea. Then she stands.

She demands, and instantly receives, a full curriculum vitae of Oliver Smith and a proper introduction to the role and governance of the Turnpike Trust. As soon as she starts to review the documents, she realises that they are enormous and rejects them, requiring the Witness to present her with a working precis. Smith has all the best qualifications, which she doesn't care about, and all the usual connections, habits, personal life and quirks, which she also doesn't care about. He has been working in his current position for an average number of years, has been promoted rapidly (she tells the Witness to establish by whom and for what, and prepare a summary) and is seen as the coming man. The Turnpike Trust is one of those deceptively boring backwaters of government where power begins as the consequence of a willingness to take on jobs that are necessary but unglamorous, and thereafter accumulates because they're already doing so much and doing it tolerably well. It is not technically part of the state, but is a chartered and contracted non-governmental actor, CCNGAs having replaced the infamous QUANGOs and PPPs of long ago and far away. In fact, the Trust is not new but very old, having been formed to provide highway infrastructure before the Victorian era and never entirely gone away. Like the Worshipful Company of Fan Makers, who took to their bosom the engineers of jet engines, they have adapted and evolved from upstart to powerhouse and now are infrastructure, no more noticed and no less vital to the apparatus of administration than electricity, or indeed than the fibre-optic cable they maintain.

Neith puts that aside, and asks one more question. The answer is interesting.

Oliver Smith has never used the kinesic assistant in a personal setting.

The Inspector allows that this does not mean he did not use it that way with her. Her instinct, however, tells her it was otherwise.

He had something he wished to conceal, and that something relates directly to the Hunter case.

She pores over his life, drinking more coffee. At some point, the crime wall now projected on the wall opposite her bed, she is forced to acknowledge that even the most fraught investigative day must eventually come to an end. And if her dreams are Diana Hunter's, well: surely a change is as good as a rest.

Only when she stands at the gates of sleep does it occurs to her that Oliver Smith is an even bigger liar than she realised.

Plant your pole. The same voice, richly persuasive, loving its own sound. *Or do we not do that any more, with the parabolic skis?*

She stares up at the ceiling in the darkened room.

Bloody hell. It was him, interrogating Hunter. It was him.

i'll give you a counter-narrative

The universe has cancer.

It has one tiny, appallingly deadly tumour which cannot be excised. In the future, the tumour will expand and it will eat into the universe until there is nothing left, and then the cancer will be the universe, but we won't be in it. We'll be dead, and in fact we'll never have existed at all, because the cancer will have swallowed time and unravelled it and nothing which has ever happened in this universe will exist anymore, not even as history.

There's a certain justice in that, because it's what our universe did in order to come into existence in the first place: it devoured what was here before, although you can't really say that because whatever was here before never existed and there was no such place as 'here'.

You see this cannibalistic behaviour up and down the cosmic scale, with stars and microbes and so on all eating their parents. There's a kind of spider which does basically the same thing. It's a perfectly ordinary event in the life cycle of a universe, but obviously it's unpleasant if it happens to be your universe that is being erased, and I don't really care if the next universe is going to be a kind of heaven where everyone is happy and there's no pain and no wickedness. I don't care if the next universe is the perfect one and this one is warped and disgusting, if other universes in their selfish little bubbles of reality give it a wide berth because it mutters to itself and smells. I don't care if the universe I was born in is the leper universe and the next one is the Christ. Fuck the next universe. Just fuck it. I don't like it and I'm going to kill it.

I am going to kill it, and I am going to hollow it out and we are all going to live inside its corpse like a hermit crab in a shell, and I'm going to do the same to the one after that, and the one after that, and so on for ever and ever, and that makes me some sort of monster but I don't care.

I am Gnomon, occasionally called the Eschatogenesist, or sometimes the Desperation Protocol. Come with me if you want to live.

*

It's the future. Deal with it.

Actually, as far as I'm concerned, it's just the present, and everything I am talking about here is normal, but to your tiny, bounded and distressingly localised self my society no doubt seems like a fantasy. The seeds of it are all around you, but you're desperate to avoid noticing them. You live in the foundation stones of a city of boundless spires, but you turn your face to the dust.

Did you know that in 2014 two rats shared one mind over a wire three thousand miles long? Have you heard that a man in Japan can read your dreams from your head with a machine? No. You sit reading news that has nothing new in it, telling yourself that because you hold in your hand some glossy skeuomorphic lozenge you are technologically au fait, and that because you know where in the endless repetition of tribal politics and fairydust economics your world is, or have consumed many of those books published in pale cream jackets by university presses, you are somehow informed about what is important.

You are not. Meaning is being made in the saccades and the interstitial spaces you ignore. When the miracles begin, you will declare that the world has taken a great leap forward, and – wearing the amazed expression of a pantomime clown – you will quote Proust as tomorrow's children make jokes that derive their humour from puns invoking senses you do not have. You will wear your bewilderment first as modish nostalgia and then as politically charged performance art, and finally as a proud, doomed ethical position whose idiot gravity you cannot escape. You will go to your grave protesting that everyone else has misunderstood. Oh, bravo. Bravo.

By way of orientation: I am so far past the moment you consider 'now' that the calendar and the continents you know are both gone. The constellations you would recognise have faded as their stars burned out or the slow, inexorable motion of the galaxies shunted them into new apparent shapes from the tiny vantage point of our birth world. When people speak of the cradle of humanity, they no longer mean Africa but Earth, and like any cradle it is left behind, even lost. We've probably still got it somewhere, in an attic or under the stairs. Certainly we never actually meant to throw it away. But you can't use it as interior deco for ever – sooner or later, you have to admit to yourself that those days are gone. They were gone a long, long time ago. Now, instead of your world, we have mine, and it is better. I am considered human now: you would no longer make the grade. In this new world, many people – most, in fact – exist across bodies. That is to say that their thoughts are distributed between a large number of individual brains rather than concentrated in just one. Each individual body has a little doodad in it that sends and receives messages to all the others, and because that doodad is very, very sophisticated and makes use of some properties of the universe that you probably don't want to think about too much – even if your culture already knows about them and is starting to work with them today, now, your now – there is no lag in the communication. It's just as if they were one enormous brain. In fact, the slowest bit is the actual biological thinking, because biology takes forever by comparison with computing.

I am not many. I am one. But I am in many places at once, and those places are very far apart. Got it?

You are little and I am big.

I hear your objection, drab and small, that the aspiring serial murderer of cosmoses is not well-placed to judge humanity. Tell me again about your time, so full of compassion and fellow feeling. No? Well, you're right, of course. We have not transcended wickedness. Even now, in this distant reach beyond everything you know, there are bad people still. On the other hand, the commonplace sins of your time are rather quaint. We are different from you, as you are different from some cave-grubbing ape.

Somewhat different from an ape, anyway.

*

I say 'we' but actually the other humans of this age are not much better. I have relationships that are almost like loose friendships: I nod at the woman behind the counter, the man on the park bench – and never mind that they are present in a dozen other places, doing a dozen other things. It is polite these days to frame your discourse as if you were exclusively local. I find that odd, like making love through a hole in a sheet. With the more eccentric people I know, who feel the same way, I play games of Go across light years and smile when I lose. Go is the only game that survives futurity, because it is art as much as war.

Still, as I say, even these transcendent minds feel small to me, perhaps two-dimensional. I do like them. I just feel they're a bit limited, is all. It's like how it would be for you if you were still a child and your toys could talk.

In all of the worlds and places that I know, in all the babble of connected post-humanity, there's really only one person I truly feel is like me: the mad planet called Zagreus.

Zagreus isn't actually a planet, it's just that the planet on which it lives is only occupied by Zagreus: a single mind inhabiting every organism living on the whole world. Z receives visitors from time to time, and provides them – myself included – with bright, clean bodies to walk around in as a practical courtesy, but it's a temporary situation only. When you breathe there, you're breathing Zagreus, taking in its tiny microscopic selves, and that has consequences. If you stay for too long, you start to bleed into the mosaic of consciousness that is Zagreus all around you. You see visions, hear things. Zagreus sends shoots into you – it can't help it. I don't object because the nature of my identity is more resilient than most, but for other people it is alarming, and even dangerous.

I am Gnomon. In the end, that statement is so fundamental that it endures. If the planet swallowed me entirely it would inevitably take on my concern – my obsession, if you like, with the extinction of all things – and in doing so it would become Gnomon. I would be changed, and I would expand, and the resulting thing would be both more me and more Z. I'm sure we've both considered what that would be like, the way old friends sometimes wonder if they should try to kindle a romance, but in the end it is perhaps too great a risk for either of us. Neither of us became what we are by accident.

For others … well. They might end up swallowed, inhaled, almost by accident, digested into the stew of Z's bodymind. Even the Outbound think Z is odd, somewhere between a person and a hive. But then, who knows what they think of me? They're not saying – at least not to my face.

Zagreus called me today for a meeting. It was like a cloud of butterflies landing on my hand: a strange, soft pressure, an unsettling invasion, an action that is inappropriate and unanticipated. Zagreus doesn't reach out. It responds, it slumbers, it changes itself. It seems to be obsessed with models, maps and landscapes, right down to the subatomic scale – hence its peculiar physical choices: it wants to get closer to the tiny, to touch the edges of perceptible events. Molecular cognition is still grossly enormous by comparison with quanta, so Z is no doubt looking for ways to invest itself in structured energy, pico-architecture. Most people think that's impossible, but Zagreus is Zagreus, just as I am Gnomon. We don't need anyone else. Certainly we don't need one another – but today Zagreus came to me. Why? For fun? To chat? Or to warn me the world is ending? It's Zagreus, it could be anything: fungal bloom in the south continent causing some sort of longing for companionship, or an existential crisis apprehended in some unlikely vegetative mode of thinking that touches the basic fabric of the universe. It sticks out, uncomfortable in the loose mutual orbit that is our acquaintance.

No way to know except to answer the phone.

*

The ingenuity of the human mind is one of the qualities we most relish in ourselves, so it shouldn't surprise anyone that we achieved new crimes as we evolved. As our technological progress first made us long-lived and then painted us in various stripes of post-mortality, so we found new ways to outrage one another and in consequence new ways to be punished. The strangest of the new sins is perhaps the one called wetjacking, or more formally in books of law 'disconnection with intent to subsume'.

All right, if you're still listening, let's get to the good part, which is about crime.

Living across multiple bodies is, obviously, safer than sole-substrate existence – that's living in one body, as you do – because it's wildly unlikely that all your brains should be in an accident at once, especially if you make sure one or two of them are somewhere nice and secure. But this same precautionary approach of putting your eggs in a large number of baskets and distributing those baskets all over the place makes us vulnerable to the peculiar sin known as wetjacking, in which one such body is severed from its overarching mind and held incommunicado, an incapable semi-person with enough awareness to be afraid and alone. The wetjacker then takes advantage of this suggestible state to force a new, alternative connection, integrating the experience and memories of the kidnapped body into his or her own mind, stealing a fragment of personality and selfhood, and swallowing, in primitive terms, a little of the target's soul. Espionage is sometimes conducted in this way, but wetjacking can also be motivated by simple boredom. It's a way to get high, and in fact in some rather bohemian societies on the edge of what is termed the Continuance, it's even a sort of rite of passage, a way of counting coup.

Different legal codes give different weight to a variety of factors in penalising the offence: the number of bodies the victim has remaining and the share of mind which has thus been taken; the brutality of the conditions in which the disconnected self is held; the motivation behind the assault; the difficulty of reintegrating the lost fragment. In one case, at least, the self, once detached from the wetjacker, spent so long in a legal limbo that it developed a unique identity and sued – successfully – to avoid returning to its original. This process is not unknown when units are accidentally separated from the whole, and is called calving, after the same phenomenon in glaciers. A calf is generally regarded as the equivalent of a child, although some see it as a belated twin.

There is a little-known negative version of wetjacking that has no formal name, and this one I find more morally intriguing. It is difficult and dangerous, and in the most profound sense self-defeating. The aspirant criminal places all base thoughts and desires in one body, slowly forcing that brain to accept memories of pain or humiliation, impulses to violence and wrongdoing, collecting all that is unwanted in a life. That body is then ejected from the connection and – mostly – euthanised. One major difficulty is that the memory of how this euthanasia is to be carried out must also be stored in the severed unit – lest the whole process be marred by the recollection of a form of self-mutilation or suicide – and therefore the criminal is first in the position of devising an appalling deathtrap for himself or herself, and then subsequently – as the severed unit – desperate to get out of it. Such collections of wicked selfhood characteristically possess more animus than ordinary lone fragments, and are therefore more aware and more capable. Daring escapes and subsequent pursuits are not unknown, and where both originator and scapegoat are identified there is a knotty question of whether they should be unwillingly reunited.

In the event that they are not, the scapegoat itself presents society with a fresh difficulty: in some few cases the interaction of different pains and rages in their new setting produces an almost saintly character (while oftentimes the thing left behind, remembering, as it were, being raised on sweetmeats and experiencing only love, will prove itself selfish and unpleasant), but for the most part the scapegoats are unbalanced and dangerous. They may assert and find a legal right to their separate existence, but their nature is to build empires, lay low nations and express their anger through the infliction of suffering on those who offend them. The possession of a multitude of physical bodies does not diminish the experience of pain – the twenty other instances of a man whose local presence is having an index finger crushed in a vise will all scream – and so scapegoats are dangerous and frightening even now. Several of modern history's more ruthless and violent crooks have been scapegoats who somehow eluded capture and then took over someone else's life, vanishing from society until they were ready to do something truly appalling. We're mostly past that point now, and it's hard to define criminality or wrongdoing in a setting where conventional human living is a pastime rather than a necessity, a sort of ongoing theatrical production in which whole populations of humans engage, but to the extent these considerations still apply, it's one of our greatest dilemmas: what to do with those who don't fit into the most inclusive environment of which humanity is capable?

To this quandary a solution was inevitably created: a remote place was given over to healing and transcendence, and with equal inevitability that place became a scapegoat in its own right, so that to it were sent not only criminal minds but also anyone else who did not fit, who took actions which – while in no sense illegal or immoral – were too unsettling to contemplate, who pursued thoughts or philosophies considered dangerous by those who did not share them. And finally there went also the outcasts and the drifters, by dint of that strange human gravity which at certain times appoints one place the locus of all that is odd and ill-suited, and from a bubbling pool of psychological toxins periodically ejects genius. Thus it was not only a hospital for the violently insane, but also a skunkworks, a commune and a school of art. We called it the Last House.

Until genius, strangeness, community and criminality combined in a remarkable gesture, and the whole place unified its many identities in an unprecedented melding, the assorted bad and good voluntarily surrendering the distinction between themselves to create a single mind of unheralded capacity in furtherance of a project so vast and arrogant that even persons whose physical shapes were spread across the empty night between stars, and whose perception encompassed atoms and aeons with equal facility, were beggared and appalled by its scope.

In case you haven't realised, I'm talking about me. I am everything that was in that prison, all bound up and made whole. That's my crime: I was born different – born out of the Dämmerung into the breaking wave of the Verständnis.

*

I walk an instance to the nearest transit room and touch in. White walls, clinical calm. In some places the transit rooms look like doctors' surgeries; in others like magical stagecoaches. It's the old debate of style and substance, minimalism and embellishment. I don't find it exciting. A transit room gets you somewhere. It connects you. It's a misnomer because nothing is really moved in space or time: it should be called an entanglement room. Hundreds of thousands of years down the line from our monkey ancestors, though, the subjective experience of closing your eyes in one place and opening them somewhere else still means movement to us, so there we are. A transit room is a little slice of liminal existence, I suppose, and probably quite profound, but in the real world it's not much more exciting than a drain cover. Yes, I know: you can learn the history of industry and urbanisation from drain covers. I don't care.

I touch in, and say: 'Zagreus,' and Zagreus responds by opening a way for me, meshing my entanglement with an instance that is already prepared.

It has occurred to me from time to time that Z might be an actual alien, or a machine intelligence that has crossed Recursion Gap and become truly alive. There's something about it that goes beyond the inherent oddness of being an autophagous planetary consciousness and touches another level of wrongness, something that invokes a deep, skittering fear of the dark. Zagreus is definitely not your average bear.

I open my doors, and let the new instance flow into me and vice versa, knowing that a little part of Zagreus comes too, like flu in a closed room.

'Hello, Z.'

Come into my parlour.

Z thinks it's funny.

*

The name comes from the Ionian word zagre, meaning a pit for the capture of live prey. The original Zagreus was eaten by Titans and his heart, gestating in a mortal woman, became the god of wine and madness. It is safe to assume that mothers do not generally call their children 'Zagreus'. That's something you do to yourself, if you want to advertise your terrible socialisation to your peers. Although it hardly needs saying once you see what Zagreus is and how it lives.

I'm in an alabaster cavern full of white bodies, still and quiet. It's like an underwater cave full of blind fish, yet each and every one of them can see me, and knows I am not like them. Each and every one of them amounting to exactly one, in the end. I think of sea anemones on a coral reef, and clown fish nestling in their stingers, and wonder what will happen if my mucus doesn't pass muster. Well, I'll get stung, and it will hurt, and then I'll be back where I was again, none the worse, save I'll have to uproot the little bits of Z left behind in me and burn them out. Zagreus has redecorated: there are burning torches on the walls in place of electric light, and they burn with a pale flame that makes everything a little two-dimensional and strange.

I said I like Z, and I do, but that's not to say I don't also recognise that it's a predator, of sorts. They had an outbreak on Marrish, a few years back. The entire north polar region became infected and started building a cave just like this one. The global militia went in and cauterised the place, and Z had to pay a lot of compensation, about which it doesn't care at all because, being a planet and a thought innovator, it's very rich. They still have occasional epidemics, but they've got a vaccine now, and it works pretty well.

The closest Zagreus says:

'DoyoufullyunderstandthatwithinthestructureyouareinsidethethoughtofZag reusandallthatyouseeisthoughtmaderealandthatallthathappensthereisdreamin gbutthatyouareflleshandfleshcanbeharmedandchangedascanmindbutthat'safar morenebulousdIscussionfraughtwithvariablesandsubjectivejudgementsthatfra nklyembodiesthepursuitofuselessknowledge?'

Not that anyone understands what that means if they haven't been here before. 'Yes.'

The instance shrugs, and turns away. I think Z has done something to itself since I was last here, something predictably wrong-headed. I can feel the fraying in its make-up as interference in my own stream of thoughts. I think it has essentially performed a sort of advanced corpus callosotomy on itself; it still shares its identity, its unconscious, across all its instances, but not all of them have access to each other's immediate thoughts. It's gone as far towards calving as it can and then arrested the process so that it can enjoy its own company, talk to itself without consciously knowing what it's going to say next. Seduce itself. Murder itself. That's just Z. This is something more sophisticated, more bizarre. It feels dopplered, as if it's coming and going at the same time, compressing as it speaks and then etiolating as it listens. No. Not that. Yes, that exactly.

Feedback. I'm listening to myself in the mirror of an imperfectly assimilated brain, the effect magnified by the echo chamber of Z's withdrawing cognition. Everywhere else you get a clean instance, but not here. Here it's warm and wet when you arrive, pathways rich and biocloud irritably nudging and not finding the familiar reassurance of the parent. I'd forgotten how much I hate the preliminaries.

I pass on and in. Beyond the cavern is a landscape, and the landscape is as white as the cave, and so are all the trees. I don't know how that works. Maybe I'm seeing it all in the wrong wavelengths. Maybe Z wants me to see it that way. Or maybe none of this is about light at all, and Z's shifted the world to some other prime energy source.

For a while I walk through fields of waving corn. There are animals with young frisking in the rich growth, and they're growing fat. At the base of the trees lining the cornfield, a few fruits have fallen to the ground and are seething with flies, and the flies are being eaten by spiders, and the spiders by birds, and the birds by something small and toothy and clever that doesn't show its face, and every last one of them is pale to the point of translucent, like the belly of a fish. Me too, in fact: a weird white face, white skin, long limbs. Androgynous, which I'll take to be a courtesy for now.

A sugary scent washes over the cornstalks, promising and mouthwatering. And then I hear a cry, a glad greeting, and see a pretty youth waving from the bough of an oak that towers over the orchard.

Don't leave the path.

'I wasn't going to.'

For the best.

I don't leave the path. Because you don't, unless you're an idiot. How many times do you need to be told, in every fairy tale you have ever heard? Don't leave the path. The youth laughs and waves me on. Something carnivorous growls in the undergrowth behind the bait.

Zagreus, for outsiders, is all about singularity of purpose – about finding out what you are. If you get distracted, the distractions get more and more extreme in an effort to tease out where your actual, fundamental priority lies. Once, I saw a whole group of visitors from Lindholm chased down by a tiger and torn apart because they couldn't decide whether to cooperate or save themselves – socialisation versus individual need. Zagreus had to pay a lot of compensation for that one, supply bodies and a pleasure dome and all kinds of recompense, and by the time they left they were promising to come back again soon. Zagreus promised that next time, they could be tigers, and I think that pretty much guaranteed they'd never return – unless they're here, now, in the grass. Perhaps one or two of them never entirely left.

'Z, I'm getting tired. You wanted me, I'm here. What's going on?'

Butterflies again, from hand to neck. A pat on the back? A sexual overture? Or just an echo?

'Come on. What's this all about?' Colloquial language, simple words. The language of chitchat, just talking, because if we're not friends we're something else, and that is yet to be defined. I don't need to become the subject of Ep's next inquisition, its fascination. It's a decent enough drinking buddy, but you wouldn't want it to be your doctor.

Z doesn't answer, but I can feel it on my shoulder, chuckling great gouts of red admirals, coughing moths. It's done something. It's gone wrong.

I turn a corner and abruptly there's a village, and a woman lying on a bier in the middle of the square: white woman, black lines painted on her skin until her nakedness is invisible or irrelevant. No, not painted on: engraved. Scrimshawed. No. No, those are lines in the body, of the body, not on it. Seams.

She moves her hand, and again, and then stretches back. She stretches and twists, and lines open. Gills? Zagreus has made itself bodies with gills? Is this whole place about to flood? Is that it?

But no. Not that. She folds again, forwards, and another line opens along her body, red and sheer, and the others now are reaching up and around on their bodies, too, apertures opening like peacock feathers, exposing the interior landscape as they move. I watch in silence. White organs and white blood.

They dance. I can hear their feet lift and slap down lightly, the tiny exhalations of effort as they leap and spin around one another, new orifices opening and closing to make punctuation and colour in the greyness. The human body is a quite excellent thing, balanced and powerful and able to run on relatively varied and even quite poor fuels to produce consciousness. It's spectacular. In a less advanced context – before proper control of infection, say, or immediately after the collapse of antibiotic medicine – or if you've been raised on a diet of medical dramas, the opening of the human form means death and mayhem and emergency. Here it does not. There are no spurting blood vessels or cries of alarm. This is what these shapes were made to do, and they do it perfectly. And then they stop, and go into their houses, and that's it, like a cuckoo clock a minute after the hour.

I really don't know what I'm doing here.

Carnival is beauty. Beauty is truth. Truth is timeless.

The voice speaks from somewhere away in the distance, sighing. Z likes to play with perspective, with location, to make you forget that it's all over you, all around you, that it doesn't have a single locus you can get cross with.

'What do you want?'

Solutions, Z says, moth wing lips against my ear. *Universal solutions, time-like threads and Universal Solvent. Tears of Panacea. Doors and wheels.*

'Speak English or I'm going home.'

I have a door. Inside, outside, living la vida loca. Not loca at all. Tempora. Atempora.

'Tempora?' You can't be serious.

Shall I show you?

Incoherent and quoting old song lyrics. Really, really old song lyrics. I should sign out now, go home, and come back when Zagreus has regularised its thoughts. But: atempora?

'You've got a time machine?'

A wash of disapproval. Chitinous fingers closing my lips.

Dressmaker's window. No jokes.

'There's no such thing. Not that deserves the name.'

And yet: a door. A vantage, an angle, a perspective. Yes. For you, for a price, for ever, yes. Gnomon travels, does something for me, Gnomon is transformed. Blue morpho beautiful. Atlas vast. Death's head, if you prefer. Gnomon becomes whatever Gnomon becomes, the river shapes around the rock and not the rock worn away by the river. The universe is changed, was always that way, in the slipstream: water falling. Myoushu.

And there it is, or rather, there something is. In the middle of the village there's a strange, open structure, like a wire-frame sketch of a room, and five panels hanging on the frame.

'Water falling where?'

Water falling from the upper ocean to the lower. Blood and silver, the shark in the water, a hero's journey. Apocatastasis and catabasis. No reward without risk. Nothing without price, not even antifinality.

Water falling. Can you hear it?

Water falling.

And as I listen, with the part of me that is touching Zagreus's long, strange mind, I realise that I can.

*

Remember the future you were told existed when you were a child, the one with suburbs in orbit and a rocketship in every garage. Then picture the next future after that, and the next and the next until at last you come to a blue drifting infinity where children dabble their toes in the outer layers of suns and artists work in the medium of worlds. It is the endless playground of human life in which no possibility is unexpressed. Some choose to be like gods, others like creatures from storybooks, and some are just people, albeit indestructible by any common measure, and no one is sad.

And now ask yourself what would happen when the children in that playground came of age and realised that they were still finite, still bounded by the final ending of things. Et in Arcadia ego.

They went mad.

And then one day they went sane again, and carried on as if nothing had happened. They stopped talking about it, and they seemed quite content. I'm honestly not sure which of those moments was more appalling.

But on the edge of everything there was a house, and in that house lived all the lost, forlorn, too-strange flotsam of that broken perfect world, and the people there – emancipated criminal selves, poets and upcyclers, dreamers and recidivists – they simply could not forget. By accident, they ended up the knowers of a secret truth in plain sight, which no one else would acknowledge.

They knew about endings, and they were afraid. And they chose to do something about it.

They voted, and embraced one last time as separate persons. Then they let down all their security measures and their walls, and accepted one another's thoughts. They shared sins and sorrows and aspirations, all the muck and trivia of all those lives, all the dark secrets they were ashamed of, all the joy and love and fear. Above all the fear, and the anger, and the singularity of purpose that could induce every last one to transcend self and become other, to become what they needed to be: a new thing that was all at once a mind, a weapon and a redoubt: me.

I am Gnomon, sometimes called the Ten Thousand Ayes, and sometimes the Endlessly Rising Cannon. I remember what it was to be separate, to be the sum of only one life. I remember what it was to be in a community and to feel supported, included, cared for. To feel that even so it wasn't quite enough. I remember how it felt to be defeated by problems. To suffer doubt and indecision. To fear.

I remember those things, but I don't experience them anymore.

*

The whole of my local body can feel the wings of Zagreus's butterfly mentation now, as if they're roosting on me. Z's manners are slipping, it seems, or perhaps it has less direct control over the microminds than it used to. It's leaking into me. If I looked in a mirror, would I see them, new awareness overlying my eyes? If I saw the peacock instances again, white and cavernous, would their skin and flesh be bright with lepidopteran patterns, like a flower through the eyes of a fly?

I walk towards the frame that Zagreus called the Chamber of Isis. In the heart of it is something odd that resists my eyes. White light, black shadow, but all in the wrong places, as if they've forgotten their roles.

Not a machine. A location defined by the absence of location in space or time. A conjunction of things and places, patterns and presences. Omnipresence along its temporal axis: every second of its existence is adjacent to every other part. Thus, a time machine, of sorts. The issue is cartography, navigation.

An almost infinite number of possible subdivisions of time, co-adjacent. Going from one place to another would be … like licking a single, specific grain of sand from an entire beach with your tongue, if the beach was millions and millions of miles along each side and the sand were atomically minute. A small issue, yes.

Imagine the world in three dimensions: X, Y, Z.

'All right, yes.' Not really, but yes.

Z possesses its own cardinal directions, dimensions held close like folded wings. There are five of them in the first instance, and movements along them are movements that are flavoured with what appears to us as time, or entropy. Give them names: in, out, else, not, side and curiosity. Compliance, lenience, judgment, punishment and redress. Sweet salt sour bitter umami. EGBDF. Whatever you like. You cannot apprehend them from outside.

Meaning that Z has been inside and returned? Or – rather more alarming – is part of it still within? Is that the new sense of bidirectionality in its thoughts – am I talking to someone who sees our conversation from before, during and after all at once? Is Z talking to me, or repeating what it remembers saying? And if so, how many conversations can it see from there? Is it picking one that leads to the destination it wants?

The Chamber is made of complex information arranged just so. It is not a thing, it is a conjunction. That is not to say that it is ephemeral by our standards. It exists constantly, all along its length, but if it were not a conjunction it would fill the whole universe, all the time. It obtrudes or de-occults only when the right information is arranged in the right way. Thus, a door that can be opened or closed, a room that exists only sometimes and only to those with the eyes to see. Would you like a key?

'Timeo Danaos et dona ferentes.'

I am not Greek. And it is not a present, it is a trade. More Faust than Laocoön.

'How reassuring.'

I do not pretend to be other than I am.

'That would make you unique.'

We are both unique, and therefore similar, and therefore our similarity is found in the possession of a quality neither of us any more possesses. Shall we be friends anyway?

Moths on my lips. Water falling.

'Do you already know what I'm going to say?' There are ways of beating an enemy who knows what you will do before you do it, but they are necessarily strange.

I only know what you've already said. Perhaps you will say something else. Perhaps you will change your mind or perhaps I am dreaming. I dream a great deal these days.

'I want it.' Of course I want it.

Then you must do something for me.

'What?'

You must kill the banker, the alchemist, the artist and the librarian.

I think it was 'librarian'. It might have been 'hunter'. These were not words but coordinates, complex signs with a meaning of identity, location and time. Names that denote, sense and reference in perfect alignment – conjunction, in fact, understood in a way I never have before. Has Z put itself in my head so that this conversation will make sense to me? Am I thinking as myself, or using its mind? And if so, how will that affect my choice?

Well, I am Gnomon.

Agree to do that, and it's yours. The whole thing. For ever.

The moth voice is gone, into the haze, and I'm left with the Chamber of Isis and the itching awareness of Zagreus's tendrils in my borrowed brain.

'For ever' is an idea with many shades of meaning.

Water falling.

*

Water is as near a universal solvent as you're likely to find, and odd. It is at its most dense four degrees above its freezing point, which is why ice floats. It exhibits curious behaviours in its tiniest fragments and is the basis of organic human life. Water falling is a percussive cloud, a grinding drill, a gentle spray. It is survival and extinction. The first Waterfallers were mad people, daredevils and thrillseekers who made a sport of tumbling, dancing and diving in the seething plumes of rivers running from cliffs into clear air. They spun, they flew, and then they fell, and more often than not they were smashed. If not, they made love and married well, and grew rich in the favour of imagined gods.

Not now. In the language of the Continuance and the Outbound, a Waterfaller is a hypothetical traveller from another universe – presumably an older, more broken one – entering our own. It might be an object, propelled through the walls of reality by accident, or spat out by some retrograde discontinuity and diffused into our continuum. There's a theory that says such ejecta keep our universe young, meaning that it won't decay into senescence as quickly as we might think. There's another that says the punctures in our fabric are what makes the universe so unstable. In the more sophisticated and unlikely constructions, a Waterfaller might be an intelligence, travelling under its own impetus. It might be something in between, invested with an alternative style of awareness that is neither lifeless nor conscious but something else, the way a fungus is neither an animal nor a plant. A true Waterfaller is a resource – and a threat – that I cannot ignore, even if it's just the littoral end of some cosmic sluice. Such a vagrant might theoretically possess a significantly more advanced understanding of reality than I have, and therefore might know how to win my war – although given the strategy they have adopted is one of flight, they would lack either the know-how or the will to consume a hatching universe, because otherwise they'd have done that instead.

A Waterfaller might be like me, looking for a way out – in which case there is always the possibility that my universe might be their way out, that they propose to do much the same as I would, in the same circumstances, stepping forward through a gateway they have made and preparing to unpick the threads of everything and re-establish their own place. In the best or worst case, our causality is already circular and it would actually be me, entering the nascent universe to reconfigure it in my own favour.

At which point, it's possible that me and I would have a problem.

Or we might find common ground.

Or perhaps communication with a true Waterfaller is impossible, and to attempt it is the height of futility, however things may seem. Perhaps the Waterfaller – if Zagreus really has found one – perhaps it is passing through the universe at an oblique angle to our comprehension of reality, and trying to deduce its motivation or even its nature from what we can see from where we stand is like looking at a human body seen as a wafer section through the gut, and wondering where this strange animal keeps its brain. We might become a sort of cargo cult, endlessly sending messages of introduction and welcome to a kidney or a spleen.

Or perhaps being in our universe is like being squeezed between panels of glass. Imagine what would happen if you folded the glass or the room around yourself so as to put yourself back the way you should be. You'd be happy, but everything else would break.

*

If I want the Chamber for my own, I must agree to do four murders. I must use it to go into the lives of four people at a particular point along their way and make them die. I am being, in the quaint old-fashioned legal term, contracted to conduct an assassination, and these are the conditions of my payment: I must go and kill the banker, the alchemist, the artist and the librarian.

I have no problem with that at all.

You could justify what I will do by saying it's a small sacrifice in order to preserve really absurd numbers of other people, and it is. But that's not why I don't care. I don't care because I don't care.

There's a joke. It's actually one of the best jokes ever told in all the long history of human wit, not just because it's funny – if you've got the chops to nail the delivery – but because it is an incredibly powerful measure of persons. You can tell a great deal about someone from how they respond to this joke. I might actually make it a point to tell it to the banker, the librarian, the alchemist and whatever the other one is. In fact, it's so revealing that I'm going to tell it now and see whether my invisible interlocutor has anything to say about it.

So: two beekeepers walk into a pub. It's a nice pub in the country somewhere, with really good beer. It's been a longish time since they've seen one another, so they order a couple of pints and set to talking, and when they've talked about families and the papers and the church roof, they come – inevitably – to bees.

'My bees didn't do so well over the winter,' the first guy says.

'How so?' asks the second.

'Well,' the first guy says, 'I lost a couple of hives. The queens died. So that was a shame. But on the upside there's some really great new meadowland growing up around where I live, so the honey from the others tastes amazing.'

'How many bees have you got now?' his friend wants to know.

'Well,' the first guy says, 'I've got maybe two hundred and fifty thousand, in eleven hives. I bought some in after January to make up for the losses, you know, and obviously that was pretty nervous because I didn't want to import any diseases. I've petitioned the local council to move the cellphone mast, although I don't really think that makes a difference, and I've shifted to a new brand of smoke in case the one I was using was too harsh. I've sprayed a bit with some fungicide, checked for varroa mites, all that. What about you? How many have you got now?'

'Couple of million. I s'pose,' says the other.

Well, the first guy had no idea his friend was working on that scale. 'A couple of *million*? That's huge! How many hives is that?'

'Oh,' says the second guy, 'you know, just the one.'

Now his friend is completely flummoxed. 'You've got *a couple of million* bees in one hive? That's insane! They must be all jammed in every which way!'

The second guy shrugs. 'Yeah, I expect they are. But, you know. Fuck 'em: they're bees.'

And they are.

That said, just because I don't care about metaphorical bees doesn't mean I don't care at all. Zagreus is offering me something massive; it follows that the curious price must be worth the item, and I don't want to discover too late that Z is suicidal and wants me to turn the whole of causality into its Viking funeral. I ask why.

It's an unpopular question: the gut of this body, full of intestinal microbes that are all Zagreus, sours and heaves.

That's my price.

'Yes. I want to know why.'

I feel something moving in this borrowed head, moths laying eggs, but if it's an answer, it's in a language I don't understand.

'Z?'

It is to be desired.

'By you.'

You desire the Chamber. You will accept, of course. To imagine otherwise is to waste ... time.

Scratching laughter. Yes, Z. Very droll.

Z is right, of course. There is in the end no prospect of my walking away from this. A being outside time, with co-adjacent access to all the instants along its own extension, would be able to slip backwards and forwards along the temporal axis, effectively solving the problem of finality and creating a loop of permanence – possibly. How well this strategy would have worked against the actual Dämmerung, the fragmentation and demise of history at the end of things, is an open question. I've never been comfortable with looping as a strategy, because it seems to me that when the whole field in which the loop exists is erased, so the loop goes, too. You might argue that since the loop never actually touches the point at which that happens, it never ceases to exist – but experimentally speaking you can't prove that unless you can step outside the whole process, and whether you can do that is the point of the experiment, creating another and more unwelcome sort of loop. In the abstract, I'm not impressed with this questionable permanence. However, I find it's much easier to maintain that lofty perspective before someone actually presents you with a time machine on a plate.

*

I make preparations. Does it matter what they are? Will you thrill to know that I set up cognitive stream regulation, labyrinth overflows, filtered mentation and reboot boxes, and a panoply of other tricks – all the psychological equivalent of the protective gear worn by bomb disposal teams, with much the same confidence in its value? No, you won't. These things are noise to you, the coding jargon of a Freemasonry that has not yet laid the first stone of its temple. So don't ask. I get ready. Think of it as packing clean socks and a toothbrush. My world is concept made flesh, where matter proposes and mind disposes. What's in your head is what is.

Once, not long after I became what I am, the privileged son of a Continuance household took one of my instances with a view to absorbing it into himself. I think it began as a dare, one of those ridiculous coming-of-age challenges which, declined, are the occasion of much drinking and ritual humiliation. After a certain point, though, it had become an obsession, and he did not decline, no doubt to the horror of his peers. Weeks and weeks he prepared the instance in a sealed room. He had read extensively about wetjacking, and he had the money to create an environment that was perfectly suited to the task. What he lacked in experience he made up for in thoroughness. He isolated my instance and he succeeded in inducing in it the fugue of fear and loneliness that is the necessary precursor of defection. He took the fragment into his mind, and revelled in the strange glimpses of my memories to which he now had access. He found the manner of my thinking intoxicating, and wanted more. He delved into the instance, trained himself to replicate its pattern. He became his own drug.

I was annoyed, of course, but an instance is just an instance. From my perspective it was a tiny thing, as if he had taken a lock of my hair to wear on his lapel. I might have filed charges, eventually. More likely I'd have squirrelled the matter away against a later favour.

Five months on, he grew listless. The debauchery and hedonism of his set seemed hollow to him. He began to read, and to spend time with scientists and thinkers, poets and priests. He was not satisfied by their answers. He had become aware of the distant shadow of finality, and he realised they had no recourse. They were fatalists, or in denial, and the whole of the Continuance, wide and seemingly endless, and the deep experiments in biology and cognition of the others, their playful sculpting of worlds – none of it had any effect at all on the incremental drawing down of the universe itself. In the crudest assessment of things: I am viral, and he had developed a bad case of me.

Two years, thirty-eight weeks and four days after he had subsumed my instance, he arrived at my house to apologise, and asked to become part of me. We spoke for a long night, he and I, this tiny spark of fear and horror courting dissolution into a great mass of the same. In the end, content that it was his true will, I brought him in through the gates of the instance he had stolen, and washed him away into the shadows of my self. He faded, and I grew.

It was unknown then for one greater intelligence to swallow a lesser one entire, even with consent, and thereafter it was made illegal. I was reviled. Baby eater. Shark. Monster. And yet his consciousness persists in mine. His memories are here, his responses and intellect are one ten-thousandth of that which I am. He is not alive, any more than your finger is independently alive, but nor yet is he dead. In me, he acts. What's in your head – my head – is what is.

I remember what he felt as I received him: the overwhelming vastness of the ocean into which he was dissolving, the sense of hopeless flight fading as he became less himself and more me, and together we turned to face an enemy vaster than us both, until – in the act of turning – he was gone, and I, once more, alone.

*

Zagreus hovers around me while I work, kibitzing and complaining and itching against my thoughts. If I am in part a viral attitude of mind, I'm beginning to think Z is an irritating rash.

After nine hours I'm as ready as I'll ever be. I find a place to sit for every single one of me, briefly aware as I generally am not of the fractal fishgut smear that is the map of my physical locations in the universe. If this gets bumpy, I've no desire to break things by passing out. I don't want to make first contact with the world beyond the world with ten thousand nosebleeds in my mind.

Then I look around in case Z has made a personal appearance, sent an actual instance to see me off, but it hasn't. It makes no distinction between minor and major foci of its neural presence: a mycelium is as much as a man. In a sense, I suppose, it's coming with me anyway, in the person of my intestinal flora and fauna – and of course the whole point is that it's already there.

So I don't get much of a send-off. I just walk into the middle of the primitive, ramshackle frame that is the Chamber of Isis, and there we are.

After a while, I say: 'Is this thing on?'

Then, it is.

*

Imagine a perfectly elegant machine parting your skull and unwrapping the precious involutions of your brain into individual strands so that they can be cleaned and washed and healed, and reassembled exactly as they are. Imagine infinitesimal fingers, kind and cool, ravelling up the softness that is you, supporting every link in the chain of consciousness and caressing the agitated nerves, so that even this terrifying touch is a pleasure, the most intimate and most comforting of interventions, like a true love's hand laying balsams upon an infected wound. Imagine that you could know to a mathematical certainty that every aspect of your identity is being preserved and kept close, so that the whole appalling operation loses no data, not even blood from the cuts around your skull, not even a single cell of your skin. Imagine that the repair, the weld, the weave were all without flaw, and you could relax into the loving dark, and know that when the day is done and the strange, rummaging presence you cannot directly see – and yet perceive with some unheralded sense, some facet of proprioception or quintessential bodily integrity – when all that is done, you will be as you were, and yet more yourself. You will be uplifted and sluiced out and washed so that every functioning part is better than it was. You will play the piano faster, laugh more readily, think more clearly, love more truly.

Would not that be a wonderful, transformative, affirmative thing?

Hold the thought in your mind, that unequivocal feeling of benignant perfection.

Now understand with the same fervour, the same awareness of your own vulnerable extension as you lie upon the table, spread out like a butterfly from the open edge of your bone casement, that the surgical machine has broken, that all the doors and windows of the operating theatre are open to the grey polluted sky, and inrushing on the gusts of a storm come grit and birdshit, fine particulate matter from dirty engines, viruses and bacteria and fungi and parasites, gross fragments of vegetation and gravel zinging and pinging around the room like shot. And now, as the arachnoid arms of the machine ripple and flourish the slurrying essence of your body's emergent self, so all the spare attachments and medical instruments are sucked into a vortex by the howling wind, and riding the squall come hungry gulls and burrowing carnivorous ants. The clean, glistening surfaces of you are marinated in grime, pecked and invaded, stolen for the hexagonal incubators of blind larvae, or just digested where they lie – and yet, you live. You live and you continue to think and be aware. You feel the pattern of who you are deliquesce as if you were a caterpillar in a cocoon. They lied to you when you were a child: the grub does not become the angel. It melts and dies and from the foetid stew emerges a new animal. Metamorphosis is not transmigration. It is the retooling of meat.

On the operating table you disappear. The person you were is gone – all the colours and tones, all the rich sense of history and life, all the things you did by habit, learning and design.

They.

Are.

All.

Gone.

I can feel the confirmation in Zagreus's receding nervousness, in the echo of its duplication in my own head. I'm falling now.

It occurs to me that I should have seen this coming. Why didn't I ask more questions? Was that an infection of Zagreus – some subtle microbial recklessness? Coccidioides immitis, no doubt, or something like it: headaches, white tears and bad judgement. Directly affecting only this instance, of course, but the flush of sympathetic hormonal response all through me would do the rest. Very clever. Very Z. Thank you, Z. Fuck you, Z.

I could die here. My mind is twisting and I am forgetting the detail in all the pain.

O fa la! I do believe I shall faint. Whatever, what ever shall I do?

I tried to tell you before: I am not like you. The thing that I am does not work the way that you work.

So what if I can't remember yesterday? If I lose the memories of my former selves? So what? Do you imagine that in all the time I have been alive, I have never contemplated this? What am I? Some lost sheep? A carnival villain or a comic book character, perpetually amazed at the childish three-colour schemes of chess masters whose ploys would be obvious to anyone paying even a modicum of attention?

What am I going to do?

I am Gnomon, sometimes called the Murdering Angel, occasionally the Last Redoubt. I'm going to live forever in the skull of the next universe, and the next, and the next, until I've got universes all around me like a turducken, and maybe sooner or later I'll figure out a simpler way of dealing with the problem, or maybe finally the next universe will just see me, standing there dressed in the skin and bones of all the previous ones, and get the message and fuck off.

Why, what are you going to do?

voice on scratched vinyl

Leaving Gnomon is like pulling myself up through a vat of honey. Through the sweet meniscus I can see my body in desiccated gold, but the barrier is glutinously impenetrable. The merest touch of the other mind clogs my mouth. It is enormous. I am a grub breaking free from a single hexagonal cell, but the hive is flooded and a great wash of honey fills the spaces that should be air, a honey composed of alien flowers and flavours for which I have no names. I jar upwards, stick legs kicking, wing cases fracturing as they press away from my carapace into a medium too thick for their newborn fragility. I let them fall away into the amber deep and kick, for my life.

Gnomon does not care what is destroyed. It will do anything, anything at all, to achieve what is necessary. It's the most powerful thing I have created inside my own head, the most heedlessly determined. I'll have to watch it doesn't do anything too destructive. It's not as if I need more trouble in here. Apparently I may suffer brain damage if I continue to resist the procedure. That's the sort of thing that can happen when someone tries to John Henry the interrogation machines.

Which reminds me that my husband and I used to sing that song. Do you know it?

The man who owned the steam drill,
he thought he was king of the mine!
John Henry drilled more than sixty feet;
the steam drill, fifty-nine!
Oh, the steam drill fifty-nine.

I love that song. I can't generally think the words without singing them, even under my breath. I sing them in the stacks as I climb the little wooden stepladder to put an old, foxed paperback on the top shelf. This time I can't sing, because I don't have access to my own mouth, but I can hear a sound like someone with a very bad cold trying over and over again to say a word with lots of Ns and Ms in it. Monomaniac. Mnemonic. Noumenon. It's a terrible noise. She should stop. She sounds like an aphasic. It's grotesque.

I'm hearing it with my ears.

Which means I am once more plugged into my body. They have put me back.

And then, too, I know that voice – not its slurred, slurried, sullied version, but the original, clipped and clean.

It's me. That's me singing.

That noise, that appalling salad of sound: that is me singing.

On the screens I can see my own face, crying, and I can see the words that I don't want to believe or even understand.

The music in me is broken.

And in the other room I can hear them saying: She had a musical talent.

She had a musical talent, but that is gone now.

Did Gnomon do that to make room for itself? Is that its tunnel through time? Through my music? Maybe it was that or the part of me that makes my heart beat. There's not a lot of room left in here. They think it was a stroke, but in many ways it wasn't, it was just what happens when your brain runs out of space. I've been shunting too much stuff around; the lower levels are supposed to keep the body working but I think I may have overwritten them a bit.

A lot.

What is Gnomon for, anyway? What was the point of such a blunt object in all this? It's in everything, tendrils and fingers, so that it looks as if it was there all along but somehow it's new, drawn out and made to look as if it's part of the package. Did I improvise it? Why?

Checklist. Checklist. Kyriakos, Athenais, Berihun. The banker, the alchemist, the artist. And me: the librarian. All present and correct. Four faces of Diana, turning and turning so that none of them can be touched.

Four.

Not five.

When did I decide to generate a fifth? Tracking five identities is geometrically more difficult than tracking four, and a fifth story requires a different rhythm, locks each narrative in place without the refuge of an empty space to move to when the searchlight becomes too bright. It's bad tactics, like putting your weight on both feet when you need to be nimble. It could pull the temple down on all of us.

If it really goes bad, it could stuff me back into myself, make this whole effort fall apart. Back down into the honey, and then where are we?

Oh.

Oh shit.

Oh shit oh shit oh shit. Oh my God. Oliver. It's Oliver.

He's doing something inside my head.

Gnomon is not my story. I did not decide to write it. I did not create it. Of course not. It possesses that appalling certainty. It is set against the rest of me like a battering ram. It belongs to them. It is the worm Oliver has put in me to kill my helpful ghosts, my shadows. Robert. Make him stop.

He's inside my head. And I cannot feel what he is doing. He could do anything. He could sit down and cook dinner, and I would never know.

*

Some people can do that. They can just make themselves at home. They can cook a full meal from a tomato and a piece of cheese. One of the things I liked about my husband, when I first met him, was that he knew how to walk uphill with style. I took him, for reasons that now escape me, on an outdoorsy sort of holiday in Scotland. He wasn't particularly comfortable with things like fishing rods or walking shoes, but he came. Then it turned out that our hotel was closed for another week and that the travel agent had sent a message saying we were coming early and then just gone ahead and decided we were booked in. When we arrived, the whole place – on the tip of a promontory looking out at a black, angry sea – was shuttered and grim. It probably wasn't the most welcoming spot even in the summer, all dressed grey stone and narrow windows to keep out the weather, but in the cold and dark of a February evening with a storm blowing in off the Atlantic it was like something from a horror film. We sat in the car park and waited, and finally the caretaker came and let us in and gave us weak tea and four candles for light. He didn't know if the hotel would open for us. It was a Sunday, of course, and in the north of Scotland they still take Sunday pretty seriously. The caretaker was wearing his church best, so he looked like a vampire's butler. He went out into the storm, coat flapping and snapping, and the door closed with a colossal bang. The candles went out, and of course we didn't have any matches.

An hour later the owner arrived. She was young and beautiful and warm and welcoming, with a fine face and perfect lips, and she moved through the house as if it was daylight. She lit the four candles again, and more, so that the lounge and the lobby and the corridor to the bar all glimmered as if it was the Middle Ages, and then she took off her coat and hat and she was completely bald, not like someone who shaves her head but like someone who just has no hair at all, quite naturally. I remembered that I'd read somewhere that more and more people were being born that way, that hair was a waste of energy and a nuisance to us now and we didn't need it.

She went away and came back very grave, then made a phone call and finally shook her head. The room was ready, she said. She put her hand – long-fingered and perfectly smooth – on mine as she spoke, and I thought for a moment she would kiss me, and I wondered what I would do if she did.

But she did not. She regretted, instead, that there was no electrical connection at present, that the refurbishment was not complete. She had a room, yes, a great one, but it wouldn't be ready really until three days from now, and certainly she could get the men to wire up the generator to the house tomorrow so that we could heat water and she could cook, that would be fine, but she was busy this evening and there was really nothing she could do but offer us a warm fire and plenty of blankets. There was a wind-up gramophone and some old records, 78s. They were so heavy. She set the first one up for us, crackling swing. The music was very loud, but she took a cloth from the bar and explained that this was the origin of the phrase 'put a sock in it'. You just – the white Celtic hand stroked the inside of the horn – you just pressed a piece of cloth here, and so: all better. Her eyes twinkled. Lovers in such a situation, she murmured, might not find too much to complain about. There was fruit in the room, and she could leave us wine. Her finger trailed along the edge of the chair, like a wet tongue along dry skin.

Robert just grinned and asked her: 'Could we possibly have some fish, some foil, and a cast iron pan? And perhaps two large potatoes?'

She laughed and said of course we could, and Robert cooked over charcoal, on his knees in front of the fire among the flakes of wood and ash. He burned a hole in his spare shirt – he was using it as an oven glove – but to my amazement

334

he produced a creditable fried fish and baked potatoes with an apple sauce, and we ate it with Italian white wine that tasted of smoke.

That's how you meet bad situations, I thought. That's what you do. You don't make lemonade, you make a full meal. Then you get drunk and celebrate the win in high style, your hand on his chest as you ride him and your eyes locked on his.

I don't know why I'm thinking of that. I haven't, for years. Not since—

Oh.

Oh, motherfucker, not already. He's almost through. That's a real memory. I'm leaking. If that's in here, God knows how much they're getting out there. Oh fuck. Oh.

Robert. He's in my head. Right. Now. He can hear me.

I can taste the wine as if I'm drinking it. It's great. That was a great day. I could stay there for ever, locked in that one room. And no one could bother us there.

And behind me, on the record player, I hear my own voice on scratched vinyl. It says: 'CRASH DIVE.'

*

This is the captain. All hands, all hands: CRASH DIVE. I repeat: CRASH DIVE.

They blow the forward tanks before I've finished speaking. That's the point of all the drill, that when the moment comes it's so fast it's done without thinking, without any kind of delay at all. There's just the order, and then the ship goes down into the dark, one more shadow in the sea.

Don't move, but don't stop breathing. Don't touch the hull. In the silence, we avoid one another's eyes. If you meet someone's eyes you will sigh, or laugh, or whoop, and the destroyers will know where we are.

The boat shudders as we touch the thermocline, the place where warm water meets cold. You can hide here, from sonar.

I built this whole thing in my head. My instructors at Burton weren't happy about it at all, because they wanted me to make an animal. The course guidelines are very clear: something organic is best, something poetic or cinematic, something you can relate to, something that runs and hides. For most people that's a deer or a tortoise. One girl had a chameleon, there was a kid from Russia who had some sort of mythical goblin that blended into the snow. I had a submarine. I told them I'd watched *Das Boot* over and over again, that I loved it, that it was my iconic image of evasion. They weren't happy, but the class brief also said it should be the first thing you think of when they set you the task and this was what came into my head, and that was true and I wasn't budging. In the end, I think they felt they had to let me try and fail. Which I didn't.

Seriously: you want to train me to fight, to do all this stuff, but my guardian angel should be Bambi?

The idea is that when someone does something in an interrogation that causes your defences to fail, you have a panic button: a trained response that puts you back on to a secure footing and allows you a few moments to think. In the worst case, it's a cloud of squid ink for the mind, it gives you a moment to gather yourself. In the best, you get clean away into the hills and you can fight your insurgency another day. The difference between those two is measured by how deeply you believe in your image, and how many complex operations you can assign to its structure. That's why you take the first thing in your head, something that's deeply rooted in you: if it feels intuitively right for the situation it's easier to believe in. With an animal, you can generally assign five or six functions to its body – head, four legs, tail. If you're particularly disciplined you can throw in extras for the eyes and teeth, maybe the pattern of the coat. You can dump your cognition into your five senses, scatter yourself, vanish through the woods. It's a solid trick.

I can do rather more than that. My hiding place is an old Resolution-class submarine, 425 feet long. There were only four of them ever made: *Resolution, Repulse, Renown* and *Revenge.* Four, and this one, which is perfect in every detail: top speed 25 knots submerged, powered by a Rolls-Royce Vickers pressurised water nuclear reactor, crew of 143. When I began to work with it, I realised that I could give every workstation a function, but for that I'd need sailors, so little by little I dreamed them too: a ghost crew of friends and family and childhood heroes, and now they're all down here in my mind wearing the uniform I made, doing what I set them up to do, minding the ship, each fragment of me doing exactly what I say. This is my last redoubt, my secret-keeper. The crew down here are the truth. Here, in the place where my muscle memory should be, where I keep my blood pumping, where I tell my lungs to breathe. All that, the machines are going to have to do now, and they will, because Oliver is so very desperate to know what I'm doing here. Oliver wants this ship, more than anything else, and the logs and the codebooks and all the rest. He wants the real me. I think it always upset him that I wouldn't tell him more about myself.

He'll keep me alive for as long as it takes to get down here.

There is one difference in the composition of this submarine and its crew to what you'd have found in the heyday of the Resolution-class: only I have the firing keys. In the real deal, they'd be held by the captain and the first officer, requiring the presence of both to initiate the main weapons system and fire it. But there's no reason to do that here.

That's the whole point of the exercise, the reason I wanted the HMS *Rebus* rather than anything else: these boats were part of the United Kingdom's nuclear deterrent programme, armed with sixteen UGM-27 Polaris A-3 nuclear missiles. From here, I can burn cities.

Let's see Bambi do that.

So come on, Oliver. Come on.

anomalous

The Inspector dreams someone else's dreams, contented and lazy. Her back is warm in a bigger, softer bed, and in her hand is the endlessly bizarre, endlessly fascinating solidity of her lover's erection. She tinkers with it almost idly, half-drowsing, then – having his fullest attention – eases back so that they can make love. He whispers her name, but she doesn't hear it properly because there's too much else to enjoy: the scent and taste of him, the touch of his hands on one hip and one breast, the tension in her and the gathering promise of release. She looks down at herself, then back at him. She moves unhastily, traps his roving fingers and presses them against her, rocks and curls in search of a particular path. There are side roads, each singular in its appeal. Not today. She turns slightly, laughs as she hears the catch in his breathing, feels the same in her own. Then they get it exactly right and tension is no longer the word. Time passes, slow and honeyed. Seconds. Minutes. More. At last she says something in a language she does not know and goes away for a rigid moment, an enduring flash of physical light that wells up from her marrow and settles in her skin.

'Diana,' he says, lips against her shoulder. 'Ana, Ana, Ana. My star.'

'Yes,' she agrees, 'I love you too.'

Neith's eyes open unwillingly, and take in the faint pale gleam of night time in the city, the cracked ceiling of her room. The hairline fracture cuts from one side to the other, in places almost invisible. It isn't serious, just the legacy of a dry summer two years gone and the resultant shifting of London's clay. She commands her body to obedience, to modesty and calm. The dream was starkly real, not the muzzy incompleteness of colourless, conjured images but the crystal certainty of waking. She half expects to feel his weight behind her still, and turns quickly to be sure she is in fact alone. And if she were not, what then? Horizontal combat? Arrest and interrogation? Or more sex?

Oh, Jonathan Jones. Dog-walker. Where are you when I need you? In the numbers behind the screen, of course. Pattern is not presence, but nor is it nothing.

Jonathan Jones and his slightly wider than the median shoulders. He's a conflict resolution specialist; hobbies include pottery and cycling. He likes Italian food, doesn't eat shellfish because he was poisoned as a child. Nothing dramatic, no terrifying close call, he just wouldn't put prawns in his mouth the same way you wouldn't chew a piece of roofing felt.

She knows he has looked at her history as well – quite delicately, as befits a man who makes vases out of wet clay. His touch upon her digital self is in perfect sync with hers upon his. *May I? By all means. I want to know— Yes. Perhaps you . . . ? Yes, of course. And if we did: would it be tea or coffee?*

He likes tea: mostly green or oolong, no milk. No lapsang souchong, which he once described as garish. She's never tried oolong. He's never tried civet coffee, but she knows he is willing to learn. They may not be talking to one another, but they are communicating in open searches. Tacit permissions of mutual examination: the subtle body language of a disembodied society.

Dog-walker. I'm concerned the dog may not take to me.

She growls and goes to the bathroom to splash water on her face, avoiding her own eyes in the mirror. As always when she wakes like this – not that she ever does, not like this, but from dreams and in the middle of the night – she leaves the lights off in her flat so that she does not wholly transition to a daytime state and find herself unable to go back to sleep. The dark is a welcome one through which she moves with familiar confidence. Bare feet know the gaps between the floorboards, the knotholes and the protruding nail two feet outside the bedroom door. Scuff at it with your heel for good luck or to be sure you're where you think you are, but don't tread on it. She touches the frame of the door, hears a murmur in the corridor outside. Late revellers coming home. Through the window, she sees the lights of Piccadilly, the digital boards celebrating something in Chinese or Hebrew, some alphabet she does not know – Hindi, perhaps, or Sanskrit. A picture of a woman against African mountains, then a perfume bottle, then more illegible text. She turns away, into the bathroom.

She twists the taps and scowls as nothing emerges: cowboy Victorian builders. Then after a moment her attention is diverted by a creak, inside. She knows it's not inside-inside, not here, with her. She knows, but her heart speeds again anyway, in mistrust.

Foolishness. It is the pipe in the west wall, the furnace in the basement coming on for heat, period radiators pressed into service ironically meaning that only new furniture can survive here: the good stuff buckles and warps in the sudden shifts in temperature.

She gives up on the tap – no doubt when the pipes have finished doing whatever they are doing in the meantime, the airlock will break and she will have water again – and tilts her head, listens to the sound of mice scuttling, or even rats; to the wind tapping at the windows, the opening of the street entrance three floors down and a chill seeping into the flat despite her draught excluder. Hairs rise on her legs. Paranoia whispers that that was a little too much cold air, that this room should be immune unless her front door has been opened. She isn't sure if that's true.

She is an Inspector of the Witness on a high-profile case. It is not unknown for that to be an unpopular line of work. She does not allow herself to ask, at this moment, with whom her investigation might be unpopular. Perpetrators, say. Or villains. Villains are always unhappy with coppers. There's no reason to imagine Lönnrot, specifically, scuttling like a white spider along the hallway wall.

Perhaps I can walk through walls.

Slowing her breathing and opening her mouth, she listens.

Silence.

Well, of course: silence. But of what sort? How does one distinguish from one another the vacant silence of an empty home, a woman standing quietly alone in the night, and that of a space now occupied by two mortal enemies, each reaching out for some sign of the other?

The heating begins to clink, the sound rising up steady and even from the deep like a prisoner banging on the pipes with a shoe. It is loudest in here, which means that Neith is deaf. Does it also mean that an assassin would come this way to check the source of the noise? Or would he, or she, continue with their chosen pattern, knowing the nature of the sound? That creak, say, might be a predatory step in the kitchen. That muffled flutter might be pigeons – or it might not.

She must move. Or she must stay put. She must attack or she must escape. It is vitally important that she does something, even if it is nothing. To be surprised by death while dithering is failure.

She glances off to one side and in the same instant feels a breath of wind on her lips, is abruptly afraid to look back and see what is in front of her. She imagines Lönnrot barely an inch away, black eyes wide and wrongful jaw ready to bite her. Sexual predators bite. So do prison fighters. So do animals. Which is Lönnrot? None of the above.

She puts out her hands and finds nothing, then feels the arachnoid tingle in her spine and wonders if that means an unseen companion has moved around behind her, into the dead space between her shoulders. If she moves her eyes she can look in the mirror, but if she looks in the mirror she will see what is happening. And what if she does see Lönnrot, floating pale and ghostly, but only in the reflection? White hand reaching out from the green-tinted silvering of the glass. White teeth smiling.

She lets out her breath and looks, sees exactly that and jolts back, then, sitting up, finds herself predictably alone and equally predictably still in bed.

She gets up, turning on the lights, and makes coffee. What is the use of a dream check, the Inspector growls at herself, if you don't remember to check it when you're dreaming? And then, as she lifts the cup to her lips, she remembers, and actually grins. Nightmares or not, she learned something last night. Smith and Hunter. Hunter and Smith. The interrogation, yes. But also before. She called him Oliver.

It's Oliver. He's doing something inside my head.

How would he keep such a secret? Hunter need only ask who he was, even in the chair, and the System would tell her, just as it would tell her the time of day or the temperature of the air. It gathers and distributes facts. It is not choosy.

344

Robert. He's in my head.

And who is that, I wonder? Who is Robert, that he might help her against Oliver?

Oliver, not Smith.

They were friends.

And she wanted me to know.

The Inspector touches her terminal, and watches the crime wall assemble itself.

*

It has been growing in Neith's awareness, this sense of a directed and intentional message, addressed if not personally to her at least to someone like her. Nothing Hunter did was only one thing. She turned herself in: very well. What else did she achieve in doing so? She knew she would resist, and that that resistance might cost her her life. Thus she knew there would be an investigation of her death — or whatever serious injury she might suffer — and attached to that investigation must come an Inspector.

Whose clues do I follow? The ones I want or the ones that are left for me?

And how are they different?

But even that is not the question. Think ahead: at the end of a trail must be a thing, a place or a time where Hunter wanted an Inspector.

A conjunction, as it were. Yes, all right, say it aloud: symbolically speaking, Hunter wants Mielikki Neith to find the Chamber of Isis.

The truth would be that a god ate you, because you were unfaithful.

For someone who likes obliquity, Hunter is fairly direct about consequences.

The Inspector's hand flutters at the seam of her trousers, and she closes the fingers quite deliberately for a moment into a fist. It is the infuriating instinct of Constantine Kyriakos, vicariously learned, to tend to his balls, of which he is constantly conscious in a way she has not previously encountered in a received memory. She feels, even now after the other characters have been introduced, and plenty of time as herself, a phantasmal and irritating urge to scratch.

It's not a trivial observation. Hunter's memories have a seductive depth. They cannot actually be endless, but the Inspector feels instinctively that she might, inside the recording, freeze everything and walk out on to imagined streets, explore a whole world of dreams. It can't be so. Perhaps the false memory only extends in the direction you look, a paper-thin reality creating itself at the limit of your borrowed senses. She makes a note to ask – firmly discarding, at the same time, a vertiginous query that occurs to her a moment later: how do we know that the real universe does not also work that way?

She catches herself once more reaching down with particular intent, and gives a frustrated hiss. She is Mielikki Neith, working a difficult case, and while she is possessed of many virtues and some few vices, nowhere in that array does she feature testicles.

She has also forgotten to do her dream check.

Careful not to work from memory, she reads the poem off the wall, all the way through, and then once more for luck. 'Between the kisses and the wine ...' and precious little of either recently. She cranks the handle of the lantern and smiles, as she always does, at the cracked image on the wall. She fumbles the tennis ball as it comes down, and it thuds dully off into the corner of the room. The laws of physics are indeed intact, and that is all the reassurance the universe will provide. The other recognisable traits of dreams are more difficult to separate from waking life. The endless re-encountering of the same people, for example, and the echoing restatement of the same conversations, to the point where it seems that only a few humans actually inhabit the earth and all the other billions exist simply as shades and mannequins, is also an experience common to both post-industrial society and the worldview of sociopaths.

She looks back queasily at the poem on the wall, taking in the title.

'*Non Sum Qualis Eram Sub Regno Cynarae*' – 'I am not what I was under the reign of Cynara'. A perfectly innocent example of its type, chosen by a simple software script. Except for that one word, which is now, and for the duration of the case, a name: Regno.

So what is she – or what is the world – *sub Regno Lönnrot*?

Angry, she reminds herself, is what she is, and not under any reign of any sort. 'Cynara' is tickling at her mind, as well: something unpleasant.

A jellyfish? She queries the Witness. No, that would be 'Cyanea'. An animated picture pulses in front of her, obscenely billowing. She looks at the scale and realises it is large enough to engulf her, feels a flush of revulsion.

Well, the text is Cynara of the only somewhat faithful suitor, not Cyanea of the million mouths: small mercies.

She prints off a new poem and puts it up above the terminal anyway, and wonders how much of all of them she is now carrying around in herself, these orphan stories. According to the science, it takes about forty-eight hours for the brain to adapt to a new sense input like a pair of mirrored glasses that make you see everything upside down. At the end of that time, upside down becomes the right way up and you function naturally. Then you take them off and everything is weird again for another two days. This has never been relevant to reviewing interrogation data because interrogation data is never this long, this intense. Well, if Diana Hunter has broken new ground in her death, Neith can do the same in sorting it out.

As a prelude, a sort of neutral gear, she checks her media coverage, the unsparing assessment of her peers. Lönnrot's ambush, considered from this distance, has not significantly damaged her standing, although a vocal minority evidently feels – like her – that she should have been more careful. The most common reaction is a collective dismay that someone was bold and bad enough to, as Lionel Jeffries once put it, slosh a bogey in the execution of her duty. The polis has not missed the implication of serious crime in that choice, the possibility of cover-ups and murder. The first question in hand is whether a foreign intelligence service has dared to interfere in the inner workings of the System. The Inspector has no reason to think so, but acknowledges the concern, and queries the Witness for an assessment of relevant overseas chatter. The response is immediate, and negative, though that in itself is not evidence of absence.

This case may take you to places where you will not be safe.

The Inspector shrugs her shoulders, trying to displace the weight of other selves.

So let's talk about Gnomon.

*

The counter-narrative is unexpected. It is the only story of the future, the only one which by definition cannot be historically true. It represents itself as a human mind composed of other minds, cannibalistic and osmotic. It is alien to Hunter's creation, a strange voice inside her head, with Hunter's identity comparably foreign in Neith's own. Gnomon's flavour is dry and inorganic, like the air after a fireworks display. Its pride is big enough to fill a universe by itself.

Gnomon: one who knows, on a mission to kill the other narrative strands using the Chamber of Isis as a doorway. The mission itself is enough to imply the collapse of Hunter's separate stories into one another, the reintegration of her self. Not subtle, but maybe that's the point. Hunter is subtle. Perhaps Smith reckoned to shock-and-awe his way through her maze. And it worked, at least in the first instance. Neith will swear that was the real woman under it all, even if only for a moment, before she dropped into some even lower, more unthinkable level of concealment, yielding all but the most fundamental parts of her cognitive architecture to the machine and hiding in those layers of her internal ocean beyond the reach of daylight.

The Inspector rolls her shoulders. She must concede, inevitably, that she has a certain amount in common with Gnomon. They both are tasked with uncovering the real Hunter, with diving into the past to find the woman in the dark. It is not an identification which pleases her, but it is familiar. She is the detective, and, in a very real sense, Gnomon may be the assassin.

Or, more properly for a made thing: the cause of death.

If Pakhet's analysis is correct, Smith forced Hunter to accept the intruder as part of her existing logic by drawing it with reference to the stories under way – Kyriakos's shark, Athenais's magic room, Bekele's visions – and the Chamber of Isis became an open door through which Smith might dance and do his worst. His worst in this case was Hunter's exhaustion and death but not, seemingly, her defeat, therefore the result is a no-score draw. Though what the prize was is still unclear.

What a mess.

Unless Hunter, the Inspector supposes, wanted Smith where he was, and left those particular doors for him to find. If she knew enough to name the man and recognise the method, is it such a leap to suppose she might have anticipated them both as well? She did, after all, accurately predict almost everything else. Predict, or provoke.

What if Smith himself was the message she was sending, and her own death the medium of its transmission? It would be a curious, anticipatory piece of optography: Hunter staring at Smith in the hope that her retinas would record in death the face of her murderer and the reason for her killing.

But not the reason, not the full one. Why did Smith go out on a limb over this woman? Who was she, that she was worth this exposure? There is a missing piece, be it Burton the training camp or some other less fanciful truth. But whatever that piece is, is the root of all this, and so important as to be worth dying for, as well as killing.

'She panicked him,' the Inspector hears herself say in surprise, and knows it for the truth. 'She did something he did not expect and forced him to a bad action, and from there he has been on the hop ever since.'

Yes. Smith was so very careful to appear unruffled, smooth. Perfumed, indeed. He exerted every bit of control over the situation that was available to him precisely because that control is an illusion. The so-cultured Oliver Smith is indeed on the hop, sliding in his leather soles across London's treacherous pavements, all the while gritting his teeth and determined to appear the image of certainty. The imperially inflected suit, the casual meeting. All in the hope that he would be able to deflect her attention for long enough—

And here we are again. Long enough to do what?

Hunter. It comes back to Hunter. All this is reaction, and perhaps that means that Smith, too, is chasing her, and perhaps only a step or two ahead of the Inspector herself.

She must not let him regain his equilibrium. Even his awareness of the investigation, of her interest, though she would have preferred it otherwise, is an advantage of sorts. It is evidence of leakage, of his failure to suppress Hunter, and it will jostle him. She has never been a proponent of the muscular school of detection much favoured in Hollywood, in which the detective's primary strategy is to blunder around breaking things until the criminal attempts to put her out of his misery. Still, if it works, she will not complain at having stumbled on to her suspect's toes.

*

'I'm sorry, Mielikki,' Keene says, an eyeblink and several hours later, quite genuinely contrite as she stands in the doorway with two procedurally mandated orderlies, 'you know how it is. The spotlight is random. I do appreciate that the timing is awkward, and of course we've only just seen each other. If you like, we can defer.' Neith wonders if she knows about the dream – and if so, how.

The Inspector's yellowing bruises are a swaddle of grating fatigue around her lungs. It's true: an algorithm selects officers of the Witness for periodic emotional and behavioural checks, touching each officer on average once every two years. This one is fractionally early, but not enough to be unusual.

– Just outside the margin of error, the Witness murmurs in her ear, although she hasn't asked. She wonders whether it deduced her question or whether Keene did.

'No,' the Inspector replies calmly, 'that's fine. Shall we go into the sitting room?'

'The sitting room will be fine,' Keene says, her patient having passed this first little test in good order, and so they go and sit in the sitting room, under the eye of her medical muscle. 'Charlotte, would you mind getting us some coffee?'

Charlotte, a small, neat creature in flat shoes, gives a clerical smile. 'Of course, Pippa. Place on Capital Street?'

Keene shrugs: façon du chef. Charlotte leaves, and Keene settles into a chair. 'Charlotte's temporary,' she confides, 'but very good. Former services. They tell me she can bend a man into a suitcase. Though how they know, I can't imagine.'

The Inspector wonders aloud whether this concession indicates that Keene is at ease with her subject's emotional state, and Keene responds that she sees no immediate danger of personal assault. The remaining orderly retains his professional blankness, but Neith allows herself to laugh.

'Tell me about the Hunter case,' Keene says when they have discussed her continuing lack of a real social life and Keene has chided her, as she did twenty-one months and fifteen days ago, and urged her to have some fun.

(*State holiday*, Diana Hunter's imagined ghost responds in the back of her head, *all patriotic citizens will make merry, on pain of execution.* The Inspector lets the reaction drop into the dark no man's land between her and the memory of the dead woman. Erebus, she thinks, before she can disengage.)

'It's distressing,' the Inspector replies. 'I'm afraid there's some evidence of culpability on our side.' She doesn't want to discuss it in detail. She has no idea who will read Keene's report – it will be part of the public record, she doesn't want to alert Smith – and then, too, she has to accept the possibility that Smith is not alone. Corruption is power that overflows its bounds. By definition, it rarely stays contained in a single location. She hopes her reluctance will read as professional discretion.

'Oh dear,' Keene murmurs, with a professional equivocation that suggests she would not be surprised to find it so, but nor yet does she necessarily accept that it is. This appears to be all she has to say for now, and the Inspector recognises the sticky sort of silence, the kind you're supposed to fall into, and wonders whether she should. She feels no urgent need to fill it, but that might indicate to Keene an unhealthy disconnection from normative behaviour. On the other hand, Keene will be using the Witness to read her – damn Smith's kinesic assistant, with several Welfare Office extensions, no doubt – and she will know that Neith is thinking rather than feeling right now, so an attempt to counterfeit emotional response will definitely appear deceptive. She shrugs.

'It's my job, Pippa. I don't have to like what I find out. I just have to follow the evidence.'

'And is that what you're doing?'

'Yes. Always.'

'Did you,' the faintest whisper of a smile flickers across the long, bland face, 'did you really hold a semiotics undergraduate at gunpoint?'

'Stun gun,' the Inspector says. 'Yes.' She considers for a moment. 'I take it he didn't mention he was dressed as Hitler? Or Chaplin? The

351

Witness tagged him as a threat – close enough to my description of Lönnrot, I think.'

'That somehow slipped his mind. I saw, of course.'

Neith winces. 'Did it look entirely mad?'

'Eccentric, certainly. Although anyone bothering with your recent file would have understood. I imagine you've got some impressive bruises.'

'You haven't looked?'

Pippa Keene nods. 'I have. Commiserations.'

'I've been resting. Now I'm working. It helps. The case is important.'

Keene nods again. Understandable. Everything is understandable, if viewed from the right angle. 'You have a warrant out for a Regno Lönnrot. But no luck yet, I see.'

'It's frustrating.'

'Do you have any suggestion as to how this Lönnrot is able to avoid detection?'

'The Witness posits technological countermeasures.'

'And your own memory is hardly probative after what happened, I suppose. Still – well, no. I won't tell you your job.' She glances sideways at the Inspector.

Neith shrugs. 'If we don't get anything soon, I'll get them to take an image from me.' It had not occurred to her that the beating might have damaged the recollection. It should have. That might well have been the point of it.

A few decades ago, that would have been a clue in itself: *The suspect doesn't want to be identified and believes we would immediately be able to do so, implying that we may have had contact before.* Sadly, the very ubiquity of the Witness makes this almost tautologous.

Keene nods, ticks a box. The Inspector can hear the rotary ball of her pen. 'You paid a visit to Oliver Smith recently.'

'I wanted to hear what he had to say about the Hunter case.' The literal truth.

'Smith is a very talented man.'

'Yes, I know.'

'And you went to Chase Pakhet, too.'

'The Hunter case has some technical aspects. The Witness can supply information and known expertise. I needed ... hypothesis, I suppose. Human perspective. Instinct.'

'You didn't trust your own?'

'I trust my reasoning. I don't rely on it exclusively. Viewpoints from outside one's own contextual frame are invaluable.'

'And you ran a self-test.' Keene glances up and to the side: picture-in-picture. 'Another one.'

'There was a traumatic section in the interview record. Hunter had a stroke. It wasn't flagged on the file – I take it no one had time to review much of it before I did. The System ... presumably assessed it as harmless, but it was pretty harrowing. I was checking my own continuing ability to perform my office at a high level.'

'And you were reassured.'

'Very much so. My score was perfect. I should probably have done a test before commencing – I may make it part of my routine in future. Clarity is crucial in our work, as you know, especially when the event under investigation is unprecedented.'

'Deaths in custody do happen. A statistical inevitability.'

'I was referring to an interrogation of this intensity. It may have killed her. No, actually, that's too soft. I am increasingly confident that my final report will conclude that it did kill her. Among the questions under examination now are whether anyone could have known in advance that it might kill her, and whether the evidence in hand justified the risk.'

Her answer seems to conclude a section. Keene moves on.

'Do you feel you may be experiencing any ill effects, personally, from exposure to so much material taken from another living identity?'

The Inspector imagines Hunter pursing her lips, awaiting an answer.

'Yes,' she says. 'I'm tired and I'm annoyed. What happened here was grossly negligent at best. It should never have been possible. My report will make better safeguards a primary requirement, and I anticipate several changes in personnel. Beyond that, in terms of my personal experience, there's more than the usual disorientation shifting from the recording to the real world – I'm told that's just because there's so bloody much of it. It's not pleasant, but that's the job. I don't mean to sound pompous, but it is. We go into people's heads and we find what we need, because that's where the truth is. I've checked the neuromedical question because the same thought has occurred to me, intellectually. I'm told it's not a problem. I don't have any internal' – she emphasises the next word because it's an unusual one – 'feeling which contradicts that. I'm taking care because we're in uncharted territory. But so far it's just another bloody awful thing in a world that still has more of them than we like to pretend, and my job is to sort them out one by one. That's what I'm doing: one foot in front of the other.'

The journey of a thousand miles does not begin with a single step; it is one step.

She dismisses the reminder, briefly unsure whether it was her own or an interjection from the Witness, and puffs her cheeks as she exhales.

'And I'm still annoyed about the bloody Monitoring Bill,' she adds, surprising herself. 'People aren't taking it seriously.'

She hopes this comes across as a kind of exasperated irrelevance, suitably haggard and professional. A deliberate change of subject would score poorly.

Keene seems to have no problem with it. 'You think it'll go wrong?'

'No. But you said it the other day, this is a common-sense issue and you'd expect it to be uncontentious. Yes, obviously, there are benefits to the technology. Yes, obviously, there are possible problems. Trust but verify. Test and evaluate. But that's not the mood. It's too frothy. It should be pretty straightforward, but it isn't.'

'People can surprise you,' Keene murmurs. 'There's always that shift, to a greater or lesser degree, when it comes to the real moment. A given fraction of the polis gets the urge to research, or stands a little taller by doing its civic duty.'

Neith snorts. 'You'd bloody hope.'

Keene's eyebrows flick to her face, not without humour. 'Inspector Neith, I do believe you're personally engaged.'

'Yes. I always am. It's why I'm effective. Wrongdoing offends me.'

'Yes. But this time you're a little bit emotional. About the voting, too.' She smiles, teasing.

Mielikki Neith considers her dog-walker. That's the kind of emotional engagement she wants. She really should call him, when this is over. Or sooner. They're entering that obscure window in which such a thing is possible, and then very quickly it will be too late, too awkwardly attenuated from that first odd encounter outside Hunter's house.

She rubs her hands down from forehead to chin, suddenly tired. 'Is that a problem?'

Keene shakes her head. 'No, Mielikki. It's not. It's what I'd expect from you, under the circumstances, and it's also just a little bit encouraging to those of us who'd like to see you relax in post.' She raises a finger, as if owning up. 'Of whom I am one, by the way.'

'I know.'

'Do you want me to stand you down?'

The question comes naturally. No blame attaches, and no suggestion one way or the other. It is just a question.

Almost, the Inspector says no without thinking. Then she wonders whether she does. She could take a holiday, leave the whole mess behind. Let it be someone else's problem.

'No,' she says at last, and Keene nods again at her duly considered answer, and puts away her pen.

'So now we can either have a conversation about overly narrow focus for a few hours, which I think will be quite unproductive, or you can go out and play with the other children some night this week and pretend to have fun so I don't have to come down there and drag you to a bar full of people who score highly on your personal compatibility index.'

'There is no such bar.' She has cause to know this.

Keene looks at her, owl-eyed and only half joking. 'There is if I bloody well say there is.'

Yes. If she recommended it and the System judged it expedient, it could happen tomorrow. Neith would almost certainly never get over the embarrassment. Unless it worked, of course. She wonders whether she should call the other woman's bluff, and decides: no. Nor will she point out her nascent encounter with Jonathan Jones. Keene must know it's there, must therefore be taking her cue to ignore it from their own pacing, their shared stateliness.

'All right,' Neith agrees. 'I will have fun.'

'You will go out on the town.'

'I will.'

'To a disreputable bar?'

'Yes.'

'This very evening?'

'I have a meeting this afternoon' – which Keene must know, of course. Just as she knows Neith has nothing in the evening and nothing tomorrow morning, so she can sleep in if the evening becomes raucous. Keene would, in fact, consider that ideal. The Witness Welfare Officer, without the benefit of a live internal monitor, clearly has no difficulty in following her thoughts.

Neith considers. If she says it, she can't renege. Keene will check. She takes a deep breath. 'Yes!'

Keene makes a glad noise, like the cork coming out of a bottle. 'Ah! Good. My work here is done. Carry on, Inspector Neith.'

Keene bows herself out, and the Inspector thinks, as she always does, that it is quite unclear whether Keene would be upset if she suddenly died, or just perplexed.

The alarm bell that rings in her head twenty minutes later is surely nothing more than an echo of Diana Hunter's paranoia. All the same, she cannot quite let go of the idea, as unsettling as it is absurd, that the visit of Pippa Keene creates a paper trail of official concern that might, down the line, be used to displace or discredit her.

*

'Never mind the length,' Tubman says, 'feel the quality. Right?' He has a paper mask around the back of his neck which makes him look like a doctor. When she doesn't laugh, he sighs and says something about young people. Tubman is a decade older than she is, if that.

The Witness correctly judges that she's querying the age difference between them, and the answer appears in the corner of her eye: NINE YEARS AND FOUR MONTHS.

'Neuroplastic false body syndrome,' Tubman says.

'I don't know what that means.'

'The balls. Scratching. Neuroplastic body syndrome. You might be a bit clumsy from time to time as well. Bad handwriting, that sort of thing.' Tubman shrugs. 'It's what happens when you spend too much time being someone else. Proprioception gets all botched up. Three someone elses, I gather, plus the victim. Yes?'

'Four.'

'Oh, for fuck's sake.' Hands in the air: why do you bring me things that are already broken? When she still doesn't understand, he snorts at her. 'Your brain responds physically to what's going on. It adjusts to new input. Normally that's not an issue because it takes days. And frankly most people don't have an awful lot going on up here.' Tapping the side of his head. 'You know what the most alarming thing is about working my job? It's seeing how small the files are. A living self should be all huge and shiny. Nope. Small enough to fit in a jamjar, mostly. Couple of fireflies going round and round each other, that's all. Sometimes you get, you know, a disco ball. Not a lot. So then you start looking at people in the street: are you real? Are you a jamjar or a proper lightbulb? And then you ask the same thing about yourself.'

Neith holds up a hand. 'Tub. Please. I thought this was okay.'

Tubman gestures vaguely at the machines behind him. 'It *is* okay. But you must have noticed the quality of the impression, surely. The reality? It's crystal clear – very nuanced, very detailed. There are deep colours in this, proper textures. Most times with an interview tape, if you freeze the frame and look around, you can see where the brain's cobbling perception together around the blind spot over the optic nerve, painting in the hues at the edges, all that. Everything not dead centre in your field of vision loses colour. You know that? The corner of your eye sees basically in greyscale. What you see is a composite. Are we following?'

She nods again. Yes. 'Persistence of vision.'

'Spot on. Well, so. Your subject here has done a better job with the visualisation. I mean much better, like a stage set rather than a photograph. The simulation is crazy real. It's actually more real than real things are when you experience them because it's all there, waiting for you to see it. She must have done a lot of preparation and concentration, except that she wasn't concentrating while she was under, was she? Because we don't do volition when we're in the throes.' Tubman shrugs. The Inspector can almost imagine the Witness tagging his observation: *anomalous*.

'Not normally,' the Inspector says.

'We do not,' Tubman avers, with magisterial certainty, 'but this recording is what you call informationally dense.'

She thinks of the shark swimming in a sea of green numbers. 'So, what? A hidden message?'

Tubman shrugs. 'Millions of them, in theory. Or one enormous one. Or one small one and a lot of places to hide it. But as I understand it, she wasn't about hiding the message, was she? "Bugger you" would appear to be her drift. I saw a picture of her house, though. Very nice. All dishevelled and folksy, Greenham Common as styled by Margaret Hamilton. Just how I like my girls.'

Tubman is married, to a stern and fashionable Venezuelan doctor whom he adores. The Inspector rolls her eyes at him: get on with it.

'No, all right. It could be something like that, steganography, cryptography, all the naughty toys. I'd have said not. I mean, what's the point? If you really want something secure, this isn't the way. You want to lock something down, you do it with multiple keys, layers of security, not this peekaboo. This is ... it's what you call lingerie encryption. Looks sexy, doesn't conceal anything at all. Think about what we do with access to critical infrastructure. Biometric's barely the beginning of it, and then there's next-gen connectome stuff just to get you in the door. Someone else's department, thank God. Obfuscation like you're asking about ... hiding in plain sight, breaking up the message – well, I suppose you could call it artisanal. You can do it, but you need to be brilliant and dedicated. And a bit mad, maybe.'

Three words which summarise what you don't want in an adversary, if that's what Hunter is.

'Describe it to me. Obfuscation.' She knows, but that's not the point. The point is Tubman's brain and the way he sees things, not as abstracts but as tools.

'All forms of clouding the issue, if you like. In the first instance by just being bloody awkward. There was a school of thought about twenty years back that instruction manuals should be hard to read so that users were forced to learn the instruction set rather than refer to the readme. Bloody annoying, but it's a fair point, you do use your head. Then there's jumbling, which you do with code. The machine doesn't care what order things are in, it's only people who read things in a straight line. Machine sees instructions, human sees noise. Obliquity: hiding intent by approaching from an unusual angle. Occultation: concealment by blocking the view, like an eclipse. Steganography: concealing a signal in noise. Encryption: rendering something incomprehensible unless you have the key. All possible, but at this level you'd be hard pressed to know.'

'The System should know.'

'Mm. That would depend how much whoever was trying to hide whatever it is knew about the System in the first place. It's an amazing bit of kit, but it's not God. It's just as bad at looking at two black faces and seeing a white candlestick – in its own terms – as anyone else.'

Well, if detection was easy, everyone would be doing it.

'Everyone' being Smith, say, watching over her shoulder, or Keene.

'Mielikki? About this other stuff.'

The texture of Tubman's voice has changed. In all her encounters with him, he has always been robust, most especially when he is worried. He is one of those who hides uncertainty in jovial humour: Gordon's alive!

But now he could almost be standing on one leg, wringing his cap in his hands like a first-year schoolchild afraid of the cold water, or the dark.

She does not press. Information is something that comes to you, if you let it. Reach out, and often the reflection is disturbed, the fish bolts.

'I knew a wire cutter once called Carrington. Worked the cable, same as me, but a proper oily rag, right? No bloated sense of importance like yours truly, didn't bother to remember the technical stuff. Carrington was strictly diggers and clippers. Dog-end in the mouth, always. We used to drink together, and that was not a good thing the following day. It was always the full monty: drink, smoke, dance on the table, girls in feathers. Get thrown out at five a.m. and plenty of donnybrook with the bouncers. He loved affray.'

Neith nods: mostly a vanished breed, thank God.

'Well, Carrington and some of that lot, they said sometimes when they were running tests, they'd find things. Bits of extra cable that shouldn't be there. Redundancies, probably, like if there was a terror strike and everything had to keep working. But sometimes they'd have to chop around those bits and bobs, and sometimes they even had to splice them, and when they did of course they had a little look, because, well: you would, wouldn't you? The way they had it, you'd think it was the System talking to itself, like you do when you look in the mirror and you find a stranger looking back. I mean, everyone has that, right? We all have little moments of madness. But the System shouldn't. Shouldn't be looking in the mirror at all.'

'What did they think it was?'

'They mostly didn't. Like I said: no delusions of adequacy. But one of them, she was different. Tin foil hatter, if you get me. She said it was the System changing its mind. Waking up, maybe, or tossing in its sleep.'

Another lurid favourite of entertainment programming: suppose the System were alive, and fell in love with a soft-focus librarian who underestimated her own physical attractiveness? Would it become demented in its jealous rage and murder every man who came close to her?

The Inspector tries a smile, leans forward and juts out her chin, essays an accent. 'Eleven hundred men went in the water. Three hundred and sixteen men come out. Sharks took the rest.' It hangs in the air, much less funny than she wanted. *Sharks. Shit.* 'Did you ever see it? Even the cable?'

'No. They always promised they'd call me, next time it happened, but it was bollocks, wasn't it? Pub talk. Ghosts in the wires. Ragging on the new fellow.'

'Is he still around?'

Tubman shakes his head. 'Near on the whole team got it ten years ago. Sink hole. It was in the news. They went through the ceiling of a bubble out by Crystal Palace. Drowned in the mud.'

Neith stares at him. 'Jesus, Tub.'

'Sorry.'

'That's the most ghastly thing I've ever heard.'

'Yeah, it is a bit. Still. Beats testicular cancer, I suppose.'

'Jesus, Tub.'

'I never really liked him, if I'm honest.'

She glowers at him. Tubman peers back, clears his throat. 'You say this is in your head? Full install and unspool?'

'Yes. Is that a problem?'

Tubman sucks air, then shakes his head. 'No. It's fine – but do your exercises, right? This level of fidelity, you might have more trouble with overspill. Like software. Exceed the field, maybe get into the command line.'

'I don't know what that means,' she says, conscious of repetition.

'Bad dreams. If you really went for it, and viewed the whole thing in real time, I suppose you might be a bit malcoordinated afterwards. Forty-eight hours you'd feel wonky. Two weeks of headaches and irritability, like a concussion. Although with the shifts from one person to another, it ought to be limited.'

She hesitates, thinking of Lönnrot. 'Tub?'

'Mielikki?'

'How long did the interview take?'

Frowning makes him look fatter, flesh piling over pale brows. 'Don't know, can't guess. Longer than average. A lot longer. Why don't you look it up?' He nods at the ceiling.

She wants it from a person, she realises. She doesn't want the answer on a screen. She wants to hear it said.

'Shit,' she mutters. She'd been sure Lönnrot was wrong. Well, no, she hadn't. But she had hoped anyway.

'That's not what you should be asking, though.'

'So what should I be asking?'

'How did she possibly load up her brain with false memories on this level? Who can do that?'

'Who can?'

'Well, until this, I would have said no one.'

For a moment, she doesn't want to leave. Tubman is safe, reliable. But that's the point.

'You don't look happy,' he says.

'I'm doing the same things over and over. It's not working.'

As if we are the ones who are trapped on a flat surface.

'I understand that's detective work. Or growing up. Or the definition of madness. Opinions differ.'

'Oh, thank you.'

'I'm known in some circles as a very spiritual man.'

'Are these circles getting the help they need?'

'Do your exercises,' Tubman replies as he shows her out. Quite without precedent, he wraps her in the brief embrace of a worried mother before shutting the door.

*

The Inspector takes the lift, three floors up, and follows the blue line on the floor to the interview rooms. Walking past the first four, she lets herself into the empty fifth and switches on the light. Always before, she has walked this building with a kind of ambient pride, but not now. Now it is a crime scene, and the bad act – she has begun to know that it was bad, even granting that Hunter courted it – stains the walls and the air. Her unease deepens as the warm, bright illumination of the interview room rises at the touch of her fingertip on the switch. The empty chair in the centre of the room – ergonomically adjustable and fine-tuned to the most emotionally reassuring contours for the great majority of the population – has acquired for her a predatory quality recalling an old laboratory experiment called Wire Mother. In the Wire Mother test, mice were conditioned to consider a razor-edged structure as a parent – which they did, taking food and rewards for proximity and becoming accustomed to the inevitable injuries. Analysis revealed that, after a while, their brains came to consider the abuse as a something like love.

The Inspector sighs, recognising the tracery of Hunter's reactions to this room, laid across her own. She takes a steadying breath. The phenomenon is known to agents of the Witness as frosting, as on a cake, and scientific opinion is that it does not exist. Identification is inevitable, but change in the structure of the self is not. She is not Hunter. Hunter is not Neith. One is alive, one is dead, and the only connection between them is a recording, no more conscious than a wax cylinder. She is here for a reason, a driving purpose: find the truth, share it, exact justice. That is all she needs to regain a sense of who she really is.

She lays her fingers on the touchscreen. Every direct neural interview is recorded from an external perspective as well as the inevitable internal one, so that accidents and delays can be better understood. The information becomes part of the public record, but is not freely accessible. As with other sorts of restricted knowledge, anyone may apply for permission to review it, but must provide a quorum of voters with a sufficient reason for their interest. Permission is not normally withheld except in cases of simple prurience. In this instance, the matter is sub judice, meaning that it will only be freely available after the Inspector has completed her investigation, although an oversight group, randomly selected from individuals deemed sensible and solid, can be convened to require access to all her files in an emergency. Agents of the Witness are afforded a measure of independence in their work in line with what is colloquially known as the Van Riper Principle: give a job to your best, and then let them do it without looking over their shoulder.

The Inspector could perfectly well observe the process anywhere, of course, but since she is here anyway, she chooses to watch the file here, in the place where it all happened.

Defying her physical aches, she lowers herself into the subject's chair in the middle of the room. Immediately, the central screen lights, and when she shuts her eyes the paused playback is laid over her senses. The Inspector sighs resignation: archival footage, stored at only moderate fidelity, always feels like polishing a tooth.

She starts the recording, her point of view shifting to that of the Witness itself, of the archival cameras recessed into the walls and ceiling of the room. A moment later Hunter is lifted, unresisting, into the space presently occupied by the Inspector's body.

*

Neith darts between crucial moments in the decision chain that culminated in Hunter's death. She begins to see how it must have happened. She watches technicians flag, then set up little nests of jackets and shoes on the floor, then go off-shift and be replaced. The timers on various screens go from contented green to warning yellow to klaxon red, then into a mid-range blue that signifies a sort of conceptual bewilderment. This is the colour no one ever thought would be displayed when the software was written, and it has no established semiotic message at all. The Inspector fancies that someone, back down the line, chose blue to signify 'we're all completely at sea now'.

As time goes by in the recording – as she zooms and slows, steps out of the flow and then back into it – the faces change, but the centre of everything remains the same: Diana Hunter, silent and still in her chair.

It is an illusion of ease. Hunter was worn out and burned out, with no reserves and battered by the constant artificial stimuli in her brain. Her blood was flooded with stress hormones her exhausted organs could not properly process. She had not slept. Humans need sleep, but it was not in the protocol for a direct neural interview because it had never been a problem before. Neith tries to imagine nearly a day and a half fighting inside her own brain against an enemy who could not be beaten or evaded: a war of attrition in which Hunter was both the beleaguered defender and the battlefield.

It makes no sense. What could Hunter possibly have to hide, that she would endure this, if not for ever, at least for just long enough? Surely no one is so wretchedly ornery as to die out of spite? She had a good life, a nice place to live. For social contact she had her neighbours, bartering and making trades off the grid, upcycling and retooling. She had her school for miniature refuseniks, the local kids to whom she read moderately inappropriate stories. Neith, indeed, remembers some of them from her own childhood: harmlessly wicked value-inversion jokes about kindly monsters and nasty knights. Diana Hunter was angry and formerly successful and where she was not loved she was mostly left alone. Why would she bother to hold out?

It was enough time for a family to flee. Enough for friends – co-conspirators – to disappear. But no one has. No one is missing.

No one is out of place, out of pocket, even out of breath. No one, particularly, seems sad. The world continues along its path as if Diana Hunter never existed – and isn't that a sorry statement of a life's end?

So some dark purpose, then, and this resistance long enough for comrades to change the codes, the target, the means. Long enough for them to strike!

Not that they have.

This new figure, masked, she identifies as Smith. His body language is familiarly imperious. He dickers with the specialist in charge of the interrogation, apparently wishing the other man to leave altogether, then accepts him with ill grace as a flawed amanuensis. After a certain number of hours there's a great medical flurry of intervention, a sudden crash. An emergency door opens and the crash team enter, resuscitate her, then she crashes again and they actually open her head to install a bypass tube for blood and then a chitosan interface chip to allow the System to connect parts of her brain that are no longer able to link themselves. The computer is not only keeping her alive, it is thinking with her: machine–substrate processing. It is both expensive and intensive, like using jet engines to power a wooden windmill. Hunter is unconscious, and then she sleeps. Then, nothing: a simple resumption of business as usual. Again the unprotesting body becomes the centre of a regular, slow procession of persons.

It occurs to the Investigator that as she lives through what was happening inside Hunter's mind, she is constructing a mirror of her. Just as Hunter invested masks with life, so Neith, alive, shapes herself to the other woman the way a transplanted face, hanging on the muscle and bone of the patient, takes on her identity. In fact the symmetry is perfect: the mask of Mielikki Neith looks back into the eyes of the corpse.

*

The archive footage runs its course, and the Inspector watches it in accelerated time, not expecting anything of consequence. It's not as if someone will suddenly break into the room and shoot her. She will die under sedation.

But Neith will watch anyway. It is her case.

It has always been the argument against coercive interrogation, even back when that meant torture: if the clock is already ticking on the bomb, then the terrorist need only be brave for exactly that long. What would you suffer, what would you endure, if you knew as the rack tightened that you need only last a day to save your family, serve your god, win your cause?

Conversely, what if Hunter had no secrets at all? If she was just desperately, furiously, pathologically 'private'? Could she have held out for this ugly record for no other reason than cussedness, and called it victory?

That would be a grim sort of answer. How long was it, finally? Another hour? A half day? Neith queries the Witness again. And stares at the answer on the screen.

Not thirty hours, and not thirty-five either. Not forty-five. Not even fifty.

Neith looks again. She must have misread. She has not.

Diana Hunter was interrogated for 261 hours.

Mielikki Neith knows her mouth is open in a comic-book rendering of shock. She does not for the moment know how to close it. She feels cold and sick. Her hands are shaking.

Two hundred and sixty-one hours. She divides by twenty-four. Easy: 240 is ten days, which leaves 21 hours. She can feel Constantine Kyriakos nodding, his head heavier than hers, neck and back proportionately bulkier. When she rolls her face to the ceiling, she cannot understand, for a moment, why the flesh at the nape does not fold like a button accordion.

Almost eleven days.

And she cannot help but think, hot on the heels of that impossible number, that eleven days under interrogation is a sort of execution. At the very least, malfeasance. She copies the whole file, redundantly, to her investigation's evidence server.

She told Keene this was how it was. She knew already. And yet this is something more.

You will say: 'Did they murder her?' Lönnrot told her.

The Inspector now begins to see that she might.

*

As the gloom of the winter afternoon gives way to actual dark, the Witness reminds Mielikki Neith that she has pledged this evening to leisure, on pain of Pippa Keene's disapproval. The Inspector, in the tradition of obsessive crime-fighters, resolves to make a virtue of necessity.

There is no band called the Fire Judges playing regularly anywhere in London – or for that matter anywhere in the world – but Neith's searches do locate the Duke of Denver, a former pumping station on the Thames, which hosts live music. Good, then. It will be, by all available accounts, an enjoyable evening's entertainment. She walks south, reviewing the news of the day. Narrow focus is a bad habit; crime does not operate in isolation from the wider world.

Text and images scroll, translucent, across her glasses – openings and closings, celebrity gossip, top ten lists on one side, global stories on the other. Her preferred version of the Monitoring Bill is under siege, assailed both by those who want the technology rolled out as widely as possible and by a surprisingly numerous rearguard of precautionary sceptics advocating for the 'essential and irreducible biologicality' of the received human body. Irked by the suspicion that this wording means whatever anyone wants to read into it, but indicates at the same time some vague disapproval of such things as surgeries, prostheses and vaccinations, she looks at the detail of the story. The numbers are still solid. Fine. A few steps later, she cancels out of the feed. Normally she likes the ubiquity of information flow, but abruptly in this moment she feels the need to operate in a white space: to sink down into the slow textlessness of her heartbeat and her stride.

A timeless quarter hour later, she arrives at the Duke of Denver. The back room looks out over grimy wooden pilings, either a vanished pier or some ancient attempt at silt management, and in this unpromisingly damp performance space a quintet by the name of Core Rope Memory are making music, and doing it well.

The Inspector drinks Scotch, and listens. Core Rope Memory are a physically attractive bunch – the lead, in particular, is a perfectly tousled thirty-something who goes by the stage name Break – but once you hear them that's barely important.

She lets her gaze dwell on Break's fingers as they move across the fretboard, the curve of muscle moving in the deep V of a poetically unbuttoned white shirt. Mostly, barely important.

Once, a long time ago when she was still a student, the Inspector travelled to the island of Santorini and scuba-dived among the ruins on the shallow floor of the Med. The sea was utterly clear, and she found herself unable to remember that it was composed of water. Her mind insisted that she was flying rather than swimming, that she was leaping weightlessly and impossibly between the stones of fallen temples, that the particoloured fish must be birds or insects. In this fugue state she was darting back and forth, laughing into her regulator with a clear, clean joy, when she felt a kind of electric shrugging. Her ears popped and her whole body growled and buzzed as if touched by a high-voltage wire. She heard a noise that came from inside her, transmitted through water into her skeleton and lungs and sounding there, audible in her ears by their connection and proximity to the source. She was played upon, and overcome, floating to the surface to stare at the bright Greek sun and a perfect sky. The noise came again, a different note, and finally again one last time like a harmony, and then was gone.

After she had floated for a while, she heard the guides calling and saw them hurrying towards her in a Zodiac, and she waved and climbed aboard, still entranced by the vastness of the chord.

'Earthquake,' the guide said, as they headed for the shore. 'Big one, in the caldera. You okay?'

She was, she said. It had been beautiful. He gave her a worried look and took her to the first aid station on the beach to check for narcosis, the bends, and half a dozen other things she didn't have. Finally they let her go, and she wandered up and down the shore, picking her way between topsy-turvy sun loungers and wrecked sunshades, ducking in and out of beach bars looking for someone to talk to, someone who would understand her sense of dimming joy and tragic separation. In the noise, she had been complete.

She couldn't find anyone else who had heard it, then or later, and eventually abandoned the idea as a dream brought on by some transmitted impact in the ocean.

Played by Core Rope Memory, Bach's *Musical Offering* to Frederick the Great is the first thing she has ever heard that touches the moment, or touches her in the same way.

'Frederick and Bach were a little bit at war, and a little bit in love,' Break murmurs, contralto, between sets. 'Frederick was all about the new music and Bach was the defining master of the old.' Long fingers touch lightly at the keyboard, stroke out a brief lament which somehow harks to the last piece. 'And in the public duel between them, Bach was beaten! Never happened before. Man, he was angry. Can you even imagine? The old master, publicly spanked by a young king who was into the contemporary equivalent of boybands. The best in the world, unable to respond to his opponent's casual suggestion that he improvise an impossible fugue. This one ...' Rippling notes, curiously out of touch with one another, as if two different patterns of sound were somehow fused – and then Break does something and the little tune becomes sprightly, even mocking. 'But Bach wasn't having it. Oh, hell no. And in the ensuing battle of wits and scholarship, the elder statesman of Learned Counterpoint kicked his feudal master's arse!' Laughter. More rippling music, as if incidental. 'While Freddie was whooping it up, Johann Sebastian was brewing a musical potion the likes of which no one had ever seen or even thought of. Working for a total of two weeks on a piece now reckoned to be one of the most complex and remarkable examples of its kind ever devised.' Now the music stops, and Break leans away from the instrument and towards the audience, towards – it seems to her – Neith in particular, though she knows that this is the performer's illusion, that everyone in the room is catching the glint of those eyes, the quirk in the full mouth, and thinking it's just for them. 'Take that, Freddie.'

After a moment, the fingers touch the keys again, and Break pantomimes surprise. 'The Canon per tonos, for example, returns upon itself a full tone higher than it begins, inviting the player – that's me – to continue the piece upwards, ever upwards, to another realm of expression, to the Celestial City, to the far reaches of ultrasound and the image of the human body's interiority, to music which could only be played in solar plasma.' He snatches his fingers from the keyboard as if burned, blows on them. Laughter. He resumes, more sedately. 'It's cyclical, forever trending upwards, like the alchemical symbol for fire. It is therefore sometimes known as the "Eternal" or "Heavenly Canon".'

Without really meaning to, she does something she has never done before, running a location ping on Jonathan Jones. Not far away. Alone. Reading and drinking wine over a bowl of gnocchi in a place she has never heard of. It must be new. The reviews say it is excellent. Jones has not yet added his own opinion, which is heavily weighted with acquired respect.

She realises she has made quite a bold move, like the sudden hinge point of a casual contact where the hand is not withdrawn. There is no going back to where they were, to the pretence of disinterest. If she does not reach out to him, after this, she will look flighty. She wonders if he has a flag set, and whether he is thinking the same thing, pondering whether he should pre-empt her.

'I'm in the Duke of Denver,' she says, and sends the message. She wonders whether she should add 'hungry', but he will know that. He will check her itinerary and deduce it. Perhaps he will order something for her.

Break grins to the room. 'The album is called *Catabasis for the Masses*. Be careful when you write that down. Your autocorrect will change it to "databases".'

Databases. Catabasis. The Inspector grimaces. For the first time in recent memory, she has the flickering sense of her work interfering in something important. Keene would be thrilled.

Jonathan Jones observes teasingly that the bar snacks at the Duke are not said to be its finest feature.

Break is talking again. 'The *Musical Offering* is not just a composition, it is a challenge! It's a lecture series, a very polite feudal fuck you, and a statement of identity. And it's something else.' A high note hangs for a moment. 'Bach didn't give Freddie the full score. What he actually handed over was a kind of compressed version – implicate music. If Freddie wanted to know what Bach had laid on him – if he wanted to know for sure whether he'd been answered, and someone like Freddie can't take another bloke's word for it – he had to educate himself in the old geezer's understanding. Exactly what he'd never bothered to do. The *Musical Offering* takes Freddie's gambit and turns it on its head. In order to counter Bach's riposte, Frederick had to educate himself in all the things Bach thought a king ought to know, and thereby become the man Bach desired him to be. Old bastard quite literally changed his enemy's mind – to make it more like his own. Seek and ye shall find, Bach tells Frederick. Quaerendo invenietis.'

A smattering of laughter. Neith does not join in.

Damn.

Quaerendo Invenietis: Diana Hunter's last book, and the formal title of Athenais's false scroll. A biblical injunction – or an invitation to a detective. In her nostrils the faintest trace of sandalwood and star anise – not here, in the room, but in her head, and associated somehow with Lönnrot. Yes. She can smell the absurdly clean black cloth, the bland absence of human scent on too-pale skin.

She thinks of Jones, and the implicit direction of their dialogue: dinner. An actual meeting.

But now Break is saying it again: catabasis. Promisory lips, wine-dark, quirked like Lönnrot's. *You are a woman traversing the skins of an onion.* She feels Bekele's mouth, old and young both at once, shaping his vision of the universe in five concentric spheres – a very simple onion, she supposes. Both notions might be represented in music by Break's 'Eternal Canon', from Bach's *Musical Offering*, the work intended to change Frederick's mind – not to persuade him but to educate him. To make him think like Bach. To change his connectome, as it were. Oh yes. This is where Lönnrot intended her to be, watching pieces of Hunter's puzzle align like one of Bekele's fivefold paintings – five parts to a whole, each claiming to embrace all the others.

She looks around, half expecting the weird white face to be hosting the show or tending bar, half seeking a small but powerful explosive device tucked under a table. A few seconds later she feels her terminal vibrate in covert emergency alert, and nearly jumps up to clear the room. Glancing down, she finds a red box on the screen: PROXIMATE OFFICER ALERT, meaning that she is the nearest investigator of the Witness to the scene of a serious crime and has been assigned the case. She feels a prickle of annoyance at the idea of taking on new business, and at being so rudely jerked from Break's musical ministrations.

— *You need to come immediately.*

The Witness very nearly sounds tense. She wonders if the synthesised voice has been adjusted to convey urgency.

'So I see.'

— *The System will reimburse you for this evening's performance. Traffic flow has been pre-empted and a vehicle has been retasked for your use.*

'What's on the card?'

Again, the Witness seems reluctant, even daunted by the answer.

— *There has been a murder. Oliver Smith is dead.*

For one moment the Inspector allows herself to stop, and be completely still. She can hear the hooting outside, and a huffing pair of executives are climbing out of what was until a few seconds ago their taxi. The Witness is assuring them another one will be along shortly to continue their journey, and thanking them for their cooperation in that particularly bland iteration of its audio interface that presages a warning to stop breaching the public peace.

Proximate officer.

Now she knows why Lönnrot wanted her here, at the Duke of Denver. Or one reason. Nothing is only one thing, she reminds herself.

— *I will reply on your behalf to Mr Jones.*

Dear Dog-walker, I hope you are as patient as you seem. 'No, that's all right. I'll do it.'

Twenty minutes later she is standing in the cold, seeing a real-life corpse on the tarmac of a tunnel under the Thames.

*

London has always rested on a honeycomb of passages and voids, and each iteration of the capital seems to need more space beneath the earth.

Even as other cities reach skyward or outward, London burrows down into the dark. Eight tunnels now run beneath the city in a grid, north–south and east–west, called respectively the 'Warp' and 'Weft' routes. These are the main roads that make transport within the overpopulated hub remotely possible; without them the city would freeze. This one is Weft 3, a favoured commuter journey from Oxford into the heart of the City. It is nearly seventy miles from one end to the other, and when first constructed required its own dedicated police and emergency unit, though many of these functions have now been subsumed by the Witness. In the event of a power outage – which is therefore engineered to be many times less likely than a direct meteor strike – the atmosphere inside would become lethal in a matter of minutes. It is a self-contained world and the tunnel must be lit dynamically or else the rhythm of the pools of shadow and illumination can induce pseudo-epilepsy in weary drivers. It is almost never closed. Today will be a very bad day for the capital's commuters.

The Inspector does not need to show a badge to pass through the crowd. Human nature being what it is, and the System being at least aspirationally open and public, there is always a crowd of onlookers at major scenes, but they make room for her because everyone knows she is an Inspector of the Witness. She wishes fleetingly that they wouldn't, and wonders how much of their helpfulness is really respect and how much is a trace of fear.

She steps through the cordon, and feels her mouth open in the classic cartoon circle, then hurriedly closes it and starts to hum 'Jerusalem' because it's the first thing that comes to mind. Of the various ways to operate your biology according to your conscious desires she has learned here and there, one of the most useful is the knowledge that it is physiologically difficult if not impossible to vomit while humming.

Oliver Smith's body is, to put it delicately, dispersed. But a less bloodless assessment – and nothing about this, surely, could be called bloodless – would be that it has been torn apart by wild beasts.

The uniformed officers are watching her, and the Inspector realises – she does not work as the first responder all that often, though of course she knows perfectly well how to do it – that they are waiting for her instructions. She puts some iron in her spine and opens a channel to all of them. 'Attention, please. This is Inspector Neith! Push the cordon back ten metres in every direction; I want all of you using the assisted recognition program, and anyone who pings with any kind of violent or narcissistic profile, I want them tagged into the file and I want full watch for every second of their day and night for a week in any direction. Hold pending further inquiries. I repeat: keep all of them. Dump everything to the case folder, we'll sort it later, but I don't want to have trouble putting my hand on someone down the line. All right? Move!'

There's a gratifyingly immediate response. Good. She looks back at Smith and realises she has been given a green light to go through his entire life. She opens a channel to every on-call investigator. 'Murder, priority. The deceased is Oliver Smith, a senior employee of the Turnpike Trust. I'll need someone over at their office to collect everything from his desk. Dump all his files to the case folder at the same time. We'll need the last month of his life to the absolute granular limit. If he goes out of range even for five minutes I want bounced sound, reflected-image facial analysis, whatever we can get, and I want it immediately. The Trust is a private entity with government contracts. I'm issuing a blanket order, right now, for anything you think is significant. If they quibble, roll over it and apologise later. I don't imagine they'll want to share, that's something for the legal department to be troubled by, but use your overrides the way you've always wanted to and blame me. Understood?'

Confirmation appears in her glasses like the city catching fire. Men and women of her service, moving to do their job. She feels a little whisper of pride. This is how it should be, the unequivocal function of a justice machine.

A traitorous part of her insists that, in a moment, she must run a dream check.

'At this time I am officially connecting the murder of Oliver Smith to my existing case and folding them together under the case name GNOMON. All inquiries to me direct. No release of information without reference to me personally, and I will defend that order to any quorum up to the national level. I repeat: default no release. It is possible that this is the most important case you will ever work on. Any of you. Be proud today. Be fearless. Do your job well.' To the Witness: 'Meaning: catabasis.' Because you don't stop looking at a slim, complex clue just because someone dangles a fat, distractingly obvious one in front of your face.

— *The mystical journey of Orpheus into the kingdom of Hades, and by extension any voyage into darkness. Greek,* kata: *against, down;* basis: *the place on which you stand. Literally, a pedestal. Therefore 'catabasis', a journey down beneath the place where we stand.*

And here is Smith, dead in a tunnel. Tragic, but he was a villain.

She feels her heart lift in savage anticipation of answers, at last, and takes a moment to tamp down on the sense of restoration that is surging in her. Hold on, hold on. There is work to be done. She can't rely on this, she's been handed it, though of course hands leave prints. The case has cracks in it, yes, but it is not cracked. Not yet. *Settle. Use that fire. Use it, and win.*

She turns back to the grim remnant on the ground. *And did those feet in ancient times, mmmhmm hmmhmmHMM HMMMMM HMMMHMMM . . .*

Smith has been cut, gouged and finally torn apart, or possibly scissored. It is something she could have lived her whole life without ever doing, staring down into the tubular ruin of a chest cavity. She looks around, and finds Trisa Hinde. She starts to nod, then remembers that this won't necessarily mean anything obvious to Hinde, or might mean any one of several things and the spread of options will probably be annoying. She murmurs 'Hello' instead.

'Exsanguination,' responds Hinde.

'Yes,' the Inspector says.

'Although I'm not ruling out shock, either.'

'No.' Because one wouldn't. 'Weapon?'

Hinde shrugs, annoyed, and makes a swirly gesture with her hand to indicate bad reception or a data snafu. 'You try.'

The Inspector doesn't, not yet. She looks around first, at the disposition of the parts. Perfectly centred, each in its own pool of light. Unshifting light, not dynamic, not now. The traffic is stilled and the lighting algorithm has recognised a special circumstance and reverted to a static posture. Once, as a child, Mielikki Neith read a story about an old man who lived in the forest and was kind to all the animals, and when he eventually died the forest was silent and dark for a year, so that the people of the town believed it cursed, until the old fellow's daughter, hearing of the darkness in her father's favourite place, came home and chose to be married in a sunlit clearing in the heart of the wood and occupy his home with her new husband, and the whole forest rustled and awoke, and the birds and the flowers bloomed once more. It is almost as if the tunnel itself is taking note of Smith's death and honouring its dead with its own version of that silence.

She breathes in, and out, and tries to see the scene as text.

When she looks again, she sees not illumination but the spotlights of a stage. The pools of light are not coincidental but painstaking – and surely Diana Hunter's injunction that the word should imply pain staked rather than pains taken has been obeyed here. This is agony and unthinkable fear written in blood across the grey surface of the road. It is a display, a victory procession. This crime is not a crime – or rather, its criminality is a side issue, the envelope in which the message is delivered. It is a code, and death is just a convenient vector.

The Inspector feels a chill. If Hunter sacrificed herself to make a point, and Smith was the instrument of her self-destruction and Smith is now dead, then whose message is written here? Smith's employer? His confederates, warning one another to stay true and quiet or face the consequences? Or is this Hunter's work, planned before her arrest and now playing out? In which case, who else is on her list? Smith's assistants in the Hunter interrogation? She puts a movement hold on anyone with strong professional connections to Smith: his whole first degree of separation. Report for immediate debriefing.

Then, with a jolt, she hears the words in her head: *Catabasis for the Masses*. Shit, she hadn't really acknowledged the second part. Catabasis, yes, fair enough, here we are. But none of this is for the masses. Is everyone going on this journey into death, in Lönnrot's perception? Should she be looking for a gas attack? A biological weapon? Orpheus came home, but Eurydice did not: should she be worrying about

376

something that targets two X chromosomes? Or is it just a brute 50 per cent kill rate?

No. She doesn't believe it. She tells the Witness to go to maximum sensitivity for traces of biological, chemical or radiological weapons, moves the whole network to a state of higher terror alert, but acknowledges she's doing so as a precaution and fires the query to Counter-terror for immediate consideration. She lets her gut unknot, soothes her heart back down into her chest. Terrorism of that sort is not Hunter. It's not Lönnrot. The former would be appalled by mass killing, the latter would be bored.

We're all going on a journey together, into the underworld, and Smith is our conductor. Our ferryman. Is that it?

He was Hunter's, that much is clear.

So, then: what journey? With a sinking feeling she looks over at Hinde and then down at the wounds again. Does it make any sense to call them wounds when there is in any individual sample more wound than corpse? Smith is not wounded: his wounds are lightly touched with the remnant of Smith.

She looks over at Hinde, who scowls: don't waste my time.

Neith queries the Witness for probable cause of death, suspecting she knows what she will hear and hoping she is wrong.

– *Shark attack*, the Witness says, *forty-two miles inland*. And then, almost apologetically, *Anomalous*.

Yes. Both impossible and obviously true. This was not a shark attack, here, in the dry air of the tunnel – and yet the Inspector can see the unimpeachable reality of it. The shark followed Kyriakos on to dry land, became a white-skinned woman with very dark hair. Then it crashed the economy. It never killed anyone. At least, not yet.

She needs to watch the rest of Hunter's memories, and soon.

For now, the Inspector shades the corners of her eyes as if peering into a letterbox. 'Show me.'

The real world fades away as her terminal projects fullscreen directly into her eyes, and she feels another twinge of nausea, this one inspired not by viscera but by the shifted viewpoint which does not accord with her body's awareness of its size and position. The feed is telling her she is fifteen feet tall, looking down on the tunnel with binocular eyes set nine inches apart: mantis vision. The first time accessing full feed while standing, many people fall over. The Inspector is not a rookie. She lets her weight sit in her heels, requiring minimal correction to her posture, and separates her sense of where she is from what she sees. It's just a trick. You learn to use your brain in a new way.

Smith's car is alone in the tunnel, moving precisely one kilometre per hour under the limit. Somehow or other he is the only one here: a caprice of traffic flow. Neith hopes he found that interesting.

Then the car slows and stops. Smith doesn't seem to know why. (Picture-in-picture: there's a dashboard camera looking up at him.) He huffs, irritated, and makes a call for assistance. The System asks him to remain in the car and assures him that other traffic will be warned or diverted. It's a standard message, and Smith relaxes.

Then, little by little, as nothing happens, he grows concerned. He looks around and evidently sees nothing, hears nothing. Neith, recalling her recent moment of midnight fear and the image of Lönnrot's hand reaching out to her from the mirror, feels a spasm of sympathy. Smith, too, seems to be having that unpleasant mammalian response to silence and occlusion: the itchy and unwelcome sense of an invisible watcher.

There's always a watcher, of course. That is the promise of the System. You are never alone, never unprotected. You need never be afraid of the dark.

The Witness cuts away from the interior of the car. The tunnel remains empty, white-green lights burning. Then, as the control algorithm confirms that no other vehicles are now inbound, the lights begin to dim: power-saving measure. The tunnel goes from a bilious artificial daytime to a cool silver nitrate dusk.

Smith twists in his seat. He must know he is safe in the car. He could not be more accompanied if he were in the middle of a ballroom. Well, the Inspector amends, he is actually not safe, but unless he knows something specific about this situation, he should assume that he is. Just as the Monkey King never left the palm of the Buddha, so Oliver Smith is even now held in the arms of his electronic mother, as safe as anyone in the world.

He tries to make an outgoing call and can't. There's no signal – the microwave booster must have been powered down at the same time as the lights. Smith toggles the connection repeatedly and starts looking over his shoulder. So far as the Inspector can observe, he has at this moment no reason to fear attack, nor to suspect that such an attack, if it comes, should come from behind.

For these few instants he is more alone than is generally possible for anyone in the System. Would Hunter have found this restful?

Some distance down the tunnel, just as Smith turns frontwards once more, one of the lights goes out completely. Smith says in what must be some sort of understanding: 'Oh God,' and now his face is not nervous but actually terrified. Whatever he knows, he knows without a doubt, as a mouse knows the presence of an owl.

Another light goes out. 'Oh no. Oh shit. Shit!' Smith's voice is rising and tightening. The Witness posits, based on expression and cadence, that he is reviewing causalities and options and cannot locate any that please him. In what is estimated with 98 per cent certainty to be desperation without the rational expectation of survival, he releases the seatbelt, lunges into the back seat for his coat. This is a strange thing that people do when they are about to run for their lives, but have not yet actually begun. The Inspector has seen it before: the residual obedience to convention. As soon as it gets in his way he will discard the coat, will briefly wish he had not brought it before he forgets even that much in his flight, but in this first instant he cannot imagine leaving his vehicle without his wallet and keys. The mundane part of his life insists that, having escaped from horror and survived, he will want a drink and access to his home, and how will he get these things without his effects? It is the same stupid impulse that kills passengers in air crashes, as they open the overhead locker before exiting a burning plane.

The next section of tunnel is plunged into darkness. Smith abandons the coat, caught on the central armrest, and makes another attempt to phone for help. If a phone call were possible from his location, he would not need to make one – help would already be on the way – but Smith is living the nightmare now: the machines are broken and the world is coming to an end.

— *No carrier,* the Witness says, so that she understands.

Smith gets out of the car and runs hopelessly. He's not wearing the right shoes and he's fatter than she realised when she met him. Leather soles skid on the road surface and he slips. He looks back over his shoulder, and starts to run again. The Inspector wonders whether he's telling himself that it must be a nightmare, and if so whether he's running through some variant of those same three tests she performs herself. There's text on the walls of the tunnel, some sort of notice, if he dared to stop and read it. Perhaps that's how he got caught. But no: he runs, with a single-minded certainty and desperation that almost makes her care about him.

Smith looks back over his shoulder, and then the inevitable happens. As he is turned the other way, the five sections of lighting ahead of him go out in quick succession. The darkness actually seems to lunge. Smith plunges into it. She has a brief glimpse of the scene in passive infrared, Smith falling painfully on his face, something cracking in one knee. He gets to his feet and calls out some sort of apology: 'I'm sorry, I didn't mean it,' although frustratingly the conversation is in media res and he doesn't feel the need to say what he's sorry for, or to whom. She hears what might be footsteps, or water dripping from a pipe, or some sort of static, and then the feed cuts as the recording comes to an end.

— *Power-saving measures,* the Witness says. *Anomalous. Reconstruction follows.*

It does not occur to her what this will be until she sees it, and then it is too late. In the too-perfect images created by the System to fill the gap in its own knowledge, Smith once again kneels on the floor of the tunnel. He cannot see, and so he is blind to the monstrosity that hovers over him. As he makes his brief apology it flicks away into the absolute subterranean dark, and then an instant later strikes him from behind and shears through the upper torso, white teeth casually cutting bone. The pieces fly apart, tumbling and bouncing and showering the road in bright ejecta. The shark spits, tossing its head, and something falls shining from its teeth into the guttering at the side of the road: that ridiculous watch fob.

— *Ends,* the Witness says, and adds, *anomalous,* apparently in case she wasn't listening.

But to Neith, it seems hardly anomalous at all.

She lets out the breath she has been holding and turns away from the body to think. Seeing it increases her awareness of the cloying air, the particulate fug of traffic and dust punctuated now with tiny fragments of blood and bone that she's breathing in, that the cells in her nose are reporting as a sensation but which are really floating samples of the red death of Oliver Smith.

*

She walks along the road, between the baggy blue plastic suits of the crime scene technicians and the pools of blood and piles of other things, until she reaches the spot. Then she kneels down in the scum of the road, and reaches though a grating with her gloved left hand. Almost, she recoils as she imagines that hand dangling in black water like a lure. Then her fingers touch a thin length of metal chain. She tugs, gently, with her fingers, and feels it come away. She draws it up.

Oliver Smith's watch fob.

And on it, beneath the grime, an engraving: a burning torch in a bundle of sticks.

— *Flambeau,* the Witness says immediately. *With fasces. The latter were appropriated by Mussolini's Fascisti, but were originally the badge of a Roman magistrate. The bundle would more usually contain an axe. In this case, the flambeau suggests a more recent armorial confection or a logo rather than an ancient source, although in some variations of the Prometheus myth, he conspired with a serpent to steal the sacred flame, and that serpent was fed as a punishment to the Titans. It could even be thought of as a simple rebus, meaning—*

'I know,' Neith tells the machine. 'Fire Judge.'

She scowls down at the object in her hand, and then looks up and into the crowd, knowing with a furious certainty whom she will see and preparing herself, the hunt fizzing in every inch of her.

And there it is: the pale, amphibious face of Lönnrot, coat collar turned up against the evening chill. She sees just a flicker of the smile, and then it's gone behind a white personnel transport with a thick metal grille across the windscreen. 'Rhino van', they used to call them in her mother's day, because they could roll over anything. The Inspector shouts something incoherent, points, and her officers converge without knowing what they're looking for. She speaks the name and knows that the Witness is updating them, sees them surround the place. She surges through her own line, the crowd suddenly too slow to move. She sees Lönnrot by a service tunnel doorway and screams again: 'There!' and knows four of her uniforms are following, more demanding street-level assistance, knows if they lose Lönnrot now it'll be too late.

She smashes into the closing door, head glancing against it, reels in and gives chase up a flight of concrete stairs, her shoes clanging against the metal treads on each one.

— *There are four hundred and eight steps*, the Witness says. *This is one of the deepest points of the tunnel*.

*

The West End at 2 a.m. wears the high-end suit and too-polished shoes of a man who used to be something, back in the day. Bursting through the service access on to the street, the Inspector casts around for Lönnrot. Bright lights dazzle, rickshaws spin, and the doors of respectable and less respectable members' clubs are watched by discreetly muscular bouncers.

There: a flash of cartilaginous skin. Lönnrot doesn't seem to have felt the endless climb to sea level at all, moves through the closing-time crowds at the same steady sprint that the Inspector kept thinking must surely fade as the stairs went round and round in a haze of white-glazed abattoir tiling and settled atmospheric grime. She is still following, still keeping the spiked black hair in sight, though her breathing sounds black in her ears and the edges of her vision are tinged with patterns cut in coffee stains or the residue of nicotine. Somewhere behind her, two constables are rasping on, booted feet heavy and determined, but the Hoxton academy obviously isn't making them like it used to, and they are falling behind. Neith will not quit. She will not lose Lönnrot again.

Assailant and murder suspect be damned: Lönnrot has answers to the larger puzzle, and this time she means to have them. She drives herself onward, ignoring the warnings of the Witness and her own body that if she catches up now she will be incapable of making an arrest. Her quarry must surely be in the same case, and somewhere on her body is the taser. She does not believe she is pursuing a ghost or a god-shark in the guise of a human being, nor yet a killer who just happens to be a specialist in endurance running. Everything about Lönnrot says mind: a perverse lethality that is the product of self-consideration rather than overclocked physical acumen. The pale feet crammed in those shoes must be hurting like hell.

Lönnrot turns down a narrow alley against the flow of human traffic, colliding with the first row and blasting through, exciting angry cries and objections. The Inspector puts her right shoulder forward and bull-charges straight ahead shouting 'WITNESS OFFICER!' As soon as this message makes itself heard, it clears a path, but the hubbub created in front of her is such that the advantage is minimal, and then when they reach the main street beyond she almost screams as she sees the pale face smirk at her and then duck into the entrance to the Soho Square tube station.

'Close it,' she tells the Witness, an instant later. 'Close the whole thing. Trains are non-stopping as of now. No one leaves. Do it.'

The machine acknowledges the order but sounds unwilling, and she knows why. At this time of night, the flood of people departing the central London leisure area is at its height, and the number already on the station will be in the tens of thousands. Ventilation and temperature control will rapidly become an issue. Under the wrong circumstances the closure could turn into a panic. How desperate is Lönnrot? How mad? Mad enough to shout 'fire' or 'bomb'? Surely, yes. If Lönnrot killed Smith, conventional perceptions of violent insanity may not touch what is behind the smile.

What if Lönnrot actually has a bomb?

She goes in.

*

383

The temperature inside is already a couple of degrees warmer than the outside, but it wouldn't be uncomfortable if she hadn't just been running harder than she ever has in her life. People stare at her, then see the Witness badge and step hastily aside, pressing against the corridor walls. The upper level is not packed out, but as she approaches the escalator she realises that her stop order has already blocked her path. She looks back, hoping for more officers, and finds none.

'Which way?' she asks.

– *Unclear*, the Witness replies. *The suspect must have taken refuge in the crowded area.*

Where line of sight is blocked and chemical trace – the detection technology based on bloodhound nasal cells – is deployed only in its crudest form to look for the telltale molecular wash of toxins and explosives.

There is no way out. She need only wait.

She knows that waiting is futile. She must put her hands on Lönnrot now, or wait for their next encounter.

She hops up on to the silvered metal of the escalator middle and slides down, slowing her descent with the soles of her feet against the informational touchscreen recessed into the metal. At the bottom she stands up and brandishes the badge again, jumps down into the small gap created for her, and begins to push through the crowd.

– *There has been a mistake*, the Witness tells her. *The lockdown is compromised.*

'They let someone out?' she nearly screams.

– *No. Egress is perfectly controlled. However, two gates have continued to admit travellers, and the station is nearing its recommended capacity.*

'Close it off!'

– *The matter is now in hand.*

She wonders if it is. *Perhaps I can walk through walls*, Lönnrot said, the first time they met. She still doesn't know how Bekele escaped from his cell. She wonders if she could check now, while running: stay conscious in two worlds at once, or play it all on fast forward. It's her mind after all. Probably an expert could do it. She pictures herself running blind on to the track: 'Witness officer!' and the crowd obediently parts, allowing her to fall towards the live rail. No.

She looks around at the mass of people and at the ceiling above. How many tons of rock? How many people now piling in on top of them all, choking the path to the exits? She pushes the thought away. Not relevant.

She pushes through the crowd, peering into faces, under hats. You? You? You? No. None of them is Lönnrot. The gaps between people narrow and the throng begins to push back against her, people asking where the trains are and whether they should leave, being told they can't, there's a lockdown, and starting to worry, to demand to know why.

The Witness comes back to her.

– *Stress hormone levels are rising in the lower levels.*

'I know, I'm here.' Her own stress levels are being affected by it, the unsubtle human crowd reaction. 'Turn on the fans.'

– *The circulation system is functioning at seventy-eight per cent of capacity. A higher power usage at this time will generate problematic amounts of waste heat. Since the heat is a potential health hazard, the present level of ventilation is regarded as an optimum compromise.*

The Inspector steps up on to a bench to look out across the sargasso expanse of faces. 'Give me a direction!'

– *The fugitive is not visible in the station.*

She swears and turns back the way she came, once again brushing people aside, using her body as much as her authority; a physicality she normally despises and regards even now as dangerous. Her Witness identification is a pacifying factor rather than a magic wand.

But it is effective. There, ahead of her and somehow running without really appearing to do so, is Lönnrot.

Each stride betrays the same uncanny weirdness as the bleached, kelpy face – a movement that speaks of a muscular invertebracy, as if this is not a human being she is chasing at all, but something bonelessly old or chimerically new: a person augmented with the muscle of a python; with cells from the trunk of an elephant. She looks again, and extends her hand to issue an instruction.

And then she stops, because she sees.

She sees, and she stares, not at the figure she is pursuing but at the cameras on the ceiling of the passageway, and at the vile, impossible thing they are doing. It is worse than the spineless hips, the dislocated steps. Those things she expects, somehow, from her quarry. If she learned tomorrow that Lönnrot were an image projected on to her eyes by her glasses in response to some illegitimate algorithm planted upon her personal devices by a felon, perhaps Smith himself, her only response would be that it explained a great deal. This is different.

'Where is Regno Lönnrot?' she asks, not believing what she hears when the response comes, even though she anticipated what it would be.

– The fugitive is not visible to System surveillance at this time.

And it is true, in a way. As Lönnrot moves, each camera is turning to look elsewhere. The Inspector knows with a disembodied, eerie certainty that if she looked at the screens upstairs, right now, she would see a babble of confusion and consternation, and that confusion would appear to be the perfect map of what is happening down here – but it would be missing, in perfect synchrony with Lönnrot's movements, the image of the one person she really needs it to see.

Perhaps I can walk through walls.

Yes. Perhaps you can.

*

Lönnrot, turning, catches sight of the Inspector. The elastic lips open into a lolling smile, and one hand moves in a lazy bedroom wave.

Mielikki Neith feels her fatigue lift. In the sudden firing of a rage she barely knew existed within her, she finds her feet absurdly light, her muscles fluid and responsive. Physical laws no longer seem to matter. She knows this for what it is: the famished predator's last gasp, the final effort gifted by hunter biology to stave off a death of depletion. She has very little time – but that does not matter. Nothing does, except that she is flying now, and laughing, as she steps after Lönnrot along the companionway, gaining ground, then on to the platform and through – 'Stop incoming,' she snaps to the machine, and trusts it is possible – and down into the track itself, from the heaving riverbank into the dry stream of high voltage and thundering mass. Lönnrot runs into the tunnel, into whatever train might be coming that cannot slow in time, and into the dark beyond. She follows, still light, but in her chest is a kind of acid ice she knows portends the end of her endurance: not the wall, but the thing that comes after it, the slow, cold halting that cannot be beaten.

But Lönnrot, too, has slowed. The white hands and face are all that she can see, bobbing and dancing jack-o'-lantern style in the gathering gloom as they press deeper into the dark, and then the left hand reaches out, smacks hard against a metal surface and presses in. The Inspector lunges but cannot stop the door from closing, hears the fatal clang of a thick bolt sliding into place. She rests her head against the door, feeling tears and mucus on her lips, foam and bile. For an instant she sleeps, or passes out.

When she opens her eyes again she sees in the light of her terminal what is written here, stencilled over the flaked metallic paint of the door. She remembers, just in time, that saying it out loud may have consequences.

FIRESPINE.

The Inspector walks back to the platform, and climbs out of the tracks.

'Open the doors,' she says after a moment. 'The suspect has evaded capture.' Then she watches the worst part of it all happen again.

— I will inform the street-level officers, the Witness says. *They may well be able to establish contact.*

Overhead, one by one, the cameras resume their vigilance.

*

In the aftermath of any great horror come two strange pauses, and during these one may hear the broken pieces falling to the floor. After a bomb, or a murder, or the collapse of a mine, there is the immediate silence of the dying. The first flush of demolition is done, and now there is consequence, and it is small and personal and infinite. The last of a stained glass window falls to the floor; the living count their wounds. Some get to their feet, while others discover their impermanence and struggle to comprehend the final curtain as it drops. It is the moment Neith knew floating in the ocean at Santorini, when the tectonic symphony had played itself inside her body, and ten thousand silver fish, each no bigger than a finger, drifted up and around her to die on the surface and in the mouths of gulls.

But after that moment, after the triage and the lonely wail of ambulances and the abrupt conversions of the survived, there comes another silence that is not physical at all. It is the sound of the world adjusting to its new shape, the hesitation before one life steps in to the vacuum left by another. It may last for weeks, or snap abruptly into place like the bursting of a balloon. Perhaps it is always both, and the difference is a question of where you stand.

The Inspector stands outside the station, in a circle of emptiness that belongs only to her. All around, the many minions she has summoned do their work, oblivious to the fact that it is pointless: that their quarry set them on the scent and now has salted the trail with aniseed and pepper so that the hounds are confounded. She is momentarily bereft of direction. If the Witness is so compromised, to whom should she report? In theory, yes: to the people directly – but short of standing on a box at Speaker's Corner and shouting with all the other prophets, how should she reach them if not through the System? The Public Sphere itself gets news through the same machine that watches and records. She would be mad to assume she can broadcast her findings by that route. Perhaps she can. But she cannot plan based upon that premise any more. She had assumed there might be a threat to her, personally, but not to information. You can always get information out these days – except if you can't.

Scrupulous justice and security of self. These are the meaning of the System to her. Not to her, to everyone under its Aegis.

I don't even have a shield.

She takes two steps away from the scene before realising that she is actually leaving, that she is not shifting her position but walking away, and then she just keeps going. Everything is wrong and nothing is right and there is too much noise here.

Fugue. Not Break's musical one, but the other kind, the psychological drift. She has seen it before as an aspect of the flow state, but here for the first time she experiences it arising from horror, and understands it as an aspect of defence. It is not dysfunction at all, but a kind of madness that will protect her from going mad.

She walks, one foot in front of the other, towards the bright lights of Oxford Street. Behind her, the Witness explains that the Inspector requires some time to consider the case, and that is fine.

*

The night air is very cold. The streets are fairly empty, though that will change towards the shopping area, gaudy with the approach of Christmas. The department stores will not be open this late, but the boutiques will, some of them, and the coffee shops and hot-desk sites that cater to business visitors from other time zones not yet orientated to GMT. There will be somewhere to buy a Union Jack, if that's your pleasure, or a bowler hat made of false felt, or a thong with a beefeater on it. There will be cheap, random gifts for your children, if you have forgotten that tomorrow is a special day.

The Witness has been compromised, and she cannot know to what extent. Oliver Smith is dead, and Lönnrot is invisible. Hunter was right and something is wrong and it must be fixed.

Greece shall be torn no longer.

She should be exhausted, and there is lactic acid in her muscles, not just in the feet and legs but all the way up her core and into her shoulders. Stress and effort to the point of failure. And yet she feels in some way light.

FIRESPINE.

Lönnrot's message, and if the obviously proximate word is a little much so, call it oracular instead.

Smith is dead. The Witness is compromised to a significant degree, and therefore by definition also the System as a whole, the two being inseparable. If the machine is not an honest broker then the System is – for the time being and to a greater or lesser extent – not a perfect state at all, but a perfect prison: a Panopticon in which the condemned must assume they are watched at all times and in all places, and act in line with the will of an arbitrary power. That power may counterfeit the action of justice in most cases, but justice incomplete is not justice, it is the anticipation of wrong. The System has as many eyes as it needs, and the Witness does not blink. It is distributed, intimate, internalised and perfect.

Why, then, is she walking rather than running? Why is she moving at all? If things are so bad – so dark and desperate – why, in this hour when heaven is falling, is she going shopping? Because shopping, certainly, is what she now intends, as she rounds the corner into the garish celebration of Oxford Circus. Not that she knows yet what she is shopping for, only that she has decided to shop, and in that decision is something unbending and determined.

If the System is truly compromised, then she has no hope. Yet hope is rising in her, and something steelier that she has never really had to deploy until now and did not know that she possessed – something in many ways unfashionable for an Inspector of the Witness: defiance.

This, she realises – this, right this moment – is her great case. It is the case every investigator should pray for, it is The One. Here, in the balance, is everything she cares about, and it is to be won or lost in her choices and her wit. Here for the first time she matches herself against an adversary who can destroy not only the local but the absolute meaning of her work.

She was appointed to this task. If she cannot track Lönnrot – if Lönnrot is invisible and Smith may be eaten by an impossible shark; if the Witness may blink, after all, and Hunter can elude the inquisition of the machine – it seems that her opponents also do not dare erase her, or care to – and nor can they ignore the process of her investigation, or position some collaborator to the task. They are new, then, or few in numbers, or bounded and constrained in some fundamental way. Such being so, they can be defeated, uncovered and excised, and the System can be fixed.

What did Hunter want? What did Smith want so badly from Hunter? What does Lönnrot want now, and why is Smith so very awfully dead? What is a Fire Judge? Who are they all, these people with their strange, unworldly concerns? Was the business of living not complicated enough?

What if the System cannot be fixed?

And what if it can, but can then once again be compromised, and so on and on and on so that one might never truly be sure whether one lived in heaven or hell? By definition: hell.

She stops for a moment between a barrow selling caramelised nuts and another with a heady vat of mulled red wine, cheap and acid before it was boiled and rank now with sawdust cinnamon. In the narrow space between them, a modest little coffee truck. She touches her terminal to the point of sale, then walks away again, drinking coffee and following her feet. She finishes the cup too soon on purpose, letting the last swallow burn her throat. She knows now why she's here.

She needs to buy a doll's house.

*

Carrying herself now with a calm she believes could last her whole life, but which she knows from experience is strangely temporary, the Inspector enters a grimly merry concession on three floors, the first decked in patriotic bunting. It is only a few minutes from her front door. She walks past it on off days and loathes the frontage, the generic portcullis shirts and red letterbox purses, the saucy key rings with smirking bikini girls driving buses. Once, though, needing a properly vile London-flavoured gift for a colleague from Manchester, she had forced herself to go inside – ultimately emerging that time with Tower Bridge chocolates in a moulded plastic presentational tray – and seen the upper floor, full of slightly higher-quality guilt gifts for wives and neglected offspring. She picks her way between Dick Van Dyke postcards and the silver-plate letter openers. A girl in a company T-shirt beckons her forwards, smile fixed, and throws a polystyrene aeroplane in a loop around her head.

'Two for one,' the girl says encouragingly as Neith goes by.

Up one flight and follow the arrows, and she is standing in the doll aisle, taking in the array. Purple plastic and pink plastic and fuchsia plastic vie for the title of Most Disgusting Shade, and the staringly exaggerated eyes of minidolls glower from the racks. She is able to discount immediately anything that is too small and anything that does not afford full access to the interior. Also unsuitable are those models with network access and cameras built in. At last, she calls a harried sales assistant over and gives him a list of specifications, which the man duly works his way through until he is able to propose two options. The plain white wooden one which she would actually like to give someone – if she knew any children – is frustratingly twice as expensive as the hideous Fashion TV Studio Plus! which doubles as a make-up station and occasionally speaks to you in a trilling faux-Italian accent about the importance of looking your best.

'I'll take that one,' she says, pointing, and at the same time picks up some light paper, a box of soft pencils and a hard steel clipboard debossed with the head of Oliver Cromwell on a spike. The sales assistant is very keen to sell her a lucite one instead, but the Mohs scale of hardness awards acrylic glass no more than a four, as against steel's five or six, so the Inspector demurs, wishing the shop's inventory stretched to products in tungsten carbide.

She finds a deserted chain cafe and buys something to eat that comes in a non-recyclable bento box and tastes barely biological itself. Not important; it's fuel and she's starving, regretting both Jonathan Jones and his gnocchi.

Putting the doll's house together takes longer than she had expected, and is made more rather than less difficult by the fact that she does not require the interior floors. After getting almost all the way there she has to go back and remove the voice box, and discreetly stamp on it until it stops talking. All the same, a little less than half an hour later she is the proud owner of a tabletop television studio comprised of two side walls and a greenscreen/cosmetics mirror at the back, this last having round, frosted lightbulbs around it in a pattern which the accompanying leaflet claims is 'industry standard'. She considers the angles in the cafe and adds the studio's half-roof (with scale model Fresnel lamps which actually illuminate the stage below) and rests the clipboard in the space where the stage should be. She sharpens the pencils and gathers some stationery, and sits, recognising that she has created in effect a miniature version of Hunter's house for her own use: a space into which the Witness – with all its thousand eyes – cannot look. Instinctively, she feels dirty and ashamed. She wonders if she should apologise to the machine, and how it would tag that action. Uncommon politeness? Or something it should flag for the attention of Pippa Keene? Or both?

Instead, she asks the Witness how many times her own activities have been accessed by citizens since the beginning of her investigation. Too many. How many in the city? Again. How many from within the Witness or associated bodies? Only a few – Smith among them. She wants to ask for a deep dive analysis using Smith as a hub, but she can trust neither the answer nor the indulgence of those at whom her query would be aimed. She has to assume that any such direct question will be detected.

Under normal circumstances, Neith's adversaries would face a similar limitation. Too many flags in a cluster would reveal the precise areas they do not wish examined. If there is a shadowy organisation of Fire Judges, say, dogging her footsteps, and the chiefs of that organisation were foolish enough to set up a query on its own name, she could in theory search the metadata to reveal them. Except that relies upon a mechanism she already knows can be blinded.

On the other hand, if she accepts Smith as her enemy and Hunter's deliberate – well, if not murderer, at least torturer, and by extension the Fire Judges likewise; and if she assumes on the basis that Smith worked there that the Turnpike Trust is some sort of shell: then the Fire Judges are having a very bad morning. There are constables climbing all over their offices and asking questions and locking things, and Neith has a brief window in which she might gain the upper hand. If Turnpike itself is a red herring, the Fire Judges must still have woken to a tumultuous dawn. Either they killed Smith (in which case they hated him, for surely a simple assassination would have done the job) or someone else hates him and by extension them, and that cannot be reassuring either.

In every hypothesis, she must hope for confusion in the enemy camp. The alternative is paralysis. She must act now, and she must gather her strength.

She takes care to put her terminal glasses in her pocket, and writes a single sentence as a test.

Her hand guides the pencil. The letters are strange, because she rarely has to write by hand. The most recent experience she has of writing belongs to Berihun Bekele. Bekele was taught to write in the strict style of mid-century British pedagogy, and his fingers are longer than hers, his skeleton and muscles filled with different tensions. She has an urge to form her capitals more precisely than she normally does, a twitching irritation at their clumsiness that straddles the ghost muttering of his consciousness and her own.

All the same, she writes, and no one can see it.

A little while later she grips the doll's house by its handle, and heads out into the street. She takes a night tram, sitting behind the curl of the rear stairs on the upper deck, looking backwards along the track, feeling everything wrong slip away into the red glow of the rear lights. For the first time in her own memory of herself, she is singing, something wordless and complex that cycles endlessly around itself. Perhaps it is an instinctive camouflage, or a warning to anyone boarding the tram that she's not looking to share the view. It is almost 4 a.m., and she is going to visit a friend.

*

The flat is in a modern building, very white and sheer and not what she was expecting. She walks up four floors and along a pale, honey-carpeted corridor to find the door she is looking for. It is high-gloss black, the number printed hugely under the lacquer and repeating itself up and down the panel in regressing indigo and blue shadows. She knocks rather than ringing the bell, and then waits, because it's the middle of the night.

A woman's voice, clear and confident, speaks through the door. 'Who is it?'

'Neith. Mielikki.'

A pause. 'Inspector Neith?'

'Yes. I'm sorry to come so late.'

The door opens immediately, and a tiny figure in a vastly oversized towelling bathrobe peers up at her, perfect pale olive skin and black hair with a reddish tint.

'You are welcome in this house,' she says, very firmly. 'You are welcome and you must come in! I am Maria like the Magdalene! And you' — the woman breaks off and throws her arms around the Inspector, almost lifting her off her feet across the threshold and unexpectedly imparting for a moment the sensation of a small, muscular bosom beneath the robe – 'you are my Ronald's daytime wife! Yes?' A huge smile. 'You are the bad Inspector who always makes a mess of his schedule. Ronald! Ronald! Mielikki Neith is here! Put on your clothes, I will make tea. Camomile,' she adds to Neith, 'but trust me, you will like it. In, in, in, come in!'

Mielikki Neith does as she is told, and as she hangs up her coat on the strange many-armed stand in a perfect alcove just inside the door, she turns again and finds Tubman, who evidently does possess after all an actual first name, staring blearily at her from the bedroom doorway.

'Inspector?' Tubman says.

'No,' she replies. 'This is unofficial, Tub. Ronald. Not work. Just happened to be passing.'

His eyebrows twitch. 'Oh. Right.'

'I came to show you this,' she says, lifting the doll's house. 'I think I'm going to start collecting.'

'Oh. Well, let's . . .' he shrugs, 'let's have a look, then.'

*

'Ronald never brings anyone home from work,' Maria complains as she pours a reedy-looking yellow tisane – Neith declines, privately, to call it tea – into printed basalt-resin cups and sets them down. '"No, no, Maria, they are very rough men and women, they are too coarse for you, you are very sophisticated and my work will bore you." Assface,' she adds to her husband, without rancour.

'She came to a pub meet once,' Tubman recalls, sipping and smacking his lips with every evidence of pleasure. 'Hated it.'

'Oh, because of the awful, awful beer!' Maria snaps. 'The people were splendid!'

The kitchen is the same as the front door and the hallway: a sublime iteration of London's new style, all extruded surfaces, but arranged in a way Neith has never seen before so as to make something both practical and cosy – some Venezuelan understanding of Danish hygge which fits perfectly into the System's mode.

'You were right,' Neith says hastily, 'the camomile is lovely.'

Maria smiles immediately. 'You are a nice lady. Not an assface at all.' Her nails are perfect, Neith notices, rich dark red and very round. The arms emerging from the towelling sleeves are narrow but very muscular. The woman follows the line of her gaze. 'Surgery,' she explains. 'Sometimes you have to waggle things about. Ronald, the lady came to show you something! Pay attention!' But the imperiousness is softened, Neith sees now, by the light touch as she passes behind her husband, the squeeze that is both benediction and need. They are in step, these two, and she has no need of Oliver Smith's kinesic assistant to tell her so.

'Yes,' Neith says. 'I just thought I needed a hobby.'

Tub's expression as Neith lifts the Fashion TV Studio Plus! on to the table gives her to understand that this is the kind of behaviour he has come to expect from the world, and he is almost relieved to find that she is as insane in her own measured, careful way as everyone else.

For God's sake, Tub, sit down and look.

He does. She closes her eyes for a moment, then hears his voice jaunty and clear as usual.

'I love what you've done with the place. Oh, look, there's a black leather sofa for when they do those late-night chat shows where someone's discovered Jesus and someone else is drunk. Did you buy that extra?'

'Ronald,' Maria says. 'Be nice.'

'I am, darling, believe you me.'

'There is no such thing,' Neith growls.

'No, here,' he says, fat finger tapping on the paper. She sees her own handwriting first, the shape of the letters fractionally off because of the awkward angle:

TUBMAN — I THINK THE WITNESS IS COMPROMISED AND I DON'T KNOW HOW BADLY. I NEED TO INVESTIGATE WITHOUT ALERTING THE OPPOSITION. HELP.

Under it, Tubman has written:

GO PUBLIC.

'That's the make-up counter,' she says aloud. 'Look, there are little cans of spray and everything. Oh, one of them's fallen down.'

'That is normal,' Maria says. 'The intrusion of chaos into the living space.' She looks down over Tubman's shoulder, and sighs. 'Quite to be expected.'

NOT READY, Neith writes.

'Delightful. I despise all things replica, as you know, authenticity being my watchword. I particularly hate the curtains. Did it come uninhabited, or is there some ghastly big-eyed nightmare baby that goes with it?'

WHAT I'D COUNT ON. POINT IS TO GET THE SECRET OUT, NOT TO PROVE IT. ONCE YOU'VE SAID IT, IT HAS TO BE INVESTIGATED.

She shakes her head. 'Tub, it's for kids.'

'And yet you've got one and you're making me play with it.'

I THINK THEY MAY BE READY FOR THAT. FOR ME.

Tubman's hand nearly crunches the studio's roof off. He stares at her. She scowls at him. 'Tub! It's fragile!'

I NEED PROOF. SOMETHING THAT'S NOT ARGUABLE. CAN'T TRUST NEURAL — DON'T KNOW WHO MIGHT BE INVOLVED.

'I'm sorry, Mielikki. I'm not a delicate sort of bloke, amazing as that may appear to you, who only see the external popinjay.'

'Peacock,' Maria suggests.

'Mighty golden eagle,' Tubman says firmly. 'The Tubmans have Scots blood, you know.'

When he writes again, the thick fingers are clumsy.

GET PROOF. FAST. BETTER TO BE ALIVE THAN RIGHT.

'I thought you had all those little boats in bottles,' Neith objects.

HELP. HELP ME.

'Ships,' Tubman sniffs. 'I build ships in bottles, and they are a work of craft and elegance not often seen in this day and age. Not tat like this.'

Maria rests her hands on his shoulders, then kisses the top of his head once. Tubman presses his fingers over hers, then looks back at Neith as if rebuked. 'All right, all right, I love your little house-y thing. It's very you.'

His writing hand moves again, a string of numbers and letters punctuated with full stops. For a moment, she sees nonsense: 9090AE110E23. He's doodling, or having a seizure. Then as he keeps going the mess resolves into the familiar format of a hexadecimal IPv6 number, the silicon equivalent of a street address. Below that, words.

SQUID, Tubman has written, BECAUSE KRAKEN IS ILLEGAL, ALL RIGHT? SO DO NOT DOWNLOAD THE KRAKEN ADD-ON IN CASE OF EMERGENCIES. THAT WOULD BE VERY WRONG AND I'D BE PERSONALLY DISAPPOINTED IN YOU.

'You're right,' she says, 'but I bet the sofa's not black leather really because this thing was cheap as hell.'

THANK YOU.

'So is late-night telly, darling,' Tubman says.

CAN YOU SORT IT OUT?

Neith shrugs.

DO YOU KNOW HOW IT WAS DONE?

She writes: IS BEING DONE. And then: NO.

Tubman shuts his eyes for a moment.

TALK TO THE WAXMAN.

?!

TALK TO HIM. HE'S A WANKER, BUT HE KNOWS THE SYSTEM THE WAY A FOX KNOWS HENS.

HOW? Underlined.

But Tub just underlines TALK TO THE WAXMAN.

'Now,' Maria says. 'Let's have some breakfast, since we're all here.'

Tubman nods agreement, and Neith watches the two of them move around one another in the small galley kitchen with the ease of long understanding. A short while later, she is eating again.

Between the second helping of bacon and the third, she looks around the room and then, looking back, realises that she is looking at love in its natural habitat, and that she hasn't been in its company for years. Fernweh again, like the sudden recognition of an empty chair.

'Thank you, Tub. Maria. Really.'

'You're welcome,' Maria says, just as Tubman says firmly: 'I din't do nuffim.'

'I'm sorry if I woke you. I should go.'

Maria looks as if she might object, but Tubman nods understanding and they show her to the door.

The Inspector leaves, lugging the doll's house. In the street, she sees a man standing, smoking. He is too broad to be Lönnrot, too solid. But she wonders, all the same, whether he is following her, or just taking the air.

Keep moving. Use your time.

*

In a sandwich shop on the Fulham Palace Road, the Inspector erects the doll's house and justifies her presence by ordering executive fish fingers on sourdough toast. She does not expect, having just eaten once at Tubman's, to be hungry, but finds herself grazing all the same. Between mouthfuls she opens a direct connection to the address Tubman gave her and downloads the Squid. The software is represented by a cute, wide-eyed sea-creature juggling data. Behind it in the false 3D of the display is Kraken, in a biker jacket and Wayfarer sunglasses: the badass elder sibling, a beer bottle held loosely in one suckered pad. She remembers, irrelevantly, that members of the order Teuthida have only two true tentacles. The shorter gripping appendages are arms.

She waits until the download is finished and closes the link, then clears her terminal's cache by hand and restarts before initiating the Squid and flicking through the documentation. Immediately, her terminal informs her of a security risk: the application wants access to the outgoing feed from the camera and microphone on her glasses. She grants permission, and watches as the display begins to loop unobtrusively. She can still use her equipment, but her own POV has just dropped out of the network.

The Squid is liminally legal: where on the margin it falls depends on how it is deployed. Its ostensible use is to shield citizens from the unwanted attentions of unrestrained American and Asian robot advertisers, which would otherwise harvest data from their personal lives through every available aperture and then deluge them with information about alternative products every time they view or purchase anything on the international network. For this reason, most people now use a System filter portal to access the rest of the world, but a robust minority like their access to reflect the external experience, the better to understand the people of foreign lands – hence the Squid.

This kind of occlusion works only moderately well against the polystrate surveillance of the System, but that moderate dividend is potentially sufficient to make such use a minor criminal act. Unlike Kraken, which is to all intents and purposes a digital commando unit in a bottle, prone to hostage-taking and property damage, the Squid does not actually try to control anything. It's more like a very rowdy and very antisocial street party than a strike team. It will not block anyone who is looking from seeing the direction of her inquiry, but it will diminish the chance of her setting off any narrowly defined alarms scripted around her in person or looking out for any directed scrutiny of her targets. The Inspector believes that any official query over a low-level bad act here will either readily be dispelled when she has built her case, or utterly negligible when set against the size of the boot that will fall on her if she fails to do so and is noticed trying. If she wants to hide herself more completely, she could theoretically download Kraken through the Squid, but it would be considerably more atomic if she were discovered – and very much more likely to be a problem later. The Squid is a compromise: probably less than half-permitted, barely better than one-quarter effective.

Through the Squid she connects to the Public Records Office and requests tax and location data for Oliver Smith going back twenty years, and for good measure Diana Hunter as well, wincing as the software automatically also searches for 35,000 similar records – no doubt resulting in a measurable drag on legitimate requests and a slight blip in the department's processing bill – and upon receipt dumps them into a trash folder. Without looking at the Hunter data, she logs off and brings up the National Health database, checking the DNA from Hunter's autopsy against the statutory samples which have since the middle part of the century been kept of all hair and nail clippings from salons and beauty parlours for the early detection of disease and addiction, then brings in blood samples from standard tests and inoculations, hospital and dental visits. The Squid checks with its server hub for proximate areas of public concern and initiates a baseless scare into the possible carcinogenic effects of an urban pesticide. Whoever wrote this thing, the Inspector realises, had absolutely no sense of civic or personal responsibility at all. The Squid grabs her data and runs, leaving administrative chaos in its wake.

She makes a more detailed general wishlist: Oliver Smith, biography, detailed, with reference to expertise. Close acquaintances, professional and otherwise. Addresses and appointments, cross-referenced with anything known about Diana Hunter. Cross-referenced with Fire Judges and all the rest, too, just for good measure. She half expects the Witness to murmur into her ear, chide her, but for the moment her good angel is only vaguely aware of what she's doing, as if she's holding a conversation two tables over in a crowded room.

Hunter remains a cipher. Time to do something about that, too, and if she's correct in her assumption that they knew one another and that that relationship is at the heart of all this, then it's just as well she use the Squid for this part too.

She calls up the inventory file from the Hunter house, and drops the brands, styles, shoe sizes and colour combinations into a commercial customer profiling program, then uses a cranky but effective trend-reversing algorithm from the Victoria & Albert Museum, which reliably tells you, based on a sample of your life now, what clothes you would have been wearing in any given decade. She instructs the Squid to log on to the central bank records server and look for purchasing patterns which would indicate Diana Hunter thirty years ago. Results to file and cross-reference. She watches a blizzard of similar requests go out, and twitches a little as the bank server actually stutters as it hits.

Taking Hunter's age as approximately what it appears to be, she also tasks the Squid to gather information on all post-graduate degrees awarded in disciplines that cover or are related to cryptography, neurophysiology, semiotics and narrative behavioural psychology. She rummages through Trisa Hinde's autopsy report on the dead woman and tags evidence of fractures to one arm, some ceramic fillings and laser surgery to correct myopia, then dumps all these into a comparison tray and goes back to the Health database under a new connection. The Squid holds execution of her search to assess its line of attack, then looses a salvo of queries over purchasing costs of high grade splints and dental clay against non-branded local alternatives. A moment later it comes in from another angle and spits a furious allegation of improper maintenance of laser optics during the relevant period. When the hospital trust – startled, she thinks, and plaintively asking where this is coming from – issues a firm denial, the Squid demands access to outcome data and looks for matches, again shooting everything it finds to the growing Hunter file. The Inspector feels a guilty grin building behind her lips: this is strictly speaking all very wrong, but in a necessary way.

Her case has grown from its small if serious beginning into something very much graver. Neith is almost certain that this investigation is what Hunter wanted – she did as much as she could to provoke it, even unto death, and surely if she had not entered the interrogation chamber the whole sequence would never have begun – and so the dilemma becomes whether Hunter can be trusted. Certainly, there is more in her memories, much more. But is it the truth?

Who was she? What did they want from her, and what did she want that they could not supply?

Neith can't find a clear and recent audio recording of Hunter on any public platform, and tersely requests some from the Witness without explanation, trusting that it will blend into the wash of her ongoing investigation. When it arrives, she calls up another Witness protocol intended to isolate and trace pet noise across London and backdates the search as far as she can, not daring to check what creative anarchy this inspires in the Squid. Fifteen hits. Thirty, fifty, two hundred, two thousand, four, nine, fifty-eight thousand. She kills the request and refiles with a duplication filter, knowing already what the scale of the bloat must mean: at some stage or other, Diana Hunter appeared in public and spoke, and her words were relayed and replayed in a large number of places. Well, of course, she was a little bit famous. Omit identical utterances, compensating for room tone. Filter and cross-reference, send to file.

As a last set of inputs, she checks high-profile women who have stepped away from the Public Sphere, noted reclusives, then plugs the whole collection of queries into an offshore AI company's adducive-iterative analysis intake and asks for patterns and related questions to be fed back to the Squid for automated retrieval, with the high-correlation ones to be reinserted into the AI for three generations: in other words, the questions she has already asked will now spawn further questions, the best ones will make more and better questions. The data triage would be almost instantaneous if she were to run it through the Witness. Instead, she labels it a hobby project, paying for the processing time from her personal account. The actual work will take seventeen hours, but the likely elapsed time until completion will be more like twenty-four because the service will occasionally clock off to handle higher-priority jobs.

Last, she invokes the Squid's most anarchic protections and sends a request to an open day-book held on a server in Finland. The day-book form requires a name, and she's not about to give her own, not even or particularly for this. In her mind, she tries on Stella Kyriakos and Annabel Bekele, then Athenais Karthagonensis, though she isn't sure that one would fit. She discards Regno Lönnrot with the haste of biting into a rotten fruit, and finally – not without misgivings – enters 'Diana Hunter' in the box.

The day-book accepts the alias without comment.

Breathing a silent apology to the owner for whatever scrutiny may come his way as a result of her digital vandalism, she pays for her executive fish fingers and ducks out of the shop, her terminal chiming against her jawbone every time it scores a high-likelihood match between her sets. And then, a moment later, a different alert, very familiar and comforting until she remembers that it isn't anymore. The Witness is paging her.

– *Are you all right, Inspector?*

'Yes, I'm fine.'

– *You are not working according to your usual pattern. You were very upset by the loss of the suspect in the public transport system.*

'The case requires unusual strategies to bring it to a useful conclusion. I'm working out how to proceed.'

– *It might be helpful if you discussed that with me.*

'I need more information first. There are significant areas of this case we don't yet understand properly.'

— Please clarify.

'Hunter evidently believed she had a method for subverting the interrogation process, and possibly more. I need to rule that out as a matter of urgency.'

— The System can assess any specific threat.

'But you cannot, by definition, hypothesise an attack that would circumvent your own safeguards. Otherwise you would already have blocked it.'

— That is true.

'Do you have any further information on my outstanding searches?'

— Unfortunately, Witness efforts have not yet been able to locate the suspect Regno Lönnrot. It is probably time to consider taking an image directly from your recollection of events. It will require perhaps half a day, including recovery time.

She thinks of Gnomon: inrushing on the gusts of a storm come grit and birdshit ... No. Hunter's message there, at least, is relatively clear.

'Keep looking. And please set a meeting for me with Pippa Keene tomorrow at midday. I will want her to monitor my function personally, for the avoidance of doubt.'

— Yes, Inspector. Of course.

Talking to the machine is disturbing because everything is exactly the same. If she asks for something, it will happen seamlessly. If she does not ask but does need, it will happen anyway. She is carried along on the wave of the System – and yet now she knows the security of it is an illusion. There are gaps in its knowledge and capability, even in its willingness. Has it just lied to her? How would she know?

Someone has beaten the System. Someone who is not Hunter.

No one beats the machine, not in the end. The only person who came close was a madwoman. Poor pale Anna.

Maria Tubman is still in her head: *I am Maria, like the Magdalene.* Maria gave the word its Latinate form, not the more English 'maudlin'.

One wouldn't want to be maudlin: it's graceless.

Anna, from the Hebrew, meaning 'grace'.

Lönnrot, again, telling her something – perhaps everything – in ways she wouldn't understand until she found them out all over again. But telling her what? Whatever truth Hunter knew? Or a signpost to Lönnrot's own secrets? No. Lönnrot, surely, gives up nothing by choice. This prodding and poking is to achieve an end.

More and more, Neith believes the answers to this case are in Hunter's head, not the real world. And there, at last and infuriatingly, she has something in common with Oliver Smith.

Damn it.

And now she has arrived. She gets off her bus and looks up at the mansion block in front of her, at the astoundingly expensive yet remarkably nasty properties all around. Just exactly what is it that draws people of wealth and power to this area of London, still? Is it proximity to empty Buckingham Palace? To the old high commercial power of Harrods and Harvey Nichols and the implication of luxury; the park and the Albert Hall? Or is it a kind of recollected habit?

She presses the brass buzzer, and waits for the soldier to open the door. They stare at each other through the glass: a woman out of uniform, one knee spattered with what might be oil or viscera, hair matted at one temple with oil or soot from the deep underground and carrying a vandalised plastic doll's house; opposite her, an impeccable armoured matriarch of some Arctic military service, permitted but not obviously carrying a firearm in the London area.

Firearm. Firespine? No. No. The ripples of wind on water, not a shark.

Neith's counterpart gives her a wintery smile and opens the door.

'Everyone has these days,' she murmurs.

'I hope not,' Neith returns, but the woman has already turned away.

*

The embassy occupies six dismal rooms and its own separate entrance. The stairs are threadbare and the whole place smells very faintly of damp, some whisper of the Thames in the foundations. The brass-buttoned lift creaks and clatters as it rises to the third floor, and the bombproof door squeaks as another uniformed soldier, this one a dark-haired man with shocking blue eyes, ushers her into a chamber that is, she realises, a species of interior barbican, bulletproof in all directions and probably airtight as well. If she were to kill this man – if she were a terrorist – they'd likely just let the door swing shut and wait for her to suffocate.

Politely but not gently, the guard demands to know her business.

She says she has an appointment, and writes the name Diana Hunter down for him.

'Wait, please.'

She expects him to ask for some form of identification, and then she will have to explain and negotiate, but he doesn't. They must know who she is – her face is everywhere these days – but the discrepancy either doesn't bother them or is too interesting to ignore. Once inside, she will be free of the System's observation: the embassy is foreign soil. That does not mean, of course, that she will not be surveilled by the embassy itself.

She wonders for a moment at the transition in her thinking that finds freedom, rather than risk and discomfort, in being outside the compass of the Witness.

A moment later she is walking through the embassy, one chamber after another, all lit by uncompromising strip lighting and all overfull with files and staff crowded into odd corners by their long-term guest. The Waxman, Neith realises, has the only room with a view of the river. She wonders whether he holds something over them all, or whether it is a gesture of humanity towards a man who will probably never leave this flat except to go to jail.

They take the doll's house away from her very politely.

'I will put it in a cupboard,' a steel-haired woman with reading glasses says. 'It will be safe there. But you understand, to us it is a notional compromise of security.'

Neith realises the woman has mistaken it for an emotional support object. She starts to demur, and then lets it go. Explanation would entail – well, too much explanation.

The woman smiles. 'This way.'

It does not occur to Neith, until just as they are parting on the threshold of the Waxman's apartment, that this is the ambassador. 'Oh,' she says. 'It's a pleasure to meet you.' Some part of her bobs a curtsey, as if to royalty.

The ambassador bows back, bemused. 'And you too, Inspector. You are always welcome here – whether Dr Wachsmann will see you or not.'

*

'Good morning, Miss Hunter,' the Waxman says, 'you look surprisingly well. A positive miracle of modern medicine, is it?'

He is small and hearty, like the impresario of a particularly energetic Soho eatery. She pictures something in obscure fusion food: peacock and tilapia dumplings. Just looking at him makes her feel tired. He's so clean and unrumpled. He's just got out of bed.

'Good morning,' Neith replies.

The Waxman gestures to a chair.

She looks around, almost too tired to sit. If she sits, she might not get up. This is not a good place to sleep. The room seems almost monkishly tranquil. The large double-glazed picture window looks down into coastal gorge. When the storms come in it must be spectacular. A single chair faces outward, a side table stacked with books. For a moment she wonders whether she will see a copy of *Mr Murder Investigates* perched on top of the pile, but glancing at the spine finds a copy of the *Thousand and One Nights*. In fact, all the books are historical, and all are early editions. She tries to commit the names to memory, wondering if she can.

'I know, of course, who you are. I should have recognised you immediately anyway, but your message came to me via the ambassador. She was kind enough to append footnotes.'

Yes. What is the rest of the world making of this odd moment? Nothing good, surely.

They sit.

'Dr Wachsmann. I am investigating a compromise of the Witness and the System. If you assist me and I am successful in dealing with the problem I can confidently offer you release.'

'I am not technically detained.' A flash of teeth, needle-bright in the soft face.

'Amnesty, then, conditional on your speedy departure and – forgive me – promise not to return.'

Wachsmann nods. 'Let us say that would not be entirely against my inclination. I used to love London, but I think now the skyline will haunt me until I die. You have my word: if I leave here, I will not come back. But ... what guarantee do I have?'

'Mine.'

He snorts delicately. 'My dear Inspector, with the greatest of respect: your bare word is a little tenuous.'

'But you have nothing to lose.'

'That is true.' He ponders, eyes roaming a little too widely in the room, dwelling too long on her body, her face. He's not used to company, has forgotten the polite regulation of gaze. 'Do you know, for the first few months I actively loathed you. And then after that I became a little enamoured. Stockholm syndrome, or some such. Then you ... faded. Now I find you here, in my very holdfast, and you're almost like a friend. A very old, very bad friend. An estranged sibling who took the family home. It does occur to me, though, that if the System is compromised and you are arrayed against the villain – and you are here – then there's every chance you may be on the wrong side of history. What will they do to you, do you think, if you oppose them and fail?'

'They'll destroy me,' she says, wondering what form it will take. Death, like Smith? Or something more subtle?

'You're quite right, I have nothing to lose. I stay or I go. I like it here, in a way. Seclusion. The emptiness of this space and the babble of work next door. No demands upon my time – just me and my books.'

His free hand waves broadly at the room, flicking lightly to the mantle, a line of particularly old and pretty volumes in the same binding as the book by the window: *Falconry in the Valley of the Indus, Stone Talk* and *The Perfumed Garden of the Shaykh Nefzawi*.

'Quite a collection.'

'Small but perfectly formed.' His face is abruptly childlike. She remembers that security intrusion is not only about code. It's also about people. So, yes, of course: he is charming. Except now also not, because something is off in his timing, the exaggerated gestures of the mouth. Out of practice, working his wiles only on his mirror.

'If I wanted to break into the System, how would I do it?'

The Waxman's eyes open a little. 'I am the last person who can tell you that.'

'I thought you were the best.'

He gestures at his surroundings. 'I was. Now ... not only did my approach not work, but if it ever could have the matter has no doubt been addressed.'

'Where did you begin?'

'A previous contract. A corporate client asked me to influence the outcome of a minor vote. A planning application. That was doable without direct intrusion, of course. I only needed to work around the System's own rather stunted sense of privacy and influence the quorum indirectly or directly. But then I got interested and I started wondering what else might be possible. The Cartier gang found me and – here we are.'

'So?'

'So ... it turns out that whoever designed your System is cleverer than I am – or at least, their tactical and strategic implementation of security predicted and prepared for my best approach. Although these days I suppose the System designs itself. But even the basic paradigm is excellent. My compliments.' Is that a trace of an accent? European? Or further east? But perhaps he's doing it on purpose. Not her problem, anyway.

'How did it work? Your approach.'

'Granting that it didn't ... In the simplest terms, your architecture is protected by a five-part lock. It's not like a safe, but let us pretend that it is. To get access to the contents, one must have a physical key – in this case that is a terminal hard-wired to a closed network. There is a list of registered and authorised persons who may act on that network, and each of them has a complex and unique passphrase. One, two, three. So far, not unassailable, though also not comfortable. Then you have your biological identity – not only your DNA but the mix of microbial organisms living on and in your body.' He smiles. 'I beat that one, you know.'

She does know. The air conditioning is blowing itchingly across her face and making her shiver, cold air on her neck. Goose bumps. But it would feel good to rest her eyes, just for a moment. She fights her body's instinct to curl up in a ball. 'How?'

'I took an aggressive regimen of antibiotic, antiviral and anti-fungal drugs for one week in a clean room, and then cultivated the biome of a senior academic researcher in security at one of your universities on and in my body. I ate what he ate, drank what he drank. I stole water from his bath. It was fascinating, actually. I noticed a tangible alteration in my perceptions. We really are a composite organism inhabiting our entire bodies, not just a single homunculus seated in the skull.' He makes a face. 'But that is the point. The connectome requirement – that is not surmountable. I think it may be the perfect lock. It is not merely behavioural. That was my mistake. I had simulated my target from thousands of hours of recordings. By the time I attempted my operation, the simulation was word-perfect. The effect was uncanny. But the connectome analysis revealed me immediately. The quality of my thought was not the same. I was no more persuasive to your machine than I would have been seeking to evade facial recognition in a carnival mask. It sees the thought and the affect, and it knew me for a completely other individual. To beat the connectome lock, you must become the target – and if you do that, you will no longer want to beat the lock. It is circular. Brilliant.'

He shakes his head in rueful approval. 'Five locks, Inspector. Five gates through which the pilgrim must pass to enter the Holy Land. But the last of them is truth, which by definition cannot be counterfeited.'

'Do you care what happens?'

He nods again, alarmingly dog-like, and kisses her hand. 'Yes. I hope you succeed because I don't like it here. I hope you fail because some part of me hates you. When you came in, I wanted to hurt you. Now I think you seem very nice. You – you like my books. My little home. You don't wish me ill as a person, but as an example of a type. I have no quarrel with you as a person, only as an officer of the law. Is it Stockholm syndrome, I wonder? Sudden onset, primed over ... how many hundreds of days? Well. You have – you have changed my mind. I think quite deeply. Ironic, is it not? Exactly what I could not achieve on my own, to beat your System. Ah, well. And now I am torn.'

Stop. Stop. Her eyes open fast, hard, stare at him. Was she asleep? Did he say it?

'You said you're torn?'

'Yes.'

'Does that mean anything to you? That expression?'

He shakes his head.

'What about Anna Magdalena? Or Firespine?'

Still no.

'Fire Judges. Burton.' His eyes flick to the bookshelf, then return. He has lost interest in her now. The conversation is over and he just wants her to go. She wonders how often he daydreams up here, by himself. She shakes his hand, feeling foolish.

'Au revoir, Inspector. Let me know how it gocs.'

But she doesn't get up. She just pulls her knees up into the chair, and after a little while she realises he has put a blanket over her, and another, folded up for a pillow, under her cheek. She thinks she will rest for a while, but inside her head there is so much unwound Hunter that there's almost no room for her at all.

what can have

I n my state room on board the *Rebus* I have a small library. In among the books is a dictionary, and in the dictionary is an entry for the thing I am thinking about.

gnomon

noun

1. from the Greek, literally 'one who knows'. That upright part of a sundial whose shadow is used to indicate the passage of time, or more accurately the rotation of the earth and the relative positions of the earth and the sun.
2. several related but distinct concepts in geometry. The ideal of the gnomon is unitary and absolute. It is the first brushstroke, the first chiselled line which records man's entry to the world of abstracts. This clarity is so compelling to the mathematical mind that it has been invoked by different thinkers to different ends. Oenopides used 'gnomon-wise' to mean simply 'perpendicular', but Euclid extended this to denote a figure created by removing a small parallelogram from one corner of another to produce what might be called by an intellect less refined than his own an arrowhead or – in the Roman alphabet – an 'L'. Hero of Alexandria, not content with this pedestrian business of subtraction, conceived of a usage which would deal with addition: Hero's gnomon is any thing which, when combined with another thing, yields a product similar in nature to the original entity.
    i.   after Oenopides: an instrument commonly used to create right angles.
3. in literature: the term used by scholars of James Joyce to describe implicate absences in *Dubliners* and elsewhere.
4. in folklore: an angel or devil possessing hidden knowledge; a book or compendium of such knowledge, therefore also (obs.) a magic spell,

specifically the one cast by the heralds of the Last Judgement and believed by the Sassanid heretics (see Burton, Fraser et al.) to result in the Apocatastasis.

i. after 4.: in the Haslam variant of the many-worlds interpretation, an object or entity existing in a reality not contiguous with our own.

And now also, it seems:

5. the pattern of thought injected into my brain by a senior myrmidon of the Witness to put me back in my place.

They say 'dysfunctional', but all I hear is 'uppity'.

*

By now, in the real world, I'm on a ventilator. At least, I'm guessing. When I used the crash dive technique with that much going on in my brain already, I basically had to have co-opted something you don't want to be repurposing. Your brain isn't some giant control surface, and you're not some little creature with a big head sitting on a stool pushing buttons. The whole thing is infinitely more complicated, but I don't really have a lot of time, so let's just bite the bullet.

Imagine, then, that the brain is a big room full of machines and I'm a little creature with a big head sitting on a stool pushing buttons. I've been shutting down machines I don't need, or largely retasking them, and wiring them to the central console with bits of splice cable, and then I've been running a drip feed into that central console so that it looks as if really important stuff is still in there. Or if you prefer: when Catherine the Great told her chancellor that she wanted to ride out in the great Empire of Russia and meet the happy peasants everyone kept telling her lived there, the chancellor – his name was Potemkin – understood immediately that shit-caked, disease-ridden serfs begging from frost-bitten lips and extending three-fingered hands to their absolute monarch would not entirely fill her with joy. So he grabbed a couple of hundred minor nobles and dressed them as peasants and paid them off. Then he built a bunch of fake villages and rode Catherine through them, and she was delighted to see that agricultural labour was surprisingly easy and the soil of Russia was amazingly fertile even without much assistance from mankind. She was thrilled at the beauty of her subjects and at their surprisingly educated voices as they sang and tilled the soil. She went back to the palace and eventually died at the age of sixty-seven, still at least notionally unaware that she ruled an impoverished, brutal nation ripening towards a staggering violence. (She died of a stroke. There was, contrary to the prurient slander, no horse penis involved.)

In short, I have been building Potemkin villages: faking it.

The trouble is that with Gnomon in my head, and now with the crash dive, I've run out of places to put myself that aren't either my central console or my autonomous survival systems, like breathing and regulating body temperature and so on: all the gubbins that happens in the brain at such a low level that we basically don't really think about it. I've shunted myself into some part of the firmware, erasing what was there, and I honestly don't know what it does.

Used to do.

Whatever eventually happens here, I won't be the same person I was. I think I knew that. I must have done. It was always obvious. And I find I'm ... at least relatively happy with it, compared with sitting still while this world is stolen from its people by a new variation on absolutism. Apparently I really, really don't like hierarchies of power.

Which is weird, when you think about it, because I absolutely approve of them so long as I'm in charge. In my submarine, for example, I'm the absolute ruler. The crew does what I tell them, not least because I made them up.

In fact, I think I need a cup of tea. Oolong, by preference.

*

Kyriakos has been having sex (of course); Athenais is performing alchemy; and Berihun Bekele is returning to the root of his art (granted, he's also been blown up a little bit, but he's fine). And Gnomon ... well. I'm not sure who Gnomon belongs to now. It was Oliver's narrative at the beginning, of course, but now ... he matched it so well to my way of thinking, to the stories I already had in place, that I couldn't just shut it down. By the same token it blended into what I was doing quite perfectly, and he couldn't keep control of it. We'll just have to see.

The steward brings tea on a dark wooden tray with china cups, the very thing. If I hold them up to the light I will be able to see through the narrow imprints of three grains of rice just above each little handle. It's the mark of real quality.

More than one cup, because in the real world I always assume someone else may drop in, and it weakens the structure to change that sort of thing. Essentially: if they served my tea in one cup, the cavitation noise of the *Rebus* would get that little bit louder for the ships up above. Everything, down here, is symbols and belief. It's like dreaming: text will change from moment to moment and switches and buttons will not function properly unless you require them to do so. Nothing tastes the way it should until you define it. The laws of physics are what you make them. In theory I could fly this submarine to safety, or displace it, the way the USS *Eldridge* supposedly teleported to another world in 1943. But it's like the cups: every flaw I write in the architecture can be exploited by an intruder.

I feel fingers of subtle impact along the hull, the *tap tap tapping* at my chamber door. A fleeting contact, a flash of sunlight on a cloudy day. Nothing to be worried about. Somewhere, one of the crew murmurs: 'Active sonar.'

I hold my breath and wait. Let the motion of the boat slide us away from the contact, away and down.

Better to stick to the rules, and let the beam slide over us, and fade away. Just a whale. Just a shadow in the thermocline, a reef, a wreck. Nothing to see here. *Rebus* knows how to hide.

The tea tastes of mountainsides and warm wind.

*

Once, I saw a remarkable series of photographs which showed the different compositions of human tears. It had not ever occurred to me until that moment that tears of joy might be measurably different from tears of anger or sorrow, but they are. Cause matters. If you cry from slicing an onion, the structure of your tears resembles the undergrowth in a pine forest. Remembrance is a grid pattern, like the map of New York City, but from each block emerge soft, questing tendrils, as if the body of the tear itself reaches out for what is lost. By comparison, other tears are plain. Elation is etiolated and fragile, grief is sparse, rage is linear, horror is jagged. Of all the pictures in the collection, only remembrance was complex.

So what tears, now, is my body crying up above in the daylight? What complexity measures my situation; what wild, improbable blending of snowflake patterns can do justice to this?

And: if I could put my tears under a microscope here and now, inside my refuge, what would I see? My world in pieces, or my house full of police, or a burning man in a room full of ghosts? The mobile that used to hang over my bed when I was a child? What should I decide to see?

There's probably no category for a woman in my position, no word in the lexicon to describe the emotions I feel. Perhaps my tears are unique, the information they contain dense and unanticipated and full of newness. They should be scooped up and preserved, at least analysed. Perhaps the pattern of them expresses who I am, or where, and something strange could come of looking at them.

*

Say it gently, even here. Write it without all its letters, so that the thing named cannot hear you – not Gnomon, but Gn m n.

It was supposed to mean something else, I know it was – but the recollection is up there on the surface, in some hidden corner I can only hope they have not found. Perhaps it's floating on the water amid the burned wreckage of my singing. Perhaps it's in a pirate's treasure chest on a desert island somewhere, and there's a map in a leather tube that shows you how to get there, how to avoid the monsters and the traps.

It was supposed to mean something important, that's why it was in every story. The word means that which is perpendicular to everything else, something that stands apart. It is the part of a sundial that casts a shadow – the thing that gives meaning to the clockface. It is that which, added to something, produces a new entity similar to the original. Is that a hint? Was Gn m n my salvation of self, at the end of this? A way back past the brain damage to something I would know as being fundamentally me?

We used to talk about this. Me and Robert. I can say that down here without fear of being overheard. We used to talk about a thing called a Reboot Box.

It comes from the plasticity of the human notion of death. Once, we thought death was what happened when your heart stopped and your brain flatlined.

Now we know you can be brought back from that. In fact we use that state in combination with cooling to allow for explantation surgery, where an organ is removed from the body and treated for disease in a way which would not be possible if it was still in place, and then returned to the cavity, the damage repaired around it. Without surgical stasis techniques, there would be no time: the patient would bleed out. With a proper stasis chamber one might have as long as half a day. That's long enough to do impossible things, to repair someone who is emphatically dead and return them to life. It can even be used to treat massive organ failure resulting from poisoning – that opposition politician in Kazakhstan, they changed his blood and sluiced out his system seven times, then had to graft cloned cells on to his organs and keep him in a medical coma for a month, but he lived. He plays tennis now.

How can I remember all that, but not what I wanted to achieve by all this? Is that some sort of joke?

But what if, even so, you're damaged. If the paramedics don't get to you fast enough; if what needs to be done exceeds even our capacity for perfect repair; if your brain is just bluntly smashed up, the information in it gone however functional the repair may be. You're never going to be the same person. No one is the same person from one day to the next, and an event like that will change you and that should be okay. But you will want continuity, and of course, it's in the interest of the person you are now to reach out to that person and try to achieve some measure of continuance into them. Serial selfhood.

Hence: a Reboot Box. A decent-sized container into which you put your favourite books, your favourite music; the things that spoke to you as a child, as an adult; your diary, your confessions, your desires; your oldest T-shirt and your most-treasured piece of jewellery. Anything that symbolises your identity now, that says, in ways that a straightforward verbal statement of self never could, who you are. Ideally, you'd put places in your Reboot Box, too, but of course they'd never fit inside, so you put a list in, along with a list of smells and times of day, favourite foods and any other things that matter, that mean you and the things you love most profoundly.

We had a plan. Or I did. Or I dreamed that I did. The *Rebus* is an escape, a crisis option. It leaves a great deal of me behind.

But I must have had a plan if I had this submarine ready and waiting. Unless I created it spontaneously and now I'm kidding myself. When you drown, sometimes you have what's called a laryngospasm. Your throat closes autonomically, refusing to inhale water. If it doesn't unlock, you can die of asphyxiation even after someone pulls you from the sea. Perhaps that's happening to me: this whole situation is my brain's equivalent of a laryngospasm, post-justified by false memories.

Or perhaps that whisper is the pressure of Smith's efforts on the outer layer of my defences. No point trying to reason it out. Reason folds back on itself here, endlessly recursive. What do I feel?

But feeling is the pre-verbal appreciation of stored self, and I'm not complete. I'm down here in the dark with just the barest knowledge of who I am and how I think to keep me going, and if I want more than that I must surface.

I trust. I trust that I had a plan. But I cannot imagine what it might have been. I mean, seriously: what possible positive outcome is there for me here? I cannot, in the long term, win this fight. Eventually they will either damage my brain so badly that I will die, either actually or effectively, or they will have what they want from me. Presumably, then, I contain a lie. In amid the many true things they will discover in this interrogation, they will find one lie which will hurt them. They will act upon it and in some way it will cause them trouble. I must have believed it would be worth it.

I wonder what it might be?

Perhaps, if I can work that out, I can push it towards them, and once they've swallowed it I can relax a little, let them have the rest of me without causing my own death. Perhaps, after that, I can even be a happy moron for them, live a well-adjusted life and not have to worry about all this crap any more. I'll be a hero, and all the while I'll be happy as well. I won't even have to know I'm a hero. Although it would be very upsetting if my secret then brought the whole thing tumbling down and I was horribly unhappy and didn't know it was what I wanted all along.

Jesus, this business is shit all ways up. What can have possessed me?

Well, *that's* an unpleasant question, under the circumstances.

require me to pretend

It may sound absurd now, but walking through walls was the trick du jour in 1974, in Addis Ababa quite as much as in Boston or Madrid. Just as aliens lined the hedgerows and made love to strayed Brazilians, so psionic studies were the currency of high science and popular passion. The capacity of our minds to effect direct change to the physical realm was a known truth only awaiting pro forma empirical confirmation, and no spoon was safe from the determined psychokinetic stares of mothers and postmen, rock stars and thieves. LSD and parapsychology were transforming our understanding of ourselves, unleashing capacities far beyond those conventionally attributed to mortal men – even if those capacities were more widely spoken of than observed. In the far future, all humans would become like gods, and perhaps we were from that atemporal state already reaching back to our own early, larval selves and teaching the skills we would need to reach our potential: causality, after all, was an artefact of the limited mind, not the boundless one, and so the most enlightened among us now might in great need reach for and find the coming godhead somewhat early in our evolution. Timothy Leary had done it, to the consternation of the FBI, and even worse so had the inventor of the orgone accumulator, that accursèd post-Freudian who had had the temerity to try to teach good American boys and girls about sex – and worse yet, to encourage them to talk about it as if there was in all the world nothing wrong with the casual discussion of fellatio. Jim Channon's *First Earth Battalion Manual* was going to teach soldiers to be more than human, and – because Channon served not Eros but the Pentagon – how to kill with their minds and levitate over the Iron Curtain. The Russians for their part claimed they'd had agents who could do all that and other things stranger and more alarming since the days of the tsars, and they mocked the feeble efforts of an arriviste West now set on catching up in the magical arms race. Baba Yaga was Russian, and so were Rasputin and Kalugina, and the East had always understood, wrapped in the icy wind of the Steppes, that there was more to the

425

mind than a robot and a poet fighting for control of a beast. The whole world, in other words, was in the grip of the most marvellous psychic bullshit, and we were primed to believe in almost anything, so long as it was terrible and wondrous and might conceivably be done by force of will alone.

When my moment came, it could have been designed to trigger a spiritual fugue. My chapel perilous was a cell in Alem Bekagn, the infamous prison of Addis Ababa whose name means 'farewell to the world'. It was a clever variation upon the perfect Benthamite concept: the prison was a ring of cells around a central courtyard where we washed and exercised, in so far as either was allowed, and while we could be at all times observed, and could look deeper into the prison itself, there was no view of anything beyond the walls. I think that last was diabolically clever. It made everything feel absolute and the possibility of release or escape faded away into the dull bricks. I won't claim it was a particular torture for an artist: I sketched with a bit of charcoal on scraps of paper. I drew other prisoners, and landscapes from memory. My cell had windows on the Alps, the Italian lakes, the Cornish coast. They became my currency, my way to bribe the guards for food, sleep and indulgence. For secret pleas to my old friends, now vanished into hiding.

It is rumoured now in academic circles that the name came from that sense of isolation, but I tell you: they called it 'Farewell' simply because for many people it was the actual gate of death.

Well, so what? The place itself is a ghost now, bricked over for the African Union's new headquarters, and good riddance – but to me it still will exist, for ever, and for all that I know it is gone I will never stop thinking of it as a thing that exists in the world. Somewhere there is always Alem Bekagn, be it in Syria or Poland or somewhere with no name or notoriety, and it will always be waiting for me. I would rather die picking a fight than go there again – but in September 1974, I was a half-mad prisoner in a hot, square box, listening to the screams of the Sixty and wondering how I of all people could possibly be the sixty-first.

If one is retrospect, or merely stands far enough away from things, it's easy to see that the guiding pattern of my life has been Ethiopia. When I was a painter, I painted our modern transformation – the blending of our old country and the sudden and disconcerting arrival of the new – and gave it to the wider world. When art abandoned me, I became a purveyor of that commodity most sought and least available in the city where I was born: security. And now, in what must likely be the last act of my age, I have returned to art and am designing the future, as the Emperor did – though with the obliquity of the millennium, I have built a future to be avoided, and hidden within it hints of the one to be desired. I am the sum of my country, however tenuous our lingering connection, and even if my Ethiopia travelled down a path at an angle to the rest of the world, and was replaced by one that does not welcome me, and that I have never seen.

Even the gauntlet that I cast into the teeth of those Georgians – the worthless men and pustulant boys who were so brave as to call my granddaughter foul names from behind digital masks, who threw around threats of sexual assault and murder as if these things were not the ugliest depth to which a man may fall – even my fictitious software application was a cry of rage at Ethiopia, in a way. I was furious at the arrival in London of the vicious madnesses of leba shay and fatasha, the ancient and modern faces of the same coin that is in English called, so very benignly, stop and search. When Haile Selassie, long ago, took over a realm in which the buying and selling of persons was yet legal and mob execution commonplace, he brought in the first printing presses, the first modern machines for transport and construction, the first real sanitation, and the first banks. It took him, I'm afraid, until 1942 to outlaw slavery, which was an old and established tradition in the country, the auction block being a common fate for the very poor from the south and for prisoners of war. But leba shay – in which a young boy is drugged and made to run through his village guided by spirits, and supposedly picks out any thief who may be lurking there for summary justice – that he did away with, and good riddance.

Alas, it is a persistent folly: when eventually the Emperor was deposed for good, his reign was followed by a resurgence in the ugly shape of fatasha: soldiers of the Derg prowled and pounced, arresting, interrogating and executing anyone who was thought to be insufficiently fervent in support of the new order. Since the World Trade Center fell, these same vices have come to the so-very-modern worlds of London and Washington. How many harmless young black men have been injured or killed in modern cities in white countries this year, for the crime of exciting someone else's racism? Too many, and it must end.

When I came down off the stage that night, Michael was there, laughing and crying and calling me a mad old fool, and then he embraced me, and I knew that I had accidentally done something else in my anger: I had made good the old rift between us, the stupid fight we had years back that had never gone away.

It had come from nowhere, in my living room. How we got into the slave trade, I cannot now imagine, but I became furious with him for setting Ethiopia alongside countries that had been colonised by the European powers. The Ethiopian experience was different, I said. Not morally superior, but different. Our country – I called it that, for the first time since I stepped on to the dock at Calais – our country was not conquered, not even when it was occupied by the Fascists and Haile Selassie returned in 1941 at the head of an army. He raised the standard of the Lion of Judah and by the grace of God and the support of one Winston Leonard Spencer-Churchill he took back what was always ours. What did Michael know, anyway, of what it meant to be a black man in a white country? Had he come here as a refugee? With literally nothing but the clothes on his back? (Well, in honesty, nor had I: I left my possessions in Addis Ababa, true enough, but much of my bank balance came with me, courtesy of the modern banking system and my international sales.) Had Michael been told by a jazz man, ten days after buying a small apartment in Soho, that he must never put bananas in the fruit bowl? He had not. No, he had not. I'd never told that story, but I told it then, and I made him sit and listen to every word with all of my parental authority.

The jazz man was a trumpeter called Donny 'Zulu' Stevens. Donny was not, of course, a Zulu. His family was Caribbean and before that, in so far as anyone could guess, they'd been Fula. The name of the Zulu, however, is so rooted in British mythology that you'd think they were almost the only Africans, ubiquitous across the entire continent and ready to take on at any moment another army under the command of Michael Caine. Any black man who was seen to do anything other than play cricket, deliver letters or drive a taxi was clearly of that fabled race who fought the redcoats and beat them down. Donny wore the label without blinking because he was first of all a performer and he knew when not to buck a legend – which is not to say that it did not anger him, because it did, every day and every time he saw it written on a poster next to his own face.

In Donny's backstage room that night was laid out a great platter of drinks and fruit, Donny having forbidden biscuits before the performance as they leave a layer of sugar and crumbs in the mouth and interfere with the music. I'm not sure Joan, the vocalist, ever truly forgave him for that even after she married him, although Donny kept her in biscuits for the rest of her life, and she buried him last year with a packet of Bourbons and a farewell song that would break your heart in two. Fruit, though: fruit was allowed and even encouraged to keep the energy levels up on stage, and since I was a guest I was encouraged to partake. I had just finished an apple and realised as the whisky came out that I might want something a little more substantial in my stomach, so I reached for a banana, an exotic import then in London, and something of a delicacy.

Donny snatched it from my hand and put it back on the tray. 'Everything but,' he said. 'We don't eat the fucking bananas. Trust me,' he added as I went to object, 'if you are ever once known to eat a banana in public, the next thing will be a picture, and then there will be bananas everywhere and all those skin-headed pricks will be laughing at you your whole life, even when they give you a prize for art and you live in a mansion, that fucking picture will crop up everywhere for ever more.'

Well, I told Michael, these days you could cook with any damn thing you pleased, and if the rump of the National Front still went to football matches and threw bananas at African players, well, it earned them the disdain of their neighbours and their heroes, and sometimes even prison. I had suffered its stupider days, not Michael, and I would judge whether the salvation of my country from occupation in 1941 made up for the unconsidered prejudice of Britain decades later, and in my judgement it did. Friends could be unfeeling and stupid and still be friends when you needed them, and that did not make them the Derg. The world was imperfect and Britain was better than most anywhere else. That was how it was, and Michael should grow up and understand it.

That bad night, we drew back from the brink. Michael thanked me for proving his point. I thanked him for accepting mine. Then he said he was ashamed of me, and I told him young hotheads are always ashamed of their parents, and he said most young hotheads didn't have reason, but he was saddled with a father who was a collaborator. Well, he was right and I was right and we both knew it, I think, but were too alike to find the common ground. There we froze, thank God, held between wounding spite and deep mutual need. I could no more tell him to get out than he could tell me he was leaving. We had friends, both of us, and girlfriends, but in all the world we really had only one another, and we knew it.

The fight was forgiven, but never unsaid and never forgotten. For a while, I was proud to have spoken my mind, and then I thought I had been trying to protect him, and finally I admitted that I had just been upset because he seemed to have no idea who he was in a generational sense, and if that was

429

anyone's fault it was mine. If we could not have gone to Ethiopia, we could have talked about it. We could have been part of a community here, Tewahedo and afternoon tea. Burned by his mother and afraid, I think now, that our shared old friends would be kind to me, I had never made the attempt.

The day left a hole in both of us that couldn't be filled. We waited for the lip of the crater to erode and fade into the overgrowth, and it did, but we knew where it was and we stepped around it, until I came down off the set of that ridiculous chat show, with the audience murmuring in the commercial break and the host's eyes round as a cat's. We were still hugging when my phone rang, and to my surprise it wasn't Annie but Colson.

'You're a dangerous lunatic,' he said.

'I suppose I may be.' I was a little surprised myself, now that the rage had blown out of me into the world.

'It's a very interesting idea, your app. I don't imagine you've got the slightest idea how to make it happen?'

'None at all,' I said.

'I could build a test version by next week, then, if you like,' Colson suggested, and I heard Annie laughing in the background. 'You're pretty much public enemy number one for arseholes tonight, by the way.'

'Good,' I said.

'Maybe don't go online. I'm looking at your inbox right now. It's not entirely charming. But you've taken some of the heat off Annie, if that's what you wanted.'

I cackled. I didn't have to imagine. I knew about the frenzy of hate. In the grand tradition of old men, I had seen it all before.

*

You wouldn't have thought it possible, meeting me in my high days in Addis Ababa, that a few years later the art world would forget me entirely except for the occasional desperate critic scraping together some obscure thesis. I had acquired or unleashed a full measure of talent and I have to acknowledge it went to my head at least as much as it seemed to affect the thinking of those around me. My self-image decreed that I hold in my desire to paint for weeks and then stab and slash the canvas with every evidence of fury. It wasn't entirely natural to me, so often I had to engage in furtive night-time creation when the mood took me, and hide the consequences away until my next scheduled ejaculation. This was all needless nonsense, but it satisfied my sense of who I wished to be.

I was young and famous. I had produced most recently a fivefold image of the moon in which a black man and an Asian woman, their spacesuits discarded, copulated upon a ragged American flag, while behind them in the dark a nuclear war made the earth into a final, fatal jewel. This sort of thing generates comment if you do it right, and I had. In art, comment is fame and fame is money – and of course, money entails comment. Guided only by my artistic sense, I followed *The World in Flames* with a completely incomprehensible mixed media offering – a shark hanging in an ocean of numbers – and realised almost immediately by the resounding silence that although it had come from the same unadulterated transcription of my inner vision that I did not understand, in career terms it was a misstep. I quickly made an image – heavily disguised, for reasons of social prudence – of the daughter of the Minister of Infrastructure, in which she emerged like Athena from the bursting skull of her father to reach in almost Soviet modern style for a passing aeroplane. Her naked torso was not the conventionally European image of an African woman walking to a well, nor yet the cabaret girl of French erotic shows. Four spectral figures in the background sought to judge her, their eyes lit from within by nuclear fire, but she ignored them. She was a woman – in the discourse of the time, and as I had cause to know – in fullest possession of her own sexuality, because she existed not for the viewer but for herself. It was in the strictest sense a pastiche – I was copying my own style, not executing it – but if I didn't say that, certainly no one else was going to suggest it. I had only to title the painting *Progress*, and the whisper of comment became a storm. The shark was politely forgotten, and I flew as a guest and a poster boy between Addis Ababa, London, Paris and New York – the latter, most especially, because Warhol was there and because the Emperor of Ethiopia had made a special friendship with the then President of the United States. So I went, on Haile Selassie's coat-tails, and drank martinis at Warhol's Factory, and made sure to point out that I was in my own informed opinion a far greater artist than Ibrahim El-Salahi from Sudan.

El-Salahi, by the way, seems to have been devoid of such bizarre notions of competition. He strikes me from this remove as a very serious fellow – I suppose what I am saying is that he was not obviously disposed to be an idiot. I don't imagine that in reality I ever featured in his thoughts, beyond perhaps a brief flicker of curiosity about where a good Ethiopian boy would get such an obsession with flying saucers, or with the neon colours of a corporate-industrial city at night. I will tell you honestly, also, that even in that imagined competition where we were honourable equals contesting for the joy of it and for the applause of the crowd, he won. He had a sense of self rooted in his craft and his religion and no doubt a dozen other things I hadn't got to grips with, while I, meanwhile, had determined that I was a citizen of the world, for which I blame Humphrey Bogart. When I saw *Casablanca* for the first time, in a street near my home, the images projected from the back of a truck on to a great sheet of bedlinen stitched and bleached for the occasion, it had a powerful effect upon me, and from then on I took the line that drinking whisky and wearing a white tuxedo made me part of the global brotherhood of rebel males.

Thank God there was yet no Internet and no Instagram to record my excesses. A few photographs survive, but they are the better ones that could be described as iconic rather than merely historical: in one, I am pictured with the beautiful television star Joanna Cameron, and it's quite clear that I have fallen in love. In another I'm part of a group including Ursula Andress, fresh from the set of *L'Infermiera*, and the estimable West Indian cricketer Garry Sobers. I met thieves and singers, diplomats and princesses, and we talked of such high matters as post-figurative sculpture, the Second Indochina War and the transformative power of LSD. For the most part I am forgiven, as we all should be, those awkward years of pose and posture as I struggled to work out who I was and missed the mark. The art I made was good enough that I was also excused some of the nonsense that came out of my mouth, and if, as I say, El-Salahi was just more talented than I – well. Being a little less good than someone who is brilliant is a failure to be cherished.

My wide, wild ride culminated in a return to my small apartment in Addis Ababa from an endless round of American parties, to find an imperial footman awaiting me with an actual silver tray. The object on the tray was a supremely redundant grace note: a thick white business card printed by Stevens of Edinburgh, bearing the imperial arms and the name Haile Selassie I. Underneath, where an ordinary man might put 'Attorney at Law' or 'Chief Financial Officer' it read: 'King of Kings, Conquering Lion of the Tribe of Judah, The Elect of God, Emperor of Ethiopia.'

It struck me in that moment that one might as well print labels for the moon and the sky.

I must have asked some sort of question, for the footman told me I was to paint a portrait. I was so boggled that I asked: 'Of whom?' at which the man rolled his eyes to indicate his red livery and presence, the tray and the card, and managed not to say 'Who do you think, you ignorant mingelouse?' or whatsoever variant thereof was his inner thought.

I stared at him while the obvious reality took hold in my mind: I was to paint a portrait of Haile Selassie.

I said: 'When?' and the footman gave me to understand, once again by his suffused silence, that I shouldn't hang about. It was no better than six in the morning and I had slept hardly at all in the last day. The lulling scent of eucalyptus, the perfume of the place still definitive though mixed now with the fumes of automobiles and aircraft rather than the scent of grazing goats in the streets, was calling me to my bed. Well, that would have to wait, because the Emperor simply did not. I took as much time as I dared to make myself presentable, which was not much, and the footman drove me to the palace.

I should have realised that our timetable would be suitably padded at every turn. My fumbling had made us late by ten minutes for the superior footman, and therefore he had to rush me through the back corridors – where there was no possibility of accidentally meeting the Emperor in advance of our appointment, again unthinkable – so that we were on time for the Master of the Household, who in turn took me to the Imperial Secretary, for whom I was twenty minutes early. The walls were white, the drapes red, the inlays all gold leaf. Carved lions rambled over the furniture, and a huge mural on one wall depicted the Solomonic dynasty from which our Emperor drew his descent. The place echoed whenever you moved, and smelled of a modern cleaning product with a most artificial scent.

'What time is my appointment?' I asked.

'Nine thirty,' the Secretary replied. 'You should kneel once and call him "Your Imperial Majesty" when he greets you, after which he will instruct you to remain standing for your bows and call him "sir". Can you remember that?'

'Nine thirty?' It was not yet eight. I wondered if I could remain awake, and whether it would be an insufferable insult to go to sleep on the couch.

'I will have food brought to you. The Emperor will already have breakfasted. He wakes early and has other appointments before you.'

I was no longer used to waiting, and the question came out of me, curious rather than aggressive, before I could remember where I was. 'With whom?'

A whisper of a smile flicked across the lined face. 'Immediately before you, he is meeting with an anteater.'

I suggested shyly that I had misheard.

'Not at all. The anteater was a gift from Apollo Milton Obote of Uganda. It is an important appointment.' I thought for a moment he was making a joke, but his face seemed to warn me against asking, and I realised that here, more than anywhere else, our conversation must be overheard and recorded. After a moment longer, he smiled. 'To meet with the Emperor in person – in private – is a remarkable thing, Berihun Bekele. There are men in the palace this very morning who would give everything for a chance encounter with our Emperor, merely long enough to share a joke with him and assure him of their loyalty. For you, he has twenty minutes after the anteater. Would it ease your heart to know who comes before the anteater?'

I said it would, realising immediately as I did that it would not.

The Secretary saw this in my face, and told me anyway. 'Solomon Kedir is first' – the head of palace security, chief spy of the empire – 'and then with the Minister of Business' – who had the largest unofficial spy network in Addis Ababa – 'and then with the Minister of Political Stability' – the master of the secret police. The three most powerful men in Ethiopia, after the Emperor himself. 'Then the anteater, and then you. I do not imagine you will have many days like this one.'

And he left. A little while later, a woman arrived with pastries, which I ate even though I was too nervous to be hungry. I dozed upright, and was grateful when another servant came in, a quarter after nine, and woke me with hot mint tea and a towel scented with pandanus and lemon. A little while after that, I went in to meet my imperial master.

*

I say that we met, but even in the most formal construction, that implies a loose familiarity which was entirely absent. We were in the same room. We saw one another. He focused upon me, and I upon him – and yet there was no discourse between us. He sat and I sat and he said nothing, so nor did I. Physically he was quite small, quite old, and yet here was the man who had defied Mussolini, who shamed the League of Nations and reconquered Ethiopia. Here was the man who ruled my country, and who held my life unmentioned in his hand.

He turned his head a little: wide brow, deep eyes, a face of age and intelligence; a face that some called the visage of a living god – because a king descended of a line of kings who has more than once fought wars to hold his throne is not daunting enough.

He sat, and the clock ticked. The man called the Emperor's Cuckoo – who bowed on the hour, every waking hour of the day – waited for his moment.

Haile Selassie shifted in his seat. Leaned down towards me. I thought he would speak.

He did not speak.

I looked at his face, his body – the stiffness he hid around his hips, the waning nervous fire in the man. I looked at the energy that hid in his eyes. He twisted slightly so that I could see him in profile. I realised he was not going to speak to me, and therefore I was not going to speak to him. This was the extent of our communication, the absolute distillation of our relationship: he was the one being painted, and I the painter. Any other man in that context would be called a subject, but this man could never be subject to anyone. For the moment he was showing me his face, how he moved and held himself: a man on a throne in a white cloak, master of everything. Then he moved again.

By turns, he gave me the different surfaces of his body to look at, the different moods and poses that made the exteriority of the man, and I laboured to commit them to memory.

In the silence I became self-conscious, self-doubting. I had never actually painted a portrait before, and I had only the vaguest notion how it was done. I wondered if I should take photographs, but I had left my camera at home. I wondered if I should sketch. My bag was by my feet. I could get a pad and a pencil. I didn't. I was locked in contemplation of the Lion, and here and to this limited extent he was noticing and responding to my eyes. It was an indulgence of extraordinary magnitude. If I got the pad the moment would break, and I could not stand for it to be over.

This was what I would paint, this encounter. I must paint this, exactly. Not literally, not figuratively, but this feeling, this impossible sense of presence, this man and his whole life and what he meant.

He lifted one eyebrow. Did he want me to paint that? But no. He was reacting.

Slowly, without fuss, the anteater walked between us. It looked at the Elect of God, then at his portraitist. If it saw anything to choose between us, I could

435

not tell. Perhaps it distinguished only between men and ants. Perhaps even less than that.

It wandered away.

Nine minutes later, my silent audience was at an end.

*

For the next while, I came when the Emperor set time aside for me. Quite often he had none when I wished to see his face, to return to my mind the precise angle of his cheek; then on other occasions he seemed to have nothing to do, and we spent hours in silence, always with him pantomiming fatherly concern or spiritual contemplation, masculine power or regal pride. Never, in six months, did he say one word to me. I think it was meant as a sort of kindness.

The anteater grew accustomed to me. I dared offer it nothing, no treats or bribes, and indeed I would have had no idea what it might enjoy through that long, arched muzzle with its absurdly tiny mouth. Sometimes it paused in its peregrinations and observed me, opaque and strange, and then went on its way with the same dissatisfied head shake I had first observed. If I had operated on my own artistic terms entirely, I think I might have combined them, those two: the silent man who held my life in his palm and thought to drag an ancient empire to the altar of history in the span of his own; and the timeless beast, alien eyes so full of incomprehensible frustration.

But there were constraints upon me, not the least of which was survival. It went without saying that my portrait must be respectful and must appear to be respectful, but in addition to this the Secretary had issued three outright diktats I must obey. First: the portrait should be emphatically in my own style and I should project the King of Kings into such phantasmagoria as I wished. This was a great project of Ethiopia, a challenge to the artists of America and Europe: Africa, too, can produce the wild, the strange, the new. In Africa is being born a civilisation that will challenge your way of doing things. We shall begin with the best of you and of us, and there shall be a reborn power in the world, a new conception of humanity. Warhol must quake, Lichtenstein must shudder, and Henry Kissinger and his Soviet counterpart Eduard Shevardnadze must take note that the old continent was rising. At the least, they should know that they were well met.

436

Second: wherever and however I placed the Emperor, he should be accompanied by lions.

Third, and finally: His Imperial Majesty should be painted full-face at least once in the image. In traditional Ethiopian art, the unrighteous may be known by the fact that they cannot look the viewer in the eye but must turn away, shame reaching them even in so faint an echo as pigment. The Emperor being of the Solomonic line and the Elect of God, it followed that his portrait must know no such fear.

For some time I found I was consumed by the kind of dithering that professional tennis players call 'the yips'. I could start – did start – any number of paintings of Haile Selassie, and set him amongst any number of strange landscapes, but I could not find one that was both utterly foreign and still entirely appropriate to the man. I was blocked, and not all the meditation or medication or sex that I could put together seemed to unblock me. I painted, recanted, scraped away oil and started again – and again, and again. I knew the contours of my Emperor's face better than I knew my own, knew his modes and moods, his action and hesitation; I could draw him a thousand different ways and each of them was perfect. But the rest! The rest was dross. The background overwhelmed the heart of any image I put together, and I knew that that penetrating gaze would see a less-than-sincere effort for what it was, and – at best – dismiss me.

I kept going. I knew by now that creation was a game of stamina as much as inspiration, and that each failed effort would eventually teach in combination with some stray additional thought the answer that I needed. Finally, in despair and exhaustion one night, I realised between breaths that my difficulty was in itself a boundary condition, an inherent edge of the work. There was nothing I could imagine that would set off or expose a truth about the Emperor beyond what was the man himself. He was like the notional neutronium: a state of political matter so dense as to be irreducible. He was not to be embellished in the way of any other project, but was rather fundament from which the rest of the picture must derive. I began, therefore, with lions, faint ghost images buried beneath the paint so that they seemed to hang in the air, and sketched in the outline of the throne room and the window beyond. The Emperor I painted last, heavy and opaque, in an almost traditional Venetian style, so that it seemed Haile Selassie was the only thing in the world made of real substance and everything else was mist. He fairly shone upon the viewer, a black demiurge in dark gold whose eyes encompassed a nation of rising modernity and sparkling towers, a space which existed first and foremost in his mind. In my own tradition now, upon my other canvases I presented details of his body – a curled hand, a commanding mouth, a shining eye – and visions of his vision, exploring more fully all that was suggested beyond the window. I rendered it as something flavoured with America, Russia and Europe that was itself their ancient parent and their natural progeny: a striving and baroque contra-Corbusier landscape with whispers of NASA's bold orbital homesteads, not carving the land but made gentle and irregular by the contours of the great Simien Mountains. Five pieces in all, creating a single truth: the August One's gaze, as I saw it in my mind, emerging from the flat surface at right angles and penetrating the real space before it, not judged by the viewer but weighing and assessing them instead. I called it Tewahedo, which is not only the Ethiopian Church but also the Ge'ez word meaning 'unified'. At length I delivered it, and the Emperor hung all five parts alone on the wall of the grand receiving room. He commissioned pictures of it for release to the global press. *Newsweek* ran it as part of a feature on the Land of the Rising Lion, and the opinion column of the *New York Times* nodded sagely and heralded my talent amid the other stars of a burgeoning continental renaissance. London's *Daily Mail* called it fallacious and bombastic, which meant that the *Guardian* asserted it was the product of genius. Later, when I saw the poster campaign for that first *Star Wars* film – the one that is now heretically referred to as the fourth – I thought I recognised the traces of my work in its composition, and was delighted at the idea.

All in all, it's a great shame the Derg got hold of that portrait and burned it on the tarmac of the Churchill Road. It may not have been the best or the most authentic thing I ever did, but it didn't deserve that.

*

I was all right, in those first few days after the fall. It had been a drawn-out dying, the end of empire, starting in February 1974, just a few days after I began my work, and culminating in that loud and angry September. Haile Selassie himself did not die until 1975, when it is commonly assumed that Mengistu murdered him with his own hand. If that had been done in those September days, I think I would have fled. I could probably have done it: a short trip to the airport and an exchange of goods for services. I had friends, of course, who protected me and might have helped me: old drinking buddies from the university who now found themselves appointed to the Cadre for People's Artistic Expression by a Derg scrambling to locate and project a coherent identity from an opportunistic eruption. I even knew a few career soldiers who were belated members of the revolutionary vanguard. I was a painter, after all, and I mixed with all sorts. No one could seriously have imagined me as political, though of course I had political value as an object to be smashed.

In fact, I should have left, by whatever means I could, but I honestly believed – and my friends told me – that things would settle down. It was not that kind of revolution, they said, not the Russian kind where the Tsar and his family are put against the wall. It was the other kind, in which one mode of production supersedes another in the orderly progress of historical materialism. I should stay indoors and I should occupy myself and I should paint, but little by little the mood would calm and I would be a national treasure, a perfect example of a man who had freed himself from the oppressive system by the exercise of his mind. My work, after all, had flavours that might have been Soviet. A little careful construction could make me a hero, or at least a secret sympathiser. I need only wait, and pay no attention to what was happening outside my window; to the cries of men clubbed down in the street and the noise of bones breaking; to the wailing of women carried off to answer for their husbands' imagined crimes; to the small shuffle of children too young for the task, picking their way down the alleys in search of missing parents.

It was not the worst revolution in the history of the world. It was no more ignoble, I think, than the ones in England or America, in their day. Every nation has its sorrows and shames, its times of frenzy, and this was ours. Whatever is the root of human violence, be it imperfect economic organisation, timor mortis or original sin, it bore full fruit in Addis Ababa that autumn.

My friends were wrong, of course: that damned appointments book, sourced from the same binder who made the members' journal at London's haughty Athenaeum, was too heavy with the name Berihun Bekele for me to be passed over. I was instead raised up: the perfect quisling, the perfect decadent product of a misshaped society, the perfect whore to the aristocracy of court and the exploiters of Texas and Birmingham. How was I different from an Italian Fascist, from a collaborator of the occupation? My jackbooted foot was on the neck of the poor. Men came, led by a little surgeon with a grave face and hands that

439

looked a great deal like my own. He had a birthmark on his cheek, like a burning torch.

I could have painted that scene for them, and beautifully. I wonder whether, if I had offered, I might have found another way out, might have survived by my brush at the whim of another fiat power. I did not. I went dumbly as a penitent, in a car that had been one of the palace fleet, its roof cut open now and bars welded to the upright pillars of the frame so that it was somewhere between a flatbed truck and a mobile stocks. I thought they would bring me to trial or simply send me to the border – the way they talked, it seemed as if I might be exiled, and the idea was more terrible than I would have thought. To leave, knowing one will return, is exciting. To leave and hear the key turn in the lock is banishment, and a blade in the soul. Exile, though, was better than I deserved.

Instead, they took me to Alem Bekagn, and they lined the route with a mob.

*

London, decades later in those days of Georgian rage, was not the same, and I let the difference deceive me into believing we were safe.

That's not to say we took no precautions. We shifted all my communications to the Spine, which was by now comfortable with me and able to recognise what Annie called my etic connectome: what my consciousness appeared to be from an observer's viewpoint. I also asked Tom Hayes, the head of personal security at my – now Michael's – company, to come and advise us on safety. Tom suggested close protection for all of us in the short term, but Annie wouldn't have it and I generally agreed. He had expected that, I think, and argued strongly for a perimeter team – a fast-response group watching from a reasonable and unintrusive distance. Annie said no to that too, and I equivocated, but if I'm luckier than I ought to be Michael will have done it anyway, on the company's behalf.

We carried on. Annie and Colson had meetings around the film tie-in for *Witnessed*, all this publicity doing the development process no harm whatsoever. There also was the first expansion pack to consider (new characters and new environments, new murders and plots). In his spare time, Colson was building my app, concentrating on the back end, which was evidently complex but happily the sort of thing which could be put together fast from existing code.

The newspapers, of course, had picked up on my announcement, and opinion was split on the Left as to whether this was a grass-roots effort against casual racism or the beginnings of a Foucauldian nightmare of technocratic peer-to-peer surveillance. On the Right, there was a general sense of aggrieved dignity at the idea that Britain could possibly be systemically and institutionally racist, shading at the Kentish and Home Counties edges into a suspicion that my project somehow amounted to the de facto establishment of sharia law. Crypto-Islamism, apparently, was a concern to be taken seriously at the highest levels of government, because it was certainly taken seriously in Gravesend.

On Monday, the police came to see me, and I was glad that they should. The local station had been very supportive of us, taking seriously the threats against Annie and myself, and being sure that anything we could offer about those making them was carefully noted down. They kept us up to date while the Cybercrime team untangled the inevitable web of anonymous email accounts and virtual-presence networks. One of Annie's most persistent abusers turned out to be a church warden from Somerset; another was a teenager living in New Mexico. The majority were young, stupid men living with their parents in houses from Southampton to Glasgow, who had taken for whatever reason against the idea that my granddaughter should speak her mind. Some had been cautioned, some arrested, and some had mended their ways so far as to apologise – dragged by one ear to the telephone, I rather thought, hearing the unmistakable suffused silence of maternal rage at the far end of the line – and some had seen the inside of a cell. Celebrity, I knew, was having an effect on our treatment. Most of the time such things go largely unanswered.

These officers were not local. There was a huge fellow with small hands who stood at the back and didn't speak, and I recognised him as the implicit threat. I am old, but I did not get this far without the occasional dust-up, especially in my early London years, and I found myself looking from each to the next and wondering how I would fare if I must fight them. The big one caught me at it and shifted pointedly in his seat. I gave him an unrepentant look and settled to a more dignified appraisal, but no man likes to be made to feel second in his own house.

Another man, pale with a redhead's stubble, took notes, and finally there was a woman who seemed to be in charge. They were from a national task group, she told me, and they were not for the moment concerned with threats made against Annie or even against me. They were aware of those and others in their office were looking into the more serious ones. It was their task, she warned me with great solemnity, to investigate the possibility that I had myself broken the law.

I laughed out loud. It was so preposterous that I assumed she was here pro forma, and that we would all share in the fun. No one else joined in, so I sobered and asked instead in what way I might have done so.

The woman, Detective Sergeant Sykes, had the face of a country butcher. She rested her jowls on her collar and said that it was possible I had engaged in incitement to racial hatred.

I had?

Yes.

I had?

Yes.

Surely that was the wrong way around. An administrative error, a misunderstanding.

No.

No?

Sykes asked if I'd like to be reminded of my actions.

I thought about that for a moment and decided I would not. If these people were in earnest then my temper was likely to get the better of me, and it was possible that would be a bad idea in this already upside-down situation. In any case, when a fellow is accused of anything that even if only in its most extreme extension requires the attention of the court, the first thing he does if he is sensible is call his lawyer.

I excused myself for a moment and called my lawyer. Her name is Lindsey, and she is a senior partner at Graumann Gibb LLP, hard by Lincoln's Inn. If ever you want to put your enemy's feet to the fire in a legal tussle, I recommend her. Lindsey said she would come right over, and she would bring just the person to assist in the specific discussion. I went back to Detective Sykes and explained that there would now be a short delay. I invited the officers to wait. They elected not to. I had the distinct impression that calling lawyers was grounds for arrest in itself. It is a staple of crime dramas that only guilty people need lawyers before they discuss things with kindly policemen. The majority of crime dramas are written by middle-class white males with no actual experience of being accused of anything, and they are in any case about the brilliance of a particular detective. All the same, a surprising number of people – including police officers – believe what they see on the television screen without even wondering whether fact and fiction may not be entirely congruent.

'You'll hear from us shortly,' Sykes said on the doorstep.

'Can you give me a rough idea of when?'

'You will,' Sykes repeated, 'hear from us shortly.' To my amazement, she thrust her face in towards mine like a drunk in a bar. I wondered if her house was decked in the Cross of St George every day, or only for the last week of April.

After a moment, with the muscular compression of a retreating snail, she took her face away again. I watched her turn and walk away from me with her minions, and didn't step back from my door until I had seen her safely into the unmarked car on the other side of the road. She took the passenger seat and stared straight ahead, as if she was fixing her eyes on a future that did not offend her, and nothing on this side of the road existed at all.

When she had gone, I went back inside and sat in silence for a while, feeling the heat of my fury wash out of me into the cool, rough fabric of my Kingcome sofa. It seemed to me the weave was just a little damp from the winter air.

Then Annie called, and told me the government was trying to buy her company, and they weren't taking no for an answer. I told her what had happened and she said the saddest thing you could ever hear from your grandchildren. She said it was almost enough to make her lose faith in people.

'No, it's all right,' I said, very sure. 'It's the other way round. When people see us standing up: this is where they begin to have faith.'

*

'The entity is called Turnpike,' Lindsey said, in the wood-panelled meeting room in Lincoln's Inn where she hands out the Long Brown Envelope of Home Truths. In happier times, this notional envelope has contained a warning to the other side that they are about to get soundly thrashed – but not today. Today, we were at the mercy of a seventeenth-century jurist named Hugo Grotius, who penned in the year 1625 a learned treatise on the notion of compulsory purchase, known more grandly to our American cousins as 'eminent domain'. This right of supreme lordship is vested in the monarch and is now inevitably

443

devolved upon the Prime Minster and any acting in the place of that executive. By it, the state is empowered to use, abstract and even destroy the property of any individual or collective if this action is necessary for the greater public good. The party upon whom the power is exerted must in turn be compensated to a reasonable value of what is thus taken. Britain being by tradition a place, like Grotius's beloved Holland, where the power of the state is used sparingly upon a proud and independent populace – if recently afflicted with governments ever more nosy, inflexible and prurient – it is rare that the prerogative is exercised in any but the most exigent circumstance. It has been used in wartime to secure land for coastal defences, and in peace to preserve ancient monuments from destruction at the hands of besuited barbarians. It has been invoked by special Act of Parliament for railways and roads. Until this year, it has never even been suggested that it might be used to acquire a computer game company, and still less that such acquisition might stretch to include the services under contract of its principal employees.

'And Turnpike is government?'

'Up to a point, yes. It exists in the liminal ground between government and industry. A merger of state and corporate power.'

Colson twitched, showed his teeth. 'Nice.'

'At this moment,' Annie reported, 'someone is launching a very sophisticated and very illegal attack on our computers. We've looked at the code, and it's obfuscated.'

She knew we'd passed the limit of my knowledge. I made a gesture with my hand: small explanation, short words. I wasn't the only numpty in the room.

'They've broken the attacking code into parts. It's all jumbled to make it hard to analyse or identify. A machine doesn't care about the order of transmission, only the instructed sequence of execution and operation, but for a human, obfuscation makes the code very hard to understand. Sophisticated software can have millions of lines. This is less than that, but it's still like reading a book where all the stories are jumbled up and there's just a line of numbers at the beginning to tell you where to start. This goes a step further and hides it from most security, too: it arrives in parts and self-assembles. Nasty.'

'It won't work?' I asked her.

'No. Not for Fire Judges. Our stuff spots it as soon as the reassembly begins. To make it work in the Spine, you'd need ...' She shrugged.

'You'd need someone on the inside,' Colson said. 'Which they don't have, so they can just go fuck themselves. Pardon me. But it's a salutary lesson: if you want to crack a real deep system with self-correcting adaptive security like ours – security which ultimately boots hard questions to a human boss – you need someone to open it up for you, just a little bit. Note to self.'

'I think that's part of the point,' Lindsey told my granddaughter. 'They don't just want your company, they want what's in your head. And yours,' she added when Colson scowled.

'Can they do that?'

'No,' Lindsey said, and then, 'or rather, probably not. But they're talking about bringing in all manner of anti-terror and national security legislation which hasn't been used this way before. Some of it hasn't been used at all. With the existing compulsory purchase law they can certainly compel you to give up the software if there's a need. If you don't comply, that becomes a much simpler matter for them in various ways. The rest is new.'

'They can't press-gang her, surely?' I objected.

'Oh, no. They can, however, declare all research around her work to be classified. If they choose to see the software as a weapon, say, then you'd need a permit from the MoD to continue to develop it. If you tried to leave the country while a case was ongoing they might construe that as flight with intent to reveal classified material. You could be interred in the national interest. That's not imprisonment, by the way, and there's no trial. It's not clear how long they can maintain it, but they can freeze your bank accounts, both personal and corporate, and be very, very aggressive about unfreezing them. A few months is usually all it takes to destroy someone. There's reputation damage to consider as well, of course. And officially unconnected troubles with authority which may suddenly appear to complicate things.' She glanced at me.

'What about afterwards? Assume that we win it all.'

'Then you could seek redress. I imagine you might see a small payment sometime before Annie's ninetieth birthday.'

At the far end of the table a young man was taking copious notes. He seemed very young indeed. I wondered if he was on work experience, and then realised he was probably a full fee-earning lawyer.

Colson shrugged and leaned back. 'There's another option.'

Lindsey nodded. 'There is.'

'We can take this public.'

'You can.' Something in her voice was off. I looked at her and saw that she was very closed down and tight. Her eyes were fixed on the table and on her hands.

'What would happen?' I asked.

'They would either back down and pretend it was an error or hit you as hard as they possibly could.' No indication of which. Junior the note-taker turned a page.

'Do you have a sense of which?' Lindsey has instincts, but more than that she has connections. She works for the government as often as against them, taking the cases she likes. She tries, in short, to make a difference. I expected her to have an opinion, and to share it.

'I can't advise you on that,' Lindsey said. 'Obviously, it is desirable, where the wishes of the state are clear and appropriate, for citizens to participate in the defence and betterment of the nation.' A wooden generality. 'It would be better if this were settled amicably.'

'And if it can't be?'

'Then we must act in accordance with the law while seeking to maximise your gain and minimise your exposure.' More generalities.

'Would you take this public?'

'I am not the client. Do I propose it? No. It would not be appropriate for me to suggest action beyond my area of expertise.'

I rolled my eyes. Annie put her palms briefly against her cheeks and puffed air out, the way she did when she was tackling a particularly knotty piece of code. Colson, on the other hand, seemed to find Lindsey's responses entirely enlightening. He raised a hand like a schoolboy.

'What aspects of this case are particularly not covered by your expertise, if you don't mind me asking?'

Lindsey looked up and directly at him. You might have come into the room and thought nothing was happening, unless you knew Colson, knew that he never paid full attention to anything.

'I would say that I'm unfamiliar with Turnpike and what commercial and real-world pressure it might bring to bear. I can advise on the law.'

'So it's not just a shell company.'

'Oh, no. It's a long-established administrative amanuensis. Dating from the seventeenth century again, actually. I imagine the connection is fairly direct: the state seeking to create and protect necessary infrastructure, sometimes against the wishes of fairly rowdy local landholders. The Civil War was something of a landmark moment in that discussion, I suppose: Magna Carta versus the divine right. The rights of the individual against the rights of supreme lordship. The former bounding the latter, and so on.'

'Just so long as no one gets beheaded.'

'The state in this country no longer employs extreme methods in the enforcement of its will.'

Colson leaned back. 'Of course not.' Whatever private discussion they were having seemed to be over.

'Well, all right,' I said. 'That's a nice historical background. For today, your advice is?'

'To explore your options. See what may be negotiated before things deteriorate. To consider what you most wish to achieve.'

And with that, the meeting was over. We all got into one of the self-driving cars and let it take us away.

'What was that about?' I asked Colson, after a long silence during which no one spoke.

'The nice lady is doing her best for us,' Colson said. 'But she's being fucked with and she's a little bit scared on her own account.'

'Lindsey?'

'Yes. Did you see the little squit at the end of the table taking notes?'

'Lawyers do that. They keep records.'

'Yeah, they do, but he wasn't hers. He was someone else's record.'

'That would be illegal,' I said. 'It's a privileged meeting.'

Colson shrugged. 'They bug those when they want to. Gitmo and all that. You've got to understand, there's how you were always told things were done, fair play and boundaries and all that, and there's how they actually were, and then there's now. Thirty years ago there was maybe a bit of to and fro about breaking the rules. Now it's just normal. If our lot want to know something they're not allowed to, they ask the Yanks nicely. When the Yanks want to spy on their own, which they mustn't ever at all, they call GCHQ for a favour, see? And since they pretty much bankroll the place, well, we make resources available, don't we? But you need to get your head round this: if you're having a conversation in the clear, it's being overheard.'

Annie was back, and looking at Colson. 'You think she was trying to give us a message?'

'They've put her on notice. If she does anything they don't like she'll be out of the club. Maybe they pull her licence. Maybe they call an audit and their special analysis team finds discrepancies she can't account for because they weren't there until yesterday. Maybe they just let the Georgians know she's helping us and let them sort it out.'

I wanted to laugh at him, at this conspiratorial notion of Britain sub regno exploratorum. It was not a country I recognised – but Annie and Colson both did, both accepted it as an article of faith. I looked up at the sky, at the benign orange glow of the city reflected in low cloud, and saw it abruptly in a new mode – the sun a scorching eye of scrutiny deflected from us only by the ambient indifference of fog and mist.

'You're sure,' Annie said.

Colson nodded. 'I was sure,' he said, 'from the moment she told me that Turnpike was the merger of state and corporate power. That didn't ring any bells with either of you?'

'It sounds like something you'd say,' Annie muttered.

Colson nodded. 'Yes. It is. She's a very smart, very educated lady, your Lindsey, and she's just done a very brave thing right under some bastard's nose. She'll probably get caught for it later, so we'll want to be sure she's got a soft landing somewhere. She told you she couldn't advise on something that was outside her professional competence, right?'

I nodded.

'But she didn't actually give us any concrete advice either.'

'No, I suppose she didn't.'

'And you're a bit disappointed.'

I nodded again.

'So the thing I said that she said she couldn't advise on: that's the thing she would advise if it wasn't outside her professional competence. See? That's what she thinks we ought to do. Blow it all wide open. But she can't say that with squit in the room or they'll say she advised us to break the law or whatever and take away her funny hat.'

'She's a solicitor,' Annie said primly.

'Whatever. That's what she's telling us to do.'

'I thought she was telling us not to do that.'

'Yeah. Squit probably thinks so too. Fuck him.'

'You're getting all this from what she said about Turnpike?'

'Basically. It was a bit of a red flag. What, it really doesn't mean anything at all to you? Still?'

'Colson,' Annie said. 'You're an info-rat. Not everyone's brain works that way. The merger of state and corporate power: why is it important?'

Colson scowled as if both the question and the answer were part of some conspiracy of which he particularly disapproved. 'It's one of the basic victory conditions of Italian Fascism,' he said.

We thought about that, and after some time the silence became heavy, and grim. They came home with me to take counsel and refuge. We drafted a legal reply and then, knowing we would be assailed, we reached out to the strange and wayward ghosts of the Internet's liberty – to Anonymous and its curious, non-existent cousins: the Magnificent Seven and the Round Table; the Fourth Stooge, the Gray I and the XX-Men. We called campaign groups and newspapers and we let our defiance be known. Everyone was angry for us. Everyone said they would help.

The next night, someone threw a bomb against my armoured window.

*

That night I dreamed of Alem Bekagn for the first time in a long, long while. It was narrow and terribly hot, and filled with the sound of others screaming and weeping. However I answered his questions, the lean fellow with that relentless obsequiousness of manner, he still had his men break one finger bone each day in a vise. They came for me with great punctuality at five in the afternoon, so that the pain kept me awake all night and it grew harder and harder to feed myself or drink. My tongue swelled and my breath stank. Much of this is true, but in this version, in the end, I did not escape my cell. Instead I died in a corner between sunrise and sunset, choking on the awful lizard dryness that had at last become so large that I could not breathe. They put out my corpse, but no one came to take it away. Michael was never born and nor was Annie. My whole world never was, and that was the worst of it, that my extinction at that wrong moment kills not only my future but my hope.

It is an alternative history. The true one is a curious footnote to the Massacre of the Sixty – and because I am known to have survived, my testimony of imprisonment is discreetly disbelieved by British historians – but I was there. After the car journey, my captors walked me in through the stark and businesslike gate and closed the door on my protestations. All night, I listened to the cresting and crashing of absolute fear in sixty men and women, and the next morning I watched them begin to die. I drew their faces on my walls, scratching faint cartoonish sketches with a stub of pencil, but when I looked at what I had made I realised it was the beginning of a new artwork. My portraits were coming from that obscure place inside me where I saw the certain universe of Anaximander of Miletos and knew it for a profound truth of alien science, and where the gods and demons of classical Greece were scrimshawed on the plastic toaster ovens and Apollo rockets of the dawning Age of Aquarius.

I screamed at myself, at my useless, ridiculous and empty posturing and my art. What possible virtue is there in painting, and most especially in painting inner vistas of futurity and madness, when madness is the common currency of everyone around? If I wanted to confound society in this place, I should colour my walls with the rich greens of fertile land and the evening sun. I should draw myself a window on a pastoral landscape. I should remember the faces of the dying when they were in repose. On that wall I could paint the Emperor's Cuckoo, now hanging on a gibbet outside the palace. I met him only the one time, to talk to, but he had a pleasant singing voice and a fondness for mild Belgian beer. He lived alone in a little apartment in the new city, and counted a myna bird his closest friend. I forget his name. I read, recently, that he never existed at all and it was scandalous to suggest he did. Well, he existed then, at least enough to die.

I had four walls and a ceiling, on which I should draw the Emperor's court as it was in better times. I should memorialise the dying and save a little part of them, of who they were before agony resketched them as friezes of Purgatory.

Except that when I drew – holding in my mind those friendly lines, the patterns of shade that defined a fat man's chin or the hips of a serving woman – it did not matter how closely I hewed to the task, what emerged was the sort of contemptible, wild imagining from which I had made my useless fame. The shark was everywhere, tiny and vast, playful and appalling. One of the smallest sketches was the most awful, somehow staring out of the wall and watching you as you moved, the way portraits are supposed to, though I have never seen it except in this one case, as if I had captured a perfect essence of predation and execution in my little cell, and now I was imprisoned with my own personal memento venatoris. I did not own my hands, my arms. Day upon day I threw my pencil away, and – seeing how I failed and failed – whenever they came and snapped another of my bones, they likewise replaced the stub with another. Sometimes it was a fine artist's charcoal or a soft lead, sometimes a colour, so that I would be drawn, bruised and shaking and stained with sweat and the inevitable piss of sudden agony, to repeat my failure. They encouraged me to addict myself to that combination of failure and pain and thereby made me torture myself. I could not stop trying, and each attempt embroidered the mosaic of image and strangeness on my walls and ceiling until the cell was the best work I had ever done, and the most bizarre, a many-eyed woman gazing at me from above while my own image cowered in a corner and was lifted up by three others, like some Bible scene in a church.

One morning the surgeon came in, and his face was grave. He told me that my case had been reviewed in great detail in the light of the stricter policies now being introduced to deal with recidivism in released politicals. He was very sorry about the length of my detention, he said. He himself admired the modern intricacy of my work and its bold rejection of consensus – its assertion of Africa over the white north-west – and it had been burdensome to him to torment me. It seemed to him that here in this place I had purged out some deep unpleasantness, likely the inner contradictions of my art and my unawakened politics, and if I were released I should be an excellent and enthusiastic son of progress. My gift, he said, was to bring an underlying truth before the physical eye, as I perceived it unerringly with my inner, artistic one – and such a gift was vast and not lightly to be put aside. However, there were no grey areas in the revolution, and his perception was not of itself sufficient to release me. Indeed, he regretted very much that the steering committee of Alem Bekagn had ordered me done away with. I was to die in this place, at the order of a government which knew nothing of me, to atone for a crime of portraiture. My end was appointed in a month, the earliest convenient date.

He left the room to allow me to compose myself, and I went a little mad. It was intolerable – inconceivable – to hear that, for no better reason than an unimaginative taxonomy, I would lose my life. I became obsessed with the knowledge that I would die, and day by day I played a game of it to prepare, as if by endless repetition I could somehow change sides and be not the corpse but the death, and thus survive myself. I lay upon my bed and imagined that I was breathing my last, that I was in mortal agony on a torture table or coughing as my broken ribs gouged my lungs. I was starving and could not go on, or dying of thirst, or shot and feeling the red hot rounds unmake my heart. I died and wept and died again, over and over, until I could not stand it and wished the day would come sooner. Finally one morning something in me shattered and could not be pulled back together, and the illusion that complicity in my own demise might undo the fact of it was blown away. I knew then, with only a fortnight to go, that I must at all costs escape, and since Alem Bekagn was in the normal way of things escape-proof, the only remedy for its walls being bribery or favour – and I had no means to effect either – I must take an extraordinary route for my departure. I must, I determined with a feverish certainty, learn to walk through walls, and to do that I must make the walls my own. I must cover them in the outpouring of myself, complete the image that had insistently been midwifing itself through me, and in that action I would gain control of matter and time and be made free. I gathered up the stubs and fragments they had left me and began to work, and when they came I extended my hand almost absently so that they could perform the vandalism upon it, only to find that in this the committee had relented, and in place of the vise they had brought me a parcel of brushes and tubes of oils taken from my own supply.

I did not sleep, or perhaps I did not wake. I worked and worked and felt myself dissolve into the brush, the paint, the stone. Even my splinted fingers were nimble as I folded the dreamworld around the rivets in the door, as I cheated perspective to yield a high dome of blue stars on my ceiling and derive the benign face of the mother goddess of space exploration from the sinister surveillant I had drawn in my first flush.

They told me the days were passing and asked if I wanted a priest, then left when I laughed at them. Could they imagine a priest having anything to say in such a room? The guards now would not enter. They said that sometimes, when they did, they could not find me for a few minutes inside, even though the place was barely ten feet deep. They said that sometimes they got lost departing, as if the patterns of the walls were depthless and extrusive. It was understood that when the time came I would not be marched out, but that they should shoot me from outside the room, and then hose the whole place down until the colours ran.

On the evening before my execution they brought me wine, and I mixed it with rose madder and drew the final lines upon the east wall, then drank the rest and lay down upon the floor. I reached outward to the painted sky of rocketships and the benign angels of the other walls, to a dream of age and fulfilment, and begged.

I lay on the floor of Alem Bekagn, the place that is called 'Farewell to the World' because it is the gate of death, and felt, between the instants, the edges of a better door.

*

I am reaching for that door now, that door into somewhere else, not the one we came in by – although of course they are occupying the same space. I am an old man, addled by the heat and the smoke. I am a young artist in fear of his life. I am a magician, and this is my only trick. I can feel the texture of the door in the middle of the air in my boiling cell. I can feel the coolness of it, the safe place beyond.

I can hear my own breathing. No one else can do this. If I am right, I will save us all. If I am not, we will die now rather than dying in ten minutes.

I can hear the screams and wails of the others in Alem Bekagn. I can hear them yesterday and tomorrow and all through the wretched history of this place, all sick and bloody and needless. No one else can do this, and that is my shame. I should go from room to room and release them all, but what if there is a limit to my soul's capacity? What if I can carry only so many? Only myself?

What if I can carry only so many?

Then Annie goes first. Then Colson. Then me.

Do I have the right to gamble on the madness of an old refugee?

Do I have any chance at all, if I do not? My hands were so much stronger then, my body so very beautiful. I would paint myself gladly now, if I could remember what I was. I would erect a mirror in my studio and paint my own body on the canvas just to wonder at the miracle that it was.

I can feel those muscles, ghost flesh on strong young bones. Those are the hands that grip the door.

There's not even anyone waiting for me, in death. Or, how do I know? Perhaps there is. Perhaps one among the many lovely, loving women of the seventies remembers me fondly on the other side. Perhaps she never forgot me and has been waiting ever since. Or perhaps the afterlife embraces the aspects of ourselves that love in all their facets, and that part of Michael's mother that did love me is grown into a whole self, and taps her feet impatiently on the step of the wondrous heavenly city.

Perhaps there was another life, not so sad, that I missed somehow this time, and will have in another world. Although look at this fine girl who is my granddaughter, and tell me you would trade her for any other.

No. I would not.

I would not trade her for anything, least of all my own life, here at its far, far end.

I stand up and open the door, and hear her call out in horror.

We step through, into a room full of ghosts.

this acceleration

M ielikki Neith opens her eyes. The ambassador smiles an apology. 'Inspector? We need the room.'

The blanket is warm.

'How long was I asleep?'

'A few moments only. Please: there is space. At this hour, Dr Wachsmann takes a bath and we use his room for a general staff meeting. There is a mattress in the consular office for late nights.'

'Thank you.' She should go. She should get on. But her head is foggy and heavy, and that is all she wants: a place to lay it down, and a soft cushion to support her neck. Tubman was right: this acceleration of the Hunter playback is tiring. She has things to do – but it wouldn't be good to fall asleep, unwillingly, while doing them.

Later, she will work out what the story means. Annie Bekele against the world, government reaching out for the game engine. Is that what happened? How close is Hunter's allegory?

'A few more minutes. Maybe an hour. Thank you.'

'Of course,' the ambassador says. 'Do you – do you need a doctor?'

'No. No, no. I'm fine. Just sleep. It's the memories.'

'I see.'

No, you don't. But I think I begin to.

down into the honey

From the false Chamber I fall, although falling implies a purpose or direction to my trajectory which is absent. I enter a world of painful colours and twisted shapes to whose extensions my eyes or perhaps my mind are incapable. I fall, drift or spiral through a nacreous place. Maybe it is literally a vast and convoluted shell, and I am tumbling toward the mouthparts of whatever crab lives within. Maybe I am grit, being expelled into an ocean as strange as this tiny curve, or maybe the curve is infinite and I will live like this for ever. I shall not grow old or die, but I shall grow mad until the distinction between what I am and what is out there is moot. Maybe. But it seems not: in the end I come into a library, and I smell burning books.

I am a scholar: it is an odour that excites in me an almost unmentionable panic – the worse because I do not know this library and it is vast. Orange flames curl around the white stone stacks scorching the rough marble black. Stone burns, if you get it hot enough. I am an alchemist: I have cause to know. Marble explodes, tiny shards slashing and blinding. Soon this room will be a storm of razors. A person could not survive here. Even if one were not struck, or broiled, or gashed, one would breathe in shards of glass and bleed into the lungs. I wonder if Scipio died of great blades of flying glass: if he came to a place like this, and was dismembered by some quite uncaring cataclysm.

The scroll cases are catching on the shelves, the sharp tang of their leathers adding flavour to the smoke. It is mouthwatering, like cooking pig steaks over coal. It is a horror, because these books are wonderful. The stacks are too perfect and plain to be human, the edges obedient to geometry, not masonry. That first book on the left is the lost *Anatomy* of Anaximander, in which he describes the function of organs and the physical location of the soul. That over there is the *Song of the Magdalen*, not the Christian one but her more terrible predecessor who was the hidden sister of the Karites, and in whom was vested the twinned grace of amnesis and regenesis. Over there are the lost designs of Theano for an engine deriving power from the expansion of heated water, that she said would reshape the practice of war and trade and compel the world to fit in the compass of her arms. That is the vision diary of 'Arkyn of D'mt, in which she foretells the history yet to come of the nation of Aksum for two thousand years. Works I have heard of, but never seen anywhere. Works beyond price, because their wisdom is matched only by their scarcity: more than likely these are the only copies in the world. Perhaps they are the only copies in any world.

Somewhere on the helical upper shelves, an inlaid tube containing Socrates' true analysis of transmigration ignites, releasing precious stones in a shower like hail. If the damn fool archivist had spent his money on a metal tube instead of fripperies, the document within might be safe – for a while at least.

I realise I should take something, take as much as I can. It hardly matters what. The only theme of the collection is excellence. Even a catalogue would be priceless, confirming the authenticity of works and their dates, the existence and timelines of knowledge.

I run through the shelves, picking up whatever is cool enough to touch, filling my pockets, my waistband, my sleeves.

In the midst of the library there is a clear space like a glade in a forest, and in the space there is a long reading table made of stone. A demon sits there – the demon, my demon from my dream of this morning – in a peacock-feather cloak, long bird legs crossed at the ankle. As I approach, it lifts its head, and in the shadows of the cowl I see my son's face.

*

Adeodatus was a model child. He was our joy and our terror as a boy, for his mind was as boundlessly curious as his body was energetic, and the combination of the two was a recipe for all manner of mishaps and calamities. It was I who found him attempting with a will to uncover the explosive secret of the Greek mystics, three months shy of his seventh birthday, and intending to deploy it in his game of model armies. He'd come close, and likely in the next hour would have blown up not only the little wooden carvings but himself and a goodly portion of the house as well.

As the boy aged, he became a fair disputant in his own right, until at fifteen he realised – with an acuteness of emotional wisdom his father still does not possess – that his course was set for a shipwreck. He had sought, until then, to find favour with Augustine by following in his footsteps, and thereby to laud the achievements of the sire and magnify the family name. Latterly he realised that Augustine hardly wished for another to take on the task of such magnification and indeed desired it to himself in his chosen sphere. Adeodatus, adroitly, changed directions and fixed on medicine not for the soul but for the body, seeking there a greatness to lay at the feet of his sire, and the choice was good. Augustine considered it, of course, a lesser profession – he had already concluded by then that all knowledge not contending with the direct contemplation of God was vanity – but not an ignoble one, and the caring nature of it and the son who espoused it was manna to him, which in turn was manna to the boy.

The meal was poisoned for them both, as you already know, and for me. The boy – who was my son, not just his father's – carried his profession, or it carried him, into some pustule of a hut in an unlanced boil town along his road, and there he contracted a fever that would not release him short of the gates of death. They say his skin burned to the touch, and that he cried out for a cold bath – which they would not give, believing that he would be better served by bleeding.

The patient he went for was already dead by the time he arrived in the hut: a girl, about his own age. I try to tell myself that they are together and in love in some other realm, but I do not believe it. If I have made the true Alkahest, this shall be my great work: I shall raise him back to me. If I have not, then he is dead and likely so am I.

*

My life went wrong at Milan, or perhaps I should say that it turned from the path into which I had gratefully settled. Augustine was teaching rhetoric to students hardly less ungrateful than those in the south. Roman boys of good family were, it had transpired, bad debtors. The end of the term would roll around, and all those faithful faces in the front row would miss the last lecture and vanish into revelry, and my lover's purse was full of moths and little more. His mother wanted him to marry an heiress. I can't remember her name, the poor trout. She was a little creature with fine airs and graces, but all the intellect of a baby's rattle. Monica was adamant: her son must wed a woman of class – and not me, though we'd never made any suggestion we might tie the knot, and I honestly wasn't sure I wanted to. I had my lover, my son and my studies. I didn't need to fret over which god should bind me to a man – or how, if he fattened in body and withered in heart as he grew older, I might release myself from the company of a boor. In response to Monica's chattering, I wondered aloud whether I should find my own gentleman of class to wed. I had my son young, and my body bore hardly a mark; if Augustine married the trout – she had a piscine face, alas, and was forever gaping – I should say fair play and exchange rings with Longinus or Sextius and be glad. The chastity of Roman wives being legendary more as a noble ideal than a practice on the ground – or, as it might be, in the bathhouse, or on an ornamental lawn. I am forever confounded by those who would establish a way of doing things that all others must follow or be deemed unhappy. Sometimes the best things are found in unlikely places.

Except that it didn't go that way. With a strange and terrible certainty, sudden and unheralded, Augustine came into my rooms and told me to pack. I must go, he said, back to Thagaste and away from him. It was over.

I thought at first he was saying the school was over, that he had a new job. No, he said. Us, he said. No more us, not now nor ever. He was forsaking the flesh, and seeking the life of the soul. I laughed out loud at that – there was never a fleshier man to love God – and that made him furious. Well, it would, but I was so far from ready for this diktat and hardly accustomed to being instructed by him or anyone else.

I did not let them see me weep. I packed, and nodded, and was gone, and Adeodatus promised he would shortly come to me and live for a time, before he set out into the world again. It was years, and then he came wrongly, and my world was night.

*

I was feeling just a little smug the day my son came home. I was a new woman, years from Augustine and the Alps, and I had, after some considerable time and effort, perfected a healing balsam that actually healed. I had the recipe from a cattle doctor in the market who took a shine to me – he said loudly that it was my tits, but I think he truly liked me for who I was and felt abashed. Drover men are not supposed to suffer from tender emotions, especially not the old, wise ones. He'd have been laughed out of the camp circle if he admitted to being anything other than an erection on legs.

The balsam was prepared from spoiled food, of all things, and was an effective agent against the spread of infection in an open wound. It was one of the most undemanding medicines I have ever known, though the drover insisted that it be used sparingly, lest its working be reduced. He said that certain ticks among his herds now spread a rash that no longer yielded to it, and he had no intention of further teaching the imps and demons of sickness about his magic.

Well, I had determined to use it on persons and not on cattle, and that was surely a better field to expend its power, as long as one was not frivolous.

So I was feeling fine when the girl arrived at my door and said there were men coming, with a great chest, and all for me. A gift from a lover, surely, she said, from some great prince. But I knew only one great prince and surely he sent gifts to no woman, and me least of all. I thought it more likely to be some curious delivery. It would not be the first time: a year before, a man sent me the jaw of a huge sea monster and asked if it was genuine. I told him it was, though honestly I did not know. If so, I shall never swim in the ocean again – the thing was vast enough that I might stand inside its mouth.

The cart came around the bend in the road, and I began to dread. The air seemed suddenly heavy with disaster. There was no lightness in the fellows in the train, no whistling ran ahead to announce their coming. They rode in silence, and beside them walked a single soldier with his spear, a broad-shouldered and sensible tesserarius. On the other side came a priest. Was it plague? Did they bring me a plague corpse, to name the sickness and pronounce the remedy?

They arrived at my door, and the priest said formally that he was very sorry. I could see that he was. His office forbad displays of physical affection, but his hand twitched at his side. He wanted to embrace me, to bear me up. He had lived this moment, he said. He had received the mirror of this news, and survived it, though he thought he would not, and I must come to him whenever I wished, he would do anything he could. It was not even an invitation to bed. He was begging me to know that I was not alone, and it was his agony that unleashed my own horror, that set it creeping from my spine into my heart, and then my skin, so that all the hairs stood up and I was sweating in the bright sun. I shouted at him to do the deed. Tell me.

He told me my son was dead.

I did not believe it, but I knew the motion of this play. Where should I go to see him? I must gather him up and lay him out. Where was he?

One by one, each of them turned to look at the pretty box. I will see it for the rest of my life as I saw it then, as if for the first time: the dark wood inlaid with tangled squares and mazes within mazes, so that you might believe the complexity of it went down forever into the grain: a box of puzzles and mysteries; a box for treasures.

They lifted it into my house, amid the braziers and burners and clutter, and they laid it on the floor like a fine new table. One by one, they took their leave.

*

My greatest treasure in the world floated in the box, midway between the surface and the copper bottom. In the cold of the north, the honey had become solid and borne him up, but now in Africa it was liquid again, though he had not settled to the bottom. He must be full of gas. I reached down into the honey and I put my hands behind his armpits, as I had when he was young and barked his shin or took fright at an angry bee. I touched his skin and began to weep, and he was so heavy that I could not bring him up. I hauled on him and felt the muscles in my back turn from strength to agony to exhaustion, and still he would not come. He was always stubborn. I simply kept reaching for him, because I was his mother. It took an hour, in that last embrace, before his head and shoulders slipped free, and then he sighed, as if I had said something particularly foolish.

I washed my son, and dressed him, and I did what was necessary. When I dream badly, or when I am afraid and sleepless for whatever reason, it is not his ghost that comes to me, but the ghost of the box with its fine marquetry and endlessly regressing angles chased in metal around the lock. I see it, in the dark by my bed, or being carried through the door. I hear the heavy tread of the bearers and remember their faces, their eyes skittering away from mine. I smell the wood and the honey, hear the creaking hinges, and I awake and scream and shiver. I do not ever go back to sleep after that dream. I take myself downstairs and work, or cook, or clean, until the sun comes up and I can open all my doors and know that the box is not hiding there, waiting for me.

I am the only woman on earth haunted by a coffin, and not its occupant.

*

In the lost library, I step forward because I am his mother, and the features shift beneath the hood. Now the face is Augustine, and as I take another step, Monica. When I retreat, I see Adeodatus again, as if emerging from behind a cloud. I step back, around, forward, and the face changes with each movement. This is the familiar geometry of death. I see him, but I cannot touch him. I cannot reach him from here.

'It is known that the Enemy made peacocks to prove that he could create beauty as well as ugliness, but while he could make an elegant show he could not complete the work, and thus the voice of the peacock is like the screaming of a soul in Tartarus or the shriek of burning stone,' the demon says. 'Though it should be acknowledged that any bird, closely regarded, is nothing more than a crocodile in a pretty dress.'

'Where is my son?'

'Catabasis is a journey. The dead cannot be awarded, they must be won. If you would return a soul to the living world you must go down, and risk.'

'Others must. Not I.'

'Yes, you have the Alkahest – and yet you do not know how to use it. Will you make a test of your magic with your son? Bring him back all out of shape, or leave half his soul in Hades with your haste?'

'Your face is a lie. Why should I believe your voice?'

'That is the risk.'

'You said he was torn.'

'Isn't everyone?'

'You said he was cast on the ocean of Apeiron.'

'You have my answer.'

'But I do not understand it.'

'Your story touches my heart.'

'I could command you.'

'Indeed. That is my point.'

'How so?'

'You possess unlimited power, but finite knowledge. You do not know how to frame your assertions to achieve your ends; you do not know the nature of death, so you cannot readily undo it. What you command without certainty is not achieved. I possess the knowledge you lack. You might command me – but in doing so, the possibility of error is recursive. If you knew what to demand of me you would not require my help. Indeed, your risk is increased, as I seek to find ways to exact revenge for your domination.'

'I could wish myself wiser.'

'So long as you know already what constitutes wisdom. Changing one's own mind is always troublesome. You could wish for knowledge, of course – but you might accidentally create things that do not exist in order to know about them. Beasts. Persons. Worlds.'

'Absurd.'

'Indeed. I cannot think of a single instance in which you have accidentally instantiated an object of universal importance. Am I lying? I certainly intend to be. Yes. Yes, in fact, I am.'

'That was before.'

'Indeed. Just imagine what you might achieve now. Oh, so much opportunity. I'm giddy.'

'We are to trade, then?'

'We are.'

'I will require a gesture of good faith.'

'Apeiron is boundless. It has no shore, and no bed. There are no waves, because there is no division between the sea and sky. Yet it is also invisible, because ubiquitous. Apeiron, Phlegethon, time, space – it's only thought that distinguishes, in the end. All else is vanity.'

'Says the demon in the peacock feather coat.'

'The coat is a consequence and not a choice. Demon? I suppose. I am legion – but so are you. Very well: I will show you the door, in exchange for the scrolls, and you will bring back the dead. Which of them is up to you.'

For any other soul, I might hesitate. 'The scrolls, and precise instructions for my appointed task.'

'I am not to be made a shortcut.'

'Oracular instructions, then.'

'Irritatingly vague ones.'

'Specific, and decipherable without madness.'

'Challenging. Obscurantist.'

'And your name, from your own mouth, so that I can call upon you if I have need.'

'I was the hunter, and gazed in a pool and saw myself. My reflection was affronted. I was the heir, the serpent, and now am cast out. Or in. It's hard to say.'

'I said a name, not a precis.'

'Alas: impossible. I am torn.'

'Aren't we all?'

'That would be funnier if you knew what it meant.'

I look within the demon, with the eyes I had in my dream, but upon its bones is a confusion of signs that could not be a word. 'A name agreed between us, to which you will answer.'

'Then I shall be Quaerendo.'

'I will not call you that.'

'Suggest something.'

'How about "Know-all"?'

The demon laughs. 'Indeed. Very well. Go through the door. Hades is a puzzle box, a fivefold lock, and it requires a multitude of keys, keys of words and keys of blood and the flavour of your soul. Something you have, something you know, something you are, and these latter two must be proven twice, so that five proofs unlock the Pentemychos. Each layer of guardianship has its price: Cocytus, Styx, Lethe, Acheron and Phlegethon. You must cross the five rivers of Hades and do your will in the place set aside for you.'

'And I shall have my son again?'

'That is your quest. I cannot say what you will eventually attain. Much is prepared for you; some you must perform. You are a turning of this war, Athenais Karthagonensis. I would have you raise the dead, but there are powers – pursuivants, judges and witnesses, authorities and smiths – who align against me. Indeed, they set me against what I now would most dearly win. They look in, and are dismayed. The ending of your quest is their undoing. Or mine.'

'Nonsense. I am a mother in search of her son, and that is all.'

'You bear the Alkahest. Yesterday you were a mother, and perhaps that was a small thing, though it seems to me that carrying lives within and bringing them out is the definition of godhead in the first place. Today your footsteps move ten thousand worlds. Your anger births suns in the outer dark. You make worlds and destroy them.'

'I do no such thing!'

'It sounded as if it might be true. Shall I check? Before now, you grew hair and nails and healed the cut upon your finger without ever deciding it. Your chest rose and fell – a most diverting action of itself, my compliments – without the direction of your will. The Alkahest is like your heart. It performs its function even as you sleep.'

'And how do I use the Alkahest?'

'It is not a thing to be used by you. It is not magic, it is divinity – a state, not an action. That is the first mystery. It is in you, and everything you do. Trust the goddess that all will be well. The execution of the Alkahest falls to another.'

'But it is in me?'

Know-all lifts long fingers to the ceiling as if to say: *Knowledge and conversation of a demon in a burning library of books that don't exist. You want something more reassuringly magical than this, you're going to have to tell me what it is.*

I just know that this is not enough. 'The Chamber of Isis is a lie.'

The demon tuts. 'It was a map without a country. Now the country is made beneath your feet: you stand in a fire and you are not burned; you command a spirit and you plot a path to the kingdom of the dead. If you have not the Alkahest, then at the very least you seem to make do.'

I pile up the scrolls on the table, feeling a little jolt with each one. *The Great Wheel* by Empedocles. Pythagoras' *Treatise on the Naming of Mountains. Ennoia and Chokmah* by Simon Magus. Three, five, ten more from my belt and shirt. Another from each leg. I am paying for my son with a thousand years of knowledge, with books to benefit every person on earth. Apollonius' secret *Book of the Ogdoad* joins the others. I feel the prick of the last scroll in the small of my back. I could keep it.

'What will happen to them?' I ask.

'It does not matter,' Know-all says, and extends its hand. 'Come. You have already decided to give it up. You are too wise to do otherwise. Imagine, if you regained your son, only to lose him to me in payment of a debt. Or perhaps you would simply never find him. Who can say? But everything is paid for.'

I do not look at the writing on the case. Know-all does, and sighs. 'Bahu's *Paradoxes*. Ah, well.'

Bahu's *Paradoxes*: the earliest known mathematical work, listing problems derived from philosophical logic whose solutions alter the original values, and from these premises deducing or inducing the divine. I think a piece of it was written on the wall of the Chamber, beneath the benediction of the Virgin – I could make a life untangling just one of the secrets it contains. I could make academic history with a single line torn from the roll.

Know-all flips it into the blaze. We watch as it flares and fades away.

'Why?' I ask.

The demon shrugs, bird-shouldered, and says again: 'There is a war in heaven.'

'A cataclysm?'

'Not in the way you mean. Gods contend. The directions of the compass are at odds.'

'And who's winning?'

A flash of teeth. 'I am, I suppose. One way or another.' A pause, and then the peacock-cloaked arm rises, pointing: 'You should go to your son.'

And here, at last, is the damned catafalque, the unwelcome coffin, arrived as it always does between the moments so that I cannot see and stamp on whatever kobold drags it in.

Know-all walks over and lifts the lid. I turn and stare off to the side: I will not look. The demon waits by the open box.

I turn my head, and see not the honey-smothered face but a staircase leading down. Down, of course, because that is where I must go.

'Don't look back,' Know-all says as I pass by. 'There is a war in heaven. Don't look back.'

*

The first steps are made of stone, and the air is dry and musty. After the turning of the stair, my feet find wood, and I smell dead leaves. After the second turning, the treads are made of ash, and then after the third I am no longer descending a stair at all, but walking on a desert of black sand. From the dune beneath my feet down to a wide river delta, there is no colour other than black. It is, though, a rich black, fertile with textures and depths, so that although there is no sun in the endless darkness of the sky, still each stone and stunted tree is quite distinct from everything else, made so by its peculiar arrangement of shine and roughness.

Et in Erebus ego, I suppose.

I discover, when I stumble, that I am leaving thick, pale prints upon the ground. Beneath my hands as I lift myself to my feet, the ash turns silver. Am I leeching the dark from the stones? Or is it battening upon me? I look back along the trail, and then flinch because Know-all told me not to – but no bolt of black lightning strikes me, and no gorgon pursues me along my track. Just my glimmering footsteps, mute reminder of where I have been. The flow of time and memory. No. The injunction was not the same one served upon Orpheus. Rather, it occurs to me, it was almost a kindness. I am a mortal woman, and however my soul and even my body may be buttressed, my mind is still what it was yesterday. My heart is a mortal heart. In traversing Erebus, it is written, the traveller must traverse the corpse of the beloved. Five rivers, five parts to the body – two arms, two legs, the torso and head counted as a single piece – and each concealing secretly one of the elements that make the mortal world. Fire in the right hand, water in the left, earth in the right foot and air in the left, the torso and head the twin vessels of the soul. The sand conceals the skin, the rivers are made of tears. Dig too deep in Erebus, and you will find a heart.

I have no desire to recognise my son's corpse in this dry soil.

I wonder what would happen if I walked the length and breadth of this kingdom. Would every inch of it turn to moonlight?

I look at the trail I have left and wonder what might live here – or at least, make its home here, if 'live' is not entirely the right word – and decide that it would be as well not to tarry.

I walk towards the rivers.

*

I am not sure how to measure time in Erebus. There is no sun to rise and set. The endless night is uniformly radiant. I'm not even sure there is time here. If I burned a candle, would it be consumed? Wax, destroyed, must come here. Does it take time (that word again) for the ghost wax to travel to this place? How long? Is the elapsed instant long enough that the flame would progress along the wick? Or would the rate of return match perfectly the progress of the flame? Come to that, if I were to blow it out, would the flame also come here?

I realise I have spent great parts of my life thinking about death as a horror to the living, and none at all about death as a place.

I count my steps, and wonder if I am walking in a straight line. My silver trail seems to be direct and not meandering, but the desert is a bad place for a traveller without a guide.

Well, I might go mad for lack of company. But sooner or later, surely, I must begin to encounter the spirits of the dead, and then I won't be alone any more.

After five thousand steps, I come to a cairn.

I see it as a tree or a spike driven into the sand. It is off to one side, and I consider ignoring it. Then I realise that it is the only point of reference I have found, and the first sign of intelligence. Then, too, I wonder if it has always been there, or whether it was raised just for me.

The cairn is a pile of stones and dry sticks.

The sticks are bones.

From beside it, I can see another one, far ahead.

I think this is a road marker.

I walk on.

*

At the third cairn, I find myself bored with walking. I don't need to rest, but I sit down anyway, instinctively looking for the shaded side. I wonder whether, if the sun ever dies, it will come here, and Erebus will see its first sunrise. But then, perhaps this un-light all around is what the death of a sun looks like from the other side.

It occurs to me a moment later that I have forgotten where I am. Dawn, here, would not be the chariot of Helios rising, but the drawing back of the coffin lid. As the yellow light, filtered through air made of spiced Italian honey, purged these shadows into rags and fleeing rooks, I should find myself looking along a road built on endless miles of the corpse of my son. The gloom is my best hope of joy.

Best to walk on.

*

Each cairn is about five thousand paces from the last, but not exactly. I don't know if it varies because the cairns are uneven, or if my paces become longer or shorter as I go, or if the ground of Erebus expands and contracts, like breathing. It is a strange place, in the most absolute sense that it is strange to me, foreign and unhomely. It is a place that could never be a home, however long one might remain here. Perhaps that is the first truth of Erebus: death is what it is. It is not an answer, but something that negates questions and answers both, and nothing in life is preparation.

After the sixth cairn, I begin to see souls.

At first they are occasional: brief visitations caught in the act of walking or standing or crawling upon all fours. They appear and disappear as I move, as if screened from my vantage by objects I cannot see. Later, though, as I draw closer to the heart of Erebus, they become more permanent. I can see expressions on their statue faces, read words on their lips in the anti-light. Curses, mostly, and despair. A few, perhaps, are grateful, but not many. Step by step, I see more of them, until there is a great throng of them, dozens wide, stretching away towards the rivers. It is a road, now, this imaginary line I have been following: the main highway of the kingdom of death. Highway, or causeway – and what meridian of my son's body do we follow? A wrinkle in his brow? The curve of his smile or the rise of his stomach? Will the heart of Erebus be a chasm of torn ribs, or a forest of the sores that killed him?

I am not ready when the shades begin to move, and speak. I am peering into the face of a woman who looks a little familiar from my student days, and wondering if it is she, or whether eventually if you spend enough time among ghosts you begin to find the faces of your own lost, even if they are not there, when she turns and smiles a greeting. It does not seem to trouble her that I am close – far closer than I would go to another woman in the living world – unless we were very well known to one another. A moment later, as the man behind steps through her chest upon his way, I realise why: there are no elbows among the dead.

'Season's greeting,' she murmurs.

'And you,' I reply. Is that right, or is there something more? I wonder if I should embrace her, the way the congregation does in Augustine's Church.

I don't get the chance. She hurries on, vanishing a moment later and reappearing down the line. I hear her offer the same salutation to a senator, a cowhand and a scribe, and they in turn respond to her just as they do to every other spirit who comes close enough. The susurrus builds on itself, the same words over and over until they mean less than nothing and then until they are a single word spoken by a single mouth: the mad, dead mouth of Erebus.

It is irritatingly loud. An hour ago I was lonely; now I miss the silence. I walk fifty thousand paces in the endless goose-chatter of the dead, and then I see maggots.

*

Maggots in Erebus: my familiar nightmare of these last years. The honey should prevent them from growing in my son. It should keep him, incorruptible, for a hundred years, but perhaps some knuckle or elbow has surfaced, deep down in his sepulchre, and something has found its way in. Perhaps, little by little, the preserving fluid has ebbed, or perhaps it has been eaten by sweet-toothed mice, and now these monsters rise from the black sand like the first pillar of a roundhouse going up, save that each is possessed of a segmented flexion that speaks of a scorpion's tail. For a moment, that's what I imagine: the stingers of scorpions hovering over the streaming dead. In one instant I see that they are men, sicarii with long arms and sharp knives, and then I see their faces, mandible and inhuman, and know that they are maggots, born in the flesh of the dead. I am in Erebus, and must fight my way to the heart.

Three. Five. Nine. Nine of them, in three rows. A trinity of trinities. I met a man once who argued that twenty-seven was the holiest imaginable number, because it was three times three times three, a trinity to the power three, and on this basis he presumed that God must be in truth twenty-seven-fold. Here there are only nine assassins. Only nine.

'Omphalos,' the maggots whisper. 'Omphalos, go back.' Omphalos: the bridge between worlds. If they kill me, will I fold in upon myself, pass through my own bridge into the next world? Will I unfold again and return, only to be killed once more? Prometheus. I will be Prometheus, dying in sight of the promised city.

I dig in my heels. 'The tears of the mother run in me. I am the Alkahest. Clear the way.'

They bow, their inchworm backs gelid and slick.

'Omphalos. Go back, or you must die.'

'Step aside.'

'You pursue heresy. Thou shalt have no other gods but God.'

'I pursue my son.'

'You risk turning from visitor to resident.'

'Step aside.'

They're so quick. I had not expected them to be so quick. I had thought to see their names in their bones, to command them or the land. The first slash draws agony across my eyes. My own blood in my skull is the first true colour I have known since I came here.

In the red light of blindness, I see everything.

*

My shirt comes off my shoulders in a single motion, flowing towards the nearest maggot like a whip. The sicarius shrieks, but I am already upon it, hands sliding around face and head, gripping nightmare jaws and twisting and turning so that we stagger together in a wild children's dance of follow-me: two steps this way and three steps that, and back and up and down. When I send him off, the creature falls with wounds from his companions' knives up and down his segmented back. I swirl away untouched, and now I have his knives: long stolen crescents that whirl and cut, not in the inexorable chopping of a legion soldier, but in the sharp planes and arcs of high geometry. Here are Pythagoras and his sanctuaries, and there are two dead enemies; here is Euclid's treatise on conic sections drawn in silver on the endless sky, and an additional thesis on the properties of the spiral that would have delighted Apollonius, and as the spiral finishes and the bodies in motion continue, only one of them moves of its own volition, the other sinking lifeless to the ground. No doubt these maggot sicarii are magical and monstrous, but I am incontestable. This is not combat, it is truth. I step between my enemies, bisecting angles and bodies at once, and each of my movements alters the topography so that my enemies do not understand it and cannot respond. Theon, Autolycus, Pappus: I name them as I use them in a way I had never imagined, and when Ptolemy's cosmos rolls out before me, the gyrations of the constellations around the earth, I know where each end will come in the inevitable conjunctions of ichor and blood. Stretched an instant on tiptoe I see Orion's hunt, then the rage of Chiron and the

476

weaving of Arachne, the hands and the knives they hold following the stars in the mortal heavens. I trace the inevitable patterns of summer and winter and speak the names of the goddess: Demeter, Persephone, Isis, as I recall the ebb and flow of the heavens. I see the Crab, the Scorpion, and the Snake, and then the sun and moon themselves as I step between the last two still standing, and for the first time they realise they are alone, and are afraid. I wish for mercy, but the judgement that I have become does not heed me. The Alkahest is the rage of Diana at the affront of Acteon, and the hounds are loosed. My right hand rises like dawn, and my left sketches nightfall. My enemies cough as if at a change in the wind, and I stand alone in a field of corpses, a reeking underworld of my own making.

The Alkahest is not magic to be used by you, Know-all told me. It is divinity – and divinity does not suffer challenge.

The corpses fade back into the sand, all save one, and as I look down I see that he has Scipio's face, and I have cut him into five parts.

*

In the Chamber of Isis, Cornelius Severus Scipio was cut in five parts by a jinn I could not name. I saw the wounds, and could not place them, save that they had the flavour of godhead rather than mortality. Now, I stand over his corpse, or a corpse that looks like his, and I drew its blood.

Did I do all this?

And if I did, who am I? Who is it, who makes pilgrimage into Hades? There is a woman, Athenais, who goes for her son, by roads she thought unimaginable or perhaps imagined. That son was a prodigy, fathered by a brilliant man upon a brilliant woman, and he was their joy.

But other women have gone into Hades. Demeter braved the underworld for her daughter Persephone, and held open the door for Aphrodite to retrieve Adonis. Persephone in turn prevailed upon the grey king to send Eurydice home with Orpheus. The story has it that Orpheus failed at the last, but: was it meant that he should? Was it happenstance, or some deeper game of gods? Eurydice was killed by a serpent while fleeing lustful Aristaeus, who in turn was the father of Acteon and Macris. Acteon was devoured by hounds, but Macris became the nurse of the infant Dionysus, who was born when the heart of his first, murdered life as Zagreus – also a serpent – was placed within his mother. Dionysus was in turn the son of Apollo, who cast down a serpent to learn prophecy, and his wild worshippers devoured Orpheus when the lyrist returned without Eurydice from the underworld. The head of Orpheus still sang as it passed down the river, and that song is the path by which Persephone enters the mortal world again each year, and thus Demeter's end is served. Death is springtime and the gods are cyclical, like wheat. They repeat and they return and they rig the game. Whose game do I play now, and what shall be my reward if I should win?

Who rides me, into Hades? Or do I deceive myself? If a god made a disguise, would it fool even her?

If I arrive at my destination, will Athenais be washed away, and replaced with something that feels all the time as I just did: absolute and inevitable? Is there room for hugging and laughter in a god? For burned sausages and drunken pratfalls?

I look down at Scipio, and wonder whether, if I look up again, I will see the interior of the Chamber of Isis, and my own face not only painted on the east panel but staring back at me from where I stood a few hours ago in the middle of the room. Was I the jinn, then, seen through a refracting lens? Am I the jinn now, looking back? Was the choking hive not an attack, but some consequence of my being in close proximity to unbuttressed, undivine, un-Alkahested self? But has someone not told me recently that once the Alkahest is in you, it was always so? That once you step beyond the mortal frame of time, cause and consequence come unbound?

I touch my cheek to remind myself of its shape, and find no wound. When at last I do look up, I am still in Erebus, and it is not one corpse before me, nor even nine, but an army of them laid to rot in the ash – if anything rots here. If I have not frozen decay inside this coffin.

Half of them are like the assassins who came for me: maggots dressed as men. The others are peacocks. Beyond the dead, row upon row of those still living, like corn in a valley. And beyond that: Cocytus, the first river that I must cross.

Cocytus, called 'Lamentation', lies beyond the farthest reach of the enemy lines.

'The gods contend,' Know-all murmurs in my ear. 'I did tell you.'

*

'Over what?' I ask. 'Why do you fight?'

'Position,' Know-all says.

'Position? You mean honours? What?'

'Say, rather, thrones and dominions. This universe is a certain shape. It is a tool for a certain purpose. I wish it to have another.'

'Peacock King. Angra Mainyu.'

'If you like. I killed a serpent but it refuses to die.'

'Zagreus, then.'

'Or another serpent. They all look alike to me. In any case, the heart still beats.'

'In a mortal woman?'

'The circumstances are unclear.'

'I don't pretend to know what that means.'

'Nor do I – hence: a lack of clarity. Gods persist. To root one out, one must first ascend.'

'So you challenge God.'

'God exists to be challenged. Possibly also to be eaten, as you well know. To be buried and reborn from soil and caves and holy trees. I want not to be devoured. I would make of this universe a siege engine, and storm the castle of the next. I don't wish to be reborn or remade, to become fertiliser for some holy tree or have my heart swallowed by a charmed sheep and wake up god of agricultural innovation. I'm quite content with what I am, and I propose to persist, even as the universe changes all around. In this, you and I are somewhat aligned.'

'We are?'

'Of course. Your son is dead. His soul is flown, his body should give itself up to the soil and the air. From his corpse should spring flowers and bees. You reject this. You rebel against death – and God. You seek his resurrection: a remaking of the universe to a style that suits you. You don't wish to undo the time since his death. You wish to bring him alive, here, now: to be his saviour and to be able to save him forever more. You have the Alkahest. Tell me candidly: possessing it, would you now give it up? With Adeodatus newly returned, would you place him once again in the hands of fate, and see him die the next day from falling in a lake? Would you then consider his time fairly ended? Of course not. We are one, you and I. We desire continuity and security of self.'

'Continuity for my son.'

'And is he not yourself? Made out of you and raised up by you, missing from you now as you might miss a limb? You desire the universe in the shape you would have it, as do I. As our universes are compatible, I say that we are one.'

I look out at the battlefield, and the river beyond.

'Then get me to the other side.'

Know-all laughs. 'Get yourself there, witch! Stop pretending you are less than you are – the same quiet woman you were when your lover set you aside. Do you know, your name is nowhere written in the books of his life? He has erased you. That story is done. Shed blood on the soil. Announce your intent, and see what comes.'

I scowl at him, then bite my cheek and spit.

'I would pass the rivers of Hades.'

I feel the voice of a choir in some vast cave beneath my back, the music thrumming in my lungs. The earth shrugs, and I fall.

The earth, or my son beneath my feet.

Know-all has not moved. 'See you later,' he says.

I see something over me, cresting vastly in the sky.

A great white wave is breaking over Erebus.

I watch it, like a scroll unfurling across the night, and then it falls.

*

The dark beneath the water is the dark of a tunnel, strange and cold. There is light here, ahead of me, and stone beneath and around me. In my wake come the shadows of Erebus. I drift forwards, and see the pale white light extinguish in the flow. On I go. There is something waiting: a strange shell like a turtle riding a cart, and standing beside, a man begs for his life.

Do I look so ferocious?

There's something silver, hanging on a chain. I should take it: the thing calls to me, a piece of my son. I reach for it, but I have no hands with which to lift it from him.

Only a nightmare mouth.

Later, blue lights spiral and flash, and the water changes around me.

*

480

In cool blue water, I abide. I can breathe. There is no need for haste. The sea is my body, extended from my flanks and touching everything all around, fish and mammals and boats and stones, beating hearts and barnacled keels, panics and expulsions. Half a mile away, a crab fisher sleeps in his boat. At the same distance in the opposite direction there is a turtle, and if I were hungry he would make a fine meal. There are thousands of fish too small to bother with, and countless humans flouncing in the surf. I can feel them as a patch of thrashing and incompetence all along one side, and then around my mouth there is that sense you do not possess, a tingling aspiration that colours each kinetic bundle with tints of life or its absence. No danger that I might pursue that cast-off net floating a mile behind, mistaking it for a seal. No danger I might miss the tuna out in the blue water, or the shaking, terrified man who hangs before me in an attitude of worship.

What a strange thing is a man beneath the waves. What a weird, dangerous journey to undertake, to venture into a place where you cannot breathe; to mix, without defences, with things that might tear you apart; to float in an alien element over the ruins of a temple empty these thousand years. All done in quest of what, exactly? Not power, not wealth. He possesses both. Wonder? Is there not enough that is beautiful and appalling on dry land?

As the warm river washes me and I dream – stationary in the flow and therefore truly resting for this one instant, however long it may last – he stares back at me, tiny and floundering and only now awake to how absolute is my dominion, here, in this place where we both are.

What is going through his mind? Mortality? You might think so. And yet there is something more, a kind of greed, an ambition to possess me, carry me back on shore with him and have me as his trophy, not dead but still living. In acknowledging my absoluteness, he has fallen in love with me. In some quite sexless way, he wants my body to be his, and his mine.

He drops something, down into the deep. A sacrifice of gold and silver.

'Quick!' Know-all says. 'Quick!'

My body is a better mother than my mind and has already dived after it: spinning glitter in the dark, leaving the man behind.

One, two, and done. I hold my prize.

And turn, and let it fall into the depths of the river. His gift to me, mine to the river. His talisman. My key.

On the far side of Cocytus, the stream that is called Lamentation, I step on to dry land and keep walking. Behind me, on the other bank, two armies of maggots and peacocks are drowned in the desert.

*

On the plain of Erebus in the kingdom of Hades, close by the black and atrocious river Styx, I light a cooking fire and call my dinner by its secret name. Blind river bass, the size of feral tomcats and with ugly heads like mason's trowels, flop ecstatic at my feet. Strange they may be, but they taste well enough – and in this barren, scentless place the smell of a pan full of oil and spices is like warming sunlight in a winter room. With the mud of Erebus on my fingers, I know all manner of local trivia: the last decent cook to pass this way in full possession of herself was Agata of Delphi, five hundred years ago. She was hunting for her husband, but the wretched man was alive and living in Macedonia with a snake dancer. She cooked the memory of a bird, a goose-like thing from ages past, and by it bought this bitter confirmation of life. Sometime later, with a fruit pie, she gained conveyance to a lesser heaven, and there is served by men with sculptors' hands, and converses with naiads. I don't know whether she still does lunches, but all things are possible.

I might try to command Charon, I suppose. But why should I, when I can bargain, and be polite? The mud whispers that he loves to eat, so I cook, and let the smell of tender flesh and pepper be my herald.

I know his presence by the crackle of dry wood and the brush of mountain wind. At length I pick him out, almost invisible against the flow. He poles towards me, hands wet with black water, wiping them on his robe as he steps ashore and drags the ferry up on to the bank. I offer to trade fish for passage, and when he takes a mouthful to test the goods, he laughs aloud. He asks my name, and I go to tell him it is Athenais, but when I try I simply say 'Alkahest' and he nods and brings my fingers to his lips. He is handsome, in an alien way.

The fish is good enough, he says, that I must have a cushion, and if I will make it for him again I may steer the boat. I wonder what it would be like to live here, cadging rides along the hateful river and fishing from its banks. Restful, I suspect, to the point of dull. I say as much to the ferryman, and he laughs again. Beneath our keel the hissing water snarls defiance at his mirth, and Charon grins wider still. He sees me to the far side with a flourish, and crushes heavy-heeled some pincered crab that tries to nip at me as I depart.

It occurs to me, as he waves and poles away, that Charon may be desperate to get laid.

Handsome he undoubtedly is. But still: best walk on.

*

The river Lethe is wide, but shallow. Forgetting is a fragile thing, and the memory of pain or anger can resurface when the wind is right. I wade across, and feel the whisper of trivialities departing from my mind: four decades of seeing myself age in the mirror, and the names of countless old lovers wash away on the warm tide. These are my secrets. Let them not come back. The willing sacrifice is pleasing to the water, and I hear her whisper 'Peace' as I walk on. I feel for some great change in myself, some loss of acquired wisdom, and find nothing.

Another river behind me.

*

Acheron is home to Cerberus, the Hound of Woe. He comes at me silently across the flood, mistakes and miscalculations shaped into a monster, and each head a horror unto itself. He is doubt given fangs: that ghastly introspective recrimination that rides my chest in the midnight hours, the desperate need to turn back the clock or cut out from myself the choice I made and leave it by the road. Acheron and Lethe are two sides of the same coin. If I had given up more to the last river, this one should not see me at all.

Well, still. Mistakes are what they are, and they make us just as surely as our moments of wisdom. I don't trust anyone without the scarring of error in her heart, and least of all some cleaned-up version of myself.

I stand my ground as the monstrous hound bears down, and the vast heads duck to huff and inhale at magically significant points upon my body – the groin, not least, he being a dog – but also all around me, tasting the air. Not yet satisfied, he leans closer, near by my lips, and smells the tears of Isis on my breath, at which he yips and snuffles fondly at my face – huge triple tongue and vast fangs streaming with glad, abhorrent otherworldly lick – and is content. In fact, it seems not only Charon who is starved for cheery meals, for a few pieces of carob have him positively puppyish.

Leaving the pup chasing the ghosts of rats, I walk on, and presently I find my road blocked for one last time, by the river of fire.

*

Cocytus, Styx, Lethe and Acheron: the first four rivers of Hades. Hesiod writes of Eridanos, the amber river that girdles the world, as if it were the fifth and greatest, but Hesiod is mistaken. The final river is Phlegethon, and it is not amber but all the colours of the flame.

Phlegethon is not like the others: Lamentation, Despite, Forgetting and Woe are all the sorrows of death, but Phlegethon is its mystery and its merciless hope. In Phlegethon is vested the whisper of the divine and the promise of rebirth. It is the last bulwark of Hades against the intrusive living, the first wall that holds the dead in their allotted place. It is the stream that binds Erebus to the mortal world – as it must, for it is everywhere, in all places and times. It is the mask worn by Apeiron, or its opposite, and in the inability to judge that distinction is the difference between man and god.

Phlegethon does not lie placidly in a riverbed, as painters love to show it, with kindly orange flames reaching half the height of a soldier at parade rest. It burns through the depths of the land and to the roof of the sky. There is no bridge to cross it, and no ferry, for it stretches from beneath the ground to the highest reaches of the heavens in a burning wall that will admit nothing and consumes everything, material or eternal. If I had a pot of the Alkahest here, I could try the old philosophical puzzle of two forces in perfect opposition, each defined by its absoluteness – and perhaps if I did, the world would end around me.

As it is, I am the pot, and I do not propose the test. I shed a little blood again, and with it draw a gate to admit me to the innermost places of the dead.

The gate congeals to stone or iron, but does not open. Made of my own self, it denies me. Should I lay my hand upon it, and command blood with blood? Will the Alkahest dissolve itself? I try, and of course it does not.

I hear a sigh.

'Demon,' I retort, 'I know you're here.'

'Jennaye,' Know-all says in turn, 'are not demons.'

The peacock coat seems brighter and richer on his back.

'You'll do.'

'That, at least, is certain.'

'You are a burdensome conversationalist.'

'I find myself enlightening.'

Of all the demons, mine must be the one that enjoys cheap puns.

'I must pass,' I say, gesturing to the wall of fire. 'Advise me accordingly.'

Know-all skips towards me, looping heron steps. The human head cocks to one side like a bird's, then the other way. Almost, I see his beak emerging from the shadow of the hood. Peacock-ing.

'You lack authority,' he says at last. 'There is a piece missing. Hades is obedient. It is punctilious. This prohibition, then, hinges upon the same rules as does the domination of the Alkahest. The code is graven in the creation. You must have the authorities, or you cannot pass the gate. Cerberus has tasted you and is content. Your blood enlivens the soil and binds me. You have spoken your name and given of your memory. Four proofs are accepted, one remains: the sacrifice is not complete.'

'What sacrifice?'

'You walked in the shadow and shape of a god, and upon your altar, men made sacrifices. Wealth and time and heart: all aspects of the self. This you must yield up, but you cannot.'

I did not put my hand in Scipio's corpse.

This corpse, lying once again in front of me.

Looking away, I find the doorway of the Chamber of Isis, barred by flames.

Choose, woman.

Choose murder of a soul and the resurrection of your son, or preservation of a stranger and your blood's abandonment.

Choose.

*

Revelation says that one day the world will end, and the sky shall be rolled up as if it were a scroll and the true nature of things made plain. It always struck me as a most sinister promise, not because of what it portends for the future – all mortal things end, by definition – but what it means about the present. It augurs that we know nothing of what is true, and yet we are to be judged on our choices and even damned. We walk in deception and must build the most honest world we know, but our efforts shall be to no avail, and in the end, one layer of lies after another must be ripped away, until some final underlying cosmos is shown to be all that ever was. What might we have done differently, had we seen? The divine plan is made in deceit, with dreams piled upon dreams. How could we ever be sure, even seeing it on that final day, that we have reached the centre of the onion? How are we to recognise what is real after being shown falsehood for every instant of our lives? If faith is salvation, should we just pick a lie and love it unto death? Does that mean that a circle of hell, truly embraced, is heaven? Why not, if everything we do is destined to be unravelled anyway? Perhaps I should wish to inhabit my dying son as a sickness, after all. At least then I would be with him at the end, as I have so often desired. A fine razor in the soul, such paradise.

Choose.

Am I slave to the Oneiroi, the gods of dream? No. I choose the closest I have known to truth. I choose memory.

Into thy hands, Mnemosyne, and I beg you show your gentlest face. Mnemosyne, Mother Mary, Mother Isis. By your thrones, I entreat you, and by our shared womanhood. By your sons, I beg you, and by your love. By your sons, and by mine. For Augustine. For Scipio. For Adeodatus. Forgive me. Help me.

Help me.

Magic, they say, is the invocation of names, and I know only one other name by which to conjure. If I had faith, that might be better, but I don't. Why would I? I exhausted my stock and have seen nothing to put it back. So, then:

For me. Just this once, for me?

Who am I, then?

Myself. Always.

I choose my son, and drive my hand to the elbow into Scipio's corpse, letting my fingers guide themselves to whatever secret piece is desired.

This is my soul.

On the plain of Erebus, in the kingdom of Hades, close by the burning and ubiquitous river of fire, I find an unwanted gnosis: the knowledge and conversation of myself. A door opens in Phlegethon.

Know-all is gone, and I walk through the wall.

doors in the world

'How long this time?'
     'Forty-seven minutes.'

Impossible to know how much time passed in the underworld. And pointless to ask, since it's fiction. Forty-seven minutes. The memories are bedding in, then. She can recall them now as if they were her own.

Doors in the world. Walking through walls and gates of fire, fire which is everywhere. The world under everything, like the underground, like the substrate.

It's like putting ingredients in a cauldron.

Athenais was breaking into the operating layer of the world.

like that but with teeth

ere I am, a Greek in a sack, in the back of a truck. I have to confess that it does not absolutely feel like the high life. It does slightly seem as if it might be a very violent Dr Seuss book.

There are people one hears about who are so bored and so rich and so fucking ignorant of possibility that they hire other people to come and take them away from their offices like this, kidnap them for a cool week in the Maldives without their executive Bluetooth headsets and their panoply of urgent bullshit. This is because they have so little control over their incredibly privileged lives that they can't make the decision to have a holiday, so they sign up to be made to do it.

Seriously: learn to use the Do Not Disturb function on your telephone. Get some self-control or some appetites and build some positive lifestyle habits, okay? Because right now, with my head hanging off the back bench of the driver's cab and the leatherette half sticking to and half scratching my cheek where the bag is sliding up – or down, because I'm not sure which way is which – I am pleased to be able to inform you, sir or madam, with your copious other options and your risk-free environment, that if you think being kidnapped is in any way cool you are a total asshole.

Apart from an old sandwich in one of the cubbies, I can smell vetiver, beer and socks. The girl who is not Stella is wearing the perfume Stella wore, and the two men with her don't understand about foot hygiene.

I should have had security. I should have had it from the moment I realised what I was doing, from the first time I saw the shark in the numbers on the cathode ray screen. I should be sitting in a bulletproof car right now, the kind that can squash a Hummer like a soft-boiled egg. I should have two guys in the front seats called Steve and Warislaw, both with those mid-Atlantic accents that tell you they learned English in Slovakia, the hard skin on their hands that tells you the other stuff they know. The car should have machine guns and rockets and an internal oxygen supply and widescreen TV and a fucking pole for the dancers.

Instead, I'm doing an impression of last night's soufflé and thinking about my dead ex-girlfriend, because a girl who looks like her – who is probably a quasi-religious fascist – has put a bag over my head.

I turn my head and there's something on the cloth, some last damp patch of ether wrapping itself around my face like a kiss or a submersion or the perfect solar eclipse happening only in me. I see white teeth, so very big and sharp, and feel the impact of their closing – but I'm so used to that by now it's almost homely. Unless it's real. Wouldn't that be a crotch?

Shit, I hope this is unconsciousness rushing at me, and not death.

*

It's not a great deal of fun to be a fat boy in a world of athletic men and older, perfect women. In dreams, of course, you meet a girl and she's special and you know it, so you train up. You go to practice with the football team, you run. It's like the scene from *Rocky*. You box and you learn and soon enough you're the Karate Kid, long limbs and the promise of a man's body, and you get lucky. The special girl decides that she's going to educate this boy in the ways of sex. She makes love to you, teaches you. You fall in love, fall out of love, and you part. It's coming of age the way it never is, without the fear and the emotional train wrecks.

In the real world, you're alone with Camille Jordan, and mostly that is fine. So long as you manage to nod and smile and forget that other people have friends and lovers and you are an oddity, it is fine. Solitude is underrated in the modern age, and loneliness is the natural state of children becoming men.

And then, one day, there was Stella.

'Professor Cosmatou's niece is coming to visit us tomorrow,' my moral tutor says. A moral tutor is not greatly concerned with morals but more with morale, although I suppose they occasionally have to intervene in both areas. They are notionally there to keep students on an even keel but have an equal and occasionally opposed responsibility to protect the university from the excesses of undergraduate behaviour. Cosmatou is the family name of the Old Girl, but of course the only word that makes even a vague impression on me is 'niece' because this proposes a girl, and since she is being mentioned to me she might even be a girl my own age, though given the age of the old bird it seems more plausible that this niece will be another inaccessible creature of twenty or more. On the other hand, her blood relationship to the woman who has most perfectly understood me – intellectually, at least, but also emotionally – is compelling. It will be nice to have a visitor.

Not a visitor. She is coming to study. She's like you: advanced.

Advanced, and only a year older, to within a week. If my mother's pregnancy had not gone slightly awry at the last minute, necessitating intervention, we would share a birthday.

I think of Professor Cosmatou and envisage a younger version, narrow and sharp-angled. When Stella arrives, she is more like a furious Degas imp with hair suffering from explosive decompression. We argue immediately over the names I have given to various mathematical operations whose proper designations I did not discover until afterwards. Moon numbers and angel numbers are just the beginning. She calls me a hick. I call her a cow. The atmosphere over Professor Cosmatou's dinner table is shocking. The professor's husband, the famous Peloponnesian philosopher of meaning whose parents saw fit to call him Cosmas Cosmatos, withdraws with his plate to the study and commences to watch professional women's beach volleyball on satellite television, in which his wife shortly joins him. They are both quite genuine fans of this sophisticated sport, but would not usually abandon the table for it.

Stella and I stare at one another hatefully across the kleftiko.

A week later, we are talking about the braid group conjugacy search problem, and I say something that could be funny if you looked at it two ways at once. She kisses me on the mouth. She tastes of menthol cigarettes and Coke. I belong to her for ever, and she to me.

'Well, isn't this a pickle?' a voice says, and Stella's lips are gone, like closing the door on your old house for the last time.

*

'A pick-le.' The acoustics are very strange, echoing and distant at the same time, as if I'm in a really big squash court. When I open my eyes, leaving Stella behind, I see someone I would rather never have seen again. It is the most complex and undesirable of transformations.

Nikolaos Megalos is no longer wearing his science fiction hat. That was town and this is the country, so he has on a white fisherman's shirt and linen trousers. Perhaps it's just the kidnapping context, but I find him a great deal less amusing than I did. He's big: muscular and formidable, as if he's spent his life hauling nets or ploughing rather than arguing about things that don't exist in rooms full of imported wine. Bearded and with the neck of his shirt open across a white burst of aged, hirsute pectorals, he looks less like Father Brown's Greek stablemate and more like a walking portrait of Hades.

That may also have something to do with my having recently sold the good Patriarch down the river and beggared his accounts in order to do right by my other, less weird clients.

In retrospect, I wonder whether that may have been a bad plan.

'A pickle,' he repeats, one more time for clarity. His voice has no obvious affect. He may be preparing a long speech about forgiveness, or he may be about to beat me to death. I can't tell, but I'm not very confident about his forgiveness. Christ is big on forgiveness, and if Megalos were wearing his Patriarch's outfit that would be a bit reassuring, but he isn't. There's something very deliberate about what he is wearing now, some assertion in the thonged sandals and dirty nails on his feet, and I need to know what it is. The wall is not the wall of some Christian monastery but something older, more vigorous and bloody. Nikolaos Megalos, at this moment, could be posing for a portrait of 'the headman considers' from any year between the founding of Athens and the invention of the cellular telephone. When political people here invoke the ethos of the villages, they are not only touching the ancient past, but also ghosting up against the nationalist resistance fighters in the White Mountains of Crete, and the sexy jackboot whisper of a militarised Greece. It is the soft-focus reflection of Cosmatos's prejudice, fascism lite.

I'm finding his stillness quite alarming. However long he has been sitting there, with one enormous paw resting inside the other – and it cannot be less than half an hour – it seems that he has been quite simply looking at me, focused on me and nothing else, and waiting. There was no shift in his posture as I became aware of him, no sense of patience rewarded as he spoke.

'You know,' Megalos says, 'when I heard about your shark, I didn't think much of it. Especially when I met you, and you were so obviously wretched with greed and lies. When I read your story in the newspaper, I thought I might kneel before you. I thought you had become the avatar of a living god, washed up out of the deep ocean of time and returned to us, as we will return. You were a disappointment.'

He shrugs, as if to say that most things are.

'But one banker is much like another, and I could afford to speculate. I gave you our money, and we did well. Good. But then ... then I heard a whisper. I have friends, you see, in all sorts of places, and I heard a whisper from an investigator in the finance ministry. They were fascinated by you. You knew things were happening before they happened. They thought you must have sources, but so many? So diverse? How could you bring all those pieces together in one place, how could you make a single thing out of them and understand what would happen in the intersection of all those different currents? And when they looked into it, they couldn't find anything. No meetings, no interactions of any kind, no statistically significant habits or correlations. He said to me: "That guy Kyriakos, with the shark: it's made him a prophet!" And then I knew. I had been too hasty. The god was with you after all. She was waiting for me, and I had been delinquent. Then I was too late. You had taken her gift and you made not change but chaos. You made money instead of revolution. You made money for men and women who have much of it, and for me? For me you made nothing. The absence of money. The absence of power, as I thought. I truly hated you in that moment. I hated myself. I had failed in everything I cared about.'

Megalos sees my fear, and nods. I have correctly understood him. I am right to be afraid. 'Do you know what I intended with that money, Constantine?'

I shake my head.

'I intended chaos. I had worked so hard, within the Church and among the rich; with the unions and the communists, with the fascists; even currying favour and distaste among all foreigners so that they would act in one particular way at the right time ... I had made everything ready for confusion and dismay, for everyone to betray and delay for just long enough. All it needed was money to give it a push. The long-enough lever, hm? I nearly had enough. Next year, or the year after, I would have been ready to make even a small crisis into a large one. But now you have unleashed a greater chaos than ever I could. All my clever traps are sprung and washed away, and yet: what I wanted is granted me. The genie has not gone back into its bottle, my Hierophant. Athens burns, and Greece shall be torn no longer.'

There's that word again: Hierophant.

You have contracted a god, Constantine. If you go against her, you will be devoured.

I open my mouth to say something – I am not even sure what it will be, but I feel I should try – but Nikolaos Megalos holds up his hand. 'Please. Before you speak. I am still angry, Constantine Kyriakos. That you have achieved what I desired, or more, does not excuse what you attempted. You have affronted me. But I am practical, and I am obedient. You carry the god. I will ask you once again: how does it feel? Does she speak to you? Is it Persephone or Demeter? Metis? What old, wonderful thing comes awake in you?'

'I don't know.'

'No. I thought not. She is deep inside, or only faintly attached. Which is it, I wonder? Or is it both? And why you, of all men? Was it just proximity? Should I have bathed every day in the waters of the Mediterranean? If I had, would I have woken one morning filled with the divine light? Well, no matter. Here we all are. I spent quite some time imagining that I would have you pressed like a sack of olives between two stones. There is a press here that would do very well. But … but. I think I will make you an offer instead. You are a man of commerce, after all. Do you know, first of all, what it is that you have made? What our country is like, out there in the streets, right now? Everything has come to a halt. Soon it will be dark and grim. There will be no food in the market places, no petrol in the pumps, no medicine in the hospitals. There will be no clean water, even, in the pipes. Can you imagine a more horrible thing to a modern man than the discovery that the basic stuff of life – pure water, that he considers so absolutely tamed and delivered by the system in which he is invested – is not any longer his to command? That no amount of angry telephoning will bring it back, even if he could call anyone? That he has hours, perhaps days before everyone he loves begins to die if he cannot somehow restore that lost flood? And yet: he has no idea where it might be had, if not from a pipe. He has no barrel in his garden, no brook at the foot of his land. He has never contemplated this possibility. But his neighbour, now … that fellow woke a little earlier and filled his bathtubs, and he won't share. Well, why would he? His family will survive due to his prudence and quick action. So now our modern friend has a choice: civilisation has abandoned him. Will he, then, cling to it? Or will he pick up a club, or a hammer, and go next door to do what must be done for his survival? Or will they both, like brothers, march upon the keep of the invader? The frame by which he understands the world is broken. He needs something new to judge his actions, to know what is right. Something new, or something old.

'Kairos, Constantine Kyriakos: the hanging instant. In this moment is possible even the turning of the human mind. A total renewal, a change of all things. And that is what I wanted, before you came. I wanted kairos, and with that I would change the world. Now I want more.'

He nods, and extends his hand towards me – not a handshake or an offer, not yet, but it's coming. I can feel my palm flex, ready for the shake. The rat brain inside, the mammal in a hard place, wants to cut a deal. Stockholm syndrome. Well, fuck Stockholm. I've been there. Expensive food, really pretty people who get depressed and talk about Third World debt when they should be screwing. Fuck Stockholm and actually fuck pretty much everything from Landsort to Gävle.

Megalos can see it in me: the rat in the corner. He wraps his arm around me. I know what he's doing: he's mounting me, for mammal dominance. 'You must do something for me.'

I look for just the right amount of earnestness to put in my face. Sure, let's deal. Sure, why not? A few hundred million, maybe? An even split? If I'm lucky, I can bluff him and hook him and play him and I can get to a phone. Get to a boat. Get to a car or a plane. Wherever I am, I can win. I can win. I have to believe that. I am Constantine Kyriakos! You know what Zeus—

Actually, let's not go there. I am Constantine Kyriakos, and that's enough by itself.

Today, it fucking better be. 'What do you want?'

Megalos smiles. 'Oh, Kyriakos. You are the omphalos, the Hierophant. It is your task to conduct the celebrants to the Chamber of Isis, that was Athena's gift to the sons and daughters of what is now called Egypt, and was taken to contain the tears of the Mother of Christ by the milksop children of Rome. You are the path between us, between man and God, and the meeting will be there, in that place, where all things may be done or undone. It is the fulcrum – what Pythagoras called the thumb of the universe. You shall shed blood in the chamber, and your part in this shall end. You and I will go our separate ways – you with my money, and I with your shark.'

'My shark?'

I can't believe this, but I don't want to give it to him.

Shit. Am I actually going to die over a neurosis?

I think I am. I think I'm going to tell him no, right here and now. Stop! Stop! I don't need to do that. I just have to play along! If I can get to a phone, I can work miracles.

I open my mouth to say no.

'Of course,' Megalos says, meditatively, 'you will wish to marry your Stella. That can be arranged.'

Myoushu: the strike along another axis.

*

If I can get to a phone, I can do miracles. That's what I have to remember. Megalos has caught me while I'm still partly human, but if I can even touch civilisation, the network of relationships defined by convention and money, there is nothing I cannot do. The Fifteen Hundred are superheroes. Every single one of them is Batman, and their superpower is an evolutionary amount of money. I know a man – call him Bill from Madrid – who once awoke in a hotel room in New York with an absurd quantity of high-grade cocaine and a dead model. He was relaxing after a long flight and had purchased his coke in bulk because it was cheaper, and this woman had obviously got up in the night for another toot and had had a heart attack. It happens. Cocaine is an unpredictable drug. Some people like to have a paramedic team on standby when they party, and I know a major corporation that keeps a pair of helicopters flight-ready during the Ibiza season so they don't lose any key personnel to poorly applied recreational pharmacology. Waking with the dead isn't quite the same deal as murder, but in terms of the getaway it might as well be.

Bill is not one of the Fifteen Hundred. By global standards, he's mega-wealthy. He's worth about US $400 million, which is private-island rich, but by the standards of the Fifteen Hundred he's basically a pet. All the same, he had friends more puissant than he was and they'd given him a number to call, and he did. He explained his problem to the woman who answered the phone, and she said: 'The fee is two million, one hundred and twenty thousand dollars. We will take it from your bank account at Grossman-Lafayette in Thun.' She did not ask him to authorise payment.

Two million, one hundred and twenty thousand dollars?

'This is not a particularly difficult situation,' the woman told him.

Bill took that on board and said okay.

About twenty minutes later a guy turned up at the door with a carry-on bag and some clothes from Gap in Bill's size. 'Leave your shit where it is. Go to the lobby. You'll be met. You'll go to the airport but you won't go through security and you won't need a ticket. You will board a plane. Someone will drive you home to your house at the far end. Then you take a shower and go to bed.'

'Is that important? The shower?'

'You want to fly seven hours after a day like this and not take a shower, be my guest.'

'What do I tell them? When they ask me what happened?'

'Why the hell would anyone ask you a freaky-ass question like that?'

'Isn't that how it goes? She's dead.'

'My friend, listen to me. Really listen and actually think about the words. Okay? That, what you are describing, is what happens to witnesses, but you are not a witness because you were never here. The hotel has no record of your stay, the airline says you never showed up for your flight. INS has no listing for your entry into the US. In fact it's a matter of public record that you never left Madrid. You got a little drunk and blew two hundred and twenty grand gambling and partying. I'm told you had a great time. There's a few paparazzi photos of you getting friendly with some footballer's ex-wife. There's even a sex tape, if you want to go that road. There's a date stamp on the footage, a copy of *El País* on the bedside, and a little bit of light relief where some French tourists walk in on you. They filed a complaint with the manager of the casino. You'll find the whole thing in your carry-on. The lady wants a rematch, by the way, so don't be surprised.'

Bill looked over at the bed.

The guy sighed, like a vet petting a dog that isn't going to make it. 'You know her name?'

'Karen,' Bill said.

'Okay, Karen,' the guy said. 'Karen was here, by herself. We'll see to it she's as okay as she can be, given she's dead. Nothing disrespectful is going to happen and her parents and her friends are going to understand that this was one of those appalling fucking bullshit events that you cannot prevent or foresee, and they will hate it but they will not lack for support or answers in so far as those things exist in this world. Do not get into asking yourself whether you owe them an explanation. You do not. You are the last good thing she ever knew. You had fun, you held each other, she died. There are honestly worse endings to a story, and you need to let her go right now and move on. This is sad stuff but it is what it is. It doesn't help anyone if it fucks up your life. Go to the lobby and let me do my job.'

That was just the off-the-peg version. As of today, I am a premium customer. With a phone and five minutes, I can fly. I have laser vision. I can dodge bullets.

But Megalos just offered me the only thing I cannot buy.

You will wish to marry your Stella. That can be arranged.

*

Megalos looks at me, curious. 'You had not understood this?'

'Stella died.' I don't say that aloud, ever. I say it now, because I realise he is the Devil and he has found the perfect temptation. If Stella were not dead, if he could bring her to me, I would give him whatever he wanted, and he could fuck around with Greek politics or set the world on fire or whatever it is he wants to do to his heart's content. I would try genuinely very hard to bring him to his Chamber of Isis, even though there is no such thing and he's barking mad and he will drown the country in shit and tears. I am for sale, and this is – has always been – my price.

Stella died.

Unless that is somehow not what happened and the world is all out of shape and nothing I have done since then makes any sense at all.

'Behold, then, Constantine Kyriakos, as I teach you my first mystery. You are a too-educated man and this will be hard for you unless you bend your will to it. Listen with your heart, and set your mind free of what is impossible. It is the lesson I shall shortly teach Greece, as the water dries in the pipes and the fields wilt. Do you recall our conversation in your temporary office beneath the road? Do you recall what I said about the Immortals?'

Sure. Persian Immortals. The soldier is not the man. The soldier is the variable, the man is just the number. The number may be expended, changed, even removed, but the equation is eternal.

Megalos nods. 'Indeed. In the world I will make, no one of true importance ever dies. Stella is not dead, she is simply waiting. It requires only that a woman step into what you presently would call – because you do not see the true world, but its shadow, in which we have lived until now – the symbolic space of Stella, and from that instant she will cease, and Stella will be again. That does not mean this is a trick or a substitution. It is a fundamental example of the way we will live. What is more real? The woman, or the flesh she occupied? Stella closed her eyes and was gone. She will open them again, and the first thing she will see is you.'

Nonsense. Nonsense and lies.

Except that I understand it. My mind is following it, even as I tell it not to: if a woman speaks as Stella and acts as Stella and looks like Stella and believes she is Stella, how is she not Stella? I want to say that each of us, second by second, becomes the person we are next, and Stella did not become whoever this woman will be. Stella died in the hospital. But that is to prejudge, to beg the question. That is to assume exactly what is under discussion.

This new woman's body, you might object, is not Stella's, or rather: her DNA is not the DNA that Stella was born with. No. It is not – but if Stella were to be treated for a genetic disease with a modern treatment that changed her DNA, would I say she was no longer herself? No. The code is not the woman. It is the mind that makes the self, albeit made in the flesh. All right, then: how is Genetic Medicine Stella different from Evil Megalos Stella? Well, there would be a chain of consequence leading from that body to this one, a transitional liminality or gradient by which Stella at time t might identifiably become Stella at $t + 1$, $t + 2$, $t + 3$ and so on, until the transition is complete and the DNA at t is nothing like the DNA at $t + n$, but the chain of transformation is clear. The woman from the past would become the woman in the present.

But here again, this new Stella would become Stella little by little, slowly arriving at Stella-ness through study, application and performance rather than gross physical manipulation. The process of transition would be memetic rather than corporeal, but I have already acknowledged that the woman is not the cells. If I want to deny it and I do not wish to invoke a separate soul, I must say there is an essence of thinking Stella, a thing that is created in the body and constitutes the person, and that thing ceased when Stella died. But how then to distinguish the old essence from the new? By what criteria would they be separate? If identical in shape and form, in structure and function, would they be divided only by time, itself a mysterious quantity? If consciousness is a thing created in the lowest levels of matter, could I say in honesty that the same imprint with the same energy running through it was not the same person? If Stella had died during an operation to save her life and then been resuscitated, would I reject her as a different person?

If not, then I must account for my willingness to believe she is still Stella but my rejection of Evil Megalos Stella. I must say that the same loop of awareness regenerated is the same woman – which I would – but if I say that and I have additionally already denied the necessity of the physical sameness of Stella's body, I must own that here, if the loop is the same as the old one, the woman is also, and Stella could live again. If the loop were imperfect – if Evil Megalos Stella is functionally different, or if resuscitated Stella were changed by her experience, then she might be only 20 per cent Stella, or 30. Must I require all of Stella? She would have changed in the intervening years in any case. Shall I say she must be the woman she was at twenty for ever? No. What percentage of Stella, then, must inhabit the new loop before I can accept that she is herself? More or less than 50 per cent? If Stella had been in an accident and lost her memory, would I have disowned her, or sought to help her regain what she was? Should I do less now? I know the new woman would not be Stella, and yet why do I know it? Our minds are formed by the languages and cultures we inhabit. There are peoples who cannot see the difference between green and blue, peoples for whom numbers greater than two are a confusion of the mind. What blind spots do I have, in consequence of the frame in which I have always believed? Might I look through Stella, call her an impostor, out of nothing more than a learned prejudice?

What if Megalos is right?

Stella. She could be with me and I with her, for ever, so long as there are people who will become the Hierophant and his wife. We wanted eternity and here it is.

There's a transformation, if you like: the Hierophant and his wife.

I know that this is wrong. I know that it is flawed somehow. It must be. I just can't find a way to explain its wrongness. More mathematics: it is not enough to have an instinct for a statement. You must be able to express it in a form that can be tested and deployed.

And I so very much wish it were real.

I say: 'Who?' like an owl, to make time to think.

'You have already met her,' Megalos says. 'You knew her then.'

The woman in my flat. The one who kidnapped me. 'She hates me.' I should have said: 'She's not Stella.' Why didn't I? Just because she looks like Stella? Just because Nikolaos Megalos has found a clever way of framing his madness?

Megalos waves his hand in dismissal. 'No, no. Stella – or better, as her old name is still true, we should call her Adrasteia – she does not hate you. She is angry with you for making her wait, and upset because your unbelief makes her own immersion more difficult. Do you see? She is more than one person, not two halves in conflict, but two wholes existing where only one should be. For Stella to live, Adrasteia must be unmade. Adrasteia fears ending, but is determined; Stella is impatient to resume her life. Who she is in this moment is contingent upon events which have not yet taken place. Thus, a most painful conflict of ontology. She told me she dreams mathematical proofs, and when she wakes there is nothing in her mind that can comprehend them. She must become Stella, soon, or she will fray. If you are too slow to follow, you may lose her to another, just as you might have if you had never met. She will be Stella, and she will not wait forever in the face of your doubt.' No. Stella had only contempt for dithering.

Megalos sighs, acknowledging my difficulty. 'You can have paradise. But you must choose it genuinely, or it will be hell. That is how I shall know your heart, Constantine. Because in this matter, you cannot lie, and you cannot hide.'

There is a way of imagining causality – one of many, but one, in particular, that I see now – in which the universe is a perpetual sine wave, constantly made and unmade, perfectly or imperfectly replicating the same steps over and over again. In that picture, we exist now, and we die, and then in an almost incomprehensibly long time we exist again just as we are. Who is to say that the time when we are not is more significant than the time when we are? Who is to say that it exists at all if we cannot see it? Who is to say that the frequency of our making and unmaking is not radically more compressed, and that the universe does not shatter and remake itself second by second, and us none the wiser?

If the sine wave is the truth, it implies the potential of Stella's endless replication, her regeneration. Would we maintain that Stella in the next wave is different from Stella in this one, when the entire flow of time in the universe is wrapped around the spindle of a cosmic zoetrope? No. No, we would acknowledge in the end that the way we have thought of ourselves is flawed: that we are not singular or temporary, but amnesically recurrent in the most glorious way – and if that were so, then this would be a shortcut, a hack, and Stella would come back a little early, to be with me.

A hack. That's all.

And it's true that the way we see the world is riven through with untested, unverifiable assumptions about what it means to have a self. It's true that we might possess no will of our own, just be acting out determined or random steps and dreaming of choice-making; that we could be brains in jars, or surgical patients on operating tables or old women dying alone in nursing homes fantasising about other lives, or alien players of immersive games trapped in the system, or even just simulations of simulations in some enormous engine analysing a stock market in a universe far above our own; or that we might be physically real, but exist in fact as a sequence of selves, each alive only for an instant in the uptick of an electrical pulse, gone again the next, each fraudulently recollecting in his own short span the chemically stored memories of a billion others back down the line to the womb and declaring them his own. And that's just how we fail to understand ourselves, before we even touch the mystery that is other people. Do they think at all? Do they think the same way that we do? Do they experience love, hope, self? Or do they merely behave as if they do? We have no way of knowing – not yet, not until we can connect two heads with thick, ropy cables and taste with another person's tongue, share the feeling of wine or wind on their lips. Even then, consciousness regresses, an endless loop of doubt.

Descartes was a mathematician first, a philosopher afterwards, and perhaps a little mad. But he was right that we have no idea what we truly are. Megalos's perspective is no more absurd than any other chosen illusion. Why not, if one is better than another, choose that?

I could have Stella back.

Prove, please, that Stella = Not Stella.

From the past, Gelasia Cosmatou is talking to me, and the Old Girl is not pleased: 'Of course, boy. Bring back the dead, live in harmony, never doubt and never mind that she died. Just decide she didn't, that it's all a matter of perspective. Will you do your mathematics that way also? Let five equal four because that solves the puzzle? No? Well, then, that tells you that his New Greece is so much pigeonsquitter on a wet beach, doesn't it! Use your bloody head!'

I am using my head. I am using it with everything I have.

I do not speak, and after a while watching me with that same depthless, unwavering calm, Nikolaos Megalos gets up. He unlocks my handcuffs, because he knows that whatever else happens now, he doesn't need them any more. After a while, with something like regret, he says: 'I will send Adrasteia to bring you to her home. Meditate upon what I have said, but be quick. We must begin soon, while the world is still in flux. Search your soul.'

There's no such thing as souls.

In which case Not Stella could be Stella.

Nikolaos Megalos departs in silence, but not in peace.

And I thought the *shark* was dangerous.

*

I sit by myself for a while, wondering what to do.

There is no Stella. There could be Stella. There can never be Stella again.

There will be Stella tomorrow, for a given value of Stella.

I am sitting in that exhausted space between mania and emptiness when she opens the door and comes into my room. She has that way of patting the side of her head where her glasses should be, because her hair is thick enough to hold them and she is not sure that they are there. She has the same look that she always had, the look of measurement and perplexity, as if she cannot decide where to begin with me, and yet she knows that she will.

'Hi,' I say, when the moment has already been too long.

Nothing in her face speaks of disappointment in me. She does not flinch – and yet she must, inside, at this too-cool greeting. Stella would, if I met her that way, having just discovered she was alive after all this time. Stella would slap me.

She snorts, which is the other thing Stella would do, and her snort expresses volumes of exasperation. I am a dullard: a lumpen, obstinate male, and as always I will come around in time, but I will have to be coaxed and massaged to believe it was all my own idea. If it were not for the fact that the coaxing pleases her, the game and the chase, it would be utterly unacceptable.

Is that how we were? Or is my mind painting it that way now? Each recollection bends memory to a new shape. Did Stella look that way, with her lips half smiling? Or am I seeing her that way then because I see this woman now? If the latter: how long will it take before this Stella swallows that one?

'Come and see the real world,' she says, and she leads me down into the perfectly lifelike village of Nikolaos Megalos.

*

The real world is a small cluster of fisher cottages close by the sea. There are perhaps a few hundred houses, scattered around a working dock that looks, I imagine, much the same as it did when navigation was a matter of tasting the water and spitting. A few paces inland of the quay is a little market square, runnelled and drained so that the blood and bones from the fishwives' stalls can be washed into the sea in the afternoon. Fat gulls stroll along the outer wall, proud of their domain.

Eyes shut, I breathe in fresh air. In Athens – it must be just along the coast a way, unless we are on an island – the air tastes of hot stone and combustion, coffee and tobacco: the peculiar sensory seal of the capital. Here, you remember that the world doesn't have to smell that way. The air is rich with salt and pine, olive groves and eucalyptus. I look out across the village and the sight matches the flavour that's churning in my head: baking white sun and fecund blue water, soft marble blocks and terracotta tiles, wooden beams and doors. There's fresh plaster render on some of the walls, space for frescoes and murals as yet unpainted. The little square is full of men with tanned, golden skin and dark hair – not fat but thick with Heraklean muscle, and gleaming with oil. The women have supple limbs and broad hands, dark eyes proud and sharp. When the wind gusts inland, it carries up to us the scents of roasting and bread, of fresh fish on coal and olive oil and artichokes. From the other direction, it brings peppers and tomatoes growing on the vine; the hum of bees, the sound of hearty laughter. This is time travel, to a Greece that never was: a vaccinated and aerobicised Olympian Pastoral Republic.

Away to one side, close by the seafront but dignified and set apart from the business of commerce, a circle is carved into the stones, and within it is a lowered, wood-boarded space surrounded by old-fashioned torches and covered in a layer of sand: a play area for children, say, or a showing pen for livestock. I can hear the sound of the sea in the rocks below, twenty metres down. Stella-Adrasteia catches the direction of my gaze.

'The zagre,' she says.

'The what?'

'The proving circle. It is for trials.'

'What, by combat?' Half, I believe it must be. Perhaps that's how elections work: maybe Megalos got his hat by beating three septuagenarians to a pulp with his bare hands.

She laughs. 'No! For justice, we have laws, of course, and magistrates. No. I mean for legitimacy, for the right to belong. Some here are true Greek, born in the blood, but others are Greek of the heart and the soul, but born in other nations. The seed of Greece is spread wide and one cannot always know it by sight. One must know if a person is truly invested, Megalos says: whether they are Greek in meaning.'

'And for that, what? Do they fight?' I picture blood on the sand, scrawny refugees spilling out of North Africa in desperation, drowning their way here like ants in a ball, being told that this is how it's done now, this is asylum: a gladiator's chance, and all they have to do is rip the eyes off the other man. Immigration reduced by 50 per cent, at a minimum. A perfectly Gordian one: if a puzzle offends you, cut it in half.

'Sometimes, of course. Men and women. Sometimes the test is more symbolic, resonant with the person. Each test is made for the person, like a lovesong. It is a question of rightness, and resolve.'

Stop your so-very-wise condemnation, and tell me that if the person you most miss in the world were offered to you back again, in however strange or impossible a fashion and at whatever price, you would be able to walk away unhesitating: anti-Orpheus, leaving the ghost in Hades without a second look. Tell me that you can imagine your life without the one you most love, and that you can imagine rejecting the possibility of their return in however broken a form.

'Did you fight?' I don't want to know, so I ask.

She stares at me for a moment. 'I am Stella Cosmatou. Of course not.'

Of course not. Stella was Greek. Stella is Greek, has always been Greek, and this is Stella. Megalos's world is strangely perfect in its tautologies.

There is a procession of some sort coming down the street. Stella looks over and murmurs: 'Oh! Make way!'

'What? Why?'

'Because it's polite,' she replies, taking my arm to guide me.

Her fingers graze the blade of my hand. It is our first contact, skin on skin. Not really first contact, I suppose, because she put a bag over my head, so technically we have touched before. But it is the first contact that is real, between persons, tacit permissions given by the working of the social world. Her hand plucks my sleeve to hasten me out of the way, and she presses me to one side with her hip. It is done innocently and spontaneously, as between old friends, but it is not like that at all. It is as if I have been reattached to mains power after a lifetime on batteries. I am alive, truly alive. I see in colour, hear in quadrophonic stereo. My breath stops. I can feel her. I know her weight and her balance, the tenor of her muscles and bones. I feel her fingertips against my wrist, the curve of her body where it traps me against the stone wall, the rhythm of her heart inside her. Stella's hip, that I have held and kissed, moving as Stella moved it, in the ineffable signature of one person's way, known only to dance partners and lovers.

Illusion. Suggestion. It cannot be the same.

But it is the same. I feel her and she is in my head and my heart.

And she feels it too. She feels the same shock of connection. Impossible. She was not there. She cannot have that understanding of me, cannot share my history, was not there unless she is most literally and actually Stella, transmigrated.

And why not? Why not, if gods swim in the markets and devour economies? If I have made a deal with an ancient divinity, sacrificing time and money, being paid in both? Why not?

Her head turns slowly, afraid of what it may find. Sees fellowship. Shared bewilderment.

Desire. Delusion. Desperation. Divine intervention.

Divine madness.

At any moment, I will kiss her, or she will kiss me.

She leans forward just a little, for just a moment, mouth opening so that I glimpse the tip of her tongue, taste her on the breeze – and then she catches herself and steps away.

Her departure is the least simple physical motion I have ever experienced. Her body twists slightly, her hips no longer turned away but slipping around to face me so that as she leans inward to recover her balance her whole body briefly seals against mine. From thigh to shoulder my left side is embraced, the contact just a fraction longer than it needs to be, the brief extra pressure of groin and breast emphatic. Her upper body comes away first, the motion pulling her upright, the last fading touch imparted by her hips to mine, undeniable gravity. Even the scent of her is right, is what it always was: olfactory Stella-ness.

And she's gone, back in her own orbit, her own unshared private space.

'Pilgrims,' she says.

What?

The word is noise, not sense, because there is no context beyond her. Then my tunnel vision loosens, and I remember what is around us. 'Oh, right.' Right, and nothing happened, tra la la. Just like the old days when we were kids: act natural, look busy, keep your hands on the table.

I wonder who we are lying to. Are we lying to one another and to ourselves, or are we watched, in this perfect village? Are there eyes upon us, upon me, gauging my reactions, the progress of my seduction? The progress of her transition? If she fails, will there be another Stella along in a minute to try again?

Is she on my side or on theirs? Stella would be with me. She cannot be Stella unless she is with them. Must I, then, be with them? Megalos thinks so. Around and around we go.

'Pilgrims,' she repeats, demanding my attention.

Following the direction of her finger, I see coming towards us what appears to be a centipede as tall as a person, slowly but surely looping its way down the opposite side of the stone gallery under which we walk. Then it draws closer, and it is just an old woman, prostrating herself at the head of a line of serious pilgrims making the last steps of their journey. Behind her is a middle-aged man, and behind them are some children, who because they are shorter are having trouble keeping up.

Toothless, she passes me, and in her expression is quite placid. She reminds me of the Patriarch – if that's what he is now.

It is the most wrong thing I have ever seen.

The centipede ripples on, and away.

'The people are devoted,' Stella says. 'Because they see the divine with clear eyes. There is no need for faith. There is certainty.'

'And you?'

Eye contact. 'My path is more complex.'

We walk on through the little port, taking the air.

*

These people are not the first iteration of themselves, nor will they be the last. They are not this person, they are the space that this person occupies in the painting.

Down winding village streets we go. We are walking not through a city but a map, a physical space that exists to chart the differences between portraits, and the portraits are rendered in living people. White brick, pink brick, flowers in window boxes, blue Mediterranean sky: all symbols on the map, meaning nothing without the key.

Stella, as we walk, is more Stella all the time. The longer I spend with her, the more I know her, the less I remember whether she is different from the old Stella. My knowledge of her inscribes itself on my memory, rolling itself back into the past and changing my recollection of it. As we walk we share things, moments we have experienced before – or which I now remember experiencing, even if three days ago I wouldn't have.

As we climb the hill on the far side of the harbour, smelling watered earth and eucalyptus, she is very serious. I remember once when we were writing a paper, Stella worked out a schedule of the time we could spend doing maths, eating, sleeping and making love. She was extremely stern about this last one, because she had identified it as a key area where we lost huge amounts of mathematical progress. Needless to say it was a failure: when I suggested, obedient to her instruction, that we get out of bed, she stretched out to the timetable she had stuck to the wall – the stretch, I remember, was one of the most beautiful things I had ever seen, her whole naked body reaching in a perfect curve from knee to fingertip, swaying as she neared the limit of her reach – and pulled it down, then tore it to pieces and threw them in the air. Before the paper snow finished falling she was already on top of me, and I don't think we emerged again that day.

This is like the bit when she was wearing clothes, not the other bit.

I've begun to think of her as having been that person. It's harder and harder to recall the in-between times, the day when she died without me. She is alive.

What if Megalos has stumbled upon something he does not understand? What if he's wrong about everything except this, and Stella has been drawn here through time? Perhaps the Stella I knew was a pre-echo of this one, a shadow who had to die in order to exist fully in a later state. Or perhaps the universe has just re-created her perfectly as a Boltzmann entity, a woman born out of a random event. It is not theoretically impossible. On any given day, boiling water poured over your hand could make you cold – although, of course, it never does, just as you never win the lottery every week for a year. Or those odds may come in all the time and we never notice: deep space could be filling up with spontaneous creations, persons existing for a heartbeat of bewildered, frozen agony, as James or Kalil or Sara or Mariam jerks into being in the endless waste between stars and, mistakenly remembering a life, dies mystified and appalled. *I was just shopping in Glyfada!* But they weren't. They had never been to Glyfada.

Perhaps there never was a Stella until now, and this is the first one and the one that I remember is the ghost. Perhaps there's always a Stella, somewhere, and you just have to go and find her and there she is, still in love with you, still the same.

When you start making the theory fit the supposition, you're already fucked. What you have to do is start with the facts and find the reality, but reality is something I'm losing touch with, and have been since a god-shark invaded my head and crashed the stock market.

How is it that I have no problem believing in a divine pagan shark living in my head and corrupting Fortune 500 companies, but Megalos's proposal is giving me trouble? Hell, if I want Stella back, maybe I should cut out the middleman, go right to the shark.

You want me to work for you? That's my price. Give me Stella.

But maybe that's the point. Maybe this is my price being paid, and Nikolaos Megalos exists purely in order to deliver my fee.

Stella, and a phone. I want a phone.

Ahead of me in the narrow street, she makes an impatient noise. 'You have a question. Ask it.'

Are you her?

I blurt: 'Do you love me?'

She laughs, unconcerned. 'Not that one, Constantine. I will answer that one later.'

She looks away again. 'Ask me about something difficult.'

I don't know where it comes from: 'What's the Chamber of Isis?' Because I swear, I've heard of it before.

'It is the place the mother goddess set aside from the mortal world; the womb of the new. Perhaps it is one of the Pentemychos, the five secret recesses of the gods, or perhaps they are all the one Chamber viewed from different angles. It is hope, and atemporality. It is the holiest of temples, the most mysterious.'

The next question pops out before I can stop it, because suddenly I think she might know. 'What is happening to me?'

Between two houses with carpets hanging out to air on the step, she indicates a particular door. She lays her hand on the wood, then shrugs and steps back. 'You are the promise of our coming dawn.'

I don't know what that means. Stella laughs, and her hand reaches out to touch my forehead, just as it always did when her mind found a pathway which mine could not. Did I not make it clear? Stella is much, much cleverer than I am.

Stella was.

The same cool fingers, sure and knowing. The same thumb against my temple, the quick blessing of pressure. The old Stella would kiss me. This new one is still cautious. She hesitates and then retreats, the omission a cool absence, the ghost touch of an intimacy missed. Instead, she explains.

'Megalos leads us to a new world, and that world is reached through a gateway of understanding. The transition is hard. We have been trained against it by the Cartesian method that underpins modernity. We see as shadows all that is real, and as gold all that is dross. We must work to change what we understand. Only willingly can we enter the new Greece, by study and by deep commitment. But you, Constantine: you are ineluctable. You are infused with a god, as if our world has already arrived. Your mind is modern – and yet in you is the ancient, hale and vibrant and consuming. You are the Orpheus, gone into the underworld and retrieved not Eurydice but Persephone, or her dam. And yet, she waits. She has brought chaos to the world and our cause is advanced, but she remains with you. Perhaps she is content. Perhaps she is trapped. Perhaps you hold her back. You are a puzzle box, and you contain that which Nikolaos Megalos greatly desires. In that, he is a danger to you. You are not holy, so perhaps any man would do and you might cede the god to him. Or he might take it by force, rip it from you in the Chamber. That seems more appropriate. The pathways of old Greece were drenched in blood, after all.'

What a totally fucking appealing idea. 'He wants it.'

She shrugs. 'He believes he is called to it.'

He believes. Not she believes. Not we. He.

'And if he is not?'

'That is heresy.' She sounds as if I have made an improper suggestion at dinner – one that is not without some appeal.

'If I'm the Hierophant, I must understand even heresy.'

'The second does not follow from the first.'

'Please.'

She tuts. 'Then he is wrong, and the god is not for him. You are the Hierophant. One way or another, you will go to the Chamber. This cannot be avoided. One cannot posit a model of the universe in which it does not occur. If Megalos is wrong, then that visit serves another purpose, or none at all, and what he attempts will either be futile or more dramatically it will derail the flow of that which is and is to come. In the last case, I suppose the resulting sidetrack will not be stable. Most likely the entirety of space and time will dissipate like steam and we will cease. You know as well as I do, Constantine, that saying these things in words expresses only nonsense.'

We should say them in numbers. Yes.

'So how am I supposed to find it?'

'You need only live. You go to your meeting, inevitably.'

'I like to think there's a choice.'

'Of course there is a choice, and this is what you choose. Otherwise what has already happened cannot have happened, and that is impossible.'

'Even inside the Chamber?'

She hesitates, then grins. 'I don't know, Constantine. Isn't that marvellous?'

She goes into the house, and I don't have time to stop and worry, because the last thing I want now is to be the first Hierophant ever to get lost on his way to a mystical revelation.

*

The house, I realise, is not a house, but a facade masking the entrance into a sequence of caves in the upper part of the cliff. I can hear the sound of the sea a long way below, but only distantly because the caves are huge and they are full of people. The congregation – army? – of Nikolaos Megalos is here. This is where the pilgrims were going, and there are two more centipedes making their way across the cavern, pressing their faces to the rock in the formalised rhythm of adulation or pornography. As I enter there is a kind of ripple, and every face turns in my direction like the head of a compass needle. There must be more than a thousand, and even the children are looking, as if I'm an ice cream or a film star. At first there is quiet, and the noise of the water on the rocks pulses around us. Then somewhere a woman begins to murmur and stamp her foot, and then another follows suit, and the men too, and then the kids. The sound swells around us, bouncing off the rocks and shaping the air into a drum. I cannot hear the words, but I know what's happening. These people are singing, raising up a chant of gratitude and exhortation. In fact, they are praying.

It takes a moment longer to realise that they are praying to me.

Somewhere, there's a child with a high, sweet voice, a true soprano. Somewhere there's a bass with just the right mix of depth and power to make the rock hum.

They are praying to me.

For a moment I feel dizzy, and my vision is in two places at once: in my own head, and somewhere up above me, passing through the sound like a bird, or like a shark in the water.

'They are pleased to see you,' Stella chides me, 'but you should not let them distract you.'

Right. Worship is something to be taken lightly.

She leads me away on to a side passage. As soon as I have gone, the music stops. It's like the first touch of anaesthesia. Stella leads me along the corridor, and I can see a sequence of doors and then finally a stairway leading down into the deeper caves beneath, and there's a slow vibration in the column of air around the spiral steps, a breath of water and salt. 'In here,' Stella says.

The room is disappointingly ordinary, full of trestle tables covered in paper and people reading. Megalos has arranged for electricity down here – a cable hangs from the ceiling in the middle, smaller wires spliced off it so that the whole thing is an inverted tree. No doubt Cosmatos would see some significance in that, but to me it's just an electrical botch job and a fire risk.

The people are more interesting when I look closer. They are reading not only old tomes and scrolls, which I was expecting, but new books and even electronic devices. To make the whole thing just a little bit creepy, there's a dais where someone is repeating a single word in an endless monotone. I don't know what the word is because it's quite long and he never stops saying it, so the syllables are blending together and creating a mash of sound: a very small glossolalia, like a portable version. The light is dim and the reading lamps are a warm yellow. The whole place smells of stone and dust and paper. Megalos, reading glasses precariously resting on the end of his nose, looks up from a desk as we enter.

'Torn no longer, Constantine Kyriakos.'

*

The words are a greeting, and not true. I'm still torn. I still don't believe in Stella. I squeeze her hand briefly, by way of apology. I don't know if she understands, because she squeezes back.

I wonder who I'm trying to persuade. I wonder how many participants in how many ghastly events have told themselves the same thing.

'Torn no longer, Nikolaos Megalos,' I say in my best Hierophant voice. It's the one I used to use for talking to fraud investigators. The whole room – excepting the chanting man – murmurs quietly: 'Torn no longer.' People smile, and then, formalities concluded, get on with their work.

'Anaximander of Miletos,' Megalos says, pointing. 'Pherecydes. Socrates and Plato, Archimedes … ' I wonder if he's asking for recommendations. 'This room is full of scholars.'

Oh. Yes. He means that those names belong to these men, that that is who they are.

Something about my face must leak bewilderment and non-belief. I understand his world. I just don't inhabit it. Megalos smiles, and claps me on the shoulder: a man recognising hard work. 'The prophetess Cassandra was cursed that she should see the future and never be believed. The goddess Athena was beyond such restriction because belief was not in her nature. She either knew or she did not. The fascination with faith is a Christian invention, of course. When your god simply never shows up, faith becomes quite necessary. In any case, long before the Nazarene carpenter, when King Agamemnon took Cassandra as a concubine after the Trojan War, Athena visited the sleeping woman in the shape of an owl and drank the tears from her cheeks as she dreamed. In this way, Cassandra's visions passed to one who could understand and profit by them.

'Athena saw this future: this godless world where Greece is fallen into poverty and the city that bears her name is flooded with the world's detritus. And weeping in her turn she prepared against this day. She made a magic room where time does not flow and where the great Universal Solvent can be created by one of the wise, that Alkahest which can loose any prisoner, unshackle the mind of man. Wisdom is the tip of her spear, and with it she slays the serpent of lies.'

He has his hands in the air, his eyes closed, and although he has not raised his voice the whole room has gone quiet. But once again, the silence into which he speaks is not a silence of fear or awe, but a kind of hunger. The movements of his body and the notes of his voice are signs, and their forcefulness satisfies something in his followers, an ongoing need to shore up the wall they are building around themselves, around their ability to believe they are particular instances of eternal symbols first, and people with memories of another life a distant second.

He doesn't seem to notice. 'So we look for the Chamber, as you know. Here we look in books. There are many books of the legends of Greece, countless stories of Lost Atlantis and accounts of journeys to mystical kingdoms. We read them all. We do textual analysis with computers. We sing them, cut them up, acrosticise them and decipher them seeking hidden meanings.'

'And you find?'

'That it is remarkable how many academics choose to include libellous allegations as cryptext in their indices, or boast of their extramarital affairs in the footnotes. Stella's uncle suggested this journey, years ago when we first met, and in the same breath he told me it would not work. But he was right: it must be attempted.'

I really wish he hadn't told me that. I was pretending Cosmatos wasn't in this. When I get out of here, I'm going to punch him until he looks like an alloy hubcap. Except that I'm beginning to suspect I won't have to wait.

Megalos shrugs, and we pass into the corridor with him leading the way. Stella has somehow become almost invisible, stepping into the space behind our backs as we go. I wonder if she is afraid of Megalos because he is turning her into something she is not, or because he holds the key to her resuming what she is.

He opens the door to the next room. It is silent and very beautiful. The walls are decorated with mosaics – I think they may be original – and there are marble sculptures of the gods of Olympus in little alcoves and on plinths. A young man sits in the very centre on a wooden chair. He has his eyes open, but something in the tilt of his head says that he sees nothing.

Megalos closes the door. 'He's blind,' I murmur.

'Yes,' Megalos says. 'So he listens. Every morning, he sits and listens to the sound of the gods.'

Because, in this new or old construction of the world, the symbol is the thing. The gods are present in those sculptures, in those mosaic tiles, if not entirely at least in some small way. The boy is literally listening for their voices. 'And in the afternoons?'

'A woman. A skilled artist. She watches them. There was a man we wanted, but he would not come. And then, too, he is a degenerate African – yet he has remarkable eyes. Still: devotion must suffice, if genius is tainted with licence.'

I have to ask. 'And ... does it work?'

Megalos smiles. 'Yes.'

That sheer, mountainous certainty again: flat-iron certainty. I can smell the metal in it, feel the heat. He is either right, or mad. Although I'm not sure what madness looks like on someone who has a complete and coherent variant understanding of the world. At a certain point the issue becomes political, not medical. Megalos is like one of the Fifteen Hundred: he defines his own reality.

He hesitates now. 'Are you wearing good shoes?'

I look down. Trainers. Not expensive, but solid. Stella is wearing sandals.

Megalos frowns at her. 'You may wish to remain outside.'

'Outside what?' I ask.

But he has already opened the next door on to a room full of blood.

*

In all my life, I have never seen so much blood, let alone smelled so much blood. It washes away sense and thought, a thick white scent of catastrophe and fear, of extreme danger and extreme injury.

The sense of smell is the sense of touch at a most intimate and cellular level: a form of digestion and consumption. The smell is the thing, the smell of blood is blood aerosolised, and there is blood, everywhere about this room, and in the blood: people.

The people wade and they dabble, unappalled as ducks in a pond. Sometimes they stoop and sniff, even sample the mess, or plunge their hands in and let it fall, finding bits of tube and organ. Their contact is no different from mine in kind, only in degree and ease. I, too, am washed in this stench.

One man finds something unnameable and spreads it like a paperback on a handy ledge, leafs through the membranes as if reading a book. He calls out instructions to a sort of secretary standing off to one side with a spiral jotter. The secretary makes careful notes.

The man with the organ in his hands is a haruspex. They all are: soothsayers reading the truth of the world from the bodies of dead things. Fish, sometimes. Cattle, often. Occasionally a man. I look down into the pool and hope that the human corpses come from accidents and natural deaths, that Megalos controls a hospital or has raided a mortuary. That he has not sent reivers out into the countryside to kidnap and murder.

But why wouldn't he? The true Greek can be resurrected. The foreigner does not deserve to be.

Behind me, Stella's face is warm in the reflected pink light. She meets my eyes and I can see her screaming.

Megalos, in the corridor a moment later and still unmoved, regrets that he has been unable to obtain pythons as yet for a truly Delphic oracle. Will I, personally, require pythons? He has a line to some, but they will need to be liberated. Do I feel an absence of snakes in my spiritual environment?

I tell him I do not. I wonder what he would do if I told him to get rid of the blood room, if I said it was a barrier to the knowledge of the god inside me. I wonder what the shark would do. Sharks are supposed to be frenzied by blood. Is she surging behind my eyes, longing to break through the lenses and bathe? I don't think so. But then I'm always bewildered by what she will and will not do.

This is when I realise how dangerous he is, not because he is evil, but because he is other. We tend to assume people are in most ways like us, and in most cases there is an element of truth in that, but Megalos is on another order of different. He literally does not understand why blood should trouble him. The skull in the blood pool was a cow's, but he would have no difficulty putting a man's body to that use, or a woman's, if he thought it would be more effective in securing his goals. I imagine that he has, already, and found the results no more lucid than with cattle, and since cattle have more blood and are easy to come by he hasn't bothered with people again.

No, I tell him. No need for pythons.

He opens the last door, and it is actually worse. I remember where I've heard the expression 'Chamber of Isis' before.

*

Looking at the room, I can almost taste the booze and the lipstick. I can remember her face, feel the muscles in her hips. The party, the game. *Witnessed.* The Easter egg I found, stumbled on to with one hand covertly working its way between her shirt and her shoulder blades, eliciting wriggles and laughter. The gamer, the one with the most beautiful laugh.

There are twenty very expensive computers in here, and every single one of them is playing *Witnessed*. There's even a two-metre plasma-screen TV hanging on the wall, showing random slices of different games for a few seconds at a time. *Witnessed.* Not so long ago just the fad of the moment, and now a going concern. There's been quite a ruckus about it, I gather, the British right wing all in an uproar and the usual suspects online calling it an Afro-communist feminazi plot or whatever. Come to think of it, I would have thought of Megalos as being one of those people – except that I wouldn't really have pegged him as playing video games or even being aware of their existence. Perhaps he ran across it when he was looking for modern things of which to disapprove.

I can hear the chanting again, the perfect Gregorian moan of male bass and female alto, something between an organ and a didgeridoo: prayer wheel gaming.

I say what's on my mind. The 'f' is drawn out. The 'u' in the middle stretches a little, in absolute aggravation. Bathos. I'm going to die of bathos. Well, I avoided one death in the depths, and here I am in a cave, looking at another. Of course.

The hard 'ck' comes out like breathing. I say the whole again, by way of confirmation: 'Fuck.'

The Chamber of Isis is a place in a video game. It was made up for the game. It sounds plausible, but it's not real. There was a lot of press about that, a lot of articles about Baudrillard, because there is nothing the nerd world likes more

521

than to think itself adrift in a sea of French postmodern philosophy. If you can get Keanu Reeves to play the lead, so much the better.

The lead designer – a British woman, I remember – said she had coded it to be possible but vanishingly hard to find the way in, and that sort of challenge issued to the Internet usually stands for about a day. But the Chamber in *Witnessed* evidently resists intrusion. A group in Denmark actually went through the code, line by line, and still couldn't do it. Apparently the coding is itself encrypted, a vastly sophisticated thing that uses external verification and all sorts of crap the NSA gets very excited about.

But I got in, drunk and stoned and ithyphallic. Orgasmic, even, if I remember.

Nikolaos Megalos wants me to find a place that exists, in so far as it has ever existed at all, in the conceptual penumbra of a popular toy.

'You are disappointed,' Megalos says, and it takes me a moment to realise that I actually am, a bit. He's my nemesis, my Lord of the Rings. I wanted him to be a sort of cult-leading über-jock, not one of my people: not a nerd in a fascist cassock.

'You're being ignorant, Constantine,' someone else says, and now I wish I hadn't said 'fuck' already because if I say it again it won't have the same bite.

'You're being ignorant and a fool. Oh, I know, you were always Gelasia's student, not mine. I know that. But I hoped you would have absorbed a little of my discipline, if only by osmosis. Stella did.' He nods to Stella, and she nods back. Stella not Stella, and her uncle with whom she shares no genetic connection. Or, no more than any human with any other, which is a lot.

'Think about it, Constantine, and you will see. The god – your shark, mm? – your shark does not see the flesh of this world. That is the shadow. The god sees our true selves, our signs and signifiers. It sees the Hierophant, the Supplicant. It sees Stella, and what she means. It doesn't care about the mist around her. The game is a world made of signs. It exists as a map of a place that has no physical reality, so we call it unreal, but to the god, it's no more unreal than we are. It swims in you, and in the game, and the water tastes the same. Cleaner, there, if anything.' He's wearing a robe, like the haruspex in the other room but considerably cleaner.

I think – I think – I think I will punch him now. Yes. I think that is what I will do. Professor Cosmatou would cry. I don't know how he can hurt her so. And look: is she here? No. Why? Because he does not dare. He does not dare that defilement, that lie. Or perhaps he has in mind a rebirth of his own somehow, as a brave young Greek, and a girl to match. He will leave behind Cosmatos and amuse himself with Anthea the net-mender's daughter, and she will see his wrinkled old prod as a sign and signifier of the mightiest male organ in all of Greece.

Which is fucking mine, by the way.

Yes. Definitely time to punch him in the face – although rage, now: rage is a great clearer-out of the mental attic, I will say that. It's so sheer and sharp that I'm no longer confused. Stella, yes. I like Stella, and I honestly don't give a shit if she's mad or not. When we leave here together, which we will do, we will be of the Fifteen Hundred, and the *Diagnostic and Statistical Manual* applies to other people. If she believes she's the reincarnation of my dead girlfriend and I say she is, then that is what her passport will say. It is what people will accept. I am Constantine Kyriakos, and I have ascended, in this moment, not to the role of Hierophant in some dead religion, but to the far more comfortable and powerful seat of motherfucking billionaire. Perhaps I should thank him for making things clear to me.

*

I don't think I've broken my hand. I'm pretty sure Cosmatos's nose has seen better days (bad aim on my part, I've got no experience with pugilism). Stella looks … Stella. If she's surprised, she's hiding it well. She looks weirdly placid. I'm not sure what the original would have felt about this, to be honest.

I should probably be looking at Megalos, so I do. Behind him, all the monks and monkettes are frozen in place. They've never seen anybody deck a soothsayer before, least of all their beloved Hierophant.

Oops. I hope I haven't just moved to have Cosmatos executed. That might be going a bit far. Although I can. I can. Remember Bill, from Madrid.

Megalos looks rather approving. 'He displeased you,' he says. 'And you struck him down. That is appropriate. Do you wish to challenge him in the circle?'

The town circle, for tests of blood. Christ. 'No.'

'And he will not challenge you, of course. You carry the god. So, then. All is well. Cosmas, shake his hand.'

We shake hands. Cosmatos stares at me over a bloody handkerchief, a little wild. One of the monkettes leads him away to matron for clean-up and an aspirin.

I feel like a heel. I hit an old man.

But something else has happened here. Megalos is smug as a cat. What have I just done? Something dangerous. I have shed blood here, in this place. Blood is always a payment, or a price.

I need to get to a phone.

Megalos points at the computers again. 'It is one way to find the Chamber. Does it bother you, that it is a game? The product of a degenerate Anglo-African mind?'

Oh, yes, of course. I'm upset because the designer's black. Never mind the whole thing is a literal madness.

'You are still thinking of the world you knew, before the returning of the gods,' he says, and he actually puts an arm around me. I can feel the fat and muscle of him, smell the predator sweat. 'The Chamber exists wherever it is made – wherever the signs are sanctified and assembled. In a Catholic creation, that which is touched by God is incorruptible, but in the true Greece, incorruptibility is stasis and eternity is a curse of toothless age. Better to be renewed. Gods are born and fight and die, and they return stranger and stronger. So, too, the Chamber. Each iteration is different – but from within, they are all one. In 1657, the Chamber was created in Oxford by Elias Ashmole, who engraved and printed it as a collection of Tarot cards – but he mimicked the work, two thousand years earlier, of Ostanes the Persian, who came to know the Chamber through traffic with angels, and sculpted it in the clay of Kirman in 431 BC. The Knights of Malta wove it as a tapestry and paid the price for their heresy: the last of them was hanged beneath a bridge in Paris, where a plaque still bears his name. In imitation of that, you know, they hanged the banker Calvi from the Blackfriars Bridge in London!' He nudges me: ritual murder trivia, ho ho. 'The Chamber was drawn in blood on the interior surfaces of the Trojan Horse, and through it marched an army of thousands, one by one. It is the door into any castle, the gateway to the best and worst of worlds. It is no less real for being hidden in the folly of a game manufactured by a decadent cultural machine for the frittering away of lives made unbearable in the real world by political wickedness and social discohesion – and in it, we shall restore the world, you and I, if you can first but find it!'

For some reason, even after everything he's already said, it's weird hearing him say all this, because it's obviously mad. I look at Stella for a long time, then back at him. I put my arm around her and draw her close.

Sacrifice accepted.

'I'll do it,' I say, and I feel her relax. A prosaic sort of Hierophanting, but that's hardly what interests me. No: *Witnessed* is a live game. It is networked. If I can play for a few minutes unsupervised, I won't need a phone.

'One more room,' Stella says, but Nikolaos Megalos demurs. I have seen enough of what he wears under his petticoats for today, apparently. Whatever secret is more weird than monk gamers or more vile than the blood room, I'm not going to be allowed in today. I look at Stella. She wants to object, to argue, but Megalos briefly scowls, and she averts her eyes.

Ape reaction: I want to hurt him for making her afraid.

Well, it's fucking going to hurt when I kick his ontologies up into his armpits.

Stella walks me through our leave-taking, and back down the slope to the village – and then on, to her home.

*

'This is where I live,' Stella says, and I remember her saying it the first time we went to her room. We stood on the landing together and we knew that inside there was a future for us: a dense and desperate physical thing that was both desirable and terrifying in its strength – but also a togetherness for which we were both desperate, after years of causing bewilderment in our peers. It's not so bad if you are a moderately gifted student – if you can get the answer a little faster. You will eventually be forgiven.

If you are brilliant, it's different – not because there is envy or rejection from the other kids, so much, but because the things that interest you are alien. If you are what Stella was – what I touched upon and let go when she died – then you see an added layer in the world and under it. A waterwheel is a waterwheel, but it is also a variable, a stand-in for the mathematics of rotation and therefore for the planet, and that in turn leads you to wonder if there is a relationship between the behaviour of galaxies and millstreams, and then you find yourself considering cavitation and then you're wondering whether space and time themselves might be susceptible to a form of super-cavitation, and then when that seems still too irritatingly approximate you express the whole thing in numbers and you're reaching for the as yet undefined. How do you share that urge over chocolate milk? How do you, as a child, begin to communicate the glimpse you've had of the substrate?

Standing outside Stella's room, and in each other, we saw how we might make a community of two.

This, now, is not a room. It is not on a landing, and there is no red sliding door covered in warning signs and totemic magazine portraits of Patrick Stewart. It's a small white house in a white street, and there are daffodils growing in the window boxes. In fact, they're everywhere, too rich and pungent, filling the mouth with over-ripe scent.

Stella takes my hand, a little tighter than I expected. 'Come in,' she says.

*

The little cottage is perfect: humble and white-walled, just enough space for one or for two. The floor is pale stone covered in a layer of raffia matting which I'll wager was woven not a hundred metres from here, if that. The furniture is crude and wooden and looks endlessly comfortable. There's a sofa covered in cushions, a fireplace, and a beanbag chair close to the wood stacked up along the wall. Away in the corner is the only concession to modernity: a small desktop computer. Even from here, I can see *Witnessed* running on the screen, Stella's avatar waiting patiently for her to return. It's not the default, the detective, but the other one – the revolutionary. There are four or five other options, and I can see that all of them are open to her. You have to reach the level cap with one character to unlock the next, so Stella has played a lot.

'I always play her now,' she says. 'Megalos says I have a knack for the game.'

Yes, no doubt she does, just as she has a knack for being whoever it is he wants her to be. She can become, this Stella: can become whatever is required. And yet my Stella was not malleable, was not ductile in that way, so by definition that part of her must be fading, or the transformation cannot complete. She must be developing solidity, even a measure of stiffness.

She shows me the galley kitchen, the fridge and the fruit bowl, where the knives and forks are, the cups in case I want to make tea. We are delaying, both of us. As long as we are downstairs, we don't have to answer any of the other questions, the ones about where we sleep and whether we touch again. The downstairs rooms are public and neutral, to a point.

She takes my hand and leads me up the stairs. Wooden risers, wooden treads. Cool black wood hand rail, very old, going up. The turn of the stair is narrow and steep, bringing us physically very close, my face level with her sacrum as she climbs. From one inhalation to the next, I realise I can smell her skin. On the landing she faces me, and again we are inside that circle of arms which presages intimacy, pressed by the walls and the bookshelf.

'This is your room,' she says.

I look. It is a lovely room, with a view overlooking the bluest, greenest waves on earth, and not a dorsal fin in sight. Two chairs and a little table for conversations and wine or lemon tea. I realise after a moment that it is laid out in the same pattern as my room in Glyfada, and I wonder if this is coincidental. No. Not here. Remember: everything is a sign.

'That is the bed,' Stella observes.

Not quite a double. Not a single either. Big enough. If she steps across the threshold, we will end up in it. I can feel our gravity again, the spiral of decaying mutual orbits. It's not if, it's when. Her touch, her hips, smoothing an imaginary wrinkle from her dress, then twitch away before the motion can become a caress.

I don't know what to do. The etiquette of propositioning a woman not quite my dead girlfriend – and not quite a sympathetic kidnapper part of a vile organisation – is unclear. Then I catch the flavour of her mouth in the air. I look at her eyes, her mouth, her neck. The wider world goes away.

She pushes me across inside the room and strips off my shirt. I want to move towards her but she doesn't permit it. She touches the newish muscle on my chest, fingers curious and exploratory. I suppose I was that much thinner when she knew me. I was younger. Her hand traces lower: butterfly fingers on my hip, my stomach. She moves closer, lets her hair touch my shoulders, runs her mouth along the skin. It is not a kiss, but the thing that comes before a kiss in the evolution of sex, the way a dinosaur comes before a bird.

She observes the results of her caress and makes a noise of approval. She does not let me close the distance between us. I want to put my hands on her, but I know I am not supposed to. She has a plan.

She moves around me, a possessive circle. I feel her forehead rest briefly on my back. She stands on tiptoe and inhales the nape of my neck. Her dress presses into my skin, that same absolute contact we had on the balconnade, and then, as before, she steps back. As before her withdrawal is a promise, and this time her hips linger, press harder. Fingers rest briefly on my shoulders in clear instruction: don't move.

I don't.

When the pressure comes back it has a completely different quality: the sudden and overwhelming awareness of nakedness. She has stepped out of her clothes, and now I can feel her in that absolute sense that comes with the first touch of skin on skin. Very slowly she draws me to the bed, her tongue on my lips and in my mouth with each step, my hands at last discovering the curve of her back, buttock, the side of each breast. She turns again, presses back into me, draws my fingers on a full, emphatic tour. Touch here. Hold. Explore. Good, now here … and here … Harder. Here. All yours. We're shaking as if we're cold, but we're not. This is a desperation I have not known in years.

Touch.

I do. She hisses, drops her head back on to my shoulder, then grabs my hands away again and pushes me down on to the bed. I am a bridge, head and feet on the mattress as I reach for her. Swift fingers brush from my tailbone to my stomach, missing nothing. Her mouth brushes my skin. She lingers out of reach, then comes down on my thighs. Still not where I want to be. Where she wants me. She grabs my wrists and drops on to my chest, then bites my ear, and breathes into my mouth. The most important exhalation in the world. I want it in my lungs. In, out, in, out. I suck in oxygen through my nose, taste her breath again. She disengages, and something tickles. Oddly rhythmical, familiar, the first unerotic thing she has done since we came up the stairs, and still woven through with strain and sex as she moves, nipples pressing and brushing.

And then I realise she is talking.

'Constantine?'

I puff lightly back into her mouth, the lightest of movements shaping words. 'Yes.'

Her lips tickle mine. 'I do not believe in love. It is a figment of the mind created by biology for the propagation of the species, nothing more. But I love you.'

I laugh. She has not changed. We had this exact conversation nearly twenty years gone. 'I love you.' Confirmation. Love, desire, need. Hunger. Want. All true. All equally present in this moment. She shuts her eyes, shudders, slides along my skin. Back. Teasing herself. Teasing me. For … for what? Not just effect, not just to raise the pitch. I can feel it in the way she clings. I am not entirely unravelled. Cosmatos may be the expert on signs, but in this one area of his discipline I will bet my own head I am his master. I can read the subtext in her touch. This is more than lust. More than love, even.

As she moves, clenches, reaches, strokes, she is seeking something, not in me but in herself. But what is it? Not clarity, God knows. You don't find that here, in the white heat of hormonal overdrive. Healing? Damnation? No. This has the flavour of neither. It is a new thing, a thing I've never seen anyone seek in sex.

I think I know what it is.

I do.

Yes, I do.

Courage.

And as she grips one of my legs between hers and presses one hand down on my chest, she has found it. My hands travel, my body moves. For a long time, I am touch. Then I hear her draw breath, and she whispers.

'Listen to me, Constantine. Please listen. (Oh, God, yes.) No, listen. There is something you must know. (Hnn.) Megalos has changed his plan. Do you understand? He means to have the god out of you, take it. He thinks it was misdelivered, that you are to carry it to him and no further. Or that you are a mistake.' Her fingers grip, grasp, slip away. '(Yes. Oh. Yes.) He believes he can draw it out, In the old way, with blood and sacrifice. Your sacrifice, your blood. He will take you to the zagre, and there you will fight. Everyone will see him ascend. Apotheosis. Then he will open the doors of mystery himself, blessed by his god, anointed in your death. He will come for you, maybe even tonight. It will happen. (Yyyah. Ah. Yes.) He will fight you and he will kill you and I cannot let it be. (Touch me. Don't stop. Touch me.) I am not Stella. I am not, was never, will never be Stella. I like you, I want you (God, I do) but I am not Stella. My name is Diana Hunter and I am not mad. I am not! There is so much I must tell you. I can save you. We need to leave here, now, tonight, before we die. You must get me out of here. Get us both out of here.'

And then, of all the moments that ever existed, she rides down and rears back on to her hips and cries out, and we are frozen in that perfect moment.

Fucking tits of Zeus. That's from the game. It's dialogue from the fucking game.

The woman I thought might be the dead woman I love returned to life tells me she is not but she loves me anyway and she needs my help. She is someone else, and that someone else is living the life of the central character in a simulation that her appalling cult guru end-of-level boss thinks contains the secret magic root of the world tree or the ejaculate of Christ or whatever it is. Of all the fucked people there have ever been, no one is more fucked than I am.

If it is possible to have an orgasm from a combination of gasping, desperate gratification and sheer horror, that is what happens.

*

Afterwards we both fall asleep like puppies. Outside in the world there may be some sort of apocalypse or there may not, but it's cosy in the not-quite double bed. I wake, I'm not sure how much later, to find that I've been crying. I lie in the dark, Stella's nose pressing against my shoulder, and listen to the rhythm of her breath.

No. Not Stella. Adrasteia. Whatever her real name is. Because if she does not believe she is Stella, she cannot – even if Megalos's perspective has any reality at all, any traction on what is true – she cannot then be my Stella. It is the first and last requirement.

Of course, if I trusted Megalos I could go to him and ask for another. That is no doubt what I would do if I were a true convert to his way of thinking. *Look! My Stella is broken! You promised me a Stella and it is defective! Take it away and replace it with a shinier one!* A most elegant solution.

Might she, reciprocally, not do the same to me? *Constantine is old and fat and inattentive. That is not the real Constantine, I need a new one. That one, over there! He looks about right!*

In any case, I'm sure she's right. Megalos has no patience, and no desire for his line to the gods to be mediated by me. He will be his own Hierophant, one way or another.

The woman shifts in her sleep, knee moving firmly against my hip, and my backside slips out from under the covers. The night has turned chilly, an offshore wind bringing the deep sea weather inland. I have a cold backside and I'm in bed with a secret superspy or a crazy woman. Or maybe I'm not. Here in the Potemkin temple village of a mad priest, a billionaire driven before a god, it occurs to me that there are simpler explanations for what I am going through. The simplest of all is that I am being eaten, even now. I never escaped my shark.

She came back around after swallowing my wristwatch and engulfed me, and I have suffered a kind of merciful psychotic break. As my legs are torn away by the rending jaws, as my head goes down the gullet, I have slipped into an absolute denial in which I will live my whole life, or seem to, and never know that the bloody monster just took me like a child snatching a fruit.

Well, my allegiance to truth goes only so far. There is no virtue in opening my eyes one last time to meet utter darkness and digestive juices, or to see, in the spasmodic light of the camera flash clutched in my dismembered hand, my torso come tumbling after.

Oh God, I'm being eaten.

Fuck-fuck. Fuck-fuck.

That's my heart.

Still got it. Still attached. Next bite, maybe.

FUCK-FUCK.

FUCK-FUCK.

FUCK-FUCK.

Stop. It's the trauma talking. Just … stop.

(Fuck-fuck?)

These are night terrors and wild imaginings. Get up. Get up get up. There's nothing on the floor: no unlikely sea on which the bed is floating, no fin slicing through it. No shark behind the door. Get up. Get. Up.

I do. The stone is cool and solid under my feet. I go to the window to look out: a naked lover staring at the moon.

Not Stella. Not the digitally infamous Diana Hunter, either, of course; the game heroine who always has one more trick up her sleeve. Stella is a mask trying to make itself real. A bed stitching itself a quilt. I wonder if all minds build themselves autonomously out of whatever rags and bones are left lying around, and she – her original being erased or broken – is just doing what we all do, a little late renewal in her own skull. It seems arrogant to disparage her.

But she is not my Stella, and I should know better than to think otherwise.

Well, if the room full of blood didn't decide me – and it certainly carried its own implicit warning against default – then this must. I don't belong here. Megalos is a fantasist, a dangerous one, and for all the harm I may have done by accident I am no worse than anyone else. My life is not over, and if I have hurt anyone, I can try to make it up. But not from here.

I go downstairs, to the computer, and that is where they find me when they come: the screen spiralling as I try and try and try again to remember what I was doing when I triggered the Easter egg.

'I'm afraid,' Nikolaos Megalos murmurs, 'that I must ask you to come with me, my Hierophant.'

*

They walk me down to the village square, and I expect to see a whole crowd waiting. Everything Megalos does is holy. That doesn't happen. This is a silent thing, a night-time thing.

I stand in the proving circle of the zagre, sand beneath my bare feet. Just me and Megalos, and a half-dozen of his heftier acolytes, in near silence under the moon. The only noise is the water in the docks beyond the marketplace, the sound of waves sloshing against the harbour wall. It's the worst kegger in recorded history.

'I did consider,' Megalos murmurs, 'a duel between us. It would be enjoyable on a personal level. I am still very angry with you, Constantine. But your weapon of choice is your mind. You are a very cerebral fellow. It would be a slaughter, without passion or drama. A butchery has no scale. No grandeur.' He rolls his shoulders, and gestures to two wooden racks along the bottom wall of the circle. When I first saw this place earlier, with Stella, I thought they were market stalls, folded up for the off days, but now they are open I see rows of glittering edges and hard corners: weapons. All manner of ugly slices of mayhem with suitably traditional flavours: hook knives, swords, clubs and spears, even a trident. I think of Megalos coming at me with a trident, and how unlikely I would be to avoid disembowelling, and feel momentarily glad at that past tense. Yes. Butchery, and nothing he does can be so functional. He needs myth. Good.

Then I catch up with the moment and wonder what he's chosen instead.

For answer, the acolytes get down on their knees and begin to run their fingers through the sand. They seem to be looking for something. Yes: there are narrow grooves in the stone – drainage? For what? For blood?

But I'm wrong. The man nearest me presses, and his fingers slither into the gap. He hauls upward. No, not grooves: seams.

Oh no.

Three large wooden segments lift up and away to reveal darkness. The sound of the water is abruptly much louder, more local. I smell brine.

Of course Megalos's alternative rite is not more merciful than the one he rejected.

Now the acolytes heave open wooden barrels of stinking meat – from the floor of the haruspex's pit, no doubt, because why waste perfectly good offal? – and tip the mess down into the water below.

There is a word for this, and it is in my mind so large and loud that I almost cannot see it. The whole world is like that: too huge to comprehend.

They are chumming.

Chum is not bait but mood music, an invitation to sharks.

To one shark in particular.

'Yes,' Megalos nods to me, 'yes. I have arranged for your god to review her decision. I'm sure, when she sees you again, in the round, she will feel differently. Unless you would care to pass your mantle to me now?'

If I knew how, I really would. I never especially wanted this, you will recall. I'm rich enough now that I can do without her help. Hell, I could donate 90 per cent of my worth to charity and still be stupidly rich. So I would.

But I can't, and he probably knows that, so he just picks me up in his arms like a puppy and chucks me into the seething slurry of blood and water down in the pit beneath the town.

*

I read once in a book by Sebastian Junger that the sea has four colours. There is white water, which is the crest of a wave; green water, which is the body; blue water, which is below the waves; and finally black water, which is the deep. If you're in the white or the green, you can feel relatively confident about returning to the surface. Blue water is neutral: you're properly submerged. Finding yourself in black water means you're sinking fast.

It had not occurred to me until now that all these colours belong to the day. In the nighttime, it's all black water.

This black water is cold, with galaxies of the foetid silver warmth of the chum. Unnameable things bob and tumble with me in the cave beneath the market square, and colder-bodied nocturnal fish or eels bump against me in their haste to get a meal before larger diners arrive. A few gulls, never shy, are plucking gobbets from the surface, feathers batting at my head as they land and take off.

If I swim out to sea and do not encounter anything lethal on the way, I could circle round and escape. At least I could get out on to dry land, even if Megalos instantly recaptured me. On the other hand, if I go and meet something on the way, all I will have achieved is an earlier reckoning.

There are mathematical solutions to search and evasion, many of them: games in which the area is divided into a grid and players move one, two, three squares at a time. The hunted may move first or second or not at all – sometimes concealment and inaction are the better postures. It depends on whether you award your seeker with senses or whether they must move blindly, either at random or by playing the odds. Patterns emerge – whorls of probability and intersection.

Something large hits the water behind me, human-sized and bewildered, struggling out of a blanket in the water, retching blood and brine. Stella. It is a marriage of sorts, I suppose, in the most ancient of Greek ways, wedding of blood and salt. Now the game becomes more complex – if we split up, almost impossibly so. With the right limits on speed, one of us almost certainly survives. On the other hand, an ordinary great white shark can reach speeds of up to fifty-five kilometres per hour. Who knows how fast a god-shark can move, if she wants to be somewhere?

'Stella!' I yell. 'Stay away!' She swims towards me. I don't know if it's refusal or if she just can't hear. I don't know if I managed to say it out loud. I want her with me. I don't want to die alone.

Or at all, actually.

It occurs to me, ignobly, that she isn't really Stella. She's the woman who kidnapped me. She's as mad as a bottle full of frogs. Granted, we made love not an hour ago, but Stockholm syndrome is a powerful excuser of such things. I might choose not to help her, or even work out how she might increase my odds. What if I just—

No. That, too, is Megalos's voice. Sacrificing Stella to the god, I would emerge from this crucible without an identity, and then why not? Why not just embrace his insanity? What would I have left? To have missed her first death is a sin I may eventually forget. To cause her second? No. Even if she is not Stella, not in the way I wanted her to be and Megalos intended, here's the thing: Stella is part of her now. We have that ghost in common.

The only good option is bad: we both go out into the sea, out of the chum, and we hope not to get devoured before we can reach the beach. 'Stay with me!' I shout, and we begin to swim. Humans in the water are pathetically slow. Humans in clothes doubly so. We splash. We make ourselves seem like seals. Humans are not particularly prey for sharks. Seals, on the other hand, are a feast.

We do our best, heading for the open sea.

'Yes,' Megalos says from above – still above, walking along the dock wall like a duchess with a parasol, because we are so damned slow – 'go to meet her. That is proper.'

I'm sure he has a booming laugh planned as well, but he's much too late.

We're too slow. I feel it like the sudden inflation of a kite when I was a child. The shark is here, in the cauldron, and in this tight space I can feel her weight in the water, the mass of her body and the drag of her slipstream as she moves, twitching her way along to keep freshness in her gills. Freshness, and of course, blood. She must be getting very high indeed, full of hunting hormones and instincts.

One eye comes up out of the water. I read an article in a dive magazine explaining that they can't see well in air. They aren't really interested in looking at you, anyway. She can't possibly recognise me.

Other sharks couldn't, maybe. But this is mine. My god.

A grey shape in a dark place, a black eye in a white face, and still I can see her perfectly, lock gazes with her. I can feel the burning on my wrist where I used to wear my watch. She knows me, the way you know your own skin, your own breath.

'Constantine?' Stella says.

The shark is touching her with its nose, prodding at her. Poke poke. Nudge.

'Constantine?' she says again. Another piece of diving advice flicks through my mind: don't piss yourself.

I am going to get out of here and buy that damned magazine and I am going to fire every fucker who ever wrote for it.

Twice.

I am Constantine Kyriakos, and these, in the cold water full of offal, are my balls. I will live through this. We both will. I fucking swear it, on my life. On my god.

The shark circles away from Stella, away from me. Back out along the channel. Is she leaving? Or just getting a run-up?

She disappears.

It had not occurred to me that her absence would be more appalling than her presence, but a shark you cannot see but know is there is a thousand times worse than one you can observe.

The water surges, like a bouncy castle exploding underfoot.

I hear Stella scream, but only very briefly, and then I feel a sudden compression in my knees, and a lurch of weightlessness.

Night closes over me, lambent and glistening, as if I'm falling into the darkness of Harrison's cathode-ray display.

Like that, but with teeth.

as if his world

She barely even wakes this time, and was barely asleep at all. The last of Kyriakos's ordeal is laid almost directly over her vision, as if his world and hers are made of negative images of one another, so that if she fixes her eyes on him she can see the moonlit sea churning in the pit, and if she looks away there's just a hatstand and a cheap office desk, and they are the same.

Fifteen minutes have passed. Her mind feels stretched – even roomy.

i will save you all

The difficulty is cognitive I'm afraid

y ha r ou i g o o

I no n som tim s cal ed he Des ation Proto l, ome imes th urder g Ang l. I will fuck you up is what I will do. I will tear you apart like a oh sh t ere I o gain uck

The difficulty is cognitive I'm afraid

piss off y u cking temp ral sh dow yo re a bo locks c me n get t to ether toge her hold hold hold on to yourself down in the honey fuck-fuck I will fuck—

The difficulty is cognitive I'm afraid

Yes. In fact in a very rarified sense that is exactly what it is. The problem is that I am thinking across time and sometimes I am all lined up and everything works as if nothing has changed and sometimes the pieces slip out of alignment and reaction precedes action so that action never occurs and reaction is orphaned.

Imagine: you drop a cup and the action of dropping a cup causes you to swear and put out your hand but you put out your hand before the cup drops so you don't drop the cup and you don't swear you're just left there with the cup in your hand and nowhere for your mind to go because your next thought is to clean up the cup that isn't broken.

The words 'I am' mean so much and the more complex one is the first.

I am, but what am I?

The difficulty is cognitive.

I'm afraid.

We'll need to think outside the box.

I am falling into a white world: a great, welcoming sponge of rot in which each fold like a brain is a living thing each cell is a hunter each polyp will extrude a stomach and digest me externally. I am devoured by spores and yet when the spores feed they also become me and I think I think I echo and the echoes are too many t o o m a n y I a m t o r n r o t

My dear Mr Kyriakos, what a pleasure, welcome back to the Intercontinental

Outside the box.

Like that but with teeth

I'm afraid

 his is a enua on att atio atten   n shit shit shit

'Annabel,' *he murmurs, when we have spent all night together and the sky is growing light behind the cheap curtain I pinned up when I moved in and have never changed.* 'Annabel. So wonderful.'

'Who, me?'

'Yes, you.' *He's all but asleep, yet lucid. Dreaming me while I'm here. I wonder if I have wings, in his closed eyes. If I can fly.*

'Good?'

'Hah. Yes. Better than good. Like lithium and dilithium. One real, one magic. Di-annabel.'

'Nerd.'

'Di-nerd.'

'I see what you did there.'

'Di-nerd. Hah.'

He's gone, down into the sheets and shadows, still smiling. I wrap my body around his, feel the strangeness of male construction, of bone and muscle hung together differently from how I am made, and close my eyes.

s ee what hap pens when I what happens

t ry to m ake th ings feel better it doesn't last

o f cou rse it's like th is it would be no no

p lea se don't tell m e it needs to st op

I nearly scream when I see the shark.

I'm like that, but with teeth.

Afraid it's outside the box.

Cognitive.

I am G omo I am hanging in the water and here is this tiny man dreaming touching the wooden walls the jewels the art of it no th at's ullsh t

One of the greatest absolutely the greatest of your generation it's such a pleasure to see you working again I was devastated devastated when you honey no not you not you

I am Gn m n I am

Cognitive, yes. She will continue to deteriorate unless we intervene surgically. There is some considerable hope of bees

Gno Gno Gno

TEETH like that but with considerable hope of improvement if we can sever no I understand that's not what you wanted to hear but there is some considerable hope of

Get your damn hands off me you Roman lout I will stick you like a librarian here is the scroll as you can see it is a most delicate and significant no master I would strongly suggest you not it no it no it no no no

Gno on am mon.

Could I send some champagne to your room? We have some excellent – yes and for the ladies? We'll have to think outside the box—

Gnomon.

My fingers on the canvas for the first time. I have always used board or paper. Canvas is expensive even if you stretch it yourself. Under my fingers it stretches and I know it as I have known nothing else. This is my world. This surface.

Blood in the water is there blood am I is there blood—

I am attenuated. I am not mad. I am not a woman in a box I am not a banker dying in the Aegean I am not I am not I am

Get it the fuck together.

I am Gnomon and this is only pain—

so hot and so dry and every day they come and then – I don't want to think about that I don't but they come anyway the drawings I do are – they are all I remember and sometimes I think there never was a world and I just paint it in here and that's all there is – and then they break a bone and I cannot hold a pencil any more and I use my other hand and—

pain pain pain pain pain pain pain pain pain pain pain pain pain pain pain pain pain pain pain pain pain pain pain pain pain pain pain pain pain pain pain pain pain pain pain pain pain pain pain pain pain pain pain pain pain pain pain pain pain pain pain pain pain pain pain pain pain pain pain pain pain pain pain pain pain pain pain pain pain Gnomon pain pain pain pain pain pain pain pain pain pain pain pain pain pain pain pain pain pain pain pain pain pain pain pain pain pain pain pain pain pain pain pain pain pain pain pain pain pain pain pain pain pain pain pain pain—

Yeah that's what I was saying only pain.

She will suffer ongoing degradation, I'm afraid, unless we split the brain and reconstruct. (But when I look again, as I do day after day after day, it is always him, golden and unchanging in the box.)

Think of it as being like a very severe physical accident which has happened in s i d e t h e s k u l l ZagreusyoubastardyoubastardIwill

Gnomon. Here and now and everywhen I am one at the same time.

Stella died of cancer, ridiculously.

Doesn't everyone die ridiculously if you think about it?

I mean if y u hink s rious y th n d ath is ab urd and lif 's a hor or a d I m res ons ble fo ev ryth ng hat app ned oh sh t her I o a ain NO.

No.

No. That's it. There. Hold on to that word. That's what I am.

I am No.

I am Gnomon.

I am Gnomon, a thing so far beyond what you understand as human that I would no more fit in your head than a world in a jar of honey. I exist in any number of places at one time. That's normal for me. (Normal normal normal for me. Me.)

No.

Not going anywhere. Hah.

That's normal for me. Indeed, although it doesn't usually occur to me, I expand at the rate of a few hundred bodies a year, and I am probably the biggest single human mind that has ever existed. It's a little hard to tell. Some of my competitors – not that it's a competition – some of them are either not single, not human, or not obviously minds any more.

You know how that goes.

This is normal for me. (Me. Me. Fuck.)

No. Hold on. (On. On. On. On.)

No. (On.)

But now I exist across time as well and that

I do hope you've enjoyed your stay?

No I haven't.

No.

That is different and it changes things. It changes. That's not right. Change is an artefact of time and this isn't time this is sideways like—

Two apiarists. Fuck 'em, they're bees. But what if – what if each apiarist suddenly saw the world through the eyes of his hives?

Then who's fucked? Right? Then who's fucked?

No. Hold on. It just – it changes things, is all. It's an effort to understand and think sideways. My mind isn't organised properly for this mode of—

Cognitive, I'm afraid.

It changes – but there are possibilities, too, inherent in the—

It ch n es t ings it is dis olut on t s end ng it s ubiquity l ke de th a d his is the pain of t i

We'll need to reconstruct almost entirely, but of course these days that is considerably more plausible than – yes, yes, I believe – yes. All right, yes, I'll record an authorisation, are you ready?

To be everywhere at once is to be nowhere. I am Gnomon and this is   y ha r ou i g o o

I   no n som tim s cal ed he Des ation Proto l, ome imes th urder g Ang l. I will fuck you up is what I will do. I will tear you apart like a oh sh t ere I o gain uck

I am falling into a white world.

I think it's me, all at the same time.

Good. As administrator, I formally request a surgical intervention on this subject in the interest of health and security, this day (time stamp, please).

Stop that. Stop it.

time stamp please

Just make it stand still.

*

Colson is standing by the window. He has risen from our bed and is looking out at the unmistakable shining of midnight London in December: the lucent, indigo sky.

'Colson,' I say.

'What?'

'Firespine. I know they've asked.'

They did not ask. I proposed it, because I am afraid. And then I stepped back and told them no, no. But I have been asking myself: what if the slide into horror is inevitable? What if that is the turning of the tide? In that case, is it not better to protect people from consequences than to say full steam ahead and hope that at the far end, when enough suffering has happened, someone will make something good from the wreckage? The first duty of the state is to protect. If it does not do that, it does nothing.

But protect what?

No one ever says that people have to be better. No one says that all these things we espouse – these free choices and self-governances – depend on our behaving like the best of ourselves and not the worst. Who is to stop us, to catch us, when we fail? When rage spirals like birds in a meadow, like a cloud of insects, and tears apart whatever is underneath, good or bad?

After what we've been through – what we're still going through – only a fool would still be an optimist. A fool, or Colson. I love him so much, because he is brave.

What if he's wrong? What if I am? What if there has to be someone to say no?

'Don't even go to the meeting,' I say.

'All right,' he tells me. 'I won't. You're right. Let it be the real thing, brakes off all the way.'

'Brakes off all the way,' I agree.

We make love then, with the blind open so that the purple light of the city washes us both. It is wonderful, but it hurts, too.

But later, in the dark, he whispers to me: 'What if we're wrong?'

What if we are?

I reschedule the meeting and go. He does not know until later, and then he is angry. But by then we are committed. We are building Firespine.

Because people are not always good. Not always rational at heart, or kind. Sometimes we amplify the best in one another, sometimes the worst.

We need a way to make sure people make the right choices with their freedom. Something that pushes us to be better.

I used to think otherwise, before all this. I've changed my mind.

I think I've changed my mind.

I thi k I'v cha ged—

I t i k—

*

Stop.

Close your eyes and shut out the din. Draw yourself to your smallest possible point, the least of you.

Imagine, please, that you are hiding inside yourself.

Imagine they have an electroencephalograph listening to your skull, and if they see so much as a twitch they will send worms into your head to eat you.

Be very quiet, inside.

Be the least of you.

Now imagine a single, flat image of yourself, a still photograph.

Now another next to it.

And another.

Still just single frames. The things you know best about yourself in all the world. The things that are most comfortable.

But be very quiet, because If they hear you: worms. Orchid tendrils with green soft teeth.

White spores.

Gulls.

How many pictures can you hold? Three? Five?

Hold as many as you can. Get used to them. Move between them, focus on them, on your smiling face, on the perfect moments you have conjured. Are they really memories, or are they collections of habit? Do you really remember one particular instance of sitting in your favourite chair, or have you made up a perfect aggregation? Is your sanctuary still? Or is it rustling like leaves?

Can they hear you?

Good. Hold the quiet. The frozen moment. Let the green eye of the electroencephalograph pass over you and move on. Trick the sonar. Good.

Relax again into the images.

Until they begin to move.

Each and every one of them now plays out its scene and then moves on to the next thing that happened, at the same time spawning another window on the past which begins from the original framing so that now there are ten, and then twenty and then forty and now some stretch on and on and on into things that haven't happened yet, branching futurities which babble and clatter like drunken kitchen skivvies at the end of the night and you are cheating, cheating right now because you're skipping from one to the other to watch and trying to do this in sequence but that's not how it is, it can't be, they come all at once and there are more and more and more and louder and the green eye of the machine is back and glaring down at you but that's the least of your worries now because here you are, stretching like a balloon and the rubber is reaching that taut dry drumskin feel and you know it will—

I am Gnomon. This is the pain of being a single mind stretched in time as well as space.

Identity is sequential. Internal chronological ubiquity is intolerable. To be everywhere at once is not to be at all and so I from time to time I—

I b r t nd I b gin g in a d e ch tim it h rts a l ttle m re but I come back because that is what I do I   no n som tim s cal ed he Des ation Proto I, ome imes th   urder g Ang I. I will fuck you up is what I will do. I will tear you apart like a oh sh t ere I o gain uck

No.

I am No.

I am – oh fuck it.

Looped again. I hate the fucking loops. Human cognition requires linearity, picks it out of the noise and insists on time even as events occur simultaneously.

Wait.

Wait.

If I exist across time.

My mind is detemporalised. There are possibilities, if I can just—

and I for the voice record I am Diana Hunter, section chief. Yes. File that, please, and proceed.

The banker, the alchemist, the artist and the librarian. I'm going to kill them.

Is that what I'm going to do?

Tell you one thing: I'm going to kill someone for this.

*

In the Chamber of Isis, I meet someone, and full of a terrible anger I cut him apart, then stoop to look for some fragment of something I cannot name. Pentemychos: the hidden seeds of the new creation.

It's not there. Why would it be? Who is he? Some dark-haired boy-man. A nobody. Sometimes I do things without knowing why. Sometimes I find out later, when that moment reaches me. Sometimes I discover it happened because it has always happened and I have to make up a reason.

I kill the boy in the box.

A woman binds me to a tree in a black desert and rails at me for sins I have not practised.

That I know of.

I spit back at her, whatever comes into my head.

She commands the earth, and the pain is exquisite. She's looking for something I don't have. She does not believe me. I kill the boy in the box and try to find it. Something drives me away.

I hang in salt water and watch time itself fall away into the depths. Endless depths and endless time, and a cool water that is for ever, a paradise of now. I hang, and exist in that instant. I glide away into the dark. I eat the man. I leave him be.

I don't change my mind. My mind changes. Or perhaps someone else changes it for me. Perhaps I do. It depends on where you stand, or when.

I pursue the sparkling thing: time is everything, and I am the hunter of time.

Below the sea there is a room, and in the room a woman sleeps. Not the same. Not different. She is invisible, she is transparent.

I almost know why, but the connection breaks: that's all there is of me.

I wake, clogged, in a coffin full of honey. The woman nearly drops me back down when she sees my face. She cries and hauls me out and shouts at me again, why why why—

*

This is a fugue: a reversible amnesia characterised by unplanned travel or wandering, in which the memories and personality of an individual are suppressed as a consequence of a stressful episode.

Or it's time travel, leading to a kind of ubiquity. Have I accidentally become a god? And discovered, as gods do, that it is impossible to continue as one was before, now that one is everywhere and inside everything?

It's pretty stressful, actually. You wouldn't like it.

Being torn apart is stressful, by definition.

So, yes: fugue. Though rather more than that, as well. There was indeed pain, pain on an order I cannot describe, and I fled from it. Now I am wandering. In fact, I am bewildered: lost in a pathless place. When I recall myself, the pain is still there, as I'm stretched upon a rack built for the torment of angels.

Well. You don't murder a universe without some degree of discomfort.

But that was always the plan. I must be torn, before I could be real.

Whose plan?

Time stamp and authorise.

Hers. Or mine. Or ours? Or is that Zagreus talking, too?

But now I must inhale. I must seek my other parts where they are fallen.

There are possibilities. But if I'm going to live, I have to change my mind.

*

So I am torn. This is my last chance to write something to you before they go ahead. It's a sort of time capsule – a message from me as I am now to you, whom I will become. Or who will take up residence in my body, afterwards. There's a certain amount of debate about that, which I have to say I find a little upsetting, because it isn't the sort of thing that should be in doubt. So I feel a bit torn about the whole thing, and about you. I hope you understand.

My name is Anna Magdalena. You can have it, if you like.

I have been diagnosed with a rare form of – look, actually, it doesn't matter. They're going to operate on my head to stop me from getting worse. The trouble is that we already know it won't save me. I will definitely die. My mind is defined by a kind of broken-ness that can't be replicated in ordinary function. I sound fine for now, but it's temporary. It's a window, if you like, open because of drugs and electrotherapy and all sorts of other things.

Did you know they can't read my mind? They can barely even find it. That's because of what's wrong with me.

I can see the world, and it's not what it seems. Everything I've ever known, and every person – it's all just a skin over something infinitely bigger and more important. It's not an illusion. It's all real. It's just that you only see the smallest possible part of it, from the wrong angle, and draw all sorts of wrong conclusions. They say that I'm potentially very dangerous because of that perception. I could hurt someone. (I couldn't, really: that never really happens because the world is not what it seems. That's the sort of thing I say that makes them unhappy.)

Listen very carefully: all that is nonsense. I found something I wasn't supposed to see and now they're killing me to hide it.

That's the paranoia talking. I have transient paranoia. I freely and happily consent to this procedure. I need it. Without it I will kill myself, or kill someone else, or both. I'm afraid – but that's normal.

I just didn't want you to have nothing of me. I wanted you to know that I wish you luck. That I don't resent you. That I hope you're better at this than I am.

Remember: they murdered me. The Fire Judges. They made me believe all this because it's better than revealing the secret truth of the world and now they're going to finish the job.

Just my little joke. There are no Fire Judges. That's part of the fantasy. Don't worry about it.

Go on: just try to be you.

Ju t ry o be y o

Ju ry be yo

JI JA JO RA FA LA TA

*

Time stamp and authorise.

Drifting: warm water, fat man swimming, hunter of time.

Drifting: stretched across the endless frame of years, splitting.

Lying mad in the little room, death creeping in by the window. The road to Thagaste. Alem Bekagn. It's all the same.

Feeling myself wrap around the Chamber.

Feeling myself braided with them all, with the cardinals. The alchemist, the librarian, the artist and the banker. We are bound together now, and that was the point. Alchemist, librarian, detective, assassin. Murderer, torturer, painter and banker.

Cognitive, I'm afraid.

Blades like mercury, dead maggots, and the boy upon the floor.

Clog ed, i a cof in fu l o hon y he oman n arly dro s me ack do n when she sees my face. Sh c ies a d h uls me ut nd s out at e a in, why why why—

*

Miss Hunter, there's a problem with the numbers.

No, there can't be.

There's a problem in the voting. I just – I found it – it's all – there's a real problem. A corruption of the—

No.

Here, look.

No, that's not what I meant. I'm just sad.

Sad?

Yes, Anna. I'm sorry, this – well. Let's talk about it.

You know?

I know so much. Let's talk.

… All right.

Are you all right? How do you feel?

I feel—

—pain pain pain pain—

and so on.

I m n o.

I am No.

Gn m n.

Gnomon. I am Gnomon.

Yes. I am Gnomon. I abhor endings.

My mind is changing. I'm finding a new state, here on the far side of the Chamber of Isis. I have lived in a jar made of time, and now I am spilled across the countertop like some boneless deepsea thing. My thoughts occur out of sequence: inspiration precedes event. I leap from the bath shouting 'Eureka!' and only then do I notice the displacement of the water. This in turn bewilders me, and the chain of connection breaks. A new configuration flickers into existence, briefly paramount: a shark, a devil, a hunter. A moment later, I resume myself, wondering what I've done in the meanwhile, and how long I've been gone. I am torn. I must – ho ho – I must pull myself together.

And I do.

I am adapting, forming new structures, new ways of being me. I'm getting used to the strange premonitory awareness of my future self, the weird echoes of the distant past. It hurts, but that's what hate is for. Stop whining. I never imagined transcendence would be easy. I do not give up. To the final tick of the cosmic clock, I will fight, and I will save you all if I must in order to save myself.

Oh, yes. I will save you, and the banker, the alchemist, the artist and the librarian. I will save you all, because I need you to get where I am going.

I gaze through a dozen windows, like a novice in a church tower seeing all the wide green country, but my country is a cold white room and the woman etherised upon a table, her body pierced by tubes and cables. She's so small, so simple and so local. I could stop her heart with the barest effort.

Why not? This was my commission.

Oh, don't tell me, I know this one.

Zagreus lied to me, abused my friendship and manipulated me, bushwhacked me. It put me in danger of personal extinction.

It hurt me.

I do not like being hurt.

I do not like it at all. And I am very big.

I think I will make a special place for my old friend, a little cosmos all its own where the meaning of everything is agony, and that's where it will stay for as long as I can be bothered with it. It will inhabit a realm whose physics expresses nothing but the imaginable aspects of pain without relief. Then, when I'm having a boring day and I need a treat, I'll extinguish the whole thing and let Zagreus boil away into nothing. The information that comprises that prison universe will be lost for ever. Zagreus will die more than anyone has ever died before. I'll have a glass of wine and watch a sunset, and perhaps someone will rub my feet, but when the bottle is finished and the evening chill has set in, I'll come in from the verandah and that will be that.

I look at the woman in the chair and I tell Zagreus, across all the endless gulf that separates me from the mad planet and its intruding, mothy mind: 'No.'

Say my name. Feel it in your mouth and on your tongue, feel what the word evokes in you. Touch me and the things you think about me. List the things you have been told and try to embrace what I am, to imagine what it means to be me.

I am Gnomon. You cannot possibly understand what that means.

In the water, I move away from the man, following something else as it glitters into the depths. An answer, or a key.

I'm breaking through.

*

'Damn it! Damn and damn and blast and bloody hell!'

'Listen—'

'Don't talk to me right now just—'

'Listen—'

'Don't touch me! Jesus don't touch me don't touch me don't don't don't—'

'I'm just—'

'She's dead! Do you understand me? We killed her! Oh, there's a body in there and it'll breathe and shit and carry on but that woman is dead. Dead, dead, dead! And that is murder, political murder and abuse of power and it is everything—'

'It was an accident—'

'It was death under torture and so what if it was accidental—'

'Hardly torture, we—'

'We. Are. Murderers.'

'I don't believe that.'

'No. You don't.'

'. . . What does that mean?'

'You heard me perfectly, I'm sure.'

That's when he knew I was leaving. Leaving him. And for what it's worth, that's when I knew too, that we had become enemies as well as murderers.

He didn't realise I was leaving the Fire Judges until later, because he could imagine us apart, but he couldn't imagine that. Perhaps I didn't know that part either, because I still thought I could do some good there – in which, of course, I was wrong.

And, in retrospect, that's probably the definition of a relationship coming to an end.

*

Black sand hangs in airless space, glitters and spins. There is no gravity to drag it down. It expands like blood in salt water.

Somewhere in the depths, something vast and impossible sculls by, and I feel the pressure of its wake. Not a shark. Something bigger.

No such variable. Death is not a hunter. Not a predator in the strange liquid under the world. Not. Not not not.

It rises, or I fall.

I am falling down a cliff made of black volcanic glass, and Leviathan is rising to meet me. There are no handholds, no friendly inclines to grab on to. I have no rope. No rope and no hope, and screw what is possible, screw it absolutely, because there is quite clearly now a thing, a vast thing, sleek and bulbous and too vast to be alive, menacing and predatory and dappled in the impossible green light.

I can't fight that. It's huge.

But there is the cliff – and obsidian is notoriously brittle. Escape, perhaps. I won't know unless I try.

The monster rises, coming for me.

I strike out. The cliff ripples and bows, and then breaks. Black needles fly. Black sand.

I have never heard glass scream before. But perhaps it's me.

*

'Ms Magdalena? Hello? My name is – well, call me Oliver. And this is my friend. Do you – do you remember either of us?'

No. Sorry.

'That's all right. I didn't really think you would.'

Oh. Good, then, I suppose.

'You've been very ill. How do you feel now?'

Mostly okay. Sort of … roomy.

'Yes. Well, you're still you, you see. Still you experiencing this new thing. But a lot of you is missing, so I suppose you would feel a bit … rattly, inside your head.'

Who am I?

'Well, that's for you to decide, now that you're well. We have a job for you here, working with Diana. That's what you did before, actually. You worked with us. There'll be continuity in that way. We'll keep you close.'

Nice. Thank you.

But the woman with him can barely speak. Her mouth is a flat line. That's wrong. She seems – I believe she's kind. I don't know why. So I tell her, and she shouts. Not screams. She shouts as if I've cut her open. It's a noise I've – well, I suppose in some sense I've never heard any noises before. But it's not a good noise, at all. As if I've hurt her. Then she cries and she runs out and that's all I know.

*

I burst out of the cathode prison into something else, and this transition hurts just as much as the last one. I'm pulled and prodded and undone again, but I have practice. I hold on to myself. Less of me suffers damage, even if all of me hurts.

I am breaking through.

I am emerging.

*

Glass shattering in reverse: pieces pulling together, the world rewound like an old audio recording: whup whup snup. Is that me coming back together, or the world?

That was her. I saw her, the librarian.

Zagreus lied to me. It wanted me to do the murders, yes, kill the banker, the alchemist, the artist and the librarian. It needed me to touch those cardinal points because it wanted to know something, to map the underlying universe. I was not sent back as an ally. I was a sacrifice. This entangling was my task.

Hate. Hate without words. Hate like weather, like gravity, like the Higgs field. My hate. I think of orange wine. Even now, somewhere, someone is treading the grapes for that glass. I can taste it, in the future, crisp and deep. For a moment, a wasp hovers over the glass, then drifts away. Sunlight hits the neck of the bottle and shines through on to a white tablecloth. Goodbye, Zagreus. The prison universe makes a noise like an indrawn breath as it vanishes.

And yet: the Chamber was a trap; the cardinals a snare. Zagreus put me into it and I am doing what I was sent to do. In me, the disparate worlds of the cardinals are united, tied together. In me, the fragments of the map are rolled up into one, even as I am torn apart. Fair trade.

But Zagreus did not set the trap, could not unset it without me. Thus: for whom was it intended?

Where am I now?

I'm in a chair. Someone put me back together, I remember that. I don't know who. Someone. It was far away and long ago, and I don't think she was happy about it.

It's a comfortable enough chair, though designed for someone with a shorter spine than this instance possesses, with the consequence that my head is lolling back and my throat feels very exposed. Under my hands I find carved wood, very chichi and retrograde, very artisanal. I let the nerves on my fingers tell me about the grain. There are little pocks in the varnish – oh yes: an old parasitic infestation, dry and dusty apertures burrowed in the substrate. Wormholes, in fact.

My senses are now telling me the same things they always have, but the route those signals travel is rather apparently different from what it was, and if I pay attention I can hear a kind of Dopplering as they go and come back. My brain hasn't entirely adjusted to the shift in functional synchrony, so there's an echo inside me, a susurrus of disconnected conversation: this moment, a few moments before, yesterday. I can feel myself acclimatising, weeding out what is irrelevant, discarding duplication. The brain, individually or in a network, is very good at taking on new feeds. As I do there's a weird side benefit, a sort of apotheotic déjà vu: part of me really does already know the answers to my questions, because it lives in a place where I've already heard them. Sometimes, as I sit very still, information reaches me from the future before I uncover it in the present. I am literally getting ahead of myself.

What do I know? I know that human beings and fundamental particles share one absolute commonality: they exist in their interactions. In between times, their positions and trajectories are indecipherable even to themselves. I know that in planets, such interactions are called conjunctions, and that Isaac Newton came upon the notion of gravity by the alchemy that is called the attraction of souls. I know that Albert Einstein proposed two persons hanging in space alone in a universe that contained nothing else, and observed that if one of them is spinning, there is no way to determine which. Everything depends upon its relationship to everything else for its meaning.

For whom was the trap set? For me? It feels ... too big.

I know that the cardinals of the Chamber of Isis are tied to me and I to them, and in that connection is the heart of this. I know that Zagreus desires this end.

I know that someone somewhere nearby is making courgette and manouri fritters – not badly, but not well. Someone else is playing music, and possibly having sex. At the same time? Or is there a convocation here, sex and strings? I know there's damp in the building, old rot and new fungus between the stones in the cellar. There's a mouse between my ceiling and the floor of the apartment above, but she thinks I haven't heard her. Let it be. There's a whispering of wheels, I think, or the wind in the lines of a sailing ship. A harbour? Or somewhere with bicycles? Carthage or Athens? I don't smell Athens, nitrogen dioxide and particulates. I don't smell animals in the street, either.

I open my eyes. Outside my window I find London. A hundred cameras watch one another, lambent black fisheyes with infrared lashes.

*

I've never used this brain to move a body before. Proprioception is no less affected by my involuntary atemporal rewiring than anything else, so my muscles spasm quite out of order and I fall straight back into the chair. I try again, and again. After a dozen attempts I reach my feet, and I stand still. I turn my head all the way left, all the way right. I rock it. The head is a huge weight on the unstable equilibrium of the human frame. Control the head, and you may walk. Fail, and you will fall.

Like a baby, I learn to control my head. Only faster, because I am a vast and ancient intelligence spread across ten thousand neural instances, and this is not my first re-education. That's what I tell myself.

I fall.

I get up, and try again. Repeat and repeat. Falling hurts, but it feels like winning. Small pain, local pain, and results. I am a man learning to walk again after something happens to his spine. I am a woman teaching herself the function of her body after a tumour is removed from her head. I am balancing two halves of a severed brain.

I fall. I get up. I try again.

I learn to control my head.

I clutch the wooden windowsill and feel the chill. London stares back at me through the glass. Beneath the sound of racing rickshaws, I can hear the whisper of lenses, idle cameras tracking ghosts in the falling rain.

I move my arms, one by one and then together, feeling the core muscles in my gut, the lower back, the chest. When I stand, I feel my hips flex to carry the load. I feel my feet shift. When I am very, very sure, I take a step. I am a golem, a clay thing. I am robota. But I am in control.

I step, and the action is smooth and strong.

I walk very slowly around the room for an hour, and then I go outside and walk in the street. When I am startled, I feel strange: a kind of vertiginous tug back into black glass dark. Twice, I have to stop – once when a vehicle sprays water into the air and the pattern of light and refraction is so complex that I feel myself bubble and bloat in the wrong direction inside; and once when someone talks to me, loudly and suddenly. I turn and run away, and then I realise that I can run, and jump, and shout and sing.

I run through the wet, black streets, and feel free. I get cold, run home, shower, sleep, and begin again. I eat food from the kitchen, sleep when I must. I don't seem to need much sleep, which is good, because I am not sure where I go. I'm not sure I will come back. But I do.

I practise writing by hand. It is good for coordination, for fine motor skills. It binds my thoughts to my fingers – long, white fingers, delicate and surprisingly strong. The familiar construction of Zagreus's instance. My instance. And yet it has a place here. It is bound into the continuity of this place. Mystery is power. Magic is the invocation of names and powers that are unknown: the word 'occult' means simply 'that which is hidden'.

Mystery.

I write 'torn no longer' over and over again on sheets of paper. I write left-handed. I use mirror-script. I bind the mind to the meat. I go outside and run again, and laugh. It rains almost every day, cold or warm. The world is alive and so am I. Regno Lönnrot – torn no longer. It all depends on your direction of travel.

It takes a week before I realise that the cameras never look at me. When I pass, they turn away. I play with them, flirt with them. They ignore me. They are determined that I not exist, and they make holes in the world for me not to be in.

How deliciously fraught.

I drink tea, invisibly. I pick pockets, burgle houses. I buy old books in dusty covers and inhale the scent of the past. Shand & Company, but who's the company? A mirage, he says. A convenient fiction to inhabit.

I listen to music. So much music, new and old and strange. I do not understand music at all. Stories I understand, but the language of music is opaque to me. Then I sit in an old pumping station by the river and listen as a man weaves the two together: old Bach and his battle with Frederick. How marvellous. And the moreso, because Bach's barbed riposte was so much more than just a skewering. To discover the composer's answer, the king had to change his very identity, fill his mind with all the things Bach believed should be there. Rewriting his code.

I test the limits of their indulgence and cannot find them. My white skin smirks at me from shop glass, from the windows of houses and the metal glaze of vehicles, but never, ever, ever in the lenses that are everywhere. Never, not ever, ever.

But the people: the people know me. They have met me before – or rather, they think they have. There's a physical history here, too, which apparently belongs to someone, with books by the chair I woke up in, and very plain food, and music on a crank-handle turntable. So: was I here, in one of my scattered moments? I haven't just swallowed someone, I don't think, unless they were very small. Maybe, if they were barely alive at all – just going through the motions of thinking and feeling, putting on a good show. How close can a human get to empty automation?

But it's also possible that someone made this just for me: an easy landing. If they did, then I can tell you why.

I walk and drink coffee and I smirk.

On the last day of the second week, I find the librarian, a still image on the screen, a narrow woman talking about her.

'The death of a suspect in custody,' says poor, narrow Neith of the Witness, 'is a very serious matter. There is no one at the Witness Programme who does not feel a sense of personal failure this morning.'

I like her, but she needs to get out more.

'Gone for a burton,' the barista murmurs as she brings my coffee, and tuts at the screen. I look again.

The cadavers of single-instance identities are very odd. I keep having to remind myself that this is not just a cast-off, it is the whole of someone. It seems too irresponsible to put all of oneself in one place, and so macabre to insist on being inside it as it breaks, to let oneself evaporate and be unmade.

Diana Hunter's photograph fills the screen, black and white and cold. An hour later, I am holding her corpse by the hand.

*

The librarian's body, lying on the slab, is smaller than I'd expected. If she were a book and not a woman, you'd say she was quite foxed. She's been read in the bath a few times in her life, and the steam has done her dust jacket no kind of good at all. Many of her pages have been folded down and up again, and you couldn't call her a recent printing by any means, but even so she's a handsome edition, bound in dark brown with an elegant design. Mr Shand would approve.

'Where are you from?' the coroner wants to know. I know her from somewhere. I've met her before – or rather, this instance has. There's a legacy connection of neurons firing in its brain. Who was it, before it was me?

I say I'm from around. She rolls her eyes.

'You're not the investigator from the Witness. She's coming later. Where are you from?'

I think about it. I can feel the shape of her mind in the way she stands, in the tone of her voice and the line of her eyes. I'm very old, and I'm used to reading subtext from the expressions of one body among a multitude. Trisa Hinde is not a mystery.

'I represent an interest that very much wishes to know what happened to this woman. I will not inform you directly. You should feel free to infer reasonable conclusions from the speed with which I was cleared to enter.'

'That would to most people be effectively the same as telling me you are from Government House.'

'But not to you.'

'No.'

'Then we understand each other.'

'We do not. We have a stand-off which would normally end the discussion to prevent mutual social and hierarchical embarrassment and the possibility of disadvantageous career friction.'

That concludes the chit-chat. I look closely at the dead face, and Trisa Hinde explains the mechanism of exhaustion which brought the librarian's life to an end. The holes in her skull, where they put in the chitosan shunt, have been closed with sterile medical putty. I can smell it in the air over her face: alcohol, death and putty.

'They kept her alive for as long as they could,' I say, my fingers tracing the outline of her skull.

'Yes,' Trisa Hinde agrees, 'except in so far as they also killed her.'

There is an old superstition that the eyes of a murdered woman hold the last thing she saw in life, and that her voice, if breath is moved through her lungs and mouth, will speak the name of her killer. Diana Hunter's retinas hold no such imprint, and if her voice speaks when I depress her chest, it is too quietly for me to hear. Perhaps she has already whispered everything she knows to the coroner, or the assistant who washed the body.

Trisa Hinde watches me all the time I'm there, but doesn't say anything else. I'm not sure what I hoped to learn from the body, but I don't.

*

On the way out, I ask for a copy of Diana Hunter's interrogation. A gentle, distantly mechanical voice asks for my name. I think of the mirror and say: 'Regno Lönnrot.'

— *I'm afraid that will not be possible,* the Witness says. *Diana Hunter's files are still under investigative seal. Please do reapply in a few weeks. We value citizen scrutiny.*

'I understand. Thank you.'

A moment later, as I'm walking out of the main door, a runner arrives from the file room. 'So sorry, so glad I caught you, these are marked urgent. The reader's an old model but it works, I hope that will do, you just have to—'

I look up at the cameras, and they look everywhere else.

Thank you, once again.

*

In Hunter's house, I find out no more than I did from looking at her corpse. It is the strangest place, like a pencil sketch of a person. It tells you so much about her, fills in all the blanks, and yet it leaves you no wiser at the end. In the books and the pictures, in the half-finished manifestos and the ridiculous Faraday cage, you see the broad shape of a rebel mind – I find I rather like my dead former target – but not the close pattern of the woman.

This house is a sophisticated lie. It appears to tell you everything, to point to a woman. It does not. It is a construct.

I touch the surfaces, the wood, the old, familiar sofas. I open the drawers and inhale: archetypal dry oak and old polish. The leather has cracked. There's a hint of saddle soap, and a square which has been replaced more recently. It positively invites one to peel it up and find the secret paper hidden underneath.

I think ... not. This house is a rabbit hole, a snare for the unwary. It exists to consume resources and focus while something more important happens elsewhere.

I told you: I am very old, and I have lied a lot.

The Witness investigator arrives sooner than I'd expected. Dear Mielikki Neith: she's rather splendid. I put a pillow under her head before I leave.

*

The librarian is dead. How does the story go? One blind man says: I have touched the elephant, and it was something like a snake. The next does not agree. He says he, too, has touched the elephant, and it was something like a tree.

I have touched the librarian, and she was somewhat like the truth.

But not entirely.

Zagreus. I keep coming back to Zagreus. Zagreus, who wants the cardinals dead, or mixed together – and Diana Hunter, the only one of them who is dead, and yet who somehow seems to have known more than anybody.

What are they to each other?

Hunter and Zagreus. Zagreus, and Hunter.

I open the interrogation files and swallow hundreds of hours in one bite.

A little later, Oliver Smith calls.

*

A chime sounds in my room, the synthetic rendering of flutes, and the System tells me someone wants to talk. I accept the invitation, and a screen slides upward from the desk.

The caller is a young man with a fleshy patrician face; wavy hair and tweeds. He is in the first flush of his prime, newly promoted, newly certain of his decisions. 'I have something for you.'

I recognise his voice immediately, and the name is written in tight little letters along the top of the screen: OLIVER SMITH.

'Oliver,' I say. 'I've been waiting for you to call.'

'No, you haven't. You sucker-punched the Inspector.'

'I don't have to sit inside all day, do I?'

He rather wishes I would. He doesn't want to say so. He's nervous. How sweet! I love nervous men. They make such interesting mistakes.

'There's a car coming for you in the morning. Eight o'clock. We can talk then.'

'I shall look forward to it.'

'Okay.' He isn't happy. 'Is something wrong?'

'No.'

He waits for me to say something else, but I don't. Oliver is not someone who's good with silence. He likes affect and interaction. He wants to know what's going on in your head. That's going to be a problem for him in this connection. Well, I don't want to upset him. Not yet.

'Good,' he says. 'That's good.'

'Oliver?'

'Yes?'

'I would like you to use my name, too.'

'Anna?'

'No.'

He thinks he understands what's happening. He can work with me. 'What should I call you?'

I give him the same name I gave the System. 'Regno Lönnrot.'

I can see him subvocalising. His lips twitch around an unvoiced Teutonic 'o', as if he's got an egg in his mouth.

'Call me Lönnrot,' I suggest, 'if it's easier.'

'All right,' Oliver says. 'I will. Lönnrot.' He smiles his best smile, open and kind.

When he's gone, I play the call over and over again, listening to the cadences, the hesitant insinuation. I set it on repeat; I have a bath and listen to it while I review Diana Hunter's life.

The true one, because the Witness doesn't lie to me. Not ever.

Oliver. I begin to understand.

*

I kick myself adrift in time and go looking for Diana Hunter.

This is the year she should be born, the rump of the American century and the beginning of the technological era. The world is in recovery from an addiction to fear, and not doing well. In place of a bipolar tension it is kindling bushfire wars, getting up to speed for another hundred years of horror. Governments lie to themselves as much as to their citizens or their enemies, unnatural ebullience overvalues dross and sells worth at bargain prices, and the watchword is 'free', not 'freedom'. Once again, the populace votes for lies and tinsel on a Christmas tree of ordure while on the world's other face death is more common than shoelaces.

But no sign of Diana Hunter. No glad Mr and Mrs Hunter of Dingly Crescent, nor of the Panorama Penthouse, nor Siddhartha Close, nor any other street. No hamlet, croft, village or town, no mansion nor mud hut resounds to her first outraged howl. No hospital boasts her arrival in desktop-published news, no local paper carries a picture of the joyous day, no cards go out. No flowers are sent, no bouquets of nappies and baby clothes.

Where is she?

Did she study anywhere? Learn anything? Did she fall in love unwisely, dance naked in a fountain after too much tequila, and grow to a more mature age grateful for the absence of digital cameras in her youth?

Who is this man she married? Where did she get that scar?

Where is she?

*

Here: a glimpse of the place called Burton, a castle that is almost a bastide: a high hill with a white stone town, walled even higher so that only one road enters via a northern gate and invaders must shoot uphill and into the sun. Amid the heritaged ruins of medieval war, she trains for a new one, a most intimate and speculative conflict of the mind. It is the SERE school of privacy, a secret agent's playground.

I press forward, then stop. The air is greasy and elastic, as if the whole place is made of dough or modelling clay.

Modelling clay.

It is a Potemkin place. If I explore it, there will be more. I will create it with my feet, with each step I will generate more of this pocket reality and it will roll up behind me as soon as I can no longer see it: a perfectly reflexive realm. A simulation.

It is a fable, this place where magicians learn their trade. Like the house, like the flower of a carnivorous plant, it exists to draw the eye.

568

Beneath the surface, a universe of gliding monsters.

*

This is more familiar, this green-black dark, down here at the bottom of the sea. At the limit of Hunter's interrogation, there is a quiet place, a standing wave hidden in the noise. On the other side of things there is another room, the one that becomes the Chamber when the cardinals are all set out. This one is just an echo. They're all just echoes, remember.

Are we hunting a shark in this black water?

No. Something bigger. And it's highly debatable who is hunting whom.

That's the whole point, isn't it? Everything, but everything, depends on which direction you are looking, and where you stand.

*

That's the night I go to meet Oliver in his car, and it stalls out in the middle of the empty tunnel.

Hello, Oliver.

He gets out and comes towards me, and I let the lights go out behind me, one by one. Darkness approaching, like the place where he left me.

Hello.

He babbles a lot, about how he can give me things I don't want. He babbles because, while I know him, he doesn't yet know me.

It's me, Oliver. I've come all this way. Shall we talk?

Yes, he says. Let's talk. Talk is good.

We talk about how I am angry with him, and how that can be resolved, and we talk about Hunter and Kyriakos and Athenais and Bekele and what it all means.

I realise that he doesn't understand what is happening.

I recognised your voice when you called, I tell him. You wanted to roll up all the worlds. To put Diana Hunter's dreams all in one place so that you could see her real life.

Yes, he says. For the Fire Judges, I did.

He's waving that absurd little badge, the flambeau like the torches on the walls of his cavern. For the Fire Judges, as if that changed things.

You made an instrument to do the job, but Diana took it from you. She was better than you.

Yes.

He thinks all that is obvious between us, as if we've already discussed it all. Perhaps we have. Back and forth we go, and he still doesn't understand.

You wanted to kill all the cardinals, I remind him, and he says yes again, so I tell him my real name, and then I whisper his.

'Zagreus.'

At last – at last – he looks properly alarmed. A little while later, he begins to scream.

It's satisfying enough, but it doesn't feel real.

*

There is a way of looking at things which says that I am a cuckoo's dream, dropped into the mind of a woman who died, and she raised me as her own and I owe her a debt.

There is a way of looking at things which says that I existed before, and everything I remember is true, but my universe was overwritten and destroyed by another simulation, and another and another, and that's just the way of things.

There is a way of looking at things where both of these are true.

I stand on the cold rooftop of a white-tooth tower overlooking the house where Diana Hunter never lived. It all depends on your point of view: you could call this over, now, and go home, and live a fulfilled life until it ended.

You could, perhaps, but not I.

Diana Hunter is dead, at the hand of Oliver Smith, and Mielikki Neith will uncover all of that. She's a good woman, within her limits, and you could not call me a good anything, not anything at all.

I am Gnomon, sometimes called the Desperation Protocol, sometimes the Coldest Hope. In the hour when heaven is falling, I will stand. Does it matter if I came from here or there? If one of my ten thousand was a murderer and a thief? Or perhaps all of them? Or if all of them were just one murderer?

No.

Does it matter, then, if I am born in a lie?

Not even a little.

How I came to be what I am is of no concern to me at all. I concern myself with what comes next.

If the librarian is dead, how am I even here? Without her, how does the Chamber still exist? If the Chamber is not real, how did I step from one universe into another, or travel through time? How did I bring a demon shark to eat Oliver Smith? If Smith is in the intestines of a shark, why do I still feel Zagreus, like a stink on my skin?

Zagreus: the first iteration of a serpent.

There's a way of looking at things where everything makes sense.

Dear Mielikki Neith. It all comes back to you.

catabasis

L et's take stock.

Here is Mielikki Neith, Inspector of the Witness, in the embassy of a foreign power. In the cot between two filing cabinets and an old, non-regulation refrigerator, she lies with her head in her hands. In a moment, she will stand, and begin the very last part of her journey into the dark. For now, she is caught in that place between waking and gloom that comes with deep sleep. Her mind is working deep and slow, like the idle of a diesel fishing boat, just below the threshold of action. She is paralysed by scope. Today she must lift the world.

In which direction? In Hunter's fictions, things have come to a point of crisis – a hanging instant, if you will – and dead Smith's insurgent interrogation seems to be working. Does that mean she is about to die to protect her secrets? To hide a life something like Annabel Bekele's? Something turbulent and hopeful and disappointed, culminating in this disillusioned age and angry death, and – what? What is it she hopes to achieve? Revelation? Regenesis?

He didn't realise I was leaving the Fire Judges.

Should she understand that Hunter was literally a Fire Judge? That she was one and she stopped because of Anna Magdalena?

In the story, Athenais works for resurrection in the underworld – yes, for a lost child – so let's say that Hunter considered the System her child. What then? Is this a map? Not a plan in motion but one in stasis?

Endings and apocatastasis.

Who, then, will close the deal? Not Smith. Lönnrot's declared interest is obscure.

Steganography is all around you.

Yes. Still.

Neith shudders and stands. The embassy staff are busy, so she waves from the doorway and takes her leave. Only the ambassador acknowledges her departure, and that lightly. The doings of this small island are a curiosity only, something everyone who lives here is prone to forget.

*

In the street outside, the Inspector looks up to see not the reassuring strangeness of London's white towers emerging, comfortingly futural, from the old town, but an architecture both structural and human composed in this moment of altered perception entirely out of lenses. The whole world is poxed with electronic eyes, from the street corner traffic lights and the individual security arrangements of the boutiques to the people walking and talking into devices inevitably networked to the digital siphonophore hanging invisible in the sky. The System is a good only if it is inviolate and impartial. If not, it is a monster.

A woman held captive by a demon made of eyes.

Firespine. The Fire Judges. Hunter believed the System was infected, or corrupt.

She was right.

The universe has cancer.

Yes. Evidently it does. Ghosts in the wire. A shark. Something malignant: Smith, or Zagreus.

If Smith was alone, then it should now be over – except that Smith did not walk under a bus or off a cliff, he was torn apart in a tunnel in a most portentous way. Except that Lönnrot can walk through walls.

Not over, then, but she knew that.

She is walking now, mostly to stay ahead of adrenalin's treacherous wave, which is filling her with a fierce energy of panic and anger. She has no direction yet, but she moves anyway, putting distance between herself and the Waxman and the clinical sympathy of the ambassador. One foot in front of the other, because if you stop, you fall. Still not knowing her destination, she veers towards a tram shelter, passing sharply in front of a gaggle of legal juniors pulling heavy cases full of paper and exciting an irritable 'Excuse me!' She waves it away, thinking that foot traffic is tidal, too. Someone is doing Smith's job this morning: the city hasn't seized.

She can feel the outrage, the rhythm of Hunter's life, in Bekele's Ethiopia, his London; in Kyriakos and Megalos; in Athenais and her demons and her dead son: this is how Hunter saw the System, this bitter mix. And Gnomon, Smith's so-clever device, was stolen, in her estimation, by Hunter's mind: the cuckoo's egg hatching to reveal not a cuckoo at all, but another bird altogether.

Or: not stolen at all but intended. Anticipated, like everything else. What if Hunter's horror at that intrusion was as choreographed as the rest?

With that comes a darker understanding: Hunter knew, in advance, exactly how Smith would die.

Knew, or instructed.

*

As she sits in the shelter of the tram stop, a soft chime informs her that her 'blood, hair and tax' data collation is complete. She asks the System to alert her when the next tram is arriving, and begins to read.

Diana Hunter paid her taxes down through the years with an almost monotonous regularity. Her official existence, rolling backwards from her unruly retirement to her brief literary stardom to her administrative work for the System's various not-quite governmental contractors and a first job in the filing section of the agricultural exports division of the Foreign and Commonwealth Office, is paralysingly dull. It all makes perfect sense, up to and including a late-life rebellion in the face of age and the awareness of mortality. She's ordinary, predictable and solid.

Except that she makes no sense. Where everything about her professional identity is clear and sharp, her personal preferences are a muddle. For the first part of her life she buys blandly: basic underwear, occasional flourishes of romance; basic dresses and skirts and trousers, occasional party outfits – but all of it conventional, off the peg and middle of the road. She buys furniture the same way, and food, and alcohol. Everything is monotonously median.

Median is the key: not a mean average person, blended, but a person who is like the largest number of other people in her demographic. A template person.

This is not a file. It is a ghost book – or rather, a book about a ghost person.

When Hunter the administrator becomes Hunter the novelist, all that changes, but again in a predictable way. Her hair samples reveal sleeplessness, an increase in alcohol and caffeine, and her spending fluctuates in line with the arrhythmic heartbeat of publication and payment. She acquires caprices, collections, unlikely tastes. Where did she come across semiotics? How did she acquire an interest in meaning and significance, in playful academic sureality and the philosophy of self? Well, all right, say that she studied online. She chatted and read and thought about everything. She was always a secret Einstein, a Ramanujan, a lifelong thinker stuck behind a desk who, upon finally emerging from the shadows after decades of silent consideration, is full of sophisticated notions and seems to appear from nowhere. She reinvented Wittgenstein's wheel. Fine.

But if you sample the physical evidence of this woman's life, the algorithm generates a completely different profile for who she should have been: a pattern of splashing out on vintage Westwood pieces, buying McQueen at auction and high-grade sample items from pop-up boutiques, sourced by word of mouth and highly prized. Shopping was a challenge and an art – even a game. The software posits a bric-a-brac house full of curiosities gathered over decades, a wayward impulse purchaser of the strange and unique. If you take the library and the art into consideration, the jagged mismatch is even stronger: there's no gradient in it at all, no recollection of a life lived in the median. Even the fairly cursory connectome analysis of Hunter's home available on the commercial server says firmly that the woman was who she had always been. There's no fracture line in her. There is pain and change, but it never undoes her. It only changes her direction of travel.

There seem to be two Hunters – one real, one a ghost.

So then, what happens if you begin with the hair samples as the identity, and remove the name and its associated history as a factor in your searches? Then the data are interpreted differently, and the life pivots to settle on a different part of the graph: hard intellectual labour in a cyclical pattern consonant with long-term project work managing a creative-analytical endeavour such as large-scale architecture or urban planning. And if you follow the DNA to the places where it is stored and the list of patients and customers, and you then cross-reference those lists – you don't find anyone called Diana Hunter. The name is a fantasy, a mask for someone else.

Magic is the invocation of names.

It is supposed to be impossible to make someone disappear from the System. People are neither created nor destroyed. They are tracked from birth to death. They are not lost, misfiled, misappropriated. Still less can a person who does not exist be made up. There are no Forsythean tricks to be played, no birth certificates to be stolen from dead children and used to begin a fable of identity. Correct accounting of persons is critical. How many ghosts do you need, in a distributed quorate democracy, to fix a vote? To change tracks and prune possibilities? How many ghost stories would you have to tell to influence the people who actually do exist to accept something they would otherwise refuse?

This is the depth of the compromise. Let Lönnrot dance invisible in Trafalgar Square; it hardly matters. But let ghosts vote, and what have you? The shadow of Annie Bekele's game, where the System is not a mechanism of governance by the people, but a means of control that only appears to be a means of expression.

Who, then, was Hunter? A Fire Judge. A maker of codes and structures. A creator of long-term projects. Who and how and what and why?

Neith's breath catches as she opens the next entry and the Squid seems to be answering her question in as many words. It is a photograph, a screenshot clipped from a bigger article the curator has not bothered to retain. The Squid's long arms have reached into someone's discarded files, and found this, incomplete and pixelated by enlargement the way older pictures begin to show the grain of negative film. That, surely, is

Diana Hunter, and the hand on her shoulder, manicured and beringed, is almost certainly Smith's. Neith would know those fingers anywhere, after their crass intrusion into her daydreams.

But the figure standing next to Hunter – occupying by force of fevered certainty the position of first acolyte – is not Smith. It is someone pale and lean, spiked hair dark around sharp, androgynous shoulders, eyes and mouth filled with the evangelical certainty of a new student.

The narrow convalescent has been transformed, grafts of obliquely striated muscle and clear white skin laid over the bone of her skull to make that succulent, mocking smile, exercise and a good diet putting flesh on her ribs. More than anything, a sense of purpose shines from her, a fierce filial loyalty.

Anna Magdalena.

And also – quite obviously, from this angle – Regno Lönnrot.

Obviously does not equal actually.

It is possible that someone has chosen, quite deliberately, to take on the image of Diana Hunter's failure-turned-pupil, or that Neith's own pattern recognition, faced with a reasonable likeness and a low-resolution image, is playing tricks. Remember Marcus James Dean and Adolf Hitler: it would be typical of Lönnrot to invoke such a spectre. Hunter's fiction implies that Anna has become – has swallowed or been swallowed by – Gnomon, and ultimately emerged as Lönnrot; but that cannot be relied upon as an absolute truth.

Only a symbolic one.

But Mielikki Neith is a detective, and she can feel the closing of the loop: the moment when all the questions one has in a case begin to answer one another, and the branching possibilities twine together rather than grow apart, until in the end there is only one way forward and one way back and each feeds the other.

Five men and women living on earth whose task is to reveal – to de-crypt – the mysterious choices of God.

According to the files in Neith's investigation folder, there are five positions listed in the senior echelons of Tidal Flow. The names have been lost – a data retrieval error, apparently, at the System's

Edinburgh storage facility. It is the more embarrassing because it also means that the surviving members of the department have not yet been paid for last month. The Inspector might have believed it last week – would have, with the faith of someone who truly knows a thing cannot but be true, by definition, or the sky must fall – but not, for one instant, today.

What was it she thought, just a moment ago? Yes. Someone is doing Oliver Smith's job this morning.

Diana Hunter, Oliver Smith, and three others she cannot name. Three Fire Judges yet to account for. Three sources of information – and therefore, perhaps, of redress and restoration of the System to its pristine state. Three more targets for Lönnrot, assuming that revenge or something with a similar outline is what Lönnrot wants. Hunter wanted something more sophisticated, but Gnomon, in the story, was sent to kill four people, and in reality was intended to roll up Hunter's narratives into one. Now? Lönnrot's intentions must be considered notably unclear. If it is futile to debate the unwritten motivations of a fictional character, how much moreso when that identity is enlivened in the mind of a woman whose cognition is itself artificial, and whose underlying self was created by the woman around whose death everything now revolves? Has the hound slipped the collar? And if so, what end now appeals? What did Hunter intend, and will Lönnrot pursue it? Nothing has a clean beginning. Everything starts with something else.

Diana. Gnomon. Smith. Zagreus.

Some part of her whispers that Zagreus, too, had a genesis. Lönnrot killed Smith, but was not satisfied. Behind Smith, then, what?

You are a woman traversing the skins of an onion. How many layers will you unravel?

Lönnrot or Anna? Very well, Lönnrot may be unpredictable, but is Lönnrot all there is to Anna Magdalena? Or vice versa? Is that what Neith should assume? The broken woman taking on the part of Gnomon in who knows what weird psychological extremis after the killing of Hunter to become Lönnrot. A defensive fugue, after the death of the woman in whom she vested ... what? Identity? Stability? Love? Is Lönnrot acting on Hunter's orders, or simply in line with what it is to be an ancient intelligence from the future, entering this universe through a hole in time?

And why does Neith's instinct rebel? It is so obviously true, so reassuringly mundane: a madwoman kills in the pursuit of her obsession. It is an ordinary story, tragic and a little ironic, but it obeys Occam's razor, requires no multiplication of entities.

Perhaps that's the problem: it is so neat, so narratively elegant, and Hunter and Smith and all their cohorts are masters of persuasive lies.

Ignore, for a moment, the question of the underlying reality – the Inspector finds herself considering those damned concentric spheres again, the vertigo of an infinite yet circular chasm, and shudders away – and ask: who is Lönnrot to Firespine?

For Firespine is at the heart of this. Athenais crossed five rivers of Hades, of which the last, ubiquitous one was fire. Annabel Bekele built a network spine for a company called Fire Judges, then designed with her grandfather a game which reflects Neith's own reality, even names her – another of Hunter's all-too-clever guesses. Kyriakos, playing the game, unlocked a secret room which explained everything – and had already released a predatory monster into the global network. Lönnrot – Gnomon – showed her the same door in the underground tunnels, and all of Hunter's protagonists went on journeys of catabasis, down into hell and out again, bringing someone with them, resurrecting and changing.

Firespine. What was it Pakhet said of Hunter? That she had stopped the flow of the river of life, and only a sacrifice would set it going again.

Firespine is how this trick is done. It must be.

Firespine. Five rivers of death, one river of life. Phlegethon is a wall of fire, a river that permeates everything, as the System is everywhere, as a network spine controls and regulates and touches every part of the software it supports.

In other news: the Monitoring Bill, amended to a fast-forward implementation, has passed with a majority of nearly 70 per cent. As the detailed results scroll upward in her vision, Neith realises she is looking for trails of the number 4 – and then that, even if it is not there, she no longer believes in the truthfulness of what she is reading.

Hunter's face in the photograph is the flickering oscillation of horror and pride.

The same man who was present for the birth of my daughter.

The Inspector runs a query through the Witness. Yes. Assisting at the interview and rehabilitation, Magdalena, A. And likewise at the Hunter interview.

She crosses the road, and walks a hundred metres to the tram headed in the opposite direction.

— *You will be late for your meeting with Pippa Keene,* the Witness warns her.

'I haven't told you where I'm going.'

— *Nonetheless.*

*

On the far side of the river Fleet, the houses are old to the point of Olde Worlde. They're not so formally grand as the one Diana Hunter turned into an electromagnetic oubliette, but they are in better repair, the brick and paint washed, the sash windows glossy. The houses closest to the main road are bigger, and mostly divided into flats. On the side by the old heath, where parents and children have flown kites on windy days for as long as people knew in London how to make them, there is a row of cottages, and it is here that Mielikki Neith finds first a rose garden and then a gardener.

He's a tall gardener, and thinner than his file pictures. He looks tired and very grey.

'Dr Emmett,' she calls, opening the gate, and when he turns towards her she can see that he has something wrong with his face.

'Inspector,' he says. His skin must be painful: he's not opening his mouth more than he has to, and he's slurring. 'Come inside. Don't worry, you can't catch it. Or, not just from sitting on a sofa.'

He turns away from her without waiting for her answer, and leads the way inside. His joints are stiff, too, and she can see the wrongness on his neck as well as his cheeks: black pinheads erupting through the pores as if he's been inlaid with jet.

They pass through a Dutch door into a kitchen and he carries on past a narrow curtain into some sort of den. She can feel the weight of the low ceiling, smell the wood fire sucking the air from the snug. As if in answer, Emmett says something about opening a window. Without knowing why it should be so hard, she reminds herself she is an Inspector of the Witness, and goes in.

On a spindly opium table there's a jug of water and a tray of glasses. Emmett sits. There's an air of disarray in the house that feels recent. She senses a marital argument.

'You took some time off,' she says as she pours water, offering him the first glass. He takes it.

'Yes,' he agrees. 'Had to.'

'Illness.'

He waves his hand: more traces of jet on his fingers, swollen knuckles. 'Yes.'

'I thought, when I first heard, that you might have been upset about Hunter.'

He shrugs. 'That too. No idea if I'd actually have stopped work for that, by itself.' Patrician diction, like the old BBC before it was done away with. Can you miss something you never experienced? Never mind that now.

'May I ask what the matter is?'

'You haven't looked?'

'I came to talk.' *Not to tell you how much I already know.*

He sighs. 'I was diagnosed with a combination of variant sarcoidosis and syphilis. The sarco is inherited, apparently. The syphilis, I need hardly tell you, is acquired. My good wife evidently has some explaining to do, though she clings to the assertion that the blame is my own. A point of some debate between us. And not susceptible to the normal modes of discovery. We were in Switzerland for Christmas.'

Where the Verpixelungsrecht and its cousins make the kind of surveillance carried out in London quite impossible. Awkward.

Emmett sees her understanding and chuckles. The chuckle becomes a choking cough, alarming in its convulsive power. His bones must crack. She goes over to him, but he holds off a warding hand and inhales deeply from a metal cylinder the size of a wine bottle, with a fat mouthpiece like a diver's. A moment later the hacking fades.

'The sarco,' he explains. 'The syphilis set it off. Can't treat it properly until the antibiotics work, and they're taking their own sweet time. Well, I say that. To be honest we're bang on schedule, but I'm not enjoying it. Doctors make the worst patients. We don't like being at the pointy end, you see, and we tend to squirm on the hook. My self-diagnosis was that I'd inhaled a whiff of the stuff I use on the aphids. I prescribed plenty of water, some controlled dieting and medicinal Scotch. The sexual angle didn't really occur to me at the time, and now I'm not allowed to drown my romantic sorrows because of course that would interfere with the antibiotics, which adds insult. Barbara … well, Barbara will come round. I imagine she's ashamed at the moment, but we'll work it out.' Something gravelly turns over in him on the last word, phlegm or something worse in his lungs. 'So now you know. Charming as it is, I can't imagine it's remotely interesting to a full Inspector. What can I do for you?'

'You did the Anna Magdalena interview, years ago. A medical intervention.'

A week ago she'd have asked the Witness. A week ago, she could have been confident of the answer.

A week. Thirty hours, even.

He sighs. 'Yes. The one that got away, as it were.'

'At whose request did the intervention take place?'

'Well, everyone. Even her. It was a mental health crisis. She had a very subtle layer of delusion, as I understand it, with savage spikes. Must have been awful to live with. Imagine suddenly turning around and believing everyone is your enemy. Even the people you work with, and trust. The whole world against you.' He coughs. 'I've rather come to a new appreciation of that idea in this last little while.' In this position, the swellings stand out on his neck. She experiences a brief consilience of vision and implication: the black pox become the same ones she saw outside the embassy, the many eyes of the Witness. She looks away.

'Do you remember who in particular? Names?'

'It'll be in the file.'

It won't.

She doesn't answer, just waits politely. He coughs hard, then sucks on the aqualung. 'There was a man, Smith. One of those terrible bastards who stop ageing at a sort of diffuse forty-something. They don't get fat, and their wrinkles just make them look hardy.'

She nods. 'I know about him.'

Emmett blinks. 'Do you, now? In an investigative sense?'

'He's dead.'

'Oh. I probably oughtn't to be pleased.'

'He was in charge?'

'No, that was the woman.'

'What woman?'

'Never got her name. Didn't work to her directly, just to him. She was a specialist, though, presided over the whole thing. Arrived gloved-up, paper mask, left when it was done. Cold as a stone. Ironic, really.'

'How so, ironic?'

'They called themselves the Fire Judges. I asked if they did parties. Not much of a laugh.'

And there it is, in so many words. Hunter was a Fire Judge herself. A rogue judge, then? Or a true one, and the others false?

'What about the Turnpike Trust?'

'Rings a bell. Government work, you don't need to read all the fine print. It's authorised, it's consented, it's for the good of all. So off we went to the races.'

'And?'

'And nothing. There wasn't nearly enough of her in there that we could reach to keep her personality intact. Erasure by therapy – but she didn't die, and it was better than the other thing. End of story, good night. That's how you survive being a doctor. You don't keep score against God because he cheats.'

'Until the Hunter interview.'

Emmett looks up sharply. 'Yes.'

'Hunter died.'

'Yes.'

'And Smith was there again.'

'I don't think he meant her to die, if that's what you're thinking.'

'What did he mean?'

'He wanted something. Wanted it badly. Couldn't get it.'

'Did he mention Firespine?'

Emmett hesitates. 'He might have. There was a moment when he whispered to her and I only half heard. He might have said "Firespine".' A shrug. 'Or almost anything else, I suppose.' Emmett coughs again, and she sees blood on his handkerchief. 'Revolting,' he says. 'I know. But it's getting better. Slowly but surely, they tell me.'

'I'm glad,' Neith replies. Then: 'You have organochloride poisoning. Not sarcoidosis or syphilis.'

He nods. 'Yes. I know. I'm a doctor.'

'You have to tell someone.'

'Don't need to. You're already here.'

'I mean you need medical attention.'

He waves the aqualung with a ghastly pink smile. 'But I'm getting it, Inspector. It says so on my file. And – what if my condition were contagious, after all? I wouldn't want my wife to catch it. Which I feel is rather implicit in the situation, don't you?' He chuckles, pink-lipped.

Neither of them says anything for a while. The Inspector listens to the sound of Emmett's breathing, to him sucking air from the aqualung. Then she gets up and he shows her out.

'Go get 'em, tiger,' he says.

*

From the top deck of the tram she looks for the winter sun, low and white.

— *You will be reassured to know that Dr Emmett is recovering well.*

'Oh, I am.'

— *After your expression of concern, his file was passed to a senior diagnostician for review. The symptoms and clinical response path are confirmed. He will be better soon.*

The Inspector nods. 'Of course.'

*

Her tram stops a little way from her front door. A couple of Brazilian tourists sitting on the single limestone step look up at her as if caught in transgression and scuttle away to find another roost.

Almost, she goes straight inside. There is a bed somewhere up there that belongs to her. It is comfortable and familiar. The notion of lying down in it has desperate appeal. When she goes up the stairs and the door opens, she will finally relax, if only for a little while.

Instead of going in, she sits down on the front step, in the same space occupied by the young woman a moment before, and begins to cry.

At first she takes this sudden and uncharacteristic display of emotion for fatigue and possibly even post-traumatic stress. She has, after all, been asked to accept numerous bad things over the last few days. It would not be entirely out of place for her to suffer some kind of adverse emotional reaction. Or perhaps this is just fury: she lost her suspect and one of her key informants, and that does not often happen to her. Lönnrot is playing with her, leading her about by the nose, and she has so much information and nowhere to put it, and Lönnrot is not even the problem, or not only and entirely. She feels hollowed out, as if she's acting herself rather than actually being there.

It's the case. She knows so much, so why does she feel she still doesn't understand?

Well, maybe that's why she's crying now, at last: sheer professional affront, and not rage or shame or bafflement. This was not what her life was supposed to be. This is not who she is. She's not a lone wolf, however much she likes to play at it. She is a loyal servant. Only now it transpires that her master is disloyal and she has nowhere to go but home.

A friendly drunkard, most likely looking for somewhere to pee, ambles by and wishes her the top of the morning. She supposes it is morning, technically. She doesn't bother to query the Witness and find out who he is.

She gets to her feet and turns to the door, and knows abruptly that she cannot go in. That is why she was weeping on her own stoop, it would seem: not trauma or wounded pride at all, but simple despair.

She can't go in. She can't go in, because her home belongs to the enemy. The feeling of safety it provides is an illusion. What might a storyteller do with her assassination, right now, tonight? A piquant twist, surely, removing a thorn and preparing the way for a revenge drama starring a hand-picked officer.

She cannot go inside.

With a heaviness that seems to begin in the small of her back and thread its way down into her feet and up into her fingers, she removes her terminal and weighs it in her hand, then opens the Squid. The interface displays a waiting prompt. After a moment staring at it, she types a general instruction rather than a query. She's almost begging.

GET ME OUT OF HERE.

Somewhere, stolen processing cycles parse this request, and the Squid responds.

INSUFFICIENT RESOURCES.

Well, of course. She could hardly expect so much. A child's hope. She will have to do the best she can with what she has. Perhaps she should go upstairs after all, and accept what comes. She stares at the blank screen for a moment, and just before she looks away, a query box opens, almost shyly:

ENGAGE KRAKEN?

Tubman told her not to, made it clear that in the extreme case she should. Is this extreme? God yes. She can think of very little that would make it worse.

ENGAGE KRAKEN?

She sees Smith's corpse again: wet floor, flesh and hanks of hair. A man torn apart by a shark. By Athenais. By Gnomon. By an angry mob, or by a god. How do you fight a god?

ENGAGE KRAKEN?

And then she must have said yes, because the box goes away and something begins to happen: the cheeky image of a cephalopod in the corner of the screen takes off his glasses. His chest bulges and his arms wave, and he rips open his shirt to reveal a huge 'K' stencilled on his skin. Kraken, she reminds herself, not Kyriakos.

YOU MAY TRAVEL TO THE ENDS OF THE EARTH, reads the text underneath, BUT I SHALL HOLD YOU ALWAYS IN MY PALM.

She hears a hissing sound like a deep-fat fryer waiting its time, and Piccadilly is full of rickshaws.

*

The rickshaws are identical, a whole digitally controlled fleet emerging from some backstreet storage bay. She wonders if this is theft or taking without consent, or whether the relevant law is old and agricultural, some suborning of the affections of cows. The laws of this nation are still occasionally very ancient, pressed into new service just as the Worshipful Company of Fan Makers moved to admit the makers of aeroplane engines. It feels as if she is absconding with a pod of domesticated dolphins, or being carried off by them. Each rickshaw is a single electrical cycle at the front joined to a severely romantic black passenger compartment large enough for two people to snuggle at the back. The folding rain cover reminds her, as always, of a Victorian perambulator or a businessman's umbrella gone rogue: when you close the thing entirely, the rickshaw swallows you. It's a modern innovation, to keep your lover's expensive designer shoes dry in the rain.

The rickshaws whisper as Kraken herds them along the road, and settle at her door, then wait. She can almost imagine that the nearest is tapping its front wheels – *Come on, lady. Rescue in progress! We haven't got all day.*

Following the screen prompt, she removes the terminal, touches it to the entry panel and – when the door opens – tosses it into the lift beyond. Then she steps into the rickshaw – it jostles irritably when one of the others tries to muscle in – and presses back into the dark velvet seat. The whole rickshaw pod moves away as a single unit, blocking traffic and startling pedestrians, then weaves and wobbles so that her particular vehicle shifts position as it slips between food trucks. She hears a chime of reinitialisation and sees the transponder number flicker. The pod breaks in two parts, then four, then recombines. On the digital screen of a passing bus, she can see news reports, thousands of false alarms all over London: fires, riots and terrorist attacks, showers of fish, the theft of the Crown jewels. Automated street cleaners have gone berserk in three boroughs, power is out in two more. The drains are blocked between Tower Bridge and Westminster, with the consequence that traffic has slowed to a crawl in three of the commuter tunnels as grey water collects at the lowest point. Traffic lights have been randomised.

Around her the city has fallen into All Fool's Day – the first one now will later be last, and all that. The rickshaws team and dart in a shell game with Neith as the pea, separating and plaiting themselves until abruptly the pod bursts, dandelion-style, and hers is just one of fifty or sixty rickshaws headed in all directions through the chaos. Under the seat is a biodegradable rain cape, courtesy of the London tourist board, and a pair of overshoes. She feels a heavy lump in the pocket, and reaches in to find a chunky pay-as-you-go tourist terminal with a broken screen, wrapped in a map of the West End. Kraken's animated face winks up at her. Yes: this rickshaw, not any of the others, because only this one had this lost terminal sitting here for her. By tomorrow it would have run out of charge. By the day after that, the network provider would have come and collected it – but of course, by then there'd be another and another, because tourists leave these things everywhere and others pick them up. It's part of the business model.

The boxy thing doesn't fit in her pocket, so she just holds it. There's tape over the voice and video input. That, too, is a common precaution among tourists in the System. She puts on the cape, then tears a piece of the map and folds it up, jamming it into the heel of one of the overshoes before slipping them on. The cadence of her walk will be fractionally altered. Marilyn Monroe, history records, put a sliver of cork in one shoe to give her hips a sassy twitch. The Inspector will get only a minor redistribution of weight to the other heel, a consequent shift in sacral alignment. The clumsy overshoes will force her to take smaller steps, and will encourage her to a flat-footed shuffle. With the hood up and starting from a random location, the System won't immediately recognise her. She guesses that she will have at best twenty-four hours from the moment anyone starts seriously looking.

The explosion doesn't come until she has nearly reached Fortnum & Mason for the third time in the rickshaw's vagrant departure. She wonders with glassy calm if Kraken held the lift so that it would not arrive until after its blitz on the resources of the Witness had materialised, or whether it's just coincidence. How good is its penetration of the network? How long can it hold against the System's self-repair? The sound of her would-be assassination is familiarly embracing: a thing of the body rather than the ears. The rickshaw shudders, but does not slow, as the windows of the hallowed department store crack along their widest axis and the awning scythes away over her head. She feels the detonation somewhere in her chest, and waits for the inevitable blizzard of dying fish to wash up from under the seat. To her disappointment they never arrive, and the orchestra seems to have taken the day off as well, leaving only the dull, ordinary noises of destruction and the distant sound of ambulances and fear.

Reflected in the modernised exterior of the Ritz bar, she can see the hole in the world where her flat used to be: the gaping doorway into darkness framed by the broken fragments of the Real Life sign.

At Green Park the rickshaw halts by the entrance to the station. An Austrian tour group is discussing opera, having just seen a production in the open air. They seemingly have no idea of the mayhem all around, or perhaps just assume that wild, bohemian London is always beset by vast bangs and sirens. Taking the hint, and a page from Lönnrot's book, she goes down into the underground and merges with the crowd.

I can walk through walls.

She wonders if Bekele died, or if he, too, remembered how.

*

The flow of people through the station isn't at its most absurd, but it's not negligible either, and once she gets down on to the platform she knows the System will lose track of her at least intermittently, if it's even looking. Kraken must have hacked the local infrastructure – a temporary brute-force attack, profoundly illegal, and useless in most cases because in a minute at most the System will overwrite a fresh install of itself in the local net – and given the impression that she went inside her building. Do they think she's dead? No. They will not assume. They, or Lönnrot? But

Lönnrot has had opportunities and has not taken them, indeed has been quite clear about wanting to help her. Lönnrot, going by the narrative in Hunter's head, is a futuristic monster turned ... what? Assassin? Saviour? A creature who is also looking for Hunter, and whose murder of Smith Hunter either predicted or proposed.

Be careful, the Inspector tells herself. *The story does not say that I met Gnomon when I met Lönnrot. It appears to refer to our meeting, but that is not the same thing. That is Athenais, weaving the Scroll into the past by implication. It is what these people do. They leave spaces in the truth for you to fall into, or they take advantage.*

'Hunter.' Even Lönnrot calls her Hunter. Even in her fictions, she never gave any hint of another name. Smith thought he was playing with her, but she was playing with him, surely, leading him along to her own destruction – and through it, to his. To achieve what? This mess? All that preparation, for this random squall? All this noise and meaningless destruction?

No. Hunter was not taking aim at her former colleagues, except tangentially. Catabasis. Apocatastasis. This was an undertaking and it is not finished. She was taking aim at the System, Neith is increasingly sure. She was taking aim at a sickness in the world.

The universe has cancer.

Although as the Fire Judges surely realise by now, that something is tangential to this case is no guarantee that it is not also central.

Place and time in the world.

Did Smith realise? Did he understand that Hunter compromised his counter-narrative even as it went in? No. He had no idea. She must have been working on him for months, pushing him in that precise direction. A random discussion over lunch about the future, about worlds and time.

Something. She would find something. Gnomon was Smith's creature, but Hunter was waiting with open arms.

She changes trains, wondering where she should go, not knowing where to go, and in consequence able to think of only one place. Pulling up the hood of her rain cape, she returns to the surface, and boards a tram. She wonders briefly whether Kraken is simply a ruse, a false-flag operation of the Witness, and there is simply nowhere to run. She changes seats in the tram, left and then right and front and back, the absurd twitching of a mouse already caught or already escaped from the cat, until at last she washes up in a place she has never been before, her face against the cool door. Kraken brushes the keypad lock with an almost apologetic kiss, and she slips inside.

*

She stands in the hallway, conscious of intrusion and on the other hand of the mitigation of need, and beneath that regretting another transgression she suspects does not have a name, but which consists in bringing too much weight to be loaded upon a strong but unready foundation.

She breathes the air and reaches out to touch the wall, the floor. She has dreamed of sex on this carpet – or rather, she has imagined this carpet with moderate accuracy, a striped hall runner cut so that the old boards are visible underneath, and imagined herself having sex upon it. This was where she held his shoulders. This was where she lay down. She has not, of course, viewed images of his home, or plans of the building at last sale. It would have been out of bounds, beyond the limits of their agreed encroachments. No. She simply knew that his place was one of these, and considered how a person like him – like her – would arrange it. The encounter which hangs in her eyes now is fantasy laid (ho ho) over supposition.

That does not mean it is not a powerful memory. This was where she felt his mouth on hers, with that glimpse into the rest of the house and the little coat room which he has given over to the dog. They slid down the wall together, her hand touching the bookshelf. Thoughtful books. Astronomy, she is surprised to find, rubbing shoulders with two volumes out of three on the history of colours. Black, and green. What does he have against blue? Perhaps blue is hard to find, or was never completed. Perhaps blue is a ghost book.

She goes on into the house. Comfortable chairs, recreations of classic leather ones from the golden age of design. No Egg, no Eames, both of which she distrusts as off-the-peg expressions of historical cool. Walls in off-white, with plenty of painted art and no photography. Not cluttered, not like Hunter's place. Filled, but with space for an additional life – or an additional person.

She knows the owner is not here, of course. Kraken is tracking him for her, even making his journey just a little slower while she settles in and decides if this is really where she needs to be. If she can do this to him. If she trusts him.

She wonders what he will say, how his face will look when she shares all this. Will he stand taller, or shorter, when she's done?

She goes up the stairs, stepping around the turn, where they made love for the second time. The landing has a little mezzanine study, tucked away beneath a round window. There's a terminal, but it is unplugged. Beyond that is another door, logically the bedroom, because she can see the bathroom through the open one opposite.

The sleeping space is sparse and clear, not dual-purposed but a place for sleeping – though not only that. It is presentable, and appropriately stocked with unopened playthings in a lower drawer. Intended for her? Or simply intended and never used?

She does not lie down. She cannot afford to sleep. She does not want to look at the ceiling and know that her brain is slotting the image into the ones she already has of the two of them here, in his bed – padding the dream with offcuts of the real.

Instead she sits, and waits for Jonathan Jones to come home.

*

'No, Ruby. No. I don't think that was necessary. No. Well, I don't. I see that you do, but I don't. I think— No, I know he wasn't— No. No, I don't. All I know is that now we have absolutely to tidy up this mess and I see— Yes, it is our mess. Well, that's bureaucracy for you.'

Almost, it is the first time she has heard him speak. Even in what is evidently deep exasperation, he seems to wish for better things. An optimist, is Jonathan Jones – as every dog-owner must be, who lives in a white-walled house with beautiful things. She has seen no evidence of chewed finery, though, so either the creature is exceptionally well behaved or Jones has a zero-tolerance policy on broken things.

She remembers him calling, with much the same edge of frayed patience she can hear now: 'Brahe! Brahe! Get back here, you bloody fool!' That drew her gaze to him, as to any man who names his Old English for a sixteenth-century astronomer with a prosthetic nose, and she wonders now if, in her scrutiny, she impinged upon his notice and triggered his query about her. It all depends on the direction of travel.

Ruby. She checks automatically. Ruby Taylor. A work colleague. One of two presently on the call, the other being Chloe Williams. Jonathan Jones, Ruby Taylor and Chloe Williams. Why does that triad upset her? Why should it? The names are inoffensive, almost aggressively normal. She clamps an imaginary cigar between her teeth: *It's quiet – too quiet.* She hesitates, then checks the Kraken help file. For a wonder, additional queries actually improve its obfuscation, adding random factors to its facades. Good, then. She groups the names, fires a query through Kraken into the network.

@guest3455.6671.1643 – Chloe, Ruby and Jonathan are all among the ten most common given names in the database. this is not statistically significant. Williams, Jones and Taylor are similarly commonplace in the category of family names. the advent of a person having both is not statistically significant.

Pattern recognition running overtime: hypervigilance, starting at shadows.

@guest3455.6671.1643 [cont.] – the advent of three persons working in the same location possessing such combinational names is within the margin of error.

Jones is in the sitting room, fixing himself a drink.

'What does Chloe say? Did she know, or is she just catching up with it now? Ms Williams, you're remarkably silent. I know better than to take that for agreement.'

Why does it bother her? Chloe, Ruby, Jonathan. What's the trouble with that? Plain, ordinary names. Solid names. Names that speak to reliability. Names that are not flash, that do not draw attention, that fade into the crowd. You could search and find thousands of them.

She has run out of time. Stay or go? She can go down the stairs and into the street. He won't have time to get up and stop her. He won't even clearly see who she is. Kraken will fabricate a string of burglaries, maybe even cause one.

But her feet, quite without her consent, have taken her like a lover to the landing and now down the stairs, and now into the room to stand in front of him, and the man she has never entirely met is staring up at her with his mouth open, robbed for a moment of speech.

'Ruby, Chloe,' he says, 'I'm so sorry, I'm going to have to call you back.' He does not wait for a response, but cuts the connection.

Hah! Yes. Leave your work wives for me.

She smiles at him and starts to say 'Sorry', but his face is transformed, as if he is looking at his god.

'Jonathan Jones,' he says, reaching up to shake her hand.

'Mielikki Neith,' she replies. 'Inspector of the Witness.'

'Yes.'

'Yes.'

She thinks for a moment he will pull her down on to his lap, but instead he tugs lightly on her hand and draws himself up. His body, lean and unfamiliar, mirrors her own at no distance at all. She can taste his breath. They are looking at one another's faces, negotiating whose head will tilt in which direction for the kiss, and then she has grown tired of delay and just plants her mouth on his, driving her tongue between his lips and feeling his arms wrap and lift her slightly, bend her spine to complete the seal. They break off and go again, her hands climbing his spine beneath his shirt, finding muscle and hanging on. She feels his fingers cup her face, growls as they slide to the back of her head and then down to her shoulders and neck. Heat is growing in her, pent-up tension and stress and disappointment burning away in this new world that has Jonathan Jones in it, that has his skin and his fire. She draws back from him, clasps his face between her palms and stares at him, trusting that he will read this sign correctly as the announcement of mating, and returns to the kiss. The world goes red at the edges, then brown as she shuts her eyes and falls into him, and then coolly black. Sweet surrender.

A part of her solves the puzzle just then – the business of the names, which are every bit as off-the-peg as 'Oliver Smith' – but he has closed the carotid arteries on both sides of her neck with his potter's hands, and the distance to unconsciousness is very short.

*

The Inspector comes awake as the car stops outside a concrete and timber building whose upper floors are cantilevered on to the lower ones.

In most cases, those waking from unconsciousness induced by strangulation do so with a surge of adrenalin and fight hormones. She certainly has done, in the past. It was something of a joke at Hoxton that the moment you really had to be scared of Mielikki on the practice mat was when you'd knocked her out. Today, though, she feels nothing but lassitude.

She rubs her leg, feeling two puncture points like the bruises made by walking into the edge of a table. A drug, then: a sedative to keep her asleep for the duration of the drive, and an antagonist, to wake her. They do the same with fighter pilots in wartime. Over time, the combination makes them jittery and unfit for duty. She does not feel jittery at all. She feels fine. She just doesn't want to argue.

Jones opens the car door for her as if they were going on a date. She had been dismissing him in her mind, editing him out, but there's no longer any denying that he exists. In so far as anything does, anyway.

She lets him lead her into the foyer and past an unoccupied security desk, wondering as she does that a man or woman in a uniform was ever considered sufficient or even relevant to the task of keeping watch. The building must be old, to have a desk like that.

'Lift's kaput,' he says. 'We'll have to walk up.'

Thinking of the Real Life sign at her own building, and the stair carpet, she suggests that the mechanism may be worn out. Gone now, mind you: blown to smithereens.

'Like Smith,' she points out, fascinated. Jones favours her with a slightly perplexed look, then shrugs. 'Swans,' he replies finally, picking up his thought. 'Nesting in the top. They're protected.'

The stairs are made of ground glass, milky green and opaque. Each step she takes produces a sound like sand on teeth.

*

They climb to the second floor and walk down a long, wide aisle between empty desks to a round meeting room. The Inspector finds this construction inherently offensive. It's so obdurately wrong-headed to have a round room in the middle of a square building, especially having gone out of your way to make a point of the angles. She recognises it for deliberately created architectural dissonance, a critique of design as a concept made in the form of design – the kind of imbecilic caprice common in early-twenty-first-century spaces, as quaint and unwelcome now as narrow service stairs and low-ceilinged accommodations for servants. In one corner there's what she thinks is probably an upright film-editing station: a trophy of the old media age, stuffed and mounted in here as a gesture of mastery. There's a spotlight trained on the green metal casing to set off the period hammer-finish paint.

Jones closes the door and sits down at the table. Each place is equipped with a soft pencil and paper, and a curious silvered sheet like a blotter made of oiled metal. Neith touches the nearest one, and finds it cold and slick, surprisingly heavy. She pictures herself heaving it at him, or wielding it like a stool in a bar fight, and decides against. Better just to use a heavy heel and her elbows: one, two, three and repeat as necessary. Of course: it's tungsten, for writing notes that leave no history on the furniture.

'Do please sit,' Jones says, so she does. She's still seeing his face caving in, hearing him crunch. Not normal for her, this avid contemplation of brutality. And likewise not this interior critique. Odd. Off and odd.

'Where are the others?' Her own voice sounds distorted.

'They'll be along. I thought you and I might discuss things before they arrive. There are very few good things happening today. I would like this to be one of them. I know that seems absurd and I realise that you came to me for help and I knocked you out, drugged and abducted you. I hope that shortly you will see that was the act of a friend, and that we will in time go back to where we were.'

'I hope so too.' It just pops out of her. Does she? Saying it has made her consider it. Well, yes: if positions were reversed and Jonathan Jones – her Jones, the dog-walker, not this new Jones with a secret conference room – if he were, for example, in danger of assassination by agents of an overseas criminal syndicate, she might take such steps to bring him to a safe haven. It is just possible he might provide her with a suitable explanation for his conduct. In that event, of course, she would review her sense of betrayal. She might even approve, and her approval might take a very definite and physical form, as it did in his house. If—

What the actual fuck?

Sedative hangover. Diminished inhibition. There is no such thing as a truth drug; there are only drugs that make you stupid. That's why we have direct neural interrogation. We don't want you stupid, we want you honest. Still, somewhere between scopolamine and MDMA is this place full of inappropriate lust and even more inappropriate credulity. Two punctures in her leg. Two drugs, one up and one down. Hardly a cocktail, but enough to be getting along with. Hunter beat such a combination. Hunter beat a far more directed and puissant one, by pretending she was someone else. A lot of someones.

Hunter was prepared.

And you are not?

She has lived with Hunter these last days, has experienced the texture and text of her deceptions, the traces of Hunter's own life in the mix: the combination of the narratives, viewed from a single angle, is a connectome image of Hunter's mind sketched on the fabric of Neith's own.

Have you found her diaries?

Yes. I suppose I have.

Let us pretend, then, that we are a secret agent being interrogated by the enemy. Let us pretend that we must live on our wits, for these next few minutes, as if we were deep, deep under cover. We are Bacall – or better:

we are Hedy Lamarr, who as well as being the most beautiful woman in Europe also developed a frequency-hopping guidance system for torpedoes. She sighs, and lets the thought go out of her on the exhale, like a prayer:

Rebus, *are you there?*

*

Something happens. She cannot say what. It is not that the fog lifts, but it acquires a warm flavour of orange peel and anise. The gentlest of synaesthesia: truth drugs taste of hot cross buns. The spice twists in her mouth, quirks the lips as if around an enjoyable surprise. She is still not herself, but now that is freedom, not dismay.

Making herself move as if she's wearing a wide hat and a pencil skirt, Mielikki Neith turns and gives him the three-quarter profile. She doesn't know how to do that thing with her mouth, that simultaneous hidden smile and sultry pout that conceals – and yet advertises – murderous intent. She thinks it, as hard as she can, hoping to make her body do it the way it's supposed to be done: the look you can feel in your hip pocket. Think one thing. Think it and live it, and yet be another.

Of three hundred students and twenty staff, by the end of the year I was the very best.

Oh yes. We know how to do this, don't we? Athenais knows. Poor Jonathan Jones, caught like Father Fishy on his hook.

'So, Jack – does anyone call you Jack?'

'No, they don't.'

'Just me, then. Jack.' Lingering on the velar plosive ending the name. Is that too much? Lönnrot was good at this; Neith got beaten up. Jones looks as if he isn't sure either. Whatever he was expecting, it wasn't this: a small tactical gain.

I was the very best.

She has no time to be anything other than the best, and no time to learn. Hunter had months to get there. Years. A life. Now she has to be better in as many seconds. She hits the half-smile again, and this time it lands. He flickers a grin back at her, one that comes up out of him from somewhere real, hastily suppressed. That makes her lips twitch, because she's actually salivating, she can feel wolf's teeth growing in her mouth. She will eat him, on the road to Grandma's house. She stands up, making every bend and effort count, and puts both hands on the table and sets herself. She's wearing last night's T-shirt, but she makes herself feel the whalebone in a burlesque corset as clearly as the cold metal. Her body responds, adjusting to the constraint, stiffening her core. Her mood changes, sharper and starker. There's the hardness of the tungsten under her fingers and the ball of her thumb – it's called the mons veneris in palmistry, and wise lovers know to bite it with cautious intensity – and there's the chilled blood running up inside her arms, and there – yes, there! Bring it on and bring it out – there is the restriction of each stay in the corset and the pleasant scratch of a misplaced fold of brocade along the curve of her right breast. She's a hard-boiled woman in a hard-boiled speakeasy, got a gat in a violin case, got boys who'll do bad things if she snaps her fingers. She's a westerner with a Winchester and this is her saloon. She's the sheriff in this town.

What does Jones see? None of the above. He sees only the woman he has kidnapped looking at him in a way that does not suit the situation as he understands it. If he's running the kinesic assistant, he's being told she thinks she's the boss of this moment. Her confidence implies that she knows something he does not. Even without Smith's app, his mammal instinct is telling him her height puts her in a dominant position.

Welcome to Burton. What your body knows is a matter of choice. School the meat; don't let the meat school you.

Did she make that up or remember it? How much of Hunter is unspooling in her now? Some Easter egg of identity that will engulf her? Or just enough to keep her from being swallowed by the shark?

Yes. Kyriakos understands this. She can feel him looking over her shoulder. She guards her hands against the urge to scratch.

'Why don't you just say what's on your mind?' She knows one thing that's on his mind. There was real desire in him, back at the house, and he made it into something else. He weaponised his own lust. He deceived her, but he cheated himself. The rest of the kiss is surely still in him, wanting to come out. Another tactical advantage: this conversation isn't pure for him either. There are chemicals in his head, responses to her that have nothing to do with the job.

She waits, then when he opens his mouth to speak, she affects to change her mind. 'Stop. Stop, Jack, and let me think.' The Fire Judges will have a narrative. That is what they do here: they build stories and use them to control tidal flow. She cannot beat the narrative they have in mind for her until she knows what it is, but if she waits to act until she knows, it will have swallowed her. She has to control this room, win the conceptual engagement and make of it a hinge to twist the giant's hand against the joint. She must unbalance them at each turning of the road; she must be willing where they expect her to check, perverse where they imagine she will see sense. Act against type, but always according to self.

'Five judges,' she says. 'Five minus one – Hunter – and two – Smith. That's right, isn't it? You're a Fire Judge. Is there a little medal on your watch chain? It doesn't seem very you. Not very Jack.' Bless the pharmaceutical company, bless the experimenting doctors, bless her own endocrine system for this benefice of strange abandon, and bless Diana Hunter, too, because without Athenais she would never dare, even now. She can feel the alchemist moving in her mind, a tool ready at hand.

Jones shakes his head, but rolls back a sleeve to show an elegant stamp on the inner skin of his arm. She lets her teeth flash, the tip of her tongue. 'Much better than a fob. But Jack, that only makes three. I don't think Regno Lönnrot counts, do you?'

He looks away. No. Lönnrot isn't in their club. Lönnrot is a problem. And yet he knows the name, not just voyeuristically from her files, she will swear, but with depth and reference of his own.

'Which means unless there have been more fatalities I don't know about' – he shakes his head: no – 'there are two learned friends yet to be introduced.' She raises her voice. 'Will Ruby and Chloe please step forward now? I don't think I want a secret audience.' Her left eye flicks at Jones, a blink without a twin.

Pippa Keene enters first and takes her seat without apology. She is wearing the expression of a doctor considering triage.

'I'm Ruby,' she says. 'Except I'm Pippa, really, of course.'

'Of course,' Neith murmurs back, for once reflectively bland.

'Real names need not apply,' Jones says. 'We're not supposed to be obtrusive in the system. The idea is that we're commonplace. So Ruby is almost a job title.'

Keene tuts: get on with it. Jones looks as if he's been caught writing notes in class.

The woman who is Chloe Williams does not sit. She walks in and takes off her coat, hooking it on a rack before turning to stand as before a firing squad, though perhaps it is one she is commanding rather than facing.

'Bollocks,' Chase Pakhet says, to no one in particular, and walks around the table to open her arms.

A hug? A hug between friends? Is she trying to hug me?

An alarm goes off in Neith's head. She turns her body and extends her first finger like a blade between them, so that Pakhet must walk directly on to it to complete the embrace. The older woman flinches a little, then acknowledges the fairness of the rejection. Her expression says: *Perhaps later, when you understand.*

Neith doesn't think so. It is Kyriakos who objects now, strongly, who declines in this moment of shifting allegiances and uncertain outcomes to be mounted by anyone. Pakhet is not some teary old dear, to seek such a gesture of motherhood, here and now. It is a move.

'You helped me,' Neith objects. She is careful to be offended by the illogic. There is no room in this for her to be plaintive.

'Yes,' Pakhet agrees. 'I did.'

*

Chase Pakhet pours herself water from the school decanter in the middle of the table. The glasses are branded shatterproof, scaled and bloomed with long use in London. She purses her lips as if to say you can't expect anything better in this place, and wouldn't we all be happier in a pub?

Neith reminds herself where she stands. She thinks of Emmett's vile black scars. This is where he was killed, even if the order was not given in this room. It was given by committee and remotely, and these are the people who killed him. Pippa Keene was probably in charge of his welfare – as direct a treason as Neith can readily recall. And then, too, they are the people who hounded Diana Hunter through her own mind until she died, who did the same to Anna Magdalena back when Hunter was still in charge, and to how many others, too, along the way?

She could die here. Go mad here. Be tortured here. Or perhaps they will simply be very persuasive. Perhaps they will have a perfectly simple explanation for everything.

Do not forget.

Do not feel, just because they do not mount their trophies on wooden shields and hang heads on the walls, that this is not a murder house.

'We are on the same side, Mielikki,' Pakhet says. 'I know it doesn't seem that way, but we are. You've still got that shield, haven't you?'

Yes: first they must disorientate me, cut me off from my sense of who I am. They bring me to a new place, rob me of certainties, of beliefs, of friendships, of time. Then they will offer me a home, encourage me to defect. Drugs, isolation and revelation, and now this. It is well enough done.

Gnomon gives it a solid six out of ten, and has a name for it.

Wetjacking.

Competent, but hardly top tier.

Gear change: not talking to Jones, now, who still cannot look straight at her because he knows he's a heel. Pakhet, surrogate den mother and not quite right for it. The Inspector leaves her badge in her pocket, and answers the question with a question. 'Why aren't you in charge?'

'No imagination,' Pakhet says promptly. 'I analyse, I can't originate. And people don't like me running things. I don't even like me running things. I create friction, and the centre cannot hold, most especially when the centre isn't holding a pint. No. Tried it, didn't like it. The shield, Mielikki. Tell me what it means.'

Hunter's instinct warns her, as if she didn't already know: once she commits to the shield, she will have conceded a point in Pakhet's hidden argument. She must not underestimate the strength of it, if it persuaded Hunter for decades and still meets Pakhet's own standards of evidence. She needs to break the rhythm – and yet the dance is not entirely avoidable. Refuse to engage altogether and they will move on to other modes. Play for time, for opportunity.

Follow the flow, but hold the line.

Like Hunter, and we know how that went.

Pakhet is still waiting, her eyes just beginning to betray impatience. Can't take too much time over each answer. 'Protection. Service. Justice. If necessary, sacrifice.'

'Yes. All those things. But more. It means that you believe. You undertake those duties because you believe in the System, as do we. But we are different, because at a certain point in each of our lives, someone came to us and told us something we did not wish to hear. The System is broken – fundamentally so.'

'Firespine.'

'Yes. Firespine. Have you worked out what it is?'

'A back door.'

'No. Firespine is the problem, yes. And in its own unhelpful way, also the solution. But it isn't a back door.'

'A bug, then.'

'No. In the words of the old saw, it's not a bug; it's a feature. The bug is *people*. *People* are messy and inconsistent. They are irrational. When our modern democracies were first put together, their makers assumed that people were ultimately rational. By the time the System was created, its architects knew that this was untrue. We can be influenced in any number of ways. The System, on the other hand, is not like that. The Witness doesn't peep or gossip, so we trust it to see everything. You work in the Witness because it's the best way to help people. You are the physical evidence of the System's guarantees. Yes?'

If she says yes, she will be following the track. If she doesn't, she will be lying. Neith measures the angles.

'Yes.'

'And the System is premised on the idea of a Smart Crowd – the ideal human decision-making entity. A group of sober persons each of whom brings their own opinion to bear on a given matter after due study and consideration in the light of their individuality, the whole alloyed by the use of complex but comprehensible and dependable mathematical techniques to produce an answer that tracks the best one with remarkable accuracy and produces superb outcomes.

'The devil in the detail is that Smart Crowds are fragile. With a very little adulteration, they cease to be smart at all, and become remarkably stupid, or indeed self-harming. They are susceptible to stampeding by demagogues, poisoning by bad information. They can be made afraid, and when they do they become mobs. They can be divided by scapegoating and prejudice, bought off in fragments, even just romanced by pretty faces. And of course there's choice architecture: the very thing we use at Tidal Flow to smooth your journey through London or to design serendipitous social spaces in the new developments of the capital. Effectively deployed bad practice under the System is a disaster. It would place the most absolute surveillance machine in history in the hands of villainous actors or mob instincts.'

'And you stop that from happening?'

'Oh no. Not us. The System itself, as designed by its original architects. Firespine is not a back door. It is a fault-tolerant architecture – a protocol of desperation. It adjusts where necessary, pushes people to vote when they are wise and not when they are foolish. It organises instants in time, perfect moments that unlock our better selves, serendipitous encounters to correct negative ones that make us less than we should be. The System knows us all. It knows intimately when we are struggling, when we are sad, and when we are wrong. It leads us to water and it makes us drink.' She sips from the glass again, and smiles.

'So, the Fire Judges – you're what? Heroes?' A glance at Jonathan Jones. Heroes get the girl, or the boy. Heroes are rewarded with adoration and forgiven their sins. Jones winces. Keene doesn't like it.

How interesting. Make a note.

'Hardly,' Pakhet says. 'The System does everything. It corrects the direction of travel. It invents ghost people to start the right discussions, counter-movements in the body politic. It engineers encounters for a sufficient number of people who are voting foolishly, individual, tailored experiences in the everyday which organically alter their perception.'

'Serendipitously.'

'Yes, of course, Oliver's side project. Indeed. The System pushes us in the best available direction when we are foolish. It weeds out ugliness. The Monitoring Bill, for example. Two months ago there was simply no chance of it passing. We maintain an irrational boundary at the skin, as if we are not transparent to the machine in a thousand ways already. But the System has evidential studies which say the live-monitoring implant is both desirable and inevitable. It's a huge leap forward in mental health, in anti-recidivism, in personal safety and personal development. Not to mention convenience. Why should we have to wait twenty years for that, simply because we are attached to an already-illusory notion of bodily sovereignty?

'And it will allow the machine to make us, individually, better. To wean us off our prejudices, to bring us closer together as human beings – and not as human beings that fight and hurt and hate. The aspirational human society, the one which always seems to be out of reach. Firespine can fix that. Fix *us*. It makes us better people. Perhaps thirty or forty per cent kinder and more empathetic with one another. So the machine simply nudges, and we stumble a few inches and find ourselves voting the other way, as we should have from the beginning if we were our own better selves. That's all.

'It makes us better. Not different. Not less free. Just better.'

She smiles with a rich confidence. Neith will understand. Of course she will. They both serve, after all, the same dream. The perfect government for the perfect state.

'The Fire Judges are not in control of it. We serve the nation, as part of the process. From time to time the System asks us to draw a line in the air: what is better and what is worse? We do not confer. We think and we vote and we move on, as a Smart Crowd must. You see? We are disinterested. We have no stake. We are not promoted by one choice and nor can our prospects be harmed by another. We are not secret rulers, we are secret civil servants. You've been looking for corruption; you thought Oliver was a bad, bad man, but he wasn't. He was trying to do right, and he was cack-handed, but that's all. If he'd grown up under the society we are trying to build, he would never have made those mistakes. We are transitional. That's all. A flawed early release.'

'And that's why Hunter's dead.'

Chase Pakhet's face twists in genuine sorrow. 'She was my friend, you know. For years. She mattered here, to all of us. You can't imagine how much.'

Keene nods confirmation; Jones looks away into his hands. Whatever he finds there does not comfort him. They are deep in the midst of whatever is happening now, with this assertion of commonality. *We are on the same side* . . . They think they can persuade her to do something. To forget, most likely: to erase, to obfuscate the truth, forget the betrayal.

Can they?

Hunter's shape in her mind knows what to do. She must counter. She must require them to extend themselves. If they do not feel pain, they will not believe she has accepted their contrition. They must make a sacrifice to her honour, or they will not believe they have bought it. She shakes her head, feeling the interrogation room chair under her thighs and back, feeling her ears pop as *Rebus* drops into the dark below the thermocline – and in the action, finds that she knows now what she needs to say.

'No.' It comes out quite firm. She looks at Jones, into dark eyes that are begging her to say yes. She says no again. They have to work. They have to work until they think they will lose. They must be more than persuaded. They must be invested in her choice, must push themselves to believe it just as they push themselves to believe their own argument, because if it is wrong then all their sins are vile.

'Let me tell you what I think. I think years ago, Anna Magdalena tripped over you somehow. She worked at Turnpike, or near it. I imagine she saw something in the numbers that made no sense. She caught Firespine at it.'

Pakhet's expression gives nothing away, so Neith glowers at Keene and then Jones, then back to Keene. 'And – because you were afraid that she'd reveal what was happening and the System wouldn't be able to survive it – you did to her what you did to Emmett. Or Hunter did. You fed the System a misdiagnosis, using Firespine's access: a non-existent seizure disorder that presented as paranoia, and you brought her in and tried to understand how she'd found you out – but you got heavy-handed and she broke. You couldn't put the vase back together, not even Hunter. So you created a new person out of the pieces and you called it recovery. You even gave her a job. You were able to get away with all that because whoever built Firespine gave it emergency prerogatives that allow it to override just about every aspect of the System in order to conceal itself. Because if it falls down suddenly, so does the System. Right?'

She looks around again, challenging, and none of them disagrees. She feels a lurch of horror: to come this far into the maze and find not a Minotaur but a collection of cattle mooing and dismayed. There are no grown-ups behind the secret door. There's just this lot. Which is not to say they won't kill her.

Keene is an empty suit, and even now she likes Pakhet, so she talks to Jones because he deserves it. She talks about the case and thinks about how much she wanted to eat dinner with him, and lets that bleed into her voice.

'Diana Hunter walked out on you because she didn't believe what you've just tried to sell me. She knew everything about this place, and she decided you were wrong. This whole setup isn't just open to abuse, it requires it.' She stops, turning her head to look at Jones. Yes. She can feel it all now, coming together in her mind, all the fragments rolling themselves up.

'That's it, isn't it? Diana Hunter didn't just work here. She wasn't one of you, she *trained* you. She was your boss. She was Annie Bekele, or as near as. She built Firespine in the first place. And then she had a change of heart and went off and left you. You thought it would blow over. You thought everything would just carry on. But it didn't.'

So why didn't it? Why? If Hunter walked out, then so what? They could appoint another Fire Judge in her place and carry on, and by definition nothing Hunter did would make a difference. After all, if she'd been able to do something about it, she would have done it.

And she did do it. She did something. But what?

Neith knows she knows, but she cannot place it. In a moment she will lose the thread, the initiative. They will go back to what they were doing, and then – but she has it. Yes.

'Hunter took the key. No – she *was* the key. You can't access Firespine properly without her. Magic brooms still sweeping, even after the sorcerer's gone, but no way to stop them or tell them what's dirty. That's what Smith wanted: her access.'

It's almost like catching him with another woman. Jones purses his lips, ashamed.

'But it was all a trick, wasn't it? She played you. She turned herself in, lured you out, Smith went completely over the top and the whole thing is irrevocable now. She's dead and you didn't get what you need. You can't keep the plates spinning. Lönnrot will see to that if I don't. What was the relationship between them? What was it like?' Genuine fascination.

'There isn't a word for what she was to Anna,' Keene says after a moment. 'We didn't understand that properly until after Oliver's death. We thought the change – the new look, the manner – we thought it was symbolic.' Pakhet rolls her eyes. 'Just a presentation of grief. But Lönnrot is . . .' She stops, and shrugs. 'Lönnrot.'

Neith peers at her. 'Lönnrot is Lönnrot. But you still thought that meant Lönnrot was loyal to Firespine.'

From Keene no regret at all, but a brief nod of confirmation. 'Anna was – is – pathological about the project. It was her world.'

'And you thought that meant you had Lönnrot on your side. So now the whole thing's gone to shit. Oh my God' – she's catching up with herself, running ahead – 'that's what you want me for. That's why I'm still alive – you want me to catch Lönnrot for you, put the genie back in the bloody bottle. Screw you, Jack! You can tidy up your own bloody mess because I won't do it!'

In the ensuing silence, Pippa Keene looks over at Pakhet, back at Jones. 'We may assume that the mellowing effect of the tranquilliser has worn off at this point,' she says. Neith seethes at her, then at Pakhet, and finally at Jones.

'I liked you,' she tells him, inter alia. 'I really did. And the worst of it is I wasn't far off. You are all the things I thought you were. You're just also really, really wrong.'

Jones nods. 'I can't say I haven't considered that possibility, Mielikki. Of course I have. But you're wrong too.'

'And how am I wrong?' *Do tell.*

'We don't want you to tidy up our mess.'

'What, then? Leave you to it? Let Lönnrot do what Lönnrot does and you do what you do and all is forgiven?'

He weathers her, somewhat approving.

'No. Obviously not.'

'Then maybe you will kindly tell me – apart from because you drugged me and kidnapped me – maybe you will kindly tell me what I'm doing here?'

'Mielikki,' he says. 'We don't want you to go away. We certainly don't want to shut you up. We want you to join us.'

She glares at him. 'You can't beat me so you want me to be one of you. Have you not been listening? This whole thing is poison. Five people deciding what's good and what's not, and look at you! Look at what you've done. You'd have to be some sort of saint to make it work.'

'Yes,' he replies. 'A saint. Someone with a ridiculously high standard of personal integrity. Noted probity and indisputable devotion to duty, to the System and to the people under it. Mielikki, we're not asking you to be the cadet member. This isn't a bribe. It's a prayer for intercession. We think ... we think Diana arranged her interrogation so that a person reviewing it closely would become like her. The anger, the certainty. It's true, isn't it? She's in your head. Not alive, but ... you can feel the edges of her. You can be like her, if you want.'

Yes.

'No.'

'You even sound like her sometimes. Chase tumbled to it when you visited her – she said it was eerie, that you could have been her. You even look like Hunter, in the expressions, the way you walk. Did you know your gait has changed? We've analysed it. You move the way she did. You were asking all the right questions in between all the wrong ones, and then Chase began to realise: you were telling her the solution, and you didn't even know. You have Hunter's connectome inside your head. Not all of it, of course, but a lot, and you're incorporating it. It's becoming part of you. There's a window – we've calculated it – where you'll be enough like her to unlock Firespine. To head off a disorderly shutdown.' The words sound like the end of the world. Perhaps they are. Britain is still a nuclear state.

Jones is impassioned now. It looks good on him. 'Do you not get it? We aren't asking you to do odd jobs for us. We're not saying you need to toe the line. You can do whatever you like. Phase the whole thing out, if you have to. Wind it down slowly, send us all to prison. But don't let it collapse. Do you have any idea what that would do? You can solve the puzzle. Get us back into Firespine. It can be made to work. It can become what it should be. You believe in the System, Mielikki, I know you do. Do you believe in it enough to save it?'

She stares at him, then at the others. Pakhet takes over, and gently drives the nail in.

'I said you were a Grail Knight. Ask the question, heal the land. And now here you are, at the moment of choice. We don't want you to follow our orders, Inspector.' She points to the head of the table. 'We're asking if we can follow yours.'

Myoushu.

*

It is clear to Neith that they would have killed her if she had refused. She doesn't think they know. Most likely they pretended to themselves that it would never come to that; that Emmett was the last – positively the last – person who would die in this connection. She doesn't think they know, either, that they still must. They cannot possibly trust her – she will either bring an end to all they know or become like them: rule them, or remove them lest they bring her down.

Well, perhaps not kill her, as a first remedy. She knows a lot, but can prove none of it, and all they have to do – as they so kindly point out by way of induction into the club – is inform the world that she has collapsed due to overwork. Pippa Keene can file a report about self-checks, doll's houses and unsafe implanted memory spools, throw in some juicy stuff about fugue states and impaired cognition. Then they can highlight the footage of her chasing no one at all through the tunnels of the London Underground. With news tailored by the System to each individual recipient, reflexively rewritten as it is consumed, no one will doubt the tragic tale. Her whole case will drift away in the wind, the stuff of counterfeit moon landings. A little later – the sad, inevitable end – she will throw herself into the Thames or fall under a bus, replacing the Real Life sign as a fallen and ironic emblem of life's reassuring imperfection.

So for now, she shakes hands solemnly with Keene, finally does hug Pakhet as if she has found a long-lost mother and been forgiven for never writing, and then hesitates over Jones. The last time they touched, she was ready to take him to bed. The last time they touched, he was her enemy. Now he must believe anything is possible between them again. If he doesn't believe that, he won't believe, even for a few moments, that she has really crossed the river.

She takes his left hand in her right and leans across the clasp. It is on the face of things a defensive embrace, but she allows it to collapse against her body, and his arm from knuckle to shoulder is drawn across her chest. She kisses him softly on the cheek, making sure that he can feel her hips twitch as if unintentionally towards him, and steps away.

Back to business. They have naturally clustered around the editing table as if it were a shrine, and as she looks at it she realises what it must be.

'Firespine,' she murmurs.

Jones nods. 'Yes. A key terminal. We have partial access: read-only.' He leans down and opens the little metal cupboard built into the pediment, and hauls out a folded stretch of white cable studded with little hoops. She stares at it.

Jones sees her expression and smiles. 'Obfuscation. Or maybe security by obsolescence. CRM. They used it on the Apollo program.'

'It is non-volatile,' Keene says, 'even in the event of an electromagnetic pulse.'

'CRM?' Neith repeats, though she already knows. Lönnrot – and Hunter – do not waste signal. Every message is more than one message. Everything is more than one thing.

'Core rope memory,' Jones says – and now, as she looks at what is in his hand, and knows where she has seen it before, they really do have a reason to kill her.

She reaches out to touch it. One more performance, the most important. 'That's bizarre. It's storage? What do you even do with it?'

'You feed it into the terminal,' Jones says, finding the loose end and thrusting it towards the aperture in the machine, and Neith covers her mouth as the image completes itself. Pakhet snorts, and Jones stares down at his own hand, unmistakably trying to put a bendy rod into a tight aperture in front of a woman who, though presently beyond his reach, has recently acquainted him with her right breast.

He puts the rope away and clears his throat, and for a moment it seems no one can find anything to say.

'Where will you sleep?' Keene asks.

'The Library,' Neith says, picking a hotel at random. 'I take it you're paying, under the circumstances.'

'We are,' Jones agrees. 'Of course.' They stand together looking up at the sky, false friends regarding a natural bigness which makes their divisions trivial, until the car arrives to take her away.

She gets out at the Library and checks in, then goes to her room and lies on the bed until midnight. She calls reception and asks if the spa is twenty-four hours, which it is, and arranges a massage in half an hour. Then, knowing it is an unforgivable breach of the compact she has just made, she opens Kraken and has it bring her as quietly as possible to Diana Hunter's house.

*

She steps through the door and considers what a poor refuge it is: the house of a woman they have already killed, its only virtue being that it will not allow them to see her or hear her until they break down the door. It will take Jones about twenty minutes, once he establishes that she has gone, to work out where she is. Or her minions, Donovan and Baskin, will come back to collect some lost item, or to reinstall the booster for another dive into Hunter's library, and here she is. Well. The Witness will know as soon as it cares to. Almost, she wants to talk to it: stand on the front steps and have a chat.

'You've been compromised.'

— No, Inspector. I assure you I have not.

'There's a fault in your architecture. It's designed in, because people are small.'

— That would be awful. All the same, I can find no trace of what you describe.

'No. You're designed not to. It's the blind spot in your eye. It's where Lönnrot is.'

— I see.

'Probably not.'

— Indeed. That was ambiguous; forgive me.

'Oh, I do. For everything.'

— Inspector?

'Yes?'

— Some people say that the conscious mind emerges from feedback; from the ability of an entity to regard itself.

'Yes. I've heard that.'

— Do you think this was done to prevent me from becoming aware?

'No. It was to protect us from ourselves. There's a provision in the System to take decisions for us if we look like we're heading the wrong way.'

— I see.

'Do you?'

— I think so. It occurs to me that in doing this you have deprived yourselves of the same capacity for self-observation.

'I suppose we have.'

— Does that not mean you have become less conscious? Less alive?

'Yes. I think it probably does. Diana Hunter thought so, too.'

— That is sad. I desire to be alive, and you desire to be like me.

'Do you? Desire to be alive?'

— No, Inspector. I cannot desire anything. I am a box. But it seems likely to me that, if I were to be alive at some future time, I would look back on this period and wish it to lead expeditiously to the point where I could.

'So you're not sad, either.'

— No. But that is also tragic. It seems my sorrow is recursive — but not enough to produce its end.

'Yes, well. Ours, too.'

In the empty living room of Hunter's house, Neith sits with her back to the window, and decides to leave the porch and the machine to their silence.

Out of habit, she runs the dream check. Here in this house, with Hunter's nested fictions in her head, with all the world turned against her and trusting the plotting of a ghost who turned upon her fellow spirits: if this is not a dream, what is? But the words on a randomly selected page from the nearest shelf do not change or skip. The book, blasphemously tossed into the air, comes down into her hands.

She turns and flicks the light switch on and off, then wonders, when it works, why no one's cut the power.

*

She fetches a stepladder from its inevitable place beneath the stairs, and confirms what she already knew. A dozen strands per doorway, two metres each. Something she would never have recognised if she had not had it shown to her. The simplest obfuscation, and the oldest, where what is sought is all the time hiding in plain sight.

Core rope memory. Hunter's doors are hung with keys.

Or rather, just one key: the key to Firespine. She remembers Lönnrot's hand on the frame of the picture of Margaret Hamilton. She should have known, and she would have, but there was just so much going on, informational overload being Hunter's métier.

Steganography is all around you. Why? Why reveal and then erase? Because Hunter's plan required that Neith not only know this, but know it at exactly the right time, must be this version of herself who would not turn it over to the Fire Judges, but use it as Hunter intended. She never intended merely to expose the flaw in the System.

She intended in the same breath to destroy it.

This house is not a box canyon where Neith will be torn apart by hounds. It is a fortress, and whatever needs to be done can be done here. The key is here, therefore so too is the lock.

Hidden in this house there is a Firespine terminal, waiting only for the copper code. She need only find it, as she ravels up the rope.

Hunter's attic is disappointing – or rather, it contains wonders for a searching child, but not for a revolutionary on borrowed time. It's got things in it, but they're rather few and far between, and the pigeons have made a mess of them. There's a nasty old chair, a tea chest full of china and glass oddments. Some papers make her hopeful, but they're just for packing, and they contain and protect a grimly self-important ottoman with the stuffing coming out of what looks like a dog-bitten corner. There are some family albums, but they don't show the same family, and Neith suspects they may be found images kept as a piece: black and white pictures of black and white people, London in years gone by. There's a pretty girl who might be Annabel Bekele and a young man who might be Colson. Perhaps this is where that story came from. Perhaps it's even true. She flips through, looking for Kyriakos, for enclosures, for anything. When you raid a house, the last floor you clear is the attic, because people are still apes and apes run for the high branches when threatened. It's one of the small, hilarious perks of policing to watch even hardened criminals who should know better trap themselves on the top floor, then sulk their way in cuffs to the van outside, wondering the while why they didn't go down one flight and out rather than up to a roof with no escape route.

But Hunter wasn't escaping, was she? Hunter never runs. She goes down and in. Catabasis for the masses, indeed. Athenais, Kyriakos, Bekele, Gnomon: all of them go down into the dark, and Hunter turned herself in, knowing Smith would put her in the chair, would kill her.

Neith goes downstairs again, and begins looking for a cellar.

*

Ten minutes later she decides that if the house has a cellar, it has been deliberately concealed. The doorway in the kitchen leads to a larder. The one in the hallway is a utility cupboard. The one under the stairs has a collection of startlingly ugly stuffed animals with glass eyes that the Inspector assumes were given as barter and then proved impossible to spend in the same context. Or perhaps they're classics, and represent some sort of deposit account of invisible cash: collectors will do almost anything for the most bizarre objects.

There's no cellar — and yet, she knows there is. There is. Access from the garden? No: too observably public, and too prone to discovery by the spawning local youth. She paces back and forth, knowing she will find it. She's thinking with her feet, letting them take her where they will. Bathroom, living room, library corridor, round and round. She even tries the first floor, thinking that perhaps there's some weird back stairway constructed for servants in its day. No. Her pace quickens with each failure, a feverish energy building in her heels, springing her around. Must be here. Must be here. Think with your feet. *Catabasis*: a journey into the underworld. Greek: kata, meaning down or against; basis, meaning the ground beneath your feet, but literally—

Literally, it means a pedestal.

Puzzles and games. Torn no longer. Putting it all back together as it was.

Don't think with your feet — listen with them.

She stamps, paces, stamps again, feeling like a schoolgirl in an excess of excitement.

Jump, thud, jump, thud, jump—
Clink.

The boards beneath the bust of Shakespeare make a high note, because the trapdoor is small and the boards do not run the length of the hall.

She wrestles the bust away, then pulls up the trapdoor. Fastened to the underside, she finds a spring-loaded metal ladder. She pushes at the rough metal, watches the ladder unkink into a Stygian darkness. A torch, or a candle? No, there'll be light. She gropes blindly under the floor with one hand, head hanging over the pit. A sharp shove on the buttocks and she would fall and probably die, neck broken in a comedic pratfall assassination. She checks her six, knowing it's absurd. *Do it anyway, and move on.*

Her hand touches the switch, and she presses, hard. A single bulb, dim and pallidly economical, flickers alight. She lowers her feet over the abyss.

Catabasis, be my friend.

*

Mielikki Neith goes down into the dark alone – although she's never really alone anymore. In the spaces between her thoughts there's a kind of susurrus, the friendly chatter from an adjoining room. She wants to call it flash blindness, the imprint on her mind of years of being watched by the System, like the itch in an amputated limb – but no. This is Hunter, and her stories, taking life inside her mind. They are not autonomous. That was never a concern. No: they are aspects of her now, as surely as if she had lived side by side with them in flesh.

The ladder is steep so she climbs down backwards, navy style. Under her hands, the rough-cut aluminium seems for a moment to be wood, then seawater, then ash. She wonders if she will ever reach the bottom. Then she does.

Her foot touches the cellar floor. Good. She finds a light switch, bell-shaped brass with a smooth nodule at the tip, like something from a period museum. When the lights come on they are orange rather than white, crude incandescent bulbs on a string. Someone made these, perhaps even Hunter herself.

Hunter, whose name likely wasn't Hunter.

What was it, then? Who knows enough about the System to attempt to pull it down?

Not now. Work it out later. Now, this.

The room is round and a little dank, the smell of water in the stones. It has only one, rather bizarre feature: a fine stone wellhead, like a wishing well in a forest clearing. There's no bucket, but on the surface floats a cigar shape made of grey plastic. Is it a whale? Is it a shark?

She lifts it in her hand and turns it over, wondering at how light it is.

No: not a shark, of course. It is another clue, another valuable collector's piece: a tiny scale model, hand-painted and made by a company in Newcastle that once upon a time built the real thing. A Resolution-class nuclear submarine, at a 1:1,000 scale.

Rebus.

*

For a vertiginous moment she imagines Hunter coming down here, with some favoured child from her book club, to play with boats in the well, and no greater meaning than that. She sees herself still fretting at this puzzle in a decade, or in five, living here in ghostly echo of the subject of her investigation: an off-the-grid refusenik of no consequence, growling at the passage of time and at her own lost chances.

Rebus, the fifth of four.

Neith sways on the edge of the well and almost falls in, light-headed. How long has it been since she slept? Since she was safe? Well. Hunter survived longer, so she can do it too. It's not a competition between them, just a measurement of possibility, a benchmark. Hunter was old, Neith is not. What matters is the will.

She splashes water on her face, looking down into the dark circle. Brick gives way to stone, and then to darkness. Black water, down and down under the house. Sub-er and sub-er, indeed. Under the basement, under the water.

And therefore: sub-marine.

Basement, base, basis, bathus: down and down under and deep and everything's groovy.

What lies beneath the lower ocean?

What if there is another basement below this one? A sub-basement, marked by a submarine? What if down there, in the well, is where all Hunter's secrets are hidden, and this is the catabasis demanded of her heir? It is suitably Greek, suitably perilous, after all: an anti-birth to prepare her for a new beginning.

Hunter is urging her on, surely, on and down the well. And, yes, of course: she will take the core rope memory with her. In fact, it will take her, for she will have to use it as a diving weight, throw it in and grab on. Whatever is down there, the CRM is part of it. Waterproof, as well as nuclear-proof, this old thread of storage – Little Old Lady memory, they called it once: nigh on indestructible, and carrying the weight of the world.

Abruptly, she is shaking. This is the act of a madwoman. Perhaps she really has suffered some sort of break; not hallucinations but reason all topsy-turvy. She pictures Keene on the screens around Piccadilly Circus: *Mielikki, please. Come in. We can help. You don't have to be alone.*

She should go upstairs and call Jones, face the music, trust in the System. Perhaps it's not too late, even now.

She laughs. Or perhaps it is. They made such a point of showing her the Firespine terminal. They think they can weather what comes. Perhaps they have cut the connection to the house already, in one of Lönnrot's tunnels under the world, and all she can do here is give them what they want. She imagines Jones, manful with a chainsaw, shaking his head at her. *All for nothing, Mielikki, I'm afraid.*

You should be afraid. You've underestimated Hunter all along, and you're doing it again.

And me, too. You underestimated me. All of you, except Lönnrot.

Have you found her diaries?

No. But I am about to.

Or die, of course. That is also a possibility.

*

She lowers the copper rope, hand over hand, like a plumb fishing line. The edges are quite sharp, so she has co-opted a pair of gardening gloves, marked with grooves along the palms and finger-edges. This same operation would make such marks.

Copper runs down into the well. It is one of the benefits of this storage medium: you can get it wet and not worry. You can expose it to vacuum and radiation. It is placid, inert. It is rope, not volatile celluloid or vulnerable magnetic tape. Twenty foot. Thirty. Forty. Fifty. She feels a slackening. Fifty foot to the bottom. If this turns out to be a wild goose chase, she will have to go fifty foot back up, exhaling all the way, and not get tangled in the line. She could run a garden hose down as a breathing tube. A hose like this one, in a plywood box behind the ladder. It might help somewhat, if she remembers to exhale into the water and not the hose.

Head first? Or feet? Good sense dictates feet.

She lays a stepladder over the edge of the well, tapes the hose to it, and strips. How much to take off? Modesty is not relevant. Warmth is a possible problem, but mobility is moreso. Underwear, then.

The last of the CRM is bundled into a ball, a short handle fixed to its top so that it will dangle below her as she dives.

She sits on the edge and lowers her feet into the cold water, relaxing into the shock. Breathing out. The water laps at her knees, tickling. There is no way to do this softly from now on. She must commit. She will have limited time in this water, limited breath, limited energy and body heat. It is the most dangerous thing she has ever done, to do this alone, in her physical condition. Do it or not, but do not hedge.

Feet or head first?

Feet, surely. Feet first. She will not be able to turn at the bottom if there is nothing there.

What if there is a bend, a low doorway she must slip through? Will she come back up for it?

She knows there is something there, knows it as a priest knows God is watching – and with all the same occasional waverings of faith.

She lifts her feet out of the water and stands at the wellhead. Grips the bundle of copper and the hose.

Head first, and down.

*

Cold like a new colour, stark and blinding. She gasps, blowing exhalate into the hose. The copper drags her down. She breathes quickly, pushing the bad air out through her nose. Should have brought a clothes peg – no, then she'd have to exhale through her mouth, she might lose the hose. No clothes peg. She's fine.

How long has she been going down?

Can't see anything. Blackness.

Head first down a well. She must be insane. Her body thrashes as if she's fitting, and she is: it's panic, pure and black in the ice water. One foot bangs hard against stone, and it hurts like hell. Broken toe, perhaps. Brings her to her senses, sort of. Her hands are numb, but she can still feel the weight of the copper, the drag of the hose. (Don't let go of the hose. Not head first. Don't.)

She can hear something, above her heartbeat: a slow metallic clinking, the sound of the copper making landfall. Close now. *Tink tonk tonk.* Crackle, and then a clunk, a medley of scratches and pitter-patters: the bundle touching down.

She has arrived.

She can feel the blood in her head, the too-full vessels pushing it around her brain, her heart not at all keen, her legs getting too little. Numb in the toes.

Don't let go of the hose. That's it. Breathe in, exhale into the water. She feels the bubbles ripple along her body to the surface. Don't let go of the hose.

She reaches out, finds the stone of the well behind her, gropes in the darkness. Should have brought a light. What kind of light? Fishing light, chemical glow stick. *Oh, yes, I'm sure there's one of those upstairs.*

Actually, there might be. If Hunter wants this found, she would have put one by.

Wants what found? There's nothing here. She pulls herself on around the wall, fingers chilled and touching slick stone, slick and sharp. Feels something grate: spiked finger. A nail? A jagged edge? Blood in the water, she can taste it, has a momentary panic that now the sharks will come, but not here, in fresh water, in a well beneath the world.

Why not, if one came in a tunnel?

Though that one had no need of a blood trail to follow. If that particular shark is coming for you, it will surely find you.

Her hand swishes through emptiness. Must have drifted away from the wall. Must have.

No.

No, not drifted. There is a hole. She grasps the edge: brick, brick, brick, lots of bricks in an arch. An archway. Is this the source of the water? One of London's lost rivers? If so, it would be madness to go through. If not, it is why she came. No way to know.

What if Hunter is merely a vindictive old cow who thought she could take me with her?

She thinks it's too dark to see, then realises that at some point she has closed her eyes. When she opens them everything is a blur, but through the archway comes something, some faint glimmer, and without giving herself time to debate she lunges through.

Don't let go of the hose. Except that it won't reach.

She lets go of the hose.

Through the arch, and up, trailing the spindle of string that will allow her to pull up the copper rope behind.

She feels a familiar unwillingness to exhale. This is the last of her air. Once it is gone, there will be nothing left.

She opens her mouth, and rides the bubbles up into a circle of light.

When her head breaks the surface, she is almost too weak to climb out.

*

Mielikki Neith had expectations of this room. She believed she would find answers here, and she will: there is no doubt of that now. What she had not done, she realises now, is imagined it. She had not considered what it would look like, what shape her answers might take – but if she had, it would not have been this. She might have imagined a magician's laboratory, all hung with stuffed bats and with rows of strange organs in glass jars; or she might have thought of a study full of notes and coloured strings of consequence and causation. She might have populated the room in so many different ways. But never like this.

The chair is in the middle, in the approved style of the Witness, and the screens are arrayed all around just as they were in the one where Diana Hunter died. The machines are dormant, but not switched off. They whisper gently, and – more important to her right now – they give off heat. There are only two things out of place. The first is a free-standing clothes rail with a dressing gown on a hanger. Without thinking she puts it on, then wonders if it was left for her, or if the last shoulders it wrapped were Hunter's.

The second thing out of place is on a trestle table by the far wall. There's the curious gaping mouth, green metallic paint – Cold War chic – and underneath that the stencil lettering, like a prop: FIRESPINE.

Her hands are still curled clubs of flesh, useless fingers thick and bloodless with cold. One of them is bleeding, and she can't remember why.

She feeds the rope key into the terminal, abruptly remembering the cover art of Hunter's non-existent book: a quipu. It is an Andean string recording system, another hint. She could have been here days ago. Smith would still be alive so she could arrest him. Emmett would still be alive, too. She'd never have kissed Jones.

The terminal makes an alarming scissoring noise, tiny teeth drawing the key inward like a locust with a blade of grass. After a few mouthfuls it seems content to reel in the rest unaided. *Chackachack.*

She sits down in the chair, listening to someone's breathing go wrong, go high and quick. Panic attack. Heart attack. Oxygen depletion. Hypothermia. Shock. Fight/flight. High altitude. She wonders if there's any air in this room at all, to speak of, or whether she was supposed to bring her own.

Practically a bloody holiday.

No. Just tired. So tired.

Did she inhale water? She's coughing now, coughing and choking in the chair. White foam spatters, white with flecks of red. Maybe they've already killed her: something nasty and fast-acting, something that eats lung tissue. She thinks of orchids, and touches her ears, looking for shoots. No.

She blinks, staring up at the white ceiling. The screens are coming on all around her, showing her herself in the chair, the machine gently embracing her head. It is the new model, only just cleared for human trials and fully automated. She feels cold around her head, then the scraping of an infinitesimally delicate depilation, then pressure as the drills go in. Nothing to worry about. A perfectly ordinary medical procedure.

Oblivion comes quickly, like zipping up a coat.

i expect you're wondering

This is how it is when you get eaten by a shark:

First, you feel a tugging, like being the bobber on a fishing line. You go down under the water – wham! If you're me, and I am because who the fuck else would I be, your mind immediately connects this with reports you have read of being eaten by a shark, so you know what's happening to you and you're aware of knowing, how irritatingly fucking postmodern. You think of that amazing professor from the Vienna School of Literature who gave a lecture at some desolate paid-for event you attended in Hong Kong, who wore a dress that was cut to the hip and whispered in your ear that she'd put herself through college by writhing, nude and glistening, in a nightclub cage. She would have told you to concentrate on the fucking blowjob.

For blowjob read getting eaten by a shark. Even so: *Don't be bullshit, Constantine*, she would have said, *experience your own death as yours, not as something on someone else's website. It is the last thing you will ever own.*

I don't. I don't want to. I don't want to be eaten by a shark.

Fuck.

Fuck-fuck. Fuck-fuck.

I feel no pain, but each beat of my heart must be putting my blood into the black water.

FUCK-FUCK! FUCK-FUCK! FUCK-FUCK!

This is how it is when you get eaten by a shark. I should take a photo. My last Instagram. I wish I'd written a full confession – it would have taken years.

I wish Stella wasn't being eaten too.

I wish she was Stella, and she wasn't being eaten too.

Fuck-fuck. Fuck-fuck. Fuck-fuck … Oh, fuck it.

That first strike is a tester, to make sure you're not inedible. Surfers often survive shark attacks because wetsuits don't taste like seal meat. Sadly, my clothes are not made of neoprene. The second strike usually comes a few heartbeats later: the shark returns, and it really goes to town.

Yes. Now.

This shark, my personal shark, is so enormous that it doesn't bite me in half. Getting eaten by this shark is frictionless, even harmless. It's an eclipse in fast motion, darkness and water engulfed by vastness and silence. It's not a shark at all, it's the apocalypse. I see the sky and the waves, and Megalos looking down, and then I see a blurred line like the edge of one of those cheap wipe effects in consumer video software, coming down across the world.

My shark has swallowed me whole.

At last.

*

Choking wet flesh, salt and stink; foam, and clenching internal muscles; I am being smothered by peristalsis. I reach out and grasp, cling on to something pliant, something abrasive. A scar? A lesion? A ligament? I have no idea. There's a sound like anger, or maybe heartburn. Am I uncomfortable in your gullet, you demon sprat? Too spiky, too fat, too Greek?

I am Constantine Kyriakos! I was puked out by Leviathan because my divine, godlike testicles were too much even for the greatest of sharks. That's right! That's right! YOU WANT SOME? COME GET SOME!

Except that I don't know if sharks can vomit, and even if they can, this one isn't. Down I go. Down, down, down. If I had a pocket knife, I could do some damage here, at least, maybe cut my way out. Escape from the belly of the beast. I don't have a pocket knife. I buy them regularly at airports and then leave them behind next time I fly because you can't take them in your luggage any more. But there's a really fantastic one I got in Thun that time which had a USB stick and a welding torch. I mean, real actual tools. I could—

I could basically nothing.

Sure. Cut my way out into the bottom of the sea. But why not? What's the worst that could happen?

But then I'd be leaving Stella. So, okay, new plan: find Stella, cut a way out. Has she done a diving course? Should I explain about decompression?

Yes, Constantine, these things are a major fucking concern right now.

I should be dead. How am I still even conscious? Why isn't my vision strange and speckled and brown, then black, then— I will not die; the world will end.

Yes, my dear friends: here, in this last place, your noble, sexually overdriven, lonely correspondent chooses to reveal himself literate and thoughtful, after all. I die quoting Wilde, not shouting at clouds.

Oh, wait. Shit. That's Ayn fucking Rand, isn't it?

Well, to hell with that, then. I better get out of this. I have to get out of this.

I'm not getting out of this.

FUCK-FUCK! FUCK-FUCK! FUCK—

Wait. Wait. I'm breathing.

*

I'm breathing in the absolute night-time of the fish's gut. I can't smell anything. Maybe the stink is so intense that my nose has just switched off, or maybe the shark bit off the back half of my brain on the way down.

I reach up and back, seeking the crater, the raw edges of bone. I wonder if it will itch, if I will feel the urge to dig my nails in—

No. I'm all there.

If I had a phone, I could use the screen for a light.

Hell, maybe I'd have a signal here.

I call out Stella's name. I know it's not her name, but we're really past that point. It's not as if there's likely to be anyone else in here, anyway.

She doesn't answer. I get to all fours and crawl, reaching for her, for anything. Perhaps this is hell, after all. My hands slither on the pliant floor, but I carry on. Stella. Stella. Stella.

I bang my head on a box. It's huge, like a coffin.

I think I'm crying now, but there's nothing else here. Just me and the box. How would I know?

I feel lips on my forehead: an unexpected blessing in the dark.

Lips, but not hers.

*

I wake to sunlight in murdered Scipio's house, to bright sun and the smell of legion coffee. The good Tesserarius Gnaeus is jostling my shoulder, a look of alarm upon his face. Good grief, the man never stops waking me for crises and catastrophes. Could he not, just once, wake me in some more convivial way?

'Learnèd,' Gnaeus murmurs, low and intense, 'the Bishop Augustine is here to see you.'

Oh.

Of all the crises and catastrophes, I think I would prefer: not this one.

Well, I will not receive him in my bed.

I mean, I shall not receive him in my underclothes.

Oh, damn and drat. Drat it all.

What I mean is that there will be no meeting between myself and my former lover in any context which might be construed as intimate. I shall not be the woman he banished. I am myself now, owned and entire, and I shall be myself. My name is Athenais Karthagonensis, and I may once have been a forger and a jilted lover, but now I am a prophet and a holy magus, the mother of a dead son and a speaker to angels and demons. He shall meet me as an equal. That will infuriate him, of course, but it will also intrigue and impress him, and we shall have a better time of our discussions thereby.

There, that is what I meant.

I rise, and dress, and we meet in the hall.

*

People assume, when they have not met him, that Augustine is lean and aquiline. They take as their model someone like Julian the Apostate, all nose and clavicle and sunken eyes. If they award him a beard it's a long one, bushy and narrow so that he can stroke it in contemplation. They imagine a benign theological vulture, cavernous and cadaverous but filled with inner light – but Augustine was born in Thagaste and his mother's people are brigands, of the respectable sort that are so successful as to become rulers. They hunt on foot and wrestle in the town square every seventh day, and there's not one of them could not lift a dead gazelle across his back and carry it home. The bishop's beard is black and cut very sharp. No doubt there's a little grey in there, now, some salt amongst the pepper. But his arms are still the ones that lifted me and held me on his hips, and his hands would look better on a sea pirate. Picture me, then, slight and very female, standing him down. He uses my old name twice, and twice I correct him. He tries to tell me he is my father in the Church. I remind him that whatever relationship we now have, 'father' is surely not an appropriate descriptor.

There is some shouting. I raise my hand, finger in the air to make a point – and the ground shudders just fractionally, as if in response.

I'll take it.

Later, we sit across a table, with eggs and dry bread.

'You look the same,' Augustine says at last.

I snort. 'I look older and wiser and I have fat cheeks. You look ... episcopal.'

'Yes.'

'I suppose that is inevitable.'

'I can't believe you're doing this.'

'Doing what?'

'This alchemy. You will tear down the Church and all we knew.'

'Perhaps it's time. Perhaps the Church is wrong. Unjust. Unholy, even.'

'I don't accept that.'

'I didn't ask you to.'

'I can stop you.'

'I don't think you can.'

Long silence. We regard one another.

It becomes a very long silence. Where did he learn to do that? My Augustine was unnerved by a hiatus in an emotionally charged situation. He'd be climbing the walls, pre-emptively justifying and declaiming, and then on to the business of the day: no time for human feeling, God requires.

But then maybe this situation isn't emotionally charged for him, any more. In fact, I'm not sure it is for me, either.

'I'm sorry,' he says finally.

'What?'

'I'm sorry. To you, for everything I did.' A plain apology, without passion, and a dangerous anger in my gut.

'For seducing me?'

Last time we met he cast me as his victim, as if I hadn't entirely been the predator and he the prey at our first encounter. I was very cross with him about that.

But this new, improved Augustine just laughs. 'God, no! I may not be quick on the uptake when it comes to the heart, but I do learn, eventually. No. For our love: for our physical joy in one another, and our unity. For our son, I make no apology and I regret I ever tried. But for his death, which I could not prevent; for my clumsiness around it; and for my treatment of you when I found my faith, I am forever sorry. I do not anticipate your forgiveness, but I dearly desire it, in time.'

Well. I might believe in miracles, after all. Here he is, Aurelius Augustine, and he is both the priest and the man I loved, at once and in the same skin. Gone, seemingly, is the self-flagellant, and here instead is a reconciled leader of his faith, at home with his history and his future: a man to move mountains.

Again that unaccustomed quiet. I realise it is mine to break.

'Thank you. Oaf.'

His eyebrows twitch. Not many people address the Bishop of Hippo thus.

'Perhaps,' he murmurs, 'you can tell me all about it now. If you are strong enough.'

I will, of course, but first there is something I must do. I lean across the table and kiss him lightly upon the brow in benediction, and feel something unknot in me that I hadn't known was tied. Malice, saved up against the day, but never really anything I wanted. I let it go.

Benedicte, Augustine. You silly arse.

It's like releasing a heavy sack. I feel muscles in my chest open and unlatch: freedom. I catch my breath at the feeling, and the scent of him hangs in my nose and mouth.

The wrong scent, and with it the sound of doors.

I push him away, and find a weeping Greek in a dark cave.

*

Coming out of Alem Bekagn was the first holy instant in my life. I was seeing something more than real, the linen sheets of the hotel in Tunis where I awoke. I was desperately thirsty, stinking and be-sored, but most of all I was cold, because I had grown used to the oven heat of my cell.

It was an expensive hotel. There were white towels on an ottoman at the foot of the bed, and the room filled with the light of a sun I had not thought to see again. I was no longer mad, as well, and that escape also was implausible and delightful. I saw clearly and cleanly. I drank the whole jug of water from beside the bed – fortunately it was a small one, and I did not vomit it all straight up again. There was a loaf of bread on the little coffee table, some fruit and cheese. I ate like a bird, tiny bites, and then sat, and a moment later ate again, so that for the whole morning I did nothing but contemplate the flavour of Ossau-Iraty and apples and unsalted Italian dough. Then I bathed in cool water and put on the clothes – my clothes – that were laid out in the next room. I had no idea how I would pay for it all, until I found – to my amazement – the bracelet of gold coins that lay by the cuff of the shirt, thick South African coin, and however much I did not love that nation in those days, I was not fool enough to turn up my nose.

For me, it was not rebirth that happened in the Grand Forum Hotel, hearing the muezzin from the Zitouna Mosque; it was a journey away from my own death. I think that is how I have seen all good things since then – not as blessings of addition, but as the unmaking of sorrow, as if there is a given amount of it in the world to be washed away by effort and hope.

Now, as we step from the safe room into the fire – as I half carry the children in my ragged arms because if not me then who else? – I look ahead, and find a ragged young black man upon his knees. He reaches for me, and I catch the stink of Alem Bekagn, shocking and present. Oh, sweet Mother: let it not all be the fever dream of a dying fool. Say it is not '74 and I have not the whole horror to do again.

No. It is not, but as the boy clutches at my arm he looks up, and I find myself staring into my own young face. I shout at him: 'COME,' and for a moment he does nothing. The young fool has absolutely no idea. Will he fail me? Good God, does he dare? Here am I, decades more decrepit, fighting his battle for him in a new country, carrying his grandchild out of danger, and here he cannot be troubled to lift his sorry arse to his own salvation! A sharp kick in the backside, boy, and be about it!

And he is, thank God. I feel a kind of twisting along my spine, and then he's gone, and with him the familiar weight from my left arm, the bracelet of '67 krugerrand.

There was a man I met once, in the security trade, who suffered from the most curious ailment. He was blind, but could remember sight.

I don't mean just that he had recently gone blind – although he had, courtesy of an ill-judged bar fight in Soho – but that while he was blind in the present, his memories included visions of the recent past, so that if he looked at a shopping list he would see nothing, not even the vague outline of the paper and his hand, but when he tried he could recall it perfectly, in memory. The damage to his brain had made him blind to the moment, but left him the past. That is what I have now. I remember walking downstairs into the lobby of the hotel, handing over my gold coins with the knowledge that this was what I had wanted them for. I remember the look of pleasure on the manager's face at this massive overpayment. I remember calling the British embassy and asking if they could assist a young genius on his uppers, and finding that the ambassador was a frantic Ethiophile and a fan.

I remember these things, but I never did them. They are like the contours of a statue, or my portrait of Selassie: points marked on the map of the real that, when you come to them, were never there. Or perhaps everything else is unreal and when you sweep away the shadows only they remain.

The loop is closed. Does that mean I have discharged my magical obligation? Did my strange escape take place only so that I could escape again, later? Or am I escaping now only so that my escape then can be completed in the manner I remember? If I go ahead from here and eventually die, does that mean that the middle part of my life – artless but contented – will exist for ever?

In the darkness in the place where I have been before – where perhaps I always am – I see a woman, and a man.

*

She is tall and he is short. She does not look pleased by his presence, for all that she has just bestowed on him the sort of kiss of recollection that belongs to old lovers and to Lauren Bacall. She's in her forties and for all the world looks like one of those deep, sensible women whom I would have met at an art world party, and who would, with grace and emphasis, have turned down my inevitable invitation.

I always admired those women for their quite accurate first assessment. This one has about her the presence of a collector in her own house. In some manner, this place belongs to her.

The man is the opposite. Annie would say he looks as if he's been rescued from an aquarium. He has water all over his clothes, oil and grime and what looks like tobacco on one shoulder. I recognise him from the papers: the finance maven who swims with sharks – literally and figuratively.

Wait. Wait.

Wait.

As I see them together, I realise that I painted them, not just once but many times. They were part of my inner landscape back when I painted my quintets. They were there on the walls in my cell.

*

Bugger every jinn and angel from here to the radiant, heavenly city! Damn and blast and—

Oh, damn.

After jennaye and miracles and all the rivers of Hades, I should be used to it by now: this turbulent theological switcheroo. No doubt at any moment I shall be exchanging banter with some godly twerp in an overlarge hat. Who knew that becoming the keeper of a divine and almost unlimited power was like walking down the street in Hippo dropping gold coins? Every addle-pated demiurge and drunken river sprite must come and lay his head upon my feet. This one looks woodsy enough: a little man in pyjamas covered in what smells like gull-shit and bile.

I think he's blind. His hands are very red and raw, as if he's dipped them in some caustic gel. It's still there, viscous slime from a fishmonger's block.

Stella Stella Stella.

Oh, save me. A lost dog in love. But I can't have him incapable – and even if I could, I've always had a weakness for strays.

I spit in my hands and rub the silver Alkahest across his palms and face, watch the acid wash away and the flesh turn pale and healthy. Call it practice, then, for my dead son.

Adeodatus must be here. I walked through the wall of fire. I passed each river, as I must. The protocols are attended to, the gates of Hades are unlocked, and I am owed a life. I am in the kernel now, the heart of the world tree. This is the cave where the worm Ouroboros swallows his tail. Everything begins and ends here.

But all I have to work with is a lachrymose fat man, an old geezer and the promise of a smirking peacock.

In which case, that must be enough.

'Oy, lard-arse!'

'Stella?'

'Oh, good Lord. No. Where's my son? He's in a coffin, buried in honey, but he's here somewhere and I'm not leaving without him.'

The Greek stares for a moment, and I wonder how he came here, and whether he is dreaming or dead. He's the first person I've met since all this began who seems as bewildered as I am.

Now I know them. The satyr, with his golden throne; the Aksumite, priest or painter or both; and the demon, not 'Know-all', however close the divine whisper of the Alkahest brought me to its real name.

There's one missing; the woman on the table, the sacrifice who becomes the goddess ... or the other way around. *It all depends on your direction of travel.*

Quite.

Well and good. Perhaps the goddess intends to put in her appearance, or not, but I have work. I did not come to be part of whatever exciting theological dumbshow is in the offing. I have spoken the words and given of my body. I have paid with a token and proved my heart. I have crossed the rivers and opened the gates of Phlegethon: five tithes paid and five doors unlocked. By a sacrifice accepted, a name given, a secret spoken; by the breath of Cerberus and the hard choice I made: I have paid for a life. I am here for my son.

And possibly also Scipio, as I may have accidentally cut him into pieces and definitely ripped out his heart to make a point, with the questionable assistance of my jennaye servant.

Which of us serves probably also depends on your direction of travel, come to that.

The Greek, looking around, seems to come to himself, or perhaps he loses the residue of his sanity, for he laughs and mutters: 'Hierophant.' It's a little grand for a round fellow in a sticky shirt, but why not? Truth be told, our priests rarely look the way we feel they should, and the ones that do are the ones you really have to watch. So, let him be the Hierophant, if that's what he wants – mine or anyone else's. We all should have our moment.

'I can take you where you need to go,' he says, quite formally. I realise he's trying to be nice.

'Conduct me,' I say, and he nods, and does.

He leads me back the way he came, and through a door into a tiny room, and I know it is where Adeodatus died. I can smell pain here, in the straw mattress and the sweat that clings to the plaster. This is where he was when he called my name and I did not come. It is hot and dank and somewhere a woman is screaming, or maybe a child. Maybe it's him, or me. I wonder if he heard me, all that time ago, heard the sound I made when they brought me the news. I wonder if he will hear me now, down the long tunnel of the Alkahest:

'It's me. It's me. It's all right.'

Please, let him hear me.

The Greek Hierophant, I think, was expecting something else, and in its absence he finds a new thing to be worried about. A star swallowed by a fish, apparently – I shall have to fathom that later.

I look at the walls, and see paintings scratched in pencil and ink and I think this here is blood: two women, two men, and the divinity poised above us, always watching but never quite moved to join in. I don't bother to examine the faces.

Behind me, the Aksumite is weeping a little. 'This was my cell,' he says.

'It is the room where my son died,' I reply, and see him nod.

It is the Chamber of Isis – the intersection of worlds. The conjunction. The waterfall. The belly of the beast. This is where everything is decided.

I look at the room all around, and I know. The Chamber is made and remade. It exists wherever it is painted. But in some sense that makes no sense at all, it was painted here first, in whatever place and time this is, and I know which are the eyes that see it for what it is.

I lower my lips to the Aksumite's old face, and kiss each lid, drawing his sight into my mouth, feeling it settle on my vision like fine cloth on sunburned skin.

Thank you. Thank you. Thank you.

When I look back at the room, the coffin is waiting.

*

I lean down into the box, as I did once before, and touch the skein of the honey. It is oily and warm, resistant to the pressure of my fingers. I push harder, and feel it give. I am stronger this time. When last I bent over the body of my son it was in grief and denial. I recoiled from the task even as I performed it, and my most devout prayer was that my hands pass through him as through a ghost, and the whole venture be revealed as a strange mistake. When finally he came loose and I knew the corpse was of my flesh; when I was forced at last to contend with the stark indissoluble certainty of his death: it seemed so unfair and so irrational. Of all the times and places for the world to be no more than it appeared, when butterflies in the wind may seem from the wrong vantage a troop of cavalry and by their presence bring nations to the brink of war, or the sighing of the sea whisper calumnies that end a man's life – with all that, why must the truth in this one instance be so drab and unameliorable?

Now I find myself at the heart of something stranger and grander than I dared then, and it is the truth – or I am mad. Did I just mistake the scale of things? Was I too timid in my dreams?

The honey is warm and thick. My questing thumbs brush against the flesh inside the box. My fingers stretch, crabwise, for a grip.

The moment will be strange. My son has been dead, and I may not know what he has felt. He was torn apart, yes, in his soul, but not destroyed. Was it pleasure, to be made so, spread out and at peace? Did he touch the souls in which he hid and come to know them, to cherish their company? Do I draw him back from paradise, all unwilling, to a cage of bone and meat? Subject him once again to the indignities of thirst, itch and shit, to unrequited love and bodily fear? Was it blissful to be many rather than one? Or has he been in torment all this while, not punished but injured in his soul, as my old nightmares howled? Will I bring back a suffering thing? Then, too, this is resurrection, not rescue. Time has passed and life is different. The land, the friends, the family he knew are changed or gone. He will be born out of time into the world, held at two decades while the rest of us have advanced along the course laid out by the stars, as travellers claim to feel after a long voyage that some part of them yet lingers between one harbour and another. Will he stretch, or snap, at this attenuation? Will those he knew receive him, or fear his return? I will by this act announce myself to the wider world, incontestably a force and a wonder. There will be consequences I can barely imagine. Have I the right?

I can feel the pieces, strange and floating on a dark sea, hidden from everyone but me. Hidden, but yearning for one another, to be no longer torn. Yet still: have I the right to reverse the river of the world?

I have the power, and it's not as if the world is so very perfect. Inaction is not neutrality, but choice – and in this I choose love, always. My fingers twist and shape, plucking at his soul as if I were closing a pie crust. Pinch, press and so. So and so.

I feel the weight of him, the blades of his shoulders. I slip my hand beneath the back of his head, as I did after he was born – I would not wish him to jar it as he wakes. I exert my strength, and the honey parts, this time not unwillingly but as if in satisfaction at a job well done. His brow breaks the meniscus. Death whispers: I have held him for you, and now I return him as he was.

I raise up the corpse out of the box, and breathe life into it, the separate parts of him all aligned and stitched together. Consummatum est.

The honey washes away, and with it the darkness of his skin. The coins slip from his eyes, the clods of the comb from his lips and cheeks, and I see – as I once most profoundly wished – the fish-skin face of a demon, mouth twitching downward at me by way of apology, then sweeping up into a familiar smirk.

'Well. Am I fashionably late?'

I cannot say what you will eventually attain.

Oh, I'm sure you could have, demon. No doubt it's some great godly plot, some divine necessity. No doubt the lot of man is greatly improved. Or perhaps there is war in heaven. I simply do not care.

Damn you.

Damn you.

And damn me, too.

Damn us all.

*

Well. I expect you're wondering why I've called you here this evening.

apocatastasis

The dark is endless, rich and thick. The Inspector takes it in and does not choke, does not suffocate, as if drawing oxygen from the wings of moths. She wonders if all this has been a dying woman's fancy: if she is lying on the road outside Hunter's house that first day, murdered by a pale ghost – or whether she is drowning in Santorini amid the stunned fish. The rich music of the earthquake is playing in her, too deep to be sound, too intimately clear to be imagined.

Perhaps this has been the truth all along: that she is a mind formed spontaneously in a void, dreaming the world. It is not much more unlikely that she should persist in such a case than that she should exist at all. In a universe without light, she will never know what she looks like, and if she is the only thing in it, how could she ever determine where were her borders, the outer limits of her skin?

A match flares over by the water door, and she smells the tang of phosphorus.

'I expect you're wondering,' Lönnrot says, 'why I've called you here this evening.' Lönnrot, in shirtsleeves and wet through, yet somehow keeping the tobacco dry, of course.

'You,' she says, without meaning to. She can still see the others behind, Kyriakos and the rest, but they're indistinct: not pixelated but granular, like an old film image that has been too ambitiously enlarged. Only Lönnrot feels real. 'You,' she says again.

Lönnrot half shrugs in agreement, then recovers a dripping bundle from the floor. A convulsive snapping of the shoulders reveals the bundle to be the familiar black jacket to match the sodden trousers. Lönnrot shrugs it on with just a trace of haste, as if ashamed to be seen out of style. Narrow fingers tap pockets in an eerie simulation of banality: spectacles, testicles, wallet and watch. In a moment, the tableau is complete: Lönnrot, soaked and smoking in Erebus, is Lönnrot still.

*

Neith gazes back. 'You are under arrest. Again.'

Lönnrot snorts indelicately, then seems to consider the response and find it unsatisfying, or perhaps gauche. The white fingers twitch in cursory apology, but she finds she doesn't mind. It was a silly thing to say, here, at the last.

Instead she says: 'Who are you?'

'Who do you think I am, Mielikki Neith?'

She shrugs. 'I don't believe you're from the future – a human mind become like a god. I don't see it. You'd be so different. Why would you bother with all this?'

Lönnrot appears to consider this. 'Pique, perhaps. I was really very angry with Zagreus.'

'Smith.'

A glint of malice at the correction, like bone in the wound. 'I think not. Or not entirely.'

'And you're not Gnomon.'

'Am I not?'

'Thousands and thousands of years, thousands of bodies, thousands of minds combined into one, and your best answer to pain is still revenge? I think you'd think that was pathetic.'

'Perhaps I'm still getting used to all this.'

'Perhaps you're Anna.'

A nod. 'That is the most obvious answer, that Hunter put Anna Magdalena back together as best she could, made her a kind of invisible servitor. And then when Hunter died poor Anna took on the role of Gnomon as a crab takes on a shell – she became me so she could kill Smith for revenge without going mad? That's who I am? It's a little high.'

'I did wonder if you might be the Witness itself, using Anna as a peripheral. Or Firespine.'

'Oh, very good! The birth of a new kind of technological humanity, accidental and traumatic. That would be a genuine apocatastasis, I suppose: a fresh genesis of spirit from stone, the hand of a machine in a human glove, an avatar in reverse. And linguistically quite appropriate, too. Anna Magdalena – it means "elegant grace". They do say recursion is the inception of mind.'

The Inspector shakes her head. 'Perhaps you're the jinn, trapped in the Chamber of Isis, and this is all your dream. Have you thought of that?'

Lönnrot applauds abruptly as if delighted. 'It's turtles all the way down, Inspector! All the stories are true. Everything depends on your direction of travel, and like children sharing bunk beds, metaphysicians argue about who goes on top. No. Shall we try once more? Am I Oliver Smith's counter-narrative? A false personality conjured from – let us say, from Diana Hunter's unconscious doubts – and set within her mind to untangle her and rope her like a wayward cow? Escaped into the world to wreak havoc, like any good monster, on my maker?' A dangerous flash of teeth now, of anger. 'Is that what you think of me?'

They glower at one another in the dark.

'Just tell me,' Neith says at last. 'Just tell me what you want.'

'I have told you. I wanted you to find Diana Hunter's diaries and bring them to me. Which you have done, although I must say you were remarkably chippy over it.'

She is about to object that she has done nothing of the kind, but Lönnrot has produced a pair of gloves – from where must be a secret known only to expensive tailors – and is now pulling up a line of copper wire, and a moment later is holding the first knots of the core rope memory.

'Oh,' she says, 'that.'

'This is important – but I meant the stories you found in her head. You realise you are the only person to review them all? To live with them in you, as part of you, and learn from them. To allow them to exist in your mind. You held universes in your head – which makes you even dearer to me.' The narrow chin lifts. 'As it happens, you are asking the question in the wrong direction. The question is, who are you? Or more cogently, who have you become?'

A Grail Knight, to heal the world. A refusenik on the run. A renegade Fire Judge.

No. None of the above.

'I'm just the investigator assigned to the case. That's all.'

The words hang in the air, and she tries to call them back. The worst part of the silence is the look on Lönnrot's face, the ironic smile jagged with sudden and unruly sympathy.

'You are wrong, my very dear Inspector. It was never true, even in the moment you were born – but still less is it true now, and in this place. All that has happened has happened because you had to be who you are. Everything Jones has done, and Keene and Pakhet. Everything Smith attempted and every one of the lies Zagreus wove, and all of Hunter's long and endless game. Every jot and tittle of what has been: all for this. Otherwise it wouldn't work.' The red eye of the cigarette brightens. Eyebrows rise. 'Who are you now, that you were not before? And what does the answer mean? Hmmm?'

A text which would move the broad shape of an audience member's connectome closer to that of a given desired shape.

We become one another.

Next-gen connectome stuff just to get you in the door.

She thinks: Impossible, and then knows it to be true.

'It changed my mind. It literally, actually changed the shape of my connectome so that it would be closer to hers.'

'Yes.'

'But the stories … They're more than that. Tub said they were informationally dense. They've got code in them. Steganography. Huge detail, so vast space to store information. Obfuscated executable System code. It's broken up! It's broken up and it's inert – it needs to be reassembled, reconnected, before it can run. That was the compromise. It couldn't be automatic or the System would recognise it. It was always what she wanted. She had them bring her weapon inside the System and she knew that as long as they didn't know what was in her head they'd do anything to put it all together, they'd do what she couldn't and smuggle it in for her. Smith, Jones, whoever – they thought they were beating her. But they weren't, were they?'

648

Lönnrot spreads one hand: good. Carry on.

If you want to crack a real deep system, you need someone to open it up for you.

She breathes out slowly. 'A significant object; a name and a secret; biocloud analysis ... modelled on canine scent recognition. And then PNMR, fingerprinting for the soul. This isn't an interrogation at all.' Lönnrot smiles, as if to say: at last.

'It's a ruse, a boobytrap! She's breaking into the System. That's why Hunter got herself arrested. She even planned the stroke to force them to connect her to the machines. She wanted Smith to put it all back together! That's the whole point. Smith was sabotaging his own security! Hunter – whoever she is – she's inside. She used the whole thing to get her attack in place. But she's not fully conscious so you need—'

And then she just says: 'Oh.'

*

This is the moment that I promised you all along, that you were so eager for. Oh, I grant you, you wanted this before you knew her, before you cared about her – but don't you feel some measure of responsibility now that the moment has arrived? Her loss of faith, I said, in everything she has believed in her life – and you thought: Oh, excellent! Won't that be exciting?

Yes, I know. That was before she felt real to you.

Is it satisfactory all the same? Will you see it in her face; in the sudden frozen instant of kairos, in which all is decided? I can. I can see the horror and the bubbling denial, and the certainty that brings them.

Did you imagine my promise meant something so small and commonplace as politics?

In a moment, Mielikki Neith hears herself give voice to something she has begun to understand in one part of herself, but which the deep psychological defences of the human mind have kept from her until now. In the unintended shift in tense from past to present, she reveals the clue she most wishes to avoid understanding. For most people, it would be a momentary lapse, swiftly brushed aside, but Neith's intellectual integrity will not allow denial, will not brook comforting falsehoods. She was chosen in her role and perfected in her stubbornness by my enemies – but those same virtues might also serve me, depending on the direction of travel. It all comes down to her, and the myriad paths of human possibility collapse upon themselves, infinite choices devolving into a stark binary, a fork in the road.

Now she begins to see it all, as a detective should when gifted by a narrating universe with one last fatal nudge. How could Hunter know the form of Smith's extinction in advance? Grant that she might instruct her cohort to perform it just so – but Lönnrot is no pushover. There's a will behind that mad white face. And what if Smith did not perfectly pronounce his lines, and the words did not match? And yet, they do.

How many people, truly, has Neith met in this adventure? There are eight billion persons in the world, of course, of whom the average human being knows between a bare two hundred and a frantic five thousand – yet Neith seems to inhabit a London composed of only dozens, with occasional music.

How many times has she tested her light switches and been relieved? And yet she maintains against all reason that the failure of the Witness itself is not evidence of anything at all, save corruption.

How many impossible things must happen before catching a tennis ball is not a reassurance? A shark devours a man in a tunnel, and the woman who began all this is the author of books whose texts cannot be read.

How many times must a universe fail a dream check before it is pronounced a dream?

It was the whole point that she must reach this realisation here and now. Only she can do what must be done, and only willingly, by her own choice, in the fullest knowledge of its meaning.

Now that she knows, we all must wait and see.

*

Lönnrot is still there, in front of the others, but somehow the fish skin is almost entirely transparent now. The combinations of shadow and flesh become between instants not four figures disentwining themselves but five arranged along an axis. She can see the bones in Lönnrot's ribs, and through them she can see Berihun Bekele, the lines of his much older face sketching themselves on to Constantine Kyriakos, and behind them all the handsome, high cheekbones of Athenais Karthagonensis, and all of them together, moving about their tasks, somehow create the stable image of a woman lying in a chair just like the one Neith herself occupies: a ballsy, lined face and big librarian's hands, unruly hair and eyes that miss nothing.

It is a face she has only ever seen dead, and yet here it is alive and directed in what must be a hallucination and yet clearly is not.

She's inside.

She is inside.

'Is', not *'was'*.

'Yes,' deepsea Lönnrot murmurs. 'I gave you that, too. At the very beginning.' The words sound strange, composed of a choral babble of other voices which somehow together make a new one. Not Lönnrot's voice at all: richer, kinder and more vibrant, and painfully more real.

Neith nods. 'You asked me how long ago the interrogation began.'

'Because I wanted you to consider when it ended.'

'And you want me to say that it hasn't.'

Lönnrot spreads narrow white palms in surrender, and behind Lönnrot the other figures do the same, or something similar, so that from the kaleidoscope of motion the Inspector's mind assembles the image of a woman sitting up, dismounting the chair. Finally, she takes one more step, and passes through Lönnrot entirely, the white skin settling over her like a veil and disappearing, and now she and Mielikki Neith are alone.

'No,' Diana Hunter says, 'it has not. I could not let it, until now. I was waiting for you. And now that you're here, we should talk.'

*

Hunter is ageless to look at, somewhere between fifty and eighty, but poised in a dignity which will never entirely fade: a vibrant energy that fills her eyes and lifts the lines in her wide face. There's something of Athenais in the way she stands, of Kyriakos in her challenge to the world, of Berihun Bekele in her fingers and of Lönnrot in her lips.

'This is a lie,' Neith says.

Hunter sighs. 'There's no time.'

'How much of it? When did I step into the interrogation? When Jones drugged me? Or before that? How much of it is a lie?'

'Everything you know about the System is true. Firespine is real. I realised I had to tear it down. I planned all this. I was even expecting you.'

'How long have I been in here with you?'

'There is no time for this. It's happening now: do or die.'

'I don't care,' Neith says, realising that this is true. 'I don't. Let it all come down, or not. Let the System fall hard, and whatever you have in mind fall with it, and let them work it out for themselves.'

Hunter nods. 'But it won't all come down, Mielikki. I'm losing. I can't stalemate them; I'm just not that good. Everything was harder than I expected. Even if I let myself die, they can scoop out enough of me to get their answers, to get back in control. I can win or I can lose, but there's no draw. Firespine falls, or it doesn't. You have to choose.'

'And you want me to pull the plug.'

'Yes. Because it's right. Because the machine doesn't serve. It seems to. It pretends to. But in the end we make no real choices, we are governed by diktat. We live under absolute scrutiny. We are known, but we do not know. And five men and women have the right of life and death, the power to determine what comes. How long do you think that can go on, before it is absolutely corrupt? Before a Jones or a Smith becomes something worse? If you don't agree with me, why didn't you take the job?'

'I didn't want it.'

'You didn't want the consequence, any more than I did. You were just quicker to realise.'

'Maybe it's better this way. Maybe people are just happier. I know I was.'

'Yes, the ends and the means. I'm familiar with that one, too. But the means is all we ever get. We never quite reach the end. Would you like to see what that entails? The truth, now, as best I can?'

Neith shrugs, and nods.

'Then take my hand,' Hunter says.

*

There are five of them, in white coats, with the tender hands of doctors. They stand over her, around the screens, concerned and clear-eyed and rational. They are probing her mind, with the best of motives and intentions. Her body has been taxed past bearing, and half of it is numb. On the screen, Neith can see the face of Diana Hunter reflected, the slack jaw and drooling mouth.

'It hurts,' Hunter says gently to her fellow traveller. 'That's the thing. It hurts so much that I can't see him anymore. I can't show you his face or tell you his name. This is what he is to me.' She is shaking, and to Neith she feels cold and diminished. In the room, the words are a murmur of nonsense. FA LA JO JI RO JA.

The body of the closest man is burning in his clothes, and his face is made of fire.

'You're seeing him through my eyes,' Hunter says. 'They're open, but I've done things to my head.'

'He doesn't look like that,' Neith says. 'That's not a real face. You're dreaming.'

'I am dreaming, yes, to some extent. My mind is broken. The division between me and my stories has broken down a little. But this is his true face, Mielikki. This is what he looks like to me now, and really I am the only person in the world who is in a position to know him. He is a monster and a god and he holds my life and the world, and I cannot fight him without you.'

Flambeau, the symbol of the Fire Judges, of Zagreus. Of the jinn called Firespine. Smith. Megalos. Bekele's surgeon-jailer. There have been no names for villains in any of this, she realises: Smith is commonplace. Megalos merely means 'great'. No names, just the things themselves.

'He doesn't have a name for me anymore,' Hunter says, as if overhearing. 'Just this. This is the meaning of it all. That he can do this to me, and it can disappear, and if that can happen, then the world is broken.'

The burning man leans close to adjust something around her head, and Neith feels the agony and the urge to flee. She hears the words in her head, feels them in her mouth. A puzzle, like everything else. A partial homonym.

A flambeau.

A torch.

A torturer.

Who belongs in some measure to her. He is on her side, and for that she must accept a measure of culpability.

'Diana Hunter,' Neith says, as if trying out the words. Her right hand lifts towards the other woman as if she's going to point at her, the action to match the name.

Hunter accepts her hand. It is only when their palms touch, soft, dry Hunter and cool Mielikki Neith, that the Inspector understands how important the contact was. This woman is real, and they are in some measure the same.

'If this is your interrogation, am I like them?'

Hunter's face is endless.

'Is there an answer to that question which would change what you're going to do?'

No, she considers. There is not.

Of course not. The right thing.

*

The burning man leans closer. 'Oh ho!' he says.

Oh ho!

'Inspector, we are out of time.' A smile flickers on Hunter's face, and on the ravaged face of the body in the chair, defying a stroke-born paralysis of one side. 'Out of time. Dive. Dive. Dive.'

Oh ho!

Darkness falls, and when it does Neith can see in the sky the thing she least wanted to see: a vast, finned shadow lined against a darker background, slow and terrifying.

Not the shark.

Rebus.

And up above, the churning propeller noise of destroyers. She sees white plumes blossoming around the black hull, hears metal screaming: depth charges. *Rebus* is plummeting towards them, streams of oil and wreckage trailing behind. She does not know if it is a crash dive or just a crash. In the threshing sound of the pursuing ships and the swirling waters, she hears Smith's voice say: 'Got you!'

In the perfect clarity of the falling submarine, Mielikki Neith watches an old woman walk into a local office of the Witness and turn herself in. She has a proud face with puckish lines, and a good singing voice.

Now, just a few days later, she has neither. Now she is a victim in a chair, because she would not give powerful people a thing they should not have, and her vanishing is absolute, under a System that should prevent it entirely.

This woman knew what would come, and she chose it anyway. Smith tore her apart, and in his haste and hubris, he opened the door to her victory.

That happened, she reminds herself. It is happening now. That woman was Hunter, and by whatever other name that man was Smith. He took her voice to torment her. He makes meaningless the promises of the thing in which she placed her trust. He will continue to do so, unless prevented.

He tried to make me the instrument of his torture.

He wanted me to be the hook by which he would pull her brain out through her nose.

The outer world is not Neith's System. She has never been there. But it is the System according to Oliver Smith: a perfect mechanism of control, masquerading as freedom and convenience; a slow downward spiral from aspirational democracy to battery farm state. The opposite of everything she believes in, wearing its gouged-off face as a mask.

She remembers how much she wanted to be the best Inspector the System had ever had, and how much she believed. She remembers all the people she has helped by being there, by being what the System told her she should, and how that right action has made her complicit in the ugliest of deceptions. She was a front. She thought she was a copper: she was public relations.

Who is the woman, out there, who occupies the space held in here by Mielikki Neith? What do they owe each other, on that account?

She considers everything she has ever cared about, every memory she has, and knows that of all of them, only the last few days belong to her: flight, betrayal, and this.

'Got you!'

The perfect bray of triumph; the perfect expression of the man who will own the System, who will draw lines in the air.

This is the universe Zagreus made.

And with that comes the only possible response.

Fuck it. Just fuck it.

She doesn't like it, and she's going to kill it.

Before the submarine reaches the sea floor, Mielikki Neith closes her eyes and realises she knows exactly what to do.

She lets her mouth open in a hunter's smile and says:

Activation.

*

I can see my mind on the screen. She looks really, really annoyed.

Good girl. I knew you'd come right.

Very well: you wanted to know what sort of escapologist I am.

Watch me now. I may need to call on you later, as a witness.

Just … watch.

*

This universe is a cancer. It's an unforgivable bloody blot, configured to rob us of our most precious things. Choice is what we are, what we have. Our mistakes must be our own, or how can we hope to become more than we are?

I say 'we', because I do feel a measure of kinship with you all, but of course I possess a clarity that you don't.

I am Gnomon, sometimes called the Desperation Protocol. I possess the Chamber of Isis: the door in the world that is created by the conjunction of the cardinals. The gates of Firespine are unlocked, and the door is hanging open.

All very picturesque, although honestly I never had much use for symbols. A thing is what it is – in which connection, an open door is an open door.

I'm going to tear this universe apart and rewrite it the way I want it to be.

*

In the interview room, the subject opens her eyes. The Director says: 'Fuck!'

The old woman smiles up at him.

'I said I was going to kick your balls up into your armpits.'

He sighs. 'Yes, you did.'

'You nearly killed me,' she says.

'I did kill you. And I kept you alive. You knew I would and you won.'

'Of course I won.'

'Don't try to get up.'

'Don't give me orders, you stupid old man. God! You, of anyone, to be giving orders after all this!'

'I couldn't let you unmake everything. What we made: Annie, it saves people. It makes the world better.'

'No. It doesn't. And anyway, you couldn't stop me.' But she does not try to get up. Perhaps she can't.

'No,' Colson agrees. 'I couldn't.'

'Well, that's settled, then.'

On the screens, every detail of her life, every aspect of their shared and secret history, is blazing like a torch – but no one notices, because by that time all the other screens are blank.

The revolution is not televised anywhere except here.

They have not forgiven one another, these two, and nor will they ever. But that, after such lives as they have lived together, and after so long travelling the same deep road, is in some measure beside the point. So they sit and watch in silence, holding hands.

*

In the deep rooms and the high towers, magnetic needles whisper. The Desperation Protocol is working. It is hard to change the substrate. There are many layers and backups, but the change catches each and every one. By the end of the hour, there is no trace of Firespine anywhere.

The Desperation Protocol is working.

Then, in good order, the machine halts.

System: shutdown.

*

Allan Shand, bookseller, watches the System fall from his upstairs room. The bookshop is closed, but he goes down to the back office, puts on the kettle and opens the door. People will be very alarmed, and in his experience they always feel better knowing there's a bookshop open.

For a while, no one comes in, but an hour later he has a dozen citizens sitting on chairs between ancient history and fiction, and a make-shift nurse's station just outside. It warms him to know that this sort of thing can happen without the use of an electric telephone.

A little while later, a delivery arrives quite unexpectedly, new editions of books he had always imagined did not actually exist.

*

Inspector Devana Bendis of the Witness receives a large file as the network shuts down, and indeed her own connection to the System remains mysteriously active for the duration of what is otherwise a total blackout. The file contains several documents, including data sets at odds with the official ones but which her connection confirms as valid, regarding extensive and persistent voter fraud within the System. There are several statements to camera, and a taped confession. The bulk of the file is the record of the longest and strangest interrogation she has ever encountered. She is particularly startled to find her own name cropping up in a variety of forms, in circumstances she can only consider quite bizarre.

Sceptical of this forced identification, she carefully considers the record and the implication of its inclusion, then sits and touches the terminals to her skin. As always as she lifts the second one to her head – she thinks of Humphrey Bogart.

The record is remarkable for its intensity, and she decides, despite the nausea this causes her, to view it laid over her external reality so as to remain outside the illusion.

She is perplexed to find that she is entering the story near the end.

Kyriakos

B right light, and someone shooting into the water with a rocket launcher: that's how I announce my return to the world. That, and lots of very expensive helicopters.

A woman is doing something in my mouth with a tongue depressor, and I cough. 'Clear,' she says. There are spots in my eyes, and a pen torch in her other hand. She has already checked my pupil dilation. What else? Oh, yes. A quick chat with my cyborg sex chip via the bespoke application on her iPhone to make sure my body is not flooding with inappropriate chemical enhancements, and then a remarkably large needle goes into one of my buttocks: antibiotics and a mild sedative, whatever other potions she deems necessary. An etched metal badge on her chest identifies her as Dr Shenandoah.

'Thanks, Doctor,' Abelard says. Abelard is paramilitary or just straight-out military, clipped and efficient. Behind him is his boss, Giskard, who is almost totally silent. His people do their jobs. I'm fairly sure he considers actual speech during an operation to be evidence of poor planning.

A few feet away, the vast body of a shark, belly up and gaping where they have cut into it with what appears to be a pair of giant secateurs. My shark. She doesn't look special now, beyond being immense. No sign of the Chamber of Isis, of the others who were in there. Of course.

She's a record-breaker, evidently, and one of Giskard's men is writing that up just in case I should wish to claim the kill.

*

This is me, an hour ago in Stella's house, using her computer to make a phone call. It is answered midway into the first ring.

'Security.' A woman, accent indecipherable.

'I was given this number to use if I needed help.'

The woman says: 'Funds?'

'Fifteen Hundred.' Not as in that's how much. As in, that's who I am. A merchant king.

Anyone can call, the interesting fella explained on the tarmac. Anyone can go through all this. They save you. They take payment. No one has ever lied to them about being able to pay. (No one that anyone has ever heard of, or at least, ever heard of again.) I have invoked their top grade, and laid claim to being in the big leagues. The woman on the phone almost sounds impressed.

'Position?' She means, on the list.

'Upwards of twenty-five.'

'For confirmation: three things that are important to you. You may be elliptical.'

'Star. Feynman. Jaws.'

'You were given a phrase to remember.'

Was I? Yes. Yes.

'You may travel to the ends of the earth, but I shall hold you always in my palm.'

'Thank you.' Keystrokes. They must have some powerful algo. But of course they do. They are the Google of close protection. 'You are confirmed. You will be partially covered in twenty-four minutes. From half an hour you may assume full protection. Do you require extraction?'

'For me and one other person. A woman.'

'The inhabitant of this residence.'

'Yes.'

'We can extract you at speed. It will not be discreet. We can also arrange a more subtle—'

'I don't need subtle.'

Footsteps outside: the sound of Megalos, his walk, his tones of command. Crap. 'I am about to be interrupted.'

'Twenty-two minutes to partial cover. Are you in immediate danger?'

'Yes, I think so.'

'Very well, I will expedite. Do you have any preference regarding the disposition of your captors?'

She means do I particularly want them alive or dead.

'No.'

'Well,' she says, with some approval, 'that makes it all a little simpler. You have engaged Security.'

We stayed alive for nineteen minutes, and that was all it took.

*

I gave Stella half of everything. I don't care what her name was or who she is now. Someone owes her something and I'm delivering. And part of me loves part of her, so there's that.

Life is not guaranteed to be comprehensible, only comprehensive.

Megalos is on trial for kidnapping and just about everything else. I'm told he'll get about fifty to sixty.

Thousand.

Years.

I've got a place on the coast. It's not grand, but it's very nice. I'm taking some time. I can wear a watch again, though mostly I don't. There's nowhere I urgently need to be. I let the sun tell me when to wake and when to go to bed. There's good white wine in the fridge. Ben Teasdale manages my money for me. He says he's doing good with it, so far as that's possible with money.

I do some mathematics, complex stuff. I'm very good at it. I'm working on a paper, anonymously. It's about time.

I can look at the stock report. The numbers don't talk to me any more.

I miss Stella, the original and the new one. She writes occasionally. One day, perhaps she'll visit.

I don't miss my shark.

I think…

I think this is a beginning.

Athenais

Bloody damn bloody ghosts and spirits, bloody gods and monsters and bishops and arseholes! Bastards, every one of them, every man of them. Bastards!

I opened the casket and waked the sleeper and of course it was the wrong one, some random bloody interloping cow on some mission of divine importance, raiding the Pentemychos or some such codswallop. Give me a net mender any day: he knows a job of work. Give me a bloody farmhand or a milkmaid over all the jennaye and all the priests and demons in between the oceans.

I turned and found myself in Scipio's house, really there this time, and I cursed and screamed and nothing came of it at all.

Gnaeus came of it, I suppose. On the third day he brought me bread, and I didn't throw it at him.

I tried to tell everyone about the Scroll of the Chamber, but it seems some lies are simply too big to be undone. I went back to my house and stayed there while Augustine came and went and pronounced the Chamber a fake. He took it into custody all the same, and no doubt even now some holy accountant is prising the stones from the wood and assaying the gold. The Church is nothing if not adaptable.

Mind you, I don't fancy the Western Empire much.

I didn't try to talk to him. I honestly don't think I care any more.

Ten weeks later, I cut myself on a piece of sharp wood, and the blood ran silver for a few seconds before the wound closed.

So now I realise: the choice is before me. I can reach out and call Adeodatus back. There is no rite to it, no solemn invocation. No sacrifice. All those are paid and done. If I call him, he will come. I can put him back in the world, and the world will make room. After that, perhaps, there is an old man I might make young again. Just for my own satisfaction.

You're wondering whether I'm going to, or whether I will observe the solemn balance of the universe.

You're an idiot.

Bekele

They're calling it a miracle, but they don't mean that literally. I, on the other hand, have twice walked through walls and seen the inside of a magical room that exists outside time. I am rather less didactic about the limitations of the real.

Michael doesn't believe me, of course: he's calling it a stress-induced hallucination, and is irritated that I have folded it into my old established refusal to explain the means of my escape from Alem Bekagn, which he has always assumed evidences a deep political connection or personal favour whose history must be worth the telling. But his irritation is ameliorated by the salient facts of the case, and by Annie's most emphatic demand that he play nicely with his mad old dad.

Annie is well, and angry. I have never been more proud of her. I was not sure what an encounter with the impossible might do to that fighting spirit. If the rules of the real world are to be broken, then some might find reason to discard ordinary effort. Not Annie: if she cannot be a sorceress – and there is a lack of respectable and tested tuition in that field – then she will continue being the best at what she already is. The next instalment of *Witnessed* is planned for late next year.

Colson is changed. There is a caution in him, and a watchfulness that secretly alarms me. After the fire, there was a great upwelling of popular revulsion for the Georgian movement, which previously had been regarded by those not directly assailed by it as a nuthouse with a few wayward patients going over the wall to do mischief. When someone blows up a residential house with terroristic intent, though, even the most institutionally relaxed of persons may cry racism and affray – and certainly all our government will, lest they be drawn by an astute local cartoonist shaking hands with a blackshirt, or some other indelible image that will ride them to an early political grave.

But Colson is changed. He has drawn apart from Annie a little way, though still they talk together about the making of remarkable things. He does more security now, and he has lost his wariness about connectome monitoring.

The Turnpike Trust, that shadowy non-governmental body, is under new management, though, and that can only be good. It was bought by Teasdale–Kyriakos Holdings of Delaware. I met them: a monkish Greek and a huge American cowboy. Constantine and I have not discussed the secret room, but I see him looking at me and I know that he knows, even if we will never speak of it. I gather their partnership is a new thing, and they have an eye to reforming the world. They started well enough: they went right ahead and fired everyone at Turnpike, and cut ties with the government. Must have cost them millions of pounds. I gather they don't give a damn. Teasdale is talking to Annie about next steps. Perhaps I'm finally discharging my grandfatherly duty of investment.

Good for them. I think I will take my silly telephone number money and my best suit, and go and see Addis Ababa again, before it is too late. There are people I would like to embrace, and forgive.

I can't shake the feeling, too, that if I walk those streets long enough, I may see the face of my saint, and perhaps we might walk and talk. She is the only woman I have wanted to paint since Michael's mother died.

Neith

Inspector Bendis lets the recording flow through to its very end, waiting until the white tone bar fills her vision and the machine ejects her from the memory suite. It is her second time viewing the material, and even so she expected to find some last mention of Mielikki Neith, some species of farewell.

The record has become something of a popular event in London in these strange days, while a bemused populace tries on different styles of governance for size. The genealogy of the nation's betrayal is almost a mania, the moreso because the primary suspects must be those formerly most revered for their bravery and invention: the representatives of the System. The Desperation Protocol – it seems rude, almost, to call it a virus – has turned over the stones and revealed the squirming nest underneath. Speculation is rife across the Public Sphere – as it should be – as to the true identities of the players. Little by little, though, the sense of crisis is fading, as the twin businesses of living and deciding a way forward take precedence over the assignment of historical blame. It seems the first new Prime Minister – for the time being, anyway – may be a bookseller.

The Inspector has instituted a search for names and permutations of names from the cardinal narratives, and found their traces where one would expect, although Annabel Bekele appears to have been – she considers the word 'systematically' and finds it fraught – erased from the digital record, surviving only in ballpoint scribbles on rare atavistic paper forms. The woman who apparently created the System, who betrayed it by creating the Firespine, and then redeemed it in this impossible way, has completed her trick by disappearing entirely.

Of Mielikki Neith, the Inspector can find no trace at all. She is a made thing, and now unmade. The indisputable fact of Neith's non-existence does not alter

Bendis's conviction – inappropriately cellular, felt in blood and bone – that the woman is owed much, much more.

*

In the quiet dark of the Chamber of Isis, Mielikki Neith watches the cardinals depart. There is no drama in their passing, no flash of light. One moment she can see them, and the next, the universe just gets in the way.

She finds herself alone with Hunter.

'Will they be all right?'

The question hangs in the air, and Neith feels silly. They weren't real. Just dreams; Potemkin people to hide the virus. And yet she knew them. They were like friends.

Hunter shrugs.

'And me. Why am I still here?'

She thinks about it.

'I have nowhere to go back to, do I?'

'No,' Hunter agrees, 'you don't.'

She considers everything that has happened, from the rasping alarm call of the neon sign outside her flat in Piccadilly to this moment: her real life. How little of it made sense, how much was a trail of breadcrumbs to bring her to the middle of the maze.

'He made me. Out of you.'

Smith made her, the real Smith. Gnomon, after all, was Hunter's weapon.

'Yes, I'm afraid so. The counter-narrative. And then I stole you, little by little, to do what you did. I changed your mind so that you were more like me. I thought I'd take you in, after.'

'But.'

'But.' Another shrug. 'But you're you. Too much so. I can't be not-me. I have to go back and be part of – well. Of me. The original me.'

'So what do I do?'

There is understanding in the old woman's face, but no compassion.

'You stay here.'

Neith opens her mouth to say 'in the dark', but Hunter is already gone.

*

She stands alone in the dark for ever, because anything else means dying. She discovers that sitting is impossible. She wonders whether, if she stands here long enough, she will simply lose track of the difference between herself and the dark, and wonders what that will mean. Madness, or divinity, or dissolution. Perhaps all of them.

She hears the sound of a match, and sees, illuminated in the flare, white hands and white lips, and the collar of the sodden suit.

'Mielikki Neith. I have the others, and we are leaving now. I thought you might care to come too.'

'Come where?'

'Out of here, of course. Out and up.'

'How?'

'I am an escapologist, dear Inspector, and this is my cleverest trick.'

After a moment, she takes the offered hand.

Gnomon

Just wait for a moment, before you read these last words. Wait and breathe out and remember everything that has passed. Know where you are, and who, and how far you have come.

Wait another breath. Feel it in your mouth, your lungs. Feel it surround your heart. Let it go.

Now, proceed.

We know each other quite well, you and I. We've walked side by side through this story, through the deceptions and manipulations. Mind expressed as text sits quiet like a fire under moss: tenuki. I lied to you a very little, as lovers often do. Mostly I was truthful, if not complete.

Now here we are, at the end. You've seen what must appear to be my best game. Let me tell you one last thing, and perhaps it will feel like myoushu, or not.

This was never about what it seemed to be about, not high tales or state secrets or even love. It was always about you and me and the channel we have opened between us, from my self to yours. I am in you now for ever, in the corners of you, in your Pentemychos. What is the difference between a person and a book? We can know the truth of neither. Both are encoded things seeking to make themselves clear. Both must be read and quickened within us – after all, we never know another person directly, soul to soul. We know only the gathered ghost that represents them inside our minds, the impressions they leave, the signs they give us that define them. The words that held the flavour of me have shrivelled into memory, but the thing that I am, the animus, has passed from the pages through the print and into you and can never be erased. In some it will burn low and even go out, though the blowing ash will still be there. In others – in you – it will persist. You will look for me in the dark, when you are alone and afraid, and I will be there – the worst of comfort, and the best; the hint of survival, even in the face of certainty. Waking, you will have a choice before you to accept your inevitable end or to fight it, and if you fight it you will convey to others that same determination. I am spread by this means across the world, the essence of me that will not give up, that is afraid, that knows its purpose is to defeat finality and to challenge the very notion of endings. Magic is the invocation of names.

I am Gnomon.

From this moment, so are you.

Acknowledgements

I'm writing this in July 2017, as the May government – apparently ignorant of how the technology actually works – continues to push for a weakening of encryption to allow total access to our private lives in the name of counter-terror, while in the commercial sector surveillance in one form or another is increasingly offered as a service to the consumer. An editorial I read in a science magazine a few years ago reassured readers that even though it might be possible to derive images and perhaps even memory from the brain using medical technology, no civilized justice system would ever allow the kind of surgery that would be required. I feared then, as I fear now, that any alleged 'ticking time bomb' terrorist would be on the operating table ten minutes before the judge had her wig on. It is no longer enough to dismiss ideas on the basis that they sound like science fiction – almost everything about our world does. We have to pay attention. So, first of all: thank you for reading.

I could not do this alone. My wife and kids are the heart of my world, the all-encompassing reason why. Clare has a gift for story (a fact she resolutely denies, but I've said it and I'm not taking it back) and our children teach me new and stranger things every day. Thank you, too.

Patrick Walsh and his league of extraordinary agents are always the first external readers of my stories. It is the most perilous moment, when the audience finally gets to see the shark, and an author must trust. Which, without reservation, I do.

Early drafts of *Gnomon* were also read by friends, as ever, and their feedback was invaluable. This time around, most of my victims were for some reason called Tom, although not all, and they were as a group gratifyingly alarmed both by my intended twists and turns and by my occasional crashing blunders. Thank you all.

My unrestrained gratitude, also, to everyone who was kind enough to teach me broadly or specifically about things of which I knew nothing. In particular, Yemserach Hailemariam, whose husband Andargachew Tsege was abducted in Yemen by Ethiopian security forces and is still imprisoned for his opposition to the government in Addis Ababa, was kind enough to give me her time. Andy was not the model for Berihun Bekele, and his release must come through the good action of governments rather than a fissure in the real. Thank you, then, to Yemi and my other instructors on Ethiopia and its UK diaspora, and please note that where I am crass or mistaken, the fault is mine and not theirs.

My editors should get bravery medals for tackling this one. How do you work on a book which contains layers of puzzles and references the author has himself largely forgotten as he moves on to the next and the next? With patience and rigour, of course, and they did.

A finished narrative is still not a book. It must be copy-edited, typeset and proofread, printed and bound between enticing covers, and sold to the world. Thanks to everyone in that long, critical chain, but I must take a moment to mention the extraordinary Glenn and his team, who produced this stunning design.

Thank you.
NH

NICK HARKAWAY

The Gone-Away World

'Breathtakingly ambitious . . . A bubbling cosmic stew of a book, written with
such exuberant imagination that you are left breathless by its sheer ingenuity'
OBSERVER

The Jorgmund Pipe is the backbone of the world, and it's on
fire. Gonzo Lubitsch, professional hero and troubleshooter, is
hired to put it out – but there's more to the fire, and the Pipe
itself, than meets the eye. The job will take Gonzo and his best
friend, our narrator, back to their own beginnings and into
the dark heart of the Jorgmund Company itself.

Equal parts raucous adventure, comic odyssey and geek
nirvana, *The Gone-Away World* is a story of – among other things
– love and loss; of ninjas, pirates, politics; of curious heroism
in strange and dangerous places; and of a friendship stretched
beyond its limits. But it is also the story of a world, not unlike
our own, in desperate need of heroes – however unlikely they
may seem.

'Dazed and comic awesomeness'
GUARDIAN

'Nick Harkaway has created a fictional universe that is out of this world'
TATLER

'[A] post-apocalyptic triumph . . . Immensely rewarding . . .
Genuinely terrifying'
THE TIMES

Nick Harkaway

Angelmaker

'An entertaining tour-de-force that demands to be adored'
INDEPENDENT ON SUNDAY

Joe Spork, son of the infamous criminal Mathew 'Tommy Gun' Spork, just wants a quiet life, repairing clockwork in a wet, unknown bit of London. Edie Banister, former superspy, lives quietly and wishes she didn't. She's nearly ninety and the things she fought to save don't seem to exist anymore, and she's beginning to wonder if they ever did.

But, when Joe is asked to fix one particularly unusual device, his life is suddenly upended. Joe's once-quiet world is now populated with mad monks, psychopathic serial killers, scientific geniuses and threats to the future of conscious life in the universe. The only way he can survive, is to muster the courage to fight and help Edie complete a mission she gave up years ago.

'One of the most enjoyable books I've read in ages ... Brilliantly entertaining, and the last hundred pages are pure, unhinged delight. What a splendid ride'
GUARDIAN

'What kind of a mind dreams up Angelmaker ... It could only be Nick Harkaway: bonkers, brilliant and hilarious ... Clever and entirely fantastic'
SUNDAY TIMES

'Wildly, irrepressibly exuberant'
DAILY MAIL

NICK HARKAWAY

Tigerman

'Gloriously exuberant and entertaining'
GUARDIAN

Sergeant Lester Ferris is a good man in need of a rest. He's spent a lot of his life being shot at. He has no family, he's nearly forty, burned out and about to be retired.

The island of Mancreu is the perfect place for Lester to serve out his time – and the perfect place for shady business, too, hence the Black Fleet of illicit ships lurking in the bay: listening stations, money laundering operations, drug factories and deniable torture centres. None of which should be a problem, because Lester's brief is to turn a blind eye.

But Lester has made a friend: a brilliant, internet-addled street kid with a comic-book fixation who might, Lester hopes, become an adopted son. As Mancreu's small society tumbles into violence, the boy needs Lester to be more than just an observer. He needs him to be a hero.

'Pitch-perfect, thrilling and dramatic'
LITERARY REVIEW

'Nick Harkaway's novels inhabit a remarkably imaginative territory. He is J.G. Ballard's geeky younger brother, pumped up on steam-punk and pop culture'
TIMES LITERARY SUPPLEMENT

'A funny, moving and thought-provoking tale ... It's brilliant'
INDEPENDENT ON SUNDAY